Ceremonies

CEREMONIES

by

Dwight Cathcart

Calamus Books
Boston, Massachusetts
2002

Cover design: Will Cook
Photography: Tobias Allen

This is a work of fiction. Names, characters, places, and incidents are either the product of the author's imagination or are used fictitiously, and any resemblance to actual persons, living or dead, events, or locales is entirely coincidental.

First published by Calamus Books
92B South Street
Boston, Massachusetts 02111

Printed in the United States of America

ISBN: 0-914852-17-5

Library of Congress Control Number: 2001099906

First Edition 2002

10 9 8 7 6 5 4 3

In memory of
Charles O. Howard
1961-1984

Ceremonies

Prologue

Timothy

This is what happened on Saturday, the day of the dance. In the afternoon, the boys were sitting on the railings along the bridge, yelling at us and laughing.

"Ooooo!"

"Hi, sweetie!"

"Lookit the girls!"

"Wanna date?"

They all try to sound like girls.

There's also a lower voice. "Wanna suck my *cock?*"

"Don't hurry." Bernie whispers. "Don't ever hurry. Walk." He glances at me and at the pavement and ahead of us, toward the end of the bridge and safety, but he never glances at the boys. "If you don't look at them, and if you walk normally, then it never gets worse than this."

I'm scared and excited and I want to run, but Bernie keeps up this steady pace, and the boys keep to the railings. Bernie has this trick of being able to look right at somebody and not see him, and he does this, going over the bridge, looking everywhere and not seeing any of them or even hearing any of the things they are yelling at us, just as if he and I are the only two guys on the bridge, or anywhere in town. This guy on the railing says in a loud whisper, "Wanna suck my dick?" and I start to grin—I can't help it I'm so afraid. Bernie keeps on chattering to me in a voice too quiet for him to hear. "If you start to run, or if you let them know you are afraid, then, honey"—he rolls his eyes—"watch out!" He shrugs and throws his shoulders back. "There's something about a flying fairy that inflames the passion of teenage boys." He takes my arm and leans down. His eyes narrow, and he whispers to me, "If you run, they'll chase you. They can't help it. They're like dogs. And if they catch you, they kick you." He looks away into the water beyond the bridge. "I know faggots who've died that way." I think maybe he is trying to scare me more, and I don't know why he would want to do that.

Their laughing and yelling are behind us when something hits me in the shoulder. I lurch and start to run, but Bernie holds my arm tight and goes on talking. "Take it easy, honey. Safety lies in being calm." It was a rock or a piece of dirt, and I feel it fall against my leg. My shoulder hurts, and Bernie's fingers hold my arm and make me walk on with him toward the end of the bridge. I think they are right behind us, and I am afraid they are going to hit me. I want Bernie to let me go. I feel like crying and I'm grinning and my heart is going like crazy. "Keep calm," Bernie says. "The end of the bridge is right here. We're OK." I don't believe that. He leans down and whispers in my ear. "You're beautiful when you are afraid. Your eyes get very big." Bernie is always telling me how pretty I am. I'm grinning and I'm crying, and I don't want to hear that.

Then we are at the end of the bridge and can turn up the hill to Bernie's place. He says we are safe. Bernie is twenty-three and knows a lot. I am almost seventeen, and I am learning from him. In his room—he lives in a house at the top of the hill—he asks me if I want tea. I never had tea before I met Bernie. I look at some magazines he has with pictures of naked men, and he makes tea and we smoke and get high. After a while I forget about being scared. It's good being around Bernie. It's exciting. Things are always happening, and it's never boring. It's fun being queer around him. But I think it's fucking dangerous too.

Bernie turns on the light and puts his face close to the mirror and stares. "I think I need to do my face again." He begins to make a thin line just inside his eyelashes. Bernie is taller than I am. His hair is blond, and sometimes when he puts on makeup he looks like a girl. He finishes and turns to me. "How do I look?" He closes his eyes and turns his head a little away from me, and then he opens his eyes real slow and looks at me from the side. "Am I pretty?"

I don't know. Bernie does not look like the men in the magazines. They are big and strong-looking and all of them have mustaches and none of them wear makeup. I think it is exciting to look at them, but I think it is exciting to look at Bernie too. Bernie wants me to say he is pretty. "Would you like me to do your eyes?" I don't know. Bernie comes over and sits down on the bed with me and takes the pencil and tells me to look up. I like it when he tells me what to do. He puts his finger on my cheek and pulls the skin down a little and runs the pencil along my eyelid. I wonder if I look like a girl. I want to look like a boy, but I want to look like a girl too. I want to be pretty. When he finishes, I stare at myself in the mirror. I look different, but still like me—only with dark lines around my eyes—and I am not pretty like Bernie, no matter what he says. He is standing behind me, looking into the mirror over my shoulder, his hands on either side of my neck, smiling. He thinks I look pretty. I don't know whether to believe him. He kisses me underneath my ear, and later we lie on the bed and he feels me all over. We take off our clothes and I get excited and he makes me come. Bernie is good at that. Then I'm tired, so I go to sleep.

Bernie is smart. He has everything figured out, and when he came to town in the spring, everybody got to know him right away. One day we were hanging out together and we went to the mall and he went in this ladies store and began to look at ladies dresses. I was scared about the lady who worked there and I wanted to get away, but Bernie kept taking these dresses down from the hangers and holding them up to him and turning around to me and saying, "What do you think, Lucille?" so I would have to answer. People began to come around and stare—these ladies with blue hair—and I was scared, but I thought it was funny too, the looks on their faces while they watched this boy try on ladies dresses and look at himself in the mirror and see how he looked. Once, he went into the dressing room and came back out in this red dress. He had on tennis shoes and he looked real funny, and he didn't pay any attention to the ladies staring at him, their eyes real big and round and their mouths open. He turned to me to show off and cocked his hip out, and then he turned and showed off for them too, this great look on his face. And then he said, "You can scream now!" I started laughing and I couldn't stop, so I ran away. I liked that, because I am scared most of the time, and Bernie isn't.

Bernie was the first boy I ever saw in a dress, and after he did it, everybody did it but me. We were having a party and smoking and getting high at Jack's and there was this clumping up the stairs outside and the door opened real fast—real wide—and there was Bernie in this black shiny dress and high heels. I guess everybody was so surprised they didn't know what to say. Bernie put his arms way over his head and kind of tucked his chin down on the side, next to his neck, and then everybody started to clap and cheer and everybody got up and ran over and started hugging him and pinching his titties—he had put toilet paper down there—and slapping him on the butt. He called everybody "darling" and kissed us, and when he got back to me, he stuck his arms out straight and put his elbows on my shoulders and kissed me real gentle and said, "Hi, sweetie. How do you like this?" I got embarrassed.

After that, everybody did it. It was like Halloween sometimes. Somebody would have on a dress and high heel shoes but his face was just regular. And sometimes somebody would wear a wig and lots of makeup and jewelry with just regular clothes. It wasn't exactly like Halloween because everybody laughed a lot and nobody was trying to fool anybody. I don't think. I don't know what they were trying to do. They were trying to look like ladies, but I don't understand that because regular guys like ladies and queers like boys. Sometimes I thought Bernie was trying to look like a lady so regular guys would like him, but mostly I don't think that. All the queers liked Bernie when he looked like a lady. I liked Bernie when he looked like a lady, too, but I don't know why. It bothers me some.

They tried to get me to wear drag, but it upset me and I wouldn't. I kept thinking of my mom and my dad, and I wanted to cry. I wanted to be pretty and have all the guys hug me and see how that felt. They teased me and told me I didn't have the guts and I was embarrassed. I got mad and was glad if nobody showed up in a dress or a wig or whatever. What Bernie has figured out is how to make people like him. He knows how to do that. I don't know whether wearing a dress or not wearing a dress is the way to do that. Whatever I do it doesn't seem right.

When I wake up, he is holding me and it is dark. Sometimes, when he is holding me, I wish it would go on forever. But he gets up and puts a can of spaghetti in a pot on the burner and begins to make supper. The boys on the bridge know who we are. They go to the school, but I think they don't go much because they are always hanging out at the mall and downtown on the bridge when they should be in school. Every time they see us, they call us faggots and fairies and laugh and Bernie ignores them. He tells me that you have to be what you are. He says all the time, I am what I am. He says you have to be brave. I am not brave. I don't know what I am. I don't know how to find out. When he holds me, I like to forget all this.

Like, he isn't a lady, so why does he dress up like a lady? I like to forget that I am not brave. I like to be held and not think about any of this. That's why I like to smoke.

There is a hill above Main Street where you go to meet people at night. It's where you can get stuff if you want it. You kind of hang around on the corner and then men walk up the hill and you talk some and then they tell you what they would like you to do or what they want to do to you, and you can ask them for money or stuff. You can go behind the buildings up there or go with them in their car. That was the only way I knew to do it before Bernie came. He said, "Whew! What scumbags! You get AIDS that way." I started hanging out with him and met a lot of the guys, and it was more fun, just like he said. You didn't always have to do what the other guy said. And he introduced me to young guys, too, and I didn't see so many of the old men in suits any more. I started to like him, but I think Bernie doesn't really like me. He likes me just as a friend. He's still looking for the other. Bernie tells me not to go back to the hill and not to get so fucked up, but when I need money for something to smoke—or just when I get bored—I go back to the hill. Only I don't tell him.

After we finish eating, we decide to go to the church, which lets us get together and dance there. They don't mind us. Bernie cares a lot about how he looks. He spends a long time after supper fixing his hair. He parts it in the middle and it hangs down all around. It is kind of long and he washes it a lot. He has a hole in his ear and he wears a silver chain through it, and he does the lines around his eyes again, and he doesn't seem to mind me watching him at all. "I am going to catch something fabulous tonight," he says. I like to dance with him. We put our arms around each other and dance real slow. It's romantic, being with Bernie at a dance, and it's not at all like being with those old men on the hill in their suits, going down on them in their cars. This feels more like real love.

Bernie turns away from the mirror and puts his hands together over his head and turns around and around. If he had on a dress, it would swirl out straight, but he is just wearing jeans and tennis shoes. He looks happy. I don't see how he can be happy. Bernie never mentions his mother and daddy. It's like he came out of nowhere when he came here. Like he wasn't related to anything. I wish I wasn't. My mom told me I better not come home as long as I smoke marijuana. She says I make my Dad so mad that the only peace she gets is when I'm gone. I feel real bad about that. If she knew I was queer! I don't know whether I'd like to be straight or queer like Bernie. Seems like I wouldn't like it either way. If I was straight I wouldn't know Bernie. Bernie says I'm fucked up.

Bernie comes over to the bed and crawls on top of me and puts his head on my chest and blows on my neck, and I laugh.

He kisses me and I can't stop laughing.

"I want you to be pretty for the dance."

He wants to do my eyes some more. I don't know why he wants me to look like a girl. That's what those guys on the bridge said we look like. People just laugh.

"Don't you want to be pretty for me?"

I want him to like me. He fixes the light so he can do my face. Then he gets the pencil and makes the lines around my eyes again. We smoke some more and get high, and he gets out the powder and puts some on my forehead and my chin. He gets very far away, like the room has become very long and he has very long arms and his voice comes from somewhere else.

"I think you are going to be the most beautiful boy at the dance."

I think about dancing around and around with Bernie, my head on his shoulder. The music never stops. I wonder what it would be like to be a girl and to dance with my head on Bernie's shoulder. I think if I were a girl Bernie wouldn't like me.

Bernie gets on the bed and holds me. He runs his fingers through my hair. Bernie is talking.

"When we grow up, we'll live on an island where it's warm and we'll go around all day in nothing but cutoffs and get tanned. We'll eat mussels and clams and lobsters. And around the dooryard, there'll be roses climbing over the fence and over the front door and we'll have lots of cats. I'll have a husband who is big and strong with a beard who'll split the firewood and love both of us. And I'll be your daddy and love you forever, just like you are, and we'll be happy ever after."

For a long time my mom did not have a husband. He drank a lot and they used to fight, and she used to get beat up. He went away, and she said I was going to have to be the man in the house. I liked that. But I still wanted to be her little boy and sit on the floor next to her chair and put my head in her lap. I wanted to be a girl and grow up like her. I didn't want to grow up like him. Now he's back and she only pays attention to him, so I left home when I was sixteen last year.

I haven't lived any place special since I left my mom's. I stay with guys I know. Sometimes if I don't have any place to stay, I'll go home with somebody I pick up on the hill. I can get money that way too. It sucks not having a regular place to live. I lose things. One time I lost a whole bagful of stuff because I forgot it when I was running away from this man's house. It had some good things in it too. I say, "I need some money. Can you give me some money?" And they give me ten or twenty dollars, and I have to say, "Can't you let me have more than that? Another twenty?" Sometimes I beg. Sometimes they beat me up when I ask for money. If I don't ask, I don't get money. If I ask, sometimes I get beat up.

I dream about how it would be if Bernie and me lived together all the time. I think I would like it to be the way he describes it. But I don't think it would be that way. I don't see how you can be queer and be happy unless you have lots of money. Then you could just go away to somewhere far away and do whatever you wanted to and there wouldn't be anybody who knew you and who could yell at you and beat you up. You'd have your own place and you could close the door and pull down the shades. That's the trouble with being around Bernie. It's like he was being queer out in the street all the time, when he ought not to do it except indoors when the shades are down.

"Would you like an earring?"

Bernie says it won't hurt much. He gets an ice cube from the refrigerator. He's going to do it himself. I know it is going to hurt, but Bernie wants me to have an earring, so I let him do it. He holds the ice cube to my ear until it gets cold and I don't feel anything anymore, and he pushes a needle through my ear. It hurts a lot. Then Bernie gets an earring and he pulls the needle out and tries to push the earring in.

"Shit!"

He has a worried look on his face and he is biting his tongue and he keeps poking the earring at my ear, but he can't find the hole the needle made. My ear isn't so cold any more and it hurts a lot and I think he must have made about a dozen holes in my ear. Finally, he relaxes and smiles.

"There!" He puts his hands on my shoulders and pulls back and looks at me and smiles. "Look!"

I think I am going to be pretty, but I look in the mirror and I see me again with powder on my forehead and chin and dark lines around my eyes and a gold earring in my ear with blood on it. I want to cry. I don't know if I look good.

Bernie says it is late, and we go down the hill and cross the bridge and up the other side to the church. The only people we pass are people going to the movies because all the stores are closed in the middle of town. Bernie calls them breeders because they are regular people and have children. Bernie doesn't like breeders, but I like my mom, and I wish I were with her sometimes. This is the hill where you go at night. Most of them are old and all they want is for you to suck them off, and they don't even take their pants off. I think there must be something wrong with being queer because they don't even take their pants off. I don't think there is anything wrong with being a regular person, but I don't tell Bernie that. I like my mom. Some of the women going to the movies look like my mom. The men look at us.

People notice Bernie. Even when he doesn't have anything strange on, they look at him in the street. When I am by myself, nobody seems to see me, but when I am with Bernie, I see people coming toward us and their faces stay straight ahead but their eyes slide over to the side like they were spies, and then when we get past, they stop and stare. Sometimes I think it is the way he walks—he rolls his bottom from side to side—but sometimes he doesn't walk that way and they still stare. Sometimes they smile or laugh. Sometimes it's just that their eyes get big. Bernie never notices, though. He goes on walking down the street, his head way up—he has this real long neck—and turned to the side a little, so that if you reached out to touch him, the first thing you'd feel would be his cheek next to his nose. He keeps his mouth shut like he's just said something important and didn't expect you to say anything back. He looks in the store windows and points to things and says stuff to me and never notices the people looking at him.

I like this sometimes. When you are with Bernie, you feel like you are rich. But if the boys are out, Bernie stands out so much that they see him, and then they call him names, and I get scared and wish I weren't with Bernie. I think he wants to make people look at him. I guess he even wants the boys to look at him, but I don't know why, since they call him names. It's like he's on show and he wants us all to clap. And he must have just decided sometime not to hear if what they did was what the boys usually did, call him cocksucker. But I heard. When I am with Bernie, I am always afraid, except when we are alone. But I want to be with him anyway, because he is the best friend I ever had.

We go to dances a lot now that I know Bernie. There is one every other Saturday night at the church and one once a month at the university. At the church, they push back the chairs in a corner and there is a stereo. People bring records, if they have them. I don't have any. Everybody comes. Bernie and me and Jack and Mickey and Robbie and some older guys and one old man. There are girls too. At first, I thought that was weird, but it's OK because they dance with each other and leave us alone. Dykes wear leather jackets and cut their hair in crewcuts. I used to think it was weird to be in a room where the girls dance with each other and the guys dance with each other.

In school, the guys all dance with the girls. I used to watch them. I wanted to be one of the guys dancing with the girls. They were popular and had nice hair, and the girls liked them. They knew how to dance so they looked real good. I wanted to be a girl and dance with the guys so they would know I liked them. I guess it is better, here at the church, where nobody can see us, and the guys dance with the guys and the girls dance with the girls.

The song they are playing is called "Gloria," about a girl who is fucked up. They've played it all summer. When it comes to the part where it goes, "Gloria, where you been so long?" everybody sings. Jack puts his head back and makes an "O" out of his mouth and looks like he is going to spit water straight up when he says "Gloria."

Bernie dances with Jack, and they are having a good time. I watch them. Jack is handsome. He wears a leather jacket even when he is dancing. I like the way his hair lies close to his head and curls out at the ends. He looks real masculine. He doesn't wear makeup. I dance with a girl some. She is short and fat and has short hair that stands up and isn't like a real girl. I am not having fun. She has some stuff and we go outside and smoke and get high. She talks a lot. There are cokes and things, and we drink and eat some, but it is boring. Bernie is with Jack, and I am with her. We smoke and get high and I wish I were somewhere else. When I get high, it's like I go somewhere else and be somebody else. Sometimes I think I am this kid Gloria that people like, and I'm dancing with some cool guy. And the music is easy for me to dance to.

Mickey and Robbie dance together. That's mainly what they do, and they dance better than anybody else. Every time one of them does something, the other does it too, only backward, so it looks like one of them is dancing in front of a mirror. I like that, but it makes me feel weird. I think it is really weird that they are so happy. They don't seem to care about anything. I've been to see Robbie where he lives and met his mother, and she seemed real nice and didn't seem to mind us at all. She gave us something to eat at the kitchen table. I wouldn't know how to cope with that. My mom tells me I'm nothing but a pain and a heartache to her.

I like to listen to music when I am high. It's like you're down inside the speaker and the music is all around you and nothing else matters. It's like floating underwater where the only thing you feel is the gurgle sound in your ears and the cold on your skin. My teachers put me in the slow section at school because they said I don't think as fast as the other kids. When I am high, I don't think at all, and I like that.

I dance with Bernie, but it is a fast dance. When Bernie dances a fast dance, he forgets the person he is dancing with and closes his eyes mostly and dances by himself, turning around and putting his arms way out. When I'm high and listening to music, sometimes all I can do is giggle at everything. I can't even talk. Sometimes, though, all I feel like is crying.

Then Robbie and Mickey come back with the things they bought at the 7-Eleven. They start telling everybody what happened.

Mickey is real excited and mad. "They were in a car stopped at the light and they leaned out and began to yell at us, and Robbie, damn him, yelled back at them."

"I told them they were assholes," Robbie says. "They were calling us cocksuckers." Bernie and me quit dancing and go over and listen. "So they opened the door and two of them got out, and we began to run, and they ran after us, and the ones in the car drove after us too. We ran as fast as we could up Second Avenue to the 7-Eleven." Bernie said not to run.

Everybody quits dancing now and crowds around, and Robbie and Mickey have to tell how it was, over and over.

"One of them was behind me so close I could feel his fingers on my shoulder."

"Who was it?"

"The same guys."

"We saw them on the bridge today." This is Bernie. They threw something at me and it hit my shoulder and hurt.

Everybody is excited and forgets about the music, which stops playing after a little bit. And everybody begins to talk at once, telling about these guys and what they did. Jack wants to go find them. I don't want to find them.

"I want to put this right in their face," Jack says, holding up his fist. He is very mad, and when he gets mad, his face gets white and his lips get thin. He moves his hands a lot. "Fucking assholes. Let's go get them!" Nobody answers him. I want somebody to answer him.

"Bernie, let's you and me go get 'em," Jack says.

"What would I do if you found them, honey?"

Jack is impatient. "We'd fight."

"I don't think I know how," Bernie says.

"You're chickenshit."

Jack asks some of the other guys. Then he asks me.

"Timmie?" He looks right at me. I would go with him because I want to go somewhere with him, but I am afraid to go looking for the boys. He is looking right at me, and I want to tell him

I will do anything for him, if he'll let me, but I am afraid to go after those boys. I can't look at him, and I look at the floor.

"Leave him alone. He's fucked up." That's Bernie. He puts his arm around me. "You smoke too much of that stuff."

I can't answer. I want to talk to Jack and tell him it is OK, but he is very angry and won't talk to any of us and goes over and puts a record on the turntable. The only reason I can think of for not going is that I am afraid, and I don't want to have to think about that. I want to go over and tell Jack I think he is real brave, but I don't know if I am right, so I don't go. Jack can be mean sometimes. He says I am just a dumb fairy. Bernie can be an asshole, too, when he says I get too high. I like getting high.

Nothing happens. Somebody starts the music again. The older man asks me to dance. He comes up behind me and runs his hand down my back and down to my bottom. In a way, I like that. I stop thinking about the boys out there.

"Hi, cutie."

I smile at him because he is real attractive. He is a lot older and he is not fat. I only see him at these dances.

"Why are you standing all alone?"

I don't know how to answer that. We dance for a while. He doesn't dance very well. He looks at me real close and I think he wants me to go home with him. I think I would just like to lie in his bed and have him hold me. He looks strong. He ought to go fight the boys.

"You're cute."

He won't just let me lie in his bed and hold me. He'll make me suck his cock and then he'll fuck me.

We stand around, but I don't say anything, and after a while he goes away to get a coke and doesn't come back.

Everybody has somebody to dance with, and everybody is over being scared, so I leave and go up on the hill and talk to a man standing under a light. He offers me a smoke, and we get high, and in a little bit we go to his car and I suck him off. He has on a sweatshirt and isn't too fat. I suck off another man, too, in the alley, and then I walk back by the church, which is dark. None of the men on the hill wear makeup. My ear hurts, but nobody said anything about it. Nobody mentioned the lines around my eyes.

I walk down the hill toward town. It is warm but getting a little cool, and I feel bad. Bernie and Jack are having a coke at the 7-Eleven. We talk some. Bernie says I ought not to be walking around alone with the boys out. I tell him I don't give a shit. He tells me I am going to get AIDS. Jack tells me I am too dumb to breathe. That's not so. Jack is going home, and then he is going to come back to Bernie's. Jack talks a lot and I feel dumb around him. I feel scared, too, just like I used to around the guys in school. He smiles a lot and everybody likes him. He's as tall as Bernie but bigger, and he has muscles and that nice hair. I would like it if he liked me. I don't know what makes people like people. There was a man on the hill who said I was sweet, but I don't like that. He wanted me to go live with him. I wish Jack would go on home. He tells jokes and makes Bernie laugh and they are always putting their arms around each other. I stick my hands in my pockets because it's getting cool. It's hard to talk.

Bernie asks me what I am going to do. I don't know. I don't give a shit. I don't have a place to stay. I can go back on the hill and go home with one of them. Bernie tells me to go with him. I don't want to be there when he is with Jack, but he tells me to go home with him, so I say I will. I am really bummed out. I feel like crying all the time. I wish I had a job. I wish I had a place to live and Bernie was just with me.

When Jack left, Bernie and I walk down to the river to look in. It looks cold.

"Poor kid." I am a poor kid. Bernie puts his arm around me. "You're so pretty. You looked pretty with your eyes and your earring. What did everybody say?"

"They didn't say anything. Nobody noticed." They thought it was weird.

Bernie is quiet, looking into the water. I am cold. I want to go home. I am really fucked. Today seems like all I wanted to do was cry. I am all inside my head and Bernie is coming from a million miles away and real slow. I put my head down on Bernie's chest and Bernie holds it there while I cry.

"Poor kid. Doesn't want to be queer."

I don't want to be queer.

He strokes my head for a long time. It seems to get real cold. Bernie swings me around so that I am more in front of him, and he puts both arms around me and I put my arms around his neck and hold on there. I put my head on his chest.

"Well, you are. And there's nothing you can do about it."

I cry some more. I want to get high, but I don't have any, and Bernie says he doesn't either. I am fucked up and bummed out and coming down all at the same time. That's the worst thing. I am afraid.

"What are you afraid of?"

I don't know. I am just afraid. I need to say something, so I say, "My dad."

"That's OK. You'll get over that," Bernie says.

Bernie is braver than me.

I think sometimes I'll give up smoking and go home and live with my mom and dad again. And I'll give up being queer. I tell Bernie this.

"Look." Sometimes Bernie talks to you like he dares you to say anything back. "You can't give up being queer. That's what you are." He puts his arm around me. He strokes me again. "Poor kid." In a little bit, he lets me go and leans up on the railing and looks into the water. "I wish you weren't so fucked up."

He thinks I am so fucked up I don't know what he's saying.

"I want to be beautiful," Bernie says. I think he is already. "I want to be graceful and lovely." He puts his arms in front of him. "So that all the guys will come to me and fall in love with me and want to dance with me forever." He is quiet some more. "I want to plant flowers in my garden, peonies and daffodils and roses and lilies of the valley and things that bloom very late, so that in the fall when it gets cold and everything is dry and brown, there will still be something growing and blooming." He turns to me. "And I will cut a blossom and give it to you." He looks at me.

I look at him. "What about being queer?"

He doesn't know what I mean.

"You're not going to have any garden," I say. "You're not going to have any of those flowers."

"Someday I'll have a man in love with me, and he'll give me a garden."

"You're queer. And you live in a rooming house and you don't have a garden and you don't have any money and no way to get one. And that's the way it's going to be for you all your fucking life."

He strokes me while I cry.

We lean over the railing together and look into the cold water. "You shouldn't get so fucked up. Be brave."

Across the river everything is black except for the tiny white lights that shine but don't light up anything. "I am not brave."

We hear them up in the street behind us.

"Ooooo! Lookit the girls!"

"Oh dear," Bernie says. He lets his arm slip away from my shoulder.

"Hey! Cocksuckers!"

We are in the dark down by the river and they are up on the street in the light and the light shines down on us. I want to run away, but there isn't any place to run to that isn't past them. I could die.

"Be calm."

Then he starts walking up the embankment toward the light and where the boys are in their car.

"Be calm. Remember. Don't hurry."

It is shitty to have to walk slow when you feel like running and your heart is going so fast.

"Hey! Cocksuckers!"

But they don't get out of their car, and we get up on the street and walk right past them toward the bridge. I am grinning like mad.

The car comes behind us, its lights really bright behind us.

"No matter how bad it gets, it's important to remember how good it can be. Didn't we have fun at the dance?"

I can't remember the dance. The headlights are lighting up everything in front of me and I can see my long shadow and Bernie's. "Talk." Bernie sounds mad. "Talk about the dance." He turns to me. "Wasn't it fun dancing?" Bernie looks at me. "Why do you have to get so fucked up?"

I can't help it. We are walking along the street and the car is following us. They blow the horn, and I nearly jump out of my skin.

"Oh, God." He sounds awful. "I love being a faggot. Nobody knows how much I love being a faggot."

I hate it! I am so scared. The car seems so close I think it's going to get my heels.

We get to the other end of the bridge and we step off the curb and then the car nearly hits me. I feel the heat. They blow the horn again, and I nearly go crazy. It sounds so loud I jump, and my heart beats so loud I can't hear anything else.

"Oh, Bernie." We keep walking across the street to the other side. "Do something. Make them stop."

"I am a beautiful person. Don't you think I was pretty tonight? I was Queen of the Ball." He turns to me. "You were pretty tonight, Timmie. There's nothing we can do."

We start up the hill.

"Hey! Cocksuckers! Where's you going?"

I don't know how many of them there are. There must be a lot. I am going to get beat up. I am going to get hurt real bad. Oh, shit. Oh, shit.

The car isn't following us anymore. It stopped at that street. A car door opens and I hear somebody get out.

"Come back here! We want to talk! Hey, cocksucker!"

"They're coming, Bernie! Run!"

"Don't run. They won't hurt us."

I can't help it. I know they are going to hurt us. I grab Bernie's hand. "Come with me. Run with me. Oh, Bernie!" I start to cry. "Oh, Bernie, come with me!"

I start to run. I run as fast as I can up the hill, and my heart is going like it is going to break it hurts so.

But Bernie didn't come with me and the boys are not following me and I look back over my shoulder and see that they are around Bernie, all around him, lots of them, and I can't even see Bernie anymore. There is a house there and a yard and I climb up the embankment and hide behind the tree and watch and try not to cry too loud.

They are yelling down there, and I hear Bernie's voice, but I can't hear what he is saying. He sounds scared. I want to get help, but I don't know where to go. I don't know what to do.

Then I can see Bernie run away from them. He doesn't have his shirt. They run after him, all of them. He stumbles and then he runs down the street along the river, stumbling and running.

"Let's go get us a queer!" they are yelling. And they are laughing too.

They all run away where I can't see them anymore, and I go back on the street and look. The car is still there with its lights on, but there is nobody in it. I run after them.

Halfway down the block, I see them all again, laughing. I get up as close as I can. I am crying and then I am screaming, but they don't pay any attention to me. I don't see Bernie anywhere, and I think they must have caught him. They are kicking him and hurting him. I scream, "Don't! Oh, don't! Run away, Bernie!"

"Take his pants off!"

I hear Bernie screaming, but I can't see him.

"Run, Bernie!" I want him to be safe and not be hurt.

I am jumping up and down and screaming, "Run, Bernie!"

And then he is away from them, and the boys run after him and I run too. I can see Bernie now, his skin all white in the street light, running and stumbling. They are all laughing and calling out, "Run, queer! Lookit him run!"

"Don't do that!" I am so afraid.

Bernie runs down a little side street by the river, where the warehouses are and the election posters, and there aren't as many lights, and I think he might get away, but the doors are all locked and there is nowhere for him to hide and I can see him in the light at the next corner, naked and shining, coming back toward me, the boys right up behind him yelling and laughing.

His arms are up and his head is back—I can see his hair shining in the light—and his knees coming up and going down. They're on the bridge again, and they have Bernie. I hear Bernie scream, and I see, above the heads of the boys, down this long dark street onto the bridge, Bernie's white body fly up in the air in the light. He seems to just hang there for a moment, with nothing holding him up, and then he is gone, and everything is quiet, and I can't stop running. I run right into the boys, all those big boys, and I am crying and I start to hit them and hit them and hit them. But they

21

go away, and I look for Bernie. I look everywhere on the bridge, but he isn't here.

He's in the water. They threw him over the railing into the water. I look down into the water. It is black and it runs fast underneath the bridge. I can't see him. He is too far underneath the water for me to see. Oh, Bernie. I want him to come up where I can see him.

What am I to do? Where will I sleep? He doesn't come up, and I want him to hold his breath, and I know he is drowned. I look into the black water for Bernie, and I know he is drowned.

"Stop screaming!"

The man is shaking me and yelling. He should go away.

"Stop screaming! Stop screaming! Stop screaming!"

They come and lean over the railing, and they keep telling me to stop screaming. I kneel down and hold onto the railings and look through at the water. I don't know I am screaming. I can't move. The rocks in the street cut my knees, and I can't move, and they tell me over and over to stop screaming.

1

Carole

When I was a child, I sat in the pew next to my father and held his hand. The priest, in his homily, told us to be good Catholics, and I associated in my mind the priest and my father and God and the warmth of my father's hand and the comfort of sitting next to him, and I determined to be good always. Later, when I had grown up a little but had not changed, my friends thought that was a joke and laughed at me. But I had been a good child, and I had pleased my father, and I had found a way of life suitable for me. I preferred to continue in the manner I had begun than to please them by some new departure.

I'm all right as I am. I've done all this long enough now to know how to do it and to have reaped the rewards. I am respected in my profession and here in town. I have friends. I enjoy what I do and where I live, and when my investment income reaches ninety thousand dollars a year, I will have achieved my goal: I'll quit and move to London and let go. That will happen in six years, in 1990, and in the meantime, I'm forty-five and my life is OK. I am sitting on the right side of the center aisle of the largest, oldest Catholic church in town—the stained glass windows here are famous—where I am chair of the development committee of the parish council, listening to the priest blather on. I am the most prominent woman in the parish and, arguably, the most prominent woman in the diocese. Ordinarily, I find, in any gathering in town which is called to conduct some sort of business—the church, charities, cultural activities, industry—there will be the men, and there will be me. I find that enormously satisfying.

The priest is in the middle of his homily, and around me is Catholic New England on a summer Sunday morning, solid people who admire those who go about their duty. What empty seats there might have been are filled with tourists, coming here for the sailing and the cool summer weather, dressed in casual clothes. We listen attentively. The priest is a fool. One of the attractions of the church is that it is so hard-nosed about things—what's sin and what's not, who's in charge—yet it attracts people like Father O'Meara who is all squishy soft in his thinking. I suspect, actually, he never thinks. He merely reacts to what his senses are telling him, and his sermons are

Carole

successions of little cries of pleasure or pain, strung together like balloons filled with warm water. The whole church is drifting in his direction, and Vatican II is the cause. He has a soft face, and when he tries to articulate some bit of dogma or other—why women cannot be priests, say—he makes a mess of it by trying to make it palatable. He ought to say, "Because the pope says so." And slam the book shut.

Deborah loves him. She is sitting two pews ahead and over to my left, her head tilted up adoringly. I have known her for years— all my life in this town—and her discourse is like his, composed entirely of little effusions uttered under her breath. So polite. Deborah is two years older than I am, 48, and entirely gray. Motherly, even grandmotherly.

I tint my hair. I have it done once a week in a sleek pageboy, and I always wear the same jewelry—a thin gold chain at my wrist, a gold watch, small gold disks for my ears, which are pierced, and a gold brooch. The brooch has my initials on it in large old English lettering. I established a style for myself my senior year at Smith, in 1961, and I haven't found a reason to change it since. People take you as seriously as you take yourself, and I find gold is about as serious as you can get.

Deborah called this morning about the article in the paper, all aflutter. A man drowned last night in the Passadumkeag Stream. He was naked, it seems. Deborah needs someone to take care of her, and I do. Her fluttering encourages a calmness in me, and when she said on the phone, "It's appalling," I said, "We don't know that yet." Of course, I think it is appalling. He was naked for some reason and not just for sex, which would have required only that he drop his pants. What is appalling is that a tiny bit of the underside of things has been allowed to surface—even if only on the bottom of the last page before the classifieds—and now all of us are going to have to grit our teeth until things quiet down again.

I never tell anybody anything they don't need to know. This is a small town—thirty-thousand—and if you start telling people bits of truth about yourself, this one this little bit and that one that little bit, these little bits don't go away. They stay in the air like dust, and then they settle, and suddenly everybody in town knows all about you. I find that people will put you in a slot as soon as they can find one they think fits, and it makes sense to control the flow of information just so you're the one choosing which slot they're going to put you in. One of the quickest ways to oblivion is to express any kind of interest in why a man was naked at two in the morning on the State Street bridge. You get labeled weird just for noticing. Deborah should do what I do: When I am in church, I never let my eyes wander from the priest's face. I don't blink. And I never take public notice of anything that has to do with sex.

I always go to church on Sunday. I like the stained glass windows—they are nineteenth century, and the figures are large and clear and the story emphatic—and I enjoy the music. I don't believe in God. I accept the way things are, and I find a way to make them work for me. The world is a heterosexual place, dominated by men, and I have learned how to secure my place here, how to act, who my friends should be, what to say. I come to church because it is expected of me, to speak to people in the small social way people speak at church, to maintain ties, to present myself to be seen as being here. It is one of the things I do.

Father O'Meara finishes his sermon, his yellow teeth exposed, murmurs the lines and then retreats to the chancel and the altar and the offertory. The English mass lacks authority. It was a great mistake to abandon Latin. Everything now is relative, shifting, and we are in the hands of translators. My father used to help me make things in the basement. He taught me how to hammer, and he told me there is a right way and a wrong way. It is a disease of our time that we experiment. The right way is difficult and requires discipline and practice. People now take the easy way. They smile and have good will and hope that things will turn out well. Stupid. Lazy.

When I leave here, I am going to invite Charles Preble for brunch. I don't think I can bear Deborah right now. I must drive across the bridge on the way home. Why would a man have taken off his clothes and left them "strewn" along Ferguson Street in the middle of the night? The paper says the police have no explanation. I wouldn't wager on that, dear heart. When I leave here—when I retire to London—I am never going to mass again. Nor am I ever going to a meeting with men. I am deeply grateful that it can be said that there is an end to everything.

In a moment we will be called forward to take communion. I will walk in front of the congregation up the aisle to the chancel. I wish we were still required to cover our heads. I like the look. Princess Diana carries them off in photographs, but hats on women in the pew next to you look silly now, as if they came in from some other dimension. I try to have no expression on my face when I go up for communion. I dislike women who look especially pious. I let my gaze wander over the congregation.

The church is filled with good middle-class Catholics. That's what they think I am. Half the people in the town are Catholic. As long as you are married, have children, go to mass regularly, you are part of the scheme of things here. If you don't do one or the other of those things, it is best to be very clever.

After mass I find Charles Preble on the sidewalk. I stand on the steps of the church where I can be seen. The sun bleaches everything, after the dark of the church, and the crowd of people milling about all look as if they were dressed in resort whites. This is, for many, the most important part of the mass: the moment when we greet each other and congratulate ourselves on being here. Charles is taller than most, heavy, dressed in a light suit. He holds his hat in his hand. He is a lawyer in his late fifties and his conservative, even formal, mode of dress on the first Sunday after the Fourth of July—the beginning of the summer season—distinguishes him from the casual folk about him and suggests why I like him. He has been useful to know.

"Carole!" he calls out to me. He waves his arm and comes along the sidewalk through the people to the steps of the church, which he takes two at a time and stops close to me. People notice. I am pleased. "I'm in need of a drink—" He takes my arm and makes to lead me away. "—and it is better to have one with you than anyone else in Maine." He puts his hand on my shoulder.

"Hello, Charles," I say. "How very nice to see you." I put out my hand. I enjoy holding back from Charles in this way, playing with him, watching him try to find a way to encounter me on his own terms.

He stops and turns to me, genial and grateful, giving in. "Why, hello, Carole! How nice to see you! How are you!" He takes my hand in a social handshake.

"I'm fine. Now. About that drink." He laughs. "Amenities, Charles. Observe the amenities."

"Yes, Carole. How kind of you to correct me."

My relationship with Charles is satisfying. I invite him to my house for brunch.

"Cook! In this heat!"

"For you, Charles." I play my part, aware of the image we present here on the steps. "We can sit in the garden if there are no blackflies."

"Are you sure you don't mind?" It is one of the qualities that makes Charles attractive that, once he decides to treat you like a woman, he becomes solicitous, even while he is allowing you to go to trouble for him.

"I don't mind, Charles." He takes my arm again and we walk down the steps through the people, saying goodbye to our friends among them, and then up the street to our cars. Charles is ambivalent about me. He does not know whether to treat me as a woman or as a colleague with whom he drinks gin. He is uncomfortable with that ambivalence, so he chooses one, and then, the method of attack chosen, all is clear with him again, and his body—his face—visibly relax. He does not live with ambiguities. We agree that he is to meet me in forty-five minutes at my house.

On the way home, I find the heat in the car oppressive before the air conditioning brings the temperature down. I prefer a closed car, even so. I get a Boston paper and scan the headlines—the disarmament initiatives and the Democratic convention next week—and then I double back along Eaton Street along the river. It descends to the warehouse district, two or three square blocks of old brick buildings from the nineteenth century, two or three stories tall. Many are boarded up. My friend Sarah Savage has two here along Tarbell Street, which she is holding for development. She is very shrewd. At eleven on Sunday morning in July, everything is quiet. There are no cars on the streets and no business activity. It is a squalid area of town. I never come here. I find the lack of activity disquieting. Here, in the middle of the district, at the corner of Eaton and Tarbell Streets, I stop the car, but I leave it running so the air conditioning will keep the car and me cool. On the corner there, the Democrats have their campaign headquarters. One wonders why they bother.

Deborah said on the phone this morning, "I know him."

I had been sitting at the table at the back of my kitchen, where I can have my coffee and read the paper and look out over my garden—my garden is doing nicely—enjoying my solitude, when she called. I dislike having my Sundays disrupted by the telephone. The dead man? I expressed surprise and concealed my annoyance.

"Oh, no! The one with him. He was a student at school. His name is Timothy Leonard. He dropped out of the tenth grade." I found it typical of Deborah that she should know someone connected with this affair. "It was heartrending," she went on. "Apparently, he had been raped." As a teacher most of her professional life, Deborah knows this kind of fact about people in town, some heartrending thing which justifies or explains some appalling behavior.

"Is he a homosexual?"

"I think so. Certainly so."

"So the naked man was too."

"I would assume so."

"Who was he?"

"I don't know," Deborah said. "I don't know who he is. Was." She paused. "He must have been a friend of Timothy's. I feel so grief-stricken about Timothy. He is a little slow and had such difficulty in school—he is minimally retarded—an appalling family life, and then everyone made fun of him, and now his friend has died right in front of his eyes. He is such a fragile thing. It must be horrific for him right now."

Well. It is now 11:15 on Sunday morning, and some nine or ten hours ago, Timothy and his friend were having sex in the street, here at this corner, beneath these buildings. The doorways along here—some of them are quite large, big enough for trucks to enter—are all boarded up. The thick brick walls make each boarded-up doorway a deep recess, and in the winter you can find men sleeping here. Poor men, derelicts, threatening creatures coming at you with rags flying. They would be poor, Deborah's student and the naked man. Poverty is public, flaunting its victimization in the street. It's permanent, too, despite the Democrats. The derelicts along here lean into the wind. Poverty suggests failure, and one failure leads to another: The failure to make money leads to the failure to keep private the things that are private. Their most intimate secrets are shouted up stairwells for all to hear. They have their sex in the street and spread AIDS. Casual, anonymous, diseased sex. What are there now—3,000, 4,000 cases? I edge the car into the deserted traffic lane and begin to move away from the corner. I wonder if Sarah Savage's building is the one the Democrats are in. The street leads to the bridge. He died right there in the middle of the span. Why did he drown? The rich don't die outdoors. Money is a great protection. My father said money is a defense against insult. This naked man has nothing to do with me.

I leave the squalor behind me and drive up across the bridge and then up the Eaton Street hill, returning to the more congenial area of middle class homes. It is a glorious day. The sun is high and the sky is deep blue and cloudless. There is a gentle wind from the coast, and the main streets which I drive along are clogged with cars towing boats, heading for water. It is the kind of day—mild, clear, brilliant, uncomplex—for which the region is famous and which makes it a place for holidays for people who have not experienced the winter here. For those of us who have paid for this glory with ten months of snow and rain, the short summer comes at a hugely inflated price. What is permanent here is the winter. Summer is mere dazzle.

Charles Preble stands at the door when I open it, holding out to me a bottle of Soave Bolla. He is always proper. I invited him this morning because he is always the way he is. His life is bounded by the social rules of civilized behavior, and his predictability forms a baseline for our relationship. When I am feeling at all formless, I need merely to be with Charles, to have all my scaffolding re-erected. I think he enjoys coming to me for social reasons—I am, after all, a woman—but I appreciate his company as a tactic. This morning, after church, when I invited Charles to brunch, I could still hear in my mind Deborah's cries and whispers on the phone and Father O'Meara's ejaculations, and I thought what I need is Charles Preble's cool intelligence to remind me that I am not the only person in town beset on all sides by fools. We have been on boards together—we were on the steering committee of the River City Festival which ended yesterday, a great success, I must say—and we have occasionally had business to do with one another, and we have brunch together like this morning, once or twice a month. We go to the movies and to the opera and the symphony. We share an attitude—the mass of men should stay in their houses with their blinds pulled down—and a tone. He doesn't surprise me, ever. And I like that.

When I have gotten us gin and tonics, we sit in the garden beneath the wisteria tree. He opens: "I was nearly killed coming from church—run down, I should say—by a 35-foot boat, a great white thing towering above the street, scraping the trees!" He raises his glass and looks through it and then takes a sip. "Great gin."

"You escaped. You harpooned it."

"Ah! He slowed to let a school of pickup trucks with caps go by, and I took a port tack and escaped." He picks up his drink again and holds it in his hand. "We've got two months of this. Why don't we run away, Carole? Maine is no longer fit for human habitation in the summer. We should live here only from November to March. Us and the snow." He pauses. "And our character."

"If you think it's fun, it doesn't take character."

"Ah! I had forgotten." This is the first time Charles and I have sat out this summer. "Beautiful day, absolutely gorgeous." He looks about the garden. "First rate! Stunning! You've done wonders. I never can believe it." He settles himself again and looks at me. "You know I played here as a child. It was a haunted house. Terrifying. Absolutely terrifying!" Charles has told me this before.

My garden is very formal with straight beds and everything clipped and pruned, gravel walks. My house is late Federal—1820s—and I rent out the top two floors, and my mother and I share the principal floors. She is old and stays in her bedroom at the front. My house used to be a tenement like the one behind. My garden is enclosed with a fence. I am concerned about the people who live behind me. They now have two cars on blocks decaying in their driveway. I can almost see them through the hemlocks at the foot of the garden. I feel encroached upon. I tell Charles about them.

"Have nothing to do with it, Carole. Call the police. Let them handle it. It's a public nuisance."

He tells me he is going to London next week. "What should I see?"

I don't know what he should see. I know what I want to see when I go next because I read the "Arts and Leisure" section of the Sunday *Times*, and I tell him what I know about the summer exhibition at the Royal Academy and the show at the Tate. I plan to see the new gallery, the Saatchi Collection, which has just opened, when I go in January. I tell him about that. Charles exclaims, "All those immense canvases with paint put on with a roller!" Charles's conservatism, in a common pattern, leads him to reject modern art while allowing him to celebrate modern conveniences like his word processor.

"Go to the Wallace, Charles. Look at the Canalettos." Charles's mind is closed to the existence of twentieth century art. He sees it everywhere, and his eyes pass over it as if it were not there. Apparently, he can only see a picture which is a picture of something else. If I tell the police, these people behind me will discover that I was the one who complained. I wouldn't want to have to speak to them. I don't think it would bother Charles. I just want the cars gone.

There are things he doesn't think about. What it would be like to have a family of rednecks angry because you don't like their rusting cars. He makes his money so that he can have one of the largest homes in town, furnished with the antiques he buys on trips to New York and Boston and to the two or three places in the state who specialize in 18th and 19th century things. He goes on short visits to London and Paris and goes to the same places—the left side of the Tate, the National Gallery, the National Portrait Gallery, the Louvre. His talk on returning is of restaurants and food. He has told me he is going to leave his house to his eldest son, who is also a lawyer, married with two children. The house belonged to Charles's father before it belonged to Charles. I don't think Charles ever thinks of homosexuals. I think if he were confronted by the idea of one, he would be more confused than disgusted. How would he be able to deal with a person for whom the lines on his family tree only go one way?

"I'm enjoying the spectacle the Democrats are putting on," Charles says. Walter Mondale, the presumptive nominee of the Democratic party in the year's presidential election, is in Minnesota, and all week the media have recorded men and women making the journey to the upper Midwest to be interviewed for the vice presidential slot on the ticket.

"Sleight of hand, Charles. Sleight of hand."

He smiles and shows his teeth. "I know. What appears to be true is that he is making a rational choice for his running mate—"

"—and what is actually happening is that he is caving in to the National Organization for Women and letting them choose." Mondale is like Father O'Meara—squishy soft and no muscles in his face. But unlike him, Mondale wants to appear to be strong.

"It's just a show?"

"Magic, isn't it?"

"Cynic."

We both laugh.

"That depends on who's the magician."

"And on who's being sawed in half."

"We should ask Ms Ferraro about that. She's been much in the public eye this week."

"Yes," Charles says. "I find that interesting."

"What do you find interesting, Charles—" I am fully coy. "—about Ms Ferraro?"

He smiles. "Early in the week, right after the convention in Miami, she was being touted as something new, a new departure, something to electrify what promises to be a bored electorate. And now," he reaches for his gin and tonic and takes a sip, "the media have it that she is not new enough, that she is politics as usual." He puts down his drink. "*Sic transit* Geraldine."

"The politics of the new. The Democrats, I think, want a permanent revolution."

"It's a shame. I like the idea of a woman. I think we are ready for that."

"Of course we are." I lean forward and touch his knee. "I only think this choice should be made on the basis of qualification, not on gender. He should choose the best person, man or woman—"

"That ought not to have to be said," Charles smiles at me, and I color, "and it is sad that it does have to be said."

"—and it's absurd to give even the appearance of caving in to pressure groups." I settle myself in my seat again and rub the sweat from my glass. "There will be no end to the demands of the feminists if they get their way."

"I don't know." He seems so offhand. "This one seems reasonable."

"They want half the cabinet too."

Charles grimaces, his handsome, aging face crinkling up with distaste and then relaxing into smile. "I was rather looking forward to their having a woman on the ticket. It sounded amusing, Carole. We could laugh. And besides," he puts down his empty glass, "they are the only ones who can do it for fun, as it were."

Charles doesn't care about the issues involved in placing a woman on the ticket. The thing is so distant from his own world—and his own world, entirely Republican and including the president of the United States—that the danger presented by what Mondale is allowing the feminists to do is scarcely imaginable to him. Men are like that, I find. They are so secure in their own worlds that some things which don't exist in their worlds—but which nevertheless truly exist—don't exist for them. They have no fear of things they can't see.

Later, in the house, I prepare a tray for my mother—a linen placemat on a mahogany tray with silver and a linen napkin and a spray of lilac from the garden—and after I take her lunch to her, I call Charles in and put things on the table. When he comes into the dining room, he comes to my chair and pulls it out for me and seats me before he takes his own place. He is such a gentleman. Charles Preble occupies the space at the end of the table heavily and familiarly and begins to serve the omelet I have placed before him. He reminds me of my father. My father was sure of himself, too, at ease, detached, uncomplicated, hard of hearing.

"How is your mother?"

"No better. She watches old movies on the VCR. She sleeps much of the time."

"You are quite admirable."

"It's nothing. I have help."

I serve Charles salad.

"A man drowned in the stream last night," he says.

"Yes. Deborah Elkins called early this morning." I suggest he pour the wine.

"Odd. He was naked." He gets up from his chair and comes to my end of the table and pours the wine into my glass and then into his. I take a sip. My mother is in her bed eating. She is old and ill.

We eat for a few moments in silence.

"He took off his clothes a block away from the bridge." He picks up a piece of toast. "What would a man be doing naked in the street?" Then, buttering the toast, he looks up at me and says, "I don't understand what makes people act the way they do."

Sometimes I throw myself into some menial task just because it is mindless. I use my brain so much that it is restful to occupy myself with something I can do with my hands. I like to do dishes. And my kitchen is good to wash them in. I have had it re-done twice since I moved into this house, the first time just general rehabilitation, with new fixtures and countertops, and the second time, I had the men take it all out, everything, back to the studs, and start over. I had them take out the rear wall and add a small greenhouse-like affair—glass wall and curving glass roof—and put in all new cabinets and a tile floor and butcherblock. I have a maid who comes twice a week and cleans, but even so, I get satisfaction from washing up. It is easy and the results are immediate. There is nothing quite like the feel in the tips of the fingers of a bone china plate coming clean under the faucet. I find it steadies my nerves.

This crystal, some of it, was originally given to my mother by her aunt when she was married. It is French, by a company no one ever heard of, but it is pretty. Mother gave me her six—when Dad died, she moved in here with me, so I have her things—and I found some odd pieces years ago to increase the set. It is very thirties. I never use it on really good occasions. I use the Waterford then. I must admit I miss my father terribly. We always thought alike. He was the only man I have ever known who seemed worthy of my admiration. Everyone else disappoints me. My father was smarter than anybody else, and I am certain he was never complacent. I don't know why I feel the way I do. Often, I wish he were still alive. I'd like to tell him how much money I'm making. But most of the time I'm glad he's dead.

When I was a child, my father was very clear about things. There were little boys and there were little girls, and you treated them differently. With girls, you played with dolls and hair curlers and were careful to treat them gently. With boys, you played ball roughly. Since the things you did with girls were absolutely foreign to him and nothing he cared about learning, he played ball roughly with me, and put out of his mind, from the time I was eight or nine, that I had ever been a girl.

We developed, from those early years, the comraderie of ball players. My most common memory of him is of the feel of his shoulders moving back and forth as we walked home across the softball diamond, our arms draped across one another. The odor of my memories is the smell of sweat. I learned from him to have a direct, steady gaze and to use spare language. I learned to keep personal things separate from social things and to keep the personal to myself. I learned not to cry, not to be weak, not to give up. I learned to fight and to win.

I found out later, after he died, he kept all my letters to him. They were marked on the envelopes with the date and the contents and the date of his answer, which was always typed by his secretary. I kept his letters to me in the same fashion. They were like owner's manuals to complicated machinery, and I have read them so often they fall apart in my hands. It wasn't until I was fully grown that I began to realize how much I had to be grateful to him for. The world is a tougher place and there are greater dangers than I had realized growing up. He explained it and made it seem easy. I discovered that what he had taught me—essentially how things work—was not merely a good way to be but the only way to survive in a world which is dark and getting darker by the moment and full of wild animals.

The view of my garden through the glass wall at the back of the kitchen is glorious: I think I'll have a drink. I fix myself a scotch and sit at the small slate table in the greenhouse and sip my drink. I don't think I really care about the Saatchi Collection—official art of the twentieth century—and I don't know why I told Charles I would go in January. I like hard-edged things, flat color. Joseph Albers squares. Large fields of color in flat geometric shapes. I have been collecting it for years, and now my home is full of it, and I don't think I want to see any more of it.

There was a time, a long time ago, when I used to like a completely different kind of thing. I used to like Ingres. I can't remember which ones are in the National Gallery. I used to know. When did I last look? Nineteen sixty-nine? Nineteen seventy. I used to know all the Ingres in New York and Washington and Philadelphia and Boston. I was young, in college and graduate school, and I went from city to city looking at Ingres. It was a silly, youthful passion. I outgrew it, of course, as my tastes matured, and I excuse it now by pointing to Ingres' classicism. I have always been a classicist rather than a romanticist. I adored Ingres' women. Their skin is white and smooth and totally hairless. It is as if they do not have pores! Ingres seems to have been acutely sensitive to the quality of a woman's flesh, to how firm they must have felt. His women are strong but, paradoxically, without muscles. It is a unique—something, in the yielding, pliant solidity of their flesh. Something resistant.

When I was young, in high school, I used to see women on the street with that quality, that firmness which is neither fat nor muscle, and it used to take my breath away. I remember being quite dazed by it. I didn't know what it was that was exciting me, and I didn't know what my excitement was all about, until I saw an Ingres in the Fogg. I remember coming into a gallery and happening upon a painting—and standing transfixed before this Odalisque. So that's what it is! I thought. He had shown me what I had been seeing on the street without recognizing it. Then, I remember being seized with embarrassment: There was something indecent about my feelings. I glanced around me, and there was nobody but the guard to see. I fled the gallery, my face aflame. I was nineteen. I had never before in my life been embarrassed.

It was my next-to-last year at school. She sat in a corner booth in a diner across from the university, reading a book. It was after midnight, and I had just left the library. I got my cup of coffee and sat in a booth diagonally across from her and began to read—it was a book on the history of the English banking system—but after a time I was drawn to look at her. I should have run. She had parted her hair in the middle and pulled it back in a smooth sweep to the back of her head, where she had a bun. Her face was oval-shaped and olive-skinned. It was unusual, and its similarity to the Odalisque in the Fogg made it compelling. Occasionally, she raised her hand and smoothed her hair against the side of her head. Her fingers tapered to oval, manicured nails. Once she glanced at me and let her eyes remain on me for a moment, eyes that were closely set together, in which the pupils were at the inner end of the eye, the lashes a heavy fringe at the other end. I made to look away, but her glance became a stare and I felt transfixed, the pages of my book rising up and turning over because of the stiffness of the binding until my place was hopelessly lost. Finally, I blushed.

I went back to the diner the next night at midnight, but she was not there, and I found myself spending my days and nights searching the campus for her, my thoughts in some wild confusion. What had begun years before as an inexplicable quickening of the breath when I saw a certain kind of woman on the street, and had become associated in my mind with the women of Ingres, had now entered my life, walked into the diner where I sat and taken life, come on campus to haunt me. I would see the sleek brown hair ahead of me in the line at the bursar's or at the dean's or at the checkout in the library, and my heart would stop, it seemed, from fear, and my breath catch in my throat. It wouldn't be her. I took over a booth in the diner at eleven-thirty every night and waited, reading my books on the English banking system and not knowing what I was doing there. What would I do were she to walk in? What would I say? What was I thinking of?

When she finally came in quietly one night and got a cup of coffee and sat down in the booth opposite me, I felt as if I had found my grandmother's diamond ring, which she had given me and I had lost. My feelings were so charged, I didn't ask myself what was happening. I didn't know whether our meeting had occurred because she had willed it or because I had. Her name was Esther. At first, we met at night, after library hours, and talked in the diner, she on her side of the table and I on mine. I suffered from the desire to move over to her side of the table and sit with her—and from the desire to get up and move to another booth, another room, another diner, anywhere she wasn't, and where she would not so disturb my world. The severe quality of her hair style suggested a personal restraint: She was quiet to the point of silence, and calm, almost placid. Yet there was a flux of sensuality in her that made her bookishness seem artificial and temporary. During our long conversations that fall in the diner, at one and two in the morning, she sat back against the seat, her arms resting in parallel lines on the table, her fingers spread out before her, listening to me talk, her steady eyes fixed on my face. I had never been so listened to. Her silence drew out of me thoughts and feelings of which I had not been aware and had no language to embody. I searched for a way to describe the conflict I felt, but since I had never felt conflict before and therefore had no words, I fumbled and was inarticulate and fell silent in the middle of sentences. She led me on with barely perceptible nods and murmurs so low I wondered if I had heard them. Where everything had seemed clear before, now nothing seemed clear, and I hated it that I felt compelled to go on and on, that with a smile or by touching my hand with the tips of her fingers across the formica she could lead me deeper into some new attempt to bring forth what dreadful thing was happening to me.

I went home at Thanksgiving and my father immediately noticed something wrong. "You seem abstracted." He asked me about my grades, my professors, the papers I had written, the books I was reading. I didn't know why I felt the way I felt. I didn't really know how I felt, except that one thing had become blindingly clear: I wanted to be back at school with Esther. "What *is* it?" my father asked, and I knew what he expected me to say, "My back hand is slow" or "I've taken a longer grip on my racket." I was dumb with confusion.

I fled back to school and to Esther. There were movies now, regular dates, visits to each other's apartments. The first time, we came in from a movie and sat down on the sofa in her apartment and stared at the pattern in the carpet until I left, neither of us saying a word. Between Thanksgiving and Christmas, I cut half my classes and stopped sleeping through the night. My anxiety level doubled, tripled, and I started going to mass every morning. There were times when I thought she was the devil. I kissed her—and went right to church to pray for my sins. I fought my feelings all during the daylight hours and gave in to them at night. By a week after Thanksgiving, I touched her breasts and felt I was so far in damnation that there could be no retreat. I couldn't confess. I couldn't tell the priest this. When I thought of it, I colored so I imagined everyone in the room would remark upon me. I seemed ugly and ridiculous at the same time, and shameful. If I had only been more self-disciplined! How could I have been so lax! How could I have let physical desires so master me? I felt weak, defeated, without character, and I was continuously afraid of her. At the end of the term, three days before Christmas, Esther and I spent the night together for the first time, and we didn't sleep all night. I wondered if I would ever be able to sleep again. I hated myself and hated her and wouldn't have gotten out of that bed to have saved my soul from damnation at that instant.

My father, at Christmas, arranged for us to have long blocks of uninterrupted time together—a day's skiing on the New Hampshire border, a day and a night in Boston after the first of the year, where he would put me on the plane to return to school—and we stared at each other in bewildered silence across tables in restaurants. I was violating everything I had been before I met Esther—disciplined, restrained, rational, steady—the qualities he and I both understood. He would not have understood the way I felt myself to be overwhelmed by what I felt, and it was a large part of my confusion that I did not understand it either. I confronted an old dilemma: I wondered, shocked and pained, whether I was turning into someone awful or whether I was merely discovering something awful about myself that had been there all along. I fought with my father: "Why is it that you have to pry so?" I cried, and he answered, "What do you have to hide?" and I thought: *Don't ask me.* I got on a plane and left him.

I had no doubts what the church says about liaisons between women. I knew what sex is for. And I knew that what Esther and I were doing, in the eyes of the church, was "intrinsically disordered." Esther, stretching her arms above her head till she touched the headboard, arching her back, smiled and murmured, "That's bullshit." But I knew that the only natural purpose for sex was procreation, and God had ordained that it be within the sacrament of marriage. Sex between men and women, within marriage, when the purpose was procreation—that was clear enough, and it put me at least three removes from virtue. It was the first time in my life that I had not been able to measure the steps between me and the girl at the head of the class and, with practice, talent, perseverance, overtake her. Girls who fall in love with men and marry them suddenly seemed irreconcilably far away, created on a different plane of existence, made to a standard of virtue against which I was to be measured but which I was constitutionally incapable of achieving. I was devastated, for I realized, as I discovered how deeply I was sexually at the mercy of this woman, that I had never been moved like this by a man.

After Christmas I told her I would not see her any more. I avoided the places we had met, and when she continued to call, I changed my number. When classes started again, I vowed that I would never again cut a class. In two weeks I was pursuing her again, on the phone, waiting for her outside her classes, haunting her paths. This madness lasted all that spring—the worst year of my life—and did not end until I graduated and was able to leave her. There were times when I lived in her apartment for weeks at a time, or she in mine. I forgot myself so much as to obsess upon her—my every waking thought was of her—but I didn't forget myself so much that I failed to feel terrible about what I was doing to myself, to my career, to my relationship with my father. I went for weeks without seeing her, and then I could stand it no longer and found myself against my will and without my conscious acting, back in her bed again, riven by guilt and powerless to be better. I was utterly out of control.

I left her only to take a job, and so survived. At the time my departure seemed like a miraculous escape. I had seemed to have no defense against my own feelings and there were days—whole weeks—that spring when I had felt I was drowning in her and couldn't come up for air and didn't want to. Looking back on it from this vantage point, however, it is necessary to give credit to my rearing. I think my training stiffened my resistance even when I was feeling most defenseless, and my character, even against my volition, saved me. All this time, I had been making straight A's—I was actually a dazzling student—and I lay credit for that on my early training. My father taught me to take care of first things first, and no matter how insane I felt over Esther, I was never so crazy as to stop going to class entirely nor to forget that it was my professors' opinion of me that was, in the form of recommendation letters to prospective employers, the most important thing that I would take away from school.

When I did graduate and took the position with the company I am still with—I saw them as offering the best opportunities for advancement of all the companies I interviewed, and I have been proved right—and prepared to move, Esther turned suddenly into a weeping female. She cried and wept and beat on the pillow, and after I moved she wrote me letters. I had admired her reserve: I had no use for her tears and her protestations. She had become as noisy as a housewife betrayed, and her eyes, resting on me, had only one message: How could you abandon me? I moved to New York, and it wasn't long before I had begun to meet the men in my office. I found, now that I had a little money, I could entertain well, and I did.

I went to the theater with the men, my colleagues, and I had little dinner parties, and I established myself. It wasn't long before I had completely forgotten about the madness in Philadelphia, so full had my life become in New York. My father visited me that fall, and looking over my apartment—one bedroom and a few good pieces of furniture—he pronounced himself pleased with my life. Since I was no longer hiding anything from him, I found it easy to be open, as I had before. In fact, all was as it had been before, only better.

I devoted myself to my work. I established patterns of working that first autumn which have remained with me, patterns characterized by zeal, aggression, competitiveness, and single-mindedness. I found that even when I was up against someone even brighter than I was, my will proved decisive and dominant. I have made it a rule always to be early and always to have an agenda. While others are still trying to find out what the issues are, I find I am manipulating the discussion and them to my own ends with my own stratagems. I am very successful, and I think that is so because I have wanted to win more than the people I have been up against. They simply have not cared as much as I have cared. Since I left Wharton and Philadelphia, winning is all I have ever cared about.

In the late afternoon, the sun comes from off to the right, as I look out over my garden, and begins to cast parts of the yard— particularly the area just this side of the hemlocks at the foot of the garden—into deep shadow. I think I will have my gardener put in a new border at the back, across the hemlocks. I think I will have a new fence across the back, something taller. Deborah is here sitting at the slate table in the kitchen under the curving glass roof, talking. She has tears in her eyes. My mother cries a great deal too. I find that awkward. Mother is old. I am not required to comfort Deborah. My function here is to listen. I have heard that tears are good for you. Perhaps cedar planking that would turn gray, strong vertical lines that would enclose the garden.

Deborah looks frazzled, which is not the consequence of her having had a difficult day. It is her look. She wears no makeup and her jewelry is inconsequential. She has been on the phone all day and is telling me what she knows: "He was running from them, and every time he stumbled or tripped, they caught up with him and threw him down and kicked him and pulled off some other article of his clothing until he was naked, running down Ferguson Street between the warehouses. I think he must have been terrified. He must have known he was going to die." She wipes her eyes with her fingers. "It's brought back every gay joke I've ever heard. I can't believe how angry I am." Her anger expresses itself in her tears. "I try to get on with it, and it comes back on me and I am sobbing again." She moves her drink on the table, leaving a wet circle. "It's not grief. I feel desolate, as if I had been run over. I suppose I am still too stunned by what has happened. Sometime later I'll know what to do." Her face crinkles up. "Then I think I'll kill."

She glances at me—she is sitting with her back to the window and the garden, and her face is largely in shadow—and then down at her drink, which she moves about. "I called Rebecca this afternoon—" Rebecca is her daughter, away at school. "—I began to talk almost as soon as she answered, and I rushed on, everything spilling out. I told her about Timothy and about Timothy's friend Bernie and about how Bernie drowned. And then suddenly I was aware of how silent she was, and I stopped for a moment, and I heard her crying. I hadn't thought how it would affect her."

I fix myself another drink and stand for a time, my back against the counter, looking at her and, beyond her, the garden. This is extremely difficult. It is early evening, Sunday, July 8, 1984. The office tomorrow. I try to remember the name of the carpenter who did my fence last time. That was years ago. Right after I bought the house. Deborah talks: "I have been on the phone all day, it seems. I called Luke. He hadn't seen the paper, but Helen had called him and told him. The Greek Orthodox use the Unitarian Church, you know, where the dance was held last night, and she had heard from Simon Herter, the pastor there. Later I talked to Helen myself and Simon too. Then I called Mickey McNamara. He was at the dance last night and knows Timothy and Bernie. I think Mickey was surprised to find me wanting to talk to him and not his mother! I used to teach him. Mickey says Bernie was a nice young man. I don't know what that means. Bernie has not been here long, they say. Luke is very angry. Everybody is angry, or incredibly sad. There don't seem to be any other emotions.

"It's appalling that something like this could happen here. This is such a nice town, so nice for children, I always thought. I wanted to call every gay person I could think of. But I couldn't think of any others that I was sure of. At least that I knew to talk to. Isn't that odd? There are probably 3,000 gay people in Cardiff, if 10 percent of the population is gay, and I don't know any well enough to call and to say, How dreadful you must feel! I can't stand having this happen and not feeling that there is something I can do."

I fix myself a drink and watch the dark thicken in my garden. My house is dark, and in the silence I can hear my mother's television set. Deborah sets my teeth on edge. Last month she made a speech in the street that was reported in the papers! I am surrounded by fools. Perhaps I shall go to Europe, but not with Charles. I am overtired. I should not have planned to spend the whole summer here. "Our group" persuaded me. They said we'd spend every weekend on the coast. Deborah is one of us, and Sarah Savage, who is hard in the way that downeasters can be hard—wrinkled face, crooked teeth, stray gray hair, a mind like one of those old-fashioned brass cash registers. When she thinks about her money, she clangs. She made two hundred thousand dollars brokering the development of the old lumber mills on the river. Eloise Steinberg is also one of us. She is a lawyer who began with an immense divorce settlement from her second husband and has made that much again off the lumber companies' troubles. Eloise organizes house parties where we play bridge and drink margaritas and congratulate ourselves on having achieved success. We are all women of substance and breeding.

The sun goes down very late in the summer. I give parties in the summer and serve on tables set up in the garden and it is unnecessary to light the lanterns until nine-thirty or so. The name of the carpenter will be in my check register for 1973. I know what it's like to be chased by demons. You wake up gasping and you don't know whether you are dead or alive. I saw the street down which he was chased. Squalid brick buildings and dirty pavement. Who is Bernie Mallett? Why should I let what happened to him disturb the surface of my calm? I have struggled for twenty years and have reached an accommodation with my life, and I have no reason now to make common cause with queers.

Deborah says the police know Mallett was attacked. I called them but they would tell me nothing. I didn't tell them who I was. I know about fear. If the papers print this, it'll be all over everybody. No one is safe from gossip. There's no way to stop small, envious minds. I have not been with any woman since Esther. I couldn't so violate my morals. The church says homosexual relations are subjectively and objectively mortally sinful. Those are the words. I color easily when I am embarrassed. I shouldn't have to be talked about. Subjectively and objectively mortally sinful. I don't believe in God, and the church is absurd, but still. It happened a long time ago, when I was young and not fully formed. She was so like the Odalisque. It's better to do what I have done and have no intimate relations of any kind than to give in to degeneracy. To so lose control. I would be the topic of common gossip. I haven't given in in twenty years. I have been good.

I have made money—I am vice president of one of the largest corporations in New England and I have made money in the market—some I made before my father died and some, a great deal more, after. I have made more than he made, but he is dead and I can't tell him. At the end he was no longer any good for me. He was old and questioning. His bladder gave him trouble, and he was offensive to be around. I don't think he cared how much money I made. He simply ceased to care. I must call about insurance. I think I must make a new inventory of my household goods. There is the Sheraton chest and the candlesticks this year. I am not a fool. I know what I sold and why. I know what I bought. I know what a bed feels like when two people are in it.

I can't see my garden. She said when she left she was going home to watch the news. How grotesque. What does she have to do with him! Wild animals and demons. God, it makes me so angry. All the things that exist that didn't exist for him. If he were alive, I'd tell him so, to his face. And Mother. What will I do with her? Europe. I'll go to Europe. My passport is up to date and in the safety deposit box in the bank. I must find a bricklayer who can build a brick wall, something high, and all around my garden.

Mickey

I hear the noise even before I am awake. I am hearing it in my dream, a harsh, loud pounding, reverberating down to me, and I follow it up out of my dream into being awake. I am sitting upright in my bed, hearing the noise of somebody pounding on the door. Somebody is outside in the hall pounding loudly on my apartment door. I shiver and touch Robbie's back. "Somebody's there!" He squirms, his arm firmly around the pillow, and burrows deeper into the sheets. He feels warm. "There's somebody there!" The knocking goes on and on. I look at my watch, but I can't see because I don't have my glasses on, and I reach for the light. "Robbie, there's somebody there!" I think the knocking will wake everybody in the house, it is so loud and so angry. It doesn't stop, it goes on and on in this loud angry insistent way. I find my glasses. It is 4:45, and I am reaching for my jeans, running toward the door, pulling them on and buttoning. In the hall, I hear him.

"It's me, Jack! Open up! They've killed Bernie!"

I unlock the locks and open the door, and there is Jack, looking the same as he did at the dance, only wild. It's crazy that Jack can say something so off the wall as *They've killed Bernie* and I don't feel anything.

"What do you mean?"

Jack looks like murder.

"They've killed him!"

Jack is walking into the living room, and I am shutting the door behind him. I lock it. Jack is talking too fast.

"The boys! They caught him and threw him into the Passadumkeag. They chased him and beat him up and threw him in the stream. He couldn't swim, and he drowned! They're going to kill all of us! We've got to go find them! We've got to kill them first!"

"Wait. Jack!" I need to wake up.

"He ran into the street, trying to get away from them, and then they chased him back onto the bridge. He tripped and they caught him and threw him in." Jack's eyes are big and his face is red. He looks like murder.

I need to wake up, and then I need to have time to think.

"One. Two. By two, anyway. Three hours ago. I don't know."

I must have asked him questions. Two-and-a-half hours ago.
I have been asleep only two hours.

"Timothy. I found him on the hill. He told me. He was with
him."

I can feel the tears behind my eyes. "Who are these boys?"

"The ones who chased you and Robbie tonight."

"The same ones." I got away. Now they've killed Bernie.

"They chased him?"

Robbie has come into the living room, his eyes swollen and
his hair wild, pulling on a pair of jeans. He looks at each of us. Jack
goes on: "They beat him too." Robbie looks at Jack. He is wondering what we are talking about. I hardly know. Robbie starts to say
something.

"They chased him until he fell—"

"Jack, wait."

"—and they kicked him. Over and over again." Jack's voice
is thin and high now.

Robbie's face is beginning to crumple up. "Who?"

"Jack, wait." I move to Robbie and put my arms around him.
He struggles wildly against my hands.

"Who?" Then, "Bernie!" He takes his eyes from me to look
at Jack.

"Bernie is dead."

"Who?" He looks suddenly crazy, like he is going to run
somewhere.

"Every time he tripped—"

"Jack, give us time." What I heard in his voice, I see on his
face: Jack is crying.

"—the motherfucker caught him and tore his clothes off—"

Now I am holding Robbie, my arms around him, his around
my shoulders, holding tight. He buries his face in the hollow of my
neck, and I feel him wince when Jack says, *and tore his clothes off.*

"—and kicked him—"

Robbie's whole body lurches at Jack's words.

"—he was trying to get away from them when they caught
him and lifted him up. There were four of them—"

"Oh, Jack, please."

"—and they threw him up over the railings into the water.
He couldn't swim." Robbie's body is pressed up against mine, jerking

with each blow of Jack's words, like those things you see in movies where the man's body is still jumping around a long time after it's dead from the bullets the guys are still pumping into it.

And while it's happening, I'm thinking, nothing in my life is going to be the same, ever again.

I stumble and gain my footing and stumble again. There are no stars and no moon, and the only light comes from my window. I gain my footing and run into the dark street beyond the light, my feet telling me holes and roots and loose gravel, treacherous to my ankles. I run to the right down a long incline, gaining speed, lengthening my stride, toward a light at the corner, my breathing hard and shallow.

I am running hard. I want to run harder, but there is the broken surface of the asphalt. I tell potholes and treeroots by the shapes of their shadows, and I run with my eyes on the ground. These houses, gable ends to the street, are closed off, paler masses in the dark lining the street. I know them all—Helen Gonsalves lived there in the gray one in high school, and there in the white, the old man and woman. At the corner, the pool of light. I had a dog who pissed at every bush.

I run into it and then out of it and into the dark again. The branches of the trees almost cut off the sky, wretched openwork. I push my stride and feel the gravel roll beneath my feet. I hardly care. Lift my knees. Lift my knees. No one can see me. No one cares what happens in the street. I lift my arms up and straight out and throw my head back.

There is the mansion the alcoholics have—men with red, runny eyes and shirts too large, smelling of aftershave. I run toward the light at the corner. Where are the boys? The large gray house on the corner? It is now a dancing school. Where, then? In what bed, sleeping, what dreams? Do they know me, running through the town? Why should they notice me—fleet, slender, sinewy runner? I don't look gay.

I am through the light and into the dark again and then I am on State. State runs almost due east, and I see beyond the trees across the valley the stream runs through a faintly lighter sky. I run to the east, toward dawn. A car's lights coming from behind cast my shadow immensely long ahead of me, but I stay in lane and he pulls out and around. I pick up speed, lifting my legs higher, moving just beyond a long lope. The pavement here is repaired every spring after the thaw, so it's smooth. State Street is lined with very large houses—French, Second Empire, Greek Revival, American Gothic. The one on the corner is a dentist's office. The world is withdrawn, hesitant, silent, complicit. I feel strung out, light-headed, giddy, immensely powerful, vengeful, vulnerable, afraid.

The street is lit evenly, lights on both sides and close enough together so there are no pools of light surrounded by dark. You can make time: light and a smooth deserted pavement. Lift my knees. Bernie lived in the big house on the corner. I am at the edge of the long slope down to the river, and as I go over the edge, I feel the momentary exhilaration of weightlessness. I run harder, recklessly, down the hill in a long, controlled fall, and I am aware that I can see beyond the corridor of light into the gray shadows which only a moment ago were black. Jack climbed this hill and waited in the dark for Bernie. It is hard on the legs. I run down into the dark town. The bridge is level and the street beyond it so it's easier. My footfalls echo from the buildings of brick and stone. My bank. The Quoddy Bank. A shop selling Indian things. I uscd to work in that building with the heavy Victorian cornice. I haven't cried since I came home. Where is Timothy? I have a friend who was murdered tonight.

The light is eerie now, directionless, disorienting in the middle of the town. It flattens things out and drains them of color. The ground is level, but a hundred yards away from the river, the hills start. I never came here alone until I was in the Boy Scouts at the Baptist Church. Union Street begins a slow rise toward the Congregational Church. I am the only person in the center of town. Main Street goes up the hill to the Unitarian Church. I am the only person awake. I turn up Union and run a ways and then turn around and run backwards, watching the center of town get farther away. The colors deepen as the light strengthens. The sky above me is drenched with violet, bleaching out to pink and blue. The sun is about to come up. I can hear nothing but the hiss of the river over the dam against the staggered intake of my own breath.

One of the oldest memories I have is of bacon frying. I knew the sound of it and the smell a long time before I knew anything about memory. This morning the heat is oppressive in my kitchen. I have taken off my tanktop, but the sweat runs from my armpits down my sides and stings. Robbie went back to bed after Jack came this morning—he wouldn't go running with me—and he's still there, one leg tangled in the sheet and naked otherwise, on his back, his head thrown back gurgling as he breathes. I kissed him when I came back from running. He snorted and swallowed, but he didn't wake up, and I didn't have the nerve to wake him. I kissed his neck, on his Adam's apple, and it tasted of sweat. I need him but I don't want to wake him.

Jack is on the phone in the living room. I told him he could wait to call people, but he wouldn't listen. I hear him now, telling the same story to everybody we know. He says, "I'm at Mickey's." He says, "I came over here after I found Timothy." He tells everybody, "You can call me here. I'll be here." Most of the time this is my life: Robbie asleep in my bed, somebody—a couple of people—in the living room doing something, me in the kitchen. This morning the smell of bacon makes me think of my mom. Right now I want her to fry the bacon. I'm going to be OK in a minute. Usually, if you give me something to do, I'll be OK.

I'm usually together—I'm about the only person in our crowd with a real job—and I think that's one reason people are here all the time. Most of the people in our crowd are younger than me by five or six years—I'm twenty-six, they tend to be nineteen and twenty—and they're like schools of fish: You blink and they're off in another direction. I'm older, I have a house—an apartment in a house—I have a job and money, I have Robbie. And so they drift here to me and to my place, stay here for a couple of hours or a couple of days—they watch television a lot, dirty movies on the VCR, play games, and talk about their love affairs—and then they're gone. Bernie was one of our crowd.

"Got coffee?" Jack is here, standing in the doorway, leaning against the jamb. I pour him a cup. When he appears without warning like this, he can be overwhelming, he's so big.

"Where's Timothy?" Jack says he doesn't know. "I think we should find him. I don't think he can take care of himself." Jack tells me who he's called and that he's invited people here later. Jack tends to move in on me when he's here, crowding me like he crowds the kitchen. I find it hard to relax around him. I'm always on edge, thinking he's going to do something thoughtless, like back up his car

51

and run over me without seeing me. I tell him I have plans for later. "What's the matter?" he says. Marian is bringing the children. He rubs his shoulder up against the wood. Jack is the best looking man I know but he never heard anybody else in his whole life. "You don't want us here?" When he finally understands, he's too late and you're irritated.

"I need to deal with the children." Jack stares at me as if he does not believe me. "They need quiet. I need to be alone too," I say. "Robbie will leave in a little bit."

"I think we all need to be together." He has set his face against me. "Everybody thinks that. All the gay people."

I would like to be in bed with Robbie, somewhere wherever he is, deep inside that dream of his, but if I can't do that, I say to Jack, "I think I need to get on with the regular things in my life. That's what's going to get me through this." I beat the eggs in the bowl and then pour them into the skillet.

"Want me to get Robbie?"

"I'll get him." This morning after Jack told us, he wouldn't go home. He sat down in the middle of the rug, cross-legged. I was feeling crazy and I needed peace, but Jack wouldn't stop talking about what had happened. He told us about waiting at Bernie's place for him to come home, and when he didn't, he went looking for Timothy. He found him up there on the hill doing tricks. That was when he found out what happened. While Jack was telling this, he pulled his fingers through the rug like claws, making dark marks, and then he smoothed them out with the palm of his hand. He made the claw marks again, and smoothed them out again with his hand. I couldn't take my eyes off what he was doing. But the shattering thing about it was his face and the sound of his voice. He was wet with tears, and his whole story came out between these long, wrenching sobs. I had never seen him cry before, this great macho dude, sitting on my living room floor, sobbing.

"I had a date with him last night." Jack has crossed his arms over his chest, and he stares out through the window through the plants over the sink. "I was beginning to like him. Afterwards, we went down on the river and talked. That was the first time with him. He was real open about being with me. He held my arm when we were walking through town. I told him he ought not to do that, but he did it anyway. I think we were both high. I told him it wasn't safe to be so open about it. He just laughed. I never liked a guy like him before. He was skinny and he wore makeup, and I don't like that. It was real romantic, being with him, him holding my arm and all. He had courage, didn't he?"

He is crying again, and I put my arms around his waist and hug him. I would cry too, I guess, but I kiss him and go and get Robbie and we have breakfast, and it is still only six-thirty. Twenty minutes later we hear a thud against the door. It is the paper and there on page 27 at the bottom, in a tiny article, we read about Bernie and how he drowned and about how he did it all by himself.

I call Marian shortly after eight. Jack is in the bathroom taking a shower, and Robbie is sitting on the back steps in his underwear, leaning back against the steps, his eyes closed, taking the sun. I am alone in the living room for the first time since Jack came. I have waited until now because Lloyd doesn't like being waked up on Sundays. Lloyd doesn't much like it whenever I call, and both of us find it easier if we communicate through Marian. That's hard on her, and I think it's dishonest, but it is the way we do. She says, "Hello?" Her voice is apprehensive at this hour, expecting bad news.

"Marian?"

"Oh, Mickey! You scared me."

"I need to talk. Something has happened."

"Are you OK?"

"—I'm OK. A friend of mine has died—"

"Oh, Mickey!"

"—he drowned. I just found out."

"How terrible!"

"He was attacked and thrown into the Passadumkeag last night."

"Here!"

"He was beaten badly, and then thrown into the stream off the State Street bridge."

"How terrible! That's murder!" Then, before I can answer, she interjects, "Who?" And then, again, "Are you OK?"

"I'm OK. I'm fine." Except that I think I am not fine, that nothing is OK. I am aware of a pause that is lengthening out between the moment we are in and the last thing I said. I suddenly don't know why I have made this call. I begin to talk without knowing where I am going to end: "His name is Bernie. He's a friend. I don't think you know him. He was attacked last night and chased. Into a street. He was terribly beaten. Then he was thrown into the water." I can't keep talking. I fall silent and wait, and I don't quite know what I am waiting for.

"Are you talking about the one in the paper—?"

"Yes—"

"—the naked man?"

"—his name is Bernie."

"What a terrible thing. How odd. Why was he naked!" But before I can answer, she says something else: "Did you know him well?"

I call her every day. Today, at 9:45, she is to bring her children to me while she goes to church. Her husband, Lloyd, doesn't like her to leave them with him on his day off, so I have two hours with the kids alone; and then Marian comes back and we have coffee. One of the reasons I came back home after school was Marian. Did you know him well? However I answer that question, I am going to destroy something. I am angry, but I don't know who I am angry at. I am afraid too.

"I want him to go and he won't, and I don't want you to and you are." Robbie stands on one leg, nude, at the foot of the bed, bent over holding a sock, his raised foot pointed down and about to be inserted into the sock.

"Marian's bringing the kids," he says, not looking up from his foot, now fully into the sock. "You want me to go." He changes feet and picks up the second sock and holds it. There are Greek statues of women in exactly that pose, only without the sock.

"I love them. I love you. I don't want you to go."

He stands fully erect and looks fully at me. "You want me to go so the children can be here."

It is Robbie's way to point out how my desires conflict.

"Where will you go?"

"Mass."

"Your parents?"

"If they saw me, they could see how murderous I am. No. I am going to arrive at exactly 10:00 and sit in the back and pray—that I get 'em."

"Come sit on the bed." As a dancer, Robbie is continuously aware of his beauty and of the ways to present himself. At this moment, he invites me to want him at the same time he pulls himself away.

"Keep your fingers off me. It's Sunday. Bernie died today. I feel like killing. It could have been us last night."

"But it wasn't. He was further out than we are."

"I hate that. I'm thinking of becoming a queen."

"Come here." Robbie stops tying his shoes and slips to his knees on the floor and turns to me, putting his head in my lap.

"Farther out, farther in. He was killed because he was gay. If the police don't do something, then we will have to."

"Look, kid." Robbie has light brown curls all over his head, and I run my fingers through them. "Go to church and pray, and then come back here and we'll spend the afternoon together. We can think of something to do."

"Aren't you going sailing?"

"I want to spend the day in bed with you."

He is quiet. He has settled himself on the floor, his head down in my lap, his arms folded across his skull. "I'm worried about Timothy. Shouldn't we do something? Something about Bernie?"

"What's to do?" I don't know what I want from him. "I want to make love to you."

Jack walks about my living room as if he were waiting for me to tell him he is under arrest. His shoulders are hunched up and his head thrust forward, and he glances at me from the side of his eyes. He is angry, and he works his jaw muscles. I shut the door behind me and hear Robbie's footsteps across the stoop and down the granite and across the yard, fading. I tell Jack he must leave. He stands in the bay window, watching Robbie go, the full sunlight on him.

"Why!" He looks at me head on.

He knows why.

"Go with me."

"I can't."

"I know where they're going to be."

"I don't want to."

"We gotta show them we can fight."

"No we don't."

He turns back to the window. "You just going to sit here? What about Timothy?"

"My niece and nephew are coming."

"You think that's more important?"

"I don't know. I don't want to disappoint them."

"Don't you think it's important to stand up for yourself?"

"I do."

"With girls and kids."

"You're a bully."

"You're a sissy."

We have few words. There's this and then there's that, and we act like those two words divide reality between them. Jack came on to me once. We had gone to the movies and were walking home across the bridge and up the hill, and when we got to my place, he said he needed to piss. I opened the door to let us in, standing aside to let him pass. I had both my arms out, one holding open the main front door and the other pushing open the door to my apartment, and, as he passed me, he suddenly turned on me and slipped his hands on either side of my head, covering my ears, and pulling my head up slightly, he kissed me.

I began to struggle, but his hands were like seatbelts—the instant he felt my resistance, he clamped down on me, and I was immobilized while he kissed me. When he finally pulled away, I hit him.

"What the shit!" He was surprised and angry.

"I am not in love with you, and I don't play games. Remember that."

The little hall was lit by a bare bulb in the ceiling, and when I looked up at Jack, it shone in my face—his own face was in darkness—and I felt blinded by the glare.

"You're acting like you're not gay, like you can just turn away from this and go on with your life." He stares at me, waiting for me to argue with him—with Jack, everything is struggle—but I let it lie, and he gets his coat and leaves. As he walks down the front steps, I tell him he can come back this afternoon if he wants, after the children have left.

I lead three lives. I move here and there among them, shedding thoughts and mannerisms and picking up phrases and gestures, exiting and entering into different plays. The wrench is clearest on Sunday morning. Usually, Robbie and I have been out the night before, and he is asleep in my bed, and I wake and know the children are coming at 9:45. I have to wake him and get him dressed and out the door in time to clean the house of his evidence before Marian blows in the driveway with the kids and I become uncle for a couple of hours. Sometimes I am holding one of the children—Josh, maybe—and I think just an hour ago I held Robbie in my arms just this way, and now I have Josh. Yet the children and Marian don't know about Robbie. And I act as if he did not exist and as if I had not held him in my arms an hour ago. I feel as if all the cells in my body are being exchanged, in an instant.

A horn blows in the street. I go to the front door, and then I push open the screen and step out onto the stoop.

She waves. She opens the door of her car and steps out. I go down and stand within an arm's length of her.

"How are you?" she asks.

I shrug. My sister is slender, like me, and tall too, and her hair is short and shingled. She wears little makeup and only small gold studs are in her ears. She is pert, cute, athletic, outdoorsy, honest. She is lovely in her church clothes.

"Did you know him well?"

I shrug again. I want to talk, but I am suddenly shy.

"Does it hurt?" She puts her hand on my arm. "It must." She stares into my face, her eyes steady and easy. I feel like crying. "I read the paper." Then she says, "There wasn't much there." She pauses again. "I wouldn't have thought you would know him, if you hadn't told me."

I have tears in my eyes.

"Poor Mickey."

Her voice is like a key that opens me to her, and there is nothing I can hold back from her in all this sunlight, if she chooses to solicit it. But she thrusts Sarah, the little one, and the diaper bag in my arms. Josh follows, oblivious. She kisses me, and then she gets back into the car. I usually tell her how good she looks. She likes that from me because, she says, she never gets it from Lloyd. This time I am not thinking. She starts the car, and then Josh notices and turns and waves.

I fix Josh lemonade and settle him in front of the television and put Sarah down in the carbed. Marian is three years older than me. It has always been hard for me to tell whether what she appears to be—she is a lovely, good, person—is what she really is. She is never not what she appears to be, and so I worry. I remember when we were kids. She was upstairs getting dressed for a date and I was downstairs watching TV, and the doorbell rang. There wasn't anyone else to answer, so I went to the door, and just as I opened it, she came down the stairs. And the guy, her date, came in and saw me just as he saw her. She said, "Oh, George," or whatever his name was, "this is my brother, Mickey." It was not the first time I had seen him. I recognized him from school at the same time he recognized me. He was the high school jock—that was the type Marian dated—and I was the high school pansy. And there was Marian making a third side of our triangle, her eyes going from me to him and back. The jock and I knew each other in a way that I doubt even he and Marian knew each other—on the football field where he was the star, all muscles and bruises, and I was the one people hated to have on their side, girlish, pretty, clean. The power of the moment there in the hall before the open front door came from the fact that he was "all" male and I wasn't. It was something men know about each other—how close they measure up to the real thing—and his awareness of it, his triumph and my defeat, was there in his eyes and joined him and me and left her, for an instant, out. When it was over—she was already taking his arm and smiling at him and asking about the movie—I could tell my defeat either didn't signify or she didn't know.

It is difficult to fathom the affection I see in her eyes. Sometimes I have wanted to ask her which it was, but most of the time, I have just wanted to let it be something I shared only with George, buried in the past. The possibility that it was the third alternative, that she knew what passed between George and me that night and had seen me humiliated and had cared, was so painful that I couldn't have continued to be her friend if I had known it to be true.

Bernie liked to have me tell him about Sarah and Josh. He came over one Sunday morning when they were here, and I introduced him to them. The next Sunday he brought me cookies that he had made in his landlord's oven. Sarah was on the floor, playing with some blocks, and Josh sat near her watching the television. Bernie surveyed the scene for a moment, then he sat down too. Sarah eyed him, and he was still while she inspected him up and down. Josh paid no attention to anything that was happening. Sarah's attention was drawn fully to Bernie—she held a block in her hand halfway toward putting it on the castle she was making—and she sat immobile, observing him. Bernie let this happen for the longest time. It went on so long, Sarah staring at Bernie, Josh staring at the television set, Bernie watching Sarah watch him, that I wanted to break the stillness, but her attention was on Bernie, not on me.

Finally, without taking his eyes from Sarah, Bernie picked up a block and held it lightly between his fingers for a moment. He held it up in the line of sight between their heads, lowered his a little, and raised his eyebrows. Sarah glanced at the block, away from Bernie, and then, breaking into a grin, back at his face. The grin seemed to be what he needed, and he placed the block on the castle. She said something—from my distance, it was a cross between a gurgle and a word, unintelligible—and I heard Bernie say something in apparent response, something also unintelligible. Then she said something again, putting a block on the castle. And then he, and then she, and the castle grew taller and larger to the accompaniment of this gurgled conversation. Since the moment when he picked up a block, they ceased to look at each other, absorbed as they were in the building of the castle, the work at hand, and I was absorbed too with their work, and, I discovered, so was Josh, who had ceased to watch TV and had turned to watch his sister and this strange blonde man picking up blocks and gurgling and talking and putting blocks on the castle. Finally, he picked up a block too and, ceasing to look at his sister and Bernie, stood up and went over to the castle and put a block on the topmost point of the tower, carefully, so that it balanced, and when it did, he stood back on his heels and turned to the two of them and grinned. They grinned back.

I am a systems analyst, and Bernie was the only one of my friends to be able to ask the second question, after I had answered the first. He said, "OK, but I want you to tell me what you do when you go to work." Bernie had an odd way of closing his mouth: It was very deliberate and seemed to be the consequence of his having thought about the question of whether or not to close his mouth. When he did close it, the ends came up a little. It was almost a smile, but it wasn't. It was conscious and as if he closed his mouth in anticipation of something. He would tilt his head down a little and then stare at you straight ahead, so his eyes were looking up a little. It was a very challenging look, and it made it seem as if he knew more than he was going to tell you. And when he said, "I want you to tell me what you do when you go to work," I felt threatened and, at the same time, excited. My work is important to me in ways, I think, that nobody suspects.

"I work with computers."

"Yes, but what do you do with computers."

Then he took me by the arm—I was standing at the sink—and led me to the table in the windows and said, "Sit down. I want to hear about it." His attention, when he turned it on me, was so strong that I felt nobody had ever paid attention to me before. Bernie had the ability to make people look at him, even when he was not doing anything in particular, and when you realized he was looking at you, the power of that was enormous.

What I told him was what he expected to hear, I think—something about computers being very orderly things, and I am an orderly person—but I also told him something I think he didn't expect to hear: Having a good job gives me money to have an apartment, which satisfies my mother, in a decent area of town among neighbors who leave me alone and let me live the kind of life I want to lead with Robbie and our crowd.

During the morning, the heat grows oppressive, and the children become cranky. I can't get either of them interested in anything. I try blocks, and I try books. They seem not to want to do anything but tear out the pages or throw things. Josh ends up sobbing on my shoulder, and I can't soothe him, and Sarah turns sullen. The phone rings repeatedly, people in our crowd wanting to talk to me or to Jack—I get the sense they want to talk to anybody who'll listen—about Bernie. Claire calls to say the police do not know who did it, and then to say they do know but are not going to arrest them. People call to ask me if I've heard, and we talk about what we were doing when we found out. I put down the phone and return to the living room rug, where both children are now, and settle myself between them, only to be interrupted by the phone's ringing. Late in the morning Simon Herter calls. He is the pastor of the Unitarian Church where the dances are held and, if there is such a thing here, chaplain to the gay community.

"How are you doing?" he asks me.

"Right now I have two unhappy children on my hands. That's enough for now. For the rest of it, I'll think about it later." I like Simon. You can talk to him when you want, and he doesn't intrude when you don't want, and he's generally supportive. The Unitarian Church has what they call a "special ministry" to gays and lesbians, and I suppose that's nice—he's nice—but I am uncomfortable with being singled out. I prefer to be treated just like everybody else.

"People are feeling the need to do something, Mickey, to memorialize Bernie, something that will help people deal with grief, and I am thinking of a service of some sort tomorrow night at the church. What do you think?"

I am wet with stinging sweat, and the children are crying or fighting on the floor, and I don't really want to deal with Simon Herter. I'd like to do something to express my grief for Bernie—I'd like to burn this fucking town down, for one thing—but I can't imagine people coming out in public and going to a church service for a known homosexual. I know I wouldn't go. I've made too big an effort for too long a time to be straight when I am in public. How many people would be there? Twenty? How many of us were at the dance? Simon says he will get back to me, and I hang up and go back to the children.

When Marian comes back, she doesn't stay. She blows the horn from the street and then comes running in before I can gather the children's things together. She kisses me and makes the sounds that mothers make to their children—"Did you miss Mommie?" "Is baby hot? Mommie'll take you home and give you a cool bath!"— odd sounds that in their tone exclude all other adults. She goes about the room, collecting their toys and diapers, leaving the room a wreck but absolutely cleansed of any sign of the children. I follow her out to the car and watch while she puts things in the back and fastens the children's seatbelts. I want it to be different than it's been. I want to have the morning over again, to concentrate on the children, on

Josh's needs and Sarah's, and my own need to spend a quiet two hours with my niece and nephew. This morning I didn't do anything well. I tell Marian that I thought she would stay for coffee, and she says it is hot and she is tired after church and, besides, Lloyd wants lunch. Before she drives away, she looks up at me through the open window, enormous dark glasses masking her face, and says, "Would you please not say anything to Mother about knowing the naked man? Would you do that for me?" Then she drives away.

So. She heard something at church. This is where it begins, the gradual collapse of my carefully structured life.

I want to throw rocks at something alive. I go back in the house instead and clean up after the children. I mop the kitchen floor—Robbie says I am compulsive about it—and wring the sponge with violent movements. I have a rage for order, and I feel crazy when I can't make it happen.

I like pressed shirts, cut flowers, swimming in a swimming pool. I like novels that have a beginning, middle, and an end, and a church that believes in a heaven and a hell. I like Robbie because his elegance is studied, and I like knowing where I stand with my mother, that I'll call every evening at six and that she'll come to see me Wednesday evenings after work, and with my sister: We're each other's best friends. I like there being rules to play by, the measure of the music, doors to separate rooms. I am not like Bernie, who floated. I have goals. I want a house, I own a car, I want to go to China and see the terra cotta soldiers lined up in their ranks. I don't drift. I know where I am going.

I want a life without seams, at least in my mind. And when Robbie comes and finds me scrubbing out the bottom drawer in the refrigerator, I want to be able to turn to him and say, "It's all of a piece, our lives." I know where Robbie fits into my life, and where Marian and her children, and Bernie, and Mom, even if some of them don't know about the others. All the figures in *The Gates of Hell* belong but not all can see each other. I know where they are for me.

As it is, Robbie stands in the kitchen door and watches me wrestle with the plastic tray for the refrigerator, silently, apparently for some moments before I even know he is there. I look up and see him—he seems irritated, angry—and what I would like to say dies on my lips.

"How is the sister?"

"Terrific," I say, fitting the tray into the slot in the fridge, "she didn't stay. It was hot, and Lloyd wanted lunch, so she got the kids and left."

"Did you enjoy them?"

I think for a moment. "No. It was hot and they were cranky. Then the phone kept ringing. Everything got in the way." I bang trays around. "I think she figured it out."

"What?"

"That I'm gay—" I am finished with the refrigerator. "Would you like lunch?"

I fix us sandwiches, and we eat on the back steps.

"What are you going to do?"

"About what?"

"Marian—"

I think for a moment. "I don't know. What can I do." I survey the wasteland that is our backyard. "There's nothing to be done. Wait for it to happen."

We sit in silence for a while.

"Church was horrible."

"Did you see your parents?"

"They wanted to know why I wouldn't sit with them."

I can't think of anything to say, so we sit in silence, eating our sandwiches and staring out across the weeds of our backyard. Everything here is perennial—weeds and grass and a few flowers left in beds planted by former tenants—and the luxury of its growth will give way in November to a desert of straw. She'll tell Lloyd.

Robbie says he went to Dominic's looking for Timothy. Timothy was in this morning, but nobody knows where he is now. I want to bring Timothy here, when we find him.

"I'd like to stay over too," Robbie says.

"You never stay over during the week. What about your parents?"

"I don't care."

I need to go to the store then this afternoon. I will have a house full—Timothy can sleep on the sofa—and if there is anybody else, I can put them on the floor. We shouldn't let anybody stay out with things as they are.

"My parents wanted to know why I didn't sit with them, and I couldn't tell them. I thought, there's no way these people are going to understand what has just happened."

"You didn't give them a chance."

"No. Cause I know. They'll think it's bad for anybody to get beaten up and thrown off a bridge, but they won't feel it the way I do. Bernie drowns, and their lives go on undisturbed. It doesn't really happen to them." He settles himself on the step, leaning back on his elbows, his chin on his chest, a glow of sweat on his face and arms. "But you know, it happened to me? They beat up Bernie because he was gay, and I'm gay, and so I am a victim here too, and I thought, when I saw my parents coming down the aisle toward me, they haven't been victimized like me. I thought, I'm a victim, and they're a part of all that victimizes me, and I can't talk to them anymore. I came away from church feeling that this enormous crevasse had opened up between me and every straight person."

"It was some boys who did it, not your parents, Robbie." He doesn't answer me, and I don't pursue it, and we let it lie. I feel too battered to. All my careful plans.

He talks about what is going on at Dominic's. Dominic Abruzzizi is an old homosexual man—he's fat and gray and kind of awful—who runs an ice cream parlor/coffee shop downtown where the kids hang out. You wouldn't call it a gay place—there aren't any of those in town—but at least Dominic doesn't run gays out. It's a place to go that's safe, and it's where you can find out what's going on.

"There wasn't anybody there but Dominic, but while I was there, four or five people came in. They stayed a minute and then left, and then somebody else would come in. Cindy came in and stayed a minute and then left. She said she was going to Claire's. Ginnie Santiago didn't even sit down. She walked in, looked around, didn't speak to me, and then walked back out again. Nobody bought anything. They just looked wild, and then they left again. Crazy. It was like all the gay kids in town were on the move, like they couldn't stay still. All this energy! Jack has been there this morning, and Dominic says he is coming back later today. *He's* wild. Dominic says he's dangerous. He's apparently carrying a piece of pipe."

He puts out his hand toward me without turning to look at me. "I don't want to be alone." I take his hand and hold it. "Dominic says the police know who did it, but they're not going to do anything about it, that they're just going to let the cause of death be accidental drowning. On the other hand, he says he's heard that the police have already arrested the boys who did it. Nobody knows."

"Oh, shit." There are so many people involved. "People going crazy a little bit. We know what happened. And the police are going to arrest them—"

"They may not."

"They can't escape this. Too many people know."

"The newspaper didn't report it the way it happened. A lot of people think it's the beginning of a coverup."

"Does everybody know?"

"Everybody who's in town. Jack called half the gay population in town from your apartment this morning before six o'clock. Jeff Fernbach heard it on his police scanner early this morning about the time it happened. I think it must be hard to be gay in this town right now and not know Bernie Mallett is dead."

I tell him about Simon Herter's plans.

"Would you go?"

"No. Of course not."

The phone rings in the kitchen. The voice on the other end says, "Mickey?" as if even after she hears my voice, she's not real sure it is me. "Is this Mickey McNamara?"

"Yes, this is me." And this lady—I can tell she is old—says, "Oh, Mickey, this is Deborah Elkins." Holy shit. What is she calling me about? Right away, before I can saying anything, she goes on, "You may not remember me—"

I interrupt her. "I know you, Mrs. Elkins. From school. American Heritage." I am waiting to hear why my senior American Heritage teacher is calling me eight years later on a Sunday afternoon.

"I read the paper," she says. "I had to call. I read about Bernie Mallett, and I know Timothy Leonard was with him—"

I don't say anything.

"—and I thought I remembered that you knew Timothy."

"Yes ma'am."

"I'm very worried about Timothy. Do you know where he is?" And before I can answer, she asks, "Do you think he is perfectly safe?"

I don't know why this is happening. I haven't spoken to her since graduation, when she gave me the award for the best essay on Changing Interpretations of the Constitution. I never even see her from one year to the next. And why did she think I knew Timothy? She knows too. And of *course* he's not safe.

I want to go to bed, but I don't know what I want to do after that. I would like to make love to Robbie, but I feel like I've stayed up for three nights and have just finished final exams: I'm too tired to make love and too tense to sleep. Robbie is off in his anger somewhere.

Later we go for a walk, and we hear, for the first time, the news bulletin about Bernie. Robbie has brought his walkman along —it's always around his neck—and we're going over the brow of the hill down into town when he suddenly stops walking, his legs apart and his knees bent a little, his arms out at about waist high, his eyes open but his concentration totally inside his head. "They're talking about Bernie!" He listens for few minutes, and then he passes the earphones to me, and I listen, but I don't hear anything but music, and he has to tell me what they said—that they have arrested three boys. Below us, Cardiff slides down the slopes of the hills to where the river and the stream come together. The town is deserted. It is the weekend after the Fourth of July and the River City Festival, and the citizens have not stopped celebrating. They've gone in search of water, any lake or stream or sand beach. And what we are doing is organizing a wake.

I have this weird feeling, hearing about Bernie on the radio and seeing his name in the paper this morning. You never see the names of people you know in the paper. And you never see the names of gay people in the paper except when something terrible has happened, when they've been caught molesting children or something.

Later on I hear the bulletin myself, and then, when we get back to the house, my living room is filled with people staring at the television set, the volume on low, and listening to the stereo tuned to one of the rock stations. There's no place to sit, and I stand against the wall, looking over their heads, staring at the TV. They talk during the music and fall silent during the DJ's patter. The DJ talks of the assault on Bernie and the arrest of the three boys.

Jack is jubilant. "They're going to go after those fuckers now!" He sits in the middle of the sofa, his knees apart, his elbows on his knees, hands holding a bag of popcorn. "They've got to get 'em now!"

What's so disorienting about all this is the angle. Gay people never watch television to find out what is happening to one of us. And we don't read the newspapers to get our news. We tell each other what we want us to know, and the television remains blind and deaf to us. And to hear the name of someone we know on the radio is like coming across a picture of yourself in somebody else's album, somebody you didn't know was interested. You thought you had it all down—these people are your friends and these people don't even know you exist—and now you discover, turning the pages of this album, a picture of yourself, taken from behind, and you have to think it all through all over again.

Robbie and I stay in the living room for a few minutes. We talk about the memorial service at the Unitarian Church tomorrow night and about who would go. Jack says a lot of people are coming over later tonight to watch the ten o'clock news. He says he expects there will be something about the boys then. "Everybody's passing the word about coming here." There must be ten people here, gays and lesbians. I wish we were all beautiful, but we're not. The tears that have been on me all day come up to the surface again. These are the people who've been watching my TV since Christmas and eating my popcorn, my crowd.

Claire—she's short and fat and her hair is cut in a brush which she has spiked up—has her arm around my waist, her head on my shoulder. We hug. She tells me no one has seen Timothy all afternoon. She danced with him last night. She wears blue jeans and a t-shirt and has a wrist band with steel spikes. "Bummer, ain't it? He oughta be here in his dress."

I am exhausted. Later I need to run by my mother's for a moment. I propose to Robbie that we take a nap. He shrugs, but he is apparently willing to go. Just as we're leaving the living room, we hear the six o'clock news bulletin.

It's one thing to be ashamed of being gay—I've been through that—but it's another thing entirely to know that you have been treated wretchedly, that you've been hurt and that people know you've been hurt and are watching you while it's happening. It's like being slapped in public. How do you turn and face the people who saw it happen? Hurt is a private thing. You learn with someone like Marian's George to close your face down and not let it show. If you don't acknowledge it, he can't see what he's done to you. You close your mouth and you walk on until he can't see you anymore. But what do you do if you can't get away from them? What do you do if everybody knows? What do you do if it's on the radio?

Going back to our bedroom, I hear their voices. They talk of the boys and how they have to be punished, what they will be charged with and how long they'll spend in jail.

"They gotta charge 'em with murder!"

The sun is coming in almost horizontally through the window: The opposite wall is all yellow with it, and the rest of the room is in darkness, lit by reflected glory. Jack is in the living room with the others. They talk of going to the store to get food. We lie in bed.

"You going tomorrow night?"

I think for a little bit. "I don't know. It may already be too late. It may not matter."

"I am. I think it matters a lot. Go and stand up with Bernie. That matters to me—"

"If I go, everything is going to be destroyed—" I think of Mother. How could I talk to her so she'd understand? She'll never let me in the house again. My whole accommodation I've made so I could have a good job and a good relationship with Mother and still have Robbie—. I don't know. It may already be destroyed without me doing anything. And it may not be any worse if I go out in public. I can't think now. There are too many big things happening, and it all seems out of my control.

"I'm angry," Robbie says.

"At what?"

Robbie does not think my question stupid. He stares at the ceiling, his hands cradling his head, and makes lists: "The boys. Because they hurt Bernie." He closes his eyes and doesn't say anything for a time. "Their parents. The police. My parents." He pauses, thinking. It is clear that he is not searching for, merely formulating, an answer. "The priest today, who is a fool. The cardinal. The pope. The president." He turns on his side and slides his hands together between his thighs: "The Baptists, and all homophobes everywhere." He smiles and waits for a long moment before speaking again. "Bernie's parents, for throwing him out. Timothy's parents. They threw him out too." The list-making is soothing. The smile on his face gradually relaxes.

"Marian?"

"Of course. And Lloyd."

"I'm angry with Jack."

"He does occupy a lot of space."

It is a moment before I can decide what I want to say. "I'm angry at Bernie too."

"Bernie!" He throws himself away from me and looks back at me across the full width of the bed.

"He was so far out—" But before Robbie can answer—I can feel his anger now directed at me—the phone rings. Robbie answers it and listens and then gives it to me. It is my mother. I feel a chill. Robbie turns on his side, away from me.

"I do so worry about you when you don't go to church. People ask where you are, and I don't know what to say." Her age has made her voice thinner, and she can less control its timbre. It wavers in pitch and sounds querulous even when she's not. But despite its decay, it's her, unmistakably the same woman who held my hand when I crossed State, fearful of the passing cars. "Oh, Mickey, I know you love Marian's children, but I think you should find another time to be with them than Sunday morning." Each thing in its place. I lie here in bed with my hand touching Robbie's bare back, and she doesn't know he exists. Each thing in its separate place. Her complaints against me are familiar as dirt.

"What did you say to Marian this morning? She is upset with you about something, and I do hate it when you two quarrel. You know how much she needs you, with Lloyd and all. She loves you so. And you know how proud I am of you." I listen with all my attention. I have no memories that, taken far enough back, don't begin with her. And when I talk to her, I put out of my mind the parts of my life which she wouldn't understand, or which would hurt her. "What have you been doing today?" she asks. "Did you get outside? It's such a lovely day." Marian hasn't told. I tell her I went sailing with friends. "Oh, that's the right thing. I do so worry about you, living alone. I worry that you don't take care of yourself." I promise to come by for a minute later in the evening. Then we say goodbye. "And do, please, call Marian. I don't know what's bothering her, but you are always so good." And then we hang up. I have never seen a reason to tell my mother I am a homosexual. I don't believe in hurting people. At my work, I never talk about my personal life. I rarely talk about my work with my mother. And my life with Robbie is separate from both my other lives. The trouble with Bernie is that he was careless. You can't be gay and be careless. You can't let anything show.

I kiss Robbie's shoulder—he still has his back to me. I would like to talk. He grunts, and I kiss him again. I want to make love to him, but he doesn't respond, even when I stroke him. I cuddle up against his back and wait, but after a while I feel that he is asleep, and, after a time, I go to sleep too, and I dream of running through dark streets, the gravel rolling under my feet.

This time when I hear the noise, I am awake right away, and I know what it is—the phone ringing in the living room—and I know what's happening when it stops. Jack has answered it and is talking in a low voice—too far away to get the sense of but close enough to almost feel, a low male rumble—and I know I don't need to get up to deal with anything. I slide back down in the bed, under the covers, next to Robbie, and feel his warm smooth skin on my chest and thighs. What could happen has already happened, and I don't need to be afraid.

Then Jack is at the door saying, "For you," and I reach for the phone beside my bed. "Hello?" It is a voice I don't recognize.

"Is this Mickey McNamara?"

"Yes."

"This is Howard Nestingen. I am a reporter from Channel 4 news. I understand you were a friend of Bernard Mallett's."

The fear is on me. "Why do you want to know?"

"We are trying to find out more about what happened last night just before he died. I understand you knew him."

"I don't think I want to answer that."

The other man pauses for a moment. "I can understand that you don't want your name on television, and I am willing not to use your name. It's just that we want to find out something about him and how it was for him here before he died."

How did he find out? "Who gave you my name?"

"I am not free to divulge my sources. Look, you can remain anonymous if you want, but I understand you were at the dance last night at the Unitarian Church and that you knew Mallett. You could be helpful if you wanted."

Even if Marian doesn't tell! "Why are you calling me?"

"I am trying to find someone in the gay community who will talk."

"Look, I don't want to talk to you." It's too late!

"I won't tell anybody you're gay, if that's what's bothering you."

"I didn't ever say I was gay. I think I am going to hang up."

"Oh shit. Why are you people like this! I know you're gay, and I won't say anything on camera that will let your secret out."

"On camera!"

"What was Bernie Mallett like? You can tell me that, can't you, without admitting anything about yourself?"

"You ask a lot."

"Not really very much, I think. What did Bernie Mallett look like? Did he wear earrings?"

I am going to hang up on this guy. I am going to hang right up on this shit.

"Did he wear makeup? He carried a purse, I hear. Was Bernie Mallett what you would call a flamboyant homosexual?"

How did he get my name? How did he find out? Who the fuck told? My mother! Robbie is fully awake, staring at me as if he had never seen me before.

Dana

A ll the way up the lake, tacking back and forth across the wind, I have had my back to where I am going. The sun and the wind come over my shoulder and blow my hair in my face and warm my shoulders and leave the rest of me cold. It is late enough in the afternoon so that at the end of every tack, when I come about, I am momentarily blinded by the sun, which sits so low on the hills that it seems to sit on the surface of the lake, turning everything to fire. Not being able to see, I steer by memory, and my mind makes metaphors of my predicament. Sailing across the lake in my dinghy, going home, I am burdened—my boat lurches in the water under the restless energy of it—by my thought, which never goes slack at the end of a run, and by my education: The freight of literary allusion, broken loose from its moorings, rolls about the bottom of the boat.

My dinghy is an old one. We bought it in the spring from a man who said he was never going sailing any more and therefore had no use for it. There was a chill of death about that. He put an ad in the paper, and the heading was "Useless Boat." Right now, it's all we can afford—we've just moved here—and the boat is here in this lake where it can't go anywhere. We've promised ourselves that it's only our first boat and that soon we'll have one big enough to sleep on, one that's not trapped down here between these hills. If my boat is going to be a metaphor for anything, it is going to have to be able to go somewhere.

For the last hour, I have sailed back and forth across the north end alone in this thirteen foot dinghy. The air has an edge to it that July in the South doesn't have: You know its going to be cool tonight—cool enough to sleep under a flannel sheet, a reminder that you're never very far from winter around here—and Marc won't be tossing and turning in the heat. I tack and come about and lose the wind for a minute—it's the hills, and you never quite know where it's going to be—and then I find it again, and I'm on my way. It's not so much that the wind surprises you here as much as it is that it is sneaky, and you can't ever let your guard down. That, and the sun blinding you every few seconds, is what life is all about.

I'm going almost due south right now on a tack that's going to take me past the opening into the finger of the lake where I'm trying to go. Then I'll come about on my next tack and be deep inside the upper end of the lake. I'll be on shore in forty-five minutes. This is our first boat. And the car is our first car. It's a first for everything: our first house, our first guest bedroom, our first garden. My first job. Our first child. I sometimes wonder if we ever did anything important before we came here. At each stage of my life as I've reached the markers, I've thought now all the preparation is over. *Now* it's going to begin. It's a way I have of denying reality. You can't turn over a new leaf or start fresh or *begin again*. You only go around once, honey. This is all you've got, and you've already begun, and the race is half over, and I'm still combing my hair and wondering how I look. Holy smoke.

It's impossible to escape the sailing metaphor: The way I feel has been coming on me for months and has to do with a sense that I'm headed in the right direction, that I know how to make everything work. The sail is set right and I push against the tiller till I feel it go hard. I'm making all the decisions that affect me. When I'm cutting through the water as fast as a boat like this can be made to go, it's easy to forget how acid rain is turning all the forests yellow between here and the Gaspé Peninsula three months early, and that there won't be a spring next year: dead trees, bloated fish floating upside down down the streams, dying deer. The holocaust will come and it won't matter how close to the wind I can sail: I'll be vaporized like everybody else. *Useless boat indeed.*

Where am I going? North-northeast so I can go east-south-east, go where I can't see, the sun, sitting on the edge of the lake, turning things in its path first black and then burning away their edges and then incinerating them. A pine tree growing up between me and the sun seems to disappear where the sun is. Where am I going? North toward home and, soon, south toward home. That whole end of the lake seems not so much to be burning away as it seems to be in the center of a furnace, too hot, too glaringly bright, to look at. I would rather look at old men dying in their dinghies along the cool, dark green shore than have to look in that direction, yet I have chosen this way to go.

Somewhere there, under all that, Marcia and Marc wait, on the cool shore, playing in the sand. The two of them are the end of at least one of my journeys. He seems to be an achievement which is permanent and which has altered our lives in some absolute way— there's a beginning for you that was unexpected—and that has nothing to do with staying home and doing diapers. We have money at last, which sounds as if it has been one of our goals. The money came with the new house and the new jobs, so to speak, and so we have the ability to maneuver. We have bought a house on the Main Road down the river—there are little towns strung out along the river bank, one row of houses deep, like green peppers on a string—and we have one built in 1870. We stripped and painted Marc's room and have plans for the rest. My mother and father visited and Marcia's mother, and for the first time nobody had to sleep on the sofa. It's the kind of thing that makes you think you've arrived, finally, like our first washer and dryer. Except that you know you only arrive etc. And anyway, arrived where? I can situate us geographically easily enough. I can tell you where I am on this lake, too, if you want to know. We're too much in the middle of things for that to be interesting. I think the question I want to ask is, *How'm I doing?*

I know Marcia is watching me—I watched her when she was out here and I want to ask her, How'd I do on the coming about? How'd I *look*? I see people doing things, sometimes—a boy on a rock watching girls in the water, his elbows across his chest and his wrists up under his chin, shivering and trying to look brave at the same time—and I want to say, "You're doing *fine!*" It's important to recognize how fine people are doing. It's hard to be *fine* in a world where any achievement that does not immediately increase your net worth brings the response, "Big fucking deal!" Especially when you know they could be selling their dinghies and moving to Florida.

Marcia and I have a room of one's own and five hundred a year. In that sense, I'm doing fine, even if I can't see down that end of the lake where I need to go. This inability to see ahead—one steers by knowing where one has been—suggests what I do. Marcia and I spend our days exploring our new state. Part of this is professional—I am looking for the names of women on gravestones—but much of it is sheer pleasure. We pack picnics and drive down country roads looking for old towns and old churches. Marc likes playing in the grass, and the dogs like to run. Marcia takes pictures: black and white camera for pictures of gravestones for my book, and color for snaps of us, of Marc chasing after the dogs. I chase after him, then after the dogs, and sometimes after Marcia. Or perhaps I run away from her, until she catches me and we wrestle in the grass—we two, and then we three, and then all of us, dogs too, rolling over and laughing and barking.

I am approaching the north shore. It's shallow here—ten, twelve feet deep, and enormous boulders which loom up out of the dark, clear water. They look like the houses of trolls. Because of the lay of the land, the wind will die, and I have to come about in an almost dead calm, and if everything works right, I'll be positioned right, with just enough momentum to get out beyond the point and pick up the wind again. I concentrate, think it all through first, then throw the rudder to the other side and change hands on the rope and slip to the other side of the boat—momentarily blinded as I go over—and duck the sail as it comes across, slack. The boat slides forward, the sail gradually fills and I pick up speed. I grin. I know Marcia hasn't taken her eyes off me since I came out here, except to look at Marc. At the end of this tack, I will be close enough to wave and for her to see. If I turned to look, all I would see is the sun.

My father said he was coming back before the end of the summer and teach me how to sail. Thanks, Dad. He should spend his money and rent something bigger that all of us can go on, explore some of the coast—Frenchmen's Bay, Castine. He'll find this dinghy absurdly small. My father likes the process of sailing: hours talking to the man at the boatyard in the spring about the qualities of different kinds of sails, the catalogues of sailing paraphernalia, the complex technology. Sailing with him is a constant trial run of the new equipment, and to the elements of the old equation is added something new: a man and the sea and a boat and *marine design*.

He and mother took us all sailing when we were kids—me, my brothers, our friends—along the Gulf Coast, but I was the youngest and I didn't learn anything about it. All I can remember is having to wear the life jacket and the rope they had tied to me, which was anchored to something on board. My father held the tiller in his hand and looked like J. J. Astor, patrician nose, no flesh under his cheekbones, wispy hair blowing in the wind, confident and stern, gazing at the far horizon, and my brothers, like monkeys, climbing forward, held to the rigging. I was too young to have been there without my mother, but she has disappeared from my memory, washed overboard, or become shrouded in fog. In my mind I move about the cockpit and look in different directions at the scene—it must have been an idyll—but I have no memory of her. I can see her hands passing out sandwiches, but not her.

I am searching for the names of women in the census rolls, as well as on gravestones. I go to Augusta a good bit, too, to read in the archives for the period after the civil war—the seventies is the period I am interested in—old newspapers, church records, the rolls to auxiliaries to the veterans organizations. I like it particularly when I can find a family plot in some graveyard where there is a woman's grave surrounded by men—her husband, her sons, her brothers, her father, perhaps. There is a woman's grave in Mount Hope cemetery in Bangor and surrounding her like the spokes from the hub of a wheel are her sons and their wives. Each of the graves is covered with a slab of marble and around the whole affair is a colonnade, a single circle of columns supporting a lintel with an inscription. The sons all died after the mother and, presumably, arranged this elaborate monument to her, setting themselves, for as much of eternity as one gets in a plot of ground set in this earth, in subordinate positions to her. My father is a prominent lawyer in Texas, but someday I am going to surprise them all and write *Mother's* biography, she of the well-manicured and disembodied hands.

The sun is near the rim of the hills up behind the lake and the cove where Marcia and Marc are is in dark shadow. I won't be able to see into it until the next pass, when I enter the shadow myself. It will turn cold, then. The wind is dying. It's a breeze now, and the boat lies almost level in the water, moving forward slowly. I come in at almost due west, the sun down to my right. We met gradually, aware of each other's presence in meetings of various women's groups, over a period of almost a year. We served together on committees and helped raise defense funds for a woman charged with the murder of her husband. He had come on to her with an oar and had broken her cheekbone, and she got his gun and put a stop to him.

I don't know that we ever dated. It just happened—I suppose I was less comfortable with that than she was—and we realized we were spending all our time together that wasn't spent in the library or in class. She began to assume, and I began to assume, and after a while it was assumed as a fact that we were a couple. It had happened as imperceptibly as the maturing of spring into summer, so slowly and quietly that I had to make sure and had to ask, "Are we a couple?" We were out to dinner in a Tex-Mex restaurant and were talking about the kind of research I wanted to do, and she was saying that when I finished my book, we should do a book together. My question made her laugh, and she said I was silly, and I blushed and that was that. But it wasn't because she said, "I would like to be." And that was when that was that.

When we are in the car going home, we will listen to PBS and *All Things Considered* and then the local news. Later, we will catch the *MacNeil/Lehrer Report*. I see them on the shore. Marcia has Marc in her arms, and they are waving. The breeze is almost gone now and I have barely enough momentum to make it to shore. I am coming in straight now. I wave at them. They call but I can't hear their words. The sky overhead is brilliant blue. The sun is down behind the hill, but it's several hours to sunset, so the blue is still evenly tinted across the sky. The hills behind me have turned golden and are so intensely lit that they reflect their light across the lake into the cove in front of me. Marcia and Marc, lit from behind by the sun and from the front by this reflected light, seem disembodied, detached from the ground they stand on.

I am much aware of images of women: The NOW Convention was in Miami last weekend, and every night on the news there have been clips of Geraldine Ferraro answering reporters' questions without giving them what they are trying to get out of her: Whether she will be the vice presidential running mate of Walter Mondale. We are becoming accustomed to her face, lit in the harsh false light of the television cameras, and to her voice, articulate, sharp, intelligent, and in a way depthless. There is in New Orleans, in the Garden District, a park. Marcia and I were there once. There is a great archway—an entrance to something, a children's zoo or a botanical garden—with a legend of a man's name in very large letters. And under that or beside it in smaller letters is the phrase, "Given by his wife." Antonia Fraser has just published *The Weaker Vessel,* and I have been reading, in a sustained attempt to become accustomed to life this far north of Boston, *Letters of a Woman Homesteader*. It is not too much to say that we homestead here.

The water narrows in the long finger of the lake, and the hills close in on both sides. The sand beach is apparent at the end, and

Dana

Marcia and Marc stand in the odd light of dusk, shadowless. I remember my mother's hand handing me a sandwich, her carefully tended fingers on the white bread, but I can't remember her arm or the rest of her. Given the circumstances of our lives, we don't need to know more about rich and important men whose names are in marble anywhere. But it is necessary to know more about a woman who calls herself *wife*. Marcia and I live on the Main Road along the river, four-and-a-half hours north of Boston and as close to Quebec City. Our friends in New York say we live in isolation. That's true, in ways more paralyzing than geographical. You read the history of this region, and it is as if it were populated by one sex only, the other cast into dark shadow, their lives—what they did with their days and what mattered to them—lost to us because nobody thought to set it down. Virginia Woolf said, "All these infinitely obscure lives remain to be recorded."

I feel the sand crunch under the bow of the boat. She stands twenty feet up on the shore. Marc sits on her hip, his legs spread one in front and one in back, supported by her arm, sitting in the cradle of her hands. One of his arms is around her neck, and the other rests on her arm. She is a small woman, slender, black hair, pale olive skin, high cheekbones, and full lips. Like many Jewish women, her most compelling feature is her eyes, which are large and round, with thick eyelashes. Her beauty seems very urban—the shadows under her eyes suggest she has been up all night—and out of place here among the pine trees and the red-and-black plaid jackets. She stands still, watching me bring the boat up onto the sand, looking uncharacteristically somber and thoughtful. Around her head her hair seems struck with diamonds: It is the reflected light, shining off the metal headpiece of her earphones. She has been listening to her Walkman.

Channing

The last flight up Sunday night is at 8:55 and arrives at a little before ten, and that means I can make the tea dance at Chaps at five and, with a little luck, pick up something right away, fuck for two hours, jump a cab for Logan at 8:15, and be home in time to stop off here on the hill on the way home from the airport for a quick blow to kind of round off the weekend, so to speak. Then I'll be in bed by one and up at seven, ready for the week. I have the girls go light on the scheduling for Monday morning in case things get heavy the night before, but usually I find all this makes for an easy weekend. Of course, you have to be in good shape. And there's safe sex.

I can go out to dinner with friends here in town Friday night —society here is straight and married and the conversation is about children, so dinner parties break up early—and make the last flight down to Boston in time to check into my hotel and still make the Ramrod thirty-five minutes before closing, easily time enough to pick up something to start the weekend off right.

All in all, I have a good life. I still have most of my hair, a tan, which I cultivate, a good body, which I also cultivate, a position halfway up the ladder at the Medical Center and a decent shot at the chairmanship of my department, a lucrative practice, respect from my colleagues, some friends. I also have a weekend or two in Boston every month, fucking my brains out. And what is the most fun of all is that I can sit in the plane waiting for takeoff next to this real hunky number in the center seat, and he doesn't have any idea that the quiet-spoken, polite, authoritative physician he's sitting next to has only one thought in his head. Breeders are such dipshits.

In the shadows over there beyond the streetlight, I think there's somebody. I think he's been standing in the doorway of that building, and he probably doesn't know he can't be seen. This is what I like: the hunt. He's moving. He's coming out into the light. He's slender, small. He's a kid. He's a beautiful kid. He's got a nice ass. I walk up the hill across the street from him. Slowly. Slowly. Let him get a good look at me. I'm something to look at. There could be a cop watching too.

I look over my shoulder at the kid. He's watching. I walk on. I hear him follow. I get in my car and lean across to open the door.

He slides in. There's always the possibility that what slides in is something that says, *You're under arrest.*

"Timothy?"

"Is that you?" He looks scared as hell.

"It's me." I put my hand on his thigh. Nice thigh. He's jumpy. He doesn't know that the danger is what you're going for. Danger you'll get knifed, arrested, humiliated in city court, publicly exposed as a degenerate on the front pages of the newspaper, or merely get the clap or, now, from the people who brought you genital herpes, AIDS! and die the most horrible death currently known to man. And all for a moment's oblivion.

"I wish you'd tell me your name."

"You don't need to know my name." I start the car and pull out into the traffic lane. I stroke his thigh. He'll come home with me. I've had this one before.

"The worst thing has happened," he says.

Derek

The water would have been cold, even now, in July. In these rivers, it comes down fast from the mountains where there is still snow, and the shock would have taken his breath away. You lose feeling in your toes when you swim in these rivers, and you're aware of your heart beating. When it is dark, on top of being cold, it is disorienting: You can't see which way is up and everything that ought to help you find yourself—the feel of the water through your fingers, the pressure against your legs as you kick—gets blotted out by the single, sharp, sense of the cold which comes at you from every direction and you feel in every part of your body. It is like *white*: It is a loss of every other feeling—but panic and fear. I was thrown in once—friends did it and I know how to swim—but even so, I thought I was going to drown. It was on a camping trip in Baxter ten years ago.

And I'm a big guy. Imagine what Bernie must have been feeling. Bernie is here on the front page of the paper—page one, above the fold—and he would have hated this picture of him. It must have been taken when he was in the eighth grade. Does anybody look good at fourteen? Teeth and eyes much bigger than your head, and a head too big for his neck. Nothing in scale. He looks a mess. Where did they get it? To a guy playing to an audience as much as Bernie did, this picture would be devastating. He'd never get an audition on this one.

I sit on my back stoop, the paper in one hand, my chin in the other, feeling the sun come up and things already beginning to get warm, out of synch with everything. Bernie was just a soft kid. He was nine years younger than me. I hike in the woods around here, and he talked about going with me, but being in the woods wasn't his thing. When we talked, the things he was concerned about were boys' things: How do I look? How can I get him to love me? Am I good? Am I beautiful? They occupied all of his mind and his feelings. It was easy, with him, to think of the things he hadn't thought of: age, ugliness, monotony, work, failure. He was a kid, and he hadn't learned to make himself happy. He talked about his parents and his boyfriends and his discovery that there is not enough love. He would have learned there's not enough of anything: warmth, pleasure, beauty—though, God knows, the world is a beautiful place this morning. He would have learned that the question is, Am I beautiful enough? He died before he had a chance to prepare himself for the harsh sensations he died from, cold and fear, which he had too much of.

I was up until three with a boy, who is still in my bed asleep. I'm exhausted, but I can't sleep—I sink into it and then wake up, clawing the sheets—and when I heard the paper hit the screen door, I took it as a sign that it was OK to get up, that life is going to go on along this curve despite current rumor. It's not even seven yet, and at eleven I have to do an exercise in a class for a friend in the drama department at the U, and nothing until then. Sebastian sleeps with his arms around both my pillows. I think I'll go put both my arms around Sebastian.

I'm an actor. I'm five eleven, Italian, curly dark brown hair, hairy, swarthy, Roman nose. My features are not refined, and there is nothing about me that is delicate, except my ego, so I can play Stanley still in my street clothes. I can play good men, solid men, *men's* men, but not men that are too sensitive or intellectual. Smart, yes: brainy, no. I am handsome in a working-class kind of way. You can trust me. I play hard to an audience, and I saw that in Bernie. He played hard to an audience, too, but the applause he got didn't sustain him. I think he expected to hear, at some point, his mother or father or, even worse, the kids who killed him, cheering his performance. People are already saying he didn't care what anybody thought, but I think that's bullshit. That chin-up-I-don't-care-what-you-think-of-me-Charlotte was only attitude, not real. What he wanted was to be loved. And he loved the clapping.

I go back into the house—I sublet the ground floor for these summers when I am here doing summer stock—and walk through the kitchen to the bedroom at the back: other people's furniture, patterned wallpaper. I don't have the motivation to fix up somebody else's house. The picture of Bernie shows how far he came. He sat on my bed on his left hip, his left leg folded up under him, his right leg on the floor. This put him in a position facing me. I sat at the head of the bed, leaning back against the headboard, my legs crossed lotus-fashion. He talked as if he were trying out a theory on me.

"I've been tinting it since I was sixteen. I did it the first time in the summer, and no one noticed because of the sun, and then I kept on doing it right on into the winter when my hair gets dark. In February you couldn't ignore it—this brilliant sun-bleached hair when no one had seen the sun in six months—and people began to stare on the street. They stepped back as I passed, and I liked that. I wanted to be brilliant. I want it to be something I had done myself. Like, I wanted to be able to say, this is something *I* created. Do you know? I didn't just want to look into the mirror and say, gee, you're pretty. I never wanted to be natural. I never could see the point in that. I wanted to take whatever was given me and turn it into something stunning. I wanted to be able to say, look what *I* can do. Watch *this*! And honey," here he put his hand on my arm and leaned toward me slightly, "I've come a long way. Let me tell you, it's a long way from Rockbridge, Vermont. Farther even than you'd imagine."

The small bedroom with its too-small windows is on the eastern end of the house and heats up from the sun without the benefit of any ventilation. The bed occupies most of the room, and Sebastian occupies most of the bed. He lies on his side, his back to me, his spine inviting my finger to trace its long, beautiful, damp curve. I need to go back to bed and sleep. I'll be a wreck later today if I don't. But I'm too hyper to sleep. Just inside Bernie's eyelashes was a fine brown line and just outside the lashes was a smudge of pale gold. He was not beautiful yet—he still had baby fat, and his bone structure didn't show—but in five years he would have been stunning. Bernie led a hard life—imagine what it took to stay alive with no skills to sell!—and I think his beauty would have decayed before it ever had the chance to reach perfection. I like the thought of that. He would have had character. He deserved that.

As Bernie would talk, he would put out his right hand to emphasize a word or a pause, touching my forearm with the tips of his fingers. It was a delicate gesture—the touch was as light as a hair—but insistent. He demanded my attention: "I want to be something special. I could *never* be a member of the chorus line. I *have* to be the star. If I'm doing something—maybe cutting my hair a certain way—and I begin to notice that other people are doing it, I stop. I am a unique individual, and why should I want to dress and act so people can think I am like everybody else?"

Bernie was the kind of boy you wanted to wrap up in your arms and take away to the bedroom and fuck his brains out. That is, he was the kind of boy you wanted to do it to. But I'll have to admit that I had this powerful need to envelop him, to say, "I'll protect you," though what I was protecting him from, aside from me, was unclear. Holding him in my arms, I kept him from getting away from me, and at the same time I made both of us think I was protecting him from some danger. In that way my relationship with Bernie was closer to things I've had with women than those I've had with other men. The difference in physical sizes—I weigh 190 pounds and he couldn't weigh more than 130—meant that a huge factor in whatever fantasy we were playing out in our heads was power.

I like that. I work out, and I'm big enough to fill the fantasies that Bernie had, along with my own—a drama which I have not yet reached the end of. Any relationship in which a man is one of the partners is founded in some way on a question of power: Who's got it? What's he going to do with it? Bernie gave in to me—I don't think that was hard for him to do—but there are times when I feel my own powerlessness. I enjoy the competition with another man—who's bigger, who's faster—and while there's something terrific about defeating him, there's also something exhilarating about struggling hard until you sweat and then letting yourself be defeated.

One of the interesting things about lifting weights is the testing of limits: *How much can I lift?* is not merely a static question of manpower—x strength in my muscles equals y weight lifted—but is psychological and even moral. The answer changes from moment to moment. The line which delimits what you can lift is also the line delimiting what you can't lift: *You can't go beyond this weight*. What you can do is known and done. What you can't do is *terra incognita*. That's a great drama. I know what it feels like to have strength sufficient to the task: 330 pounds in a bench press, say, or—in a different kind of thing—coming out to my Dad when I'm the only son and he has worshiped every fucking thing I've ever done. What does it feel like to have moved beyond your abilities into that territory where your strength is insufficient to the job at hand? Where you are, relative to the demands made upon you, *weak*? I could do what I'd like to do—envelop Bernie in my arms and carry him away to bed to get fucked. I know how *strong* feels. But how does *weak* feel? I felt his fingers, light as a hair on the muscles of my forearm, and I knew that what he demanded, my attention, I was powerless to withhold. Why were these boys so afraid of Bernie? What was it about his image as he went about town during the last two months, fey and defenseless, which was so powerful to them that they got out of their car and chased it down three streets to the bridge and, in a frenzy of fear of it, threw it in the water to get rid of it?

I think continuously of Bernie's hair. Did it float out in the water like Ophelia's? I am obsessed with the image: Bernie naked under the cold water, his hair floating out from his head, tumbling slowly along the bottom of the stream, carried along by the current in a reverie. Proust speaks of men's hair splayed out on a pillow giving away secrets. Sebastian's eyelids are slightly open and his hair, which is very long, radiates out from his head, the curls covering the pillow like the tendrils from a vine. He is lying on his back, his face toward me, one knee pulled up and over the other, his hands on the sheets. I lie on my side facing him. He is exposed in that posture and sleeps like the only lord in the jungle. I slide my fingers under his balls and hold them. They are firm and his cock grows stiff and warm. For a long time we lie still, until finally he opens his eyes behind his veil of hair and looks at me.

The paper says the boys are to be arraigned today and the service is tonight. In between times I have a class to teach—*Richard II*. The kids will all want to play him as a victim—and a three-hour rehearsal this afternoon. I must call Simon Herter. He will need help and moral support. The service tonight will bring all sorts of kooks out of the woodwork. I must get up. I won't get up yet. Sebastian sleeps, the sheet on the floor, his arms and legs stretched to the corners of the bed. It is a noble posture and suggests an attitude: *Nothing dares touch me*. As it happens, I will kiss him and then I will get dressed and leave him here to get his rest. I will leave a note before I leave, but I will not get up yet.

"I've been gay forever. There never was a time when I didn't know that. It was like knowing I was a boy—by the time I realized there was a choice, I knew already that I had chosen. I'm queer, and I never ever denied it, honey. I am what I am, and I knew that from when I was a little itty bitty baby. Everybody around me has always known, sometimes even when they didn't want to. Look, I knew right off it wasn't going to earn me any credits anywhere, but it was what I had, and I knew there wasn't any point in trying to change, so I thought I'm going to take this thing and make it fly. And I did."

I lay on my back, my hands under my head, and Bernie lay on his stomach, his head on my chest, his finger making slow circles through the hair. "I never have had any money, and if you measure me that way, I'm a failure. Gay boys who come out when they are thirteen like I did become waiters and hairdressers, not doctors and lawyers. They run away from home—or their parents run them off—and go to the big city to seek fame and fortune. And *sex*! I didn't meet my first man until I was in Boston—I mean the first man who wasn't a kid. Since then I've been too busy keeping alive to think about getting myself a place in the world. And I tell you, just staying alive has been something to write home about. You know what it's like: You're always dealing with a strut of fourteen-year-old boys in a locker room."

His fingers circled my nipples and teased them until they tightened up and the sensitivity radiated out across my pectorals. At some point, Bernie stopped hearing the boys in the locker room, the static of homophobia. The electrical crackle of other people's hate, because it was a constant, had stopped demanding his attention, and his inner ear had turned inward. When I knew him, he was kicking loose of the real world trying to float above us, defying gravity.

He dreamed that a man would take him away from all this. He saw himself as Linda Darnell in a Western, where Randolph Scott on a galloping horse, one hand on the pommel, leans down and gathers her to him, scooping her up into his strong arms, the horse not losing a stride as it leaves the little town at the other end, the closing credits not beginning to scroll over the screen until we have had a chance to see Linda's face, tear-stained but happy, looking up adoringly into Randolph's firm, satisfied visage. These movies he had never seen on a big screen. My own images were more literary. I saw him as a nude Ganymede, idealized shepherd, son of the King of Troy, lifted from the slopes of Mount Ida by an eagle, which was me in disguise, trailing his smooth flank and rosy buns: clouds of glory.

I tried to raise myself up on my elbows. Bernie smiled and his fingers, which had toyed with my nipples, straightened out and pushed against my chest, pressing me down onto my bed. He wouldn't let me move. "Not," he said, "until I have had my way with you." He had his way. Bernie was slender, and when you hugged him, there wasn't a lot there. You felt stiff bone, and he didn't melt into you the way heavier men can. It may be that he didn't know how to melt into you. I think that was what made me want to rape him. I think his life has been like an alley cat's in an alley filled with dogs.

I felt his lips on my tits. I've had it easy. I am thirty-three years old, and I am playing Orsino this summer. The boy asleep in my bed is "Sebastian." And the only thing wrong with my life right now is that, at the end, I have to kiss Viola and not Sebastian. That's the way the script is written. Someday, when I have a company of my own, I am going to rearrange things. Sebastian is going to enter, and Olivia is going to see what has happened: She is in love with Viola, not Cesario. This will leave Orsino free to discover that he is in love with Cesario, not Olivia or Viola, and that, since Cesario does not exist, he will take the proximate thing and settle for Sebastian. Only Antonio will be bereft. And with a few lines anyone can write, we can give Antonio a choice of Feste or Fabian or Viola's Sea Captain.

My parents came to see *Twelfth Night* when it opened. They drove up from New York, caught the opening Friday night and then went on to the coast for the rest of the weekend. They were in the third row, and I played to them. When I had my big scenes in the first half of the play, I could hear mother laughing at my character and his pompous, stupid, male vanity. My father doesn't laugh out loud—he thinks and appreciates—but he applauds loudly. Afterwards they came backstage and met everyone, including Sebastian, whom they took right into their affections. There was a cast party later to which they came and then still later Sebastian and I and Mother and Dad went to a bar for a drink—gossip about the director, baby pictures of me, Sebastian's nephews, laughter about Cardiff—before they went back to the motel for bed.

Sebastian is this year's beauty. Last year it was Hal, and the year before, it was Ferdinand. Before that it was Octavius. There is always someone, and when the play closes or the season ends, the "someone" fades away and suffers a sea change into "someone else." Sometimes the end of things is long-looked for, and other times I see it coming with dread. But I have given up thinking that if I were better or the world kinder, these things would last longer. Durability is good in marble, but not necessarily terrific in romantic relationships. There is no reason to believe that prolonging these things would make them finer. They are temporary, but they are not provisional, and they have the place in my life that plays have in the repertory. What endures for me is my relationship with my parents, and with some half-a-dozen friends. My parents are unfailingly attentive to this year's beauty—Mother says they are all reflections of me—and never mention last year's. When I introduced Sebastian to her, she took both his hands and looked him directly in the eye and said, "You are just what I thought you'd be," which made him wriggle and gave her the opportunity to wink at me. When I go to visit them, I always go alone.

I called them yesterday when I heard about Bernie. "Would it be helpful if I were there with you?" my dad asked. It would help but it's a long way, and I told him not to come. I spent the afternoon with Sebastian, curled up in his arms. He is turned away from me now, and I lie behind him, my body fitted to the shape of his, my arms around him.

I don't suspect, as Bernie did, that I am incomplete. I know I am beautiful enough, and the applause I have heard has been sustaining. I am strong and I really don't know how weak feels. Bernie lived closer to the edge than I ever have. He gave more of himself away, kept less back, surrendered to the necessity of things more completely than I have ever been able to do. Or had to do. He has been hungrier than I. Even his fantasies soared.

I struggle against sleep. I must get up. I have a class to teach at 11:00 and rehearsals this afternoon. He now lies across my bed like a Descent from the Cross. I draw my finger up the inside of his right leg, up across his calf and his knee and his thigh, almost to his scrotum. He bends his knee. I draw my finger up his left leg. I want to reach him inside his dream without waking him. He moves to touch my hand, hesitates, and then he relaxes again and his hand falls away to the sheet. He swallows and his mouth falls partly open again.

I am on my left elbow. I reach across him and take his cock and lay it on his abdomen so that the underside is exposed. I lean across him and kiss the little part at the front of the scrotum usually hidden by the cock. He pulls up his knees, his whole body gathers together. After a moment, he relaxes again down into the sheet.

I lower my head onto his shoulder. I am on my side, and I put my right arm across his chest and feel his slow breathing. From this perspective, his body is a nude landscape, a desert of pale golden dunes. I fall backward toward sleep, toward the image of a white body tumbling through the dark icy water, arms and legs following the roll of the torso with a wild grace, mouth and eyes partly open, veiled by voluptuous hair.

Had I been there, I could have saved him. The boys would have been nothing to me; they would have scattered like dogs before a man wielding a stick. I could have dived into the cold dark water and found him, felt the wisp of his hair across my fingers in the dark water, closed on him, and stopped his slow dance. I struggle to pull him to the surface. The frigid water paralyzes me. He is heavier than I imagined. He weighs so much. It takes all the strength I have.

I hear a voice.

"Derek."

It comes from far away.

"Derek."

He is stroking my hair and holding me.

"Derek, wake up."

Luke

I was astonished to find it on the front page of the newspaper. Normally to get on the front page in Cardiff, gays have to molest little boys. They didn't qualify "homosexual" with "alleged" or "self-admitted" either, or any of the other ways the culture uses the language to make being gay sound like a crime. I thought, we're out in the open on this one, and as angry as I have been since yesterday when Deborah called about Mallett's drowning, I felt a thrill of gratitude to the *Sentinel* for telling the truth about a gay man, for once.

That was how I felt at first. When I read it through the second time, I wondered, Why should I feel grateful to them for doing what they should be expected to do in any case? They said that a gay man was murdered in an unprovoked attack by three hooligans, and there is nothing there for me to be grateful to them for, it being merely the truth. And the proper emotion was surprise that they tell the truth now when they've lied about us so consistently in the past. It was here, in the contrast between today's paper and the paper's past treatment of homosexuals, that I got at something more fascinating. I presumed the paper remained as homophobic as it had ever been, but the editors had other principles, under the rubric of *reverence for the truth*.

Somewhere back of the lines of this unremarkable treatment of the story of Mallett's death is the paper's history, which, like a crime of passion, can't be undone now on this July morning. And reading the article again, I wondered what the reporter and the editors, "decent" men all, must have felt when their decency collided with their own demonstrated homophobia. It seemed as if I had stumbled on an unexpected drama which they were unwilling or even unable to hide from the public. As I thought about it, the article became more brazen and took on the tone of a eulogy of the dead spoken by the murderer. It was an act of stunning arrogance which could be saved only by a concurrent act of contrition. And that act was nowhere to be seen. I wondered how long they could get away with it.

This state is like the body of a swimmer: Everything shows. You're never more than a shallow scratch in the earth away from bedrock. There's no fat here, and so if you like things head on, the bones, the joints, the muscle, the sinews holding it all together—if you're a toucher—then this is the place to be. There's nothing pretty about all this. It's not Virginia, which has a fat, pastoral beauty about the landscape, and it's not Wyoming, where the scale throws everything off and you can't see what you're looking at. Confusion is the only thing you can feel. But here you can see it all, if you can stand to look at a body from which all the skin has been removed.

I'm standing in front of the p.o. boxes, sorting through the things that came in over the weekend—bills, fliers, business and personal letters—and hearing over the chatter of the typewriters, the voices of the other townspeople.

"I don't think the kid was gay," one says.

"Why not?"

"A gay boy wouldn't have drowned."

And, to the inevitable question:

"Fairies have wings." Laughter.

I don't turn around. I know the voices and don't need my eyes to tell me who is talking. I shuffle envelopes, concentrating on the paper in my hands. They know me too. They talk about the boys who have been arrested and who will be charged this morning. I turn around and look in the direction of the voices. They're gone. I go out the door and down the steps to the street. That's what I mean. This place is a kind of zoo where you can enjoy the animals up close, and that can be educational, if you stay away from the cages and avoid getting your eyes clawed out.

The court house is up the street from the post office, higher up on the hill, a ponderous gray stone neoclassic building. Cardiff is so small that news out of the court house takes up a disproportionately large amount of space in the paper and, I think, in gossip. It is difficult here or elsewhere to avoid the crimes that men do. At 9:30 this morning, the boys will be arraigned. On days when I am not doing anything else, I like to lie in my backyard in a chaise and think. If I were there today, I would like to be thinking about this: How long can this town continue to think of itself as decent, given the fact of what's about to happen to it?

I once had a lover. I know what that's all about. And I know what it's like afterwards, too, when you want to tear down every memory of the past and create a desert. Down there where the River City Festival was held last week, the town fathers in the fifties tore down every building along the stream where it runs into the river, a Romanesque stone railroad station on the river banks and three acres of red brick lumber mills, in a fit against the glory days. The whole center of town turned into a parking lot whose concrete expanse runs right up to the foot of the four-story Victorian brick office blocks. Deborah says it looks like the stretched and shiny skin of a scar from a burn.

I am retired, so I fill up my days with busyness. I do work around the church, and there's the garden club in good weather. I have my group, all old men who've found each other over the years. We have supper together and watch the video. Video is a boon to homosexual men of a certain age in the hinterlands: It satisfies a need to hear Bette Davis say, "Don't let's ask for the moon, we have the stars!" My friends are Arthur and Deborah. It's a thin way to live, and my interests and activities have narrowed to a point. Churchill said *old age is a wreck*. I don't have the energy to try and lift myself out of the sink I am in, and I feel no desire to escape calamity. I spend my life now in the orchestra stalls, watching the drama unfold on stage.

I spend Mondays and Thursdays at the historical society, keeping the door, so to speak, somebody to answer questions from tourists and take up money. We have the oldest house in town, and over the last twenty years we've been collecting things from the eighteen hundreds, back when this area was first being settled. We're making a museum. There are things to be preserved from our past. Besides the artifacts of lumbering and a certain number of old clothes, we've saved some furniture brought here by people who struck it rich when this was a boomtown. Thoreau came through here, and we have an exhibit in a glass cabinet connecting him with the river and the North Woods. I do this but I have no faith that what we save is what should be saved.

The tourist literature and the cases here in the historical society say we were at the center of a great lumbering industry that served the world. And there are going to be people to say this has happened because we're a rough town on the edge of the woods, that this is the last unraveling fringe of civilization. But whatever there was of the frontier spirit died by the first world war, leaving only a colossal statue of a lumberjack down on the river facing east, and the tone of life here—wound tight between violence and repression—is not unique. Flaubert would call us now a provincial banking and marketing center. It's an ordinary small American town with its K-Mart and its parking lot downtown. People move here now to get away from the stress of the cities of the northeast corridor: clean air, slower pace, family-oriented life. We're the biggest thing between the Kennebeck and the St. Lawrence, and we have the oldest symphony orchestra in the country. We are the last stop in the northeast for the airlines. There aren't many places in America that are good for homosexuals, but this is worse than most. Every time you come back up here on a plane, you understand you can't go farther away than this on a major airline; and you face a civic schizophrenia divided between the symphony and the lumberjack, and the astringent truth that you don't know what's honored here.

I unlock the front door and open the windows and let the air in. It's nine o'clock and the historical society is open for business. Now I wait. I will stay here until noon, answering the phone—not real business, just my friends—and then around eleven a tourist or two will show up. I don't know what they come looking for. Arthur will call, and probably Deborah. In the summer, the tourists come to be close to the water and what the water offers: sailing, sun, cool nights, lobster. One kind of tourist comes up here looking for antiques. They think they are going to find a bargain. Old furniture. It is impossible to tell what of the past can be recovered by owning old chairs. I hear someone walking across the porch.

Deborah comes in. She has a tense and fearful look, already beginning to talk when she clears the door. "You know there's to be a service tonight." She looks at me as if she's checking how much I've been drinking, then she drops her bag on the table and drops herself into the chair we keep there just for people like her, who are too tired to stand up while I'm giving them directions to the Ainsley Mansion. "I can't think that's a good idea." Her brow is always wrinkled and shows perpetual worry. I think it's a professional characteristic of high school teachers, like superclean fingernails are for dentists. "If nobody comes, we'll all feel so bad, and if there are many of us, it can't help but look provocative." Her eyes are gray, and at some moments Deborah Elkins reminds me of Katherine Hepburn in a movie like *Suddenly, Last Summer*, her eyes focused on a piece of furniture, which, you realize, is a thousand miles away. "Oh, Luke," she says, "I am so angry, I could spit nails."

"Are you going?"

She looks puzzled. "Where?"

"The service tonight, at the church."

"Of course. Where else would I go tonight?"

"It's going to be provocative just to be there."

"I don't care." Her feet are together, and her back does not touch her chair. Her hands are entwined on her lap. She perceptibly lifts her chin. "I am sick of this. I think I am too old to care."

There is a clause in the contracts of all teachers in this state that requires that they be "of good moral character." No teacher accused of being a lesbian has ever successfully held onto her job, it being held in court that being a lesbian and being "of good moral character" are mutually exclusive categories. Had I been writing the Act that governs these things, I would have let their morals go and require that they be of *sound mind*.

"No. I think of Betsy and what our lives might have been like had things been different. I have had enough of hiding."

"You've done a lot of coming out my dear, recently."

Her glance at me is immediate and suspicious.

"Your speech, dear heart."

She smiles and lifts her chin.

"They say the dead kid and his boyfriend were walking along the bridge together. Holding hands. Pretty picture."

"That's not so." She is indignant. "Timothy and Bernie were not boyfriends. They were friends. Of course, maybe they were—" She looks at me and then through me. "—holding hands. Do you know Betsy and I lived together six years and walked across that bridge together at least twice a week, and we never in six years held hands while we were crossing from one side to the other?"

I am tired of this. Most of the complaints homosexuals have about their lot are trivial: People won't like us if we hold hands on the street, wear dresses or men's suits, or whatever our tastes run to—use whips, have indiscriminate sex, get married, have our significant others inherit the leases on our apartments, wank off without fearing hair is going to grow in our palms.

Most homosexuals, particularly the men, for some reason, seem themselves to be trivial people—maybe it's that they trivialize themselves because they don't have children—interested in clothes, antiques, opera, movie queens. We have made a fetish of style over substance. We point out the injustice of not being able to hold hands in public with a man we hardly know and whose face we won't recognize tomorrow in the sun, as if being able to hold hands in public made us serious people. We have perfected our ability to play the victim.

"I feel awful right now, Luke. What are we to do?"

"I don't know. I don't know of anything I can do."

"We must begin by going to the church tonight." She picks up her bag and sets it in her lap and then roots around in it for something. "We have to show that we're here."

What we have not known is how to make the trivial facts of our lives have some high political significance.

"Will you be there?" She looks at me with her soft gray eyes gone all watery with age, the same look she might have if she were watching a person sleeping in a hospital bed. Deborah has earned her reputation for being difficult. Some people find her a little dippy. She leaves after a few more minutes: "I am going to the arraignment," she says and I am alone again at my table in the hall of the house that belongs to the Historical Association, surrounded by what's left of the nineteenth century.

Thoreau once wrote a poem to a boy. I didn't know that until two years ago, when I read a new book. For years the poem was suppressed, and then the gender of the pronouns was changed. His name was Edmund Sewall, and he visited Thoreau in 1839. Thoreau said, "I might have loved him, had I loved him less." Edmund was eleven years old at the time and Thoreau was twenty-two. I keep a book with that poem in it—the poem is called "Sympathy," and its first line is, "Lately, alas, I knew a gentle boy"—in the top shelf of the glass case with a copy of *The Maine Woods* and his other works. Nobody asks to see his poetry. Only one person in my memory has ever asked to see the copy of *The Maine Woods*, and here we are in the middle of them.

Deborah is not sure they were holding hands. She is not sure of me. I have held hands with a man in a public place. I was young, on my first trip to Europe, and he and I walked through the garden entrance of a palace in Vienna into a great urban garden. The architecture of the lobby and stairs just inside the door and the design of the landscape just outside the door, the sense one had of going into greater and greater enclosed spaces, each larger and more carefully arranged than the last, was inspiriting, and I laughed. I reached out and took his hand, and for a moment there on the terrace outside the great doors, facing the garden which fell away to wonderful huge baroque fountains composed of tritons and dolphins and an immense Neptune, Vienna all around us, we held hands and laughed.

I had met him that morning at the gate leading to the Great North Entrance of the Schonbrunn Palace. The war had been over since spring, and I was still in uniform—everyone was still in uniform—and was trying to read a prewar guidebook in German when he appeared and offered to help. He led me around, happy, apparently, to use his English, to be with an American, to show off his city. During the war I had not laughed, and now I felt, in the middle of summer, as if spring had come for me, the end of war. Everything seemed new, and I fell in love with him, in the Belvedere Gardens.

Then we separated and walked down the terrace steps divided by a few feet, of which we were intensely aware, as we were aware of the other tourists entering and leaving the palace. Part of the intensity of the moment came from the unfamiliar feel of his hand, but part of it also came from the sense of danger, of having exposed ourselves in a public place, and therefore from a sense of the extremely brief life of physical intimacy.

At some point in the afternoon, the Austrian boy stood up from a café table, marble top and bent iron legs done in scrollwork, and smiled and wished me a happy future. He shook my hand and, with a kind of bow, nodded and disappeared into the crowd along the Karntner Strasse: It was like watching a match dying down already when it was hardly lit.

What did Thoreau mean when he said, "I might have loved him, had I loved him less?" What did he mean loved him? He didn't know the word *homosexual*, which was not invented until 1869, and of course he didn't know *gay*. What were his feelings for Edmund Sewall? He called them love. I called them love, too, once. I was like this kid. I was young and slender, and I bought a dress once—I said it was for my sister—and wore it to look at when my parents were out for the evening. I have been chased, too, by the boys of my generation. My lover and I were called names once when we were walking home at night from the movies. After that we drove in separate cars and lived in separate apartments. My lover left me in 1964 to go to California with someone younger—curls and blond hair.

The phone rings. It is Arthur.

"First," he says, "I can only talk for a minute because I am leaving the house right now to go to the arraignment. Don't ask me," he interrupts himself, "I'll tell you about it when I come back. Secondly, meet me for lunch in the park, noon. *Third*, I don't understand it at all."

Arthur is excited and upset and worried, and his voice goes way up at times like this, almost to a squeak. I sit in the silent hallway of the historical society house, and Arthur's shrill voice tears through the gloom like scissors cutting through brown wrapping paper.

"It is so unlike them! If there is *one* thing we have been able to count on over these endless years we've spent here, it's that the *Sentinel* is steady, immovable, rocklike. And now! I feel adrift in a fog." Arthur has been speaking from his kitchen where his phone, an old black one on a long knotted black cord, sits on the counter. He cradles the handpiece under his chin and walks about his kitchen puttering. His conversations are accompanied by the sounds of appliances running and the refrigerator door slamming. Right now he is preparing our lunch.

Arthur and I have known each other for fifteen years. He came here in the late sixties—came back here, I should say, because his family had lived here when he was small—to look after his mother. I had, in the meantime, come north from Boston for a job with the bus line after my lover left me. We met at the symphony. In the years since then, his mother has died, my mother, his sister. We are growing old together, growing into a relationship which at first puzzled me: As we grew closer, we did not at the same time grow sexually intimate, and he didn't understand that. "I don't know why not," I said. "It would be like having sex with one's own mind."

Arthur and I talk most mornings—and most evenings too— and now that we're both retired, we see each other during the day two or three times a week. This time it's on the phone.

"It's on the radio too!"

I ask him what he's heard.

"After years and years and years of trying to get people to see that there is a massive—positively *massive*—plot against gay people in this country and after becoming absolutely *inured* to the indifference of the *world* to our plight, suddenly everyone is taking up *my* song! The leopard has changed its spots, Luke, dear, and I don't know how to arrange my face. I am going to court to try to find what it's all about."

At noon we are sitting on the grass in the sun above the stream, a little up from the covered bridge, which connects a park on this side with the strip of park on the other bank. We sip chablis from paper cups and eat the fried chicken that Arthur has cooked. The news from the arraignment has been on the radio all morning: He couldn't swim and he told them so, and as kids do at pool parties, they threw him in anyway. It ought to have been innocent fun, except that he drowned and they threw him in because he was queer, and so it wasn't innocent.

Arthur sits beside me on a checkered tablecloth, the picnic basket between us. Since Arthur was young, he has subjected himself to long hours lying in the sun cultivating a tan and now two decades after it has ceased to be glamorous, his skin is aged, weathered, dry and loose. His eyes, which are large and round and pale blue, seem perpetually astonished to find themselves amid such decay, reflecting an enduring adolescence. Arthur reports on the arraignment.

"Of course, I went. Missing it would have been like missing Jesus's trial. Imagine having been alive in Jerusalem then and having someone ask you, What were you doing last Thursday when everything, absolutely *everything* in the universe, changed? and you had to answer, *I was picking the pebbles out of my garden?*"

I imagine the scene and the three boys brought in to docket. The image of three men arraigned for killing a gay man is so bizarre, so unexpected, and yet so profoundly right, that even though I wasn't there, I can imagine it in every detail.

"It was all very grand. Very impressive. Except, did you know they've redone the inside of the court house, and the court-room is all pale wood paneling, four by eight sheets of plywood? Bland. Very Perry Mason in the fifties. Unsuitable as a setting for high drama in the eighties. The judge presided in his robes up high in front.   He was miscast too. If I had chosen the actors for this drama—"

"Arthur—"

"—I would have chosen someone with white hair. This one looked like he dealt in traffic tickets and delinquent alimony and drunks. They announced the case, and there I was, with the assistant district attorney on *my* side! I was exhilarated. I think my fear, all my life, has been to find myself in a courtroom just like that one, and to have the charges brought against *me*. Sodomy! Indecent exposure! Offense against the public morals! And here I was on the side of Justice and Truth." Arthur stops and exchanges his bone for a fresh drumstick. "And the boys! Hunky kids. They're only children. Failures already in everything that matters—all three have dropped out of school—strutting and flexing in front of a bunch of girls and beating up queers. Their one victory is beating up on girls and queers. It was pathetic. One of them is only fifteen." Arthur has his drumstick in his fingers and gestures with it as he speaks. "They were brought into court in handcuffs—I would as soon handcuff my Pekinese—their heads down and eyes on the ground. I am *sure* they had been crying. I had thought I would feel something powerful when they were brought in. I thought I would feel triumphant, *vindicated*. But I didn't."

I look at the water. Loggers used to float logs down this stream, and there were the remains of lumber mills along here until ten years ago, but the stream hardly seems deep enough to float many logs. The scene Arthur describes seems bizarre in the extreme.

"There was a reporter from the *Sentinel* there, scribbling away and listening to whoever would talk."

"Did you speak to him?"

"Oh no! She was trying to find someone who knew Mallett. She wanted to know all about Mallett."

"Do you suppose she feels that she's on the wrong side of the fence?" I think of her predicament: to have always written of homosexuals as criminals and now to find one must write of homosexuals as victims. What is bizarre about the picture that Arthur paints is that at the center of a scene we are familiar with from countless television shows and movies, so predictable in all respects, is something new: A homosexual in the middle of the proceedings of the official life of the community.

"I am absolutely *gripped*, Luke, with anxiety. And I don't know why."

Arthur has lived on the rusty edge of fear all his life. He walks down the street with his head turned to the side so he can see what's behind him, and he is ready to run at the first shadow that moves without asking him for a light. He is certain that there is no place to run to. There being no escape, he parades it like a queen.

"They may not try them as adults," Arthur says. "It seems that ordinarily people underage are tried in juvenile court, but if the charge is serious enough, the judge may decide to try them as adults. There will be hearings later. If they're tried as juveniles, they can only be sentenced to the correction facility until their twenty-first birthdays *at most*, and then they'll be set free, the evidence of this murder expunged from the record. The oldest one could be set free in eighteen months! *Poof!* the whole thing evaporates with a slap on the wrist! And I'll be *so* mad! I have waited *so* long for this!"

I stretch out on the grass and catch the sun. Arthur continues to gnaw at a bone. Below us we can hear the slushing of the water over the rocks in the stream, and downstream a little ways is the covered bridge, brought up from its original spot where the stream enters the river. Now a footpath connects the two sides of the stream, but there's no road across this bridge.

"So they have been sent home to mother."

"*Released into the custody of their parents* is what the judge said. There were some other gay people there, and when the judge announced that, the whole room stiffened. It was ghastly."

"This suggests the tack they will take."

"Yes! The judge said they're not a danger to the community!"

"What community did he have in mind?" He doesn't answer. "Were there many gay people there?"

"Deborah was there."

"She told me she was going. Carrying the banner."

He nods and smiles. "Some I thought were gay. But none I knew."

He is quiet for a time, sipping his chablis and watching the water.

"What was odd about it was my being there at all—"

"What were you doing there?"

"I don't know. I've spent my life avoiding getting into confrontations with straights. I was sitting in court waiting for things to start and I thought, I'm coming out!"

"You've been out since you were thirteen, Arthur."

"No. I've been out to other homosexuals. I've never been out to straight people before."

"That's what you think."

"Oh, I know. They may *suspect*, but we would never *talk* about it. That's what was different about this morning. I was there because I was gay, and I had come to see justice done."

"You liked it."

"Yes." He put out his hands in front of him. "Oh, yes!"

"There were you and Deborah and the other gay people and the officers of the law and the assistant district attorney on one side, standing up for justice, and on the other, these three pathetic children?"

"Yes! It was marvelous." He pauses and looks at me, his eyes wide. "Although I am ill at ease with your *pathetic children*."

"That's what you called them. What *do* you call children who commit murder?"

"Oh, Luke." He looks at me and then away. "I don't know. But *someone* must answer Mallett's death."

"If they're not tried as adults, that whole drama this morning will have been nothing but a charade."

"Surely that's not going to happen."

"The boys are not the enemy."

"I know. I have difficulty not feeling they should be petted." Arthur falls silent.

"They're going to scapegoat those kids. They're going to blame everything on them. They're going to convict them of murder and send them away somewhere. They're going to close the book and say *done*. And that's dishonest as *hell*."

Arthur stares at the water.

"They're involved in damage control."

"I was so pleased when I read the paper this morning."

"So was I."

"They call it murder so they won't have to admit that its something worse. I was pleased because I knew there would be pressures to back away even from this—"

"—when the letters-to-the-editor start coming in from the Baptists, and the Roman Catholic bishops weigh in on sodomy. I think one's need at a moment like this is to *do* something. Mount a barricade, throw a bomb, tear one's shirt, wave a flag. *We few, we happy few*, our arms raised to call to those behind to follow into the breach. Yet we don't know who the enemy is, and we don't know who our friends are, and the designation this morning of those three boys as the criminals forces us onto the same side as the police and the system of justice. I don't want to be on the same side as the police and the district attorney. Too often they have themselves been the enemy. And I am suspicious of any interpretation of these events which places me and the Chief of Police in the same camp."

The sun is directly overhead and the landscape—the stream and the rocks and the steep rocky banks and the trees—is shellacked by the heat. I suggest that we go to Dominic's for coffee and ice cream. I take the basket, and Arthur takes the bag, and we walk along the path by the water toward town. We wind our way among the bushes toward the road, which along here comes very close to the stream. We will walk along the road half a mile, past a depression in the ground where the last lumber mill once stood, past small one-story buildings with a typewriter repair shop and insurance offices, until we can see the bridge over the stream where Bernie drowned. Along here the stream has been forced into a narrow run between concrete embankments. It is swift and deep.

"I felt disassociated from what was happening. I remembered all the times I have been chased by kids, and I was glad that these kids were getting what was coming to them, but none of it reached my hurt."

"They don't recognize your hurt. Much of that, my dear, is sixty years old, and for them it might as well have happened in another country."

We stop on the bridge. We lean on the rail and stare down into the water, which is cloudy from the mud stirred up from the bottom. I imagine what it must be like to be under the water and to be carried swiftly along by the current, so swiftly that you can't find which way is up and to not be able to see through the muddy water.

"To whom should I complain? I have this powerful anger—it's been coming on me all morning and it's greater now than it was in court. I want somebody to answer for all that. I want somebody to answer for Mallett's death, but I want somebody to answer for every little slur I've ever suffered. I feel like raising up crosses in my garden and crucifying people."

"You're not going to get that need answered in court."

He laughs. "They only deal with *crimes* there!"

Arthur's nieces and nephews have nothing to do with him. He used to visit, but the children were always inexplicably gone when he arrived, and he got the message. He sent cards and money for a long time, but he finally stopped even that. He used to ask me, "What can I do to make them respond?" I've told him to tell them to go to hell, but he says, "They're my family," and he nurses the pain.

"None of this is going to be satisfactory."

"No."

"You remember what it's been like."

"Every *moment* of it."

"It's important to remember the main thing."

We lean on the railing, side by side, and stare into the water. The sun reflects off the ripples with a light that is both shimmering and blinding. After a few moments looking into it, everything loses color and the eye can only distinguish black from white. It is difficult to comprehend that a man's life ended right where we stand, that all the accumulated thoughts and feelings of a human being ended here thirty-six hours ago, like a sudden power failure which makes the screen go black and shrink to a point of light which then goes dark.

"The article this morning comes at us without context." Arthur looks up from the water and glances at me. "There have been capital sodomy laws in this country since 1636. And the difference between us and *them* is that we remember that and they don't. The paper said this was the first murder in Cardiff in nine years. So. They should have said this was the seventy-second—or whatever the number is—murder of a gay man in America this year. They should have opened their little article this way—*As a consequence of bigoted pronouncements by the pope, the president of the United States, all Baptist ministers everywhere, and seventy-two percent of the American public, among others, three ignorant boys murdered Bernie Mallett today—*"

"You're wonderful."

I scowl.

He looks away and becomes serious again. "I don't know whether I feel anger so much as grief."

"For the boy? Yes."

Arthur speaks of the memorial service. "A ceremony of grieving." He looks into the water and quotes Shelley. Arthur cries at funerals.

We walk on across the bridge, past the banks and the insurance companies, into the center of town. Two streets dead end at an angle into Main Street and create an irregular shaped square which has now been cleared of traffic and bricked in, the Victorian brick buildings with their arched windows looking something like a stage set for a comedy set in the Midwest. From here, all streets either go up hill or down and across the parking lot to the river. All of this is familiar—as familiar as my own face—but it's an old landscape and worn out.

Dominic's is a storefront on Main street, a large room with its original hardwood floor still exposed, now worn and grease stained. There are a tin ceiling, ceiling fans, formica topped tables, chrome chairs, and lying here and there on empty tables, pieces of this morning's *Sentinel*. It is the kind of place where people leave their papers for other customers. The room was part of a hotel once and now has a kind of grubby grandeur, high ceiling and Victorian moldings. People who come to town come here for coffee, bagels, breakfast, lunch. It is the only place to eat. Of course, most people go to the mall for real shopping.

Arthur and I sit at a table in the window where we have a view of the outdoors and wait for a waitress. The room is mainly empty. Out here near the windows in the sunlight, there is a table occupied by a woman in blue jeans who fusses with her son, about twelve, in a subdued strained voice. They have finished whatever they were eating. Another table across the door from where Arthur and I sit holds three middle-aged women in pants and t-shirts, drinking coffee and flipping through the newspaper. They all move their hands while they talk, and they reach across the table to touch one another to emphasize their words. They break up into laughter, and when they do, all three lean back in their chairs and cover their chests with one hand and their mouths with another. One of them holds the newspaper so the front page faces me and I see the article about the drowning and the picture of the dead boy. There are two men in the booths along the side. I see only the tops of their heads above the dividers. And in the back near the door to the kitchen, there are several young people who speak to the waitress every time she comes out.

Wherever I look indoors, I see the face of the dead boy staring off the front page of the newspapers. All around the restaurant discarded papers lie folded on empty chairs and tables, and from every side I see the face of the dead boy. The picture must be ten years old. It must have been cut out of a yearbook—a school picture—because there hasn't been time to have reached his parents and to have gotten the picture from them. He must have carried it with him. It is a small picture, across one column, and the bad reproduction emphasizes the intimacy of the expression on his face: the mouth is slightly open and the eyes are large and set close together and look upward. The eyebrows rise center and plead with the camera.

"It is as if he is looking at us."

"I expect he has more presence now than he had when he was alive."

The waitress is suddenly at the table. She is short, dumpy, and has spiked hair and a leather wrist band with steel studs. She looks down at us belligerently.

"Do you have pie?" Arthur asks. He speaks in a sweet voice which he uses with waitresses.

"You bet your sweet ass I have pie," this woman says. "What do you think this place is, the fucking post office?" The teenagers in the back stare. I feel my face flush red and hot.

"Oh, good!" Arthur whispers. "Could I have blueberry pie with ice cream? And a cup of coffee?" He is a little pale, but otherwise he has shown no response to the waitress. It may be that his eyes have narrowed, but it is hard to tell.

"How 'bout you?" she turns to me. "Same thing, pop?" I can't think of what to say. While she waits for me to respond, she tucks in the corner of her mouth and rolls her eyes. I feel my hands gripping the sides of the table.

"First, you little bitch—" I get her attention but she doesn't think fast enough to interrupt me. "—I'll have a civil tongue in your head. Do you understand?" Her eyes widen and her mouth begins to open. It must mean that she is going to say something. "If you don't apologize to my friend here, this very minute, I'm going to turn this table upside down on top of your head! And then I'm going to turn upside down every fucking table I pass as I make my way to find the manager." I begin to stand up and the table begins to come up with me. I can't imagine what I am doing. She steps back, and I lift the edge of the table enough to cause the sugar and creamer to begin to slide. Arthur, who hasn't moved, reaches toward them.

I am enraged. I feel like killing her.

She begins to laugh. She drops her arms to her sides and shrugs and grins, and then she turns on her heels and walks toward the kitchen door. I stand here and watch her back. I want to shout at her to come back, but I see her pass the kids—they watch her and me, grinning silently—and then she disappears through the kitchen door. I watch the door until it stops swinging, and then I slide back down into my chair, breathing hard and feeling cold and, at the same time, as if my face were hot. The men in the booth have turned to look, and the women, too, have stopped their chatter and stare at me, openmouthed. Even the mother has stopped badgering her son long enough for both of them to stare at me.

"I don't know what came over me."

"*I* do, my dear," Arthur whispers. "You were provoked. Mightily."

I am breathing in deep jerky intakes, and I stare at the formica and the trembling of my hands on the table and wonder what has happened. "You were provoked as much, Arthur. Why did I go to pieces?"

"You didn't go to pieces. You were defending me, my dear. You wanted to turn over all the tables." He slides his hand across the formica and encloses the back of my hand with his fingers. He smiles. "Are you all right?"

Then there is another waitress standing by table. She is blond and thin and altogether unlike the other one.

"I hope you will forgive my friend," she says, looking from one to the other of us. She is anxious to please. "I would like to get you what you want. Do you still want blueberry pie? And ice cream?" Her face is tense with pleading. "I won't charge you."

I look at Arthur. I don't know what to say.

"Why don't we?" Arthur says. "Would that be OK?"

I glance at the waitress, and then I let Arthur know it is OK.

"Oh, good. It will give you a chance to catch your breath and let your heart calm down. Then we can leave. And I'll walk you home." He squeezes my hand. "Are you OK now?" The women stare at us.

I am not OK. I wonder if I am having a heart attack.

I stare at the kitchen door and wonder if she will return.

"Pay no attention to them," Arthur says.

At Dominic's, with its layered humanity, its shifting but distinct groupings of people, we're like animals in an open zoo, space surrounded by a ditch inhabited by animals and birds common to a single geographic area—the African veldt, say—each species having staked out its own space on the ground, in the shrubbery or in the trees, separate from the others.

People have turned back to their own tables and have begun to ignore me. The waitress with the spiked hair has returned and seated herself with her friends by the kitchen. I hear them. *The boys*, they say, with no other word of explanation. The others ignore them. It is like the casts of two plays giving performances on the same stage, each unaware of the other. The kids by the kitchen door don't seem to care who hears them, but they are not heard as they talk about the boys.

The other waitress brings out our pie. Arthur removes his hand from mine and picks up his fork. One boy, a tough-looking kid maybe nineteen years old, says, "They'll have to try them for murder." Then he asks, "How do they execute people in this state?"

"Cut off their balls!" the one with the spiked hair says loudly, and the rest of them laugh.

"Yeah! Cut off their balls!" The women glance in their direction and stir in their chairs.

I look at Arthur, and he raises his eyebrow and glances around the room at the other customers.

I feel humiliated. I allowed myself to be dragged into a fight with a waitress.

"We need Rosa Parks," Arthur says.

I can't eat, and I want to go.

"We need an old black lady who tells the bus driver she ain't gonna move."

He touches me again.

"Laugh, Luke." He waits, and I don't. "I've figured out what we need," he says.

"What?"

"What we need is a television camera and Bull Connor and some firehoses and dogs. And we need for all of it to be on the nightly news."

The idea *is* funny.

"We wouldn't have any trouble making our point then, would we? Between Bull Connor and his firehoses and us, nobody would have difficulty making a choice, would they?" He leans over the table, his hands clasped together in his lap. "Or how about the Coliseum and some lions? Wouldn't that show them? Wouldn't they know then which side to be on?" He smiles and nudges me. "Wouldn't they know then that this isn't about justice? It's about righteousness?"

I want to please Arthur and let him know I have come out of the sink I'm in—I wonder if age has something to do with these mood swings?—but I can't do it for him. The paper this morning referred to the "gay community," but that doesn't exist. There're those kids at the table by the kitchen—I don't think any of them is over twenty—and there's me and Arthur, sitting at this table in the window, and Deborah is probably having lunch with somebody else right now. Who else? There must be others I don't know, people between me and that waitress. But there's no community. We don't sit down at the same table.

I have made Arthur the executor of my will, and I have left him my things. I have given him explicit instructions as to how I am to be buried. I am certain he will carry them out. I am far closer to him than I am to my brother, who I see frequently—he lives across the river near his wife's people—but who hasn't cared for years whether I lived or died. I don't want him to bury me.

I have survived a difficult life, and it is to my credit that I have never been thrown off a bridge. Arthur and I know how to survive, something these reckless kids know nothing about. I don't know what is happening to me. I don't know what is happening here. Arthur and I talked last night of going to Boston for the weekend. I have thought, sometimes, that "passing" is cowardly, lying about yourself when it matters not to lie. These kids don't know anything about history. And God knows there are more important things than being queer. I am alone now because my lover left me, not because I am gay. I am alone because I am old, and I have become ugly. People are alone.

Arthur for years has wanted me to live with him. Would that mean we were lovers? "It would be such fun," he has said. The last two dinosaurs. Later we finish our pie and walk out into the sun again, headed toward the bridge and then up the hill toward my place. We will pass the library where Deborah does work occasionally in the afternoons. I'm too old to change now. I've lived alone for more than twenty years.

Arthur has taken my arm. I have asked him not to do that. I don't like to draw attention. His hand rests in the corner of my arm and he leans on me. "Shall we call on Deborah?"

"Why?"

"Because she's one of us."

Walking through town with Arthur on my arm is comforting. I feel *loud*. I would like to find that waitress and show her. I feel exhausted. I don't care what people think any longer. I am angry enough not to care too. This is not what I wanted to happen. This boy's death!

At the foot of the library steps, Arthur leaves me and goes to find Deborah. Deborah thinks with her heart, and despite her interest in the historical society, she has no interest in history. She *cares* for old clothes, but she has never read a book on the history of homosexuality. She has never read Sappho and knows nothing of Adrienne Rich. She knows nothing of women in love with women in the nineteenth century. Her perceptions are limited by her ignorance of the relationship between her feelings and her life at this epoch. She is in that way an innocent.

I sit on the steps, which go up from the street and divide and then join again on the landing before the door. There are large bronze candelabra which stand on the stone balustrade beside me. Like the court house and the churches, the library was built at a time when this area still had a sense of the importance of public life.

From where I sit, I am halfway up the side of the small valley the stream runs through. Across from me on the other side of the valley, frame houses are half hidden among the trees, and below a street curves away from the library toward a bridge to the other side. This is a civilized, urban landscape, built by people who cared for the look of things, but it is set against one's irrepressible memory of the merciless woods which surround us. It would be easy, and one must resist the effort, to make all of this a moral tale by Hawthorne: violent passions at home in the woods breaking loose in the city streets.

In a few minutes, Deborah and Arthur join me on the steps.

"I'm glad you came by," she says, "I needed to be dragged away. I cannot read today." She sits down next to me, and Arthur descends the steps in front of us and leans against the balustrade. "We are blessed by the weather."

"I have just acted like a fool."

"Oh, Luke," she says, and glances up at Arthur and then back at me. "What a harsh thing to say."

"A waitress was snippy, and I overreacted and started my heart going. I should be old enough."

I see her glance at Arthur again.

"I haven't done that in years."

"Arthur says you were quite brave."

"I was a fool."

She smiles at me. "I wish I had been there to see it."

"I'm glad you weren't."

"I would have cheered."

"He was really quite imposing," Arthur says.

"I'll bet she was taken down a peg!"

"She *laughed*."

"It was the only thing she could do, except run."

"Or kill us both."

"You did the right thing," Deborah says.

"Rightness had nothing to do with my anger."

Deborah puts her hand on my arm and squeezes. I hate it when Deborah patronizes me. I hate it being in a position where she can. Women do that to men when they soothe them.

"I have something delicious to tell you," she says, looking directly into my eyes. "It'll make you happy."

Arthur leans back against the balustrade and smiles, his arms crossed over his chest. We wait.

"I've bought a dress."

Arthur laughs.

"You're getting married."

"Oh be still," she says. "It's beautiful. And I'm going to tell you about it."

"You bought a dress. You are so upset over that boy drowning that you went out and bought a dress."

"I want to look nice."

"You're going to wear it to that service tonight."

"I wanted to look presentable. My best."

"You're going to get yourself up in your *frumpery*—"

"Luke—" Arthur's hand is on my arm.

"Oh, Luke," she says. "It's a *dress*, only a dress." She looks away. She stops and looks down at the street and then across it at Central, which begins here and crosses the stream and then curves around the base of the hill, red brick buildings with arched windows and, in the facades, the legends in stone: *Culver Block* and *McClennan Block* and, in a gray building, *1872*.

The streets are crowded with people walking into shops and carrying shopping bags to their cars. "I haven't bought anything in a long time, and I thought it might cheer me up. I got some shoes to go with it."

"Tell us about it," Arthur says.

"It's red. I thought if I was going to be there, I might as well be in something people would notice. And you know me—" She waited for each of us to acknowledge her glance. "—everything I have is brown. *Tonight*, I'm not going to be *brown*."

Arthur is laughing again. "Of *course*. I don't know why I didn't think of it myself, my dear." He turns to me. "Luke, let's go to the mall and buy something to *wear*. A tie. A new pair of socks. God. I think I need a whole new personality for these dangerous times. I am so used to taking life on a *slant* that I don't know if I suit these direct times. Where do you suppose I can buy a new character? Does the Cardiff Mall carry them? After-the-Fourth-of-July Sale, perhaps, of *integrity*? And where," he says, rolling his eyes and putting his hands out helplessly, "can I buy courage?"

"You boys. I have been to see Carole."

Carole! "Why!"

"To talk about tonight."

"Carole won't come, surely," Arthur says. "Carole is very *grand*."

"Oh, she may! I'm working on it."

"She has too much invested in her position here."

"Carole lives in pain most of her life, and she is deeply disturbed by this."

"Carole is the most repressed woman in Cardiff." She is also the most vicious.

"I don't know that that is so." Deborah does not so much disagree with me as back away from the manifestation of it, holding her breath. We have been friends for fifteen years. "We don't know all the women in Cardiff," she says, taking my hand across the steps.

We are picking up sides. Kinsey, forty years ago, drew a line with seven points, and we were all somewhere on that line, and not all at the ends. Deborah and Arthur stand up. They turn to me to see what I will do. The picture of that boy divides us—his open lips and his eyes pleading with the camera. I think it's appalling. It's an accusation in itself. It is the face of a victim. Villains and victims, gays and straights, those who've been injured from those who haven't. It forces a response and it insists on categories, and then gets the categories wrong.

"What are you thinking of?" Arthur asks.

"Polymorphous perversity. *The Kinsey Report*. Kinsey's seven-point scale. Do you remember? Way over on the left were the three percent of us who were exclusively homosexual? And then next to them were those who were almost exclusively homosexual, but who had had some heterosexual experience. Some of us were strung out in the middle, with some of this and some of that. The categories feathered into one another and blurred." I am looking down across this town where the reason for us being here—the juncture of the two rivers cutting down through the rocks—is so insistently before us. "If you go to the church tonight, you reduce Kinsey's multiple categories to two. Tomorrow morning, there'll be just two groups in this town—gays and straights—and there won't be any bridge between them except astonishment and anger, charges and recriminations."

Deborah shakes her head. "Oh, Luke. You go to church tonight to honor the dead. Anybody could do that. Any decent person."

Deborah and Arthur respond from sympathy and grief to Mallett's drowning, but they played a part this morning in a drama organized by the district attorney, whose interest it was to focus attention on three children, when there is probable cause to charge the district attorney himself—as representative of the larger culture—with a crime of violence.

We go to church tonight and stand with the victim. And we take on ourselves publicly the stigma which the boys put on Mallett. Whose purposes do we serve here? How can we be sure that they are our own? No matter how many people show up tonight, they will be fewer than have committed homosexual acts in this town. Even with the church filled to overflowing, we will have defined the number of homosexuals in Cardiff as fewer than it is and will have made life safer and easier for those who have never felt homosexual feelings or who don't admit to them. We will have allowed a line to be drawn between us and them. I am cynical. I credit the sincerity of my friends, but it is certain that we are about to be used against ourselves.

Marybeth

I 'm always bewildered in K-Mart. If I had had time to explore the place—to wander back past the Seiko watches and Konica cameras, past gold chains and boys' sweats and yellow slickers, through plastic furniture and wood stepladders to shower curtains— if I had had time to orient myself without having any goal in mind other than finding out where I am, then it wouldn't be bad when I came here in a desperate hurry, like now. I could ignore everything and go right to the counter in the middle far right distance and find exactly what I am looking for: *lavender ribbon*. But I never come to K-Mart to find out where I am. I always come here when I am in a desperate hurry to find one particular thing, and so I am always lost in this place, and that's why I hate it. It's big and confusing and the merchandise seems to assault you and hide from you at the same time. I've already been to Walgreen's at the Airport Mall and to CVS and to LaVerdiere's. I can't find lavender ribbon. Last year there was a department store on Main Street, which had everything, displayed so you could actually see what you were staring at, but it went bankrupt, and now here I am at K-Mart.

Bernie would know where to go, to begin with, to find the ribbon, and to him the whole process would be an adventure and a drama. Bernie was a crisis himself, so he would feel at home. It was my idea: I thought, since some of us going tonight won't know each other, it would be good if we had something that could make us feel a part of the group and a part of something bigger than ourselves. Gender and class and age separate us like oceans. We don't speak to each other and barely know each other, and I thought if we each wore a lavender ribbon, perhaps we'd feel more connected.

It's 3:30. I work at Dominic's and got off an hour ago. I worked breakfast and lunch, and between now and 5:00, when Cynthia gets off, I have to find all this ribbon. I wanted to get something about an inch or an inch and a half wide, and enough of it so that each person could have a big bow on her arm, but we didn't think of it in time. We figure there will be about forty people there tonight, and if we have forty people, then at eighteen inches a person, we'll need sixty feet, and that is twenty yards, and that is a lot of lavender ribbon.

She said the ribbons were one aisle past cameras, in the third section, past hockey sticks. At first the problem was trying to find lavender ribbon, now the problem is trying to match the ribbon we've already bought. You have no idea how many shades there are. Some of the stuff they are selling is really pink, and some of it is so dark it's almost purple. The point is to make us feel a part of something, and that's not going to be any good if the lavender we have divides us along the shades of the color wheel.

I find the ribbon in a section next to thread. Each roll of ribbon contains three-and-a-half yards. That means we need six of these little rolls. There are two in the color we want. I take them both, at $1.98 each, total: $4.16. I would like three more. I search for a saleslady. I don't find one, and I go to the cash register, where I ask. I am told she is in housewares, past automotive parts. I pursue her, past automotive parts, past housewares, and find her leaning on a stack of plastic bathmats in closet and bath. "Do you have any more of this color in the stock in the back?" What they have is out on the shelves. What you see is what you get. This is all there is.

The sound system plays the country music station. It has a curious metallic sound, coming from everywhere in the store, as if all the speakers were behind tin foil. The news: "This morning, three Cardiff residents were charged with the death by drowning of Bernard Mallett—" I try not to listen. "Tonight the gay community will hold a memorial service for Bernard Mallett at the Unitarian Church at 7:00." At first it was passed around word-of-mouth. Simon started it and called people. Now it's on the radio. It's as if somebody has found a note you wrote and tacked it up to the bulletin board so the wrong kind of people can read it. I feel like getting in a protected posture under a heavy piece of furniture while the bomb goes up. I want Cynthia! I hate this.

I don't have enough time. Since I was sixteen, it seems I couldn't run fast enough to catch up with what I wanted to be a part of. I read Susan Brownmiller when I was still living in a town of twelve hundred people four miles this side of the Canadian border, and I wanted to get out of there and into a city where it was happening, and every time I thought I had caught up with what women were thinking, I read another book and discovered that what I thought was happening had happened four years ago for everybody else, and I had to run to catch up again. I've been too young and too far out in the sticks to have any real sense that when I stopped running, the ground wouldn't shift under my feet again. I know what I've been looking for though, so I'll know when I've found it. I'm looking for a place where, when I come in, they'll celebrate me.

Until I find it, I can take care of myself. I support myself waiting tables. I put myself through four years of college waiting tables, and I traveled from one side of the country to the other when I was sixteen and seventeen—after I left home—waiting tables. I don't owe anybody anything. Even Cynthia.

Gay people in Cardiff need to come together just to see how we look, now that this has happened. In *Papillon* a man has been a prisoner in solitary on Devil's Island forever, and the guards take a head count by making the prisoners stick their heads through little holes in the cell doors, and his first question—he's lost his teeth, his hair is white, and he has cataracts—is *How do I look?*

On Monday afternoon at 3:40 at K-Mart, only two registers are in operation. The cashier is a girl about my age with carefully done hair, slightly bouffant. She hits the register keys, her long finger nails clicking against the plastic keys, her lips pulled back to expose her teeth. She shakes her head and her whole body shivers. "I couldn't stand it!"

Beside her stands another cashier, an older woman, hard shiny skin and a tear of red lipstick, her hair pulled back and held flat against her skull by bobby pins. "Yeeccch!"

"They say he propositioned one of 'em," the first one says. "They say that's what they're going to say in court, that he followed 'em all around town begging 'em to let'm have sex with 'em, and these boys—they're only kids—got so scared—"

"Why, can you blame 'em?"

I look hard at my ribbons, each one sliding under her talons.

"Imagine!"

What do I say?

Clang, clickety, whrrrrr. Clang, clickety, whrrrrr. *Clang,* clickety, whrrrrrr.

"I heard it on the radio," the second one says, "that they're all going to the Unitarian Church tonight."

"It's a protest march, they say." She turns her eyes full on me and smiles. "That'll be $4.16, please."

"I can't believe this is happening here," the other one says. "Cardiff is such a quiet, *nice* place to live." She turns away, her arms folded across her chest.

I have my wallet out, and I am fumbling for the bills. I find three ones, which I pull out and put in her hand. I search for quarters and then dimes and nickels. My fingers are shaking. Three quarters. Three dimes. Two nickels. If I don't say it now, I will never be able to call myself a woman. I open my mouth and start talking.

"I heard what you said. I am a friend of Bernie Mallett's." Both girls look at me open-faced. "I know that what you said about him is not true. They killed him in an unprovoked attack. The service tonight is a memorial service for Bernie, and people who loved him are going to go. I am a lesbian. And you are a bigot." I throw down some pennies on the counter and grab the ribbons and run. It is only after I get in the car with my small precious bag of ribbon that I feel my face flush red. *And I hate you!*

I drive across the parking lot to the other end of the mall, nearly running into three cars on the way. I call Cynthia from the pay phones at the front door of Archer's Discount Beauty Aids. She's a receptionist at the Department of Human Services. I drop in the dimes and listen to the whrrring sounds as if I am trying to decipher the voice of God. Then, click, and I hear her, "Hello?"

"Cynthia?" In the sudden safety within the sound of her voice, I start to cry.

"Marybeth?" and then, "Are you OK?"

"I'm OK. I'm fucking angry. Wait a minute." I am crying. She is silent on the other end, waiting. I am glad that there is somebody to hear. Then I tell her what happened.

"Bitches."

"I could have died. I could have killed them."

"Oh, shit," she says. "Poor baby."

"I didn't know if I'd have the courage—"

"The business manager of my office told a joke about Bernie's death and everybody laughed."

"These were rednecks and I shouldn't care—"

"Holy shit," Cynthia says, "who said class governed the amount of damage a person can do?"

"I hate this." I tell her I have been buying ribbon.

"Terrific. Save several yards for me. I'm going in black leather, my arms bound behind me in lavender ribbon." She pauses. "On the other hand, I may decide to call attention to myself. Why?"

"I called Simon. It'll make the gays and the lesbians look more like they're on the same team tonight."

"That's OK," she says. "That's terrific. That ought to work."

I want to pick her up after work and take her home: "I need some time with you alone, before tonight."

"I don't know," she says. "There's not much time before the service. What about supper?" Before I can answer, she goes on, "I'd rather not. Let's just get something to eat in town and go to church early."

"Cynthia, I want to go home, even if it's only for ten minutes. I would like you to do that with me. I need that. We can worry about eating later."

She hears me. "Meet me at the front door at five."

I am to pick her up.

"Hey, Marybeth, take it easy, will you?"

I will. How can I?

"I love you, honey, OK?"

I get in the car, biting my lip and my eyes full of tears. I'll stop in Baskahegon and get supper stuff, call Robbie, and then if I have time before I pick up Cynthia at five, I'll look for more ribbon at the Cardiff Mall. I start the car and head toward the river and south. The radio comes on when the car does, a rock station. It's the Baptists who are responsible for all this. The redneck Baptists, who believe that gay people are the abomination of the Lord. What does that mean in real language? A woman's place is in the home!

I've been looking for a place since I was sixteen, and I would have taken it in my home, if one had been there for me. My job was to help my mother in the kitchen while my father sat in the living room talking with my brothers. It was, "Arnold, how was basketball today?" "Seth, how was track?" Wherever my place is, it has to be where they're going to notice me, where they know who I am, and it matters that I am there. And I thought that must mean getting to a city. I began to travel when I was sixteen.

Robbie says the memorial service tonight is going to have an open mike. Anybody who wants to can go up and say what she wants to about Bernie. Bernie was young, and he didn't have it all together.

He should have had a chance to do that. I'm going to the church to remember him. But I'm clear about something else too. Bernie was not the only victim when he was thrown into the water Saturday night. It could as well have been any of the gay men I know better than I knew Bernie. And it could have been me because I am a lesbian and because I am a woman. It is important to have some public accounting of that fact. It is important not to leave it to the court system. They are as homophobic as the rest of society and just as likely to treat lightly the murder of a gay man as they have been to treat wifebattering lightly. Sometime all this has to stop.

Since the middle of the day, they have been announcing the service tonight, and I can't figure out why they are doing that. I can't believe they want to spread the word to all the gay people in the area, and yet it is too awful to think that maybe what they are doing is telling everybody, *This is where the queers are going to be tonight*. This morning there was that big article in the paper about the three boys, and then the arraignment and then this. All day long in the paper or on the radio, something has been happening about being gay and about Bernie. It's like I'm under assault.

I think everybody feels that way. The smallest little thing sets people off. Claire was waiting on two old men who came in for pie, and one of them had this little squeaky voice, and she nearly killed them. I think she would have if everybody hadn't started laughing. I was already off my shift, and I took them for her. But I wasn't in much better shape.

Dana came in around eleven for coffee. She and Marcia are coming tonight. I think it must be wonderful to be them. They're settled with each other. They have their careers and their house and their baby. They are out. They seem to have found what they're looking for. I'm still waiting for it to happen for me. I could get a better job than waiting—I have a BA in history from the U, which I got by waiting and going to night school, and I wrote a history of women in Washington county for my senior thesis—, but I'm not ready to make the commitment yet. I still need to hang free for a while longer. It's like I'm watching to see what's going to happen. I'm trying to find something I can do that will enable me to use all my abilities—my imagination and my strength—without turning me into a man. I don't want to have happen to me what is happening to Geraldine Ferraro. I am just floating for a while until I get a handle on how to do that. Except that I'm not so much floating as jumping. From one thing to another. With Dana and Marcia, there are no hard edges. They smoothed everything out a long time ago. How did they learn to be happy when women are put down and everybody hates lesbians? I don't know how long Cynthia and I are going to last either. I wanted my last relationship to last forever and it didn't, and now I'm afraid to ask for that for fear of jeopardizing things.

Dana said, "Come to the church, tonight. That's what we all need. We need to be in one place where we can hug each other and think about Bernie." She hugged me, and I started crying. "We need all to be together so we can look at ourselves and see that we are OK."

When I left this morning, I stopped in the doorway and looked back at her, and Cynthia said, "You will be careful, won't you?" I laughed—she looked so serious and she sounded so much like my mother—and then I said, "Of course I will." She didn't mean to sound that way. She worries about me and brushes me off when I worry about her, but she doesn't mean to patronize me. I went back across the room and leaned down over her—she was sitting at the table still drinking coffee and wondering how they knew these three boys were the ones who did it—and kissed her. "And if you're not careful," she said, "would you run fast?" She made a knuckle with her middle finger and scrubbed my scalp with it.

All today I've done the same things I do everyday—I worked through breakfast and lunch shifts—but I've thought all the time about Cynthia being like my mother sometimes and about Bernie being dead in the Passadumkeag Stream. All day yesterday we all worried about Timothy. Nobody knew where he was, and the boys had been released by the judge, and since his picture has been on TV, he's recognizable. We've been thinking they're going to find him. Then he showed up this morning at the court house for the arraignment, drunk. He didn't know he is in danger or that everybody has been looking for him. He just smiles if you ask him where he has been. Mickey says he doesn't know whether he's going to get AIDS first or be murdered. Mickey has talked to him, but he just cries. He says he loved Bernie and that Bernie was going to "teach him things." I wonder about whether Bernie's death had any impact on Timothy at all. Was it just one more blow in a long succession of them, like being hit in the face after you've already been hit in the butt, the breasts, the groin? Can you distinguish the source of the pain? Robbie said he's been drunk all day. Or high.

All this while the radio has been playing rock, and I've hardly been listening. I think they play "Born in the USA" every other song. Now the DJ is talking:

"This morning three Cardiff residents were charged with murder in the death by drowning of Bernard Mallett on Saturday night. Mallett, a self-avowed homosexual, was a recent arrival in Cardiff and was unemployed. The three charged with his murder all attended local schools. The case has been bound over, and a hearing will be held on July 17 on the question of whether the three men should be tried as adults or as juveniles. In the meantime, they have been released into the custody of their parents.

"Tonight, there will be a memorial service at the Unitarian Church for the dead man."

The DJ goes back to music. Fucking asshole.

At the end of Stillwater Road, I am in Baskahegon. I will stop here and get sandwich stuff for tonight. At the pay phones at the entrance of The Store, I call Robbie at the studio at the U where he teaches on Mondays. It is 3:50 and I am beginning to panic. When I got off work, Robbie helped me look for ribbon for a while. He went in stores I didn't know were there. I'm calling Robbie hoping he has found enough lavender ribbon and that I won't be a failure. I hear his voice. He agrees to meet me at the pizza parlor.

The Store is owned by a woman we know and carries cheese and homemade bread and grains and flours. It is the kind of place with barrels sawed in half and lined with plastic and filled with different kinds of flour and beans and grains and peas. The floor is raw pine, the ceiling painted pressed tin, and the walls are covered with pine shelves.

The thing I've been driving toward since high school is discovering what it's like being with women. I don't mean merely working with them or having sex with them. I mean being in a society in which women relate to women free of patriarchy. Helen Demopoulos is behind the register in The Store and waves at me when I come in. She is about fifty, wonderful strong gray hair. She is active in the Democratic Party and in pro-choice things. She's on the steering committee of Planned Parenthood and is a volunteer with the shelter for battered women. We are in the midst of women who are living woman-identified lives: Dana and Marcia, me and Cynthia, Katherine, Sarah, Beth, and Mary Kay. And those are just the ones I know here in Cardiff. When you go down the river to Brookville and Jonesport and Kershaw and Georgetown, there are others. They run a bookstore in Jonesport and a restaurant in Kershaw. Almost all of us have something to do with the shelter, raising money for it or counseling. There's a drug abuse center down on the coast south of Georgetown that's just for women, and we know three of the counselors there. With a little care, it is possible to go for days without dealing with a man in any serious way. I feel like I have to know who I am as a woman before I can deal with men, because when I am with a man, I get blown away, like I'm standing ten feet from a helicopter with its rotors spinning, blowing my hair in my face and throwing up dust and dirt in my eyes.

I pick out crackers and two cheeses and a half pound container of falafel and some pita bread. I can get a little lettuce and tomatoes across the street at the market. I plunk all these things down on the counter and put my hands down and lean on the counter. "Ah, Helen, you have no idea."

"I bet I do, honey. It's on the radio. It's on the TV. It's all anybody can talk about when they come in here. I've never seen people so upset." She begins to drag my things across the wooden counter and to ring them up on the register. She watches what she is doing, but she talks continuously. "That is, honey, you're upset, Dana and Marcia are upset, I'm upset, Nicholas my boy is upset. Even Constantine—" Constantine is her husband. "—is upset. Maybe other people are upset too—" She shrugs. "—but when they come in here they act like nothing is happening. Have you noticed that, honey? That there are some people who are pretending that nothing is happening? I ask them, 'How's things,' and they say—" She shrugs and pulls the corner of her mouth down. " ' —So-so. Nothing's happ'n'n. The dead time of summer. Kids away at camp, vacation not till August. Nothing's happ'n'n.' I don't understand it."

She finishes ringing up my things, and I pay her.

"This thing has people uneasy, you know. I can tell that. People want to do the right thing—some of them—but they feel guilty, you know, because they're straight and it happened here, and they—I wonder if they're going to try these kids as adults. If they do, we'll know they're going to treat this thing seriously. If they don't—"

I have to get down to Cardiff and pick up Cynthia.

"You going tonight? Of course you are. Constantine and I will be there if there is no crisis with the kids."

We hug and then I say goodbye, take my bag, and walk across the street to the pizza parlor. It is 4:05. What is it like to live among women? It is quiet and caring. It is sharing. It is doing the dishes and looking up and seeing another woman drying and another one putting away, and it is feeling a part of something very deep and very old. It is giving and giving *space*. It is paying attention and listening and seeing. I feel as if my five senses have been doubled to ten when I have spent a weekend with women in the woods or on the coast. I come back in tune and in harmony. In the fall we go from house to house of our friends in the country, helping them lay in enough firewood. One of us sings while we all chop and stack. It's long and tiring work, and at the end of it, there is a huge, slowly-served meal, and then the dishes. Somebody is singing all the while. It is also reading the books. I'm only twenty-two, so I'm behind, and I don't know as much as women like Dana and Marcia know. They've not only read the books, they've lived it. They were in Washington last year for the big march. They were in Washington in 1976 for the demonstrations. I was only fourteen then.

I am confused because what the boys have done has thrown us all in the same camp with gay men, and here I am driving around town looking for lavender ribbon. Lesbians normally gravitate toward other women whether the women are straight or gay. Helen is in our crowd even though she's straight, but sometimes I feel that my being a lesbian means I have to stand with gay men, that my closest identity is with gay men, and I find that hard. When I am with men, even if they are gay, I feel like I am in the camp of the enemy under false pretenses. In the pizza parlor I find a booth and wait for Robbie.

Cynthia called her folks last night and told them about Bernie. It was after supper, and we were in the living room. I sat on the floor while she sat on the end of the sofa where the phone was. I could hear the phone ringing.

Finally they picked it up, and Cynthia said, "Mom?" and she told them about Bernie. They said things to her. Her voice took on an edge. "He was a citizen," she said to them, "and he had a right to walk along the street, however he looked."

When they had hung up, she spoke to me. "They thought it was awful. They hope something is done to catch the people who did it. They want to know what Bernie looked like. They wanted to know what he had done to make them do it."

She slid down from the sofa and lay on the floor with her head in my lap. I ran my fingers through her hair and felt the sweat on her scalp. Her parents live in the southern part of the state and write and call and visit back and forth. They want to be close to Cynthia—that's clear—and the fact that they're not is almost not their fault. It's like they are victims too. They're homophobic even though they try not to be. Then they're middle-class, which makes them value things. It is as if all these things were fences or hurdles they had to jump to get to Cynthia and me, and we watch them down the track coming toward us. They want to come to us, everybody knows, and the hurdles are not there because they're sinful or deficient as persons. They don't hate us because they are bad. They hate us because they live in a culture that hates lesbians and has driven homosexual expression of love underground, and they have never known a dyke who could show them how unreal their ideas are.

Her parents' love hasn't been enough to give them courage. It's like Cynthia is calling to her parents like they were children on diving board, "*Jump!* It won't hurt!"

Sometimes it's just when her parents have been mean that our lovemaking is the most intense. She turns to me. Me. I'm out, so people don't generally bother me about that. It's just the rest of my life that makes me need her.

Five minutes later Robbie walks in and slides into my booth. He is tall and slender and looks like a certain kind of movie star. His eyes make you think he's been getting over a love affair.

"Robbie, we're not going to have enough—"

"How much do you have?"

"I got seven rolls. Woolworth's had three, and K-Mart—"

"I have nine. And there's still Hamlin. Did you go there?"

"No—"

"Terrific. If we have to make do with what we have, we can get straight pins and give each person a six inch banner to pin on their shirts. Otherwise, I can run by Whitlock's in Hamlin after I pick up Mickey at work and maybe get some more. If Whitlock has any, we can stick to our original plan for ribbons around our arms." He pauses. "Sexy!"

"What if more than forty come tonight?"

"Honey—" He leans over toward me. "—there're going to be a lot more than forty people tonight!"

I don't think it will work, but I am too frazzled to do anything but accept his reading of it. "Cynthia says the boys are already riding 'round town in a convertible, yelling at people."

"Is that true?"

"She says they yelled faggot at Brad. I don't know."

"Everywhere you go, they're talking about it."

I tell him about K-Mart.

"Did they know you were a dyke?"

"God, I don't know. How do I look?"

"Like a dyke, honey." He smiles. "But then I know you, don't I? I don't think anybody else would guess your dread secret."

"It's not a secret any longer. I told them."

"Haaaay," he drawls. "Tha's all *right*!" And, grinning, he reaches across the table and touches my hand. When he settles back down, he rests both his elbows on the table before him, staring at me head on. "Have you heard the radio? WRVG has been calling the service at the church tonight a rally for homosexual rights."

The image conjured up by the phrase—queens and dykes parading in the streets carrying signs and crying and cheering, a kind of queer political Mardi Gras—makes my mouth go dry. I had thought—, I am not sure what I thought the service would be about, but I had imagined, I suppose, all kinds of people sitting in pews with bowed heads and lavender ribbons on everybody's arms.

"Public radio is still calling it a memorial service, but WRVG is calling it a rally. I don't know where they got that."

"Who do they talk to?"

"I feel like a rally," Robbie says, "but I thought I was going to a memorial service. I feel like standing on the corner in front of Dominic's, in the center of town, carrying a sign saying, *We're not going away*."

I don't feel like saying anything, and I wish we didn't have to fight. I hate the way I feel.

"It feels weird," he says, "to be doing something and to have the radio talking about it—"

"—and to have them disagree about what it is we are doing." We are so alien to these people, I don't think they'd understand us even if we sat down around a campfire and explained it all to them.

I ask him about Mickey.

"Heavy. His sister maybe has figured out he's gay—"

"How?"

He shrugs. "He told her he knew Bernie, and somebody told her Bernie was queer. She must've put it together. Now his high school teacher has it figured out, and then last night a TV reporter called, and it's out of control now. Whether he goes to the service tonight or not, he's being forced out of the closet, and there's nothing he can do—"

"Is he OK?" It's hard to think of Mickey out of control. Mr. I-can-handle-this.

"He's bitter. I think he's afraid—"

I think it must be fear I'm feeling. Everything seems disrupted. Cynthia and I were settled into a nice little life. We knew the people who were good for us, and we avoided the people who were bad, and everything seemed so comfortable. We hardly ever saw any men.

Robbie is silent. Then he says, "I've never thought you could get away from it, everyday in every way. I was never like Mickey like that. I always assumed that sooner or later we were both going to have to face it with our parents—"

"You're a fatalist—"

"I'm out. I did that when I was sixteen—"

"But you see you have to do it again and again, with each new bunch of people. Your parents just once. Your job. Then each time you change jobs. Every time you walk into a new room—"

Robbie is talking. "The secretary at the dancing school said she is very sorry it happened, and she wanted me to know that. She's a nice lady. She said, 'I felt so bad for you, Robbie, because I knew he must be a friend of yours—.' I was feeling so good, listening to her, and then she blew it. She acted like this was the first time it had ever happened."

He asks me about Cynthia, and I tell him how odd it is to be depending on her to keep me together, when it is usually the other way around. Then for a little bit we talk about Timmie. He seems to be slipping right through our fingers. Robbie doesn't think he's taking anything stronger than pot. What is it that destroys some people and not others?

I leave him and head back to the car and down the river to Cynthia, feeling desolate.

There are places up on the interstate that are high enough so you can see the whole valley the river runs through and even where the Passadumkeag Stream comes down to meet the river in the middle of town. The terrain here is not abrupt and harsh, the way it is farther back from the coast. It rolls and swells between the streams. From a distance it seems almost flat. There are a couple of hills about twenty miles to the north that stand out like pimples on the skin and in the winter are nice-looking covered with snow. From the air this area seems like wool cloth thrown across a bed, the wrinkles in it going every which way.

When you're up on the interstate—it runs north and south, parallel to the river—you can sometimes see to the other side of the valley and realize that down here somewhere is a river you can't see, and you are surprised because the land seems too flat to hide a whole river. And then it is even more upsetting to realize that there is a whole town down here too that you can't see. There are places where it is built up around the exit ramps from the highway, but you can't see what they lead to, even though you can see a great distance to the other side.

When you're on the other side, the road along the river bank gives you an uninterrupted view—in great detail—of Cardiff from north to south. From that side of the river, you see the railroad tracks, then, beyond them, the backs of a string of stores and warehouses, then beyond them a parking lot where the River City Festival was held last week, then the office blocks built in the late nineteenth century, which surround downtown, then against the hills among the trees, the roofs of houses up to the skyline. Everything is bisected by the Passadumkeag Stream, which runs through concrete banks the last half mile before it enters the river. From the place where the stream joins the river, there radiate out across the town and then up the hills which the town climbs, a half-dozen streets, so that it is hard to go anywhere in Cardiff without going up or down a hill, and extremely hard without crossing a bridge.

Marybeth

There are steeples and towers of several churches, arranged on the slope of the hills around the half bowl which makes the town. Until the banks were built, the church steeples were the most prominent architecture in town. Even now, we look like something on a postcard, proclaiming all the small town American virtues. All last week, that's what we did. The River City Festival was one self-congratulatory event after another, funded by the banks and prayed over by the churches, until God knows some of us wanted to puke.

The most powerful political forces in Cardiff are the churches. You have the Catholics, and you have the fundamentalist Protestants. The Catholics and the fundamentalists have the biggest buildings in town, the largest church auditoriums, schools, and the most money. They have their own radio stations and broadcast their own church services on television, and sermons you see every Sunday find that the source of all evil in Cardiff is the drug pushers, and the abortionists, and the *homoseckshulls*.

All this town rising up these hills around, and there's nothing here which reflects me. I'm twenty-two now, and I thought by now that when I walked down the street, I would see people whose lives I'd affected, see things I've done. I want to live in a town where straight women and lesbians are a natural part of public life. I'd like to hear news of women on the radio, serious women who're doing important things. Lesbian women who're accepted as lesbians and who're known for what they're doing, not for their lesbianism. But there's no news like that. There's this DJ telling about the arraignment and about the service tonight, but what I'd like to hear is that the mayor has come out and said it's awful that a gay man was thrown in the river like a sack of shit. He hasn't said that.

Entering Cardiff at a quarter of five, I face traffic leaving town. I call my mother every Sunday night. I ask her how she is, and she tells me about the house painters who have been there for six weeks, about the glaucoma and the gall bladder, about the insurance policy that is not going to pay for the storm damage to the roof, and she tells me about Frances and her children, and how little Eddie is the cutest thing in first grade and can already add, and about Suzanne and learning the alphabet in kindergarten. She tells me about Frances' husband and his promotion. And then she says she is spending a lot of my time, so she must hang up. I say, "Wait a minute! I want to tell you about me."

"News" in some families is news about children. Mother's calls are about my sister's children, and they give me a paragraph on each child. In social discourse at a certain level, children are the only fit subject for communication. Frances lives down the river a ways, and when I was out west, she wrote three-page letters, a page each about her children, and concluded with a line, "Write and tell us all your news." The truth is, I have no news which is comparable to her news. I have no children. I have much news, and news which is as important as her news, but I have no children. Women like me write women like Frances, and their answers—detailed gossip about their children and nothing about themselves—feel like a willful refusal to communicate. I have spoken to Frances about this: *When I write you about myself, I would like to hear you write about yourself.* She says, "But what I say about my children is communicating about myself."

There is a whole realm of "news" that Frances is aware of. Her husband drinks too much and has beaten her. She has gone home to Mother twice in their five-year marriage. She has borrowed money from Mother every year since 1981. These are things she talks about only when she is alone with Mother. They are secrets to unburden oneself of, not facts about one's life to communicate to a friend or a sister. It is not that there is nothing else. She is active in church, she is in a Republican organization of some kind, and she and Van take a trip about twice a year. She has "views." And when I have asked her to write me about herself, to tell me about her interior life, she doesn't answer at all.

This is the way they control us. They tell us what they'll talk about: They'll talk about love between men and women and between men and women and children. They'll talk about diapers and hemorrhoids and mortgage payments and makeup on *women* and college tuition and the Neighborhood Association to Clean up the Magazine Racks and *his* job and *her* meetings and how exhausted everyone is upholding cultural values. And when it comes to how you think about the things you are permitted to talk about, they control that too. When somebody has been married forty years, there's only one permissible thought. There's also only one way to think about all those promises in the marriage service, about casual sex and S&M and what's natural and what's not. Their words are like prisons—adultery, promiscuity, degenerate—which force you to feel things you don't want to feel. They rate things, and then say their way of rating things is the only way: heterosexual over homosexual, non-sexual over sexual, men over women, adults over children, having children over not having them, house over an apartment, long marriages over short relationships. I get tired just thinking about having conversations with my family, we disagree on so much, and it would take so long and so much energy to go back and try to explain to them how it's really only an illusion that we are both speaking English.

I find a parking place in front of Cynthia's building and turn off the ignition but leave the radio on. The DJ announces the protest rally for gay rights. When you hear it enough, a part of you dies. I think the only people who will be there will be the ones from the dance Saturday night. That crowd is the only group who knew him well enough—and young enough to be crazy enough—to brave the publicity. That means 22 people. And that means we've bought too much ribbon.

I knew Bernie only about three weeks. He was wounded. He didn't know who he was and so he pretended, and you could watch him putting on his little pretense. Sometimes when you are watching an actor you catch him doing his thing. You see him calculating and accumulating the little movements which express an emotional state. He raises an eyebrow, his eyes move off to the left, and his head lifts a little. He opens his mouth, and you can see his tongue, and you know, watching him, that all this is being created for you out of nothing. It was the same sense you had watching Bernie. He was making himself right there in front of your eyes. He wasn't an actor, so he didn't do it well and what I remember was his panic. He checked out our response from moment to moment, his eyes wary, sliding from side to side. And no fucking wonder. His parents threw him out when he was thirteen.

When I discovered I was a dyke, right away I felt a closer identification with women. When gay men discover they're queer, right away they stop thinking of themselves as men, and they have to fight their way back through all the homophobic horseshit, and sometimes when they do it—I think Bernie was trying to do it—they are covered with scars and limp and can see through only one eye because of the battles they've fought and lived through. It must be like coming home from Viet Nam.

Cynthia is late. It is 5:15. We're going to have a hard time making it. The DJ talks about the murder and the service. He makes the service sound as hostile, aggressive, violent as the murder. He makes it sound like our service is our way of getting back. Getting even.

She comes out of the building—it is a one story brick affair—holding a heavy brown accordian envelope under her arm. She is smaller than me, with small features, except for her big eyes. She perms her hair so that she has this great ruff of curls over her forehead which goes all across her head and falls down her back. It's sleek and pulled back over her ears. She wears two long earrings on one side and three on the other. Her hair bounces, and she holds her head up. Her eyes are slightly narrowed, and she looks up and down the street. She is surveying the scene, she already knows I am here. I depend on her like food. I want to grow old with her, and I wonder if that is possible.

When she is in and the door closed, I pull out into the traffic lane.

"Have you thought about supper?"

"I haven't. But I have more lavender ribbon than you could use at a coronation of a homecoming queen."

"Swell. You really need me. Some people might think you were incompetent."

"Politically sophisticated, though."

"Yes, but domestically incompetent. I think we should go by the house, clean up a little, run by the Taco Bell for food, and then go on to the church. What do you think?"

"Right. Except that I have gotten sandwich things."

"I thought you said you hadn't thought about supper."

"I bought the stuff. I didn't think about it."

She grins. "You're terrific." She settles back against the seat. "That'll save time. I am too tired to move."

"I want to lie down."

We live in the third little town above Cardiff—Staceyville, Baskahegon, Hamlin. The houses thin out, and there'll be a stretch of fields and a country store, and then the houses start up again. You can take the interstate, but we never do. The river road is close to the water and close to what's happening. Up where we live, you have to cross the river. We live in an old house with an ell on the water, and we can lie on the grass and get the sun with our feet on the rock ledge, ten feet away from the water. Hamlin has a couple of mills and an Indian reservation, and people from down the river go up there because there's a mom and pop store that sells the best home-made ice-cream in the area. It's my first home.

"I don't know what is worse, answering them or not answering them." She has stretched out, her head resting on the back of the seat, and her legs as straight as they will go in front of her. She stares at the roof of the car while I drive us north. "They told a joke about fairies not being able to drown because they have wings. And I thought today I am not interested in answering these jerks in my office—insensitive clods—and I will ignore them. There didn't seem to be any other possibility. Either keep silent or scream. I didn't trust myself—I was in no shape—to speak calmly to them, to say what I should have said, 'The dead man was a friend of mine, and you should honor his memory or keep silent.' I know if I had spoken at all, I would have started to cry, and they would have smiled."

We have left Cardiff behind and are in the little stretch of the river between the cemetery, which we have just passed on the left, and the monument makers, who are half a mile ahead on the right. Staceyville is straight ahead. Cynthia is crying. "I simply did not have it in me to deal with things today. And that is rare." She strokes my thigh and then rests her hand on my knee. When Cynthia cries, her eyes fill up with tears and then overflow and her voice gets husky and unsure of itself. It wavers in pitch and tone. She doesn't sob the way I do. When I cry, I have to stop everything else. I would kill myself and anybody I had in the car with me if I started crying while I was driving. Cynthia can go on with her life—driving, cooking, working in the garden—while moved to tears by pain.

She looks at her watch. "We've got to hurry. I wish I could spend the week in bed. We shouldn't have gone to Mickey's last night."

She stares out of the window at Staceyville—they say it was founded by a man in the nineteenth century pissed off that Cardiff wasn't named after him—and bites her nails.

"Please forgive me."

She holds my hand, and I steer with my left.

"And I hardly knew Bernie! Imagine what it must be like to have known him well!" Her voice is growlly, as low as a man's.

"You are gay." I have been working on that all day. Why is it that I feel the way I do?

"Oh, you're right. And it's not even that it could have been us. They'll try those boys for murder—if they do what they said this morning they're going to do—or they won't, and that's beside the point. Nobody's tried to murder me, either, that I know of, and that doesn't matter—"

"What matters is what the boys did—"

"—they remind you of all this hatred—"

"—it seems like you can't turn around without being confronted by it, by this hatred and disgust in this town. Only—"

"—only, honey, you knew all that before."

"—only now it's down here in my lap again. And now, driving up and down the river this afternoon after work looking for lavender ribbon, it was all I could think about—"

In this stretch of highway, you can see for twenty miles, an immensely broad shallow valley, the river hidden in the middle distance, the sun behind us on the horizon casting long shadows. Everything is in high relief.

We get home, finally, and let the dog out and the cats in, and riffle through the mail. It is amazing that ordinary things are still coming through the mail. Why is there no announcement of the end of the world?

We shower and snack on cheese and crackers and falafel sandwiches to hold us, one activity after another, without thought. It is almost six. It will be almost seven or seven by the time we get to the church.

The phone rings. It is Simon Herter.

We speak about the ribbons.

"We've been thinking," Simon says, "about afterwards and how it would be nice to walk down to the bridge, all of us who come to the church. What do you think? Down to where Bernie died."

The idea of a bunch of homosexuals walking in an identifiable group through the middle of town sounds crazy.

"Sounds great."

I wonder who he has been with.

"We thought candles would be appropriate."

Sounds beautiful. A little group of us walking down the hill from the church to the bridge, carrying candles, standing with Bernie.

"Tell Simon hey," Cynthia says over my shoulder.

"Hey Simon. That's from Cynthia."

He laughs and sends greetings back to Cynthia.

"Would you pick some up on the way over?"

"How many?"

"As many as you can find. Don't worry about it."

"I'll go to Whitlock's."

"Just get what you can and then come on. It'll be fine."

Where am I going to get candles in the hour left before the service? It's going to take us twenty-five minutes just to drive down.

Cynthia has her arm around my neck. She lifts up the hair and kisses me there. She is still steamy from her shower. I feel the moist skin of her forearm across my cheek. I kiss it. She is wrapped in a towel. "Oh, sweetie, I have such difficulty saying I need you." We have ten minutes to ourselves. And now that we have it, I can't focus on it.

Perry

Now, I think of my father: I loved him, and I hated him. There is such confusion and conflict in my brain that I get a pain behind my eyes. When my father came home from work, we were required to stand at the front door to greet him, to show respect, my mother said, because he supported us all. He was a careful man with a very straight back, and when you hugged him, since he didn't bend, you were hugging his waist, and my face got mashed up against his belt buckle. I liked to hug him. Now I come home from work, and my children greet me the same way. It's good to walk up the steps and see Harriet organizing things just inside the door so they will all be there when I step inside. We are like a picture on a card. I like having the children around me and having supper with Harriet. I like our house. It's big and comfortable and, in some ways, grand. It has a front hall that is as big as the living room in our old house. It's suitable to where we are in life, though I have trouble paying the bills. The children like having space to run in. They run all over the house just when I want them to go to bed, and I can't find them and I feel like screaming at all four of them, beginning with Harriet. I usually have a headache by the time the children are in bed, and when that happens, I can't carry on a conversation with Harriet. I think my children feel the same way about me as I felt about my father.

I love my wife and my kids. I hate it when I don't have any time to myself. I like to watch the news. That's my time, when I first get home in the afternoon from work and I sit here on this sofa and drink my bourbon and watch the evening news. My father sat in the big chair in the corner and read his paper and drank a martini, and we were not allowed to speak. Of course if anybody needs something, I oblige, if what they need is important, but now all I want to do is sit here and have my drink and watch the news and not have anybody pulling at me. I used to sit in my father's lap while he had his drink, but I wasn't allowed to speak.

It's network news and the anchorman is a little figure on a screen that glows, reduced in size, simplified and blurred in outline, in three colors and two dimensions, like an animated and skillfully done cartoon. We are so inured to what technology does to what we see that we forget reality doesn't look like that. Brannigan reports the most important story in the country tonight—Mondale and who he is going to choose to run with him—and I know reality doesn't sound like that either.

Harriet calls from the kitchen, "Has he chosen yet?"

"Who?" Harriet is interested in the possibility that Mondale will choose a woman to run with him.

"Mondale. Ferraro. The vice presidency."

"He's talking to men now."

"Men." She is a feminist.

"There's more. Come watch. He's going to make a drama of it."

"In a minute." She's making supper. When I am hungry, the drink goes right to my head. Henry straddles my instep, and I hold his hands and ride him up and down, up and down. Ride a cock horse to Banbury Cross. He squeals with laughter every time I drop my foot and he falls. Henry is three and blond. Clara is five and blond. She sits on the floor, her legs straight and at right angles propping her up, a pile of blocks on the floor between them, building a castle. The dog sleeps with his head on her thigh. Helena is nine and sits in an upholstered chair opposite me, reading, grownup. She is blond too.

The odors from the kitchen occupy the den: sauteed chicken breasts, an as yet unidentified vegetable. Other odors: my bourbon, the smell of the dog. When Harriet comes in, I'll be able to smell her perfume—light, pale, lingering. When I kiss the children on their necks, I can smell soap and powder and sweat. You might think these smells—the chicken, the bourbon, the perfume, the powder— don't go together, and if you thought that, you'd be wrong. I am moved by odors. I remember the way things smell more than the way they look. The sour smell of burnt rubber where my car skidded just before I had my wreck. The smell of high school: leather and sweat and wax on the gym floor. Hairspray. Semen. A boy in the grade above me wore his hair in a great wave, and the odor of his hair oil permeated the space around him. I used to be late for class, waiting for him to come down the hall for the class next door.

Harriet comes in and sits on the arm of the sofa next to me. She runs her fingers around my neck. Her fingers are long and cool, and I feel the tips of her nails. It makes the top of my head tingle. I lower Henry to the floor and reach up and hold her hand. I like this. Sometimes I prefer to be at the other end of the sofa. I don't know what makes me one way or the other. We watch the head of Mondale on the screen for a few moments, speaking from North Oaks, Minnesota.

"What's he been saying?"

"Hart is still saying Mondale is pandering to special interests. They say he's selling out to NOW. He says he hasn't sold out. In any case, he says he's talking to men."

"Who?"

"Dukakis. Bradley. Cisneros—"

"Neither Feinstein nor Ferraro good enough? Is that the message?"

"He's playing games. He doesn't want to look like he's pandering to special interests."

"Are women a special interest? I think he should sell out."

"He says he's going to choose the best man."

"Right."

She has known all along that he was going to betray her. "It was too much to wish that he'd be honest, honey."

"He could say, 'The time has come to have a woman, so this year I'm not going to consider any men.' In any case," she says, "what's wrong with selling out to NOW? If he has to sell out to somebody."

"Hart and Glenn say he's become a captive of special interests. What he has had to promise them—the blacks, the elderly, the poor—is going to be expensive."

She runs her fingers through my hair and kisses my scalp. "Would you sell out to me?"

I smile and pull away. "I sell out every day." Then I turn toward her and incline my head, an invitation. She leans down and kisses me. "Why shouldn't Mondale do it once? Why should he be pure?" We have made beautiful children together. We have good friends. She entertains well and dresses well. She's an attentive, responsive, steady mother. She's supportive of me. I love what she is—intelligent, graceful, sense of humor. We are happy together. She is fun to talk with. Right now she fondles me about the neck, and my alert children watch all this silently. We make a pretty picture. They are so goddamn curious. I know what falling in love means.

Perry

We settle back into the sofa—me on the seat and Harriet behind me, her arms along my shoulders—and watch the screen idly. The reporter says that Mondale has 2,067 delegates, 100 more than he needs. As I grow older sex is less important, only I think about it more. Sometimes I am with another man—maybe a business trip—and we'll be waiting in our seats for the stewardess to come down the aisle with the drinks. He'll nudge me and glance at this young stew and raise his eyebrows. It doesn't mean anything. But of course, that's a lie. It means he's letting off steam. It means she is sexy. We're both men and sexually aware, and he wants to establish a bond between us. I smile and nod and glance at the stew. These are powerful feelings, and this is the way men deal with them, by laughing and joking—raised eyebrows—diffusing the sexual tension. When my parents had parties, I used to watch my father in the corner of the room surrounded by his friends, their fingers wrapped around their drinks, telling jokes.

I have plenty of friends. Harriet and I give large parties and know everybody in town, and I do the usual things. I hunt, I sail, I ski, I go to Boston regularly to see the Patriots and the Celtics. I play handball, and I do all these things with men I know, some I've known since college, and I have plenty of friends, I live the way American men of my class live, surrounded by men I can talk to about anything—politics, religion, art, business, our wives, sex.

The reporter says that 60 percent of Mondale's delegates come from three organization—AFL-CIO, NEA, NOW. The delegates to the convention are nearly equally divided between men and women. Almost 50 percent. Kinsey says that 37 percent of American males have had erotic experiences with other males leading to orgasm at least once since adolescence. No man I have ever known has ever said to me that he had ever been turned on by another man. Men never say that. They never say, Look at the buns on that one! Nice cock! No man I've ever sat next to in a plane has ever nudged me and then glanced at a handsome steward and raised his eyebrows. He's never said, I like his hair. Is everybody telling the truth? Is nobody telling truth? I get so sick of it I want to puke. My father never told a lie in his life, and when he died, there was real grief. I haven't gotten over it yet.

Clara climbs into my lap and settles down, leaning against my chest. I nuzzle her at the base of her neck. She ignores the screen

138

and me, concentrating on the tips of her fingers, aware of me and of the anchor person only as a rumble behind her back or as a puddle of electronic color in the periphery of her vision. She smells, as children should, of soap and peanut butter. Henry concentrates on the blocks. I catch Helena's eye and smile. She looks from me to Harriet and back again and smiles at both of us. Then she goes back to reading her book, ignoring the screen.

Today the three boys were arraigned for the murder. One of the boys was dating the niece of a CPA I know. Meet my nephew, the murderer. Meet my dad, the queer. They are local boys, nice middle-class boys out for some fun on Saturday night. That's what I mean. I've seen the dead one, but I can't remember where now. What would make a man choose a life of homosexual sex? Sex and drugs. They say the men who have AIDS have had a thousand partners, two thousand each. And they're on poppers all the time. No wonder. Their immune system just gives in. I've seen them on the hill looking for each other at night, standing under the lights and smoking cigarettes. A quick grope in the dark with thick fingers. Gay life is life underground, but now they're going to meet at the church tonight. All day long the radio and TV stations have been carrying the bulletin, "All this and more tonight, six o'clock news, Channel 4. Stay tuned." They're going to come out into the light, and here I am, tuned.

Everything that matters in life happens in public: graduation from high school, college, marriage, baptism. It's important to stop at certain junctures and to present yourself to the community as if to say, 'Here I am for your approval.' To stand up and let them look at you. A baptism is like that. You stand up in the front of the church with your wife holding the baby and you say, 'Here I am.' And everything about you suggests where you've been, and where you are, and how you fit into the society you are a part of. It suggests the moment in the parable when the worker in the field returns to the master and shows him what he has done with his talents.

Before the week is out, Mondale will be standing with the person he has chosen to be his running mate—I think he's going to choose a woman—and he will present himself to us. We'll congratulate ourselves. The system works. There won't be a revolution this year. The American system accommodates itself to each new pressure that comes along by bringing it inside—the Irish, the

Indians, the blacks, the Franco-Americans, the women, the radical left—and transforming them into something they hadn't been before. This is the way Americans are made.

What the books leave out is the anger. Because this is the way it works—an Irishman gets transformed into an American middleclass WASP male, say. We end up with a Sioux model of a middleclass WASP male, or even what we're faced with now—Bronx Italian woman's model of a middleclass WASP male. Is this what's happening? It's Geraldine Ferraro selling out, isn't it? Is it? Why is she doing that? I don't care whether he chooses a woman, but I want to know, what is she getting for it? And why don't we know what's really happening?

I survey my little kingdom. This room, our "family room," was just redecorated this spring. It signifies my success. Paneled walls, brass ceiling fixture, rust shag rug, brown corduroy sofa and chair. Harriet has gotten travel posters and had them framed for the walls. Where would I go if I could escape? If I could shed my wife and kids and be free again, where would I go? Somewhere among people with brown skins and dreadlocks, standing waist deep in a carpet of huge green leaves. Some Caribbean jungle island. Haiti.

The reporter goes into a story about a train wreck. The Montrealer jumped the tracks in Milliston, Vermont, and an unknown number are dead. We are shown pictures of the sleek railroad cars piled in confusion like telephone poles along a ditch. You would be sleeping, lulled by the clackety-clack of the rails. Suddenly you'd wake, struggling up toward consciousness, knowing something was terribly wrong, feeling the berth beneath you lurch and then go over in a sickening slow arc,—you clutch at something, anything, to hold onto, and your mouth would open in the guttural beginnings of a scream—and then in mind-obliterating pain, you'd be dead. You'd die in a dream.

I like standing in the front hall—waist deep among my possessions—and welcoming guests: I have on this blazer, and this beautiful tie, and I've taken some time getting my act together. I know I look terrific. My hair is cut and combed down properly. And when people start coming, I feel excitement, pride, pleasure, satisfaction—which is entirely different from what I feel when I see the money I am making—and more important, they're going to be proud to know me. A year ago I was made a partner, and Harriet and

I had a party to celebrate. My parents were here and her parents, and the children were playing on the floor, and there were all these people from town: my business friends, people from church, everybody from the neighborhood, Harriet's Sunday school class. All wonderful people. Some had brought their children, and some were children—there was ice cream on the porch for the kids—and Harriet's mother played the piano in the dining room for people who were singing old Beatle's songs.

There wasn't a homosexual among them. Except that I think that boy was the one who delivered ice cream and stayed to play with the children. That's crazy. Why would he come here? I don't understand why that boy stayed after he had brought the ice cream. And why would anybody want to call himself gay? I am about a lot of things more than merely my sex. What would have to have happened to you when you were twelve to make you decide to define yourself by the gender of the object of your sexuality? How could you present yourself to people and say, Here I am, I'm gay. In 1973 when I got married, I chose the healthy, normal way.

"Daddy." It's Helena, looking up from her book. She talks above the noise of the newscast.

"Yo, sweetheart."

"My counselor says the way you taught me to kick is all wrong."

She is in day camp taking swimming lessons.

"What way does he think you should do it?"

"A really hard way. I think I'll keep on doing it your way. I think I like that best."

"Does he say to keep your legs together and bring your fanny up in the air?"

She grins. "He says nobody does it your way any more."

"Come here to me." She gets down and trots across the rug to my chair. I spread my legs so that she can get on my other knee. My father was too stiff. He let us sit in his lap, but he didn't touch us. He didn't care what we thought of him. There didn't seem to be any cracks in him.

I have one arm around Clara and one around Helena. Henry sits on my left foot on the floor. Harriet sits on the arm of the sofa with her hand resting on my shoulder. I speak directly into Helena's ear. "Is it confusing when I tell you to kick one way and your teacher tells you to kick another way?"

She thinks about that for a moment.

"Is it?"

She nods.

"Do you know it's OK for there to be two good ways to kick?"

She nods.

"It's OK for you to try out his way. Did you know that?"

She nods.

"Would you like to learn his way?"

She nods.

"Then why don't you, sweetheart, tomorrow!" I stroke her back. I have done everything my father ever did, and when Henry comes along, he will do everything I've done. The anchor has been presenting a long story on the disarmament negotiations. It appears the Reagan administration may be willing to resume negotiations on nuclear missiles—intermediate range and strategic nuclear weapons —with the Soviet Union. They may even be willing to engage in talks on limiting antisatellite weapons. It's a nonstory: The Reagan administration has trashed every negotiating session since 1981. I wonder if my father was telling a lie too. What makes men do this? What makes men choose, in the beginning, to take on the role of providing for their families?

It's the local news. The anchorperson goes into a story about the River City Festival. My children are arrayed about me and my wife on the arm of the sofa, facing the television screen as if it were a giant camera lens. Look at me. Pater Familias.

"Did you know the River City Festival finished in the black?" Harriet asks, not taking her eyes off the screen. "The initial accounting figures show we may have three thousand dollars. All the major bills are in."

Harriet is a member of the fund-raising committee for the Festival.

"No one expected the beer tent to make so much money."

There appears on the screen a man reading a statement. He says, "The River City Festival Corporation wishes to thank the citizens of Cardiff for having made the recent festival such a success. They can be proud—" Clara shifts herself in my lap and Harriet strokes my hair. Helena, bored with me, goes back to her own chair and book.

The anchorperson speaks directly into the camera. He is a man you might meet in some large town selling something intangible. The lines about his face suggest anxiety, not character, and there is about the hunch of his shoulders a hint of some hidden defeat. He reads from a sheaf of papers in his hands. "Tonight at seven friends and relatives of Bernard Mallett will attend a memorial service for the dead man at Cardiff's Unitarian-Universalist Church on Union Street." The screen shows the front of the church. The camera is some distance away from the church—across the street— and since there is no movement in the scene, it is possible that what we are seeing is a still photograph. Or it could be a movie still from something set in a quaint New England village.

"Have you ever been inside?" Harriet asks.

"Nhhhm." It would be a terrorist flic and the threat would all be internal.

"The historical society organized a tour once. It's 1830s, I think."

"Oh, great." While she calls herself a feminist, she lives on my money and occupies herself, aside from the kids, with volunteer work. The question is not, Am I selling out? which implies that I gave up this for that, something real and valued for something meretricious. In 1973 it was a question of doing what was right.

A car crosses the foreground, and I see the limbs of the trees moving in the early evening wind. The front of the church is largely in shadow, since it faces northeast. Clara moves again. She is restless and needs her bed. Helena has not looked up from her book, and Henry has turned himself around on my foot and now, straddling my instep, his head resting on my knee, has gone to sleep. The dog stands up and claws the floor and, circling slowly, his nose pointed at his ass, he drops down again, already asleep. The anchorperson speaks in a voiceover.

"Members of Cardiff's homosexual community have expressed their anger at the murder Saturday night of Bernard Mallett, who was beaten and stripped of his clothes and thrown into the Passadumkeag Stream off the State Street bridge. Many plan to attend the service tonight to protest what they say is the harassment of gay men and lesbians in Cardiff. According to Reverend Simon

Herter, pastor of the Unitarian-Universalist Church, physical violence against gays is a common occurrence in Cardiff, and the service tonight is to memorialize a victim of that violence and to call attention to it." Harriet has settled herself more deeply into the arm of the sofa and is now almost lying down along the back behind me. I feel her breath on my neck and smell the faint, pale odor of her perfume, a scent which irresistibly speaks of our fourteen years of devotion.

The screen now shows the head and shoulders of the anchor-person again and then changes to a camera shot of the front of the court house.

"This morning three Cardiff residents were charged with murder in the Second District Court in the death by drowning of Bernard Mallett. Judge Harold Olsen withheld a formal charge until a decision is made on whether to try the juveniles as adults. He has ordered psychiatric evaluations to be made of all three. Formal arraignment has been set for July 17." As the reporter speaks, policemen can be seen walking across the paved area between the police station and the court house. There are several of them—beefy men in dark blue uniforms—and three of them are leading three teenage boys dressed in t-shirts and jeans, their hands handcuffed together at their waists. The policemen hold the boys' upper arms. "The three young men have been released into the custody of their parents."

"I know the middle one," I say.

"How?"

"I know about him. He dated Christian Wormick's niece this year. Christian was talking about it today. Says he's a scumbag."

This time the screen shows a newswoman standing on the steps of the Unitarian-Universalist Church, microphone in hand. Behind her, the camera takes in a large white wood classical pedimented doorframe set in a rose red brick wall. This camera angle, so close to the north side of the building and in the absence of sunlight, is entirely lit by the glare of artificial light. The woman speaks: "—the word is homophobia: the hatred or fear of homosexuals—" Harriet slides her hand along my shoulder until her fingers encircle my neck.

"I don't hate homosexuals," she says.

"How would you know?"

"I know."

"You don't know any." She doesn't. In bed we bring each other to climax in a fury of fingers and palms, slaps and pinches, charged with the fear that, were she him, I would be plowing his ass with the same bewildered dumb violence.

The woman at the church continues to speak into the camera. His height, the size and shape of his hard body—he didn't seem to have ever touched anything softer than a football—the lynx-like way he moved, the toughness of his eyes, the whole hurricane of sensations which he aroused in me was concentrated in the perfume of his hair oil. I was like a dog after a bitch in heat. And for fourteen years now, I've been lunging against a chain.

I have the whole bag. I have everything, a job, a wife, three children, a house, a place in the community, everything but myself, everything but peace. By now I should have had peace. What would it be like to go to the church tonight to stand among those people?

Would I feel at peace with myself there? Just to stand there among them, even if I didn't speak to anybody? Do they tell the truth there?

"I'm not afraid of them either." Harriet says, speaking over the reporter's voice. She looks at the screen, and nods.

"Please—" I shift away from her down the sofa.

Helena has stopped reading her book, even though she is continuing to look at it. She listens to her mother without appearing to. I know her.

On the little screen, a young woman walks up the steps onto the terrace before the church. The reporter turns to her and says something. The young woman's face comes alive with indignation. She stops and fully faces the reporter.

"How can you ask that? Of course we're angry!" She glances at the camera and then back at the reporter.

"That's not very dignified," Harriet says behind my neck.

"No." What kind of anger would you have to have that you didn't mind being photographed expressing it?

Another woman walks into the pool of light behind the reporter. As she passes, she stops and stares into the camera eye. She wears a red dress. She is middle-aged, maybe older, frazzled. She seems startled, disbelieving, as if she has never seen a television camera before. Almost confused. I know that woman. From the library. She knows me. The vegetable is green peas. His hair oil was called Vitalis and came in a clear yellow bottle with a red top. I get a hard-on just smelling that stuff.

"Come on," Harriet says, rising from the back of the sofa. "Supper is ready."

Clara climbs down off me. Harriet reaches down and gathers Henry to her.

"I'm not hungry."

She stops in the kitchen door and looks back, surprised. "I've got supper ready."

"I'm not going to eat yet."

"But Perry—"

"I'm going to sit here and watch the news—" Leave me alone.

"But supper—"

Helena looks at her mother and then at me.

I strain against my underwear. I sit here in the midst of things and drift away into my own world where he is and I am fourteen standing in a school hallway waiting for him to come down past me, to see his smooth skin and fine, straight nose and his oiled hair in ducktails.

Deborah

I'm blinded by the light. When I wanted most to see, I can't see anything but suns and their coronae in the gloom of the church. I stepped up on the terrace in front of the church and turned around to see what they were doing. A man was holding up a row of them on a bar, and another man stood under them, holding a camera on his shoulder. I tried to see her, but the lights were just beyond her head. She held out a microphone, and she said, "Were you a friend of Bernie Mallett's?" but the light blinded me and because I couldn't see, I couldn't think or speak. While I couldn't see, suddenly I knew they were photographing me. This is a private moment, and I was being photographed for television, and I thought of all the people who would see me going in here on their televisions tonight. This was not what I expected. I was not prepared for that. I couldn't do anything but turn away and push open the door into the dark church.

"Deborah!"

"It's Mrs. Elkins!"

People speak to me, but I am blinded by light in the gloom of the church, and I don't know who they are. I smile. I feel I should smile because they must be friends here. It is disconcerting to be able to think and feel but not to see. Is this what paralysis is like? Where your mind can roam farther than your body? I don't feel weighted and the space behind my retinas hurts. I hear people around me talking:

"The shits!"

"Over here. We have something for you!"

"Isn't it awful?"

The great windows of the church have brilliant painted glass which seems too thin, and the sun, still way above the trees at seven, burns out the color. I look away and search in the dark for the people who've spoken. People are talking all around me.

"Go and get her."

"I could kill that bitch from Channel 6."

There is a table near the door, and two young women sit there.

"Mrs. Elkins, I'm Cynthia Rieve." She has a great mane of blond hair, all curls, tumbling down in front of her forehead. "Come over here by the table. We have something for you." They have ribbons. Lavender ribbons. On the table is a great tangle of lavender ribbons.

"She's been outside since five-thirty, setting up," one of the women says, "and when people began to come, she turned on her lights and starting filming. She's been interviewing people."

I am beginning to be able to see now and to be able to connect faces with the voices I hear. Friendly voices.

"Can I pin this on your arm?" Cynthia Rieve holds a length of lavender ribbon.

"Of course you can." I hold out my arm.

"Bernie loved lavender."

There are other people standing at the table. The door is open behind me—I can feel the breeze and see the light—and others are coming in.

"She couldn't shut Claire up. She asked her, in that nice yuppie voice, 'Were you a friend of Bernie Mallett's?' and stuck the microphone in Claire's face, and Claire turned around on her—you know what she looks like, don't you, well, tonight she's breathing fire—and said, 'You bet your fucking ass I was a friend of Bernie Mallett's, and I'm still a friend of Bernie Mallett's —'" I don't know who it is talking. They're all laughing.

The door opens again and more people come in. Around the church, people are talking in low voices. Is it too many? Or is it not enough? I have to hope it goes well. This is the first time this has ever happened, and it would be a pity if something marred it. I don't see Luke or Arthur anywhere.

"Thank you," I say to the girls at the table. Sweet. I don't think I know anybody here.

The other girl gets up from the table and comes around to me. "Mrs. Elkins, I'm Marybeth Pechinski. I met you at the Holly Near concert last fall, and I heard you speak at the Take Back the Night rally last month. I think it's wonderful you're here."

"How sweet you are to remember." She's thin, attenuated. I watch as her left hand, hanging by her side, searches for and closes on Cynthia's hand. Betsey and I would never have done that. We prided ourselves on our ability to be in the same room and never let on that we even knew each other.

"You are very brave," Marybeth says. "Could we have tea sometime?"

"That would be nice." I can't imagine. She is Rebecca's age. "I'll give you my number."

"Oh, I know who you are. We'll talk later. And I can call, if that's OK."

It is. Very much "OK." We smile at one another.

I move on into the hall. This isn't the way I imagined it. Betsey would not have liked this. Around me people are talking.

"She's out there getting anybody she can to spill their guts on television."

"I think that's great."

"We're being used."

"We're using her. We're getting our story out."

Everybody is in blue jeans. I feel silly in my new red dress and matching shoes. Everybody is thirty years younger than I. There are rows of chairs set up in the hall, and there are people in them. The Unitarians took out the pews twenty years ago and replaced them with chairs, which didn't occupy as much space, and left twenty feet along the sides and across the back of the auditorium. People cluster in that space as if they were at an outdoor meeting. On Saturday night they take the chairs out completely, and this is where the young people have their dances. A hundred years ago this church had the largest, most active congregation in town. Ralph Waldo Emerson preached here for six weeks in 1834. Now they have about forty members.

"Mrs. Elkins, hello." It is a familiar voice, but I can't place it, and I turn around to find—Mickey McNamara. I had no idea! He has become so tall! Such a fine young man.

"Oh, Mickey!"

He smiles and puts out his hand. We shake hands.

"Oh, Mickey, I had to come." He seems, in the least little way, embarrassed. "I am afraid I have done something I should not have done. I am afraid I disturbed you yesterday afternoon when I called you. But I was so upset and so angry—"

"It's OK." He looks about him. He's looking for a way to end this.

"I knew Timothy, you know. I taught him."

I feel as if I have to justify my being here. How can I tell him why I am here? There is a group of young men talking behind me:

"Sure, they've been riding around all day, and every time they pass one of us, they lean out of the car and yell faggot! They give the finger too through the sun roof—"

"—Claire saw them at the 7-Eleven—"

"—Jack says they're going to drop charges."

"—says they're coming here tonight."

Mickey looks acutely uncomfortable. I put out my hand and touch his forearm. "I should go find a place to sit. Thank you, Mickey. Can we talk later?"

He seems grateful and smiles and nods and is gone.

I stand at the back of the auditorium, and I watch the door open and shut. There is not a continuous stream of people coming in, but there is a steady trickle—two and then three and then one and then two. The chairs, which will seat perhaps eighty people, are half filled. Dozens of people have not yet moved toward the chairs. The late afternoon sun, stained varicolored by the windows, comes in almost horizontally under the vaulted ceiling of the hall. There are too many of us now for this to pass unnoticed in Cardiff. Already, there are enough of us here—whatever we do here—to be threatening to people in town. Everyone is talking in low voices. The first church on this site—the one Emerson spoke in—was burned to the ground after a sermon damning slavery. This one was built in 1853.

I see Timothy with some of the young people. He looks even more frail than he did when he was in my classes. He smiles and laughs and looks as if he is about to burst into tears at any moment. His eyes never stay put on anything for very long. I wonder if he has a place to live.

Simon Herter is near the front. He has a hand on one hip and his other hand gesturing in the air by his forehead, as if he were trying to explain some difficult but very basic bit of metaphysics. I think the fact that this is happening here, in one of the oldest churches in town, in this blaze of publicity, is the most incongruous thing I have ever experienced in my life. I think I am the only woman in the room with stockings on. And a skirt! I considered wearing a hat!

Beside me a woman is surrounded by her friends. She talks in a low voice, and I sense, after a moment, that she is crying:

"—she saw the lights just as we got out of the car, and we both realized immediately what it was: TV lights and they were taking pictures of everybody going in here, and she just stood by the car and said, 'I can't go past that! I'll lose my job.' I had to come on, and I said maybe we could find a back way into the church where you didn't have to go past the lights, but we couldn't, so she stayed by the car and I came on—" She looks around her at each one of her friends in turn. "I couldn't not come. I've never left her before—"

I am having a sinking feeling. Luke and Arthur haven't come. Perhaps they will have thought better of the danger of being here—and the publicity. There is no one my age here. I am alone, and everyone else is in groups. I miss Betsey—it's been eighteen years—but I am glad she is not here. The world is too different now. I don't know what is going to happen—or how it is going to happen, but I am apprehensive. At mass, you know what to do: sit quietly in your pew until the priest enters and starts the service. And you know where you are in the missal too. This seems very secular, very formless. I am feeling very secular, very formless right now, and I need some support from somewhere, and I am thinking that my presence here is an embarrassment and that I wish I had not come. Simon Herter is a nice man, but I think what I want right now is someone who can represent Authority for me. Simon is wearing a sweater over his shirt and tie. He moves about, his blond hair colored by the light of the windows, speaking seriously to various people. He is so young that it is inevitable that everybody calls him Simon.

Around me I hear people call out to their friends who are just entering. They hug and kiss. "Have you ever seen so many people!" Then there are the queries: "Where is—?" "Have you seen—?" Everyone seems to stand on tiptoe looking out across the crowd. Every few moments the crowd is rent by a rumor which runs from one side of the room to the other: They're outside! They're going to let the boys go! They're going to charge them with murder!

There is an energy here in the room which is unfocused and formless. People don't know what to do with what they feel. I look about and wonder who I know and who is here and who is not. Where is Luke? Arthur? What is going to happen here? I can already see that what I had thought—we come to pray for the dead—is not to be expected. There is no crucifix and no altar in a Unitarian Church, and the mood is all wrong. Grief here is still taking the form of anger. I know about that. I have been angry in my time.

Timothy is surrounded by people. He looks down at the floor. A tall young man has his arm around Timothy's shoulders, protectively. That's good. He needs that. People are talking to him, at him. I expect he's being asked what happened. He looks extremely uncomfortable. Poor child. He has never had a chance. They say he's drunk all the time. I watch the little tableau for a while—Timothy at once protected by the tall young man and assaulted by all those standing around asking their questions—and consider what to do. What should be done for Timothy? Surely, if we find him a place to live—. And shouldn't we find his parents? But that's absurd!

Then I can't see them anymore. The crowd is between us. I am surprised I know so few people. I am surprised how many people there are. Most of the seats now are filled, and the space along the sides of the church and across the back where I stand is filling up. It is still difficult to tell how many of us there are. Simon Herter is moving across the front of the auditorium toward the podium. The door is open almost continuously now, a steady stream of people coming in. I am not the oldest here, nor am I the only one in a dress. Men and women are coming in together now, and the room is not so much dominated by groups of young men in jeans and t-shirts and separate groups of young women. It begins to seem to me to be an utterly indistinguishable gathering of citizens. Many of them must be straight. It matters to me oddly enough that I know which of us here are homosexuals and which ones not. And except for the occasional standout, I cannot tell. What did I expect?

Simon stands at the podium. He is a medium-sized man, five-eight, nine, regular features, handsome in an unassertive way. He does not have the failing so characteristic of preachers—an interior energy of such high level that it constitutes an aggression upon those around it—and, in my experience, his success has been due to his reticence. He waits and the room gradually becomes still. The people around me stop talking and turn their attention to the front where he stands. It is odd. He seems to allow it to happen rather than to invite or command it. The door opens again, and Luke and Arthur enter. Simon says, "Let us pray," and they stand where they are just inside the door. Of course, it is Arthur who has made them late. There is a rustle of noise in the auditorium.

"Great Creator," Simon begins. So. "We have come to re- member our friend Bernie, who was a young gay man and who died two nights ago. He lived in Cardiff for only two months, but he made us love him during that time, and we're going to miss him terribly." There are coughs and people shift in their chairs, and it seems to me there is an undercurrent throughout the auditorium. "Bernie came to this church a stranger, but he became one of us, and it seems to me now that he was always one of us. The first time I met him he volunteered to help with the cleaning of the church, and later he started helping with the nursery school. He was good with children. We shared a common humanity—"

I am fearful of this man, steeled against his words, apprehensive that he will turn all this into bathos. People around me stare at him attentively, and the congregation is mainly stilled, but it isn't conquered by him or his rhetoric. I think he restrains himself purposefully. He talks some more—it seems less a prayer than a sermon or an articulated, collective wish—his eyes closed, his hands resting lightly on both sides of the podium. He speaks of the common decency of humankind, uses gender-free language when he comes close to dangerous ground—God is "he" and "she," interchangeably—and speaks of the terrible tyranny of those who insist that there be only one way to paradise. My mind wanders, my eyes traveling over the crowd filling the seats and the space between the seats and the walls. How would one estimate its size? I am surprised at how many people are here. I want this crowd to be huge, and I am embarrassed by that fact, for I think the confrontational mode is unworthy of me.

Simon steps back from the podium and off the dais and then moves around in front. He has a candle in a small dish, which he places on the step below the podium. "I think we should light a candle to serve to remind us that Bernie's spirit isn't dead." He strikes a match and holds it against the wick. I watch it flicker and then grow and grow steady. "It also symbolizes our shared humanity and our resolution that this shall not happen again."

Then it is over. I wake with a start to discover that the whole crowd is shifting. People cough and talk. Eight or ten people have gotten up from their seats and are forming a line over to the right. Simon has led the first one up to the podium and raises the microphone and then steps back and down the steps where he is lost in the crowd. What's this?

It is a young man maybe twenty years old.

"I'm Jack." He speaks in a gruff voice as if he thinks one of us is going to question him. "I'm a friend of Bernie's. I'm queer, like Bernie, and the night Bernie was murdered, I danced with him every dance, and afterwards he and I went to the 7-Eleven and drank cokes and talked for a long time. I loved Bernie, and I don't give a fuck who knows that, and if anybody ever tries to throw me in the river, I'm going to take three of them with me, just to remember Bernie by."

There is a young woman standing next to me—slender, blue jeans, cowboy shirt, closely cropped brown hair—and I turn to her and introduce myself.

"Of course, Mrs. Elkins. I heard you speak. I'm Dana," she said. She steps back to introduce the woman standing beside her. "This is Marcia." I think, they must be lovers. Betsey and I could never have claimed each other like that in public. I find it intriguing, and I am envious, a little. I also find it oddly embarrassing, as if I know something too intimate about them, something that strangers shouldn't know.

"Bernie was pretty. He had long blond hair which hung down in front of his eyes, and he wore an earring, and he took a lot of grief for that. I thought he had a lot of guts." The young man is continuing to talk—loudly, angrily, full of anguish—into the microphone while people begin to move about the auditorium.

Dana nods toward the podium. "Jack is a dear."

Marcia asks, "Did you know Bernie?"

We talk in whispers.

"I knew the boy he was with. I taught him. Timothy."

"Oh, that's so sad. We're all worried about Timothy."

"Does he have a place to stay?"

"That's what we're worried about," Dana says.

"I think Mickey is going to do something about it."

We are quiet again and listen to Jack.

"The thing about Bernie that you need to remember is how strong he was. He was a lot stronger than I am. He kept saying, 'I am what I am.' I learned a lot from Bernie. I'm going to remember Bernie and what he taught me. I'm never going back in the closet again." I think he's going to cry. "I'm never going back in the closet again." He can't think of what to say. He has never learned to express the emotions he has in him, and that's heartrending.

He grips the sides of the podium. His head is bowed a little and he waits. Then suddenly he says, "That's what I have to say," and walks off the dais into the crowd, which stirs again and encloses him.

Marcia has left us and I see her making her way along the side aisle between the people standing and the people sitting, to the line of people waiting to speak. The light has softened. The sun is down now, and there are no more brilliant colors through the windows.

I was wrong earlier. This is not an indistinguishable group. There are many more young people here than would be at a church service. And the way the people array themselves suggests something different from the usual man-woman pairing. There are some men and women standing or sitting together—I see Helen and Constantine Demopoulos sitting together with Nicholas, their son— but I see many more women standing and sitting together in pairs. The men seem to be in groups, without women. And there is something I didn't notice at first: the earrings on everybody, small studs on the men and very long silver chains—two and three on an ear—on the women.

Another man stands at the podium and reads a letter which he has written to the editor of the *Sentinel*, which is angry and can't be understood. I feel sorry for him. He says, "A gay life is as valuable as a straight life," but he doesn't reach the crowd, and he steps down in some confusion. I wish that he had not chosen to read and had spoken instead from his heart.

It is so clear that the crowd wants to be moved, to be given direction. People watch intently what is happening at the podium, but they are constantly looking about the room. There is a look of wonder on everybody's face. It must come from the same place my own wonder comes from. How many of us there are! The church is filled!

A young woman is at the podium. It is Marybeth.

"Bernie was a friend of mine, and I hate it that he is dead, and that he died so painfully. We were all at the dance together Saturday night, and all of us that night knew the boys were out chasing faggots. But there wasn't any point in us going to the police.

Deborah

We've been to the police. We've been to the police. The police don't listen to us. We tell them about being harassed on the street, and they don't even listen. They don't write it up. They don't make any effort to find the people who make our lives miserable." She has their attention. "We go to them and tell them we've been beaten up, and they don't listen. They see the blood on our faces, and they don't write it up, and they don't make any effort to find the people who beat us up. The laws in this country are for the benefit of the majority—the straight, white, male, majority—and the only time the law applies to us is when they arrest us for sodomy or fire us from our jobs for being lesbians, because they say we are not of good moral character. So there was no point in trying to go to the police Saturday night to get help, when we knew the boys were out looking for queers to bash, because we knew we wouldn't get help from them. This was bound to happen. I grieve for Bernie, but it would have happened anyway sooner or later to one of us, one of us gay men or lesbians. It happened two days ago here, and it's happening right now somewhere else in this country that some little strutting kids attack somebody gay or lesbian and hurt them or kill them."

She's amazing. She's thin and pale and emaciated, and I wouldn't have thought she'd have it in her. She reminds me of Rebecca.

"And nobody cares! We're the only ones who care about us!" She's been holding onto the podium, and now, she makes a fist with her hand and brings it down firmly on the wood. "We're the only ones who can do anything to protect ourselves!" Then she holds onto the podium again and draws herself up. "Come out. We have to come out and tell them we're here and that we're not going away, no matter how many of us they kill, and that we're not going to change. Bernie told us what to say: I am what I am! I am what I am! And you can't kill me because there'll be another one standing right next to me, another faggot or another dyke, and every time you get one of us, there'll be another one standing there facing you saying, like Bernie said, I am what I am! and I'm not going to change for you!"

They don't wait for her to finish. They are applauding all over the room. People are moving forward in their seats and holding their hands up above their heads and applauding with great wide movements of their arms and hands. There is jubilation in the air. People are grinning broadly and looking around them at each other.

156

Dana, who is standing alone, slips her hand into the crook of my elbow and rests her head, briefly, on my shoulder. We look at each other and smile in amazement.

There are other speakers, young men and women, who get up and remember Bernie and their lives here in Cardiff as gay men and women. They speak of the corrosive effect of secrecy, of living in the closet, of their anger at the authorities who have done nothing to stop the level of street violence. As they speak, the shadows in the pitched ceiling and the corners deepen. The sun is down and there is no light now coming from outside through the great windows. In June I spoke at a gathering like this one. They wanted me to speak, they said, about what it had been like for me here, as a woman and as a lesbian in the fifties and sixties, before the women's movement and before gay people began to come out. I told them all about it. There seemed no point in keeping it hidden anymore. I don't know where Betsey is. I haven't heard of her in five years. I don't know whether she is alive or dead.

There is a young man standing at the microphone. He waits for the applause to quiet down and then leans over to speak into the microphone. It had been bent low for another speaker, but he doesn't bother to adjust it for his great height. He speaks in a low voice.

"My name is Robbie. I don't use words very well. I'm a dancer. And I would like to dance for Bernie." And then he walks away from the podium and down the steps to the area at the right where the line had formed. The people there move back against the wall to give him room, and all around the hall people shift to get a view. Mickey has moved from where he was standing against the far left wall up toward the edge of the dais on the left side. He has crossed his arms over his chest and watches.

Robbie is a lovely boy. He's like Peter Maartens, only not quite so big and rawboned. There is no music, and while he dances, he snaps his fingers to announce the rhythm. He uses the entire space cleared for him, dancing right up to the feet of the row of people against the wall, almost into the arms of that young man Jack. His dance is jerky, unlovely, unbearable to watch. He reaches out and drags his fingers back toward him across the carpet, making dark furrows, which he smooths out and then plows again. He claws the dark furrows and then smooths them out again and again, all to a powerful rhythm marked by the movement of his body and by the snapping of his fingers. Finally he stops in the corner of the hall, lying on his side on the floor, his arms around his knees. Jack is standing against the wall over him, the side of his head against the wall, his hand up against his head.

"My name is Suzanne." Our attention is drawn to a young woman standing at the podium. There was no applause for Robbie—I think people were too stunned and they weren't given time. I look for Luke and Arthur, but I have lost them in the crowd.

"The judge says he has to decide whether to try these boys as adults or juveniles. So he has ordered them released to go home to Mother while he makes up his mind and in the meantime, these boys are free to ride around town in a convertible and shout 'faggot' at all the gay people they see." She grips the podium.

"Well, I want to say this to all you judges who think that the murder of a gay man is not 'real' murder, the blood of Bernie Mallett is on your hands!"

Dana slips her hand again into mine and squeezes.

"To all you policemen and district attorneys everywhere who've ignored the crimes committed against gay people, the blood of Bernic Mallett is on your hands!"

She has short blond hair which is brushed up and away from her face. It seems to fly away, energized, electric.

"To all you ministers and pastors who've avoided speaking out on the great violence being done to God's children, the blood of Bernie Mallett is on your hands!"

"To all you macho dudes at Cardiff High School who think it's fun to go out on Saturday night and roll queers, I want to say the blood of Bernie Mallett is on your hands!"

"To Baptist ministers, to Anita Bryant, and to all those homophobes who say we are the abomination of the Lord, who think God is as bigoted as you are, I want to say the blood of Bernie Mallett is on your hands!"

She creates a drum roll of accusation: "To the pope, who says we are unnatural—

"To all you sexist pigs who run a patriarchal world—"

People are beginning to shout.

"To all you greedy capitalists who've robbed the poor to build your riches—"

They applaud. They've become gleeful. They're egging her on.

"To all you teachers and university professors who taught your courses and lied to your students when you hid our great history from us, when you told us Shakespeare didn't have a thing for his young man—"

People laugh in relief. They applaud even before she has a chance to finish her sentence.

"—that Michelangelo wasn't queer, that Leonardo da Vinci wasn't queer, that J. Edgar Hoover wasn't queer—" They are delighted and laughing and applauding at the same time.

"When you told us in your courses that in all of history, only the Greeks were queer and that happened so long ago it didn't matter—My God, you even told Montgomery Clift he ought not to be queer—I want to say to you, you liars all, the blood of Bernie Mallett is on your hands.

"And, finally, I want to say to you psychiatrists—"

She can't finish. The crowd is cheering and whistling.

"—I want to say to you psychiatrists who told us we ought to be straight and that you could make us be straight, to you psychiatrists who gave us shock treatments and aversion therapy and put us through the torture of the talking cure, and then had to put it to a goddamn vote when you finally decided to stop telling us we were sick, there's a special place in hell for you, my friends, because the blood of Bernie Mallett is on your hands!"

I am wondering what Luke is thinking. Unhappily, I know what Luke is thinking. I don't see him anywhere. Perhaps he has already walked out.

She waits at the podium while the crowd cheers and then gradually allows it to die down until the room becomes still again.

When there is quiet everywhere, she speaks again, this time very softly. "We've been made to feel guilty about ourselves and about the way we are and the way we make love. We've been made to feel guilty about the kinds of questions we raise about our society and its various oppressions. And we've been told that people so guilty ought to die. We've been told, I thought people like that killed themselves. Well, people, that time is over. No more guilt!" She puts out her hand in front of her, her index finger pointing. "We must tell the truth and stand up and in a loud and strong voice to those who have bloody hands for the murders they have committed, we must say, I accuse you!"

The applause moves around the room. People whistle and cheer and some stand up in an ovation. I see Jack, his face still wet with tears, his fingers in his mouth, his lips pursed, making shrill whistles and grinning as he does it. Dana, next to me, is smiling and clapping, and across the room, I see Marybeth and Cynthia. Robbie, his arms folded across his chest, stands in front of Mickey, who has put his arms around Robbie's shoulders. Mickey is laughing and stomping his feet.

And then there is Marcia. She's calm and quiet and she waits for silence. She is a beautiful woman. Beautiful dark eyes.

"My name is Marcia. I think Bernie would have enjoyed this, don't you?" Everybody laughs.

"Why is there no gay rights bill in this state?" We all clap and cheer. "Why is there no law which protects us from the intrusion of the police into our homes? No law which protects us from common street violence? Why is there no law which protects our jobs from discrimination by those employers who would fire us when they discover we are gay? Why is there no law which protects us when we grow old and sick and our loved ones are prevented from visiting us in the hospital, prevented from caring for us, because the state has defined 'family' so narrowly that we are excluded from our lovers' lives at their end? Why is there no law which protects our rights of inheritance in the deepest relationships of our lives? Why is the state doing nothing to protect our very lives from the plague of AIDS and, instead of protecting us, tells us we have brought this plague on ourselves? More than three thousand people have died already. Why does the state abandon its responsibilities and tell us that we ourselves deserve to die?

"Couldn't we, as a memorial to Bernie Mallett, do something ourselves to better our condition? Isn't it time to use our numbers and our economic strength to force the changes that will make our lives more productive, more rich?"

She steps down to applause—people are exhausted and happy and they let her go without a great demonstration—and returns to where Dana and I stand. She and Dana face one another and kiss. They hold hands, and their other hands are around each others shoulders, and then I watch as they do something I find infinitely touching. They stroke each other's hair and look into each other's eyes and smile.

Betsey and I loved one another too, until she became too afraid and left. When we were alone and could fully express our affection, we were very free with one another. She had a beautiful body, even when she became older, and I loved all of her. We used to bathe each other, and I did her hair. The memory of it causes me unspeakable pain.

There are no more speakers, and the room breaks up in some confusion. There is great noise. Everyone talks happily—I know I am—feeling sustained and supported and among friends. It's odd, how you can feel grief and anger—and be happy too, among friends. I am exhausted, but I don't want this to end. I would like this feeling of being in the middle of people who love me to go on forever.

People are forming a circle. There are so many of us the circle spreads out to the walls of the room. We hold hands.

"Shall we sing?" Simon asks.

People begin to sing a song I don't know: *We Are a Gentle, Angry People.* Then someone starts, *We Shall Overcome.* I look around the room for black people. I don't think there are any.

I hear from a group of young people next to me that they fear going outside. *The boys* are said to have made plans to bait us when we go outside the church. I don't care. I think I could walk through fire unshod. At the front someone is handing out candles. People are taking them over to light from the candle Simon Herter lit at the beginning.

Gradually, the number of persons carrying candles increases, spreads out through the crowded room, and, because I can feel a breeze, I know the door is open and people must be leaving. There is a movement among us all toward the door, like sand down an hourglass. I feel sad, too, for the people not here. I think Carole would have hated this, and I am sorry for that, because it might have brought about something good in her. I told Betsey before she left that it would be all right afterwards, that the coming out was painful but that afterwards it would be better than it had ever been before, but she didn't believe me.

I find myself drawn toward the door. Dana and Marcia follow. Mickey and Robbie are not far away. I see Marybeth and Cynthia. They stand with a big man in a t-shirt and blue jeans. He looks Italian. Cynthia calls to me: "Can we walk with you?" My new friends.

When we are close enough, Cynthia takes the arm of the man she is with and says, "Mrs. Elkins, I want to introduce Derek Dellesandro. He's an actor here in summer stock." She winks and says, "He's one of us!"

Cute. "I'm Deborah Elkins," I say. "Please, won't you, all of you, call me Deborah?"

We draw near the door, and then I see Luke and Arthur. Luke is glowering, his hands stuck as deeply into his pockets as he can get them. Arthur looks beatific—he wears red cotton pants and a white t-shirt with a red bandanna tied around his neck. He looks so silly at his age, got up like that, and so wonderful. I love him. He has such courage. I have thought tonight that had Bernie lived to old age, he might have ended up like Arthur. And I would have loved to have seen that. Arthur carries a candle.

We pass through the door out onto the terrace before the church. Across the street television lights photographing us prevent us from seeing anything, but to the right it is dark—it is eight-thirty or so—and the town spreads out before us, down the hill to the river. We—the people from the service—have made a long line which goes down the steps from the church to the street and then to the right to the corner, where the line crosses the street and moves left and is lost behind the building as it goes down Main Street to the center of town and the bridge. Everyone carries candles. The flames move and dance and seem oddly at home on Main Street under the streetlights and beside the passing cars. It is a soft, warm summer night. And at the head of the stairs, the breeze is cool and caressing.

Luke has been walking beside me across the terrace and down the steps, but when we reach the sidewalk, he steps aside.

Arthur stops also.

"I am not going," Luke says.

"Of course you're going," Arthur says. "Don't be a twit. This is the time when we have to stand up. Now stop that. Get back in line."

"It's hardly my kind of thing." He shrugs and grimaces. "All this passion."

"Luke Pendergraff—" Arthur speaks with some force. "—if you don't get back in line, I will never speak to you again. Or, I will speak to you continuously until you die, whichever fate you find most horrifying. Now here is a candle. I brought it for you."

The others have waited. Cynthia and Marybeth and Derek stand by the sidewalk ahead of us. Luke takes the candle awkwardly and allows Arthur to light it for him. He holds it as if it were dynamite—or obscene. He is such a dear.

Marcia is here. "Oh, Mr. Pendergraff, walk with us, please. It would make me happy."

"Can I walk with you too?" Arthur asks, playing at being hurt, "or do you just want the young handsome ones with you?" Luke harrumphs and pretends to a disdain he may, since he is perverse, really feel.

Marybeth steps to Luke's side.

"I am very sorry for what happened today at Dominic's," she says. "Claire didn't mean—. Everybody has been so upset—"

"My dear, you wouldn't believe—," Arthur begins.

"It is quite all right," Luke says. "I had entirely forgotten it."

So, I think. She was the one. Luke has not forgiven her.

We start off again down the hill. When we reach and turn the corner onto Main Street, we can see all the way down the three blocks into the center of town. The line of us stretches all the way. In the distance, you can't see people anymore, but you can see the soft light of the candles bouncing and dancing along. Ahead of us Mickey and Robbie hold hands, walking proudly. The girls about me—Cynthia and Marybeth, Dana and Marcia—touch each other and walk arm in arm. Derek has found a place next to me. He seems like a nice man. And Arthur, behind me, has slipped his hand into the bend of Luke's elbow and settled himself there. The candles illuminate our faces. It seems like a Christmas pageant, and all of us are thirteen years old again, fresh and new. Over and over tonight I have been struck by the beauty of the young people around me, their fresh faces, hopeful, accepting, confident. Candlelight becomes them. It becomes us all. "We're beautiful in this light."

Derek smiles. "'O wonder! How many goodly creatures are there here!'"

"'How beauteous mankind is!'" I continue, and he laughs. "Can you finish?"

"Of course." He smiles, crooking his arm and taking my hand and putting it in his arm and then covering it with his other hand. "'O brave new world that has such people in it!'" He looks down at me. "I'm an actor. I've never played Miranda, but I think I ought to stretch myself and try, don't you?"

"I think you've hardly shown that you can act until you've played Miranda."

Arthur, behind us, calls out, "Oh, I agree. And I'll buy great blocks of tickets and bring all my friends. It'll be a wonder."

"You're in *Twelfth Night* aren't you?" Dana says.

"And I play a soldier in *Henry V* and am not allowed to speak."

"Ah," Luke says, "all that bombast!"

"It's about heroism of a kind. I am a man of many parts. But I haven't yet played Miranda. Thank you—" Derek leans down to me. "—for pointing that out to me. I have much to learn."

"It would have been much better if many that had spoken tonight had kept silent."

"I was moved by the young man who danced. I found it very fine."

The cars passing slow and their drivers stare. One is a truck and in the back they have set up lights and television cameras. They are photographing us for the news. We have been told that we didn't need a parade permit if we stayed on the sidewalk and obeyed the traffic signals, so we disrupt nothing. I am aware of being watched, but I am not aware of any fear.

We pass a shoe store and I glance at the shoes in the window, and then there is a clothing store with jeans and plaid jackets in the window. I could name the rest of the stores down Main Street. I could say, *and after the clothing store is a vacant building which used to house The Vogue, a women's shop with expensive things, and then the drugstore.* It is an utterly ordinary city landscape. But I have never walked down this street carrying a candle. I have never felt like this. Ahead of me down the street as far as I can see, I see the lights carried by gay and lesbian citizens of this town. There is nothing furtive here, and if any of us feel fear, it doesn't show.

When I graduated from Wellesley, all of us wore white and walked in a procession to the chapel the night before, carrying candles, down an aisle formed by two long lines of our parents. When I passed mine, I looked up from my candle—I was terribly afraid of it blowing out before I got there—and I saw them, tears streaming down their faces, they were so proud of me. I didn't understand that, then. Mother said, "You were so beautiful!" I didn't understand then why that would make her cry.

We have gotten to the first corner, and we wait for a car to pass before crossing. It seems terribly funny for us to be so law abiding! I like it too that we wear the ribbons.

"Whose idea was that?" I ask.

"Mine," Marybeth says. "Mine and Robbie's. We went all over town today. You should have seen us looking for ribbon. I was so afraid there wouldn't be enough. Now look."

"I didn't get one."

"Oh, Mr. Pendergraff—"

"I really think we would all be more comfortable here if we called each other by our first names, children." Everybody laughs. "Please call me Arthur. Or, if you like, Warren Beatty. Or Beautiful."

"Hello, Beautiful." Cynthia puts her hand on his arm for a moment. "I think I like 'Beautiful' best."

"Luke, you came in so late—," I say.

"I have an extra." Marybeth pulls one from her pocket and ties it on his arm. "Do you forgive me?"

Luke smiles painfully.

"Bernie would have enjoyed all this," Dana says.

"He was a great one for symbols," Marybeth says. "He liked to give people one single flower. We thought about that, but it was too expensive."

In a doorway, Robbie and Mickey and Jack are standing, and when we come abreast of them, they step out and join us.

"Hi, fellas." Derek holds out his hand to Jack.

"Hi, guy," Jack answers and moves to Derek's other side, away from me. They hold hands. They walk slowly so they don't rush me.

"I miss him."

"Claire said the best thing last night," Mickey says. "She said, 'What a bummer. He oughta be here in his dress.'"

Everybody laughs.

"I should go home and dress as Miranda and come back and meet you at the bridge."

"Look honey—" Marcia speaks in a mock-tough way. "—don't push your luck, hear? Besides, I got plans for you later."

I am sure I am not the only one aware of the cars driving by slowly, the drivers and passengers staring at us. We're on display, us with our candles and our lavender ribbons. I think there must be a fierce astonishment at the sight of us.

Arthur sees them too. "Imagine, children, what's happening now! All God's faggots parading down Main Street of Cardiff carrying candles! I feel so proud. Like royalty!"

"Are you afraid?" I ask.

"No," Jack says. "If any of them—"

"No!—" It's Arthur. "God looks after us!" He rolls his eyes to heaven.

"Yes. Terribly." It's Marcia.

"Who were you speaking to?" Marybeth asks me.

"I don't know. Anybody. I'm afraid."

"I am glad we're doing this together."

"If it came to a pitched battle—" Dana begins.

"If it comes to that," Derek says, "we'd lose. I'm afraid. There aren't enough of us. And I don't want to die. I don't want you to die either, Jack."

Jack grunts.

"I'm just going to run very fast," Marybeth says. "I'm good at that."

It was fear that made Betsey leave. I told her I was going to the police and was going to press charges against the man who did it. She said if I did, they'd put us on trial. Everybody would end up knowing about us. She couldn't bear that, she said. But we'd done nothing wrong, and it would have been terrible to remain silent. Silence would have meant accepting that I was guilty.

We shield our candles from the wind at the next corner when the building no longer protects us, and then we look to see how to cross the square.

"I'm afraid of what's going to happen tomorrow," Mickey says.

"What do you mean?"

"Nobody in my family—or at work either for that matter—knows I'm gay. And when I saw the television cameras there tonight, I wondered what I was going to do. This means if they haven't seen me on television tonight, I'll still have to tell them tomorrow because so many other people will have seen me on television tonight." He gestures to the street with his free hand. "I don't know who's driving along there either. Who's seen me? I think my whole life is changing tonight, and when I get up in the morning, I have to face all that."

We are across the street, and before we walk toward the bridge, we stop to shield our candles again against the wind.

"I think my sister will never speak to me again."

I have no sisters. My parents are dead. Betsey has left. During all our time together, we never told Mother and I am glad she died without knowing.

"I think my life as I have known it has come to an end tonight," Mickey says. "I'm afraid, but—"

Robbie interjects, "But you know you had to do this tonight."

"I feel like crying."

"I think that takes a lot of courage," Dana says.

"Nobody knows how much courage faggots and dykes have when it comes to it, do they now, sweetie. Let me tell you—"

"Oh, please, Arthur—"

"Let me tell you what Luke here did just this afternoon, right there—" He points to Dominic's ten feet away. "—he was a regular knight in shining—"

"I'll bet you were, Luke," Dana says, smiling. "I am glad you came with us."

"Young lady, I've been fighting all this a long time. I'm seventy-two years old. And I sometimes think the greatest virtue is survival. I don't know that this is any good. Everybody tonight is so excited about there being four hundred people in the church. What of that? Where are the rest of them? Of us? If 10 percent of the population is homosexual, then there were two thousand six hundred people sitting at home cowering by their stoves, too afraid to move or too oppressed to know that they should move. And we think getting four hundred to come out—and a third of them might have been straight in that church—is a great victory. This whole thing might be a big defeat for us. Now the paper tomorrow can say there are only four hundred homosexuals in this town that we need worry about. If you think numbers are important, then you ought to remember that their numbers are always going to be bigger than our numbers." We are at the bridge and Luke throws his candle into the water. I watch it go end over end and then, with that tightlipped sucking sound, fall into the water and go dark.

There are a great number of us on the bridge divided by the two lanes of traffic, and some young men are standing along the edge of the sidewalk warning people the police have said they will arrest us if we step into the street. There is a great crowd. Some people have dripped wax onto the railings of the bridge and have set their candles there. There is a row of them, flickering, burning unevenly, the wax dripping onto the aluminum and the concrete. I turn around and watch more of us coming down the hill. The line of us stretches all the way back up the hill to the church! The candles from this angle are more visible and, reflected against the skin of the people holding them, give off a broader light. The line of us seems endless, a multitude. This candle or that candle might bounce around, go out or flare up, but seen from down here, the line of them together seems unquenchable.

All coming to the place where Bernie died. Some of us look off the bridge into the dark waters. It happened just two nights ago. I look back up the hill at the vision of us descending to the river. The greatest pain of all has been thinking that there were so few of us.

Derek takes my arm. "It's like a vision of the dead."

Marcia stands on my other side. We look at all these descending. "It's the Israelites following the pillar of fire out of Egypt."

Dana is here too. She is next to Derek. "Look guys, it's us, four hundred faggots and dykes in Cardiff who have decided not to take it any more." She is grinning broadly.

"It's wonderful."

"It's grand. Who would've thought so many of us would come out?"

"I wouldn't have thought there were so many of us."

"More than that, more than that."

I think of Carole and the others who are not here. What is the difference between those of us here and those at home? Is it merely that we are the fortunate ones, who have been able to survive our lives with ourselves intact? Who have been battered but not defeated? But why have we not been defeated? Carole has been willing to settle for so little. Why is it that these people coming down the hill with their candles demand so much? Poor Timothy, who floats among us like a ghost!

People are happy. Arthur has his arm in Luke's again, and they stand against the railings and watch the crowd.

"Let's go to the police station," Dana says.

"Why?"

"To let'em know we're going to be watching them and the way they handle Bernie's case."

"Let them know we're here." Mickey stands very tall with his head up and shoulders back.

So I got up the next morning after it happened, and I put on a nice dress and I went to the police station. Betsey said if I went she wouldn't be there when I got home. But I didn't think she was that afraid. I didn't think she would abandon our life together out of fear. I thought she would know that there simply was no alternative, so I went to the police station. And when I returned, she was gone. You can tell when you walk into an empty house. She had packed a bag and left and afterwards all I ever had from her was a message, sent to me by her brother, to send her things to an address in Delaware.

The police station is only back along the bridge and then half a block up Court Street. People drift along. There is less of a sense now of a march than of a crowd composed of little groups of people. Some people have kept their candles. We leave the bridge and start the climb up Court Street. The court house is a large neoclassic building built in 1910, and the police station is behind it—1960s brick modern, ugly as sin.

Others are there before us. They stand in front in small groups, waiting. I look about me as we join the group clustered around the steps of the police station—I can see most of my new friends: Simon is over to the left, Dana and Marcia are with me, Mickey and Robbie a little in front, Derek, Jack behind me somewhere. Luke and Arthur are just coming. I have lost track of others: Timothy, Marybeth.

I am waiting for something to happen and nothing does. When I came that morning, the police station was still in the basement of the court house. I went in and asked to see a sergeant, and he took me into a room, and seated me at an oak table, and I told him what had happened. Betsey and I were walking along the stream at dusk the day before. The sun was down behind the trees, behind the houses, and the sky had turned pink and gray and soft. We were in love, and I reached out and took her hand. There was nobody around to see us, so I thought it was all right. I held her hand, and then we embraced.

Then, suddenly, there was a man standing there, tall and skinny with greasy hair and a horrible grin on his face. He said something awful about two women holding hands. He said what we needed was a good man. Then he came close. I think I was transfixed with fear. I don't remember what happened to Betsey because he chased me and threw me down on the ground behind a bush. I fought, but he was too strong—I remember his long greasy hair hanging down and brushing against my lips—and I couldn't resist him.

"Was a plan made?" I ask whoever would listen.

Later, I got up and tried to fix my dress. I walked toward home. On the way, along the path, I found Betsey, sobbing.

"No," Dana says. "I think most of us had a sneaking suspicion that we wouldn't get this far."

The Constitution recognizes a right of the citizens to petition for the redress of grievances. I think, if I had ever imagined it, I would have imagined it like this. A group of citizens gathered around the steps up to the door of the police station, come to have their wrongs righted.

"We ought to have a long scroll."

"Whatever are you talking about?" Luke says.

"You know. Scroll. The list of our grievances. In pictures it's always a very long sheet of paper."

"Computer paper," Dana says.

"Yes, and tied up in ribbons. Lavender ribbons." It's Arthur.

Derek bends down speaks in my ear: "In pictures the citizens are always huddled, and it's always snowing. We're wearing the wrong clothes."

The police listened. They asked me if I had proof. They asked me what I was doing there alone at that hour. They asked me where my husband was. They declined to search for the man. And then they sent me home.

I went back again. And they let me talk to another sergeant this time. And he sent me home. And I went back again and again, demanding that they do something, and they kept running me off, until finally the place between my legs healed and I quit asking. Betsey might as well have stayed. The only people who ever found out were all those sergeants I told.

Nothing is done. The glass door into the building remains closed. Occasionally someone goes in or out on business, but not our business and it seems to me even if the chief of police came out—I hope he doesn't because he is a very difficult man to deal with on committees—I don't think we have thought enough about all this to know what to say to him. We have a need and an ache, and we've brought that right up here to the steps of the police station. But we don't know what we want. I have no fear that we will fail to take it further the next time.

"We have to do something," Derek says.

"Can't let all this energy go to waste."

"Where's Simon?"

They begin to call for him.

He answers from the other side of the crowd.

Derek calls out, "Hey, folks! Now that we know how to do it, shall we get together next week and turn political?"

There is a great roar of approval. A car goes by just at that moment, and I imagine the driver in a panic for fear of his life.

"Simon?"

Simon yells back across the crowd.

"Can we have the church next Monday night, seven-thirty?"

"Absolutely!"

Derek shouts again to the crowd. "Next Monday night, everybody, at the church, seven-thirty! We need a coalition of gays and lesbians in Cardiff."

There is another great round of shouts and then people wander around a little. They are drifting away. I am thinking, *Is this it? Is this the way it's done?*

Marcia hugs me. "I love knowing you. I've admired you since we first moved here. I'm going to have fun getting to know you better." She smiles.

"Oh, I don't know what there is to admire in me." I can't think what she is talking about. I am a school teacher. But to be honest, I feel flattered because I thought she spoke best of all tonight.

"Hug me too, please," Dana says, and we do. "We're going to have you to supper." We hug again. "Thanks for what you said at the Take Back the Night rally."

"You're kind."

They say goodbye and walk back up toward the church.

I see now that some people have left their candles on the steps of the police station. Simon is on the other side of the crowd. Derek has joined him there and Jack—they're holding hands again, I see—and Mickey and Robbie. I go over.

"Robbie—" He looks up at me. It is only now that I realize they all have bowed heads. He smiles and nods, and then bows his head again, closing his eyes. Simon is praying.

"—he suffered terribly during his life. He was not allowed to grow up among people who loved him and could have supported him, and he had to make his own way in a world which hates homosexuals. We hope that by coming together tonight, and by remembering the person Bernie was and the way he died, that we can nurture in ourselves the qualities which he had in such abundance, his joy of life, his acceptance of himself, and his courage. We pray that Bernie may be the last to die at the hands of bigots. But if that is not to be, we pray that we can be shown what we must do to lessen the suffering on this earth." I stare at the candles burning down on the concrete steps.

Cars go back and forth on the street. There is a television camera and its attendant lights on the edge of the crowd. We are always watched.

Mickey comes over to me with Robbie.

"Mrs. Elkins—"

"Oh, please, Mickey. Call me Deborah." I am smiling.

He smiles too. "Deborah, this is Robbie."

How wonderful. "How well you danced tonight, Robbie."

"Thank you." He is embarrassed and pleased.

"You are wonderful together, Mickey, you two."

He grins. Then they're off.

So. That's accomplished.

"Goodnight, Deborah," Derek says. He puts out his hand. "I will see you next week?"

"Of course."

"Have you got a way home?"

"My car. Thanks."

Timothy stands alone by the door. I go over to him.

"Do you have a place to stay, Timothy?"

He smiles and shrugs and walks off into the darkness.

Luke and Arthur lean against the hood of a car parked in front of the station. I join them.

"You have on a very noticeable dress, Deborah," Arthur says.

"Thank you, Arthur."

"Thank you, Deborah, for making me come." Luke looks at the candles still burning on the steps.

"Arthur made you come. He threatened to talk you to death. Or something." I wish Rebecca had been here. She has her own life now—she's a junior at Columbia—and her own concerns. I don't think I have admitted to myself how frightened I am. Or how dangerous I think our circumstances are. I feel like I am walking into a dark and strange house, and I would like to be surrounded by everyone I love.

"Would you like to come to our house for a drink?"

"I think not. I am tired."

"So am I."

"So are we."

"Goodnight."

"Goodnight."

Luke

I am suspicious of large emotions, of getting swept away by some deep-throated hymn into believing that, for example, there is a God, who is a mighty fortress. Or of having my reason taken away from me by a throng of people holding hands and carrying candles. Joy, grandeur, *hope*. They turn the brain to soup and prevent you from working the equations of our existence. It was wrong tonight, walking down the hill to the bridge. We were doing the wrong thing for the wrong purposes, and it will have the opposite effect from what we intend. It is impossible to come together after a violent death and to be able to think clearly, to know what must be done and why. What does this death mean? What killed this boy? And why? How is one to think? In the middle of Whitehall is the Cenotaph, which is inscribed *To the Glorious Dead!*

In my kitchen is a small sink under the cabinet with the liquor. I had it put in four years ago to make drinking whiskey easier. I considered getting an ice maker but decided the chore of explaining away my purchase of an expensive, useless appliance outweighed the convenience of handy ice. So I drink my drink neat. The light from the clock on the stove casts my reflection in the black panes of glass in the window above my counter, and I raise my tumbler to a seventy-two-year-old faggot in a dressing gown: "No tears." The scotch goes down and wakes my insides. I drink moderately most of the time, and sometimes I set it down as a stated purpose to get very drunk.

I don't need light to see my house. It was built in 1870, one year after the concept of homosexuality was invented. A Victorian cottage on the edge of the park, just the size for one person: two bedrooms upstairs under the eaves. Right now Arthur, who waited around after the march until I felt forced to invite him to stay, is in one. I will sleep in the other. My house is furnished with things I inherited from my mother and my aunt—I squat among things other people have chosen—and things I've bought around here. I walk into the dining room and navigate past the chairs and the table in the middle of the room. The chairs I bought to match the table—heavy rosewood—which came from Mother. The table used to sit in her entrance hall, with a linen runner and card tray for her guests. I can remember when I grew tall enough to see its top.

I run my hand across the smooth curved back of a chair. Here are the remains of Cardiff in the nineteenth century. We know little because people didn't care enough about their lives to write it down when it was happening and before the symbol mongers got hold of it. Somebody preached a sermon against slavery in the Unitarian Church in 1853, and the next day it was burned down. Now the sermon and the fire are cause and effect, and you can understand them only in the context of the abolitionist movement and the Civil War. I want to ask, what fears did this anonymous preacher raise in the hearts of these people in Cardiff that they hoped to quiet by burning a building? We live among other people's furniture, and truth is obscure.

The newspaper this morning said, "the gay community," and a hundred years from now somebody is going to read that and think that there was such a thing. A hundred years ago when the word "homosexual" was first used, there weren't any—only people who committed an occasional sodomitical act. Now we've all arranged our lives and our concepts of ourselves to fit the word. Things are backwards, and we progress into the future with our eyes growing like tumors, out of the backs of our heads.

On the walls of the dining room are photographs in deep mahogany frames. My father was a banker. It is he in the starched shirt over the sideboard next to Mother. How could such a soft woman have kissed a man so choked by linen! When I was thirteen and fell in love with my first yardboy, we were called queers and faggots, and it was worth your life if you let anybody know you were one of *them*. We didn't "come out" then, and it was easy to mask the truth. You saved your energy for the night and for the places where it was possible to be a queen without getting a broken arm and a brick to the middle of the back. We admired ourselves for our cleverness and our style, called each other "Mary" and "Louise" and congratulated ourselves on our survival skills. During the day, we passed unnoticed, and no one, no one ever mentioned homosexuality. Now we call ourselves "gay," and everything has become serious and charged with emotion and political significance. For the last fifteen years we have been discussed in every private detail in every magazine on the rack at the drug store. I can't say that publicity has brought us freedom.

Luke

I am tired, but I cannot sleep. It is one of the conditions of my old age. Arthur, on the other hand, who is my age, sleeps like a fat dog: untroubled and heavy. Many nights I pad around my house in the middle of the night, drink in one hand, bottle in the other, sniffing furniture, angry at the decay. What can these small rooms and their low ceilings and small windows and fireplaces tell about the lives of the people who built this house? I'll wager they were cold as hell. I put out my hand in the dark and touch a cut ruby-glass decanter, which I cannot see. Mother's mother gave it to her on her first wedding anniversary. I can feel the chip in the edge.

What happened tonight is not what we think happened. They stayed home tonight and watched us on television, and what they saw is not what they think they saw. The "gay community" is composed only of those who show up, and that's different from the "black community" or the "Jewish community." One question is, Who showed up tonight? And the answer to that one is, Everybody whose homosexual feelings make them want to be a Special Interest in the Land of the Free. The more interesting question is, What about the people who stayed home? What do they do with their homosexual feelings? Do they become "straight"? Blacks who stayed home from the march on Selma didn't become white, resting around the tire swing under the pecan tree in the side yard.

It is difficult to pour a drink in the dark. But once in, it's wonderfully *clarifying*. Gays and Straights. The division exists only in theory. Kinsey dealt with all this forty years ago. Two out of five males have had orgasms sometime in their lives with other men. Twenty-five percent have had something with other men that lasted at least *three goddamn years*. Jesus, the hypocrisy! We should say, 'Look at your own fucking self.' Instead, by getting out there on the street, we've invited them to do just the opposite: Look at us.

My house is gilt and plush. I started with a chair and a love seat and then got Mother's things. I wanted coherence, so I bought a gilt mirror and crystal-drop candlesticks for the mantle, and then I got my aunt's things. This is the way life is: a piece here, a piece there, a gift for a birthday, a purchase for Christmas, and before you know it you've got the whole prison, a rigid style of red plush and gilt and crystal and tassels which suffocates you. I have trapped myself by increments, and I hate it, and sometimes I think I will sell all that I have. And then it occurs to me to ask, How would I live then?

I lower myself into a chair and cradle my drink with both hands. My chairs are uncomfortable. Because we had this service tonight and walked down the hill to the bridge, they are going to feel threatened to their roots and are going to entrench themselves deeper in their own narrow view. They'll believe even more that they are straight: After all, all the faggots were out walking down the hill! We are in for a time of moral pronouncements against us from the pulpits, editorials against us in the papers. We are exposed, and we're going to be damned. Even if we win this one—since we've let them define the terms this way—we are going to lose the strength that comes not only from saying, *We are everywhere*, but also from saying, *We are everyone.*

I see my reflection in the black windows of the living room. In this dim light I am nothing but white hair and heavy brows, a beaked nose and sharp chin. I haven't been handsome for twenty years. I have wanted to be unswayed by passion. I am a man with courage and some dignity—white hair, my mouth closed—and yet when Arthur came tonight to persuade me to go, I gave in, against every principle. I allowed him to lead me to the church. I weaken and decay, and I don't understand why that happens.

The street light casts a quadrilateral on the wall over my sofa, illuminating a steel engraving of a nineteenth century battle, soldiers lined up in their tunics and high boots, straps over their shoulders for their swords, in ranks which follow the curves of the terrain, some leader on a horse holding up his sword. The Crimea, the Civil War. We are unable to take on the whole army, so we fight skirmishes with flanking troops here and there. We have no leader and no battle plan, and we are hopelessly exposed.

We might have been Israelites following the pillar of fire out of bondage into the promised land. The image suggests victory, *with God on our side*. But now they know we are here, and they know who we are. Instead of knowing our strength, they know how few of us there are. Four hundred! And the radio said there were only two hundred. Why should they have consideration for us after tonight? That young woman, Dana, said how strong we are! There is no God and no pillar of fire and no promised land. It is my age that makes me so morose.

We have set ourselves up to be slaughtered. They will tolerate us just as long as we keep to ourselves, our ghettos in the Unitarian Church, the bars, Boston, New York, late at night *on the hill,* but if they think we are a real danger, they will be merciless. We are infected now with AIDS, and they call for quarantine and tattoos—the concentration camp—and no talk at all of *cure.* We are dying now by the thousands, and they say we'll die by the tens of thousands before it's over. And everywhere—the government, the health service industry, religion—we are told, *You brought it on yourselves.*

In 1869, they said the way we have sex sets us apart, and we let them do that to us. Now we have become vulnerable to this malignant neglect. *Know thyself.* Instead of crying for tolerance, we should cry to them—scream it from the rooftops—*Know thyself!* We make pariahs of ourselves and call it joy! When will we grow wise! When will we make *them* the battle ground, their appalling hypocrisy and dreadful lies!

We will fall to fighting among ourselves. Deborah and young Jack have different aims, though they walked down the hill together. I can't talk to Arthur. Carole is speechless. We face a civil war and internecine strife and—isn't this always the way?—our supply lines are exposed and we have no heavy industry. And we are being made to fight an enemy on our own ground who is exactly like ourselves!

I hear Arthur coming down the stairs as if he is trying to do it without being heard.

He enters the living room.

"Luke?"

"It's me."

"Must you prowl around in the dark and make me think you are being robbed?" He finds a light and switches it on. "*What* are you thinking of?"

"I was thinking of Rhett Butler and Scarlett."

"Luke, you are such a romantic. What time is it?"

"Three—"

"Sweet Mother of God. Are you drunk?"

"Not yet. I don't think so."

"Won't you come to bed?"

"I was thinking about tonight, and I couldn't sleep."

"It was such a joy, wasn't it?"

"I had rather a different sense."

He sits down on the sofa and arranges his robe. "You would, you old bear. Come sit by me."

"I was thinking how absurd all this is."

"Come sit down and tell me."

I do. I lie down and put my head in his lap, and he arranges the strands of my hair across my forehead. "The North had all the advantage in the war, and the South didn't have any—no heavy industry, no real navy to keep the supply lines open, no market for its agricultural products—and they blundered into the war anyway, full of passion and outraged innocence, convinced they were right and would win."

"And they lost."

"Even if they'd won, it would have been an irony. They fought over all the wrong issues. They thought it was state's rights and slavery, and it was really about money. Even if they'd won, they wouldn't have recognized what they won. Lincoln's Second Inaugural Address doesn't make any sense."

"Nobody wins in a civil war." He stretches his arms above his head and then brings them down again to stroke my forehead. "But everybody got to look gallant one last time."

"Rhett Butler is only in a movie."

"I prefer him to Brady's photographs."

I think of Brady's photographs, my eyes closed. The tough, ugly soldiers.

"I liked his *hair*, didn't you?"

I know who he is talking about. All that glossy black hair. In a moment Arthur asks me to fix him a drink "to celebrate," which I do. When I return, we talk on for a while about the march, about the people who were there, the speeches, that Unitarian preacher. He strokes my forehead. We talk about who wasn't there. I am riven with fear, and Arthur grows in strength as the night wears on. I am powerless to prevent him from mothering me, absurd as it is.

"What would you like?" he asks.

I think for a moment. "I think, since he has become a symbol of so much, that I would like to have known Bernie Mallett."

Arthur is surprised. "I don't think you would have liked him."

"I want to know, Did he know what he was doing?"

Arthur doesn't say anything. Then, "He's dead. The people who knew him grieve for him. It could have been me. That's enough for me."

This is not Arthur's style. He searches for my hand and holds it. "We are all alike. We don't even know that we are supposed to make them know that."

"Only they are not so clever."

He's right. Straight men are insensitive clods.

"This isn't about sex."

Arthur answers immediately, "Of course not. It's about power. Silly boy, I thought you knew that."

After a while we go up to bed.

We stop at the door to his room.

"Will you come with me?"

He puts his arms around my shoulders. He is very thin. I feel his bones. I am very thin, and I am very tired too. Our bones knock together. *Old age is a wreck.* We kiss. His lips are thin.

"Grumpy bear," he says.

I follow him into his room. He folds back the sheet neatly and then gets in and settles himself on the far side of the bed. I sit on this side of the bed and turn out the light and then swing my legs up and under the sheet. What follow are the irrepressible and urgent, bewildering demands of the flesh.

2

Dana

The reporter is talking about the memorial service last night. Behind her the screen shows the front of the church, with people going in through the large white doors. Deborah, in her red dress, walks up and turns and looks into the camera.

I turn on the VCR and push record.

Others walk up the steps, women from the university, from healthcare services in Cardiff, students, women from little towns around. Some of the women duck their heads while appearing to try not to appear to be ducking their heads. Then I see me. Marcia is on my right, and the camera gets me from the left side. A profile. I turn and glance at the camera and then at Marcia, and then we walk up the three steps to the terrace and cross it and open the door into the church. We disappear inside.

I stop the recording, and, with the remote control, rewind and replay the tape. I see the women I know from the university, the healthcare services, students, women from little towns.

Then I see me again, Marcia on my right, the camera from the left. My right hand, obscured, seems to be holding—is holding—Marcia's hand.

I turn and glance at the camera and then back at Marcia.

We pass beyond the camera's range. It gets only our backs as we disappear inside the door.

I was only within camera range for ten seconds, twenty seconds. I was recognizable. I rewind and replay the tape. I freeze it. I let it run. I freeze it again.

I have come into camera range from the right, and I can be seen in profile.

The frozen picture on the screen is of a woman in her early thirties or late twenties in jeans and a plaid shirt. Her hair is cut close to her head, and she wears no jewelry. She is still youthful—in profile her chin is firm, and there are no shadows under her eyes. Her eyes are wide, focused on the door of the church in the center of the screen, her mouth closed.

I allow the tape to proceed. The figure on the screen moves from the right toward the center of the picture, turning to glance at the camera, and then up the steps. I rewind, bringing the tape forward—she moves toward the center of the screen, glances at the

Dana

camera—and freeze the tape. The motionless figure on the screen is now caught by the camera in a full frontal view. I move the tape backward and forward and watch the figure on the screen turn to the camera and then away and then back to the camera and then away again in a closed loop.

She is older than she appears. In this view, her head turned to face the camera, her body in profile, her neck is turned and shows wrinkle lines. There is strain across her forehead. Her mouth is not merely closed firmly: the jaw is clenched, and the lips pressed together. There is the beginning of a squint—the television lights?—which seems defensive. This is surprising. This is the face of a person ill-at-ease with herself, unhappy, under considerable stress. I run the tape backward and then forward again, searching for another moment, but there are only three or four seconds in which her face is visible from the front, and the face always shows the same unhappy feelings. I am an accomplished person, at ease with myself, my sexuality, my life. I stare at the face staring at me with stupendous amazement.

Dana

I came out to myself when I was sixteen. For a couple of years, I had grown accustomed to feeling overwhelmed and foolish around girls and women with short brown hair. There was a counselor at summer camp, her hair the same shade as the mane on her chestnut horse and both blowing in the wind, her legs encased in brown leather boots, and me, standing beside her, my hand on her instep, grinning stupidly, breathless, skin aglow, feeling hot and heartbroken by the impossibility of it all. One day I read the word *lesbian* and let the magazine fall in my lap. I was surprised and confused. The feelings and the word came together and displaced me: I wasn't what I was, I wasn't where I had been.

I had planned—if I had ever thought of it at all—to be another Mom, married to another Dad. Until I was sixteen, I did the expected things. I got good grades and was popular. I went to summer camp and got an award in archery. I was against the war, smoked pot, was a dutiful daughter, and wanted to cure the ills of the world. I dreamed of being a volunteer in the Peace Corps. I had older brothers who loved me and protected me in that clumsy, goodnatured, possessive way that older brothers have. I was my father's "heart's darling," and my mother's "joy." My life had the dreamy foretold quality of a fairy tale. We were rich in everything, including money, about which I felt guilty.

I liked boys. And I liked certain girls too—particularly the ones around horses. And what I particularly liked didn't intrude on the pattern my life was forming, which was to get an education so that I could have a career, which would somehow make the world better, and to form an attachment to a man so I could get married and have children, so that I could grow up and be like Mom. My feelings, when I reached out my hand and touched, with the tips of my fingers, the brown leather of the boot of my camp counselor as she sat astride her horse, didn't figure in my life: They didn't come out of anything recognizable, like my parents' love for one another, or lead into anything, like marriage and children. These feelings, my hand on the brown leather of her instep, had no context. I was a person with a past and a future and a fully peopled present, and my feelings for this counselor had no resonance. They were like occasional forays into drugs: The trip was exciting and overwhelming and irrelevant.

Then I came across something which suggested that a woman had been in love with another woman. To be "in love with" was a different kind of thing from what I had been feeling. I began to search the libraries. I put together a vocabulary of words which I had never heard at home: lesbian, dyke, homosexual. I searched the dictionaries and the encyclopedias. The process—which occurred over half a year in late 1968 and early 1969—was like a detective fiction. When I discovered that there were other women who had had the same feelings I was experiencing, that these women had *lives*, pasts and presents, families and friends, *futures*, feelings which they were able to write about and talk about, the feelings I had took on a resonance they had not had, began to reverberate with the richness of other people's memories as well as my own.

I suspected that my feelings about my future—a house, a husband, children, somehow too a chic job—while they were still with me, would never have a resolution, would not be fulfilled. I was going to be fulfilled in a future for which I had had no preparation. I was going to have a future as rich, perhaps, as any imaginable, but *I had not imagined it*. I felt as if I were two people—the person I had always been who had no future and the person I felt myself to be now who had no past. And both of these people met in me.

It's an odd phrase, *came out to myself*. It implies that you're in two places at once, inside and outside, or that you're two people in the same place. Vivien Leigh, playing Scarlett O'Hara holding up her hoop skirts so she can run across the long lawn down from Tara: coming out. It's hard to think of her also being what she runs *toward*. The essential thing is a passage through: classically, a door. We're in a closet until we come out, trapped in the dark. But to come out, we have to have been outside the closet too, at the same time: *came out to myself*. I was inside and outside the closet at the same time. And when I came out, the me that was inside the small dark closet came out to the me that was down behind the house in the garden underneath the liveoak trees with everybody else, and I joined together.

This didn't just happen to me sitting alone in a lawn chair. The summer I was sixteen I had met a girl at the yacht club where we went every day—tanned, sunstreaked hair, cutoffs and halter—and I spent the time with her. Nothing happened at first. I don't know that I knew what I wanted to happen, but I felt the stirrings. My adrenalin was flowing and my heart pumping, as if I were on the verge of some great event.

I met her at the club every day at noon, where I found her lying in the sun at the end of a dock in a bathing suit that showed off her pelvic bones. She was small and slender and athletic, with dark streaked hair. She had the muscular body of a tennis player. She had expressive eyes which told you that she kept secrets, and she laughed when she saw me. She was nineteen. We lay there on the dock among the boats and explored each other with our eyes while the boys who worked on the boats explored us with theirs. I don't remember the moment I knew. I had known the word, and I had known the feelings too. I had figured out the important connection between the feelings and particular girls. Now I was having these feelings about this girl, and one day I was sitting up, my arms around one knee, staring at her. She was on her back, her head on one arm, and I wondered what her feelings were for me. She looked up at me and said, "Do you have any idea what is happening?"

I did know what was happening. We had a secret.

"You mean, *you* have a secret," Angela said. "I'm going to let everybody know about mine!" She made as if to stand up.

"No! Sit down." I tried to pull her down. "Oh, please." She was laughing, and I was, and I was aware people were staring, and we wrestled for a minute.

Every day we lay on the dock and talked about life and each other, swept by feelings that were new and deep and which seemed to offer the danger—or the possibility—of self-annihilation, and we were doing it all as if we were the first two people on earth. We had no antecedents, we were subject to the worst kind of censure, and we were exhilarated by our uniqueness.

"Have you done this before?"

"*What* before?" She would laugh.

"Do I have to say it?"

"You have to say it. If you love me, you have to say it."

So I did. "Loved a woman?"

"There. No. Now. Feel better?"

"Scared. Then how do you know so much?"

"College. There're groups in Austin."

"We can't trust anybody here, can we?"

"Oh, honey," Angela said, "We can trust ourselves!" She turned over on her side and put her head on her hands, as if she were going to sleep, and her eyes on me. "I watched you walk down to the ramp this morning with your brother. Your hair was still damp, and you looked as new as a baby deer. Wobbly and blinking."

I was embarrassed: "Fawn."

"Fawn."

There was a dance at the Pavilion for the Fourth of July, and I went with her. My three brothers were all in college, and during the summer worked at the yacht club and dated girls they'd met from the concession stands and amusement parks along the beach.

"Are you going?" she had asked.

I shrugged. Going to Pavilion dances had been a part of my life forever. There were always boys who wanted to take me.

"Would you like to go with me?" We were lying on our backs parallel to one another on the hot planks of the dock, and when she said *me*, she touched my hand for a moment. There was the danger: We would be exposing ourselves to attention that, if it recognized what it saw, would turn to malice. On the other hand, I felt invulnerable and courageous. It would have been an act of treachery—betrayal of myself—to be secretive about *these* feelings.

Later I asked Kevin, my brother, if we could ride with him and his date.

"What's the matter, can't get a date, you two?" He laughed at us, but he let us go with him.

At the Pavilion—it's a tin-roofed shed built on stilts over the back creek—we danced with boys until almost midnight, our eyes connecting across the dance floor over shoulders and beyond heads. Then we went out across the road into the park on the beach. I would have liked to go down to the dock—you could hear the band from there—but I knew straight couples would go there, and we would have no privacy. The park was between the oceanfront and the road which ran along the creek. It was a jungle of magnolia trees and azaleas and camellias, walkways winding among the trees, stone benches, and, in the center of the park, a gazebo.

We held hands, walking along the garden paths. We wore cutoffs and white halter tops and seemed to glow in the dark. We talked about the boys we had been dancing with and fanned ourselves with our hands. I was intensely aware of her presence. I leaned against a tree, and she faced me, leaning against the same tree.

"You're much older than you seem."

I didn't know what to say to that.

"You're a giddy kid, and then you're an adult." Angela smiled. "You present yourself in different ways. You surprise me. I like that. I want to get to know every different part of you."

She slid her hands around my neck and inched closer to me until our lips touched, and she kissed me. She slid her fingers underneath my halter and lifted it so that my breasts were exposed, and she touched them with the tips of her fingers. I had never been touched before by a woman, and I gave in to it, and for that moment, I lived only in my breasts.

"Holy shit! What the fuck are you doing!" It was Kevin. I turned around to face him, pulling my halter down, my face already red and hot. He and his date—his fly was unzipped—stood in the path leading to the gazebo.

On our ride home—Kevin insisted we leave at that moment—she and I sat in the back seat, silent, while Kevin's date inspected her nails, and Kevin kept up a stream of invective.

"I can't believe I saw you do what you were doing back there! You were feeling each other up! Holy shit! Are you a dyke? How could you do that! How long have you been doing this? Does anybody know! I can't believe you were doing that out there on the path where anybody could see you! God, what if my friends find out? What's the matter with you! I thought all the guys liked you!" Every so often, he would grip the steering wheel with both hands and close his eyes and lower his head toward the wheel as if he were beating it on it, saying, "I can't believe this is happening to me. I can't believe this is happening to me."

I knew that I was expected to feel shame. I didn't. I ground my teeth and held her hand, and I wondered, riding through town going home, if I would ever forgive him. He had lined up with the jerks. My own brother.

My secret was out. There wouldn't be any more exhilarating privacy. No lying on a dock, hidden by the people's inability to conceive of what we were doing. They would be able to conceive of it now, and they would watch me and suspect me of every awful thing under the sun.

At moments during the next day, I wanted to run away—or kill Kevin. I spoke to Angela on the phone: "What do people do?"

"Well, they used to commit suicide, honey, but I expect you to be cooler than that. Brave it out. Tell who you have to tell. Don't apologize. Don't try to explain. And remember," she said, "you can support yourself." Of course. Thanks. How. I was only sixteen.

My father, at supper that night, asked me who I had gone to the dance with. Kevin had not said anything. He had avoided me all day, and when, at supper, we had had to sit down at the same table, he had kept his eyes on his plate and on our brothers and our parents, anywhere but on me. His behavior was a threat and would have to be explained.

After supper I told Dad. "Can we talk about something important?"

We were sitting on the cushioned garden furniture on the terrace behind the house. He suddenly became serious. "Do you think," he said, "that we should invite your mother out?"

I went to get her.

When we were all seated, Dad said, "Dana has something she wants to talk to us about."

They were solemn but not worried. They had no reason to look worried. I had never given them cause.

I didn't know how to begin. I didn't want to do it abruptly— "Remember they're your parents, and it is possible to be gentle," Angela had said—but in the expanse of time that was my life, there was no way to make this seem less than abrupt. I let my eyes float over the garden to the lawn where my brothers shot baskets against a net set up under a live oak tree. Spanish moss hid the net, and in the dusk the boys' white t-shirts glowed blue-white. "I want to talk about me," I said, "and boys."

I told them about the boys I had dated—there were always several around, nice guys—and how that felt. I said, "They are like my brothers." I told them that I had had sex with some of them. That was OK. It was "nice," I told them.

"We wished that you had waited—" That was Mother.

"But I think that I probably won't end up falling in love with a guy. I think—" And here I waited a moment, trying to gage their reaction. "—that when I fall in love, it will be with a woman." They remained quiet, the shouts of the boys coming across the lawn, their blue-white tees on the periphery of our vision. And then I said it. "I am a lesbian."

They looked at each other but didn't say anything for a long time. We all looked away across the lawn, quiet and separated, the long silence broken by their questions. Mother: "How do you know?" And then, after a stretch of time, my father: "Have we done something wrong?"

My father finally came back to me and said, "I love you." He had tears in his eyes, and his voice was low and husky.

My mother came over and knelt down beside my chair and took my hands between hers and kissed them. It was the gesture that Angela made later, after we made love the first time. We talked, until the garden had grown so dark that my brothers could no longer see to shoot, and my parents' voices came to me disembodied through the summer night like thoughts from my mind.

They wanted to know about Angela. "Is she kind to you?" my father asked. They said that I was young, that it was a phase, that it was too early to tell yet, that they loved me. They said Angela must be lovely. They were reassuring themselves against this appalling shock. They said, "There's no hurry. We'll see," and then they wanted to know if I thought it was a good idea to continue to see her. And they turned to whatever comforting, mindless rituals they could find to fill up the time till bed. As I was lying in bed that night, I thought that I had never said anything to my father before that had made him cry. I thought it was exactly as if I were the parent and they the children, and I had told them something shocking and hurtful and enormously threatening. They wanted me to comfort them. That's what they wanted. They wanted *me* to comfort *them*. I told Angela the next day, "Everything's gotten turned around backwards."

During the next days, my sense of dislocation, of things radically out of joint, of being in the wrong place saying the wrong things increased. Over and over I had to tell my parents who I was— "I'm bright, I'm a woman, I'm a lesbian, I am capable"—until one night I couldn't repeat it any more. My parents gave their children a name, an identity, an education, they suggested goals, posited values, explored attitudes, and now they waffled between pleading ignorance and accusing me of mental derangement.

Dana

One night after supper, they called me into the den and asked me if I was still seeing Angela. Then they told me I should see a psychiatrist. I told them I didn't need one. They asked me to go anyway, to please them. Three days later I had an appointment. He was sixty, thin and dry, blond hair that had gone gray, rimless glasses. He said, "Would you like to talk about what's troubling you?" And I said, "No." And when he raised his eyebrow as if he knew something about me I didn't know, I said, "Nothing's troubling me," and sat on my hands for the rest of the hour, bitter and defiant and humiliated. When I came home, I told them I would never go back to that doctor—or any doctor—ever again, and I didn't and we never mentioned it again. My mother said, in fact, "We will never mention this again." It was then that they forbade me to see Angela again.

Angela said there's a joke that all gay people know: What is the difference between a Jewish girl and a lesbian? Answer: A Jewish girl doesn't have to tell her mother. Right. I had had to go to my parents who loved me and tell them who I was. I wondered how it is that good, loving parents could have raised a child that they could be so ignorant of. It is the business of children to be ignorant—they are born to parents who nurture and raise them and send them to school—and it is the business of parents to teach them. I had reversed our relationship and had become their teacher.

Which, in itself, was not irredeemable. What seemed irredeemable was my ignorance. I didn't know anything about myself. In the summer of 1969, a lesbian woman could read this about herself: "The girls like to be romantic much more than the boys. They like to kiss and fondle each other and smooch and squeeze each other. They like to have romance in their lives, and since the real thing with a man is impossible, they pretend by romancing each other. But despite this, they really aren't any different from the boys: Their relationships don't last long and are filled with fights and deceit and betrayals."

I found this in the drugstore in a revolving wire rack. The writer said, "Homosexual women are faced with the same problem as homosexual men: They are missing half the pieces nature needs for sex. Lesbians make up for this deficiency by employing a dildo, which is a sponge rubber or plastic penis. This way they can pretend to be having sex in the normal way." I had on my club gear—halter top, cutoffs, flip-flops—over a bathing suit, and I faced the revolving rack, this book open in my hands. Plastic seemed grotesque to me, who had just discovered Angela's skin.

This was in a paperback which everyone was reading that summer, *What Every Teenager Needs To Know About Sex But Usually Doesn't*, by Dr. Malcolm White. I read it in the drugstore, and then I bought it and brought it home—sneaked it in, actually, my first memory of the sneaking I was to do a lot of as a consequence of people's ideas about lesbians—and read the rest of it. It was published in 1969 and sold a million copies in *hardback* its first year. It had nothing to do with me or with my feelings. I had never been described so. What Dr. White said contradicted absolutely what I felt. I was young, pretty, attractive everyone said, intelligent. I was well-brought-up. My parents had loved me and seemed to celebrate everything I did. I had had sex with a boy—a man, I suppose—as I think most young women of my age had in 1969. But I had no desire ever to do that again. Dr. White's book was part of the sexual revolution of the sixties—it overlapped *The Joy of Sex* on the best seller lists for months—and I knew it was supposed to present the with-it, up-to-date attitude toward sexual matters that my liberal family and our class and age group were supposed to embody. And to an extent, it did that. It said masturbation was normal. It assumed that adolescents needed some sort of sexual outlet. But it said that lesbians were sick people, and I didn't believe that I was sick.

I read more. I spent the mornings in the library and met Angela at the dock at noon. What I discovered was a library full of books written by Dr. White's colleagues. In the psychology section of the library where I thought I would find the truth, I found this: The way I felt for the sun-streaked girl on the end of the dock was called a "disease." It was called a "serious abnormality," evidence of "immature sexuality," "arrested psychological development," a "regression." It was said to be evidence of a "crippling fear of the opposite sex," a "manic-depressive reaction," "massive childhood fears." My feelings were clear and clean and powerful, like rain. And what these writers said felt like hot tar.

In the religion section, I found that the Sodom and Gomorrah story was at the center of things. The men of Sodom had come to Lot's house and asked Lot to bring out his visitors, who were angels, "that we may know them." Everyone knows what *know* means in the

Bible, and the church held that God destroyed the Cities of the Plain because of their homosexuality.

Homosexuality was a sin, inconsistent with God's plan that the end result of marriage should be children. St. Paul called it unnatural. The Roman Catholic Church demanded, as pastoral goals, life-long celibacy for homosexuals and counseling and therapy to turn a homosexual orientation into a heterosexual one. The church didn't admit that love between two women was equivalent to love between a man and a woman. In fact it didn't recognize sex between them as being capable of expressing love.

The Christian fundamentalists were more direct. Homosexuals were the *Abomination of the Lord*, from a passage in Ezekiel, where the writer says the men of Sodom "committed abomination before me." Homosexuals were a serious threat to the country, and America was like ancient Rome, "which fell because everyone turned to homosexuality." The homosexuals and the Communists were the enemy, and I read about McCarthyism and the homosexuals in the State Department. I discovered you can't serve in the foreign service if they find you are a homosexual.

After I began going to the library, I asked Angela what she read. "Nothing, really. Some books girls had at school." She smiled. "Hot. But I'm not much of a reader, so I don't keep any of that kind of thing around." She didn't open her eyes or turn to me. "Why?"

"I've been reading some in the library, before I come here."

"What?"

I told her.

"What do they say?"

"That we're sick."

"Then why do you read them?"

I laughed. "That's the way you learn. You read books."

"The only lesbians those people ever talk to are the sick ones. They don't know anything about the rest of us. And what they say is just gossip."

She turned on her side and rested her head on her hand and looked at me seriously. "The psychologists and the church people are writing for other straight people. They're not talking about us, they're only talking about their ideas about us. They're not writing to us. This is no dialogue. They're just writing about us for other people who want to have their convictions confirmed. That's just gossip. And the effect of all of it is to massage egos."

I read because I wanted to know more about what I was like.

"Then ask me, dear. And if I don't know, I can find somebody who can find out."

"Do you know any poets?" I thought there must be poets who knew what this was about. I found Sappho quickly enough, and fragments from classical literature in translation with titles like "On Claudia," given by the translator. But between that and 1969, there were only a handful of poets and scarcely any more poems to represent almost two thousand years of lesbian culture.

I found *The Well of Loneliness*. I read about its trial in the encyclopedia, and then I read the book itself. I searched between the lines, read Lillian Hellman's *The Children's Hour*. My problem was I didn't know how to go about finding what I was searching for. I couldn't find *lists*. I didn't dare ask the librarian, and I didn't know how to find them without her help. I could find nothing with which I could identify—there were no romances about young middle-class girls who fell in love with *girls* advertised among the new acquisitions—but the problem was deeper than that: There being no books, I had no way to think about myself except the thoughts that occurred to me and I was aware that I was alone and my own resources were limited.

It was like looking into a mirror which resolutely refused to give back a reflection, for the thing I discovered had to do with what was not there. The Kinsey book on female sexuality suggested the loss. It was absence of comment on the prevalence of just the kind of feelings which I felt lying on the dock with Angela. It was impossible to find a nationally known sports figure who admitted to being a homosexual—no women tennis stars, no track medalists. There was no movie star, no writer. There was no presidential appointee, no doctor, or university professor. Where were the lesbians of the past? Biographies told me nothing. If the question of the identity of lesbians from history was too political a question, too loaded with sixties separatism, it could be asked another way: Where was acknowledgment of homosexual feeling among the billions of women who had peopled the earth?

In a hundred ways every hour, a straight girl catches her reflection in a storefront window, comparing herself to the mannequin inside. She sees her reflection in a mirror, in the polished marble of the post office, in the black glass at the cinema, in a piece of silver. She sees it on the page of the book in the poems written to her, in statues, in the songs, in the parts written for her, in her mother, reminding herself who she is, measuring herself against her memories and her desires.

There were no photographs in *Life* or *Time* or *Look* which showed lesbians. What lesbians did as a class of women—their occupations, their leisure activities, their families, interests, concerns—never appeared in the national press. What mattered to lesbians—healthcare, taxes on single parents, childcare, social life—were not investigated and reported. Lesbians and homosexual men were regularly covered in the newspapers and magazines only in sections and articles which dealt with crime and prostitution and drug abuse and psychiatric disorders. The stigma society put on being a homosexual was so strong that, when it had to identify a person as a homosexual, the newspaper said, "self-admitted" or "alleged," and in photographs the eyes were blacked out. It was all predictable, not in the way that arithmetic reasoning is predictable—2 + 6 is always 8—but in the way that anger follows outrage.

I looked more closely at my parents' crowd and at my own. Their parties were peopled by men and women together. That there were only heterosexual couples at their parties was no more natural—a consequence of the natural state of things—than that there were no blacks as guests. What had seemed a civilized landscape—a terrace and a lawn surrounded by live oak trees and Spanish moss, a scene crowded with men and women in summer pastels picking drinks from trays being passed—suddenly seemed confined, confining, limiting and exclusive, and I realized that I was one of the ones being excluded. I passed among my parents' friends and listened to them talk. I joined in with the ones I knew—people who knew how to talk to a sixteen-year-old—and I never heard a reference to a woman loving another woman. There was no verbal acknowledgment that I existed. In all the language that we have to describe people joined in intimate contact, these people found no words which could have included me and Angela there on the lawn. This silence was not a coincidental consequence of my parents' thoughtless choice of friends.

The culture in which I was born either damned homosexuality, or it erased every trace of it, and this was true everywhere: the libraries, the scholars, my parents' friends, my friends, the Army, the church, psychologists, newspapers or magazines, doctors, and the boys on the boats beyond the dock. And that summer I came to believe that this was done on purpose.

I was sixteen in 1969 when Dr. White published his book. That was also the summer of Stonewall. Drag queens in the Stonewall Tavern on Christopher Street in Greenwich Village on the night of June 27, 1969, were raided by the police, who were making one of their regular swings through the Village, filling up paddy wagons with homosexuals from the bars. But this night the transvestites rose up in a rage and tore up parking meters and paving stones and fought back, driving the police back into the safety of the tavern. The police called for reinforcements, and the queens got reinforcements for their side, and there was a riot. For the next four nights, the Village was torn with riots between the police and homosexuals. At Stonewall, the drag queens stood up for themselves. In a world where we are given a choice between silence or loud lies, the drag queens spoke for themselves. And when they were photographed being hauled away to jail, the papers didn't black out their eyes.

We did, of course, eventually find the books. We found Jane Rule's *The Desert of the Heart*, which we read to one another sitting under liveoaks at the end of a white sandy road down to a ramp where people put their boats in the creek. In the hot, damp Texas Gulf Coast summer, the desert of Ann and Evelyn seemed remote, desiccated, passionate, stripped of all the things that obscure feeling:

"You look uncomfortable."

"I am. I like standing up or lying down."

"Lie down then. Here, I'll move."

Ann turned her head, awkwardly propped against the wall, and looked at Evelyn.

"I sometimes think I can forecast the weather in your eyes," Evelyn said.

"What's your prediction?"

"Hot and clear."

"I want you," Ann said.

"I want you."

And, if you can't have what you need, you take what you want. Accept damnation. It has its power and its charm. You love the whole damned world in the alien, not quite accurate image of yourself.

"Take off your clothes."

"Turn out the light."

We read the passages to each other again and again, and what began to take shape for me was a way to think about my feelings, a way, even, of having them. I memorized the lines—*if you can't have what you need, you take what you want*—and found my feelings took on a force and bravado which surprised me and made me seem strange to myself. Another book, published in 1935, was by Gale Wilhelm. *We Too Are Drifting* was a kind of Hemingwayesque novel about two women—Victoria and Jan—who met and fell in love, in the middle of a lot of drinking and cigarette smoking, in San Francisco in the thirties: *Victoria turned her head smiling and then the smile hung a moment and color came as if a faint rose light had passed across her face. Why, how do you do.*

The sound of her voice was the sound of music Jan remembered and she looked at her and said, Please have tea with me this afternoon.

I should love to, Victoria said simply.

The tight muscles relaxed in Jan's face and she smiled. You're through here at five?

Five, yes.

Where shall we go? Jan said.

Anywhere.

A little place, Jan said, or a big place?

You say.

Do you know the Green Gate?

Victoria nodded and Jan said, I'll be there at five, and smiled and turned away. Walking toward the street door of the shop she felt wild and drunk. She wondered why she didn't walk into tables and upset thousands of dollars worth of china and glass.

So. Other women had felt wild and drunk. The restraints suggested by my mother's behavior were not necessarily applicable to me. The lesbians things were there, had been there all along. I discovered that summer that there were lesbian women in our town too, which I had not dreamed of before. They were hidden, and to discover them was a matter of letting my eyes get used to the dark.

Kinsey's book was a revelation. I read it with the growing sense of suspense that I used to read mysteries: There is no physiologic reason why anybody cannot respond sexually to anything. Each new fact fell on me unsuspecting, like a clue to a murder. The preponderance of heterosexual responses over homosexual responses has nothing to do with normal and abnormal sexuality. Two out of five women have had erotic responses to other women sometime in their lives. As they accumulated and as I began to foresee where they were leading, I experienced that wonderful sense of satisfaction that you feel when, toward the final chapters of a book, a mystery, click, click, click, begins to be solved. There are more than fifty societies and cultures around the world where sexual relationships between women are accepted. Most of the moral codes on which the West bases its criminal codes do not even mention women. The origin of the condemnation of homosexuals appears to be a determination by the Hebrews to differentiate themselves from other tribes in the Levant and not a condemnation of the activity itself. Cultural conditioning is the only thing that prevents every individual from being susceptible to every possible sexual stimulation. We are "homosexual" because our culture, condemning certain acts, seeks to distinguish the people committing those acts from the people who don't.

I already felt superior to the culture I had been born in—Texas Gulf Coast in 1969—but with each new fact, each new book, I was able to take a longer view. The America of 1969 was not much less provincial than the culture of the Texas Gulf Coast. The modern West was as culture-bound as the smallest portion of it. And each time I read some new fact, I found myself freed of one more of the ties that bound me to the sandy coast of Texas and which hid me from myself.

During the last weeks of the summer, under orders from my mother never to see one another again, Angela and I met each other on the creek in the maze of little sandy roads which went down to the docks where the shrimp boats were and to the ramps where the boats were launched. Back there away from the beach and the summer people from whom we were separated by a jungle of vines and palmettos, we found another dock, unused and ramshackle, the wood bleached gray and curled by the sun and heat. There we found privacy and each other, read our books, made love. I learned to move back and forth through the door that separated my several lives without leaving it ajar so that the flies got in.

The summer ended, and I drifted like smoke on a battlefield through my last two years in high school. I was beautiful, intelligent, cool, and I was almost invisible. I ceased to take part in any school activity but my classes. I spent my time at home alone, reading and waiting. By then I had found where the books were and how to get them. I knew that life would begin for me when I moved away. I had pledged undying love for Angela that summer. Like most summer romances, it didn't last much past Christmas. What had come out of it was the knowledge that I was a lesbian and the belief that I would bring myself nothing but grief if I acted on my sexuality on the Texas Gulf Coast in the winter of 1969-1970.

After Stonewall groups began to form in New York—The Gay Activist Alliance, Radical Lesbians, the Furies Collective in Washington. I eventually went away to college and found other women like me and joined groups that wanted to overthrow the government and the whole sexist, patriarchal, imperialist, war-mongering society. I spent most of my college years on some picket line or other, holding hands with another dyke. Then I grew up. I got a graduate degree, met Marcia, turned inward, searched for, identified, and satisfied my needs, settled down with Marcia, planned a book on rural women in the 1870s, planned for the birth of Marc, became, in an astonishing number of ways, like my mother.

I learned, however, that you never get to the end of coming out. On the other side of the glass there is always a new tour group coming through who haven't been here before. They start using language about you that doesn't apply, and if you're not careful, the words will begin to seep into your mind and cause damage, like water in a gas tank. They need it all explained to them, and you have to put down your business and lay it all out in simple terms.

My mother and I were having tea in the Palm Court of the Plaza one year, and she told me news of home, of my brothers and their wives, of the grandchildren, of my father and his new wife. She felt abused, she said. The rules that applied to my father were different from the ones that applied to her. She picked up a small tea sandwich from the little plate and raised it to her mouth. She bit into it and chewed for a moment, her eyes on the violinist in the distance.

"You can't imagine how it hurt to be divorced."

Last Sunday afternoon when I climbed out of the dinghy and pulled it up on the shore and turned to Marcia and Marc, standing there in the shadows beneath the hill, and listened as Marcia told me about Bernie's murder, I felt surrounded again after years of freedom by a hostile and angry world, as the lake was surrounded by hills, from which these three bigoted ignorant boys had come like terrorists.

Mickey

Now, he walks beside me, going back up the hill to my car, and something has happened between us. A minute ago, after I introduced him to Mrs. Elkins, he was quiet. We walked a block or two, then he said, "That's the first time you've ever done that." I wanted to know what he meant, and he shrugged. "You never acknowledge me." He was right.

The answering machine has messages. I push buttons. "This is your mother. Could you call me when you have a chance? Thank you, dear." Then the clicks, and it is Marian's voice: "Would you call?" Then more clicks, and Marian's voice again: "I would like to talk to you tonight. Please call me. I'll be up late." Mother: "I do so want to talk to you tonight, Mickey, dear." And Marian's again: "I really need to talk to you tonight. Please don't go to bed without calling. I'll try again later."

The sounds of their voices—Mother's thinner, older one and Marian's strong, self-aware, youthful one—take me back to the beginnings of my memories. Part of me feels four years old, hearing their voices, and I feel the continuity of things in them. Even the requests—which I must take as demands—are as old as I am and indistinguishable from my sense of myself. I can't wonder what I've done wrong.

The last message on the machine is from Dana. She has never called before. "Please call. We must talk about what's to happen next."

I sit on the overstuffed chair—Timothy is on the sofa, his hands between his legs, staring at the wall—and dial Mother. She says *hello*, and I tell her who it is, and her next word, something indecipherable, breaks off in the middle and becomes "Mickey! Oh, I am *so* glad you've called! I've been so worried about you. Are you all right?"

I reassure her. "Oh, sure, Mother. Friends and I were out tonight," formulating the empty phrases that I think she wants to hear. They are also the only things I can bring myself to say.

"Oh, I'm so glad. Did you enjoy yourselves?"

"There were a lot of us. We had a good time."

"I didn't mean to call so late. It is so late." She pauses, and then she says, "How late is it?"

"Eleven fifteen or so, Mother."

"I'm so sorry. But you know how I suffer when I don't know how you are." I keep my peace. "Perhaps we can have tea after you get off work tomorrow. Would that be nice?" There is an anxiety in her voice. I can't say it would not be "nice." I don't know if I can be careful enough to be with her. It takes a certain amount of care to be with her. She's fragile, and her strength doesn't show until she has already shattered.

I tell her I love her, and she says she loves me. "Are you quite sure you are all right?" I say the words again, and we say goodbye and hang up. I am a traitor. I make a list of people I am betraying right now, beginning with myself. There's no stopping this. I know how I got here: the boys and Bernie and the bridge and Simon Herter and the church and the television cameras. There is no way to cut *that* cord.

Marian's voice comes on the phone already knowing it's me: "Mickey? Thank God, I would have gone insane if I had had to go to bed tonight without talking to you." She is louder than Mother.

I take a breath: "Hello, Marian. What's up?"

"What is going on?" she demands. Before I can say anything, she starts speaking again: "*What* is going on? Lloyd says he watched television tonight, the coverage of that boy's funeral, and he says he saw you, and he says there was no mistaking it—"

"I was there, Marian—"

"What in God's name led you to go to a thing like that! Lloyd is fit to be tied! Lloyd—"

"Marian—"

"And Mother! I can't imagine how cruel you've been. You think only of yourself! Why did you go?"

"He was a friend. He was my friend, Marian. All his friends went. I was—am—I am one of his friends."

"What will people think?"

"I think you should lower your voice—"

"They'll think you're queer!"

This is the moment. Mother's way is to give me an opportunity, even an invitation, to lie; Marian's is to dare me. She comes on like she's training tigers, chair up and whip trailing.

"Lloyd already thinks so. He's thought that for years, and you have no idea how hard I've—"

"This is hard enough. You're not making it any easier."

"Why is it so hard? Tell me that. What are you hiding?"

Every second I wait now the lie rots the bone: "I'm queer, Marian." And the release I should feel now is polluted by my knowledge that she's had to force it out of me. "I never told you, and I wish I had." She is silent. I hope she will say something, but I am silent too. It is degrading to have to ask her to say something: *Say something, please.* "I have a lover, and his name is Robbie. We've been in love for three years." She still doesn't say anything. "I am a happy man."

Finally she says, "Well, *goddamn.*" Then, "I'm tired. It's late. I have to go to bed. I'll call you—sometime. Later. This week." I hear the click and the dial tone, and I listen to it before I hang up.

Afterwards, I pull out the sofa for Timothy and get him settled with a sheet and a blanket and pillow. He closes his eyes and crosses his arms across his chest and lets me kiss him on the forehead. I think he would accept anything I chose to do to him right now—a kiss, a blow to the forehead with an axe—since that's what he is. I want to shake him awake and make him *fight.* Robbie is waiting for me in the bedroom, on his back, nude, covered by a sheet. I slide into bed on my stomach next to him and slip my hand and arm across his chest.

"I saw you on the news. They did a tape of the march. It was easy to recognize you. They had a special, and apparently they caught a good bit of the march live."

I let him hold me while alternating waves of anger and fear keep me rigid against his smooth skin.

1

At six on Tuesday morning I leave the house by the kitchen door for my run. It is warm already and humid and cloudless. Robbie is in my bed, his body sticky with sweat, and Timothy is asleep on the sofa, his long black curls across his cheek. The dew is off the grass, the sun is way up. Even at seven, the day is already part gone and isn't new anymore. I face the day with dread. I run, already exhausted when I start, with a dogged fear, my heart so high in my chest it chokes me. When I return, I scoop the paper up off the front porch and glance across the front page for the article on us. I find it and am beginning to read as I pull open the screen door. Something on my door pulls my eyes to it. My breath comes fast. Someone has painted large red letters diagonally across the door. I feel light headed. The thing has been done sloppily, and the paint has run down the door under each letter. It seems still wet, and I put out a finger to touch it. It is dry, except in the little ball that has formed at the bottom of each run and congealed there, on the crosspiece of the molding. FAGGOT. I feel nausea pushing up against my throat. I am flushed with fear: It is there for everyone to see. I jerk around and search the quiet, sleeping street and the houses. I've lived here four years, and now everyone knows. I am naked in church.

I run inside—the screen door slams behind me—and down the stairs. In the basement on the floor behind the hot water heater is a bucket of paint Robbie and I used in the kitchen. I race back upstairs and pry open the can with my keys and dip the brush into the paint. My breathing stops. I am desperate to get the red letters covered. I do it because I feel I have to. Because I am afraid of being shamed. I don't know why I am doing it. It suddenly seems pointless. I can't paint out these letters. I didn't wake up early enough. It is too late. Too late. The anger comes and overwhelms everything, and I am enraged. I pick up the can and, whirling around in a great circle, with a violent contraction of my body, I heave it up and away from me. It makes a great high arc against the sky, spinning slowly, the paint floating out in a languid horizontal weightless lavender dribble. With a clang, it falls and there is a great slimy dash of lavender across the grass. The can bounces down across the lawn and rolls into the street. I turn back to the door with its hideous red letters, my breath coming in great jerky seizures like sobs.

Charles, my friend at work, walks by my cubicle. "Good morning," he says. He is red-headed, red faced, and stocky, quiet, satisfied, amused. I swivel on my chair and face him: "How's things?" He shrugs and grins. "Another day in the elf factory." I throw an imaginary ball at him, and he catches it and goes on down the hall.

The light in my building is fluorescent; there are no windows. There is no sensory connection with the natural world. It is carpeted in gray, and the walls are smooth ivory or dark gray. The furniture is white formica, chrome, dark gray leather. At every desk is a computer screen which glows pale fluorescent green. People speak in subdued, controlled voices and wear dark suits. We have staff meetings at eleven to discuss progress, projects, the parts each of us is to have in a project, successes, failures. I was once interested in chess, and this is like chess: Every piece has its part to play. It is absorbing and clean in a way that has nothing to do with cleanliness. And it has nothing to do with the turmoil in my mind.

At the staff meeting, the leader of our division talks about a program we are writing for the hospital. He makes columns on a blackboard—patients, staff, illness, age, race, sex, or name, specialty, department, dates of appointment, or name, diagnosis, prognosis. The hospital wants to be able to answer questions from the database: What is the incidence among American Indian patients of cancer or epilepsy in 1983? What American Indians of partial French extraction have been admitted for drug addiction by age 21? Age 24? Age 29? What is the leading cause of death among homosexual men between the ages 21 and 29? Is AIDS a natural cause of death? Charles sits across from me and listens intently. The leader has short brown hair in a brush cut, brushed back. He wears a white shirt with pens in his pocket. He is, maybe, thirty-five. The rest of us are in our twenties. All morning, I have to exhale determinedly to keep the nausea down.

I have FAGGOT written in red paint on my door. What men in this room drove down German Street between midnight and seven this morning and saw red paint dripping down my door? What route does Charles take to work? I hear Marian's voice: *People will think you are queer.* What does he think? What records in this database contain addresses which are written in red paint on a green front door? This morning the men I work with spoke to me in their usual way. They nodded when I joined them at the coffee machine and when I sat down at the table for this meeting. I can see no difference in the way I am treated today from the way I was treated yesterday. About my *subject*, there is silence. Nobody has mentioned Bernie's murder or the articles in the paper or the memorial service last night and the saturation television coverage. Did no one see FAGGOT written on my door? What are the statistical probabilities that, of twelve white male heterosexuals out of a population of thirty thousand in Cardiff, none has seen any television or read any newspapers or seen any door with red painted letters since last Saturday? I want to force an answer: What does this silence *mean*?

I pass the afternoon in my office. Charles comes in and sits down beside me and points to the screen, and we talk about what's there. "This is a pisser," he says. I stare at his calm, relaxed face. The problem we are working on does not reach him. It remains an interesting puzzle. I wonder what this serene, handsome countenance would look like were the puzzle to suddenly become a mortal struggle. The leader of my division calls me in after three to talk about my work. He makes marks on paper and crosses through things and adds figures. "Try that." He runs his fingers through his stiff hair and says, "That might work." Sure, and I wait for a second for something more, and then I leave. What am I waiting for? I get back to my office, and I play the keyboard with careless fury. I think the clicks the keyboard makes—like a bike chain dragged over a chain link fence—can be heard all over the building.

At the end of the day, I hear my colleagues leaving the building, talking. There are still four hours of sunlight, and the men are going sailing or boating, or playing ball with their kids. I get my suitcoat and join them. Charles and I talk—I find myself laughing—going down the low-ceilinged hall to the main door. We are laughing about the *Democrats*. Their convention starts a week from yesterday, and they don't know who they are. Every dissident minority in the country is parading outside the convention hall in San Francisco, demanding its plank in the party platform. blacks, women, Indians, labor, the elderly. Queers. I have discovered a stupendous secret, and—in my bitterness—there are moments when I feel I am going to laugh out loud at my discovery and at their not knowing it.

Outdoors under the immensity of the sky, a cloudbank has moved in during the afternoon. The sun, behind the cloudbank, breaks through a hole, and rays of intense golden light slant down twenty thousand feet to the evergreen forests. On such a stage, the distances being so great, movement seems impossible, and my closed and air conditioned car seems to make no progress down through the forests toward town. The car, which is a steel carapace, protects me from the heat and exposure. It is my own car, so I have not had to share with Charles or with any of the men. Had Bernie had a car Saturday night, he would not have had to share with those boys.

I am going into town to have tea with Mother. She will want to know about last night. She will seek to be assured, will invite me to lie, and I will accept her invitation as long as I can. I hate this deceit and I love her, and I can't imagine my life after I cease to have her approval. She has been the source for me of everything, and when I began to give in to my desires, I kept from going crazy with grief and guilt by keeping my two lives absolutely separate. Mother lives on the West Side. I live deep in the East Side.

Mother is sitting in the back—a screen porch that was glassed in when I was a teenager, making a den—her legs crossed at the ankles, reading. It is inescapable that I notice that she is reading the Bible. Mother is fifty-two and looks fifty-two. She is five feet three inches and plump and wears mildly fashionable clothes. She has a tired, sad, composed look on her face. It would not occur to her to try to look "young," and if you proposed it to her, she would say, "Oh, I would feel so silly." She has wanted the best for Marian and me, but she has also wanted the "appropriate best," and she has great consideration for "our kind of people."

Now, she looks up at me and her eyebrows draw up in the middle. Her eyes are watery and seem pink behind her glasses. "I've been so worried. Please sit down."

I lean down and kiss her, and then I obey her. I sit in the chair at the end of the sofa. There are large rubber plants and a television set. There are photographs in gold-hued frames on the walls, pictures of a progressively bigger me in track uniforms, all alike, pictures of Marian in tennis clothes, in bathing suits, basketball uniforms, pictures of Marian's wedding to Lloyd, pictures of the children. There is no picture of me and Robbie. He will ask for that next. In the corner is a wood stove sitting on a pad. Her wood is cut and split and in a pile beside the driveway—she buys it and has it delivered—and I will come soon and stack it in the garage. She watches me as I settle myself. There is only one door out of this room.

"How are you?" I know how she is, but the forms of things require that I ask.

To answer she has to pull herself away from looking at me and to think of herself.

"I—I'm fine, I think. Nothing at the hospital—"

She works in patient accounts.

"—I could barely think all day today." Suddenly she lurches forward in her seat. "I don't know what I am thinking of. The tea! Let me put the water on." She stands up, and I stand up as she goes out of the room into the kitchen. She returns in a moment and reseats herself. "I've been nearly crazy with worry, Michael. I don't know how to begin to talk to you, dear. We've always been so close—"

She has never known how to confront things directly. I get it from her. When that had to be done, my father did it, until he died. Marian has taken that job over in the last couple of years. Marian likes to call "family conferences."

"Were you watching television last night, the news?" I ask.

"Oh, yes—"

"And you saw me?"

"—and I saw you, Mickey, at that boy's funeral. With all those awful people. Did you know them? I hate to speak of your friends, and I apologize, but that's what they are, dear, and I'm so worried that you will be—" She pauses.

She sits with her back to the window, her face in shadow. Beyond her is the New England afternoon—sunny, almost clear skies, warm, in an odd way *earned*—that seems tenuous because it could collapse at any moment. Nothing beautiful here lasts, except the cold. The breeze causes the tree limbs to sway, and the leaves make a faint clicking sound. I feel lost, anesthetized against what is happening, sodden with anxiety.

She finds herself: "—so worried that you will be *sullied* by your association." She expects me to say something.

"I'm OK, Mother." I have never not pleased her. Her worry has been sufficient to keep me in line since I was a child. The fear of worrying her has led me to give her my life. I haven't known how not to do that. I repeat the words: "I'm OK, Mother. Those people are really very good people—"

She appears not to hear: "I can't bring myself to say what people are saying about that young man, and his friends—" She looks down and closes her eyes, her fingers of one hand touching her forehead, her elbow supported in her other hand, a gesture as old as guilt.

"Bernie was gay, Mother. He was a homosexual. Most of the people there last night were homosexual also."

209

"Oh, son, they'll think you are too!"

I cannot look at her. My eyes roam over the backyard, the small, narrow lawn back to the fence, everything neat and clipped, Mother's perennials in a sunny bed beside the garage. It seemed vast when I was a kid. I grip the arms of the chair.

"You know how wrong that would be." Then, before I can look back at her, she says, "How could you go? Go *there*? You are not one of them."

When we were little, sometimes I found Mother in the kitchen sitting at the table, her head supported by one hand, her other arm lying along the formica table top, tears wetting her cheeks. I would stop by her chair and pat her arm.

"How could you hurt me so?"

"I hate to see you suffer—" For years I thought she would do anything for me, and I spent my days in perpetual guilt at not being able to think of anything to do for her. "I love you."

She seems not to hear that. "What happened?" She looks at me as if I might not, after all, be able to explain it all away.

"I don't know. I went, Mother." What can I say?

She puts her face in her hands.

"It's OK, Mother. I have a good life. I have my friends." It seems thin and absurdly inadequate. "I have the life you wanted for me. A good job." How do you say these things? How do you say *I have a good life* and make it sound true?

The kettle in the kitchen screams, and Mother looks around as if she can't remember what the sound signifies.

"Want me to fix the tea?"

She looks up at me and wipes the skin under her eyes with her fingers. "Your father had such hatred for those people."

"Dad's dead."

"Thank the Lord." She pulls up the hem of her skirt and wipes her eyes again. I have never seen her expose her slip before. The kettle continues to scream. Finally, she speaks, "Oh, do go do the tea."

I make a tray with the cups and saucers and teaspoons and sugar bowl, some cookies she had put out, and pour the hot water into the teapot, and return to the back room. She is staring at a stack of magazines in a brass coal scuttle.

"You stopped going to church. When you went to church, you were a good boy—"

"I still am, Mother." I slide the plate of cookies toward her and put the two cups into the two saucers. "Going to church doesn't have much to do with anything."

"But we taught you to do right, didn't we?" Her eyes search my face. "Have we ever done anything wrong? The pastor talks about homosexuals."

I shrug. "I don't think he knows anything about them."

"Didn't you listen? He said how wrong it was. You knew how wrong it was."

"I did. He made me think it must be awful to be a homosexual. I thought you'd go to hell."

"But that's what they say will happen!" She looks at her fingers and then bends them back with her other hand until the knuckles turn white. "I've been reading the Bible ever since I got home, and I can't find anything in it that can justify what they are doing. It says, *They committed abominations before me.*"

"I suffered a lot because of the pastor." I am looking at the tea things. She doesn't say anything. I pour the tea. A cup of tea accompanied every event in our lives. I came home from track practice to these cups, and from summer camp, and from college. I've told Mother and Marian the story of my life over these cups. Part of the story of my life.

She allows her tea to cool before her.

"We brought you up to be a good boy."

"I am a good boy, Mother. I don't want to hurt you. I love you." How can you prove that, either?

"Oh, I am so sorry, Michael. I want the best for you. I want you to be happy. Happiness comes from doing the right things. Finding a lovely girl and settling down and having children. Happiness comes from growing old together. Oh Michael, what about your children!"

She sees her cup and lifts it to her lips absently. She puts down the cup and reaches for a cookie. She bites into it, and it crumbles in her mouth. The crumbs fall on her blouse. My tea has grown cold.

"Imagine how awful. If you were one of them, you would never get married." She has picked up the morning paper—it has a picture of the march on the cover and the headline, *Local residents charged with murder*—and absently smooths it out on her lap, as if it were laundry she were folding. "You would never have children. You would hurt me so."

"I am one of them, Mother." I lift the teacup to my lips and sip it even though it has grown cold. She stares at the paper in her lap. I don't say anything. I don't try to help her. And I don't try to help her escape.

"I should have told you when I first found out myself. But I was a kid, and I was frightened. I should have told you at some point before now when you would have had time, more time, to come to terms with this. I'm very sorry." As I talk, I watch her. She is hearing nothing I am saying. Her shoulders have become hunched. She has picked up the newspaper and holds it to her breast, her arms folded across it, her head down and forward, like a turtle's. "I am never going to lie again."

"You'll go to hell." The timbre of her voice is low and throaty.

So. I draw a breath. "I've been told that. I am still gay."

"You'll become a pariah. Nobody decent will have anything to do with you." She speaks slowly, her eyes fixed on her own interior vision. "They'll cross the street. You'll be pointed at. You'll die sterile, with nobody to look out for you in your old age. You've brought down a curse on me and your sister—"

"I am a decent gay man, Mother."

"This is a vicious sin against the Lord. Your heart has been hardened and you flaunt your vile degradation in front of God-fearing folk—"

She talks on. The moment is passing. My heart *has* been hardened. I am covered all over with scars, and I will let nobody wound me again. I have become musclebound in this struggle, insensitive and unable to respond to her pain. I don't know where my love for her has gone. I watch her going on, staring at the brass scuttle with its magazines, formulating her predictions using the language she learned in church. There are tears streaming down her checks. She is fragile, and she is frightened.

I look for my keys and find them in my pocket. I stand up.

She clutches the paper to her chest, her eyes on some middle distance. "You are degenerate. You will never have children to bless you. You will disgust yourself with unspeakable acts. You will grow old full of misery—"

I walk out through the small, close house, through the dining room and living room to the front door. The screen door slams behind me, as I take the front steps two at a time. Above, the great arching sky gives me room to breathe—the cumulus clouds are piled up to forty thousand feet—and I do, pulling in great lungsful. My hands are shaking. I back the car into the street and head toward home with the windows down, feeling the wind in my face. Queer: I am now defined by the way I have sex, and all the other things you could say about me—the things that, before, Mother and Marian loved me for—count for nothing.

When I arrive home, I find that somebody has taken paint to the front door and painted partially over the graffiti. Robbie tells me he did it, using paint left over from the bedroom. The door, which was dark green to begin with and then had the red letters painted across it, now has a large ivory splotch in the middle, partially obscuring the red letters. Robbie says he ran out of paint. "Then I ran out of desire."

Jack cut work yesterday and today to go to court. Afterwards he was among a crowd of gay men and lesbians standing outside on the sidewalk. Television reporters interviewed him, and now when the news comes on, we watch Channel 4. The anchorperson leads into the story of the hearing first thing, and suddenly we see the sidewalk in full sunlight, the neoclassic court house in the background, and people milling about. The reporter speaks into the camera: "Outside the court house, many of Bernard Mallett's friends—"

Robbie and I sit on the sofa, Robbie lying down, his head in my lap. Jack sits on the floor, his elbows resting on his knees, staring at the screen. Timothy has gone back to my bedroom. I think he is sleeping. The camera moves in closer and focuses on a group of bystanders. There is Jack, tall, handsome, male. I am intensely aware of Jack sitting on the floor in front of me. The reporter turns to him, and, holding the microphone near his mouth, says, "Were you a friend of Bernie Mallett's?"

The Jack on the screen puts his hands in his rear jeans pockets. His eyes narrow. "Bernie was my friend, sure. I'm gay. I'm not ashamed to admit it—"

There is a new picture, and the reporter is interviewing somebody else.

"She cut you off," Robbie says.

The Jack on the floor speaks. "Yeah."

"What did you say?"

"I said, *Anybody who doesn't like that can go fuck himself.*"

We spend the rest of the evening reading and rereading the paper. There were three things on us in the paper today: an article on the front page with the headline "Local Residents Charged with Murder," another with the headline "Victim a Flamboyant Gay Man, Friends Say," and a third with the headline "Memorial Service Attracts 200." We read them sitting on the floor in my living room, and we talk about them, about the things we didn't know—Bernie had asthma, which was a factor in his drowning, one of the boys in court this morning was crying, the water under the bridge right there is only 5 feet deep—and about what our lives are like now.

2

Wednesday, when I go out to run, the door is painted again, this time with a large DIE FAGGOT across it in ragged red paint. It has the effect of an expressionist painting of a war. Later when I come back, Timmie comes out on the porch with me and stares. He seems to move as if he weren't subject to gravity, as if he were painted on a background; he seems pure feeling: "Wow."

Timothy steps back and leans against me, staring at the door. By doing this, he invites me to put my hands on his shoulders. We are outdoors and we can be seen, and I know this intimacy in public is provocative. I take his shoulders in my hands and knead them with the heels of my palms.

"He doesn't want to give us any room," Timothy says, his head against my chest. "Why did he have to come over here to where we live?" He turns around and puts his arms around my neck. "It looks like they meant it to be ugly. It looks like blood."

On the table is the newspaper with the headline: "Teenagers Plead Innocent in Mallett Killing." Inside is a commentary by a staff writer and a lengthy editorial on human value, "Bernard Mallett's Life." The front page says the murder has attracted the attention of national gay organizations. "Some homosexuals in Cardiff feel that violence in Cardiff against gays is no worse than elsewhere," the article opens, and Timothy is quoted saying that one of the three boys released into the custody of his parents shouted "Faggot!" at him downtown yesterday. He is said to have told the police, but they "like, didn't do anything." According to the police chief, the charge was fully investigated and was without merit.

Robbie, Jack, Timothy, Marybeth, and Claire are sitting around the kitchen table. I am at the sink cutting vegetables. Robbie comes behind me and takes my shoulders in his hands. I lean back, my head resting on his shoulders. He feels my shoulders. We're talking about what we should do about these people painting my door.

"We're enough, aren't we," Claire asks, "to go out and take some of these dudes?" She looks around the table, counting us.

"No," I say. "We're not enough for a battle. Or for vigilante stuff."

"Well, I'm not going to sit around like some fucking coward waiting to take it up the ass from—" Jack has his jaw stuck out. "—from—"

He sits forward with his elbows and forearms on the table, his hands together. I come and stand behind him. "So far they haven't really hurt me with their words."

"No." Jack rears back in his seat. "They have hurt you."

"I know I am." Claire stares up from under her eyebrows.

"We take care of this one, and this kind of shit will stop."

"Listen to Mickey, guys," Robbie says carefully. "There's really nothing we can do right now."

Jack leans back in his chair and sticks his thumbs in his jeans belt loops. He is looking at me. "Are you saying you think we shouldn't do anything?"

I think that's what I'm saying.

"Remember the meeting on Monday. *That's* when we're going to make our response to all this—"

"What *is* our response to all this?" That's Marybeth.

"Yeah, I want to know that too. What's going on?"

"Make sure the boys get what's coming to 'em. Get whoever's painting Mickey's door."

Marybeth nods and sits back in her chair. "—a gay rights bill. We need to set that up as a goal, and then lay down ways to get there—"

I soak the vegetables and put the water on for the pasta. The truth is I don't know what's going on. "I don't know. I think we got their attention—"

Jack gets up and comes over to the sink for more coffee off the stove and then leans against the sink, sipping his coffee, his eyes little slits, staring into the middle of the table. "I went to work this morning"—he is a delivery man for UPS—"and these guys were telling the joke about launching the ferry without a license, and I wanted to kill 'em. I thought they don't know what Bernie meant to me. They're acting just like he was a piece of shit. And that he didn't mean nothing to nobody." He sips his coffee. He looks at the floor, or at the creamer and pitcher in the middle of the table, or at the wall or ceiling, but he doesn't look at any of us. "I get confused because I don't know what I'm supposed to be doing. I want to kill people. That's what I really want to do when I think about what they did to Bernie. They hurt him so bad—I mean think about it, being thrown in the river when you can't swim and you have asthma so bad—and I want to hurt somebody real bad too." His arms hang down by his side, and he clenches his fists and then opens them again and then closes them again, as if looking for something to close them around. "I can *feel* that. But I listen to Robbie or to Mickey, and it sounds so smart. I want to do something real *smart*, you know? But I keep feeling like all we're doing is being fairies and letting them beat up on us." He puts down his coffee cup on the counter behind him and then crosses his arms across his chest. He speaks directly to me and Robbie. "I think what's happening is that you don't want to rock the boat. I think you got your car and your real nice apartment and all your furniture and your good job and your college degree, and you don't want to get angry because you might lose all that stuff. And so you let 'em paint your door every night, and you don't even call the police because you don't want to complain to the boss man that you don't like the way he's treating you, while the rest of us, people like me and Claire and Marybeth—why are you talking like that, Marybeth?—who don't have all these nice things you have, are getting screwed, and you are telling us, 'Be patient, things are going to get better! Don't make anybody angry! Don't let *them* know you're angry. The newspapers're going to tell the truth, and the police're going to do their job!' You know something I think about? Bernie wouldn't have told us to *be patient*. He'd'a squawked until everybody north of Portland knew that they can't mess around with gay people. He'd'a said, *I'm fed up*, and he'd'a told me, *you ought to be fed up too*, 'cause he had courage, and he'd do what was right! I'm real confused, Mickey, but I think I'm fucking mad at you too!" Jack's eyes are welded onto me, and I am astonished and don't know what to say.

The only sound in the room for what feels like an eternity is the sound of Claire clapping.

Everything's OK. They have a place to go. They come here and eat my food. They sit around my kitchen table and talk and sit on my living room floor and watch my VCR, and when they need to go somewhere they use my car. And then they blame me when I don't live the way they think I should. Just because I have more money than they do. Now Jack wants me to be a revolutionary.

Just when I'm getting the pasta out of the pot and dumping it in the colander, the phone rings in the living room. Marian starts talking as soon as I come on: "Lloyd and I—" She is talking fast, in that planned way she has, and I'm feeling she's hitting me with each word. "—have discussed things and have decided to make some changes in our relationship with you, in response to changed circumstances."

"OK, Marian." She is making an announcement and is not trying to enter into a dialogue with me. I am thinking of the food and the guys in the other room. "Marian, I don't want to deal with whatever you're going to say."

"This will only take a minute."

"I'm sorry, I've got food coming off the stove—"

"I won't be bringing the children by on Sunday anymore. I think it best, until they are much older, that we keep a distance between them and you. Lloyd particularly wants to ask you not to come to our house without calling first. I don't mean to sever all contact between us. I just want to limit it to adults. I'll call you when I think it is appropriate for us to get together."

"Yes? You want to say more? What more do you want to say?" The food is getting cold.

"Yes. You should consider seeing a psychiatrist—"

"I am not sick, Marian."

"You could be cured—"

"No. I don't want to be cured. I don't have a disease."

"You're acting cruelly to your mother. I hope you will have some consideration for her feelings and leave her alone while she deals with this. She tells me you walked out on her yesterday afternoon. Please don't call her or go by to see her without contacting me first." She pauses.

I don't say anything.

"Do you promise?"

"No, Marian, I make no promises."

"Well, I hope you will have some consideration for others."

"I am gay, Marian. That can't be changed. What's changed is that I'm not going to be your dirty little secret any more."

I sit down on the end of the sofa. Robbie, or somebody, has served the pasta. I hear them in the kitchen.

I am coming out. I have come out to myself and to other gay people, and now I am coming out to straights. I have a compulsive need to tell people I am gay. Today I wanted to stop people in the halls and say, "Did you know my door has been painted?" I wanted to say to Charles, "Come sit down in my office, and let me tell you about my lover." I want to introduce myself all over and to say to him, "Everything you ever knew about a man named Michael was wrong. Let me tell you about the *real* Michael. Let me tell you how I met Robbie. Robbie is a dancer—" I want to tell people how we meet at Dominic's under the very nose of the straight community and they don't see us, and about the Saturday night dances. I want to tell people how clever and brilliant we are.

I have pretended to separate out my life, my life with my family and my job, and my private life with Robbie and my sexuality. I thought you could *do* that. I have pretended that I didn't hate myself. I thought it was OK to be gay and be a loving son if none of your friends ever met your mother and your mother didn't think any of your friends even existed. It turns out now that it wasn't just that I was keeping segments of my life separate from one another. I have been *lying*. Mother hasn't known the fundamental fact about me that I was never going to give her grandchildren, and my friends here have never known how much I love my mother. Keeping silent about such things amounts to deceit. And when I lied to Robbie about Marian or to Mother about Robbie, I was lying to myself about how much I hated myself, hated my cowardice, hated my inability to bring it all together, to make some gesture that was all of me.

I hear them in the other room, talking loudly. I think the only sufficient amends is a continuous presentation of myself—like a political figure, or a model, viewed from sixteen video cameras on sixteen screens simultaneously—in which no detail goes unrecorded.

I want to be seen in a completeness unimaginable before Bernie's death. I see a videotape of Robbie nude, legs together, arms at his side, staring straight ahead into the camera. He moves his arm straight out and up to shoulder height and his weight shifts on his feet. He moves his other arm, and his weight shifts again. He moves a leg out to the side and his torso follows. The movements are fluid and connected: Moving arms cause his torso to lean and his legs to shift. Movement of a leg to the side lessens his height and gives his penis and testicles room to sway. The cock of the elbow affects the set of the shoulder.

I want to feel the interconnectedness of things. There is a reason for the guys, when they arrive at work in the morning, to talk about their wives and children because there is some connection between what they do and their families. It is not just that they work to support their wives and children—they may not even do that—it is that at some root level, the need satisfied by what they do is the need satisfied by their wives and children. It has to do with need. What does one need to live? What have I needed? This thing that thing. All these things. My job, my car. I look about my apartment: the carpet and the sofa which pulls out and the chair and the lamp. My books and my pictures. I hear Robbie in the other room offering food to Claire and Marybeth and Jack and Timothy. Mother and Marian and Sarah and Josh. And Timothy on my sofa. And I need all these things. The images flip by like photographs bound in a book. They're what I am.

What if someone else—some man—were living here in my space, and he were straight. Suppose he needed all these things too, except that Robbie was a girl. Would he be exactly like me? Is the only difference between us what I do with my cock and my mouth?

We are in the living room watching the network news. The anchorman introduces stories about the Democratic party convention in San Francisco, Mondale's choice of a vice presidential running mate and the platform committee's efforts to write a party platform. There follow stories about the potential nuclear arms reduction negotiations. Then after a commercial break, he says, "In Cardiff, Maine, a town of 30,000 people, four hours north of Boston, lived a young man named Bernard Mallett. Mallett had not lived in Cardiff long—a couple of months—but he had made a name for himself there. He carried a purse and wore makeup and an earring. He was known widely as a homosexual, and according to friends he was the object of derision in the streets of Cardiff. Mallett was walking home from a dance Saturday night with a friend when three other young men got out of a car and began to chase him down side streets. These three young men are all residents of Cardiff. They caught him and pulled off his clothes. He got away from them and ran, naked, through a deserted part of town, but they caught up with him again on a bridge over a river and beat him and kicked him. And then they lifted him up and threw him over the railings of the bridge into a river, where he drowned. The boys are quoted in police reports as saying, later in the evening, at a party, 'We jumped a faggot and beat him up and threw him in the river.' The boys have been charged with murder. One of their friends has said that the three boys, whose ages are 15, 16, and 17, didn't mean to kill Mallett. That it was an accident, that they were just having fun on Saturday night. Meanwhile, two hundred homosexuals gathered for a memorial service in Mallett's memory." He turns his page over and goes to other stories.

"We got noticed." It's Marybeth. "Why did we get noticed?"

"It's the bridge. That's what makes it different."

"They didn't say it right." Jack is sitting on the sofa, leaning forward, his elbows on his knees. "They didn't say how the boys have been let loose and how Bernie's still dead. They didn't say how angry everybody is."

"Jack?"

He looks at me and waits.

"They didn't say what's happening to all of us, either."

He waits a minute, looks at the screen and then back at me. "Yeah, they should've said that too."

When I first began to know I was different, I didn't know what it meant, and even when I tried to find out, there was no one to tell me. And later, when I decided I was gay, I realized I didn't know how to do that, how to find other boys like me, how to dress, how to protect myself. I didn't know how to think about myself. And I realized there was a conspiracy out there to keep me from knowing about me.

Jack and Marybeth and Claire are in the kitchen doing the dishes. Timothy is in the big chair, watching television. Robbie is in the bedroom. On my second try, I get Dana on the phone.

"Channel 4 is doing a special on the gay community here tomorrow night, and they need some members of the gay community willing to go on camera and talk. I'm going to do it. I want you to do it too. That's the first thing. The second thing is that on Monday night we're all going to the church for a meeting, and nobody has made any plans about that." She draws a breath. "Can we get together? I can come over tonight, if that's OK, if you don't mind."

It is, as she says, "OK."

Robbie stands in the door into the living room. "You doing it?"

"You've already talked to her?"

"It's all over. We've all talked about it."

He sits on the sofa and holds up his arms for me to join him. I do. I lie down and put my head in his lap. He strokes my hair.

"I think if I ate I would get sick."

"I know. Things are out of control, aren't they?"

"Shit."

"What can I do?"

I turn over, the side of my head resting on his thigh, facing him.

"What am I going to do?"

"What you have to."

"What about Mother?"

"And Marian!"

"What about them?"

"They'll come around—"

"—or they won't."

"You can't back down now, Mickey."

He runs his fingers through my hair. "Sometimes I think they press us and press us and press us until we don't have any living space left, and then it's either come out or let 'em kill us. They didn't give Bernie much room, did they?"

He lifts me up and holds me in his arms and runs his hand down the back of my head and neck. "It's best to go on and cry. When they kill one of us, the space around all the rest of us is reduced—our freedom—until it's hard to breathe."

Later we hear Dana on the front porch. From there she can see into the living room and can see me lying in Robbie's arms: "Hi, fellas." I forget to pull the shades when it's still light outside.

When we get to the front hall, she is staring through the screen at the front door. "Some work of art."

We let her in, and she walks into the hall, her head down and to the side as she stares at the red letters on the door. "But he can't get it right, can he? Keeps coming back to do it again." She rises on tiptoe and kisses me on the cheek and then she does the same with Robbie.

"Welcome." She has never been here. Most of us have been in awe of Dana ever since she and Marcia moved here. She's older, she's been around, she knows how to do things. Most of all, none of this seems to be hurting her. She doesn't seem confused and panicked. I wish she weren't here right now. I feel apprehensive and half made up. I hug her.

She turns back to the door. "Don't you think he knew that you knew that?" She looks at me mock quizzically. I might like her. She follows us into the living room, where she lets her eyes drift around the room, taking it all in. "Nice place you have." She says hi to Timothy and then sits down. "How many of you live here?"

"Just me, but for right now Timothy is staying with me—" I slide my arm over Robbie's shoulder. "—and Robbie is hanging out here for a while until things settle down. Jack and Marybeth and Claire are in the kitchen doing dishes."

She smiles, "I see. Hunkering down with a few of the right sort until the storm is over?"

"Keeping warm."

She sits down in the big chair, we go on the sofa.

"Well, I'll have to get you down to our place. We live on the River Road south of Cardiff." She looks at us. "Do you sail?" I do. "Then we can go sailing. We have a dinghy."

Robbie pushes against my shoulder. "You're going to drown me yet."

We hold hands, and Dana takes it in.

"It's been a rough day?"

"How did you know?"

"I can see when a guy has been crying."

"I came out to Mother and my sister."

"How are they taking it?"

"I don't think either one is speaking to me."

She says she had to have a conversation with the people she works with. "There's so much of that stuff around." Then she changes the subject. "I need to talk to you about Channel 4. Have you given it any thought?"

All the people I don't know in Cardiff will know my name and my face and that I'm queer. And that will be all they'll know about me, just the one thing. Except my address. They can find me in the phone book and they can find my house. On Friday night I'll be vulnerable to every kind of hostile, malicious vandalism. Graffiti on my house, shit on doorstep.

"You've already got that," she says, shrugging and cocking her head toward the front door.

I push out my feet in front of me and stare at my toes.

"A little more or less won't make a difference." It's in the nature of a question, but no one answers.

I imagine I know what she means: As long as I tell some number fewer than the whole, then there's still the closet, however big it is. I know what's in the closet: self-hatred and fear.

Jack and Marybeth and Claire come in from the kitchen. They check out Dana. They're shy, and she's kind.

"Hi, guys. How're you holding up?"

I watch Jack, and he avoids my eyes. "I want to do something. I hate this hanging 'round."

"What do you think we ought to do?"

"I think they're going to let the boys go—"

Jack and Marybeth sit on the floor, their eyes on Dana. She shrugs and gestures with her hand. "We should get on the phone and be talking to people. People need to be thinking about what's going to happen on Monday—who they'd like for a moderator, what they want this organization to be. It's important because the coalition represents what we are, the way we see ourselves, and it'll speak for us. It's terribly important, now that this has happened, that we take control of the way we are seen—"

Later, going to bed, I feel better.

Robbie: "What's this all about?"

"We're asking the question, *What are we?* I like that. *What do we stand for?*"

He props his head up on his arm. "About time."

"Hard questions. We haven't had to ask them before."

"I have another question."

"What is it?"

"Will you conduct this meeting Monday?"

I hate that idea. "Why are you asking?"

"Somebody has to. You'd be good at it."

"Did someone ask you to ask me?"

"No. But we're all asking each other, and people keep mentioning your name."

"What about Jack?"

"He thinks you'd be good."

So. Maybe we can find ways to work together. Still. "I'd rather not. There are other people—"

"Who?"

"What about Derek? He's the actor, the one we met at the memorial service."

"I'd rather have you."

This would show Marian and Mother. And Jack too. But, I think, as I go to bed, What do I want to show them?

On Thursday, when DIE FAGGOT appears on the door, I call in to work and tell them I'll be late, and then I call the police.

Later I see the squad car park in front of the house. It is a standard American sedan, painted silver and blue, loaded with chrome. It carries a tiara of lights on its roof which are blinding, even though they are not turned on, by the sun shining on the chrome. Two men get out. They look about them as they walk around the car and stand on the walk to the street, surveying, inspecting the neighborhood. Then they turn to the house and look at the windows and the door. The men are large, in tight blue uniforms with boots that cover their legs to their knees. Their calves, encased in the shiny black leather, seem unnaturally large. They seem to need such a large car. Like the car, they have chrome all over: their belt buckles, buttons, the tip of the little rope that hangs over the shoulder and under the arm. Chrome and leather: the boots, the holsters, the wide belts punched with holes. They have pistols in holsters at their hips. They wear dark glasses and garrison caps. They don't speak to each other. After a moment inspecting my house, they walk up the walk. I hear them cross the porch and knock, loudly, commandingly. I feel as if I am about to be invaded.

I open the door. One of them has pink skin and holds a small pad with aluminum backing in his hand. The other one has olive skin and seems to be the leader.

"You call about somebody painting your door?" It's the leader.

"That was me." My breath is coming fast. "Come in."

They walk in—when they move, their leather makes creaking sounds—and stand in the middle of the room. They seem even bigger than Jack, and there are two of them, and they take up all available space.

"Your name?" The leader. I tell them. I give them my name and address and tell them who lives here besides me—"Nobody."— and who the landlord is. The one with pink skin and what looks like razor burns on his face writes all this down.

"This happened Monday night?"

"Monday night and every night since then."

"Let's look." We walk back to the front porch and look at the door. It looks recycled, like somebody who didn't have canvas to paint on used a door off some colonial mansion instead. And what he wanted to paint was something abstract and disturbing.

"What did they paint the first night?" the leader asks.

"Faggot."

The other one writes it down.

"The second night?"

"Die Faggot."

"Last night?"

"Die Faggot."

While the one with the pad is scribbling away, the leader is staring at me. His face is taut: his eyes have the beginning of a squint, his lips are closed, and the ends of his mouth are pulled back.

I let him stare—I can't do anything about that in any case—and I think I'll give him a good look while he's at it. I lift my chin.

"Are you?"

"What?"

"A fairy?"

I feel the blush coming up. Fairy. Queer. Cocksucker.

"I mean, is all this true?"

"I'm a gay man, if that's what you want to know." I pull in my chin and look him in the eyes. And I am more than that.

"You expect this then?"

I don't know where he is going. "I—"

"I mean, people see what you're doing, so they're going to react—"

The other one is putting away the pad.

Suddenly, I know where they're going. The anger comes up from way down. "Wait a fucking minute, here!"

"Watch your language, buddy."

"I don't know what law is being broken here, but it must be against the law for somebody to come up on my front porch and paint words on my front door."

"Well, yeah, but it looks to me like—"

"I am gay, and there is nothing I can do about that." I remember. "I don't want to do anything about that. I want you to stop whoever it is from painting my front door."

The men have already begun to head toward the door.

"What are you going to do?" I want to stop them, get them to declare themselves.

"Well, we don't have anything to go on. If you had any clues—" He is putting on his glasses—mirrored sunglasses—and the leather of his boots and belt creaks as he walks.

"Hey, *you* were supposed to get the clues." They have got to help me. "You could watch the house at night." I imagine them, a dozen like these two, surrounding the house during the night—in the

226

bushes, behind the trees—and suddenly at three o'clock in the morning shouting out, "Freeze!, you're under arrest!" and arc lights coming on everywhere illuminating the yard and its weeds and, in the middle, a vicious wretch, caught with the paint can in his hand.

"Sure, we'll do that, buddy—"

Then they're gone. I stand on the front stoop. I lift my hands. I want something to throw, and I don't have anything. My hands are empty, and my hands are light, and my fingers have nothing to grasp. I feel helpless, and I am enraged. I look at my front door. FAGGOT has been there since Tuesday morning. Everybody in town has seen it. It must be like those houses that have Santa Claus and his sleigh and eight tiny reindeer galloping across the roof at Christmas, and people come in from the country to drive by slowly and gawk at the glitter: *Let's go over and see the faggot's house.* The wound heals: You see faggot on your front door enough. It's obscene, and you start identifying with it, thinking of yourself that way. You stop paying attention. What's left is anger.

All week our world has depended on the telephone lines, which connect us like ganglia and which transport rumors of the police, of the court, of what is going on behind the bland pages of the newspaper. We gather around the television set where we watch somebody being interviewed, jolted off orbit by the regular announcement from one or the other gay person in the room that he or she has "had it" and isn't "going to take it anymore," which is followed by the promise to go into the "boss's office" or "Mother's" tomorrow and tell him or her that "I'm queer and you can go fuck yourself if you don't like it."

After the police leave, I am in the kitchen, and Timothy asks if he can make a local phone call. I hear him dial. I hear him say, "Mom?" There is a pause, and then he says, "Yeah, that was me." There is another pause, and he says, "Yeah, I am." Then he says, "You never asked." He listens for a while, and then he hangs up and returns to sitting on the end of the sofa, staring. He drifts through these days, suffering, his voice a monotone, his eyes unfocused, his body limp.

And yet on Monday morning and Tuesday, he showed up at the Court house for the hearings. He was sought out by the television and newspaper reporters, who took his picture and got him to repeat his story that there were a lot of boys who threw Bernie in the river. Each day the newspaper quoted him on the number of boys and then quoted the police chief, and the result discredited Timothy and makes the story of Bernie's death seem to be merely a crazy fantasy. Timothy goes in front of television cameras telling his story, and he doesn't watch the result on the news. He's being used, and he doesn't care, or know, as long as he has the chance to tell his truth. Once, he was asked if he is a homosexual. Timothy looked at the reporter and at the microphone stuck in his face. Then he giggled, and he cast his eyes around desperately at the people crowding around as if to ask, "Can somebody help me?" Timothy has become, in these first days after Bernie's death, the most famous homosexual in Cardiff. I think his life is in danger every time he goes out of my house.

I don't call Marian or Mother. I am angry and self-righteous: I see no reason to make things easier for them by going back to either one of them and begging or explaining. At the same time, I can't escape the knowledge that Mother and Marian found out about me by watching television, and I could have told them years ago. It was easier to lie than to confront the facts. Now I pay for that. Now they pay for that. Guilt gives an edge to my anger.

I am late for work today, and then I leave early: At two o'clock I am in a TV studio, hearing this being said to me: "If 10 percent of the population is gay, then the number of persons who showed up at the Unitarian Church the night before last is not a significant portion of the gay population here. Could you comment on the—"

"Wait—"

"—relatively few number of gay men and lesbians—"

"—this is misleading."

"—who were willing to come out to protest?"

I have to get the lead away from him. "Four hundred—"

"The police actually said two hundred."

"—I don't care, there were—"

"Is it possible that the death of Bernard Mallett didn't affect the homosexual community?"

"He was my friend—"

"Or is it possible that the gay community really doesn't consider itself as oppressed as you think it is?"

The lights have caused the reporter to sweat along his jaw line. His eyes dart from me to the camera and back, and occasionally he licks his lips and smiles uncertainly.

I can't be identified—the lights are arranged so that my face is in shadow—but I was unprepared for the amount of power that would give him, if I can't be seen. I must speak. I am determined, and I drive my thoughts into some coherent pattern: "When you consider the level of homophobia in Cardiff—" He opens his mouth to speak, but I am determined to override him. "—and the fact that the gay community has never come together publicly before outside of events on the university campus, it is amazing that we had as many as four hundred. Many people didn't feel they could come to the church because they would have had to come out more than they were ready for." He pulls his head back and opens his mouth again with an intake of breath, beginning to formulate a word, sweat glistening on his upper lip. But he doesn't move fast enough. I go on.

"There is no question about three things: The hatred for homosexuals in this community, the sense of oppression we feel, and the radical changes in our lives that are now happening because of the death of Bernie Mallett." There. I sit back and stare at him, my arms across my chest.

He looks at me, eyelids lowered a hair, and waits a long moment. He has on a gold and blue plaid, summer-weight sport coat, and the skin on his hands and face is remarkably clean and dry. I have beat him, have taken the lead away from him, forced him to respond to me. After a pause, he gives in and feeds me my line: "You're a young, middle-class homosexual man living in Cardiff. What is different now since the death of Bernie Mallett?"

This time I don't have to fight for my chance. "Until Bernie was murdered—" The reporter nods, a half smile on his face, his eyelids lowered. I go on for a while, my thoughts ranging over my life. I see the cameras on their wheeled tripods ranged about me like giant insects, the red light jumping from one to the other. I am not afraid of them. The reporter is repellent to me, but I think of people watching at home. I want to talk to *them*.

"I am defiant—" I don't know where the words come from. I speak as an automaton. "I won't be denied. I will say what I have to say—"

I want to say I deserve respect. But I don't know what it is about being gay that is worthy of respect. The way I have sex? I want to say I am a decent man, a decent gay man, but I don't know how to connect the one with the other. I am a dutiful son. Does that have anything to do with being gay? I am a careful worker, but what does that have to do with my love for Robbie? I love Robbie, but is that admirable? When I kept things separate, my life with Mother separate from my life with Robbie, I never asked these questions. Now it seems they are the only ones I ever think about. Can you be a dutiful son to a mother who hates what you do?

On Thursday night I read the morning's paper. For the first time since Bernie was murdered, there is no article on any facet of the case. The boys have been released into the custody of their parents, the gay community is quiescent. On the letters-to-the-editor pages, however, there are several letters, one from a child and two from adults, congratulating the city on the success of last week's River City Festival. Then there are three letters juxtaposing the River City Festival—"a proud moment in the life of the city"—with Bernie's death—"a tragedy," "an expression of bigotry," "a horror." Two of these three letters are from men and one from a woman. A fourth letter, from a Roman Catholic brother, concludes that "God does not choose to love His children on the basis of sexual orientation." There is a fifth short letter which says, "What everybody is forgetting is that these people are the abomination of the Lord. They are moral degenerates and should be hounded out of every place of civilized society in America."

We watch the screening at 11:30. The reporter, on screen, is a warm and vibrant person with attractive middle-class American middle-aged steadiness. He looks directly into the camera and, with smiles and winks and floating eyebrows, establishes trust with the audience. The person he is interviewing—me—is shown back-lighted, his face entirely in shadow. There is nothing identifiable about his silhouette: the cut of his hair, the set of the jaw, the way he moves his lips when he talks, and most particularly, the absence of moist eyes with lashes. There is no feature that would make it possible for someone to respond emotionally to him, to *grasp* him. His voice seems hostile, resentful, and aggressive. I sound even shrill at moments. This is not me. I feel exposed. I have allowed myself to be used. I feel shamed, and I hate it. I *look* shamed.

Robbie, sitting beside me on the sofa, slides down and rests his head on my shoulder.

"Hmmm, I love seeing you, hearing you. I wish I could see your face." He runs his hands through my arm. "You said what needed to be said. *I won't be denied. I will say what I have to say.* We need to hear gay men speak up like that. What's wonderful about it is that you didn't apologize anywhere." The imagery of the screen is catastrophic. I look exotic and afraid, furtive and criminal. I took refuge in the shadows. I look guilty.

3

On Friday, the day of Bernie's funeral, when I go out to run, I find all my tires have been slashed. This warfare of the paint-and-slash has the effect of causing me more psychic harm than real harm: I go to the 7-Eleven and look around and wonder who is here watching me. This isolates me. Since I don't know who is doing this, I suspect everybody, as I run through the streets. Instead of segregating me, the paint-and-slash causes me to segregate myself. My suspicion leads to a furious anger at myself. And then, what's left is a furious indifference. I call work again and a garage to take my car, and get new tires.

At work, as we are breaking up after the staff meeting, I suggest to Charles that he and I go together for a bite to eat. Charles smiles and looks at me—he is holding printouts in his hand, and he taps them into his free palm—as if it were a not uninteresting idea which had not occurred to him before. Charles is friendly and open, which extends so far as his values are not threatened. I suggest my car.

Later, headed toward the interstate where there are a couple of fast food restaurants, he admires my car. "New?"

He asks me who I have rustproof it. We talk car talk. I ask him where he buys his tires.

At the hamburger stand on the highway, we stand in line waiting to be served. At first I am in front, and then he is.

"I thought this was supposed to be fast food."

"No, No. The food is cardboard. You *eat* it fast." He laughs—I think we both laugh at it being such a weak joke—and we switch place in line again. There is a newspaper stand near the coffee urns, about twelve or fifteen feet from us. A paper shows in the plastic viewer, and there is a headline just above the fold: "Homophobia a Result of Insecurity."

We get our food and find a concrete table outdoors under a sky so blue it looks like a color photograph. I look at Charles. He has already started eating. He sits on my right, and now his head is turned down and away from me as he bites into his hamburger in his right hand. His left hand, partly curled, rests on the edge of the table. He has not wondered why I invited him to lunch.

The breeze lifts the napkins on the table and cools us at the same time the sun warms our shoulders. Around us children play in the concrete playground equipment, and parents divide their attention between the children and the recreational vehicles parked in the parking lot. We are surrounded by people traveling north on the interstate into the woods for camping.

I mean to tell him I am gay. I eat my hamburger and my french-fries, and I think what I am about to do.

He looks at me: "What about the Democrats!"

"What do you mean?"

"They already have a candidate a week before the convention, yet they're tearing themselves apart."

I grin. "That's what Democrats do best—"

His look questions me.

"—provide spectacle."

He laughs. "Will he choose a woman?"

I shrug. He has finished his hamburger and eats his french-fries with his fingers, his head down a little and turned to the right, to his right hand.

"Do you care?"

"Sure."

"I don't think I do."

"The women ought not to be excluded."

He pulls back a little, his left hand pushing him away from the table, and turns fully in my direction, an incredulous smile on his face. "You a women's libber?"

I laugh, then smile, then say, "Yeah." I nod. "I'm a feminist." I put down my hamburger. "I want to say something—"

He still has that incredulous smile on his face. Looking like that, he won't believe anything I say.

"I mean, I've been thinking the last couple of days, that I need to talk to you—"

"That's weird—"

"I've known you ever since I came to work here, right?"

He loses the incredulous smile, and he nods. He's willing to go some way with me.

"Well you don't really know me, and I feel—"

He's looking at me. "I know you about as well as I know any of the other guys." He picks up the milkshake and stirs it with the straw.

"Well, some things have been happening in my life, and I want to tell somebody at work. And you're it, buddy."

I have his full attention now. He turns to face me and puts one hand on each knee. He looks at me quizzically: "What's this all about?"

I frown. "You know the boy who drowned?"

"What boy?"

"The one who was thrown off the bridge?"

"Oh, that. Sure."

"Well, he was a homosexual—"

He doesn't say anything.

"—and it upset a lot of his friends, a lot of the homosexuals in Cardiff—"

"What are you telling me?"

"It upset me. It made me real angry that somebody—"

"Why did it make you angry?" His eyes have narrowed and he has pulled away a little bit.

"I'm a friend of his."

I am aware of the children shouting and squealing on the slide.

"You queer?" His face has crumpled up into a mask of disbelief.

"I am a homosexual."

A pause.

"No shit!" He lifts his hands from his knees and then drops

them back down again and leans on them. "You're a fucking queer!" He starts to laugh. People look at us. "Why are you telling me? You coming on to me?" He laughs. "I know, you're telling me to be careful around you, you can't help yourself, right?"

"I told you because I've been near crazy with anger and grief, and I couldn't keep that secret at work any longer, and you are the nearest thing to a friend I've got here. I am sick of not being honest."

"What a fucking surprise! You're a faggot!" He laughs again and then lifts up and drops his hands on his knees again. "You sure?"

"I'm sure." I smile.

"Are you planning on putting the make on me?" He has a broad grin on his face now.

"No, Charles—"

"You want to be a girl!" He shakes his head, grinning.

Now it's my turn to grin. "Well, no. I told you because I had to tell somebody at work what's going on with me. I want to say that being gay is OK. I have to say that."

He stands up. He puts out a hand and grasps the back of my neck and pulls me toward him. "Well, dude, I don't know about that. But as long as you keep your hands to yourself, you can do any fucking thing you want to do. Just don't tell me about it." Then he drops his hand and gathers up his trash. "I think you're an OK guy. I still think so, even though you say you're queer." His face crumples up into a question, again: "Are you sure?"

We throw our trash into the containers and walk through the kids toward the car. He is laughing the whole way and saying, "Christ! I can't believe it! You're a queer!"

On the way into town, he says that I am not to worry, he won't tell anybody at work.

Later my boss calls me in to talk about my progress—and my absence from work—and when we finish talking about where I am, I tell him too. I ask him if I can talk about something else for a minute, and he gestures toward a chair, and I sit down and tell him about Bernie's death and how Bernie was a friend of mine, and how I don't think it would have happened to Bernie if all the gay people in town had been honest and had come out. Then people wouldn't have these crazy ideas about homosexuals. So, I say that I feel that I have to tell him that I am a homosexual.

He sits through all this without saying anything: He's a straight-arrow guy with his brush haircut and his freshly pressed slacks. When I finish, he is quiet for a few minutes.

"I appreciate your telling me this. It must be very hard to talk about." Then he stands up and ushers me out of his office. "The only thing we care about here is your job performance. You're a valued employee here. I hope you work here a long time. And I promise you, I'll never mention what you have told me to anybody."

Standing in his office door, I tell him that Bernie's funeral is this afternoon and that I need the rest of the afternoon off. I hardly care if he cares.

Late in the afternoon after the funeral service for Bernie, Marybeth and Robbie and I are walking back to my car. We walk toward the television crews—they are up on an embankment on the side of the lane, and we must get past them to get to where the cars are parked. One young woman breaks loose from the group of persons and approaches us.

"Were you friends of Bernie Mallett?"

We nod.

"Could I talk to you for a few moments?" She introduces herself to us. She is from Channel 4. "How well did you know Bernie Mallett?"

"Very well," Robbie says.

"Would you mind if we asked a few questions on camera?"

We glance at each other, and then we tell her it's OK.

She calls the cameraman over. When he is set up, she turns to us.

"Could you recall for us what Bernie Mallett was like?" Robbie talks, and Marybeth.

"Most specifically, could you tell us what he looked like?" The question has been asked so many times—his earring, his purse, his makeup—that I recognize what Marybeth and Robbie are saying as they say it. I add something about his eyeliner. She also asks us what it felt like when we discovered that Bernie had been murdered, and Marybeth, who found out about it at five in the morning, tells how that was. The reporter asks whether the gay community has any plans for combating the kind of prejudice exemplified in the attack on Bernie. Marybeth talks about the underlying cause of homophobia—sexism—and Robbie talks about the right to be left alone.

It is 3:45 p.m. in the afternoon on Friday—the funeral began an hour ago—and the sun is beyond the trees. There is no cloud in the sky. The trees, great elms up against the hillside and willows along the lane, in a light breeze, rustle and cast deep shadows. The cemetery grasses are a deep, rich green, the effect of lavish care, and in the shadows the granite tombstones are gray and cool. The cameraman has turned the camera on me. At first I am aware of this only in the periphery of my vision. And then, drawn naturally toward it, I turn to the camera and face it down, talking, answering the reporter's long questions on Bernie's death and its effect on the gay community in Cardiff, on me and my homosexuality, on grief and loss, staring into the large black round glass eye. "Bernie was very courageous. He said, I am what I am. In many ways, he died of that courage." The camera's lens sees me, and in the broad light of day it takes me in without blinking.

When I get home, I find everyone there, and among the messages is one from Dana. I return the call, but she is not at home. Claire has come out to her mother and her sister. She now wears a pink triangle. Claire and Jack and Timothy have gotten off from work and gone to Portland where the gay community is having a memorial service and march for Bernie. I call Mother, and she won't speak.

On the top of the front page of the paper just above the fold is the headline, "Homophobia a Result of Insecurity." The reporter interviewed a psychologist on the sources of homophobia in our culture. I scan the paragraphs. There are religious, moral, psychological, social, and political factors to consider, the psychologist says. "The most homophobic element in our culture is the population group consisting of young adolescent males." I wonder if it's true that young males are more homophobic as a group than, say, Baptist ministers, or popes, taken collectively, or even mothers, or for that matter, psychiatrists. I let the paper fall to the floor, lost in thought.

We always lived in that house that Mother lives in now. On the West Side most of us came from the same kind of families. Our fathers worked in the shoe factory, or for one of the paper mills, or for the big construction company up the river. From the first grade, I had a friend I played with, whose name was Paul. We were in Cub Scouts together and Boy Scouts, and then we graduated to high school and were on the track team. Most of it, though, was just hanging out together: the movies, comics, television. We became fans of the Boston teams and bought caps and jackets with *Celtics* on the back. We slept over every weekend and slept in the same bed and talked after our parents made us put out the light.

We ran every morning together before school, outdoors during the good weather and indoors at the college track in the bad weather. I liked letting my stride out and matching his and running on and on down a country road and then up the hill on the other side, my eyes on the ground at a middle distance ahead of me, aware of him at my side. At some point when I was fifteen or sixteen, I fell in love with him.

In the middle of October of my junior year, there was a track meet. Paul was in the 800 meter event. I was at the finish line, waiting for him. It was a gray, cold day, occasionally drizzling. We were wet with it and miserable. He was in the final stretch, and I was at the end of the straightaway. He was coming toward me, running, his wet jersey loose and pulled away from his body by the wind, his legs moving so fast I couldn't see the muscles in them, the ends of his mouth pulled back in concentration. He came up behind the front runner and then, just as they crossed the line, seemed to pass him. He crossed the line with his arms up and out and ran on down the track for half a lap, slowing down.

Then he ran in a long easy lope back to me, his face covered with sweat and rain, like thin oil, and threw his arms out and around my shoulders and let me hold him up, his head over my shoulder, while he drew great drafts of air and his body shuddered.

I held him, feeling his thin body next to mine, while people crowded around to congratulate him, and then it was over. He pulled away and accepted the slaps and hugs of the other guys and the congratulations of the coaches.

In the end, I took it to my psychology teacher at school. She was gray haired, a little fat, and seemed overworked. She was like my mother. I told her about Paul, about the first grade and all the grades after that, about Boy Scouts and sleeping over and dating, about track and the track meet. I told her I had fallen in love with Paul. I told her I was afraid I must be a homosexual.

We were in her classroom, after school. It was almost dark—four-thirty or so—and there was a snow outside. The whole building was quiet, except for my voice going on. It seemed that my voice was as loud as the principal's over the P.A. in the morning.

"I don't know what to do."

"Have you told Paul?"

"No, ma'am."

"Anybody else?"

"No, ma'am. Just you."

"I'm glad you came to me, Mickey." She pulled down from her bookshelf behind her desk a copy of some book in a red cover. "Have you ever had feelings for other men?" she asked.

I couldn't tell her the truth. "Sometimes."

"Do you ever have feelings—sexual feelings—for women?"

I couldn't remember. I couldn't think that I had ever had anything for a woman that felt like what I felt for Paul, but I was afraid—ashamed—to tell her that. "Sometimes."

She smiled. She patted her book. "Sometimes when we're growing up, before things settle down, and when we're still in that very intense period of change that you're in now—adolescence—our feelings get confused and settle on the wrong person. You may have these feelings for Paul now, but I would imagine that in a year, you will have forgotten all about this. You will have found a lovely girl—"

She talked on like that for a while, patting the red book in her lap, and trying to be reassuring.

"You like being close to Paul?"

"Yes, ma'am."

"It must have felt very good to feel him in your arms after he won the race—"

"Yes, ma'am."

"But that doesn't mean anything except that you like him and were proud of him winning the race. Everybody—perhaps most when we're lonely or down for some reason—likes to be hugged. That's perfectly normal. Oh, Mickey, forget about this. You are a fine young man. *You're normal.*" She smiled at me. "Can you believe me?"

I didn't know what to think. What she proposed was so easy, in a way so uncomplicated. It didn't require anything of me except that I forget what I felt for Paul.

"Can you believe me?"

"I guess so. I guess so."

She stood up. "That's the ticket."

I stood up and she walked me to the door of the classroom. The long dark hall waited me outside.

She took my arm. "Mickey, one other thing. Let's keep this our secret, shall we? And I promise you, I'll never mention what you have told me to anybody."

I always knew you didn't talk about being gay. I don't remember being told that it was something you didn't talk about: I knew instinctively. Later I discovered that homosexuality had always been known to be something you weren't supposed to mention. It was "the love that dare not speak its name." In law books it was "the infamous crime against nature . . . the very mention of which is a disgrace to human nature." It was a crime "not fit to be named among Christians."

That was why I never knew anything about myself when I was growing up. I never saw a picture of a man kissing another man until I was twenty-three. And now everybody in this city knows I'm queer, and I don't know what there is that is admirable about me.

On Saturday night after supper, I call Dana and then I get in the car and drive south on the Main Road to their place. Dana says "as long as you're queer and need to be that and as long as they hate queers, you're going to hurt somebody—" It feels like we're in a war.

"—and what's so disorienting about it is that—" I look from one to the other of them, and they both have their eyes on me. "—while I feel so pressured to defend myself, I think all of them feel I am being savage, breaking up old relationships, demanding and selfish, destroying things that are important. I feel like I'm getting fewer and fewer choices."

"It's more necessary now to declare yourself—"

"What do you mean?"

"—gay or straight—"

Less room to stand on the sidelines, pursue private goals.

"It's like a battle—"

"It is like a battle," Dana says, "sometimes. It's a test of strength. Sometimes it's like open warfare, sometimes it's just us guerrillas. Occasionally we have to face terrorists—"

"It doesn't feel like that. It feels like I'm battering people—"

"You're protecting yourself—"

Marcia has been listening, and now she interrupts. "Whatever the metaphor, what's happened is that we live in a world divided into us and them—and that didn't need to have happened."

"Am I doing that?"

"No. That's their way of controlling you. Instead of dealing with you being gay, they turn it around on you and make it your responsibility, saying you're causing it—"

"But Dana, we're doing it too." Marcia speaks gently to Dana. "We're running away from each other as fast as we can."

"I don't even know what I'm fighting for." I look around their living room, which doesn't seem as embattled as mine does. "Unless it's my right to be with Robbie. Is that it?"

Dana smiles. "The beginning of it. You have to face it, gay means being subversive. That's what it'll always mean as long as our culture has the ideas it has about sex and gender and power. There's no way around that. These values oppress everybody—straight men, straight women, children, gays and lesbians. As long as our culture says, even in some unconscious way, that sex is about power, then we're going to be revolutionaries. Anarchists." She sips her tea.

I think: Queer: Cocksucker: Revolutionary.

Marcia doesn't seem touched by all this. No, that's not right: She doesn't seem *changed* by all this. She's sympathetic, she listens, she seems to care, but she doesn't seem threatened. Dana sounds like she's been through a war.

"Do you like fighting?"

She shrugs. "I do it when I have to. Life seems pretty violent a lot of the time. A battle—"

"—between two armies—"

"—yes, but in the long run, we have to go through this to get back together. It's not really about winning."

"What's it about?"

Dana pours the tea and passes me a cup. I hold the saucer in my lap and sip it. I have spilled tea into the saucer, and it drips on my shirt.

"It's about change."

I laugh. "I'm certainly changing—"

"No. The culture."

Then we talk for a while about the meeting on Monday night and who will moderate it. They ask me to.

"You know a lot of the younger crowd—they seem to flock around you. I think that would be good, a leg up to begin with. Everyone seems to admire what you're been doing this week. And we've checked around with the women and everybody seems to think they can work with you."

I hear all this and wonder what I am supposed to do. I won't lie any more, and I won't do something out of fear. I won't be *afraid* to do something. "What about Derek? Wouldn't he be good?"

Marcia frowns. "He hasn't been here long—"

"He's been through this kind of thing before, he told me, when a gay man was killed in Schenectady."

We talk about Derek and about how they want me. And we talk about how the meeting ought to proceed.

It's Saturday night. And late. I'm standing at their door. "Do you think things are going to change?"

Marcia laughs. "You shouldn't have asked that." She looks at Dana.

"No." Dana shoves her fists into her jeans pockets. "The way things are suits too many people."

We agree to talk to as many people as possible tomorrow and Monday about all this and then be back together on the phone. We will try to establish a consensus on how to proceed before the meeting starts Monday.

It is almost eleven-thirty when I hug them both—Dana and then Marcia, who has the kind of soft, wonderful womanly body that reminds me of Mother's—and then I go out the back door to my car. On the drive north on the River Road, I have the windows down and I feel the cool wind in my face. It really is a battle. It has something to do with integrity—mine and theirs—and with love. What you fight over is the integrity. What gets destroyed is the love. How did this happen? How did I get caught up in this? How is it that I have become a violent person?

The field slopes down to form a bowl which is slightly tipped, where a stream pours into the lake. Around the mown grass of the field are the dark woods covering the hills. The small lake bends around the point and disappears to the west, its dark waters now blown with whitecaps. On the lake are three white sails—the dinghies are dark and cannot be seen from this distance—which tack back and forth before the skittish wind. Every so often one of the sails goes over, and people in white and brightly colored summer clothes who are scattered in little groups across the green grass laugh and call to the wet sailor.

"Learn to sail!"

"Learn to swim!"

"Come in and have a beer!"

At the upper end of the field, just below a small cabin, long trestle tables have been set up, covered with ovenproof glass dishes wrapped in tinfoil. In a circle across the mown grass, bales of hay have been dropped haphazardly, and guitars wait players on the bales. I have parked my car behind the house and I walk down across the field. It is Sunday, just after noon, after church time, and these are people I have known since I was a child. It is a combined celebration. George and Ann Albright are celebrating their fortieth wedding anniversary—they taught me Sunday school—and Selena McKnight and Seth Brewer have announced their engagement. It is Christina Finlay's birthday—she is fifteen—and a couple who have not lived in Cardiff for fifteen years have moved back, and they are being welcomed home.

"Mickey!" someone shouts. People turn and see me, and I wave. I search the little groups for the one who called. It is Helen Eggleston.

I smile and go over and join her. I went to high school with her and dated her one fall.

"How are you?" She puts her hand on my shoulder and kisses me on the cheek. She is pretty and appears well-scrubbed and wears sandals and white shorts and a white blouse. "It's been so long! Where have you been keeping yourself!" Then she turns to a young man standing nearby. "This is Mickey McNamara, Eric." She whispers to me, "Don't tell a soul, but Eric's my boyfriend!"

"Helen, please," he says. Eric puts out his hand, genially proud and goodnaturedly embarrassed. His hand feels rough, and he grips mine strongly.

"Mickey, where have you been keeping yourself, you bad thing!"

"Working hard, Helen. Working hard."

"Making money, I bet!" She turns to Eric. "I always knew Mickey was going to be a real success!"

"What do you do?"

"I am a systems analyst out on the Passadumkeag Road. I'm not making money yet though, Helen. Wish I were."

"I bet you are and you're just not telling. Eric is doing fine, and in a couple of years, we're going to buy a place just like this." She turns and looks down the field to the lake. "We're going to have all this. Just like this. Don't you love the country?"

"What do you do?" I ask Eric.

"I'm a supervisor in the shoe factory." We talk for a while, watching the scene below us. They hold hands, and then Eric slides his arm around her waist and leaves it there, holding her to him. The sun is directly overhead, and everyone stands in the brilliance in his own shadow. I listen to the cries of children, while Eric stares at me and Helen talks of their future. She is a secretary for an insurance company, and, she says, they are to be married as soon as they have saved the down payment for a house.

I leave them and stroll on down the hill. People I know do this kind of thing two or three times a summer, collect a bunch of reasons for a party, and then organize it at somebody's place in the country. These parties bring together neighborhood people from town and the neighbors of this farm, church members, extended families—Mother is here somewhere, and Marian and Lloyd and the kids, and Lloyd's mother and father and sisters—and, less often, the people people work with. In the summertime children outnumber adults. In the wintertime children stay at home, and the adults drink more seriously.

A fat old man sits on the grass with a crowd around him, children in the middle of the circle on the grass, adults on the outside. He is talking and the crowd laughs and listens. One little girl about five leans back against her father's legs and he bends over slightly and puts his hands on her chest. She is listening seriously, a frown on her face, and her father listens with a smile, glancing at the old man and watching his daughter to see if she is enjoying it.

"—were huge, much bigger than they are now." His eyes get very big and round. "Why, a man could walk for an hour and not walk around the base of one. Some of them were so big you couldn't walk around them if you walked all day." He puts his hands on his knees and leans forward. "And they grew so tall and their leaves were so thick that you couldn't see the sun and the shade underneath them was as black as midnight!" When he says *midnight*, he jumps a little bit on chair, and the little girl, her eyes very round, jumps too, a second after. "And underneath all those giant trees lived a whole mess of creatures just about as big as those trees! Why, Paul one time came on a field mouse so big that when he dropped a rock down its hole, he didn't hear it hit bottom until the next afternoon! And Paul had come to chop wood!" The adults standing around—men with their arms across their chests and women standing in front of them, leaning against their chests—watch the children and smile and laugh with each other. The children stare, wide-eyed and absorbed, oblivious to everything but the fat old man, who holds them with a face which expresses horror and terror and amazement and with a voice as low and full as an organ.

I catch sight of Mr. Callahan, my mother's neighbor down the street.

"Hello," I say. He turns to see who it is.

"Mickey," he says.

"I might end up believing him too." I smile and nod toward the storytelling.

He doesn't smile. "What are you doing with yourself nowadays?"

"Still working."

He is a man of about fifty-five, maybe fifty-eight. He is thin and deeply tanned, and his arms are corded and the veins show. They are crossed across his chest. His granddaughter sits on the grass in the inner ring of children near the storyteller.

"Same place?"

"Systems Analysts, out on Passadumkeag Road—"

"How long has it been?" He has turned back to watch the scene and talks to me without looking at me.

"Almost three years."

"Your mother's wood needs stacking."

"Right. I'll be coming next week or the week after."

"Don't let it sit outdoors too long." He gives the scene his full attention and doesn't seem inclined to speak further.

I stand on the edge of the circle and listen for a while longer, watching the children and their parents. I can remember sitting on this grass listening to that same old fat man telling his stories of Paul Bunyan. He seemed ancient to me then. The stories were frightening—big beasts and big trees and big Paul Bunyan caught in big struggles out in the big North Woods.

I hear somebody up near the house playing the guitar and people singing. I scan the field for Mother and Marian and the children. Around the field I hear people talking—occasionally a voice sounds loud and strident calling a child or making a point—and laughing in that loose way people have when they've been drinking beer. People call to one another—"Maryanne! Maryanne! Come here right now! I haven't seen you since the Fourth of July!"—and say goodbye for a time—"I'm just going down to the lake for a little bit and cool off! I'll be right back, hear." The threads that bind them all together.

I wander about, joining people and talking for a while and then moving on. The honorees, George and Anna Albright, who have been married forty years, are being congratulated in the middle of the field. He wears white pants and a plaid shirt. His gray hair is cut short but the longer strands on top and the sides are slicked back. She is in a cotton print dress. They stand at right angles to one another, their shoulders almost touching, each talking to someone different. Standing that way, their backs almost to each other, they fend off people who have come to congratulate them and look like they are under siege. From time to time, they allow their hands to grope for each other and to touch down behind them.

A man steps forward, Reverend Carson, one of the preachers at the Baptist Church, and asks for silence. He is overweight and sleek and jolly.

"Folks!" he calls out, and people turn to him. "A toast!"

People raise beer cans and soda bottles and cheer.

"To the state of matrimony!" he cries and is answered by the crowd with another cheer. The Albrights look shy and proud. "To forty years of wedded bliss!" They cheer again and laugh with one another.

"Why, she doesn't look like she's more than a bride!"

"The dew is still on her!"

"George, how did you do it?"

A woman that I don't recognize standing next to me nods toward the Albrights and says, "I admire steadiness. Give me a steady man any day." Then she says, "Do you know them?"

Before I can answer, I hear Anna.

"—a new roof put on. They couldn't find where the leak was and Arnold finally told us that it was time for a new one anyway, so I've had men all around the house every day and in the shrubbery—" Her voice suggests the patient exasperation of one who long since has given up the notion that anything important could be repaired. She speaks to a young woman with hair swept on top of her head.

"How do you stand it!" the young woman says.

"I just go out in the backyard with the grandchildren—"

A middle-aged man, fat and jowlly, offers his congratulations to George Albright. "—a good many times, about once a month I'd wager, I wanted to kill Pauline, and I think she keeps a warrant out for my arrest on charges of cruel and unusual punishment."

"Have you had them here much this summer?"

"Oh, that's been lovely—they were here almost two weeks in June and—"

The fat man giggles and rolls his eyes. "I think I must like being in harness all the time."

Anna rises up on tiptoe and cranes her neck and then looks from one end of the field to another. "—they're here somewhere now. You know how smart they are."

"Anna," I say, breaking in. She turns to me and her eyes meet mine for a fraction of a second before she responds.

"Mickey McNamara!" She is stopped. She is unsure what step to take next. When she says my name, George turns, and then everybody does, and I find myself the center of a silent circle of people staring.

"Congratulations." No one moves. George and Anna Albright silently grasp each other's hands down behind their hips and hold tightly.

I wander about the field and listen to the bits of people's lives as I pass:

"—red hair!—"
"—she gets it done—"
"—the thing you're denying—"
"—the vice presidency—"
"—the festival—"
"—but women—"
"—manly—"
"—AIDS—"

I see Dave Donaldson coming toward where I stand, a beer in his hand, his eyes hidden by mirrored glasses.

"Hello, Dave."

"Hello, Mickey."

"How're things with you?"

He frowns and tells me he has not been able to get out of town all summer. "Once to the coast, but other than that, nothing. Sucks."

He and I were in high school together and see each other at church functions. We bank at the same bank and wave, waiting in the line for the drive-up window. "I was surprised to see the River City Festival was a success."

He says he was too, and we talk about that, about whether the beer tent actually did produce the only profit of the affair. The audit isn't in yet.

Later I sit down on the sharp grass and watch. At the lower end of the field, there is a ball game now in progress, and people drift across the field to places near home to watch it. I look for Lloyd and the kids. The players are predominantly men in their twenties and thirties. There are a couple of girls. In this heat, most of the young men have taken off their shirts and their torsos show brown skin. Now, they crouch, leaning on their knees in the outfield, brown lithe bodies, the bills of their caps giving protection from the sun and hiding their eyes from observers. Near me four or five girls sit in a row on the grass and stare intently and giggle. Occasionally one of the players will take off his cap and wave it in the air at the girls and then go back to the business at hand, while the girls, all fingers and hands and flying hair, coo at one another with wide eyes.

On my other side is a young couple in their early twenties. She sits on the ground foursquare, looking directly out onto the playing field, her elbows enclosing her knees, her eyes closed to slits in protection against the sun. He sits on one thigh next to her, his back to the field, leaning on one arm, talking intently in a whisper which is entirely drowned by the breeze sweeping the field. There is an urgency about the scene: His face in shadow, one arm around his crooked knee, the unheard words coming out to her in a strong unbroken line. His whole posture demands that she give him her attention. She responds by keeping her eyes on the field and her face, in the shadow of the sun, a mask. He uses his free hand to gesticulate, his palm out and upwards, his fingers stiff and straight.

I watch this drama, waiting for a resolution, but it doesn't come. She resists and he urges, and they don't progress. They continue, unaware of me. I lean back in the grass and feel all over my back through my thin shirt the sharp spikes of the mown shoots. I close my eyes here against the brilliant blue sky and rest my head in my hands.

"Why, there's Mickey!" I hear someone say. I turn and see a group of women sitting in aluminum folding chairs under the trees on the edge of the field. Mother is with them. She looks pretty. She is in a summer dress, and the heat doesn't seem to be affecting her. I walk over.

The one who called out to me is another neighbor of ours—of Mother's—Mrs. Simkins. I hear her say, "Ada, that Mickey of yours is such a fine young man!" She calls to me. "Come over here and talk to us old ladies!"

Mother watches me, flustered.

"He's so fine!" Mrs. Simkins says again. "Ada, you must be proud!"

There are five or six of them—older women who've done this kind of thing for years and can let the younger ones do the food now—sitting under the trees in the shade. I nod hello to everyone. They murmur and smile. I go over to Mother and lean over and kiss her on the cheek. The odor of her powder makes me feel close—intimate—to her.

"Hi, Mom."

When I stand up again, she glances at the women who have watched us, smiles hesitantly, and then fumbles with her fingers in her lap.

"Where's Marian? Where are the kids?"

"Oh—" She is acutely aware of the women around her. "—they're all together with Lloyd's people—" Her eyes dart from group to group on the field. "—down there." She nods uncertainly toward the field. I turn and look and see nothing. I stand behind Mother's chair, my arms across my chest. Everyone is silent.

"What are you doing with yourself this summer?" Mrs. Simkins asks.

"I've been working all summer, Mrs. Simkins."

"Didn't you get away at all?"

Mother watches me and Mrs. Simkins.

"Not yet. Maybe later, in August." I turn to Mother. "Mr. Callahan tells me I should come stack your wood." I try to tease her. "Have you been complaining about me to the neighbors?"

She glances around her circle and says, "Why, oh, no! I wouldn't do that! I don't think you need to hurry about the wood!"

"You are just so handsome, Mickey! Every time I see you!" Then Mrs. Simkins settles back into her chair and says, "I'll bet you want to be with the pretty young girls. You go on away now, and then come back later and speak to us again."

Mother looks up at me and smiles and frowns alternately, and then, in confusion, she looks away at the lake. "Look," she says, "somebody has blown over," and points toward the black water roughed up by the stiff breeze.

"I'll see you folks later," I say and make eye contact with each of the women and walk away from them. The stiff grass, cut short for the party, gives uncertain footing. The sun comes from back behind me now, and I cast a shadow which I walk toward. I stroll down to the water, which sends off a chill, even on such a warm day. I hear everywhere about me the voices of my people, laughing and talking and calling to one another. It is their way of touching and making sure the other one is there, of reminding themselves that they themselves are "there."

The person who had blown over has now pulled the dinghy up on the shore. Her friends crowd around and laugh as she shivers in her wet clothes. She is telling them how it happened. "—the wind came from nowhere!" and her friends nod in disbelief mixed with belief. They've had it happen to them on these lakes among the hills, where the wind comes suddenly from some new direction and spills you into the water, but they see her searching for an excuse, and their laughter has to do with familiarity with the need to blame. A young man comes running down the hill calling, "Mary! Mary!" He throws himself into the middle of the crowd around the girl—they scatter like small dogs—and sweeps the girl up in his arms. "Are you all right?" He kisses her on her neck, over and over. "Are you all right?"

"Can I take it out?" I ask no one in particular. They turn to me.

"Sure," one of the kids answers. He shrugs. "I guess."

"I'm Mickey McNamara," I say. These are high school students, and while some of them seem vaguely familiar, I don't know their names.

The whole little group of them turns to face me. "Hi," one of the girls says, then they watch silently while I take off my shoes and roll up my pants and wade in, pushing the dinghy a little ahead of me until I can climb in.

Slowly I leave the shore behind me. I find the breeze and feel the rope go tight and the tiller hard and the boat pick up speed. The dark wooded hills surround the lake, except for the light-green scar of the field with its white and pastel spots. The breeze is soft here, and I can hear the shouts from the field coming across the silent lake, the sun gilding the landscape. This is not virgin forest. It hasn't been for a hundred years. Paul Bunyan, looking for a great tree to slay, would go back to his camp empty-handed. This is not the great north woods any longer. It's been cut over and hunted and plowed and allowed to grow up again. There are spurs of track laid down through these woods to bring out the timber which have grown red with rust and now provide only pathways through the forest for picnickers. This is not the wilderness. It's the country, where people from town come on Sunday afternoon, and, if not this lake, another, on the other side of these hills. And what I hear back there, as I make my way up the lake, is Cardiff. It's domesticated, plowed and planted and mowed, and the civilization suggested by their shouts to one another follows me beyond the point where the curve of the lake prevents me from seeing them. I am alone on the quiet lake, and I can hear them, indistinct but there, following me until I can go no farther.

The sun is in my eyes as I walk back up from the lake. The ball players are taking a break. One of them I went to the university with, Ken Hadley, and I join them.

"Hello, Ken."

He turns and sees me. "Hello, Mickey." He turns back to the group. They have lost some players, and new ones have arrived, and the game is regrouping. I find myself on one side. It is hot, and I am tired, and the sun, coming from just above the trees, is in my eyes. I feel sweaty and gritty—something is in the air, some granulated dust from the soil or from the mown grass—and my armpits sting and my eyelids itch. Things like this always end with a game.

The other team is at bat first, and I take my place in the field. The players shout at one another and at the bystanders, who call back. The four girls are still there, quieter now, sitting on the grass and leaning back on their arms. There are several mothers with small children. They whisper to them and point to fathers on the field. The children wave, trying to get their father's attention. It is getting late in the afternoon, and around the field, along with the other sounds of the long afternoon, I hear children cry.

I hear men shouting and then a solid crack! and I am in a ball game. I search the sky for the ball. I didn't see the pitch or the swing and I am lost. Then I find the dark ball moving against the blur of blue sky and white clouds: It is my corner. I squint my eyes to hold contact with it against the glare of the sky and run, back up, my arm out. I position myself under it as it comes down, bouncing back and forth under it, my breath held in suspension, my head bent back on my neck until it hurts. As I follow it down, my eyes look directly into the sun and lose all vision for a moment of fear—until, with a thud, it drops solidly and heavily into my glove.

The field is silent. I glance around for the pitcher—I am momentarily disoriented—and find him and throw the ball. I am breathing heavily.

A new batter is up.

"Yo, Carl!" they call to him.

"Go home!"

251

The tone of those on Carl's team is indistinguishable from those on mine: heavy, good-natured bantering among boys and men who know each other well. Carl gets a ball that he tries for. He hits a high fly to the third base and, grinning, lopes half way to first base before shrugging his shoulders and tossing it in.

The next batter, Arnold, a businesslike man of about thirty, makes it to first.

Then the other team has a string of hits and brings one man in. One of us catches a ball to the center field and puts out a man on second, and then to first, stopping the hitter, and it's our turn at bat.

As I walk in, I pass the girls and the young, urgent couple and several mothers with children on the sideline. Some people now are trudging up the long slow slope of the field to the cabin and the cars beyond, fathers with little children on their shoulders, mothers carrying babies in their arms. Boys who, in the middle of the afternoon, had taken off their shirts have now pulled them back on, and the jersey has caught on their sweaty skin and stuck there, misshapen and uncomfortable looking. Girls run their fingers through their hair to pick out the bits of dried grass.

We have a batter up who gets on, and then another. I sit down on the stiff fragrant grass, my arms around my knees, watching. My vision encompasses, on the one end, the dark woods and the cottage and the bales of hay and then down the long sweep of the field to where we are, the green grass studded with men in jeans and shorts, mostly naked above the waist. And, at the other end of my vision is the lake, wrapping around the bottom of the field, and the dark hills encompassing all. The pitcher in the middle of all this winds up and runs forward in his classic ballet, throwing the ball, and ending up looking back over his shoulder at the batter, who takes a step into it and then, with his shoulders providing the heavy force, swings against the ball. It is a classic satisfying choreography, simple, uniting the pitcher and the batter. The batter swings, and connects, and runs. It seems so easy.

Beyond this drama I see Marian, her beauty evident even at this distance, walking up toward the cottage. The children walk on either side of her, and Lloyd's parents slightly behind. Lloyd himself walks with some men about ten yards in the rear. Occasionally one of this party looks toward the ball game, but idly, without interest or recognition.

I'm up. I get a bat from the pile of them dropped, like felled timber, on the ground behind home base and approach the base. The pitcher is a man a little older than me, maybe thirty. He is a policeman and a friend of Lloyd's. His name is Frank. He has a heavy body, and he is sweating profusely. He is a Catholic and has six children who scream for him from the sidelines. His jaw is thrust out and his eyelids are narrowed against the glare as he stares at me.

The field is silent and waits for the pitcher to windup. I feel the grit in my shoes and under my belt against my skin and under my armpits. I feel it around my eyes, stinging with the salt from my sweat. The breeze, which was stiff earlier, has dropped now and is nothing to cool us, and the lake is like black glass.

"Uncle Mickey!" Then, "There's Uncle Mickey!" I see them. I drop the end of the bat to the ground and wave. The children wave back. They have stopped and turned to face me, their legs pigeontoed, stomachs protruding a little, hands up in a kind of salute to shade their eyes. They stare for a long time, the adults pausing in the long walk up and joining them, watching me, shading their eyes with the palms of their hands.

"You gonna play ball?" someone shouts.

"Right," I say, swinging the bat casually. Then I push the bat toward Frank, and he knows we're ready. I glance around the field at the players, who gather energy from the coming pitch. They shift and move in. They squint harder.

Then the pitcher. Frank winds up, and I flex my arms and then relax. I am ready. I see it coming. It is in the right place. I lift my leg and step into it, my hip follows, my shoulder, and then my arms, trailing the bat and then swinging it faster and faster until it comes around and is there, exactly where the ball is, and there is a deafening crack! as the two meet. The bat follows through in the swing down by my left leg, and as I drop it, I begin to run. In the periphery of my vision, I see the whole field come alive, our runners beginning to move around the bases, and their players moving in as my ball makes its climb up against the sky, and then, as it climbs up and up, their men coming to a stop and moving back, backwards, their eyes in the air, looking at the ball. Running furiously, I see where my ball is: The left field is still moving back. My ball is still up, making a high slow traverse towards the woods on the other side of the field. I slow my pace. My ball begins its descent in a kind of languor. I run toward first and touch the base and then on toward second. The first baseman—Andrew, I went to school with him, his arms across his chest—stares at me. I make eye contact with him and then pass on. The second baseman has turned away. The action is in the woods now, and I run by him. After I pass third, I lift my arms and, with an easy lope, run into home, my eyes on the ground.

Vernon

It's no big thing. The boy comes in here, tears running down his cheeks, and says he'll never fall in love again, and what he doesn't know is that'll be true only if he's lucky. But if he's like the rest of us, he'll fall in love every time the moon changes. And what he thinks is a pain so great it'll kill him is really something he'll learn to live with, like his teeth in his head. I know. I'm in love right now with the boy's momma, a chick so sharp just her sighs can make you feel like you been in a razor fight—and I haven't seen her for four years. I'm in love with Gladys, who's over here weekends. She makes me feel twenty, which I was at one time, but she also makes me feel handsome, which I wasn't. It's a powerful gift she has and it makes a man want to learn to show his gratitude. And then there's the boy who lives in the attic, all cock and an ass like two pears, who thinks I can show him how to be a man just because I been one so long, and who has learned how to use everything he has, including the most agile tongue this side of a cobra's, to show his gratitude for what I'm teaching him.

Shit. I know these things don't last. On the other hand, they never quite finish, either, and the love you feel leaves you worn out, your cock sore, a prisoner, and somebody else—two, three, four other people, depending on how lucky or unlucky you've been—has the keys to the cell. The real pain comes from discovering that you got no control over any of it. I'm still in love with Tom's momma, but I'm also still in love with my second cousin, who had me under the sheets in his momma's house in Jamaica Plain in 1954 when we were both 14. That boy's fingers wrapped themselves around my cock and balls and milked me till I didn't have no will left and all of *me* was in what was about to come shooting up out of my cock. And if I'd died on the spot, I'd a been happy just because I knew I pleased him.

Young love. Then, in a day or two, Tom brings home this chick—they've been to the movies—and introduces me and gets a beer out of the fridge like I let him do it every day, leaving me in the living room lying on the sofa, the tube going on the Red Sox, this chick standing there staring. He thinks this is bringing her home to meet his family—leaving her standing staring at me watching the tube—and I thought he wasn't ever going to learn manners.

"Sit down," I say.

She shrugs and flops down in the chair.

We watch.

Only she's watching me. I like lying here on the sofa and drinking beer and watching ball games on the tube. I got my house the way I want it now. My sofa is long and the cushions are deep enough and don't crowd you, so you can have room for your shoulders, and your arm can lie by your side without being pressed in by the back. I can reach my beer on the coffee table. Sometimes I jerk off here when I'm alone and the game is slow. Sometimes the boy from upstairs comes down—he don't like baseball at all—and gives me head while I watch the game. His throat just fits my cock like a smooth, wet, soft sleeve, and when he sucks, my heart starts pumping in my cock instead of in my chest and the blood is too big for the skin, and I give up watching TV too.

Tom's girl has tits already. I remember what they feel like— still springy—but I guess when I was sixteen I didn't know what to do with 'em. I know now. If you have a good woman, she can teach you. I use my tongue. I could keep Tom's momma on the bed all morning long just with my tongue. I could use my tongue and my fingers so that her tits stood up straight and hurt. "Oh, daddy!" she'd say. Tom's girl is so young she's still embarrassed by her tits. That's one difference between boys and girls. When girls start coming out, they act like they wish it wasn't happening. Boys act like they dare you to think they've ever been any other way.

Tom has been living with me for three years. He lived with his mother before that for a while, then with me again, and then her. I have two girls too who've been with me off and on since they were born. They call and say, "Can I come this weekend?" And I say, *sure*, and they do, and then they don't leave until winter's over. Tom called—that was before he started shaving—and he's still here. I've always lived here in this house in Cardiff—German Street above the Passadumkeag Stream—and when I don't need the top floor for kids, I rent it out on short lease. Otherwise, I've got kids up there and dirty clothes in the basement and a sink full of dirty dishes and never enough food in the fridge. Or beer.

This chick Tom has brought home is definitely not a looker. She's short, and she ain't got a waist to speak of. She has a round face, and she has lines in her forehead like she's worried all the time.

I'll have to talk to Tom about his taste. Man, I would even say she is a frog!

I know something about women. All my kids have different mommas, and all of them knocked your eyes out at forty feet. This chick looks like she's studying the tube. She's a serious one. This is one you want to take away to some quiet place where nobody can see. When I am with a woman, I definitely want her to dazzle the other guys. If she don't make them want to be me, what's the point?

Tom is back with his beer. I sit up. He drops himself down into the sofa next to me and leans over and puts his hand on my thigh. "Hey, Dad."

"Yo, Tom." Tom, on the other hand, is a nice-looking kid— sharp, clean, a short haircut, like he's going places. He makes good grades, and I keep him dressed nice.

"We wanta go get a pizza."

"And you want some cash."

He grins and shrugs. I give him a bill, which he pockets. He glances at his chick, and she smiles back at him.

Then he looks over at me and raises his chin. "Thanks, Dad."

I give him enough for the pizza and to cover the movies, popcorn, and cokes. A guy needs money.

I have women in every so often—a night, week, a month, this winter—for company. Tom understands how that is. I told him when you reach a certain age, you need to have skin next to you when you sleep or else you'll die sooner. I introduce them the next morning, and he takes a sip of his coffee and says, "Lookin' good, Dad, lookin' good!" and grins. Sharp kid. Gladys is my chick now. I like to leave her some money before I go out to clean some lady's furnace and say, "Go shoppin' and get yourself something to wear. And get the kid something too." It's good to have a woman around the house, softens things. She thinks to wash the curtains, which I never do, and the kids need to hear a woman's side of things. Gladys is teaching Tom what girls like.

The girl is getting restless. She goes away to fix her hair and then comes back.

"Do we have to watch the game?" Tom asks.

"Suit yourself."

He gets up and flicks the channels. He passes the local news and a movie and some reruns of a western. He goes back and does it slower. Tom is quick, and he thinks about things. He passes the news again.

What they have on the tube is an interview program about the boy who got murdered.

"They're talking about the faggots," the chick says.

He moves on to the western. It's the one about the real rich lady and her two sons and a daughter and all their troubles.

"Go back to the faggots," the chick says.

"Dad, it's about the murder of that gay boy. Is that OK?" He looks around at me. "They're interviewing some gay people."

There's a man talking about the murder and what happened next. He is not a cool-looking dude. He is trying to be real sincere, though. He is talking to two young men and a young woman.

"Sure, kid. It's OK."

The reporter is speaking. "There was a memorial service at the Unitarian Church on Monday night for Bernard Mallett. Could you tell us why you went and what you hoped to accomplish by going?"

"Bernie was a friend—"

Tom comes back and sits on the sofa with me.

Tom's momma was hot. She was a real skinny thing and looked like a model, her hair real long and fluffed out and long eyelashes. I liked to go shopping with her. She'd go in to the room and come back out with a dress on and look at herself in the mirror and ignore me for a while, studying herself. Then she'd turn to me and ask me what I thought.

"It don't show off your tits, honey."

"Oh hush up." She'd act like she was embarrassed or disgusted, but she wouldn't buy it. She'd get another one down and hold it out to me and say, "What about this one?"

And she'd try it on, and if I grinned, she'd grin, and then she'd frown and take it to the cashier, and I'd buy it for her. She liked showing off for me. She liked it when I looked at her. I like buying things for her. I loved that woman, doing things for her.

"Hey, Dad?"

"Yo."

"Do you think those guys ever made it with a woman?"

"Who knows what goes on in people's heads?" Then, "Some of them." One time Tom went looking for me early in the morning before he usually gets up, and he couldn't find me anywhere in the house. I was upstairs with the boy in the attic—I'd spent the night up there—and I heard him walking round and I came down. He looked at me kinda funny, since he knew that I hadn't slept in my bed all night long. "I spent the night with Morris," I told him. He took that and didn't say anything more, but he looked like I had given him something hard and bitter to chew on when he'd been expecting candy. I explained that to Tom later. I said, "I'm not a faggot, hear?"

"I wanta ask them if they have ever felt a chick's tits." The chick looks uncomfortable. He turns to her and laughs, "I don't believe this," nodding toward the TV.

She shrugs. She pulls out a mirror and looks at herself.

"Why do they want to do that, go out and march down the hill carrying candles and letting everybody see them and call them queers? They act like they're proud."

I'm a furnace man. It's a good job. I meet people that way. And if I go in and do a real good job—clean the furnace and all—I get asked to stay around for a cup of coffee or a beer. Sometimes I stay over. Sometimes I stay over because the lady wants me to. Sometimes I stay over because the gentleman of the house wants me to. I can't predict beforehand what it's going to be. The difference between faggots and everybody else is that faggots never made it with a woman. Tom looks at the guys on the screen. "Faggots."

"Their friend was murdered. That's why they came out."

"Is that it, or is it because they're all faggots?"

The girl says, "Weird."

"I don't see why anybody would want to call himself a faggot."

"Yuh get AIDS," she says.

"They're all going to get AIDS, aren't they Dad?"

"The ones who're not careful."

"The promiscuous ones," the chick says. She drawls it out, *pro-mis-cue-us*, like she wasn't used to saying it.

I know what the preacher says and what all the ladies in church say: Homosexuality is the abomination of the Lord. That man closes his eyes and lifts up his head and kind of turns it to the right and says, "Pray for them, Father! Pray for them! That they may turn away from their sinful ways!" But that doesn't seem to be the right thing. I go to church for the singing and the fellowship, and I give them my money. Nobody could complain about me. But the same time, they don't know what they're talking about on this one.

I see the letters in newspaper. This morning the man writes in and says, "What everybody is forgetting is that these people are the abomination of the Lord. They are moral degenerates and should be hounded out of every place of civilized society in America." It's hard to get away from, all this. Every time you turn around somebody else is saying they know what people ought to be doing in bed.

"Cardiff has not experienced a murder in nine years, except those between family members, and part of the intensity of the response has been to the sense of the citizens here that Cardiff is a quiet, law-abiding town. It is not likely that a citizen walking down the street at any hour of the day or night is mugged or assaulted and his life threatened. We have in the studio with us a member of Cardiff's gay community who gives a different picture."

The camera pulls back a little to show a man, but the lights are not on him, so his face is dark and you can't tell who he is.

I'm on the sofa, and Tom's girl is in chair. Tom is in the kitchen getting another beer. She crosses her legs at her ankles and puts both hands between her knees. She is sitting up straight in the chair. She looks like something is really going wrong with her life and I'm the cause of it. But she doesn't look at me, she just looks toward me.

The interviewer says, "What is it like for homosexuals on the streets of Cardiff?"

"There are things you look out for. Most of the time, it's OK. You're not thinking about it, and then you see a group of teenage boys on the street up ahead of you and all your antennae go out and you're aware of the danger you're in—"

One time, Tom came into my bedroom, where I was in bed. He had just come in from a date. He said, "Do you suck cock?" He stood there, his hands behind his waist, leaning his body against the doorframe, looking at me like he didn't know what he was seeing. I told him, sure. I said, "Tom, I've done most things it's possible to do." He waited a moment, and then he grinned. I asked him if he knew I loved him. He nodded his head real slow. I asked him if he could trust me. Tom is real smart looking, and he waited a long minute before he answered. And while he was waiting, I was staring at his face and thinking how sharp looking this kid is, and then he nodded his head. I got up and we went downstairs and I fixed us something to eat out of the refrigerator. We sat at the kitchen table, and then he asked me a question: *Did you love Mom when you had me?* I grinned, sure, and then I reminded him that he knew I still did. And he did. Then we hugged and went back up to our bedrooms.

"What danger?" the reporter's voice is asking, "What are you afraid of happening?"

"Name-calling—" From the sound of his voice, it's a young man.

"Just name-calling? Is that what you're afraid of?"

"Well, obviously, we're here because the danger is something more than name-calling—"

"What do they call you?"

"Faggot. Homosexual. Queer."

"How does that make you feel?"

"You feel insulted—"

"You are gay—"

"But the words carry an insult—"

"Like nigger."

"Sure. They mean to hurt you."

The dude the man is talking to is maybe twenty-five, real college-kid type. He's looking stiff and trying to look comfortable.

"A lot of us are aware that men and women have been beaten up right here in Cardiff—"

"Right here?"

"Yeah, I know—"

"It happens regularly?"

"I don't know. I know maybe three, four guys who've been chased right here in Cardiff since the first of the year."

"What did you do?"

"They ran. They got away."

"Did you tell the police?"

"Sometimes people tell the police, and sometimes they don't. Nothing ever happens one way or the other—"

"The police—"

"They never catch anyone. They don't even seem to look. There are still kids on the street who—"

"But mainly its name-calling and chasing—"

"Well, yeah—"

"—and people don't get beat up often, or regularly, as you said—"

"—but you never know when this kid calling you 'faggot' is going to jump out of his car and chase you, when this kid is going to jump you—"

"But—"

"—you don't know when the name-calling is going to turn in to getting you killed, and it's the uncertainty, it creates an anxiety—"

"Have you ever been attacked?"

"I've been yelled at—"

"Why do you suppose you have never been attacked?"

"The way I look—"

"You look—"

"—clean cut and fit the stereotypes of what a male in our culture is supposed to look like."

"They don't—"

"They don't notice me."

"They don't recognize you're gay?"

Tom is standing in the doorway, staring at the tube.

"I'd recognize that guy as a queer any day," the girl says. "Look at the way he crosses his legs." That's his girl, the one with the nonexistent tits. "I can recognize 'em every time. Tom, would you get me a beer too?"

"Is everybody who sucks cock a faggot?" he asks, staring at the tube like he had forgotten what was on it and like he had forgotten that we were in the room.

"Tom, you are so absolutely full of shit, you couldn't find your ass with a gyrocompass and survey maps. Get the chick a beer. Get me a beer. And then come here and sit here with me. I got stuff to talk to you about."

This boy's mother told me one time I was too selfish to be married. She said, "You don't know nothing about giving anything to anybody else. All you know how to do is *take! take! take!*" She used to hate me lying on this sofa here and having to bring me beers, and when she would talk to me like that, she would stand up there next to the sofa, her legs spread apart and her feet in high heels, one hand on a hip and the other shaking an index finger at me. Some people, when they get mad, go all to pieces, but she was one of those who give a real polished performance, and when it was over, it was over, and she hadn't forgotten to say anything. And after she'd checked off all the boxes, she'd turn around and pick up her purse and go out the door. I was proud of her.

She kept trying to figure out if I was tomcat'n' around on her, even though I had told her from the beginning that I wasn't going to be faithful. I think she thought after we got married, she could tame me. She wanted to know where I was every minute. I told her I wouldn't tell her. I told her I couldn't tell her. My eyes wander just like my mind wanders, and I never can tell what it's going to end up following. And there's no way I can control that. If she coulda gotten used to that, we could have had a good thing going. We were like two cats in bed together. And look at Tom there. We made a good kid. I woulda liked to be married to her still. She's married now to an electrician in Augusta, and they do everything together, Tom says. Tom says she won't let him bring girls home.

When I'm with somebody—a chick—and I've got my hands on her like they are playing on a goddam harp, what's going on in my mind is entirely different. I'm seeing this boy who swims in the river down below here. I've only seen him twice. Both times it was late in the afternoon and the sun was coming from back behind me and shining out across the river, and this boy comes walking up toward me out of the water. He is very dark, and the water makes him seem darker—his skin is wet, the color of bitter chocolate—and his hair and eyebrows are even blacker. He's tall and has the broad shoulders and narrow hips of a swimmer—with those long, rangy muscles. I wonder what it would be like to play on *him*. He walks up out of the water toward me—toward a girl sitting near me—as if his body weren't made of anything rigid. He seemed like he was part of the water he had just left, and he acted like he didn't know that I was staring at him. I think of him, lying on his back in bed next to me, his head on his hands, my hand between his legs, stroking him until his breath begins to come fast. I imagine what his cock must feel like. I open my mouth and spread my jaws and feel it slide in past my lips. My lips close around his cock and slide up down around the shaft. I feel the head deep in my throat. I pull off and feel the head pull past my lips. Then I open my mouth and slide down onto his cock again. The softest skin is around a man's cock. I take it into my throat again. I hear his breathing get irregular and fast and hard, and his eyes close. His cock becomes very hard and, with a series of hard fast jerks, his stomach muscles clench and his cock comes. And comes. And comes.

The trouble is Tom's momma *knew* all that. And no matter how much I loved her, she wanted to be the only thing I loved. I think I must be a careless person. I drop a little of it here and a little of it there. That's why I don't have no more money than I have right now. I spend it when I get it, and I don't think ahead.

Tom sits on the sofa next to me. We watch the screen. The reporter is asking the college student, "How many homosexuals are there in Cardiff?"

I take my son in my arms. "Dipshit."

He struggles against me and laughs. "What's the matter old man?"

"You forgot to get the beer."

The college student on the television answers the reporter: "Ten percent of the population."

"Where are they all?" Tom asks.

"God knows." That's what I say.

"There's one at the 7-Eleven where I work," the chick says. "They hang out there."

"Tina knew the guy who drowned."

"What are you planning to do with your life?" the reporter asks.

"What was he like?"

She shrugs and pulls down the corners of her mouth. "Like a faggot. Like a girl. He wore makeup and had this long earring in his ear."

Dana

I tiptoe in my bare feet into the nursery, where Marc lies on his back and plays with his feet. His eyes follow me when I walk around his room, gathering yesterday's clothes. I wave. He smiles. It is early yet, but the sun is way up and lights all the rooms on that side of the house.

I woke up after a bad night—I couldn't stop thinking of Mickey and of Marcia—to Marc's crying. It is an odd sound, another person in our house with Marcia and me, which still surprises me. We reproduce ourselves, the great miracle, and I contemplate our changed place in the scheme of things: Someone is following us. I haven't finished dealing with my parents, and now I am one. When I had him on the sofa downstairs, which I shouldn't have, I unfolded his diapers, and his penis stood up and transcribed an arc of urine across the back cushions. He smiled, finding it pleasant, and we grinned at each other.

I kissed him. I gave him a bottle and rocked him. I held him against my chest, and he snuggled down and went back to sleep. I could feel his heart beat against mine, and I listened to our complicated rhythms playing off against one another. Then I took him back upstairs to his crib. The radio plays quietly in the kitchen— soft rock alternating with political advertisements. I make coffee, and then I bring in the papers, put them on the kitchen table, and scan the headlines. On the counter is Friday's edition: "It's a First: Ferraro for VP Spot, Mondale Calls Partner an 'Exciting' Choice." Another headline says, "Rep Ferraro: a Master/of the 'Old Boy' Network," and another says, "Pizazz and Risks Aplenty." Inside are page after page on what it means. Today's paper says, "Mondale's Choice of Ferraro a Bid to Harvest Diversity." It's a triumph for the women's movement, for us, and I think about it between moments when I am thinking about sorting laundry or about Marc or Mickey and his mother, the other things there are to be excited about or disturbed by, like my relationship with Marcia, which, since last night, is both exciting and disturbing.

I have become domestic, and what I do, picking up clothing and linens and carrying them to the bathroom, reminds me of my mother. I feel more like her each day as I do the things she does, run a house and give attention to Marcia and Marc and devote physical and mental energies to my job and brood on the book I am writing. Mother's eyes saw all these things that demanded her attention, all at the same time, and she never seemed flurried or anxious, and I don't know how she did that. Marcia said last night that I get more and more like Mother as I get older, which is another thing I brood over.

Returning upstairs, I gather the clothes into a pile on the tile floor in the bathroom and sort them. My mother told me how—hand things, heavy things, towels, colors, whites—as she told me how to do everything else. I run water in the sink for the lingerie. My towels are all like hers—a border with appliqued flowers—and the small framed prints around the walls are hers too: pastel flowers. We spoke quietly in our house, and the most frequently reiterated sentence from my childhood was "I love you." We all said it to one another just before the lights went out, as a way of ending a phone call, instead of merely *Love* at the end of a letter. This verbal sign—right up to the moment Kevin discovered me and Angela together behind the gazebo in the park—touched everything, like the scent of Mother's soap.

Last night after Mickey left, we were sitting at the kitchen table. "Mickey's mother is a lovely person," Marcia said. The cliché was exactly right. We met her at the hospital after Marc was born. She works there, and we got to know her before we knew Mickey.

"The only thing wrong with her life right now is Mickey, and it must seem as if he is doing it to her, willfully—"

"But Mickey's a lovely person himself—" The conflict between them shows no resolution, and I kept thinking of them last night after Marcia had gone to sleep. I've had people say—for instance at a party—when they found out whose daughter I was, "Your parents are lovely people." They could have said other things: Your father is brilliant, your mother beautiful. They could have said, Your parents are successful, or rich, or good, or conservative, or snobs, or, in their genteel way, racists. *Lovely.* At odd moments, seeing myself for a second in the mirror, I compare myself against this shadowy image. I am a parent now, and, in my way, I am a 'lovely' person. When Marcia said I was like my mother, she meant that unkindly.

I gather up an armload of the towels and take them to the basement to the washer. Mother took me to buy these towels my first year in graduate school. We shopped and compared and inspected, and I was not surprised to discover, in the end, that we bought towels just like hers at home. What does it mean: *lovely*. I am in our living room, which has already become a center to our crowd of women in Cardiff. In Mother's house on the Gulf Coast she gives teas to celebrate someone's engagement or holds neighborhood meetings to address local traffic problems. We do that too, making allowance for our differences. We give parties to celebrate somebody's union. We've been meeting all spring about the ERA, right here in this room.

As I go up and down the stairs, I listen for Marc and glance through our open door at Marcia in our bed, glimpsing myself in the mirror over the bureau, a pretty brunette woman of thirty. Once Mother visited me in Austin when I was in graduate school, and we sat on a bench in a park on the river. I asked her what it was she had tried to teach me.

"It was so clear to me when I was your age that I was to take my place in my society, do what my mother had done—make a home, have children, carry on things—" She ground out her cigarette on the flagstone, put her purse on the bench beside her, and threaded her fingers together. "Communal values." She paused. "We wanted to bring you up to take your place in society." She broke off, placed her purse on her lap and held the clasp with both hands. Then she said, "I wanted you to see the value of a home, where one cared about the sensibilities of others. There are things which are permanent, and which it is our duty to uphold and to carry on."

I pick up newspapers from the rack and replace magazines—the covers all have Geraldine Ferraro or Walter Mondale—in their pile. I hear Marc upstairs beginning to make noises again. He wants attention from me. It is easy to put down what I am doing and go to him. He is crying—Marcia is still asleep—and I pick him up and settle his small body on my shoulder. He lowers his head onto my neck, skin against skin, and I bring him down to the kitchen and put him on a square on the floor. I sit down and play, holding his rattle beyond his reach, teasing him, and when he puts out his hands toward it, giving it to him. We both laugh. Then I put him in the playpen, where he watches me.

What are the things that are permanent? My parents' marriage was not among them. I watch Marc, think of Mickey,

267

remember Mother, and wonder, *What am I supposed to be holding on to?*

"My parents make up the rules as they go along," Marcia has said, and she always laughs when she says it. She is right about that. Everything with them is *ad hoc*, and their home gives the sense of a raft floating down a slow river. They count on shared affection.

"Your mother is a gentle person—" Marcia says. "She couldn't understand that there would ever be a reason for a violation of the rules—"

"—a violation of someone else's sensibility," I say. "She has never mentioned her sexual feelings for my father—"

Time came yesterday and lies on the kitchen table. Its cover proclaims the Democratic Convention this week in San Francisco: *War or Peace in San Francisco? W* lies on the counter. *The New Yorker.* Marc plays on the blanket in the playpen. He lifts his ball and drops it and laughs. Occasionally he watches me. The room is in shadow now, the sun being too high to get in under the eaves into the house. Marcia sleeps late today. I have to get things together for the picnic. I enjoy what I am doing, the tasks having to do with the quality of food—our daily bread—with clothes, cottons and linens, the satisfying elements of our lives, uncomplicated necessaries.

In that mother-daughter conversation in Austin, Mother sat on the bench barely aware of her own body. She was beautifully dressed and carefully made up. She was at ease, her legs together at the ankles, leaning back against the bench, but she didn't seem aware. She had done what needed to be done, presented herself in the expected way to indicate her age and class and position, and then had forgotten about it. She always kissed me by presenting her cheek. Even with my father, she presented her cheek. She held his shoulders and pulled him toward her, partially turning away from him.

"I'm in love," I had said.

She lit a cigarette and held the smoke for a moment. She didn't respond.

"I'm very happy—"

She still didn't say anything.

"I wanted you to know—"

Finally, she said, "I find this very painful." She surveyed the river as if she could escape by throwing herself into it. "Why do you have to talk about it?"

"It's me—"

"Oh, it's not you. It's something you do."

"Well, it's both—."

"What is there to say about such a private thing?"

I gather together the picnic things—a couple of bottles of wine, the cheeses, and the bread and nuts—and run my fingers down the long polished wood counter. I remember Mother gathering things together for sailing expeditions, a blue and white checked cloth, thermos, the clutch of silver, the whole elaborate paraphernalia of meals outdoors. I wanted to tell her about Marcia. "I want to tell you about the woman I am in love with." Because we were women, it was something we shared. Or should have shared. I had seen her making our home—I've only just begun to understand what an effort it is to have clean linen towels in the bathroom all the time—and my making a home with Marcia made us alike. We should have been able to talk about Marcia and me the way mothers and daughters talk about men, intimately and freely—I had thought we would be able to laugh—because I saw the continuity of our family descending from Mother to me, and not to my brothers, who grew up and left. It was she who had held things together.

The bond between us was not political: She never understood my activism when I was in college, never had an understanding that it was the whole system that was infected at its root and not what she thought, that it was in the failure of individuals to be kind or thoughtful or respectful of others. Our bond was domestic—clothes and furniture and draperies, recipes and pots—and when she visited me in Austin, we went shopping for things I "needed." She brought me things from home she thought I could use, and she made a quilt and pillow covers. During her visits, we always cooked at home, and we never talked about my meetings and my marches and the women I dated. We also never talked about Dad's new wife.

Marcia is up. I hear her running water to brush her teeth. I collect the things Marc will need today: diapers, a jar of baby food, a spoon, blankets, and place them by my rucksack. I don't remember Mother doing this because I was too young—I was the baby in the household. As I go about gathering things, I talk to Marc and he gurgles back at me.

"You want to tell me what you do in bed." Mother turned away and ground out her cigarette on the flagstone.

"No—," That was not what I wanted to tell her.

If I had been living with a man, she would have known what we were doing in bed, knowledge shared between us without being spoken of.

"I couldn't bear to have to think of you that way—."

I watched the water in the little river. It was a muddy brown and swirled and eddied and rippled and occasionally a leaf or piece of crumpled paper floated by.

"I don't think of myself that way. What I did in private with your father was between us only. It was not all we had between us, not even the most important part—" She looked away. "I cannot understand how you could do this—define yourself by what you do in bed." And then she said, "I couldn't bear the coarseness of it. Like being a—" She searched for a word. "—callgirl."

I blushed. It was just because I knew what she was—a lovely person—that the thing was devastating. Her manners excluded me, and called my own into question. Worse: made me coarse. I was embarrassed for myself. My hurt was mixed with anger: The expression of Mother's sexuality, secure, though it is never alluded to, shows itself in what surrounds her, my father, in me and in my brothers, but the expression of my sexuality makes me coarse. Her judgment on me was final, and I couldn't see a way of arguing against her.

It made me wonder—I see my image in the mirror—what kind of person I am if I am not like her. Marcia, last night, said I am very much like her and said she hoped I will try to change.

I have come to hate Mother's well-bred manner, the sense she gives of always being in control, her sense of "permanent things" and "traditional values" which allowed her to say to me, *You don't speak of sex,* while her diamond catches the light wherever she is and declares all that a stranger needs to know about her own sexuality.

Marcia comes into the kitchen in her robe, her hair combed by her fingers, bringing with her an air of relaxed confusion.

"Good morning—"

She smiles at me and leans over and picks Marc up and kisses him. Then she comes to me. She smiles. She strokes my hair, holding Marc in her other arm. He leans toward me, stretching out his hand. I take his hand for a moment and smile at him. "You are wonderful—" She gestures around the room. "—the way you put it all together." She gets a cup of coffee and settles into a chair across the table from me, Marc in her arms, and reaches for a bagel. She scans the newspapers, juggling Marc—he puts his fingers to her lips—and the bagel and the paper: headlines about nuclear disarmament and the article on Geraldine Ferraro. Then she lets them drop and turns to Marc again, kissing him and speaking to me. "Thanks for letting me sleep."

I get up and take Marc from her and put him in the playpen, and then sit in her lap, where I let my head rest on her shoulder. I have enjoyed the time to myself, but I tell her, "I wanted to."

For years, Marcia has had other things to say: "I would be so happy if you could gave way a little—" She says all the time, *I am always amazed at how much like your mother you are.* Marcia doesn't have much of a sense that there's a right way to behave: Anything seems OK for her, except holding back. Now she puts her arm around my back.

What she has meant was give way to her, a little. I have searched my mind for Mother's influence on me, and I never get to the end of it. It is easy enough to see the influences of class, the sense of taste, the obligation to be financially responsible, the obligation to make a contribution to society, the respect for manners, caring what people think, a profound conservatism, but it is more difficult, and may be impossible, to discover the deeper influence: the way I think, and, beyond that, my instinctual responses. I think my mind is so much her creation that to discover the limits of her control, I would have to stand outside myself—on the moon—and look back. The relationship between my thought and my feeling, between my self and my sense of my culture is so deeply embedded that while I could study it I can never get to the end of it. In the play between Marcia and me—the exploration with lips and fingers— some part of me is still Mother's daughter, a well-bred, upper-class woman from the Texas Gulf Coast, unable to feel in terms except those associated with a White Lady.

Now she sips her coffee and strokes my back, my head on her shoulder. Her fingers encircle my neck. "I love you." What she means is, last night—and every night—is forgiven and forgotten. "I love you too." I kiss her.

She glances at my preparations.

"Almost done—" I get up and fold Marc's things and place them in the rucksack along with a handful of rattles. I doubt that last night—and every night—can be forgiven and forgotten.

I had thought Mother and I would have this in common: We are women in a world where men wield the power and set the parameters of debate. In telling her about Marcia, I wanted to give her a way of seeing that we are alike: Women in Love. But patriarchy unsexes women. What I had thought would form an identity between us actually separated us. It has separated her from her sexuality and—this was what I should have expected but didn't—from mine.

She reaches into the playpen and tickles Marc, who giggles.

I am afraid that I will never climb over these barriers to her and of what will happen if I do. I know what I am: an intelligent, fearless middle-class politically-aware dyke in the last quarter of the twentieth century, and I know about the contradictions in all that: *Fearless* is only sometimes true and seems to conflict all the time with *middle-class*. And I know that it is absurd to try to link *middle-class* with *politically aware*, much less with *dyke*. For Mother fear has to do with this: What would she be like if she had not accepted the confinements of her privilege?

Mother wrote after Marc was born. *What you and Marcia are doing is contrary to all my beliefs. I know you have not asked for my approval or advice. But I am now a part of what you have done whether I want it or not—I am Marc's grandmother. You have placed me in a position of approving—giving sanction to—beliefs you hold in order to express the love I will have for Marc. I cannot help but think that your decision is not made with Marc's best interests in mind—Think of what his future is going to be!—and that you have, instead, thought only of yourselves and your "political beliefs." I don't understand how you could put your own selfish wants above those of a child. By doing what you have done, you have placed yourself in the position of calling attention to your sexuality at every moment the three of you are together, for as long as you and Marc and Marcia live. I have lived all of my life in the belief that sexual matters are private, and that they should not be inflicted on other people—on the public!—and what you have done is an attack on those beliefs which is, I think, willful. Do you mean to be cruel?*

I have Marc now because I am like her. I have seen her when I pass the mirror in the bedroom, the genteel, well-bred, Texas lady, and the war in me—I am both parent and child—is with myself. What separates her from her sexuality and from mine also separates me from mine. That's the other thing we share.

The limits our culture places on our being sexual are placed so early—the moment we're born—that she can't discover what she would have been like: The limits are what she is. It is not like learning algebra in the eighth grade: *What was I like before I learned algebra?* What was I like before I learned to be a woman in a patriarchal world—before I was unsexed? If you want to liberate yourself from patriarchy, you would have to dismantle, piece by piece, your whole psyche. Liberation means starting over at the beginning, and it takes a kind of suicide to get there. Even with the whole feminist library to draw on and the knowledge of the hundreds of thousands of women who have done it already, there is no escaping fear. The dismantling and the reconstruction have to be done alone. It's like death. Nobody goes there with you.

We gather things for the picnic—the blue and white checked cloth, the silver—and put them in the basket. She takes Marc upstairs to change him. I hear her bustle about. I follow, and we shower and dress, sharing the bath and the dresser and the mirror, going back and forth from room to room. Deborah will be there, and Sally and Marybeth and Cynthia and Claire and the rest of our crowd, women who have found themselves and each other. I go from the bathroom to the bedroom and back again, a towel around me, drying my hair, getting things from the bureau, passing again and again the mirror and my quick-silvered image.

When she found in my things the old photographs of my grandmother and my great-grandmother, she insisted that I have them framed and hang them on the wall in our bedroom. For me they have been a reminder of what I have rebelled against, but she said they are a reminder of the continuity of things. They hang now at shoulder height on each side of the mirror, trapped in their out-of-date hair styles, staring benignly at me. We share cheeks and chins and an attitude. I can't do anything about that. It is hardly possible even to choose what you rebel against. I towel my hair again and rough it up with my fingers and stare again at the young woman in front of me, flanked by her grandmother and her great-grandmother, and I wonder what a strange creature running through a forest glade I would have been, had I been hatched from an egg by the warmth of the sun.

I stand in the kitchen at the counter, looking at Friday's newspaper and the large photograph of Geraldine Ferraro. They say she is a master of the 'old-boy' network. She and Mondale look like they are married. In the end, she comes into the kitchen, Marc on her hip, both oblivious of him and taking care of him, and grins. "Are we ready?" She glances around the kitchen at the preparations, the picnic basket, my rucksack with Marc's things, the bottle of wine, the stack of newspapers. "Bring *W*, would you?" She grabs the rucksack, and she takes one last glance around the room. "And *Time*?" Then she heads toward the door. She pushes open the screen. She turns and looks at me. "Geraldine Ferraro!" Then she smiles. "Coming?" She holds the door for me.

Deborah

D o you like it?"

"I look like I'm ready for an adventure."

"*Are* you ready for an adventure?"

"I hope so." Sally looks at my reflection in the mirror. "Would you like to go with me? We'll go somewhere hot and foreign. You'll need to carry a passport when I wear this hat."

I turn to the side and then look back at the mirror over my shoulder. The hat has a broad, floppy brim and almost hides one eye. "I think I should take up smoking and wear large dark glasses."

"If you say so—" Sally is amused and doubtful. She has been standing behind me, looking over my shoulder as I try on hats. She looks from my reflection to me.

"I *don't* say so. What are you ready for?"

She touches me on the shoulder and then turns away toward a stack of summer jerseys.

I turn my head again and lower it so that the shadow of the brim covers my eyes. "I feel like I should feel sultry—"

She is away now among the white duck pants, and I take off the hat and replace it on a stack of other hats just like it. We are in a little shop—a boutique—in a row of little tourist shops in a small picturesque town on the bay. Sally picked me up after early mass today for a day at the beach. We've stopped a couple of times already, an antiques place, and here, and once just to enjoy the view of the islands in Penobscot Bay. In a little bit we'll go down the coast to where there's a path down to a sand beach.

"Try this one," Sally says, appearing at my elbow. She is holding another hat, of natural straw.

I turn to the mirror and put it on. I am forty-eight, and I look like a woman who has never given a thought to her appearance, even though I have. Carole tells me my thoughts about my appearance have never translated themselves into any reality. In this hat I look like I'm headed for a climb on the rocks above the surf.

"Yes. You're pretty in that one. Do you like it?"

My curly hair sticks out from under the cap.

"I think so." I turn my head again to catch another angle. "It'll protect me from the sun." It has a lavender ribbon which hangs down the back, like a schoolgirl's hat.

"Let me help," she says. She places it further forward on my head.

"Oh, do you think so?" I feel less girlish, new, more purposeful.

She smiles.

"I like the ribbon, especially."

Sally smiles. "I do too," she whispers. "I'll get it for you."

This is totally unexpected.

We walk out again into the sun carrying our purchases—Sally has bought a pair of sunglasses—and get into the car and pull out into the traffic going south. Our windows are down. It is a glorious day. Ahead of us and behind are cars pulling boats going to the water. Summer doesn't really begin until now, early July. All the unstable weather is behind us, the days when it can't decide what it's going to do and leaves us feeling frustrated and uncompleted. Now full summer is upon us, and for the next six weeks, it's something we can count upon, these long warm days of cloudless skies and blue water. It's as if the stage has been cleared for some event! Even the trees have deepened from the pale green of new leaves into the dark, strong, assured green of full growth.

I reach behind the seat to the bag with my hat and take it out and bite the plastic loop that holds the tags. Sally, without taking her eyes from the road, moves the rearview mirror so that I can use it. I put the hat forward on the top of my head as she likes it and check my reflection. I snap the brim down. I have known Sally for years, in the way one knows some people in small towns—in the crowd in the lobby at the symphony, in the audience at plays at the university. I have seen her in the library and have heard her speak at the U. I have known what her name was and have spoken to her, but we have never been introduced. Now with the rally in June and the memorial service for Bernie last week, we are suddenly friends who are allowed to say we have known each other for years.

She has brought a bag of food—apparently odds and ends, some cheese and crackers, a dip, some cut vegetables. In my basket, I have brought a complete luncheon for two: cheese, an antipasto, a loaf of French bread, a bowl of potato salad, and fried chicken, with cookies for desert. I also packed a tablecloth, napkins and silverware. And glasses, in case someone doesn't want to drink out of the can.

All of this was Sally's idea. She had called on Thursday to talk about the interview, and then she said, "I was grateful for the opportunity to meet you last Monday night. Dana and Marcia speak of you. I must say, you are not what I expected. You're not a pussycat, are you?" She told me about a picnic down the coast on Sunday and hoped I would come. I did not think I would, and then late last night while I was getting undressed for bed, she called again and did something I found astonishing. She asked me to drive down with her. She made it quite plain: "Will you go down with me?"

She has a beautiful voice, low and soft, not growlly, but strong and full, like a cello. She is wearing jeans and a fuchia t-shirt, and very long earrings that I would have thought would be too elaborate for a picnic at the beach but which are just right—festive and dramatic—on her. Her forehead is covered with a scarf tied under her hair in the back like a pirate's. Her hair is black with a few gray hairs and has strong tight curls. Her skin is darker than mine.

"Several women are already there," she says. "This is all casual, all women of different ages—" She looks behind her before pulling out around an enormous boat attached to a car ahead of us. "—and everybody is bringing her own food and coming when she can. Marcia and Dana will be there, and the younger women. I think Marybeth and some others, some older women I know. Helen Demopoulos, I believe. I hope you don't mind a crowd?" She looks over at me, her eyebrows raised. "And if you do, we can leave, go somewhere by ourselves." I think she is my age, though we have not discussed that. I don't know what to "discuss" with her. I suppose I must admit I find her intimidating. She is a professor at the U, and I don't know what this invitation means.

"I feel like a celebration," she says and looks at me. I sit in the seat staring straight ahead and murmur something in reply. I have felt the most unsettling conflict of emotions all week. I know the need to celebrate. My world is measurably larger today than it was last week before Bernie died. Even more important is my discovery—can it be a reawakening?—of myself as a woman. I have spent the last ten years grading students' papers, or sitting behind a desk at the library, or in the ninth pew on the left side at mass. I feel I am coming up from underground into a world of the most beautiful people. At the same time, I find myself facing a host of old dreadful memories, which have come back on me now, leaving me morose and self-pitying. It is exactly like feeling chilled when you have a fever.

The River Road parallels the river for twenty miles down from Cardiff, passing through little villages which are very old—this area was first settled in the early eighteenth century—and which were originally farming communities. Down further the river broadens and becomes the bay. It seems at first like a broad river—the Mississippi perhaps—and then becomes unmistakably oceanic: From the highway up on the headlands, we see deep swells with whitecaps, dark forested granite islands which seem, at this distance of five and six miles, to be uninhabited, and, on the east, the Atlantic, blue. The towns down here are built around small tight harbors and have always been focused on the sea and on fishing. The road dips down from the headlands to the water's edge through these towns, and we stop for crab.

The shore changes as we move east toward the ocean: Pebbles give way to the great underlying shelf of metasedimentary bedrock which thrusts itself up from beneath the ground against the water. Down here forty miles from Cardiff and near the lighthouse on the head marking the end of land, we hear the surf fall on great broken boulders and palisades of granite.

We park beside the road on the headland within sight of the lighthouse and cross the road and a stretch of grass to the rock. I carry a bag and my basket with my lunch, and Sally carries two liter bottles of soda and another bag and the ice chest with the crab. She has thrown a blanket over her shoulder. When I reach the edge of the rock, I look for somebody—for anybody at all—and don't see anyone. I don't know where to go. And there is no sand beach.

Sally, who has been right behind me, comes up and stands on the edge and, squinting her eyes against the glare, looks up and down the shore. "There," she says, "there we are," nodding down to the right where I can see nothing.

We climb down from boulder to boulder toward the water, sometimes on flat rock exposed on all sides, sometimes on rock sheltered by other boulders, sometimes on rock slanted too steeply to stand on. We find a flat spot partially sheltered at the back, and I put down our things and sit down.

It is glorious. The wind blows my hair across my face. It is late morning, and the sun is very high: Later it will be very hot. The rock is warm, and the breeze is cool off the water. I feel myself coming alive, but I am uncertain of myself here. This feels too big— I feel exposed, as if I were too near a precipice. I think I want shelter, and I move back up against a boulder behind us.

Sally spreads out the blanket and plops herself down. "It is appropriate to be on the ocean today."

I don't know what to say.

"It's a place for strong feelings. Strong thoughts. Clear visions."

I busy myself with unpacking a little—cheese and crackers, a bag of potato chips, the antipasto. I offer her a soda.

She shakes her head. "My impulse is to take off all my clothes. Back to the land for me has always meant back to the water. Naked, if I can manage it."

It is a funny idea, and it unites us in an attitude toward a certain kind of person who moves to this state. She reaches out to touch my hand.

"You are lovely, you know."

This is pleasing. "When I was a girl—" I start to say, and then I begin again. "Do you remember the fabric they made bathing suits out of? That heavy stretch stuff?"

She laughs. "They pleated it to make your breasts look bigger and to disguise things at the same time. To confuse the boys."

"It confused me."

Sally slides off her jeans and t-shirt. Underneath, she is wearing a bathing suit of extremely thin stretch fabric. Her body is tanned and solid. I am not wearing a bathing suit under my shorts. I wouldn't have worn one even if I had thought of it.

I huddle against the boulder and stare out to sea. She lies down beside me on the rock, exposed to the sun, her eyes closed. Her fingers lightly enclose my hand, as if it meant nothing. To me it is one of the consequences of Bernie's death—Sally's attention—and so is enormous and shattering.

"One of the attractive things about you is your reticence, the way you resist presenting yourself." She rises up and sits crosslegged next to me, her hand smoothing out circles on the rock, her face turned toward me, studying me, while the wind blows her hair across her scarf. "That makes it more fun when I discover things about you."

I don't know what to say, and I look among the rocks for friends. I don't feel girlish now.

"Your hat, for example, sitting on your head like that, the brim snapped down, looks very forthright."

"What have you discovered about me?"

"These contradictions—your job, your sexuality, your child—which you insist on without calling attention to them. Your extreme difficulty in talking about yourself. How grounded you are." She allows her hand to touch my knee lightly.

The wind off the bay is chilling. A gull floats above us, motionless, waiting for us to throw food. I am in the midst of one of those vast landscape paintings with humans painted too small even to suggest the color of their skins.

"What made you give the speech?"

The sun is directly overhead now and warms the whole face of the rock. At the same time, the wind off the North Atlantic chills everything it touches. "The things that made me keep silent before— Rebecca was a child, fear of ridicule, fear that Betsey would leave, or wouldn't come back—all changed. Rebecca grew up and didn't care. And I was older, and I wasn't afraid any longer. I had become, in a way, indifferent—"

She takes my hand.

"I kept thinking, at first, I wanted them to find that man and punish him. Later I didn't care about that. I wanted to tell that story to people who'd listen. I wanted to tell how it had been, exactly how it had been, to people who could hear me. It is terribly important not to lose ourselves, our history, through neglect." Her hand tightens on mine. "And then, of course, there was the anger. I have never stopped being angry."

"You said, 'We have to stand together—'"

I did say that, but that comes and goes, I think. I think I must have felt that very early, when I was in my twenties, in college and graduate school. My friends were mainly women. Then it was a long time—ten years—before I found it again, after my divorce, when I began to go with Betsey. Then when Betsey left, I sank back into being alone again. It has only been in the last month—

Below us on the rocks I hear voices, and then I see women. I stand up to watch more closely, and Sally comes behind me and puts her arm around my shoulder. The women are laughing and shouting.

They pick up mussels and throw them up to the gull, which swoops down and catches them. They carry beer cans. There are three of them, young women in shorts and sweatshirts with the arms cut out or halter tops. They call out to us.

"Come up!"

"Come down!"

"Hello, Deborah!"

"Hello!"

"Hello, Sally!"

"Welcome to the sea!"

"We have lobsters!"

"We have crab!"

They make their way up across the rocks toward us, clambering up the face of the sloping boulders on all fours, and, when they are faced with a crevasse between the rocks, standing up and, their arms stretched out for balance, leaping across the chasm with a youthful, graceful fling, lighting on one foot.

"Isn't it wonderful?" one of them says, dropping herself down on her stomach on our rock. "Isn't it awesome?" She rolls over on her back and pulls up her halter to entirely expose her chest to the fierce sun. "Isn't it entirely awesome?" We all laugh.

The other two girls drop down beside her.

The oldest of the three, whose blond hair is in a brush cut, a slender woman in her late twenties, takes off her halter completely. "I've been waiting to do this all summer." She turns to me. "You're Deborah. Hi." She smiles. "Sally said she was going to bring you down. That's neat. I'm Joan."

"I'm Diana," the youngest of the three says. The last one is Patty. "I haven't been at a picnic in years," I say. "I think I have been alone too much."

Joan leans forward and touches my knee. "Me too. I heard you speak. You said, *We must find what our strengths are and then use them relentlessly.* I've never forgotten that. You were wonderful."

Sally holds my hand. "Did I hear you say you have lobster?"

"We bought six—enough to share."

"We've got crab—"

I have a complete lunch.

"We have corn and a gas stove to cook it on—"

"Sally," one of the younger women says, "I am reading Judy Grahn's book."

"What's the name?"

"*Another Mother's Tongue*."

"Diana is always reading."

"That's the way I find out how I want to be."

"How do you want to be?"

She is lying flat on her back on the rock. She arches her back and crosses her arms across her chest and closes her eyes, and says, "I want to know all the history of lesbians beginning with Sappho!"

She amuses us.

"Have you been to Boston to the bookstore?"

"What bookstore?"

"Glad Day. It's a bookstore for us."

Sally offers soda. Patty takes some. Joan and Diana sit up and look out to sea for a moment. Then, with a signal to each other, they stand up.

"We'll be back in a little bit," Joan says.

Diana, as she walks away, says, over her shoulder, "We'll get some wood for a fire." And they jump from our rock over to the next one and begin a descent to the water. Their voices become more and more indistinct as they get farther and farther away from us, and, when, in a few minutes, I cannot hear them at all but I can still clearly see them, their eyes down on the rocks, their hands holding on to the rocks, I think it is an odd sensation to know that they are still talking between themselves.

Patty, who has red hair and freckles and appears to be in danger of burning, has stretched out on her back on a corner of our blanket and closed her eyes. She has an exquisite body: white skin, softly molded flesh that almost completely obscures her bones, tiny waist, prominent breasts and buttocks.

Sally gestures toward her. "My bones are thirty years older than those bones."

We stare for a moment at Patty's body.

"Are you two staring at me?"

"I'm wondering what it is like to be twenty."

"Not bloody good," Patty says, her eyes still closed.

Actually, I know what it's like to be twenty: My feelings are still raw. I admire her beauty without wanting it.

"Here I lie, without a lover—" Suddenly she turns over on her side toward us, her folded hands cushioning her head from the rock. "I'll trade you my bones for your head."

That is enough to make us laugh. "Oh, no," Sally says. "That would be unfair."

"To you."

"Besides, I think I'll keep my head," Sally says. "I like my head and what's in it."

"I'm serious, you guys. I am ready to chew my knuckles off. And you two look so serene, so—, so happy! It's the worst time of my life." She turns over on her back again, her eyes closed. "So far." She is exquisitely beautiful. "How do you do it?"

"How do we do it?" Sally turns to me. She puts out an arm and draws me to her. I fall over on her and, for a moment, there is a tangle of legs and arms, and when we have sorted things out, I am leaning against her. "How do we do it, Deborah?" Then I position myself back against the boulder, as I was before.

She puts her hand carefully over my hand on the rock.

"I don't think I have it 'all' together—" I think Sally must agree with me that whatever satisfaction we experience doesn't have its sole source in our jobs, that we may even have already had that success. I wonder if Sally would agree that it is time for some radical change, and I wonder whether her silk-thin bathing suit, covering and at the same time exposing her breasts, is an indication of the distance she is willing to go in this change.

Patty turns over on her stomach again—she lies like a sacrifice to us—and says, "What I would like to discover is how to be happy alone."

The scene has the clarity of a Cezanne landscape: the colorfield of the sky, a deep undifferentiated blue from east to west, from the horizon to the zenith above my head, the ocean, a vast perspective, blue at the bottom of the frame, shading to intense dark blue at the horizon in an utterly even gradation, and here in the foreground a cubist rendering of golden rocks. We hear voices. They come to us through the sounds of the ocean, through the sibilant roar and crash on the rocks, the wind making a pipe of the surface of the waves. Their voices rise and fall, indistinguishable as words, clear and melodic above the waves.

"Listen!"

283

"—sh—"

They talk to one another, and the waves and the wind give their words an intense privacy. They draw nearer, and their words become more understandable. Sally takes my hand.

It is Marcia, and Dana, who carries Marc. They jump down from rock to rock, Marc squealing with laughter at each lurch downward. Both women whisper to him while watching the rocks under their feet.

"The ocean!"

"Yes! Water!"

"Rocks!"

Then they are upon us.

"Look," she says, pointing, "there's Sally!" She shifts him in her arms so he can see us. "Remember Sally?" She says these words, bending her head down to Marc's ear, almost in a whisper. "And there's Deborah, and there's Patty." The boy gazes on us solemnly and shifts his eyes as each one of us is introduced. "Now, down we go." Dana drops gently to her knees on the blanket and spreads out his blanket on top of ours. Her eyes move from one to the other of us, smiling, connecting, as she talks to her son. "There." She places him on his back on the cloth, his knees up. He immediately grasps them with his fingers. He blinks against the sky and closes his eyes, and Dana covers them with the palm of her hand.

Marcia drops to her knees and leans over and kisses me. "Wonderful!" We hug, and then she hugs Sally—Sally relinquishes my hand—and whispers something to her.

Patty has stood up and hugs and kisses both women.

"Will you help me fix something for his eyes?" Dana and Patty set about arranging a couple of the backpacks and a tablecloth. Dana is expert. The thing is done in a minute, and Marc established with a stuffed animal under a checked tablecloth.

"This is glorious." Marcia looks around at the rocks and the sea. "We have a salad, and we have bread—"

"There are lobsters and crab in the ice chests—" Sally says. She has leaned back against the rock next to me, and her fingers have sought out my hand again.

"We have crackers and cheese—" I lean forward to slice the cheese.

284

"Here, let me—" The wind blows her hair across her face like a veil. And she offers the cheese around before her hand is free to brush her hair away. When she does, she turns back to me and smiles. "What would you like?" She says it as if she could actually give me anything I liked, and the notion is unexpected and pleasing.

I am aware that the eyes of Dana and Marcia and Patty are suddenly upon us.

"I don't know. I don't want anything—" But I ponder what I would say, if I could speak.

Sally leans forward and slices the cheese and gives it to me on a cracker. I am suffering an immense excitement.

"Here," she says, giving me another. She sits down again, and her hand gropes for mine and, catching it, squeezes it. The many things appealing about Sally—her looks, her adventurousness, her intelligence and experience—are overwhelmed by the touch of her hand. I blush at the promise her fingers make.

The rest of them turn away, paying attention to the baby or the sea or each other. Marcia has turned to Patty: "It's OK if you're making enough money to live on."

Dana speaks directly to me in the midst of all this: "I have been thinking since last Monday night. Wouldn't it be good if you wrote down what happened to you, the story of your rape, made a long narrative of it? It would be extraordinarily powerful."

"Do you think so?"

It is a sudden eclipse of the sun.

"All of us need to know about each other—"

I drop Sally's hand and stand up. "I want to go down to the water."

"Would you like company?" Sally asks.

"Oh, no—" I need to get away quickly. I go around Patty and Marcia and step down to the next boulder. The others say goodbye. Then, as I climb and jump from rock to rock toward the water, my eyes fill up with tears, and I can't see. I have to wipe my eyes before I can take a step.

There is a chill at the water's edge. The breeze is cooler here, too, and one feels oneself getting wet—the spray from the churning surf just after low tide. I sit down to steady myself. When Betsey had been gone for two weeks, against my own will I waited for the postman, lurched when the phone rang, turned suddenly to see again some woman who had passed in the periphery of my vision who might have been—who surely was—Betsey. I felt horribly betrayed. I sat on the side of our bed and sought for something to grasp in my hands that I could hold on to which was as strong as the sense of my loss.

I had been utterly open to her. She had been inside me to a depth unimaginable in my husband. My love for her had taken the form, exactly, of a careful, delicate, deliberate, unfolding to her, and when she left, it was as if she had inserted her hand inside my breast and ripped my heart from its seat. The least of it was that great chunks of my future had been destroyed, as if pages had been ripped out and thrown away. I had opened myself to her, and I didn't know what to do with me afterwards.

"Deborah!" I look about me: Coming toward me over the kelp beds—here the rocks are covered with it, making progress treacherous—is Marybeth.

I watch her approach, picking her way among the slippery seaweed, her athletic shoes in her hand. She is entirely wet: She has just come out of the water. The sun, which comes from behind her, casts her front in shadow and turns her silhouette to silver. I sit on a rock, my arms crossed on my chest, staring.

"Deborah!" She waves. "Where is everyone!"

From her appearance, one would be tempted to say that she—this cheerful, energetic, determined young woman—has never been betrayed.

She arrives near my rock. "Where is everybody?" And then, "Are you alone?"

"Dana, Marcia—" For a moment I can't remember the young woman's name. "—Patty are all up there—" I point up to where they are hidden behind boulders. "Dana's and Marcia's baby is there too." Then I point in the other direction, to the left along the water. "I think Joan and Diana went in that direction—"

"We're all over. People are up on the grass by the road playing frisbee. Claire is up there, and Suzanne—" She sits down on the rock next to me. "I got delegated to come down and find out where people are and what we want to do about eating." She looks at me and shrugs and giggles. "We're all over this rock, aren't we! I came looking for you and found people swimming! Imagine what it would be like if you were a mermaid out there—" She spins around and gestures expansively toward the blue ocean "—and you looked back at the shore right here, you'd see dykes draped all over the shore." She giggles again, as if she can't contain herself. Then she becomes serious again. "But you can't see anything from the road." She looks at me. She leans over and kisses me on the cheek. "I'm just a tacky dyke, Deborah, don't mind me." Then she looks at me again. "Is there anything I can do?" My hands are between my knees, and she slides her arm across my shoulder and hugs me. She kisses me on the cheek. "What's happening?"

"I'm out of sorts. I'm of two minds—"

She hugs me.

"I'll be OK."

And then she is gone, climbing up beyond the kelp beds toward the rocks that demarcate high tide, in the direction of Marcia and Patty and Dana and Marc.

I stare out to sea into the harsh blue world of the sky and the water. I suffer from a failure of nerve. I take off my shoes and socks and put my feet in the water. When I was a child, I climbed on these rocks at low tide and spent my time discovering what was underneath them: starfish and sea urchins and sea anemones, clams and mussels. I was on all fours, fanny in the air, trying to reach whatever it was so I could possess it. I bought the Peterson books when I was a teenager and learned the names: Green Sea Urchin and Northern Rock Barnacle, Blood Stars, Orange Footed Cucumbers, Frilled Anemones, Blood Drop Sea Squirts. I learned the proper names at one point—the Frilled Anemone is called *metridium senile* and the Blood Drop Sea Squirt is called *dendrodoa carnea*—and drifted away into a world of tiny creatures with infinitely intricate organs and curious, secret names. It was a whole world for me, the little pool of water around the base of one of these rocks, and I felt like a lumbering giantess trying to see and not damage their delicate lives. The tide came in twice a day and drowned the whole thing: I was enchanted by the idea that things could live under water half the time and in the air half the time and was amazed that there were creatures so well equipped for so radically divided a life.

I am too old. I can't clamber around on rocks at my age. I am stiff, and my muscles have gone all flaccid. I have lost my mental agility. Leaping from this idea to the next. High above me I hear the gull cry. She sits on the wave of the wind. I feel earthbound and landlocked.

"Hello." It is Sally, who has seated herself on the rock next to me. "I came down to find you."

I turn to her and study her face. It is a strong, emphatic face. Her jaw shuts firmly and her lips close tightly around her teeth. Her eyes wait for an answer from me, and while they wait, they study me.

"I missed you." There are circles under her eyes—age and a fatigue that is, I suspect, decades old. "We have good food. Everybody has gathered. More people have just come." She touches my hand, and when I don't flinch, she takes it up. "Will you join us?"

"I was thinking about when I was a girl—"

She doesn't say anything. She turns her face toward the sea. I know what I'm doing.

"—I was fascinated by the creatures in the tidal pools. How nearly invisible they were. They were mottled brown and gray with white spots or rings."

She continues to look out to sea, her eyes narrowed to a slit.

"I thought it was wonderful that they could be so invisible. You could be right above them, a foot away, and still be unable to see them. It was only when you put your hand in and disturbed the water that they moved, and you could see them, a second after they had hidden themselves again, and it was too late."

I hear behind me, up on the rocks, the sounds of women's voices, almost indistinguishable from the sound of the wind across my ears.

"Will you teach me?"

"I would like that."

She grins.

"I like their names. One is called the Splendid Hydromedusa. Isn't that wonderful? It's a kind of little jelly fish you sometimes find around here."

"You're amazing." She looks about her. "I could bring you something to eat, if you prefer. Would that be nice? Or would you like to leave?"

"Oh, thank you. I think I would like to go back up and eat with the others—"

She releases my hand and clasps her hands together between her knees, staring out to sea. She waits for me. I marvel at her composure. I realize now that this whole day—which I thought was hers—is mine, and she has been patiently waiting all day for me to declare myself. I turn to her and glide my hand between her knees to cover her hands. My other hand goes around her shoulder, and I lean forward and kiss her cheek.

She turns to me. I move toward her, my lips touch hers, and we kiss, first gently and then more deeply. We embrace now, and I feel her breasts against mine. I stroke her back, the curve of her spine, and I smell in the corner of her neck the faint odor of her perfume mixed with the salt of the sea. I hold her against me and smell her odors and feel, on my cheek, her hair on her neck. We give in to each other. I allow myself a little time to be supported by her. When I kiss her again I am surprised to find that she has shut her eyes.

We make the trek back up the slope, moving back and forth across the face of the shore, leveling out the incline, making the giant steps up from rock to rock until the voices come from very near, and we finally can see the women they belong to.

The world is simple. There is only the sky and the sea and the rocks: solid geometry. The arch of the sky, flat sea, and these three dimensional rocks: three shapes, two colors. We have the rocks behind us and the sky above us, and we face the sea below as if it were a vast empty Attic stage. Strewn about on these rough bleachers under this searing sun are women who call out to us as we approach.

"Sally!"

"You've come back!"

"Where have you two been?"

Then another voice, distinct in tone and attitude: "I looked for you in Mount Vernon." It is Helen Demopoulos, enthroned against a small boulder, her face hidden behind immense sunglasses. "I thought you'd be there for the politicking."

I reach for her hand, and we touch fingers. "I was with Carole yesterday."

"I want to know about that."

From here, halfway up the great slope of the shore, I see below us women swimming in the sparkling water, their heads cast in shadow by the high hot sun, the water shining like diamonds on their bodies.

I pick my way among women. Dana lies on a slanting rock, her eyes closed and her arms spread out to the sun. I don't see Marcia, and Marc is playing with someone down a ways. Patty and Diana and Joan are here. On other rocks, other women—I recognize Claire and Marybeth and Suzanne—have seated themselves, surrounded by canvas bags and baskets, shirts and towels. The hard stone has sprung a soft colorful growth of women. I smell corn boiling and lobster and crab and fried clams. The odor of food comes in waves on the wind, and everyone it seems, including Sally, who stands in a space she has found for us, stretches out her hand to me.

On Monday night Sally and I sit in the church together, gripping each other's hand.

Derek, who stands in the front of the hall with Dana, has just called on Marybeth to speak. The room is crowded with people, as many as last week, who strain in their seats to see.

On my shoulders and the back of my head I still feel the heat of the television lights, even though they have been turned off for an hour. I am perspiring. It is the lights and the warm night and all the tension.

Marybeth stands on the other side. Her hands clutch the back of the seat in front of her, her eyes on Derek and Dana, her face screwed up.

"I don't *want* us to have to vote!" Her eyes beseech Derek and Dana, and all of us—I'm doing it myself—rise up in our seats to see better. I follow her eyes to Derek. He looks to Dana, whose eyes are shooting like lasers all over the room. I am sitting so near Sally that every time she moves, her energy is immediately telegraphed to me. I am in an electrical field.

"I'd *hate* that! I'd feel so oppressed!" She glances around at us—searches the room for us—for support. "It'd be just like we did to ourselves what they did to Bernie. I hate this, what this committee wants us to do. We're supposed to be here tonight to make things better, to make it so what happened to Bernie won't happen again. And it's as if we weren't paying attention. It's so traditional, so—, so—oppressive. You're going to have a president and a vice president and a board of directors of all the dykes and queers in

Cardiff. And you're going to have us vote for them! You're going to have people in power and people out of power. You're going to have a Coalition of Gays and Lesbians that's going to be all about hierarchy and competition and struggle and being in and being out." Marybeth turns around to us and speaks directly to us. "You're going to have a struggle over power, people winning and people losing, and that's just what killed Bernie, don't you see? *He was killed because he was a loser!*"

Ahead of us two men whisper to one another, and suddenly I am shocked to discover that what seems to me enormously appealing, the obvious truth, isn't being received that way by a lot of people in the audience. Men are sticking up their hands everywhere. *Men.* I suddenly am aware that it is *men* who are throwing up their hands.

Dana is impatient and calls on some gay man.

"Well, what do you propose?" His face suggests he is absolutely mystified.

Marybeth is back on her feet, speaking before she is fully upright: "Not a system where somebody wins and somebody loses. Not a system where there is a majority which rules. And especially not a system where the people who are not in the majority can be ignored, thrust out, forgotten, just like they did to Bernie."

"Then, *what?*—"

"I don't know—"

"Dear God, give her words," Sally whispers next to me. I strain to hear.

Hands go up all over the room.

"—group conscience. I don't know. Consensus. I think everything should be done by group conscience—"

She falters, and Sally puts her fingers to her lips and whispers under her breath. "Oh, *no!*"

People are waving their arms to get attention.

It is difficult to believe that Derek has called on another man, who rises languidly to his feet in front of Marybeth and turns to confront her.

"I don't see the difference between regular voting and seeking a group conscience. That's just words. Would you explain—"

"It's *not* just words! It's the difference between being empowered and being powerless—"

"*There!*—" Sally whispers, satisfied.

"—it's the difference between us, all of us, taking responsibility for our lives, now, *at last*, and us relinquishing it, giving it up again to people who say they know better. Gays and lesbians have given up responsibility for our lives to psychiatrists, to the church, to the state—How long have we done this? How much longer are we going to do this?—"

"If this goes on another millisecond, I am going to help her," Sally says under her breath, and I look from Marybeth to Dana and Derek to the gay man standing on my left, aware of Sally's profile in the periphery of my vision. People all over the room are rising in their seats to get a better view, signaling to Dana and Derek, attempting to get recognized. The room, with its enormous high dark ceiling, is a forest of gesticulating arms.

People call out, "Dana!"

"Dana!"

"Derek!"

"Over here!"

Sally's hand searches out mine. I have become familiar with the satisfying feel of her hand. It is fleshy, and the knuckles of her fingers don't seem any larger than the muscular part. My hands are thin, and the knuckles are large: Mine are not pretty hands. We held hands most of yesterday down on the coast, and we held hands all the way back to town. She came back to my house, and I cooked us supper, and then later she stayed over and didn't leave until this morning after breakfast.

We grip hands, and we listen and watch as Marybeth, roused to anger, though I think what I hear is fear, fights like a tigress. She cannot be left to fight this alone.

I raise my hand, and then I wave it so that Dana can see me.

Dana raises her arm and points her long slender finger at—at me. "Deborah!" she calls out, and I rise to speak.

As I rise, I wonder what I am to say. And when I am standing and look about me, I find the audience seems larger than I had imagined. Luke stands in the back corner, scowling, and Arthur, next to him, grins. I feel a distinct coolness, which is odd in this hot muggy room, and a clarity and distance. "Thank you for calling on me, Dana," I say. I can hear my voice, which is both familiar—the one I hear in my head—and strange in this cavernous room. She smiles at me, and I collect myself and go on.

"I can understand the consternation some people feel when Marybeth proposes that we not have voting in this new coalition we are forming. How else is the business of the group to be conducted? Voting is the traditional act of a democracy, and we call ourselves democrats. It is the efficient way to discover the will of the group, choosing between alternative proposals, people, ideas, and we want to be efficient. I think we all want this new coalition to be effective, powerful, in protecting our rights, and it is appropriate that we adopt ways to make it efficient and powerful, so that what happened to Bernie won't happen again.

"But I think it is important to analyze what it is we are doing here. What has oppressed us? What is it we are fighting against?" I look about the room at my new friends. I don't look at her, but I can see Sally's face turned up to me at my side. I can feel the power of her approval. "What killed Bernie? It is the idea that there are only a certain number of permissible ways to be, that a man or a woman must be a certain kind of thing and that, if they are not, others have the right to ridicule them and batter them and destroy them. It is a totalitarian idea. It is even a fascist notion, that we have to fit ourselves to other people's notions of us rather than make our communities and our societies and our governments fit our idea of ourselves—."

"Who are we?" I look about the room again, this time more slowly, at Mickey and Robbie, Jack, Marcia and Dana, Claire, and Derek, the persons who have so suddenly enlarged my life. "Men and women. Gay men and lesbians. Straight men and women. These traditional categories don't begin to express our infinite variety. My feelings, my self, will not be forced into categories so confining. Femme and Butch—" People laugh, and I wonder if I have used the words correctly. "—*Must* I choose between them? My *self* rebels at being compelled to choose between alternatives.

"It is one thing to create an organization that is politically effective. It is another thing, and absolutely necessary, to create an organization that does not betray our vision of what we are: inclusive, accepting, not defined by categories, fluid, continuous, obsessed with our liberty—"

293

Derek

I stand on the landing of the staircase in the classroom building at the university, looking out through the wall of glass across campus. It is almost eleven. Ten o'clock classes have just let out, and lines of students follow the cement walkways between the brick buildings, walking in and out of the sun and the shadows. From my vantage, up two floors and thirty yards from the nearest, they are indistinguishable, differences of race and class and age blurred. I share a nationality and a race with most of them, a gender with half, but these are overwhelmed by my sense of distance and difference.

A colleague comes up the stairs, a man in the drama department. He is 5 feet 10 inches, brown everything, a man who has found in this rural setting what he has sought for in his life, an intellectually interesting job, a small house he can afford on the edge of a stable community, a wife and two daughters. There are no profound challenges to his orthodoxies. We see each other every day.

"The great drama starts tonight—"

For a moment I think he is talking about us tonight at the Unitarian Church.

"San Francisco."

Yes. The Democratic convention. "I had forgotten."

He smiles. "You should take an interest in what happens around you."

"My friend was murdered last week."

He looks at me from a distance, his eyes narrowed. "A terrible thing. They got the men who did it, didn't they?"

He smiles, waves, goes through the door into the hall of offices.

And that's it. The door closes on him. There is a murder, and the police have the boys who did it, and there's nothing else to talk about. It's in the hands of the criminal justice system. The mayor won't talk about it. The governor won't talk about it. The Bishop of Portland talks about it: On Friday there was a march in Portland and a rally and speeches. There were two hundred people. In the paper this morning, the bishop is quoted saying that, while he deplores violence of any kind and of course the Roman Catholic Church is opposed to murder, still it is necessary to remember that homosexuals commit sin every time they have sex.

Under a heading "Our Readers Write in Record Numbers," in the weekend edition of the paper, there were ten letters to the editor about Bernie's death. Most of them refer to the "media blitz" and then go on to take sides. A man writes: "I am angered that any person should be murdered in Cardiff. But the murder of Bernie Mallett should not be used as a pretext for the promotion of homosexuality in our culture—" A woman says: "In all that has been written about the Mallett case, why has nothing been said about those who lurk in public parks and alleyways, preying on our fine young children and young people of our city—" In an editorial in this morning's, Monday's, edition, the *Sentinel* says that police should crack down on homosexuals on the hill "for their own good."

Tonight, at the same time we meet at the Unitarian Church to found a coalition, the convention of the Democratic Party opens in San Francisco, where most of the AIDS cases are. Yesterday fifty thousand gay men and lesbians marched from the Castro to the Moscone Center, where the convention is being held, in support of a gay plank in the Democratic platform which would address gay concerns: a gay rights bill and more AIDS funding. I watched TV. The cameras illuminated the demonstrators, oddly dressed men and women walking in circles and carrying placards, like weird fish before the porthole of a deepdiving submarine. The Sisters of Perpetual Indulgence—gay men dressed as nuns on roller skates, lascivious grins and lurid gestures—denounce the Democratic Party as criminals. At the same time, one hundred thousand union members were also marching. One said in the *Times*, "We're out here trying to show we're against the president and what he's done to organized labor." Some of the union members dropped out of their march to jeer the gays in *their* march. Walter Mondale—bland corporate liberal from the Midwest—who already has enough votes to win the nomination, has announced that he has chosen Geraldine Ferraro as his vice presidential running mate. Columnists everywhere speak of the Democratic party being a prisoner of "special interests"—blacks, Hispanics, the elderly, women, the blind and deaf, homosexuals. One man refers to the "ceaseless cries from the constituencies of the left."

I have been asked to moderate the meeting tonight. I agreed—I couldn't tell her no—and Dana will moderate it with me. It is necessary to establish that principle at the beginning. After class I will go to the gym and work out and then home for a couple of hours before the meeting tonight. My father has called twice this week and left messages. I can't call him back. Of the ten letters to the editor in the weekend edition, six were stridently homophobic, four sympathetic to gays. Their sympathy has no affect on me. It dissociates them from the criminal act of murder. Sympathy is the emotion of someone not affected for someone who is, and exactly the point is that what killed Bernie wounds us all. I don't want to hear my father tell me he is "sympathetic."

I stare at the students, their numbers beginning to thin as the time for the next class approaches. They are dressed in the careless style of summer school: shorts and t-shirts, jeans and t-shirts, brown skin and bleached hair. From this distance, as they walk along the walks under the great thrusting elms, they are an ad for athletic shoes. They grin and chatter. I have been young and beautiful like them, and empty headed. I have walked across my campuses grinning and chattering, resolutely refusing to admit the possibility of discrimination and death, hypocrisies and lies. They are members of no special interest group, except that they think everybody is like them. I have to teach them in seven minutes. The politicization of sex has already taken place before any of us came on the scene, the gender of the person I fuck the subject of laws and judgments and political commentary. To protect my privacy in my bed, I have to join with others—scores, hundreds, thousands, millions of others in front of some TV camera—to answer the question, How is America to be governed? It is one more consequence of Bernie's death that I must stop my life and turn and look into the camera—into a camera!—and tell them who I am.

After the meeting is over, the coalition founded, and the hall is emptying, Dana, leaning against the back wall, says, "It is an achievement."

"What does it mean?" I hated the messiness of it.

We had asked them to come down front and speak to the question, What do we want? What does the gay community in Cardiff want in the aftermath of Bernie's death? And they did, about twenty people, telling us they wanted justice done for the boys, they wanted their civil rights protected, they wanted a gay bar in Cardiff, a gay organization, a mailing list and a newsletter. They wanted the violence in the street addressed, they wanted the police to be more responsive to the needs of gay people, they wanted something done about the homophobia in the schools. It was random and scattershot, incomplete and preliminary, but it was a start, and it enabled us to form task forces—justice, civil rights, education, the coalition, and police.

But things fell apart when Marybeth asked how decisions were going to be made. Suddenly there were hands up all over the room, and people started shouting. The speakers divided by gender, and even after Deborah stood up and calmed everything down, Mickey had the last word: "What some of the women are telling the men here tonight is that you don't give a shit about whether or not we stay in this organization—" We spent more than half of our time together tonight arguing over how we would make decisions—whether we would vote—and the women were on one side and the men were on the other.

"We're here, we know each other now, we're visible in Cardiff, and we can't be ignored." This is Dana. "We now have the means to look after ourselves—"

"Maybe. No officers, almost no structure, no voting." I take her in my arms, and we hug. "Division among its members, and no majority rule. It's the vision of the future. And we're not going to get anything done." I sit down in a chair, and she stands beside me, her arms folded across her chest. "We are in the midst of a war. We need discipline, leaders, spokespersons, but instead, we are trying to change human nature."

I invite everybody to my place for drinks. We have wasted our opportunity, and I didn't even want to be here.

The paper Tuesday morning quotes from the peroration of the keynote speech delivered by the governor of New York at the convention last night: "—ladies and gentlemen, brothers and sisters, for the good of us, for the love of this great nation, for the family of America, for the love of God—" I can live without any of that—in fact, I have lived without any of that—if I can have Jack in my bed.

The lead editorial this morning is entitled, "There is no need for a gay rights bill." It analyzes the current feeling of the citizens of Cardiff and concludes that while Mallett's death has polarized the community between gay activists who want to see their lifestyle promoted in American society and those who want all gays to go back in the closet, there is no support for singling out the gay and lesbian population for special treatment or special protection. A gay rights bill has been rejected by the state legislature four times, and another attempt to pass a bill would be merely divisive, unwise, and unproductive. It specifically denies that Mallett's death made him a martyr to "irrational hatred and bigotry." The boys alone bear responsibility for the death of Bernie. It concludes that there is sufficient protection for all citizens in the current laws.

In a separate article, the paper announces that the governor has issued a statement deploring the murder and supporting legislation forbidding discrimination against gays in matters of housing and credit but opposing laws protecting the employment of gays. The governor is concerned that such a law might force certain churches to hire homosexuals who don't want to hire them. On page 28 of the paper, the last page of the second section, there is a small article—six inches of type—under the head, "Gays Form Organization." My name is in the first paragraph. I can take Interstate 95 South to Boston.

On Wednesday I get a call in the morning just as I am leaving to go to the university to teach my class. The man says he is a reporter for the *New York Times*, that his name is Michael Allsworthy—a name I recognize from years of reading the *Times*.

"I want to talk to you about Bernie Mallett's death."

"I'll be through my class at noon."

"Well, I need to ask you some questions now."

I think of the time—10:35—and the deadline of my class: "I'm leaving the house to teach. I have an eleven o'clock class. Can we get together after my class?"

"I'll be leaving early this afternoon. I need to ask you questions now. You teach at the university?"

"Part-time this summer."

"Can I use your name?"

I look at my watch. "Yes."

"Can I say you teach at the university?"

"Yes." I weigh, for a second, the alternatives—refusal to be coerced by this man against the loss of the chance to get my message over to him, my interior life against the public world of the media. "What are you going to do with the story?"

"What do you mean?"

"Do you have an approach?"

He pauses. "I suppose I'll approach it straightforwardly. How such a thing could have happened in such a quiet rural town—"

So. "That's not the story—"

He pauses again. I wonder if he is writing down what I am saying. "What is?"

"The story is what an ordinary thing it is for gay men to be murdered. That's what you ought to be writing about. Gay men are murdered regularly in this country for being gay."

"I don't believe that," he says in a flat sullen tone.

"Call the National Gay Task Force in New York. Ask to speak to the head of the Antigay Violence Study, which has been going on for several years. He'll validate what I am saying." I fumble among my papers at the phone table, searching for the number. "What is surprising is not how often gay men are murdered but, given the climate of bigotry, how few are murdered. Bigotry runs through all the great institutions of our culture. The Army, business, the educational establishment, the Federal Government, the churches. That's the story. The press is one of the most bigoted institutions of all, and your own paper is one of the most bigoted papers in the country. You have refused to call us what we call ourselves, you have refused to cover our events, you have declined to report our legitimate political agenda. You have declined, even, to use the word gay—"

"Oh, come on now, those are editorial decisions—"

"You have refused to give us any reality in the pages of the *Times*. You've trivialized our concerns. Why don't you write the *real* story: America's appallingly high level of antigay bigotry—" I am aware of my watch and my class and of my towering rage. "You want to write about this quiet New England village which suddenly erupts, inexplicably, into violence, right? Is that your story? That's not the story. The *hate* is the story, man, not Bernie's death! You got it fucking backwards! The *hate* is the story!" But even as I say it, I know it's pointless. I am overwhelmed by my inability to speak and to make him hear me.

Derek

"What was Bernie Mallett like?" He's calm and irritated and superior, and I answer him. And then I've got to teach. But I can't teach, and afterwards I have no memory of what I did in that class. How do you teach *Richard II* to culturally deprived kids who don't know they've ever lost anything?

In the paper this morning, there were articles on the speech given last night at the convention by Jesse Jackson, veteran of twenty years of civil rights struggles that began at lunch counters in the South and have now proceeded to this moment. Jackson has the power, by withholding his supporters, to destroy Walter Mondale. But he comes to make peace. Anchormen said that last night America experienced an historic occasion, a moment when a black man, after thirty years of effort by hundreds of thousands of black and white Americans, stood at the pinnacle of political power. They quote him: "Our flag is red, white, and blue, but our nation is a rainbow—red, yellow, brown, black and white—and we're all precious in God's sight. America is not like a blanket—one piece of unbroken cloth, the same color, the same texture, the same size. America is more like a quilt—many patches, many pieces, many colors, many sizes, all woven and held together by a common thread. The white, the Hispanic, the black, the Arab, the Jew, the women, the Native American, the small farmer, the businessperson, the environmentalist, the peace activist, the young, the old, the lesbian, the gay, and the disabled make up the American quilt—"

I think about the difficulty of forging a common identity, some common agenda out of the competing demands of men and women, of our differing ages and classes. I wonder what could be my contribution to that. At the moment my job is to be gatekeeper. My sex and these politics are still separate. I came up here this summer for a good part in a good play—Orsino in *Twelfth Night*—in resort surroundings and because it will look good on my résumé. I remind myself continuously that I am not trapped here. I can leave when I want. I can set the terms in which I see myself and in which I am seen. I will leave when the play is over. Monday night we came to the Unitarian Church to turn our grief and anger into politics, but I know that grief and anger can as easily lead to Interstate 95 South to Boston as to the Unitarian Church.

On Thursday Deborah calls to tell me that she and another teacher are talking about bigotry in the high school. The school is run

300

by "the jocks"—most American high schools are—and the worst thing that a kid can say to another one is to call him "faggot." All three boys went to Cardiff High. She and this other teacher are making plans to bring this issue to her principal. "Before this is over, we'll take it to the school committee."

The paper says the Democratic platform has been written and accepted. Under the heading *Dignity for All*, the platform affirms "All groups must be protected from discrimination based on race, color, sex, religion, national origin, language, age, or sexual orientation. We will support legislation to prohibit discrimination in the workplace based on sexual orientation. We will assure that sexual orientation per se does not serve as a bar to participation in the military. We will support an enhanced effort to learn the cause and cure of AIDS, and to provide treatment for people with AIDS. And we will ensure that foreign citizens are not excluded from this country on the basis of their sexual orientation." In the flat and deflating language, gays have joined the long list of special interests in the American political landscape.

And in a stunning return to reality—and no coincidence—the *Sentinel* says on its fifth page that a gay man in San Francisco has died after being attacked by a gang of boys. He was chased, hit, chased, and kicked, and chased again. And when he finally stumbled and fell, he hit his head against the curbstone, and the blow killed him. The report—carried on the wire services—includes the police comment that there are similarities between this death and the "recent" death of a gay man in Cardiff, Maine. Both men were gay, their attackers were heterosexual, both attacks were unprovoked. They were twelve days apart.

I move irresistibly toward the public—toward finding the conflicts, pain, joys, of my life written across the TV screen and the papers' headlines. Even at the moment that Dana is telling me we are doing something at last, I am losing control of the things that matter to me. I can deal, in a one-on-one basis, with three boys. But our opponents now are the president and congress, the legislature, the *Times*, cultural assumptions that have politicized sex for a thousand years. The scale of the scene has been immeasurably enlarged, and I feel myself grow small.

On Thursday afternoon I stand on the steps of the Unitarian Church while a photographer from Millinocket who does job work for the *Times* takes my picture. A methodical man, he has me cross my arms on my chest and look down at him on the sidewalk. He takes picture after picture, moving up and down the sidewalk and then asking me to look at him, at the sky, at the door of the church. The light at the corner turns red and then green and then red again, that odd penetrating, depthless red that traffic signals have which doesn't exist on the same visual plane as the rest of nature. Cars stop for the light, the drivers idly observing the little scene we make, and then move on. One car speeds down the hill, trying to make the light, and a male figure leans out the window and yells, "Faggot!"

The photographer, whose eye is fixed to the viewfinder of the camera, drops the camera to his chest and looks at me and then at the car, disappearing beyond the light toward the bridge.

"What the fuck!"

I shrug.

"Who was he yelling at?" The photographer looks a little crazy with fear. "Who the fuck was he yelling at!"

"Cool it. At me. At me."

"How did he know?" The photographer has *confusion* written all over his face. "How the fuck did he know?"

What is it we ask for? I am on my knees in front of Jack, who lies on his back in my bed, his knees up to his chin, my cock up his ass. I thrust hard into him, and he throws his arms out on either side, his fingers clutching at the sheets, groaning, riding me. Jack likes this in me: strong male figure with a sense of inner certainty. At his age, that is what would turn him on. In my closet are three dresses, none of which I have worn on the stage. I have worn all three, with shoes to match, and wigs, and I lied to Deborah when I said I had never played Miranda. I've been playing Miranda in certain gay bars at Halloween and Valentine's in New York for years. I know what it's like to have on your earring and your makeup and to carry a purse, to have biceps and lacquered nails at the same time.

After the grief, I feel rage. I know the rage of the Sisters of Perpetual Indulgence as they throw their images onto the television screens of all America. *I'm here, goddamn you!* See me! My liberty, paid for by my father's money and my education, seems small and bland, insular and exclusive, compared to Bernie's operatic freedom. I have taken no risks. I am in no greater danger now from hate filled boys than I was before Bernie died. What I know now is about the danger I have always been in, which reaches to the heart of my place in the world. My liberty shrinks up around me until I have no freedom to move my arms and legs and I can't breathe. There are dangers all about me, in the police, the press, the political parties, the government, the censorship of plays and books, the loss of my history. Does anyone seriously expect the choice of Geraldine Ferraro as vice presidential running mate to alter the relationship between power and sex in this country? What place is there in the American political system—even a system with a plank for gay rights—for the Sisters of Perpetual Indulgence? And if there is no place for them, where we lie so consistently about the relationships between gender and sex and power, where are they to go? Over the parapet of a bridge!

I am drawn and quartered. The grand political rhetoric of the American republic, the elaborations over two hundred years of *We the people*, is assaulted in my mind by the memory of Bernie's death, the death of the San Francisco man, the *Times*' insistence that Bernie's death was inexplicable, the people screaming at us in the court house parking lot, and by our inability to come together as a gay and lesbian people. And it overwhelms my desire to be alone and make love to a boy.

I give Jack tickets on Friday, and after the show he comes home with me. We have sex in a fury. Our sublimated anger turns it into a kind of war, and when it is over, we are both breathless and exhausted. He lies across me, my sweat growing cold on my skin, the heaving of my chest gradually subsiding. My eyes close and the need to sleep soaks my mind.

"Derek—"

"Hmmm—"

"You like to hit me."

"Hmmm—"

"You like slapping me around like that."

I can feel the breath from his nostrils on my skin. I must wake up and answer him: "Hmmm—"

"Does it turn you on, hurting me?"

He has pulled me back, now, and I am awake. "Yeah—"

"It turns you on to dominate me?"

"Sure. God, yes." I think what it feels like to wrestle him to a standstill and then to slap his rump, slowly at first and then faster and harder, until his skin turns hot and red. "You're a big guy. I like struggling with you—"

"What do you think about?"

"I'm feeling."

"What—"

"It's asserting myself. It makes me feel alive. It's a very male thing for two guys to wrestle, to struggle with one another. I won, so I slapped you. If you can win, you slap me around a little. Or hard, a lot. There's something very, very sexy about all that. There's no point in struggling if it doesn't hurt to lose." I'm looking at the ceiling, and he's got his eyes closed. I begin to stroke him. He has an incredible body. He's only twenty-two. I run my fingers down the curve of his spine and onto his buttocks. I stroke his hair. He has thick dark brown hair. And then I hold him. I gather him in my arms and hold him. He snuggles into me.

"What we're doing is making a little community for ourselves. We're creating a community which reflects what we are and what we stand for—in which every viewpoint is given serious consideration and no view is too outrageous to be listened to—separate from, insulated from, the rest of the world." Marybeth is sitting on the floor, her back against my sofa, her head leaning back and resting on Suzanne's knee, her eyes alive and searching the ceiling. "We're dykes and queers, and some people would say we are pretty outrageous ourselves—boots and leather, an occasional chain. Well, we're not. We're just ordinary blokes trying to get by." She smiles. "Of course, some of us like to cause a stir—and that's OK too. What we need is a place where we can be ourselves, be safe—" She closes her eyes and talks on, as if expressing an interior vision. "We need a *bar*, don't we? Some place we could gather and get high and meet new people? Course, I don't know where they'd come from around here, but if any were passing through, they could stop by. I think this coalition is going to be my thing, and I'm going to have a place in it and not get pushed out. Do you know," she says, sitting up abruptly and looking at us all, "how when you mention gay things, straight people will just look you in the eye and pretend they didn't hear you? You think you've lost your voice because they look at you and seem to be hearing you but nothing happens, the expressions on their faces don't change and they don't *answer*? What we need in the coalition is to make certain that we hear each other—"

I stretch out in the chair opposite her, my hands behind my head, listening to her talk of hope. Thursday night at the climax of the Democratic convention, the delegates nominated Walter Mondale to be the presidential candidate and Geraldine Ferraro—the first woman in the history of America—to be the vice presidential candidate. Friday morning's paper quotes from Mondale's acceptance speech about Geraldine Ferraro: "I've deepened my admiration for someone who shares these same values. Her immigrant father loved our country. Her widowed mother sacrificed for her family, and her own career is an American classic: Doing your work, earning your way, paying your dues, rising on merit." It is the American dream. It is Lincoln, and it is the Statue of Liberty, and American politicians know how to use the words, which come easily to the tongue. It is "your tired, your poor," and the Ferraro herself refers explicitly to it: "Tonight, the daughter of an immigrant from Italy has been chosen to run for vice president of the new land my father came to love." Tell me about that. Tell *Bernie* about that. Your tired, your poor, sure. Not, however, your *queer*. Not your *cocksuckers*. They're sent home on the next plane by the Immigration Service for being fucking perverts. Don't Come To America!

On Sunday the *New York Times* prints the article by Michael Allsworthy under the headline, "Murder of Homosexual Man Disturbs Calm of Cardiff, Maine." It is what I expected. It opens with three paragraphs on the town: It is cute, small, on the edge of the great forest, and has not had a murder in twelve years. Then there is a paragraph introducing the three boys—two from "nice, middle-class homes" who have been charged with murder. The principal says that he is "all the more upset because this kind of thing is not supposed to happen here." Cardiff is a nice little town. Bernie is flamboyantly homosexual and moved here two months ago. There are several paragraphs on the memorial service, quotations from me on Bernie's flamboyant appearance, including my address at the university, and then several smarmy paragraphs which conclude the

Derek

article quoting from the high school principal: "They are really good boys, they just weren't successful in school. They had no direction. But I don't think they went down to the bridge to kill anybody. I don't think they tried to kill him because he was gay, just because he was weak, like tormenting a drunk." There is no mention of the quotation from the police report: *We jumped a faggot and threw him in the river.* And no mention of the Bishop of Portland.

"If you expected it, why are you angry? You knew he wasn't listening to you. He had come to town with his agenda. You feel you should have spoken better, convinced him somehow to look around him at reality. And since he didn't, you feel you've failed. Why feel bad? His ignorance is chosen. The power of the *Times* to distort the truth is so great that you're powerless against it. What do you propose to do, write a letter?"

Throw a bomb. It is Dana. I say goodbye, hang up the phone, and lower myself onto the bed. I rest my arm across my forehead. Dana's intelligence is too cool for these hot times, and I am angry at her, which is not what I want.

It is five o'clock in the afternoon, and the phone rings. The voice on the other end is male, tentative, unfamiliar:

"Is this Derek Dellesandro?"

"Yes."

"Ah, did you grow up in Baton Rouge, Louisiana?"

"Yes—"

"Ah, this is Nicholas—"

He is about to go on, but I know the name and recognize, now, the voice. "I know you, Nicky. We were counselors together at Wiscassett—"

"Is it really you?" he asks.

"It's really me." We went to the same camp for three or four years and then were counselors there.

"Derek, I've been in love with you for eighteen years."

I laugh, and then I laugh and laugh and laugh. "You sweet guy. Why didn't you tell me?"

"I didn't know you were gay!"

"I couldn't tell anybody, then—" I met Nicky when we were thirteen. "I didn't know, and then I couldn't tell—" He doesn't ask me if I was in love with him. I am moved by his generous nature. He asks me if he can come to visit, and later when I am lying in bed

306

alone, just before I have to get up to get to the theater, I think of what it might have been like if we had been able to make it with each other when we were thirteen. What stopped us? What prevented me from going into the woods with him and, behind some tree, lifting his t-shirt and running my hands over his chest? What law stopped us that, by repealing it, would have let me find my way to his lips?

On Monday night at the second coalition meeting, there are only half as many people as there were last week, about a hundred of us, noticeably fewer men. The room is still hot. People mill about. They know each other better this time, and the groups divide between men and women. People are no longer looking for direction. They have their own agenda. As soon as we start, I am asked about the *Times* article.

"How did he chose you?" the woman asks, standing at her seat on the side.

"I think he got my name from the paper after the coalition meeting last week."

"I don't want you to be a spokesperson for me—" She is sullen, resentful, and, I expect, feels she is cornered. She is brave to challenge me—or anyone on this podium—from the floor.

"I didn't mean to speak for you. I spoke for myself."

"Now wait." Mickey is on his feet. "I think we need a spokesperson. I think Derek would be a terrific—" Mickey always defends the *status quo*.

"We can't have one spokesperson—"

"Wait, Marybeth—"

Marybeth leaps up, her fingers gripping the back of the seat in front of her, her eyes searching the crowd. "That's too rigid. Each of us has his or her story to tell, and we shouldn't all have to step in line behind one Official Line—"

"Well, look." It's Mickey, and he has seized the floor from Marybeth. He holds it against her will. "That's well and good, but we're getting slaughtered out there. The Cardiff *Sentinel* is not reporting the whole story, and the rest of the media is coming to town with its own agendas. We're being used. They ask one person this, and another person that, and we don't know who has said what, and the effect is the *New York Times* article. Inexplicable violence in small New England town. They use us. This thing has been going on long enough now to see the pattern: Every article has the same set of features. The boys are nice, middle-class boys, Bernie was a flamboyant outsider, the town is horrified, gays are furious. They blame the victim for the murder and then blame us for the unrest. We sound flamboyant and 'outside.' If we are not talking about Bernie's earring, we are sounding crazy. We need to appoint someone who can talk calmly and sensibly to the press about our issues: the gay rights bill, legal issues surrounding the trial, the need for a local ordinance to deal with street violence, the rest of it. Look at the local television stations. Every night they interview another gay person on charging the three boys with murder or manslaughter, or on whether they should be tried as adults, or on whether they should be allowed to plea bargain. Do we really care about what happens to the boys? What's important to us? Is it the boys and getting them tried? Is it making the connection between Bernie's murder and a gay rights bill? Do we want a bar in town, is that our major concern? We ought to find out what we are trying to say—*one thing*—and then let's everybody get in step and say that one thing—"

"Christ! That's so fucking fascist!" somebody screams. The floor erupts again. People leap to their feet and shout and wave their arms. They no longer wait to be called on. They shout at one another like enemies, while I cross my arms across my chest and stare and grind my teeth.

"—say it over and over to the press, and so no matter who they talk to, they'll get the same thing—"

"I can't stand that!" Suzanne is on her feet. "I won't have anything to do with such a fascist fucking idea. Who the fuck do you think we are? The very thing we're fighting for is freedom, the liberty to differ, to be different, to be our unique, individual selves. I'm a dyke, and I don't get in step behind anybody!"

Sally rises. "What should we focus on, Mickey? I'd like to hear."

"For one thing, we could all declare a moratorium on telling any other reporter what Bernie looked like. The gay community is the source of all these quotes in the press about Bernie being so flamboyant, about his earring and his purse and the rest of it. They use that to blame the victim. For another thing, I think the whole trial of the boys is a sideshow, irrelevant to our real interests—"

Deborah, sitting in the back next to Sally, is disturbed. Luke is furious. People come into the debate on different sides or try to take it off in new directions, some of them I know, others are new to me. People drop out, go to the back of the room for coffee, go out to smoke, and then come back to watch or join in again. Jack paces up and down along the rear wall, following the speakers and hating everything he is hearing. I am asked if I would consider being the spokesperson for the coalition, and I say *no, absolutely*. I do say that I will continue to speak for myself to any member of the media that I want to speak to. In the end, the opposition of the women to the idea of a media spokesperson prevents its adoption: We are not to have a president or a vice president or an executive committee, and we are not to have a unified response to the media.

After the meeting, Dana and I sit on the steps of the church. She pats my knee and smiles.

"You're in a bad way."

"Don't patronize me, Dana."

"Sorry. Didn't mean to." She returns to watching the traffic.

"I'm sorry. I'm pissed."

"Things are going to be OK."

"How so?"

"What you see back there happening is the creation of a community. The members are fighting it out, getting to know one another, defining what we are, what we stand for, what we want—"

"What do we stand for?" I think of Jack in my bed.

She shrugs. "I don't know." She thinks for a moment. "One thing. We stand for a kind of inclusive acceptance of people—"

"We're losing the war—"

The people here tonight were almost all familiar. The group we are reaching is getting smaller each meeting. Where are the blacks, the Indians? Where are the men? Where are the working class men? The middle-aged men? Why have I met no doctors, no lawyers at any of these meetings? The coalition is elitist. I've known from the beginning that we weren't going to get the married man down here, or the wife who has gay feelings. We abandoned that constituency at the first. But we're driving away half—more than that—of the people who might have helped us—and themselves—but won't now because they're not politically correct. We have no soaring vision that would give our need some high political significance, and we fight among ourselves about trivia.

At night, three nights a week except Monday, I play Orsino in *Twelfth Night*. I am a soldier in *Henry V* the other three nights. On Monday I am co-moderator of the coalition. Three days a week at eleven I teach a class at the university in Shakespearean Theater. I ponder questions, driving up and down the interstate between the U and Cardiff. I think Antonio, the sea captain who brings Sebastian ashore, who lends him all the money he has, who puts his life in extreme danger in order to be near Sebastian, and who says, "my love I gave him," would be a fine part to play, even if a small one. He gets to engage in sword play three times and then, at the end, to come on stage and watch Sebastian give himself away to Olivia. The man's heart is breaking open there in front of the entire audience, and he's not allowed to express it in words! But the worst of it is that nobody in the audience is watching him. The audience is engaged in the affairs of the Great Ones on stage, the big parts, the loves between Olivia and Orsino and Sebastian and Viola, required by the geometry of the play. They don't notice this single man up left, tears streaming down his cheeks. This, while they watch the little shit tell Olivia he'll marry her, whom he hasn't seen but for 90 seconds.

My brown friend meets me on the stairs on Tuesday and joins me at the glass wall where we watch the students crossing campus.

"I don't understand, Derek, what gays want. The boys who did it have been arrested. They are going to be tried. It's being treated like any other murder case. It's not being swept under the rug. What do you want? What do gays want?"

The politicization of sex. The translation of sex into a series of issues which can be laid before the electorate—or their representatives—for a vote. Eight years ago the question of whether homosexuality was a mental illness was so far politicized that the American Psychological Association, instead of running controlled scientific studies on an issue of science, had to vote the question up or down. Now, on an immensely larger scale, we propose to take the most intimate moments of our lives and present them to the electorate for their judgment. How did sex become the subject of political debate?

How is it that the whole country is not merely laughing at this? Why are there not scientists writing furiously, sociologists publishing, all saying, this is absurd.

All during the week after the *Times* article, I get letters in the mail: "Dear Sir: Please allow me to introduce myself. I am a gay man who lives on Long Island. I am 76 years old, and I read about you and about the effort of the Cardiff Area Coalition of Gays, Lesbians, and Straights in the *Times* on Sunday." The handwriting is thin and tremulous, as if the whole thing were seen from under water. *I think it is a terrible thing that young Bernard Mallett was thrown into the water from that bridge by those young hooligans. In 1925, when I was 17, boys often chased us if they thought we were 'that way,' and they would throw things at us. Sometimes it was quite dangerous to be out. I was a slight boy, and I was no match for rough boys who played football. I had a friend. His name was Lewis Zimmerman. He and I used to take the ferry to Coney Island in the summer. We were together seven years, though we never lived together. He died when boys chased him and threw rocks. Of course, the truth was never reported in the paper, for all they said was that he 'died as the result of injuries sustained in a fall.' I didn't visit him in the hospital. I pretended that I didn't care because nobody knew we loved each other. My sorrow was very difficult to hide.*

There were no organizations to protect us then, and we didn't dare march down the street. I don't know what would have happened! I didn't begin to accept my homosexuality until I was in my forties. Things are much better for you now than they were for us then. We had dear Senator McCarthy then, you know.

This is my first letter to counter the political rhetoric out of San Francisco. There are short notes enclosing checks for the coalition, and one from a woman who is a member of an organization called "Parents of Gays" in Brooklyn, and another from a Unitarian Minister in Pennsylvania. There is also a longer, typewritten letter on onionskin from Bank Street in the Village. *Dear Mr. Dellesandro: I have just read of what is happening in Cardiff. Accept my sympathies and understanding. When I was young, I knew I was 'queer,' and I had a couple of friends who were too, but we didn't talk about it. What a waste it all was! We were twenty years old and healthy and attractive, and we were all virgins and afraid even to mention to each other what we were, though of course we all knew. In 1955 they both killed themselves. There was simply no place for them here in this country which calls itself decent and moral and law-abiding and respectable. One got in a car in a closed garage. Two weeks later the other slashed his wrists. I didn't go to either funeral.*

I went to Europe and lived and worked. In my generation of homosexuals, we all hated ourselves. We were all in therapy forever, and most of us were alcoholics. 'Show me a happy homosexual, and I'll show you a gay corpse.' When gay liberation began to take hold, I began to feel different. I was living in London, and I marched in the marches, and shouted the slogans and carried a sign that said "GAY IS GOOD," even though by that time I was 53, older than all the kids, and I had wasted my whole youth on guilt.

I came back to America in 1973, and things seemed much better then. But something is happening now: Recently some boys driving along the street—in the Village, of all places—hung out of their car window and yelled, 'Fuck you, Faggots,' and I couldn't help but think what would have happened to them if they had done this in Harlem. Some black men would have jerked them out of the car and put an end to it. All the gay men on the street just stood there and suffered the children's abuse.

A few days ago, a young straight man came up to me in the street and asked me, 'Do you want to suck a big dick?' He wasn't being seductive, of course. I pretended I neither saw him nor heard him. This disarmed him, and he went on his way.

It's depressing. Discouraging. Here it is the Nuclear Age, the Space Age, and things like skin color and sexual preference and gender are still so important to people.

One doesn't know what to do.

He signs it, "Yours in the Struggle—" I read this letter and imagine myself on the street corner in the Village when the boys stop for a red light and, seeing all of us on the sidewalk, roll down the windows and lean out and yell, "Fuck you, faggots!" I feel a flush of shame. It has to do with being a man and whether I am enough of a man, and whether it is ever possible to be enough of a man, when I let them get away with their abuse, and I am ashamed to look in the eye the other people on the street who have seen the boys abuse me and escape.

On Thursday Deborah calls to tell me that last night at the school committee meeting, Richard Severance introduced a motion to the committee which has two parts: the supervisor of the Department of Schools will issue a policy statement on tolerance of divergent lifestyles, and the faculty of the high school will reserve certain times during the term for classroom discussion of tolerance. The meeting room was filled with gays and lesbians from the coalition who came to support the measure and with opponents who were alerted by pastors and other people who don't like queers. The measure was tabled. A committee was appointed to study it and report back next month and a full discussion of it scheduled for the meeting after next. In October there will be a vote. I don't know what to do with this. It is rational, measured, a considered response to our predicament. But it leaves me cold. What does tolerance have to do with the violence we have experienced this week?

On Wednesday and Thursday and Friday and Saturday, I get more letters in the mail, at the university or the Unitarian Church, from gay men in their sixties and seventies, who remember the fifties and McCarthy and the suicides of their friends, the stifling, suffocating respectability. They have the tone of those already dead speaking to those reprieved, and they carry the acid message of envy. Yet there is also something extraordinarily brave about them. They are letters home from the front: They describe events but never wounds and have the same resistance to arousing emotions. Less is said than is meant.

One man writes, "I taught successfully and with some fear for fourteen years and then changed jobs and was summarily fired from a job after 10 weeks teaching in a Catholic school." He doesn't say where this was or what decade. I wonder why he left to go to the Catholic school. He says, "I work in a simple job today and am trying to live an independent life." The lines suggest a life and a history. This is something I only barely knew before, and never with such concreteness. There has been no biography, no autobiography about a man "summarily" fired from a Catholic school who "has a simple job today." And I am only now beginning to understand the importance of having the biography of such a man. I am going to learn more about homosexual men who have "simple" jobs today and why they have them.

313

Derek

The pile of these letters growing on my bedside table suggests a huge unexplored terrain—mile after mile of rich live things from the animal and vegetable kingdoms in swamps and hot seas and red deserts—which is so near to me that I roar past it in my car and fly over it in planes and don't recognize it. One writer, in passing, says, "When the war was over—." Another mentions growing up in the Mississippi Delta. Another man writes that he holds a political office in his town and, while closeted, feels secure in his office. Why do they write? To set down the way it was so they won't be forgotten. But there is something less personal going on. They add to the communal memory. We are not born into homosexual families, and each of us has to find the homosexual community and the homosexual tradition by ourselves. I stumble on it here, in these letters. They represent riches, an almost completely unevaluated hoard of human experience. These letters demand explication, demand scholarly apparatus of footnotes and bibliography: They ask for a Guide. These letters provide the skeletal forms from which museum reconstructions are made. They should be popularized into romantic novels and become the book for musicals. There should be a section in libraries: History/US/ homosexuals/20th century. They are my past, as well as the letter writers', sent with postage stamps. I read these letters over and over. *These* letters are the ceaseless cries, and they document the failure of the American dream.

Tuesday two weeks ago, the Tuesday after Bernie was murdered, has come to be called Coming-Out Day. July 10, 1984. Looking back on it, everybody realized that they had called somebody to come out to them that day after the memorial service. Mickey came out to his mother that day. I came out to the other members of the cast. Dana went in to the chairperson of her department. Sebastian called his mother. And of course Deborah went to see the school superintendent. Each of us has our coming-out story, coming out with our rage and pride. I am beginning to see that these letters are coming-out stories too. The assault on Bernie was on our sense of ourselves, and coming out has been a way of protecting and preserving our—what?—our integrity, in the face of what amounts to a savage battering. I'm here. *See me as I am* in the face of culture that is both willfully blind and lying.

I call them "coming-out" stories, but the stories are unique, and I am beginning to see there is no way that one person could speak for all of us. The women in the coalition are right about that. No one person could be a "spokesperson" for this rich human experience. No omniscient narrator, no protagonist for this story. What we need are more letters, more voices, more messiness in the coalition, more—is this where I am headed?—more messiness in our culture. A kind of Gothic variety of human experience. Somewhere in this screech and howl of voices, in the din of it, is where we will find ourselves.

My father calls on Friday morning. Since I have not returned his messages left on my answering machine, he has called at an early enough hour to get me still in bed. I lie on my side, Jack in the hollow of my torso, his head resting on my arm, and hold the receiver to my ear:

"How are you?"

"I'm OK." I don't know how to answer him without starting farther back than I can go. "I've been busy. I haven't had time to answer your message—"

"We read about you in the *Times*—"

"He did a job on us—"

"—and we haven't been able to reach you. You haven't answered our messages, and we both feel very distant from you—"

"I have tried—"

"—as if you are trying to keep us out of your life. Your mother has stayed by the phone since Sunday, waiting for a call from you, and now she wants to drive up to see you herself. I have tried to persuade her not to do that until we can talk to you, but I have to say I would like to come myself—" His voice illustrates his anxiety—vocal chords stretched tight with strain—and hovers just this side of demanding that I open up to him. "Are you all right? Are you safe?"

I am not safe. I am assaulted on all sides by violent people, and I become violent. Bernie is dead, and I can't go back to the life I led, the "straight" actor who met his needs in the asshole of every "Sebastian" he met. There are moments when I feel an odd, unfamiliar feeling in my throat and heart which I realize only later is grief: My old life is dead. I am consumed by the conflict I am falling in to. I think of nothing else. I wait for the mail for more letters from the past, and I am driven by the notion that something must be done—some committee formed, some statement issued—and by fear of doing the wrong thing. My classes suffer, and I walk through my role in the shows I'm in. I hardly care. My parents feel a wall between us, and the little, ordinary chores of my day-to-day life go unattended to. The problem is so enormous—the distance between the rhetoric and the reality is so immense—that I am like a runner on a treadmill, exhausted, unable to keep up or to get off. My strength is ineffectual, and between the rhetoric of an Ideal American Republic and the bloody reality of this violent culture, I am paralyzed.

I am trapped by Bernie's death. There is no choice any more. What remains is how: It doesn't much matter that I preserve a private life in the face of this public catastrophe. No private life is worth much if our communal life is being destroyed. Bernie's death has brought the edge of the fire to my doorstep, and I can run now, or I can stay and fight, and it is unclear to me which is which. And yet if we don't maintain a private life—the loves we bear for parents, friends, lovers, the commitments we have to our professions and jobs, to all the intimacies of our existence—the rest, what we gain on the barricades, is worthless.

Late on Friday morning, I am standing in a crowd on the pavement in front of the court house. The sky is a flawless metallic blue, there are hot, high winds and my sweat makes the back of my shirt and my armpits wet. Around me are members of the coalition, walking up and down, carrying signs: "LESBIANS DEMAND JUSTICE" and "HOMOPHOBIA HAS GOT TO GO!" Near us are boys—not *the* boys—who stand with their legs apart and arms folded across their chests, staring and grinning and making jokes among themselves. They spot a person carrying a sign that says, "BERNIE MALLETT WAS MURDERED BY THE PEOPLE OF MAINE!" and call out, "Faggot!" "Queer!" Coalition members yell back, "Murderers!" Men in t-shirts and jeans carry television cameras, focusing first on one group and then the other. A man and a woman, slick professionals dressed for on-camera work, write on pads of paper and sometimes speak directly into the cameras, nodding over their shoulders to the scene behind them. Police move among the crowd, making a heavy, authoritarian presence, hands on their hips or across their chests. Their eyes are covered with mirrored sunglasses, and their faces are greasy with sweat.

Beyond all these are middle-aged middle-class men and women whose bodies are soft with their own virtue, who identified themselves in the courtroom as god-fearing folk come to see justice done. The women, small ladies in summer dresses, pick at the arms of the men or try to engage the police in sharp harangues on the indecency of these people marching around in public.

The judge has delayed, again, a decision on whether the boys must stand trial as adults. There are to be psychiatric evaluations. Now we are on the street, dispersing. All of us wear pink triangles and green buttons that read, "ANOTHER FRIEND OF BERNIE MALLETT." One of the task forces from the coalition ordered them from Boston, and they came this morning. I look for Jack. He is across the crowd talking to Suzanne, who has a sign. I make my way toward them. Suzanne's sign reads, "SEXISM + HOMOPHOBIA = DEATH."

As I come up on them, a boy near Suzanne calls out to her: "Hey, chick!"

She ignores him, continuing to talk to Jack and to hold her sign high.

"Hey, chick! Wanta go somewhere with me?" He grins broadly.

She ignores him.

"Chick! Why're you ignoring me? All you need is a good dick!"

"Fuckoff, kid." It seems absurdly inadequate.

The boy glances at me and then laughs at Suzanne. "Cunt."

People watch, and those who were drifting away come back. Jack is turning red, and he grips his hands by his side. He is going to explode. She tries to talk to him.

"You never been fucked?"

"Shut up, kid."

"Little shit!" She whirls on the kid, her eyes darting around, looking for a place to drop her sign.

"Wait! Don't!"

The cameramen turn their cameras on us, while people yell.

"You're going to rot in Hell!"

"Yuh got AIDS," somebody screams.

I grab at Jack, but he pulls loose and leaps on top of the boy, and then the police are here, pulling them apart.

The kid's face is red and distorted, and he is breathing heavy, his chest going up and down. "You suck cock?" he screams at Jack.

Marybeth is coming in from my right, and over on the side, I see Deborah and Sally.

"Keep your hands off our children!" I whirl around and see a thin, blond woman my age, her face red with screaming.

"Jack, you'll make things worse—" I see the angry faces, wet with sweat and pulled into grimaces with anger. "Suzanne—" I can finally touch her, and I grab her shoulder, pulling her back from the boy. "Don't. Leave him alone!" I shake her shoulder. "Get hold of yourself!"

She turns on me and recognizes me. She beats on my chest. "You're a fucking coward, Derek!" Tears cover her cheeks. "You're a fucking coward!"

I search her face. I flush cold with fear. "Shut up, Suzanne. Grow up. This is not what we're after!"

"What the fuck! Don't you see where you are?" She throws her arm out to encompass the mass of angry people.

Suddenly a woman is hitting me on my back. I hear people yelling and screaming.

A policeman, grinning, blows a piercing whistle and shouts, "Little order here, little order here!"

"Shoot 'em all!"

"You're a coward, you haven't got the balls—"

"Hah! Fucking queers!"

"Oh, please." It's Deborah. She reaches out to Suzanne and then to me, and then she grasps her hands in front of her breasts. The whistle screams.

"Get *out* of my life!" Suzanne screams at her.

"All she needs is a good fuck from a big dick—" Laughter runs through the crowd.

"I won't let you oppress me any longer!" She throws herself on top of the kid and carries him to the ground before the policeman can intervene.

"And you, my friend, you're a fucking pansy!" It is a low voice speaking to me right in my ear, and it's a familiar voice: It's Jack!

I am not smart, slow at seeing big things. I wanted a good part with one good scene—Macduff, say, weeping for his children—and a pretty boy in my bed. And I've got this instead!

I go about my business—I'm stiff all the time, you know?" He doesn't answer me. "I keep thinking every moment that somebody—I'm talking to this guy about this piece of property down in Brookline, and I'm thinking that he's going to break into what we're saying and he's going to say—. He's just going to come from way out in left field—. And the trouble is, there's no way to prepare for, to get ready for it, to steel yourself, and so I'm always wondering, while I'm listening to him, whether it's going to come from the right or the left, or whether I'm making all this up, that it's not going to come right now, it's going to come in twelve minutes, when I'm not expecting it. I'll be thinking about the traffic or getting the oil changed or whether I turned off the AC—" He smiles, just barely perceptibly. "—or thinking about whether I'm paying enough estimated taxes, and thinking about the paint peeling and making my house look like shit, and then, there it is, he'll turn to me and say—I mean, I'll be thinking, am I already dying of AIDS? And he says, out of the blue, *Are you gay*?

"Why am I so afraid?" I sit leaning forward, my elbows on my knees, in a chair upholstered in a big brown plaid. The room is small and hot, although it's still early afternoon. The whole room is tones of brown, including him, who sits slouched down in his chair beside his desk. He is a kindly-looking man, tanned, long brown and gray hair, heavy. He sits in his chair as if he has grown there, a stalagmite, his strength accreted over centuries. His facial expression suggests he ruminates, but I can't tell whether he is thinking or dreaming. His elbows rest on the arms of his chair, and he looks at me, his chin on his chest, through the arch formed by his fingers.

"And what do you say?

"I don't know what I'm doing to make him think—. How do they know? I think it's weird. It's not like we were black!" The ends of his mouth move up in a microscopic smile. "I'm careful when it comes to clothes. When I go to the store to get a suit—. I study the way my boss looks at work. I only pick out something, these brown wingtipped oxfords, if other men wear them. I don't want to be weird. I don't wear anything but white shirts, even when other people are into blue and stripes—

"I've got this anxiety that the person I'm talking to—this woman across from me in the restaurant with frosted tips or the receptionist at my lawyer's—that this person is thinking, 'This jerk is gay, and he's trying to pass—' I'm telling myself that this person is not thinking of me at all—. Or certainly not thinking of me being gay or straight, and you know what? Nobody has ever said to me, 'I think you're gay.' But I think it's coming someday, when I don't expect it and when it'll hurt the most, destroy—. Have you ever wondered about something? A guy gets run over by a train and loses both his legs, and you wonder, How did he stand the pain?—" He shifts in his chair, moving the weight of his shoulders from one arm to another. "It'll destroy—." Or is it so much that you don't stand it, that it obliterates every other thought, every other feeling—? My dad'll be there to hear, or maybe—. But it doesn't matter who hears because whoever it is will be the worst person in my life to hear.

"For the last two weeks, it's been worse. Every day there's something in the paper, and I can't escape it. You glance down and you see the paper in his trash can, and the article the paper was turned to when he threw it away had a headline, 'Gays Plan Agenda,' and I think, when he turns to talk to me, that's what he'll say: *Are you gay?* I'll be trapped, my tongue dry in my mouth and my heart pounding. There's nothing to say. What do you say when—.

"I want to say, *I am not gay!*

"The kid was thrown off the bridge—. When the kid was thrown off the bridge, then you couldn't not pay—. I think I've spent all my life trying to act like it wasn't happening, this storm of laughter all around you, because you know it was only happening inside me, the way I felt, it wasn't happening on the front pages of the newspaper, and now I get up in the morning and—I feel like every morning I get up and everything I've spent my whole life trying to hide is on the front page of the newspaper, with pictures and short headlines. I'm in the middle of that dream again, where I'm naked—. Do you remember that one?" He doesn't answer. "I'm naked, and they all know it already, and there's nowhere I can hide." Where can I go?

"I was driving down Arlington Street the night they were all out, and I drove past them, watching them walk down the hill toward the bridge, carrying their candles—. I walk down that hill at two, three o'clock in the morning most times, looking over my shoulder to see if he's following me—. And in front to see if there're people watching, cops going to arrest us—. It seemed weird to see all of them walking down the same hill carrying candles and the trucks with television cameras driving along beside them. They held candles, and their heads were up, looking straight ahead, while the cameras got them.

"I say *this* time I'm not going up there—. I'm not trapped by this—. I can live my life—. Do you believe me?" He is motionless. "Do you think I am a fearless man?" I pause. "I am fearless in obtaining the thing I'm obsessed about—. I am not afraid to go up on the hill at night to find a boy. What's there to be afraid of? A gang of queerbashers to beat me to death—. *They* were just boys. A boy! And find ten years after I've forgotten the boy that he has given me AIDS, that he has given me the chance to answer the question, 'Was this a love worth dying for?' Is this where it's going to come from? Out of the dark, out of some beautiful boy's beautiful brown eyes? What if I merely find the police, shining a light in my eyes and grinning and taking me back to the station and charging me with an unmistakable charge: *Public Indecency.* What man can survive that in this town? What life would there be for me after that appeared in the paper? I have courage. I hold my life in my hands every night I go out on the hill just for sex. But you put me in the daylight—. Put me on the street in the center of town, waiting for a light, in front of Dominic's, and ask me if I'm gay, and my courage would collapse like a blown tire. Ask me to tell Mother, an aged lady of 74—. I can walk over broken glass, but I can't tell her, the guardian of our decency!" He smiles again, that expression that exists only in barely measurable difference from the frown his face usually assumes. My hours here are measured by these small signs.

"I see them on television, screaming at the reporters, carrying their signs. They're young, vulgar kids—their language!— How have they gotten beyond the need to be decent! They don't care! SEXISM + HOMOPHOBIA = DEATH! They stand up before the whole world—. Don't they have mothers they're afraid of?

"Tell me about pain. I can't go without sex, without—. I go without sex for a week, I stop being able to concentrate. I get irritable. I can't go—. I can go without sex. I've done it dozens of times. I'm in Europe, and I don't know where to go. I was in the Army and was afraid. There've been times when I was so wrapped up in my work I didn't pay attention. I was tired, and the weather was bad, and the hill was too far to go. Sex isn't—. I mean, getting it in and getting it out again—. Find a boy with a clean ass. Getting it off isn't all that important in the grand scale of things. Think of eating and sleeping. What, two days? two weeks? you're dead if you don't sleep. Sex? It's embroidery. Stiffens the fabric—.

"Why should I have to go without sex? Why should I have to give up what nobody else in the world has to give up? Sex ought to be like taking a leak, right? Thoughtless. You're sitting at your desk, reading this book and then taking notes on this pad of paper, and then you put your pencil in the book so it won't close and stand up and go to the john, and it is only when you're shaking your dick off and pulling it back inside your pants that you stop thinking about what you're reading and think—." His face has assumed again the closed expression.

"I've read all the stuff in the paper about the gay community and how they're coming out and making all these demands—. They demand justice. They want a change in the laws. They want to be treated like Negroes. I stood in the crowd this morning at the court house—. I was walking down the hill from my insurance man to where I had parked my car, and I saw all this going on in front of the court house. I didn't go, you understand, to be there. I just found myself in the crowd, looking over the shoulders of the people in front of me. In the middle were a little group of gay people carrying signs. There were all these townspeople yelling at them, and they yelled back. They didn't care what people thought or how they looked! This kid was yelling at this girl—.

"I think, what does this have to do with my life? I go to work every morning, and I have a job and a decent salary. I have my boat.

"What I really thought was how afraid I was. People would wonder why I was there. They would wonder what business I had watching these gay people. They would even think I was gay. I didn't want to seem to be watching. So I looked and tried not to seem to be looking, you know? I'd look for a second and then look away.

"I thought, I ought to be out there with them. If I had any balls I'd be there carrying a sign. I'd make sure boys weren't going to mess with me. I thought, I could be there carrying a sign. I could stand up and say, *I'm gay too*. I'm a man with a decent job and a decent salary, and I've got my friends, the guys I play handball with at the gym, and I do my volunteer work. I could say I'm gay too. I could say, It doesn't matter who I sleep with. Sex is only part of who—. Sex is only part of what I am. But if I said I was gay, I wouldn't be any of those things anymore. I'd be a minority. I'd be a special interest. I'd be like those people on TV in San Francisco last week dressed up like nuns. Every time people looked at me, they'd see a *fairy*. I wouldn't be a man anymore.

"I looked again, around the crowd, and I saw this little skinny kid, a pretty kid, you know? I'd seen him before on the hill. Christ, I'd *had* him before! And there he was walking around carrying this sign, and I thought—. You know how sometimes you're in a place where you think something might go wrong. You're walking down a dark street, and you're looking at the doorways to see if there's anybody hiding there who's going to jump you, and then—. You know how sometimes whatever the danger is comes at you from a place you didn't expect, weren't looking for it—? You're afraid a rock is going to fall on you, and you get run over by a car? I thought the boy might recognize me. He might yell out, 'I know you, you're queer too! Why don't you have balls and come out with us and fight—.'

"I turned around and ducked my head and walked up the hill from the court house again and walked all around the block behind— I was in the sun, sweating—down by the stream, back to my car, and I didn't know which I was most afraid of—. I was afraid of both of them! The gay people walking around with their signs and the straight people yelling at them!

"I'm a respectable man, and I never wanted anything from my life but the chance to do my duty. I wanted to have my job and pay my taxes and go to church on Sundays—. I like the stained glass windows there, you know? I like to spend Sundays at the lake with my boat—and to get the respect of the other people in my town. A man is known by his friends, isn't that true? Who are my friends? When I was in college, I'd bring a friend home for the weekend and introduce him to my dad. I'd say, He's the president of the fraternity, and my dad would smile. He wanted to know what my friends' dads did for a living, and if they were respectable people. I have worked hard.

"I have this dream sometimes that I'm going into a meeting, a business meeting, and I'm not prepared. I've got my hand on the door and I know all these highpowered types are sitting around the table waiting for me, and I don't even know what the meeting is supposed to be about."

He shifts in his chair, moving his weight from one buttock to the other, and resumes staring at me under the little tent of his fingers. I want to find a way to explain to him how I feel, find the words which will be the exact equivalent of the electrical storm in my brain, so he can show me how I can shut off the current, bring on the rain, dissipate this heat. I grow tired. I stop trying to show him how I feel. I want to get him to respond somehow, anyhow. As he sits there in immobile silence, I try to convince him that I exist. The "cure" I search for, I think, could be effected by making myself heard, by getting an unmistakable signal from him that he has heard me. "What I want people to know about me is what I am: I pay my bills. I have never defaulted on a loan. I have three credit cards, and I own a house with two baths. I go to church, and I give five percent of my after-tax income. I have a boat that sleeps four. My mother always said my father was a 'tower of strength.' She called him a 'pillar in the community.' I am on the library committee and the board of the United Way. I am invited everywhere, and I always give wedding presents—." I want him to nod, now, and I wait. "—and there's nothing important about me other than those things. But I feel those things are never enough, are they? I *look* like a tower of strength!

"I've been working all my life, and what I have is never enough—. It's like I can't catch up, you know, with the rabbit? I run 'till I'm exhausted, and I can't catch up. There's the other guy in front of me, and I see the finish line, and I try to catch up with him, but he's more fleet. His feet barely touch the ground. He flies over the track. I'm horse and rider too, and I never stop using the whip. Sex is not the most important thing in my life. The 'other guy' always seems to have it easy, up there ahead of me, running so easy, wings on his feet. Is that really the way it is? This boy drowning means I can't go anywhere in this town. I go by Mother's, and she has the television on, and I see these heads lit from the back so they can't be identified, and I wonder, *Is she going to kiss me?* Is it going to come now?

"This boy drowning means there's no escape. You have to declare yourself, and anything I declare—. Why couldn't you have made me one or the other? I'm sitting in the board room of the bank, looking out across the stream at the hill rising up over there, and I think, I'm here in the daytime—.

"Everything I've ever done has gone putrid. I see it in my mother's eyes. Even if I weren't afraid to get married, what woman would have me? People forget my name—. What is there to say? What can I say to justify my life? I keep thinking, all the time, in my mind, of explanations. I'm walking down the street, and I'm saying, 'But what you don't understand is that I have this terrible sickness, and that's what's made me the way—.' But I never have the chance to make an explanation. I know what's going on around me. People write me off, assume I'm a cipher, a weirdo, and then they go on about—. You know how they never give you the chance to explain yourself? I'm standing in Mother's living room, and I'm thinking of this explanation, and then I know that when it comes, when she says, *Why aren't you married?* it's going to come from a direction I'm not expecting, and I'll be caught with nothing on but guilt. And no words to explain myself.

"They say it's self-hatred. I look for something about me that I hate—my thinning hair, the way I am in a meeting. I wish I were more forceful, more like a leader. My mind is confused. I can't think things through. I can't start here and end up there. Everything breaks off in the middle. Nothing lasts. Everything gets—. Sometimes I get through, and I give the kid some money, and I zip up my pants, and when I'm walking down the hill toward my car, I'm feeling wet—. My sweat has gone cold, and I'm feeling clammy, and I feel like I've just thrown away—. I feel I've just shown how weak—. Does any of this make any sense? I feel, like, worthless. And I can't figure out what's wrong—. I have this ache, and I have these words, and I can't get at the ache with the words." I am exhausted, and I've done the best I can, and that's not enough. What is to become of me? I stare around me at the brown room, at the closed door, the shuttered and curtained windows, the lowered lamps. He looks at me from under his raised brows, waiting for me to go on. I look at my watch. I still have twenty minutes. "It's around my heart—."

Marybeth

On Friday nights we always come to Momma's house for supper. Momma lives on the second floor of a triple-decker on Passadumkeag Avenue above the stream, where she has lived since we were little. The furniture is oak, there are snapshots of children, framed, on the walls everywhere, and there's enough room for all of us, even beds enough to sleep us all, if we don't mind spilling over the edges: me, Frances and Van, her husband, and their three kids, Arnold, my biggest brother and his wife, Helen, and their children, and Seth, my middle brother, who isn't married yet but who has the face and temperament of an angel. My brother got married out of high school, and his wife went to business college, and the first big purchase they made after they got married was a boat which was faster than anything anybody else had. When we get together Friday nights, it's a lot of noise and children running around, no different from Christmas. The men talk cars and politics, and the women talk children and food. Frances and Helen always seem to have those big gloves on for getting things out of the oven, and the house has the warm, heavy, moist smell of food.

But instead of going to Momma's tonight, I'm pulling a shift at Dominic's. Marcella, who usually works Friday nights, wanted to go skinny dipping with her boyfriend, and I told her I'd take her shift. Marcella is hot—dark skin, black hair, southern European. She has an easy way about her, both with her boyfriends and with me, and she doesn't care what other people do as long as she gets hers. She laughs a lot, never asks questions, and I have no idea what's she's like. The night shift is from five to one. At supper people are happy, going to a movie or something, and you can see it in their eyes. They expect something to happen. The mood is confident, upbeat. Later, at eleven or twelve, people drift in, and there's something else entirely going on. Some come in looking for hamburgers after the show, a few. But mainly there're the single men who come in and order coffee and smoke cigarettes. They stare at the plate glass windows which are black and reflect all of us inside. They don't say much. But the point of what they do say is they want you to notice them, admit that they're there, and I do that. There are some regulars—an old man about fifty—and every night when I say, "You're looking good tonight, George," he beams. If I forget, he asks me how he looks.

He's old, short and thin, his skin hangs on his cheekbones. His white hair sticks out in all directions. "You're looking terrific tonight, George. Have a good day?" He tells me how it was. We both know it's a lie, but he wants me to say, "I know you're there, George. How is it with you there?" I do it for him. It seems like a small thing.

Then, when it's all over and everybody's gone and I've cleaned up and then set up for tomorrow, I get to hitchhike home. Summer and winter, walking home at one-thirty in the morning through the dark streets, the only sound you can hear is your own footsteps and your own thoughts. I like to think about my life and how it's a paradigm for a certain kind of woman. There's pain in the world: Nobody knows how much George has been through. I like to think that at one-thirty in the morning, all of that's over with and everybody can sleep until tomorrow, when we can start the struggle again.

It's eight-thirty, and the end of the rush. I have only two tables left—a couple, a family of four. Tonight, just before I came to work, Mother called. Her voice is hoarse. She told me they're going to celebrate Frances' birthday tonight at her house. She said she'd miss me. I wipe up some tables and decide to check all the salt and pepper shakers. I walk around the room, picking each one up and shaking some out in my hand, putting the ones that need refilling in the big pocket of my apron. Back in the kitchen, I hear Dominic knocking pots around. Four and a half hours to go.

The couple are still eating their meal. They must be in their thirties somewhere, and she talks to him in a low voice through lips that don't expose much of her teeth. I walk around the room, wiping tables, seeing them as if they were a sculpture in a museum, from all sides. As she talks, she is watching him, except for the moment it takes to spear something else on her fork, and he keeps his head down, cutting and getting it on his fork and getting it in. He nods and seems to listen. I wipe tables and study them, the way she leans into him and he pulls back: She looks at him, and he looks at his food, his hands holding his knife and fork as he slices the red meat.

Mother tries. She tells me the news of Frances and her husband and the children. Van has been made manager of the clothing store. He used to keep the books, and now he's going to have to buy all new clothes because now he's going to be meeting the public. Then she says, "Tell me about yourself, Marybeth." She gave me the message years ago that she wants me to be married. Every sentence about my future began, "When you get married—." I was about nine, and I was going to sleep one night. She sat on the bed next to me talking, her hand on the sheet next to my shoulder. I said, when I grew up I always wanted to live with her, and she said, "Oh, Marybeth, when you grow up, you'll get married, and you'll want your own place." And now I see the hurt in her eyes.

Women get married. I think my mother loves me. She doesn't love my not being married. She loves Frances being married. I need to talk about the problems I'm having with Cynthia—I think they're normal for two people in a relationship this short a time—but it's all foreign to Momma, and I don't want to talk to a person who'd rather have me talking about a man.

The family are finishing their meal, and the man signals for me. I walk around the tables toward him. He is tall and red and weather-beaten from the sun. His blond hair is closely cut.

I smile, then I say, "What can I get you?"

"How about some desert, folks?" he says, speaking to his family. His wife beams. There are two children, about six and eight, a boy and a girl.

"Some pie?" Pie is our specialty here. Big sticky gooey slices of the stuff.

"That sounds *fine*," the man says without consulting the rest of them.

"We have pecan pie, chocolate chiffon pie, apple pie, cherry pie." They stare at me as I reel it off. Then they all look at the father, who has never yet looked at any of them.

"Pecan—," he begins.

The lady declines, shaking her head, although he wasn't looking at her and couldn't see.

"Three of them. And coffee for me."

I am tolerated in my family. I think they love me, so they tolerate the way I am. They tolerate my feminism. They tolerate my lesbianism. They tolerate Cynthia, though Momma's never invited her to her house. I make my way through the empty tables, my tray with their dishes on my shoulder, back to the kitchen to get the pie and the coffee. Dominic looks up when I come in. He's a lot older than me, big and fat, and he never talks. Going into the kitchen is like going into a cave and finding two shining eyes staring at you.

329

I carry the tray loaded with the dishes and the coffee on my shoulder, and I set it down on a nearby table and serve the desserts. The children squabble over theirs, and the mother tries to make peace. Marriage and children are so central to the way most people think of themselves that, when they look at us, we seem weird, thin, weightless, even though a lot of us have been married and have children. I give the couple their check, and then I go back and sit down by the kitchen door.

I once told a woman that I was a lesbian, and she said, "I don't care what you are, I love you and I want to be your friend and to have you be mine!" She wanted to be tolerant. But she was saying she didn't want to know what I was. Loving someone means caring what they are. I'd like to go back now and ask her, *Then how do you love me, if you don't care what I am?* Besides, gay people are different from straight people in more ways than just the gender of the person they have sex with. They've had four thousand years of oppression to deal with for one thing, and that's no small thing either.

The whispering couple is leaving. They left a ten to cover a $9.80 bill, and another dollar for a tip. She walks through the door first, pulling the collar of a windbreaker up around her face. She stares at the ground. His hands are pushed hard into his pants pockets, his eyes are slits and he stares straight ahead. I clear their table and carry things back to the kitchen, pushing the door open behind me with my buns, dropping the plates and glasses and silverware into the nickel sink with a clatter.

By the time I am back in the dining room, the family are ready for their check. The man is signaling in an authoritative manner, without smiling. I go through the tables toward him. I wait for his question—"Can we have the check?"—before I pull the slip off the pad and give it to him. The mother has already stood up and is herding the children toward the door while he pulls out his wallet and counts out bills and change.

When they are gone, the place is quiet. I put myself through the U working here at nights and going to classes in the daytime. Sometimes the other way around. I've done my reading here. I've read all the feminists' books, and I started reading the lesbian books a couple of years ago: Judy Grahn, *Queen of Wands* and *She Who* and *Common Woman*. I found *Coming to Power* about lesbian S&M and discovered that I wasn't alone there either. Gertrude Stein and

Djuna Barnes—but I got tired reading between the lines—and I read all of Rita Mae Brown's books: I've just finished *Sudden Death*. Jane Bowles, *My Sister's Hand in Mine*. I've read May Sarton and Jane Rule and Ginny Vida's *Our Right to Love*. And last year I started reading Emma Goldman. I keep a book of hers in my backpack now, all the time. I've been able to do all this because I've been a waitress, and I can support myself and at the same time teach myself about the place of women in our culture and political system. Because waiting is a skill you can take with you when it comes time to move on, it gives you freedom. They can fire me for being a dyke, but I can get just as good a job down the road later today. Of course I like the atmosphere of Dominic's, shabby, run-down, basically friendly, real. Gold flecks in the formica. It doesn't throw up decor as a way of controlling the patrons. Nobody tries to control me here, anyway.

George comes in. He makes his way to his table, his eyes on the ground. He walks as if he were still stiff from old wounds. I take him a cup of coffee.

"How're you, George?"

He looks up at me and smiles, his face breaking up into pieces. The smile costs him, and he's doing it for me.

"Better. *Much better*."

"You're looking good."

"Thanks. I thought you'd say that," he says and grins. He takes a deep breath, the air making sounds in his lungs. "I think I do too."

Then he drifts away, his eyes on the black pane and on our reflection superimposed on the city square beyond us.

"Call when you want some more." I leave him. I always say that, and he never does. He doesn't have enough wind to call across this room.

I sit at the table next to the kitchen door and watch George at the windows. I don't ask George about his life. He seems to like his privacy: He's always alone. I wonder where his family is and if it would be painful for him if I asked him. Do they know he is here this way? Could they all have died and left him?

Some people come in for coffee and danish to go, and I get their money and make change, and then I take coffee to the old man. George doesn't look up. It is ten o'clock and then it is ten-thirty, and I pass coffee again, and then the door opens and Jack comes in. His black hair is plastered down on his forehead from sweat. He wears shorts and a tank top, and he looks like he's just come from the gym. He drops into the chair across from me. I haven't seen him since this morning when we had the fight at the court house. His facial expression hasn't changed since he came through the door—a steady scowl—and when his eyes meet me they look at me the same way they look at the furniture.

"Coffee?"

I get him coffee.

"What's up?"

He looks around the room. He doesn't care what's here or who's here, and his eyes don't tarry on anything. Jack has never gotten over growing up into a big man. He occupies his body as if he had borrowed it.

"Mickey says the boys are going to get off."

"How does he know?"

He shrugs. "I don't know. I didn't talk to him. Claire says that's what he says."

"Where've you been?"

"The movies."

He wants me to ask him so I do: "What's on for later?"

"I'm going down and meet Derek after his play. We have a date." That's what he wanted to tell me. He's been seeing Derek since right after Bernie died. Everybody talks about it. He isn't content with it, though. "Do you like him?"

He looks away, around the room, and through the black glass into the street. He shrugs. "I guess."

I laugh. "Everybody says you're in love."

"Everybody can go fuck themselves."

"Jack." Then I say, "You're beautiful together." He is quiet for a while, contemplating that. His confusion shows in the way he looks around the room and then flexes his arms out in front, his fingers laced together, and stares into his coffee cup. I think he doesn't know how to feel satisfaction without having defeated someone to achieve it.

"What about more coffee?"

I get the pot and pour his cup full. I go across the room to George and raise the pot in front of him. He sees it and nods.

"I think I'm *much* better," he says, looking up at me. I put my hand along his shoulder and slide it up to his neck and squeeze.

"I'm glad, George."

Jack knows how to treat me like a waitress, but the rest of the time he is totally at sea. When I sit down again, I bring up the coalition meeting last week: "It was a good meeting." He doesn't say anything. I am on dangerous ground here. "A little tense there at times, but OK." I try to laugh.

He doesn't laugh.

"A group of the legal task force has been to see the police chief about relations with the police force. They've been talking to them about street harassment by kids, about trying to get them to see that that's a real crime. They've also talked to the assistant attorney general about the trial—"

"I am not going to go anymore."

"National Public Radio is going to be there next week. There will be a reporter doing interviews."

"I don't like that. I don't like being interviewed."

"Why not? You've been good the times I've seen you."

He stares at the tops of his fingers, his arms stretched out on the table in front of him.

"You look good on television."

Then he resettles himself, looking back over his shoulder at the room. "I don't talk right."

"Why didn't you come?"

"I'm not going any more."

"Why?"

"I'm pissed off at the women—"

"What—"

"—they always have to have their way."

"We would like things to be equal, Jack, and a lot of us thought—"

"You've kept us from having real officers and from having a spokesman for the press. Derek says we're blowing our chance to have our say in the media."

I'm thinking for a little bit and then I say, "It's better now. I think we're working together now. All of the task forces have gotten organized and are doing real work—"

Marybeth

"You women want more than your share. I don't know why you want to be like that. You don't act like girls."

I survey the scene, George at his table, the sounds of Dominic in the kitchen with his pots, the empty tables. It's oppressive just to be around Jack. He occupies all his own space and half of mine, too. While he talks, slowly, in a voice so low it's almost a whisper, he articulates his thoughts, and they come down on me like a giant collapsing canvas circus tent. I want to take Jack by the hand and tell him not to be afraid. It'll be OK if we don't act like girls.

Then I'm staring at the door when it opens and in walks Cynthia. She has been at the movies and has come by to wait until I get off work. She smiles at me and then at Jack. "Hi, Jack! Good to see you!" She settles into the seat and leans back. "God! What a movie!"

"What did you see?"

It was an Australian film about a man sometime in the future, after the bomb has gone off and after all civilization has been reduced to roving bands of thieves and murdering men, and the most precious commodity is gasoline. The man's wife has been raped and murdered, and his child killed by these bands, and he sets off to get revenge, dressed from collarbone to his toe in dusty leather, armed only with a nuclear-powered longbow. The movie is about revenge and hatred and power and winners and losers. I ask her what her plans are.

"I'm going to wait around here for you to get off." She turns to Jack with a grin. "I hear you mopped up at the court house today." She laughs and cocks her head as if she were giving away a secret. "I saw you on TV."

He looks away and doesn't answer and grinds his teeth.

It's eleven now, and in a little bit there's a crowd from after-the-movies, and I don't want her to wait. I've gotten so I can't think when she's around. "Why don't you go on home? I'll come when I get off."

"I want to wait," she says.

"It's a long time till I get off—"

"It doesn't matter, I like waiting—"

"No. I need to work. I need to do it without having you here—"

She is hurt. She's crowding me. Cynthia wants to tie me down to us. I can't breathe. The last month—since Bernie died—has not altered the way she sees her life. She's found me, and she has a decent job and a place in the community, and she's settling down. She's dropping out into the comfort of a private life.

We three are silent at our table. It's like living your whole life under Jack's giant canvas tarpaulin. You can't do anything until you can lift the tarpaulin up a little to make some space for yourself. When we marched down the hill after Bernie died, I had this sense of space, of the great sky. I walked down that hill with Cynthia and our space reached from the church to the bridge—maybe a quarter of a mile—and I found myself taking deep breaths. My time with Cynthia has been lived in a little bubble that enclosed just the two of us, like living in a pup tent. She's content with that. I need to raise the roof.

Katahdin comes up out of the ground around it like a giant surprise. It's almost impertinent, the way it comes up out of the landscape, not surrounded by any other mountains, this immense mass of rock which blocks out half the sky. And when you're on the slopes of it, you can see from horizon to horizon, the great over-arching blue sky. But you sense you're very small. Since you can see the size and shape of the mountain so clearly—you see it from the highway an hour before you begin to climb up it—you never lose the sense of yourself as a tiny little thing on the shoulder of this big giant thing. In that giant space, you're very small. *That's* not where I want to go this weekend. I want to stay here where I've got my space and I feel big.

"Is it true they're going to drop the charges?"

Jack shrugs. "That's what Mickey says."

"How does he know?"

"Claire says that's what he says."

He looks away. Sullen, cornered.

"Tell me about Derek!" She has her elbows on the table, her hands clasped together, looking to her left, at Jack. He has crossed his arms on his chest and stares straight ahead at the kitchen door.

"There's nothing to tell. He's at his play."

"Have you seen it?"

"Once."

"Did you like it?"

"No."

If they're left to themselves very long, they'll have a fight. Cynthia scorns Jack and enjoys making him feel inadequate, which she's going to do right now. She'll pick at him and find his weak spot, then, just as he gets angry, she'll laugh at him. Right now, she's going to make him feel dumb.

"Why didn't you like it?"

"Cynthia!"

She turns to me, a laugh already beginning to come up in her throat.

"That's abusive, Cynthia."

The door opens, and Frances and Van and my brother Arnold, and his wife, Helen, come into the restaurant. I turn to Jack. "I hated it too. I hate Shakespeare at that theater." I stand up, and before I go to deal with my sister, I say, "Don't go, Jack. I'll be back in a moment." I see George out of the corner of my eye. He wants me. Frances' whole table is turned toward me, broad grins on their faces, and Jack and Cynthia, unable to speak to each other, gaze at me.

I move back and forth among my separate tables, taking George his coffee and feeling Jack and Cynthia staring, silently.

"Thank heavens, it's you! We're famished," Frances says when I go to their table.

We smile and speak and laugh all around.

"You missed a *wonderful* time at Mother's." My sister is better dressed than anyone here. She wears a skirt and blouse and little flat shoes and her hair is done. She exudes a defiant respectability in these quarters, where George, in his rags and his wild and unwashed hair, is more at home than she is. Frances talks of their children: "They were so cute at Mother's. We let them eat at the grown-ups' table just this once, and we were so proud of them." Van stares around the room and then back at me, and the others watch without listening. "I missed you," she says.

She massages me with her good will. Her words are at a remove from my reality, and I hear them and wonder why these words are being directed at me. She is pretty, her hair in a long, loose pageboy, and when she talks to you her large eyes concentrate fully on your face. Her face is open, shows interest and concern, and—can I say this?—her face shows love for me. And then her words come out and have no relationship to any immediate reality. Our ship has gone down, and we're in the middle of the Atlantic, swimming toward Spain, and she turns to me and says, "The children loved your Christmas presents!"

I wait for them to make up their minds what they want. They study the menu as if it were new, and I wait, responding to their small comments. I ran away from home and stayed away for two years, calling Mother occasionally to let her know I was all right and not to send the police after me, and when I showed up one day in Cardiff and went to Mother's, the first thing Frances said to me was, *I need you to help me decide what to wear!* I took a job painting houses and went to the U and got a degree in history. I wrote my senior thesis on the history of women in Washington County. It's the first place the sun touches in America when it comes up over the ocean, and it's as poor as dirt. The women there have been in their poverty since the first woods were cut down, and I wanted to learn about the choices they had made for themselves.

Helen orders a burger.

"Pecan pie," Arnold says. "Put whipped cream on it, too, will you?"

"Sure."

"Put a lot, and I'll leave a big tip."

"You got a deal," I say.

"I think the chowder sounds delicious," Frances says. "Do you think so?"

"Sure. It's the same chowder we always have. Nobody complains."

"What do you think, Van?" She turns to him to get his views.

"Suits me," he says. "Greasy spoon—" He looks around.

"Van!" She makes a face at him of fond disapproval. Then she turns back to me. "Or is the split pea—"

"Actually, Frances, it's eleven at night, and all of them are a little old at this hour." She stares up at me. "Why don't you get a burger or a piece of pie—"

"Oh, I was so looking forward to a cup of hot soup and a salad!"

"Well, suit yourself."

"Get us a couple of burgers, medium-well, fries, coffee for me, tea for Frances." He pulls out a cigarette, lights it, and shakes the

Marybeth

match out, rests his elbows on the table, stares around the room again, and says, without looking at me, "And could you tell the cook to speed it up, I'm tired."

"Van!" she says. Then she turns to Helen, and then to me, looking at me in an intimate way that some women have between themselves. She tolerates me. I am her weird sister, the one who ran away from home and who won't comb her hair and who wears leather thongs tied in knots around her wrists. I'm her weird sister who has a college degree and insists, against all reason and decorum, to continue to be a waitress when I could have a nice husband like Van and a nice house like their three bedroom ranch in the subdivision on the other side of the interstate. I'm her weird sister who has weird friends sitting at the table by the kitchen door. I'm her weird sister who's a homoseckshul. And she tolerates me because she can call me weird and then dismiss me, secure in her ranch in her subdivision. If she were ever forced to say I'm just another person, if she had to change her ideas about weird, her whole cosmology would become merely a fable in old books. All that intimacy and kindness and those big blue eyes she throws at me, what they're really saying is *Oh God, please don't make me deal with your reality.* Please don't make me know that weird is just ordinary, and I have to abandon my fables and my fairy tales.

I am in a rage, and I make my way across the dining room floor toward the kitchen door. I see George in one corner of my eye and, ahead of me, Cynthia and Jack arguing: She has glitter in her eye, and he, turned to face her, keeps swallowing, looking for spit. When George looks at me, he needs coffee. Holy fucking Jesus, doesn't he come first! I get the coffee pot and take it to him.

"George! How are things?" I remember that Van said he was in a hurry, and I think of the pad with their order in my pocket. I sit down at George's table. "How are you George? Are you OK tonight?"

He seems to have to focus his eyes on me, and it takes a minute. Then he smiles. "You're a pretty young thing, aren't you!"

"Oh, George. Are you putting the make on me?"

He takes a minute and then is flustered.

"You're the sweetest man I know. If I were forty years older—."

338

He doesn't know what to do or say, but he grins tentatively. Then he grins broadly.

"Wouldn't we paint the town red, George!"

He nods vigorously and then shakes his head and tries to speak but can't get it out. I stand up while he struggles. I put my hand on his shoulder and wait.

"We'd never go to sleep," he finally says, nodding and then jutting out his chin defiantly.

When I was on the road, I didn't know at first how far out of things I had dropped. I had left home, and I didn't have Momma haranguing me all the time, and that felt like freedom, but it didn't tell me anything about how much freedom I had, or what it meant. I was waiting tables in Phoenix. One day I cut my foot on a nail and didn't do anything about it but wash it out and forget about it. Then it swelled up. I got red streaks up my leg, and I went to the hospital. I discovered I didn't have health insurance. In this country, to have health insurance, you have to have a job that gives you health insurance, or you have to be somebody's daughter. It made me think about my job: The only way I could get a job paying health insurance was to stay put for a while. It was an equation I hadn't thought of before, the relationship between getting what you need—insurance—and giving them what they need—a steady employee.

Well, I didn't want to stay put. I was going from Phoenix to Tucson, to the Grand Canyon, and then to Reno. On the road I had the kind of jobs where this man pays two or three dykes to paint a house. He gives them two or three hundred dollars when it's done, and we split it, and then we split, and nobody paid taxes. I never paid taxes on what I earned when I was on the road. I didn't pay social security taxes, either, or state taxes. I was free of all that. I wasn't tied down by all that.

I didn't have a checking account because I didn't want anybody able to see how much money I had, and when some man tried to pay me by check, I asked to have it in cash, please. I didn't have any identification either, no driver's license—I was too young when I left home and had no real need for it afterwards—and no phone and no steady address. In Denver I began to discover that I had dropped out of the American economy, that giant system where, if you do things the way they want you to, if you stay put and work hard, they give you things in return: insurance, credit, an identity.

I was a seventeen-year-old dyke, on the road and learning things. I began to learn how it was that Van, my brother-in-law, had paid for that shiny boat he bought and for all the other things they owned, including the house in the subdivision: He'd gone in debt for it up to his collarbone, and if he had wanted to move on, even the shortest little drive up the river, he couldn't have done it because he was so tied down by his job and the balance on his credit cards. But it was more than that: He had to cut his hair in that ridiculous way he had, too, to keep the job. And now that he is being promoted, he has to wear suits. He has to cut his hair and wear his suits to keep his job to get his credit to buy his house and get his insurance so that when he cuts his foot—. Health insurance is slavery.

On the road, where lesbian waitresses are, I wore my hair shaved on the side and spiked on top and wore leather arm bands with steel studs, and I rode on a bike behind my lover through the Rockies at night, my arms around her waist, my chin on her shoulder, my hair whistling in the wind, going so fast around the curves that I thought if we went any faster, we'd cut through the guard rail and fly right off the precipice and take off straight for the moon. And if any boss had ever said, *Let your hair grow,* I'd have said, *Fuck you,* and moved on down the street where there was a job at least as good as the one I was kicking over.

On the road, where lesbian waitresses move from job to job and town to town and lover to lover, I found I was not only outside the law—there were the after-hours places and more drugs than you wanted and there were never any taxes, and we broke every sodomy law in the west—I was beyond their reach. On the road, Momma's letters got to me only when I let her know where I was and only with my permission. She had no control over me, and when she said, *Come home and get married,* I knew I didn't have to. I was free because I had my own money. I didn't owe anything. I didn't owe them a haircut or my clothes or my life style. I hadn't taken anything from them.

While I was on a bus headed west across the Washington desert toward the Cascade mountain range and the Pacific beyond, at home the kids were taking courses in Concepts of American Democracy. It was an election year, and the liberal and conservative politicians were arguing about the country. Just east of Yakima, I discovered a hidden agenda: There was a whole range of concepts which appeared nowhere in the constitution, which underlay the whole of American society, and which, much more than the law or the economy, were absolutely defining. These concepts—the family, notions of decency, a profound fear of sex, rigidly defined gender— would control Western culture no matter what party was elected. *This* was what I had found freedom from on the road.

What I discovered on the road was a liberty unlike any described in that course in Concepts of American Democracy, nothing like the Declaration of Independence and the Bill of Rights. It wasn't until I came home and found myself swept up again in my family, that I knew what it was: It was a liberty of ideas. I could think free. It was a freedom in my mind to discover the roots of myself, and it was a courage to explore the whole Western States of my existence, unencumbered by laws and regulations and moral prescriptions, the intolerable baggage of material life and the unspoken enslaving agenda of their ideas. I had found that a lesbian waitress on the road was free to make her own way.

"What's happening to us?" Cynthia stands by the door, her back pack hanging on one shoulder. Jack is still at the table by the kitchen door, moving a coffee cup around and staring at the wet circles on the formica. "I thought it was set for this weekend in Baxter—"

"I'm not ready for that." I put my arms around her shoulders and kiss her lightly on the lips. "I wish you could hear me."

"Don't you want to get away?"

"That's just what's not possible—"

There is nothing to say.

"You don't want me to wait for you?"

I stare at her. What seemed large and capacious seems like a prison now. She can't believe that my love for her needn't lead me to marriage. There are tears all over her face. I kiss her, and she leaves.

I turn back into the room and go to Frances' table and clean up the debris they left. Frances' lipstick has left stains on her cup. She said, when they were leaving, "We want to see you. It's been weeks. Where have you been keeping yourself? Won't you come by this week?" Van stood by the door, shifting from one foot to the other, his eyes moving from table to table around the room. "You are so dear to us."

I sit down with Jack.

"Derek is going to Boston, maybe to New York, at the end of the summer."

"Will you go with him?"

He is sitting on one chair and his feet are up on another, his arm lying along the table, staring at his crotch.

"I thought if you loved each other you'd want to be together. My Dad never looked at another woman. I like being around Derek. I've been at his place every night. He's good, you know? Every night it's the same thing. We talk and then we have sex. He sits on the sofa with his legs up on the cushion, and I lie down and he holds me. Nobody has ever done that for me before. I've gotten real used to that now, talking and then having sex. Now he says he's going to New York."

Beyond the plate glass windows, through the black reflection of the dining room, you can see the street—the stoplight and the street lights and the hotel across the street. Cars go by. It's weird to see, in the glass, outside and inside at the same time.

"I told him about me. I'm not like you. I don't tell people about me, what's going on inside. I told him about telling my dad I was gay, after Bernie drowned. My dad beat me. I'm bigger than my dad now, and I could have stopped him, if I had wanted to, but I let him beat me. He took out his belt and beat me real hard. I put my hands over my head—"

It's cool. When you walk under a street light, it's very bright, but when you walk past the light, it gets very dark again. There are no moon and no stars. Jack left to meet Derek, and then George left, leaving a dollar on the table, without saying goodbye. At Dominic's, people come together, connect or don't, and leave, without commitment except to the moment. Dominic and I closed up at one. This is the part of the night I like, when all the talk is over. People go back, retreat inside their bodies. I stand on the pavement in front of Dominic's watching Dominic trudge slowly up the hill. His shoulders slope as if he were carrying a heavy burden. There are no lights in any of the buildings. There are no cars, and the town is quiet. I walk from the square toward the bridge. All the energy that has informed our lives over the past three weeks since Bernie drowned is asleep now, and there is no evidence on the street of the hatred and fear that people have for one another. From here, on the bridge over the stream, the loudest sound is of the water where the stream enters the river a quarter mile away. It sounds like the rustle of silk taffeta.

From Dominic's State Street crosses the bridge over the stream and then goes up the hill to the large gray mansion where there's a dancing school. No one is dancing now. State Street goes almost due west along the bluff above the river, past insurance companies for people with jobs and paint stores with their yellow and red neon signs for people with houses. There is a large Gothic church of stone with a green spire of copper, which speaks of the solid values of money for people who believe in a male and sexist God. I walk along State Street, taking my time, past the doctors' offices and dentists' offices in old converted houses. The big porches have been enclosed for waiting rooms. State Street dips down again near the river, near the hospital where they took Bernie's body before they took it to the morgue. The buildings of the hospital are modern concrete and glass and are brilliantly lit. Out farther the State Hospital for the Mentally Ill, nineteenth century red brick that looks like a prison, sits up on a high bluff over the road—State Street out here has become a country road, and I walk on the shoulder—overlooking the river and the cemetery where Bernie is buried among the elms and hemlocks and large classical statuary. Jack was *fine* this morning at the court house. He was right there with us. He's got possibilities if he'll just let himself learn. I walk along the right side of the road, my hands in my pockets, a backpack over one shoulder, listening to the dry rustle of the water over a log dam which has been breaking up and floating in bits and pieces down the river and out to sea ever since I was a child.

Home. Family. Sex. Materialism. Love. Gender. Capitalism. Convention. Respect for the opinions of mankind. These are the values that oppress me. We must have jobs and advance in them. We must work to have a house and make a home. We must accumulate our possessions. Men must not be effeminate nor women masculine. Majority rules. We must love one person for all our lives. We must marry. We must have children. We must be monogamous. We must have vaginal sex. Sex with many people is promiscuity. Sex and love

343

are identical. We must compete and achieve and love and procreate. We must. We must.

I am alone on a highway at two in the morning, going north. The night is alive with sounds. The rustle of water over the rocks, the buzz and click of insects in the grass. I see before me on the trees lining the road—here it dips down to the left and then curves up over a hill to the right—the dim lights of a car coming from behind. I stop and turn around and face it, holding out my arm, my fingers in a fist, my thumb up. I no longer want to make peace. The car—it is a truck—slows and stops, its tires crunching on the gravel, and, taking a deep breath, I open the door and get in.

Derek

I sit at the counter in front of the mirror, taking off my makeup. I see my face: The mascara and the heavy eyeshadow enlarge my eyes. They are dark and clear and suggest suffering. The lipstick makes my lips carnivorous and sensual. There is a brush of purple shadow under my cheeks, a hollow look. Pear-shaped pearls hang from my earlobes. I wipe off the pancake and powder and scrape the toilet tissue through my eyebrows. The enlarged stage features fade, and another face emerges: The twentieth century ethnic Italian shows through the features of the English Renaissance Italian. I can't tell whether I am moving toward greater or less artifice.

Forty minutes ago I saw Cesario for what he was and had to fall in love: "Give me thy hand, and let me see thee in thy woman's weeds!" The desire for change comes suddenly on my character, and I recognize for the first time in the play the possibility of the ambiguity of things. Four minutes later I was able to say, "Cesario, come. For so you shall be while you are a man; But when in other habits you are seen, Orsino's mistress, and his fancy's queen!" I moved toward him with a measured step. I put my arm on the small of his back, and we walked toward the center rear stage slowly, aware of the image we made from behind, two people in elaborate drag, arm in arm, followed by the others. The play is about closets and coming out. My part is the most passive one on stage. I play every scene with a ravenous appetite, a boy on my knee, mistaking him, mistaking where my affections lie, unable to cause events to unfold for my benefit, waiting for others to appear to explain the world to me, sending messengers. I have been trapped and hungry, and I have hated it.

The others have left. In twenty minutes Jack is due here: Enter Jack. I haven't seen him since this morning at the court house. This is an old play and an old town. I am watched in the theater and on the street. The stage is small, the company is small, the coalition is small, the town is small. I need a larger stage and a smaller part, and more—or less—makeup. I see now the way it is going to be: forever carrying a picket sign somewhere. The enemy is not three boys, although you have to make sure they are tried and convicted. The enemy is not the pope, either, or the Baptist minister, although you have to teach them they've misread the Bible. It's not the psychologists or the doctors, who've misread human nature. It's not the politicians, or the educators, or the media either, or the businessmen and the historians and the philosophers. The enemy is slippery, hides behind the medical profession now or the legal profession then—or the priests. Sometimes it's very rational, sometimes it merely screams in the street. I had a sudden thought this morning at the court house that I would spend all the rest of my life doing this, fighting the enemy in whatever guise he happened to choose that day. I thought that when I had finally figured out how to fight the *church*—had discovered a strategy—I would discover that now, just now, I have to fight the schools, and I would have to begin all over again. And when I was about to fight the *schools*—and had found out how to do that—I would discover my enemy was really the enacted law, and I would have to set about laying siege to that camp. Everything I ever wanted in my life—the chance to do a decent part in a decent play for an appreciative audience—would get lost, abandoned, forgotten while I fought the alligators around my hips. The Vietnam metaphor is appropriate: The enemy fights a guerrilla war, and I am lost in the jungle, shot at from all sides, stepping on mines.

I can leave. Declare a victory or defeat—it hardly matters—and go home. I have accepted a position with the repertory company in Cambridge for the fall and winter seasons. I've been there three other times—early seventies, when I was a kid, late seventies, early eighties. I was there in June for Gay Pride, and it was fabulous:

The night of Gay Pride, on all the dark narrow streets of the South End, single men and women, couples, small groups in loose shorts and t-shirts, pass under the street lights until they stand on Tremont in front of the Cyclorama. They squeeze through the door, up the stairs, and into the great circular room, out onto the dance floor. The hard rhythm of the music has already taken hold of them at the door downstairs, and by the time they get past the hordes watching, they have begun to breathe in time, their shoulders and arms lifting and settling with the movement of the music, their fingers stretching. They begin to dance, joining a thousand gay men and lesbians in a ceremony celebrating our community.

The color you remember is white: It is a tremendous celebration of spring. Tans already acquired this early in the summer are chocolate brown against the whitest white t-shirts it is possible to weave. Bodies: lithe, Greek—runners and swimmers—torsos moving against hips, every muscle and bone apparent through the thin, mobile jersey.

My hand on the shoulder of a man: My fingers palpate the articulation of the trapezius where it connects with the deltoid, feeling them move in opposite directions. I pull him toward me before we move out onto the floor. I slide my hands down his back, feeling the strong flesh. I put my face into the corner of his shoulder nearest his neck and kiss him there, feeling his hands clasp behind my waist, before the music pulls us apart and into the crowd.

There are nineteen bars in Boston for gay men and two for lesbians, and on Saturday night thousands are out, drinking and dancing. This is what it is like in Boston: In the crowded bars, the heat and sweat contribute to erotic tension. Men's clothes wilt and expose instead of covering bodies made at the gym to be beautiful and to dry all eyes. The drugs are cocaine, amyl nitrate, alcohol. But the drug of choice is sex. The men: You can have what you like. A friend says, *You can get what you want.* In any bar or bath, there are as many different kinds to choose from as there are men to choose, and whatever your fantasy, no matter how exalted or low, there is a man to fulfill it. It is a low, intense, erotic dream.

It is possible, in Boston, to slide smoothly under the surface and never to come up for air. It is possible to grow gills and stay down forever, doing a slow breaststroke in the cool half light of three fathoms. We have populated the red-brick-and-bay-window town houses of the South End and the yellow brick apartments among the students and third-world foreigners of the Fenway. We have moved to Dorchester and rented triple-deckers and set up domesticity in Jamaica Plain where we can have lawns. On Beacon Hill we wear severe, conservative suits, and the Back Bay is filled with us strolling Commonwealth Avenue, arm in arm in jeans and t-shirts, reading the inscriptions on the statue of William Lloyd Garrison. We have every lifestyle: homosexual couples, couples in imitation of heterosexual marriages, lovers, single celibates, single men perpetually on the cruise for some young man, women in couples, single women cruising. In the summer the streets are a crowded, deep relief of young men in loose white shorts and t-shirts, of an unexpected beauty which springs from deep in the genes, carrying shopping bags.

Sometimes you have to confront straight people directly: The driver of the Green Line trolley car looks straight, the woman at the counter in the Christy's in the Fenway wears a wedding ring, even the crowds pouring out of the library or in Kenmore Square after a Red Sox game. But something happens in the city: Your eyes adjust, and you don't see them. They give off a signal, something in their clothes, the leaden glance of the eye, that shuts off your retina, and what your eyes do register are the thousands of gay men and lesbians on the streets and in the shops and restaurants and movie houses, the whole electrically charged grid of us. In the city, among a million straight citizens, you can't see any but the twenty or thirty thousand who are for you.

There are so many of us that we are not aware of ourselves. There are no cameras pointed at us—SLR or video—and the newspaper has no reason to point out that we are going about our daily business. There are so many of us that when the diners in a restaurant, tourists sitting at a table next to me and my date, seem to stare, it is easy not to notice or to ignore. It is easy to forget why we are being noticed and to achieve a kind of insouciant innocence about our presence in the city.

All up and down Newbury Street and in the downtown crossing, shops and boutiques sell our clothes. The corporation that owns all the theaters in town hosts a Gay and Lesbian Film Festival in the spring every year at the Orson Welles in Cambridge, with movies from America, Europe, and Latin America. Bookstores all over town have gay and lesbian sections for hardback, serious books, and most complete magazine stands sell the major gay magazines. Glad Day stocks everything: serious sociological, philosophical, and literary studies, political studies like *The Spiral Path: A Gay Contribution to Human Survival* or *Sexual Politics, Sexual Communities;* a complete stock of current and major fiction, like Edmund White's *A Boy's Own Story;* each new translation of Proust as it comes out, current journals as well as pornography to satisfy those who don't want to go to the bars tonight: *Torso* and *Drummer* and *Manscape* and videos called *Thick and Creamy.* You stand at a bookcase, glancing at a Spanish communist homosexual's essay on the coming revolution, and one eye is on the blond number on the other side of the bookcase with three rings in his right ear and nineteen inch arms with a tattoo of a red dragon.

Money means power: Realtors and bookstores and boutiques have grown up to provide for us, and we have reached, a long time since, critical mass. Every year there's a new crop of new boys, attracted from the suburbs and from northern New England by the bars and the gay neighborhoods and the shops and the movies and the bookstores. We are indistinguishable in every significant way from every other community in America. We have our history and our traditions, our politics and religion. We have our shopping centers and our schools, our law firms and our doctors. And our numbers grow every year.

When I lived in Boston three years ago, my apartment had two rooms and a kitchen, was all white, a bay window in the living room, four floors up. My coffee table had stacks of newspapers: *Bay Windows*, happy, vapid, local, and *Gay Community News*, Boston's leftist weekly journal with its diatribes and visionary analyses. I subscribed to *The Advocate—Life* with personals—and two from New York: *The New York Native*, erratic, volatile, and *Christopher Street*. My apartment was just off Westland, and I was in walking distance to the symphony and the Handel and Haydn Society and near the Green Line to the opera. The Museum of Fine Arts was around the corner. I went to see Sargent's picture of Thomas McKeller and *Le Debardeur* by Meunier. I stopped and admired the serene handsome sons of Erin in the O'Reilly monument at Boylston and The Fenway. Where I lived, I was halfway between the Metropolitan Gym and the South End Gym, and I could go to Symphony Hall to hear the Christmas concert by the Boston Gay Men's Chorus. I was equidistant from Northeastern University and Boston University and in the middle of Berklee School of Music and the New England Conservatory, with their young men with soft eyes and curls down to their shoulders, earrings, and guitars or violins in battered black cases.

At the end of June, we all walk in the Gay Pride Parade, celebrating the night when the transvestites fought back against the New York police raid on the Stonewall Inn. All of us come above ground on that day, fifteen, twenty thousand wearing pink triangles—a reminder of the concentration camps—marching from

349

Copley Square up Boylston, down Charles, up Cambridge past City Hall, then up Tremont to Park and past the golden-domed State House, where the gay rights bill is introduced every year. At the end, finally, there is an enormous rally on Boston Common where patriots are buried.

While it is possible to join the movement in Boston, it's not necessary. The borders of our community are so distant from individual life that the struggle seems very far away. I was doing something for gay rights by living a life which was unassertively but uncompromisingly gay, at a great, even infinite, distance from family and what used to be called home—by carrying a balloon down Beacon on Gay Pride. There are times, in Boston, when I find myself thinking the struggle for freedom has already been won.

In the tens of thousands of us who have moved to Boston from Maine and Vermont and New Hampshire, Rhode Island and Connecticut, and from all the other states of the United States, in the huge numbers of us, in the interstices between the organizations and the foundations, between the boutiques and the bookshops and behind the darkened windows of the bars and clubs and baths, we have found our privacy and our freedom. Cities have always promised freedom from the conventions of provincial, parochial society. The intimacy of small towns has been like the public stocks on the Common in Salem, where we were trapped and everything about us was exposed to ridicule and punishment. In small towns everyone knows your name. Is there anyone in Cardiff who doesn't know my name now? Is there anyone here who doesn't know I'm gay and that I knew Bernie and that I have been co-moderator of the coalition for the last two weeks? Everyone knows I am queer. I remember what I sought when I first left home and moved to a city: oblivion. Cities are a kind of Illyria on whose shores we wash up. They promise forgetfulness of the past and its losses. They promise the boutiques and the bars and the baths. They protect you, and then they teach you how to be gay. They promise love, and lost ones, and reconciliation, and the end of all sorrows.

Jack drops heavily into the chair in the corner. I am scrubbing in the sink. I splash water on my face and then grope for the towel.

"They applauded you a lot, I guess."

"They liked the play."

"They liked you. I could tell." I hang up the towel and face him. He is slumped down in the seat, the soles of his feet together and his thighs wide part. "You are the one they applaud."

"They applauded me."

"They're assholes."

"Not for applauding. That's what audiences do when the play is over, applaud the actors and the company. I had a big part. They applauded me. I'm tired. Let's not fight."

He shifts in his chair. "You care more about this than about me."

I go over to him and put my hands on his shoulders. I lean over to kiss him, but he doesn't give me a place to kiss. I kiss the top of his head in the curls of his black hair. "You're jealous." Then I run a knuckle across his scalp. "You're sweet. I love you."

"You're going to leave me."

I pull on a shirt and button it. "I'm going to Boston when the season here is over. I've got a job. I got the letter today."

He looks up at me for the first time, his face tight with anxiety. "What about me?"

What about him? Jack is still a boy, and I will find a way to make this easy for him, but I can't not go to Boston. In six months I'll be so bored we won't be able to speak.

"What about me?" He waits for me to answer, and I don't, and then he looks down at his shredded paper. "Why are you going?"

I pull on my jeans and button up. No belt. Weejuns. No socks.

"You can't go to Boston just to fuck."

"Let's get a beer and then go home." I don't have to answer him. The promise of sex is enough to hold him until the end of the summer. He'll sit on his anger at being abandoned until I abandon him because he needs the sex so much he can't abandon me.

"What about me?"

What about me? I look at myself in the mirror. I am an Italian-American in my early thirties, whose working class looks suggest an unequivocal heterosexuality. I want to find a beautiful boy with soft eyes in some dark place. And dance.

He stands up behind me and slides his hands up my sides until they reach my arm pits. In the mirror, his head shows even with

Derek

mine. He is the only man I've screwed in years as big as I am. Suddenly he has me in a wrestling hold, his arms under my armpits and his fingers laced behind my neck. I struggle against him. I try to reach his head behind my head, but I can't. I twist against him, but I can't break free.

"You're fooling yourself."

I grab at his hair, but it is short, and I can't pull it.

"You're running away, Derek." His voice is hoarse with exertion. "You're supposed to stay here and help us fight." He jerks my head down, so that my neck feels like snapping. "You're a coward. If you're gay you have to fight them." He jerks it again. "You have to fight them." He jerks it down again, twice, to emphasize his words: *fight*, *them*. "Here! Now!"

I bring my arms down, hard against his ribs, and throw him off me. I face him, and before he can get away, I have one arm around his neck, my wrist held by my other hand. His face is an inch from mine. I squeeze his neck in the crook of my elbow until the veins stand out on his forehead and his face turns red. He can't withdraw his face from mine, and I feel his breath hot and damp. Then I kiss him, hard, open mouthed, my tongue reaching for his. He struggles against me. His hands clutch at my arms where they have his neck locked, groping for an opening. Then they slide, tentatively, down across my shoulders, my sides, my hips. He swings into me, his pelvis thrusting up against mine. One hand grasps for my buttocks; the other cups my balls.

352

Dana

None of us knows what we'd be like—"

"I'd be pretty much like me."

"Honey, I've *always* been just like this, hat on, veil down."

"Kinsey says—"

What they say has the confidence of the uninformed, that is, the defiance of the ignorant. "Kinsey was impressed by his own figures, but he presumed his figures would be higher."

"Well, me—*I am what I am*. I've always—"

"You'd be a different person." My mind wanders over the possibilities provided by a perfect freedom. The prospects are bewildering. "There wouldn't be a need for a gay community in a world free of bigotry. There wouldn't be gay people—"

"Dana!" Marcia takes my arm. "You're being difficult. Stop it." She puts her arm around my neck and pulls me to her.

"Hey!" I struggle free. "Don't do that!" Arthur and Luke stop and stare at us.

She laughs. "No gay people!"

"Probably not. There wouldn't be straight people either—" I put my arms around her. What follows is equal parts embrace and wrestling hold.

"Then who would I be in love with?" She speaks into my ear softly.

"With me. With me." Luke stares out through the trees toward the dark, polished lake, contemplating the impossible.

"With *you!*"

"She's not going to fall in love with Luke, Arthur. She's in love with me." My arms are around Marcia's waist, and I feel her through the thin cloth. "She's in love with me. She lives in a bigoted world, and that limits her options."

"You forget how free I am." She pulls away and looks at me. She does a little dance, and her laughing eyes make it clear that what she is for me is her own gift, unconstrained.

We stroll under the pines, the moon's pale light screened by the limbs and needles of the trees. The theater is behind us, a huge, brilliantly lit Chinese dragon squatting among the trees, breathing fire.

"No gay people!"

"I think she was speaking metaphorically, Arthur."

"No! She said, *No gay people!* Didn't you, my dear!"

"But she didn't mean it." Marcia has her arm through mine, and now she has rested her head against mine. "She couldn't have meant it."

"I meant it, guys."

"Silly!"

The theater, which is on a piece of property on a lake thirty minutes from Cardiff, was built in 1910 for vacationers who came up by train from Boston to summer here and who built large clapboard cottages with turrets and towers and many porches and spiked and jagged roof lines on broad lawns on promontories overlooking the lake. This building is of the same style, painted dark green, and in the daytime it is difficult to see, set as it is among the dark green pines back from the bluff above the lake. Between the acts, patrons get refreshments at little carts set up under umbrellas under the trees and then stroll about the grounds until a bell calls them back into the theater again.

We have seen Derek's play. He wore a white satin tunic with puffed sleeves and white tights and pearl, pear-shaped earrings. He is a handsome man in a florid, dark, Mediterranean way. It was only after the play when we went backstage that I saw him up close and saw his makeup—the lipstick and the eyeliner, the rouge and the powder. He was a caricature of a man. Now it is eleven-thirty. Luke and Arthur and Marcia and I walk about on the grounds, drifting gently down the long slope under the pines toward the promontory and a gazebo near the water, waiting for Derek to join us when he has finished inside.

"Derek does it in the classic way, of course."

"With his looks, how could he fail?"

"I think I prefer him without the earrings and the lace—"

"—What do you mean, 'classic way'?"

"He explores romance with a boy, and then he grows up and sets out to explore romance with a woman—"

Marcia laughs. "—the same person."

"Lucky for him."

"'Classic way' meaning Greek—"

"The same thing happens to Olivia—" I see the course of the conversation. "It's the Renaissance way—"

"Dana is having difficulty getting in synch with the rest of us."

"—the play suggests that in Illyria homosexual relationships were temporary. Sebastian, having had Antonio 'adore' him, grows up and marries Olivia—"

"Will he continue to wear his earring," Arthur asks, "after he is married? Will he remember Antonio?"

We are near the edge of the grove of trees. In a clearing is a gazebo, benches, a small piece of sculpture difficult to see in the dark. We find places to sit on the flagstones, our backs against the benches. Derek tonight transformed himself into a Renaissance duke and made love to a princess transformed into a boy. The image Derek made tonight when he first came on—a Renaissance voluptuary and an innocent, his earrings proclaiming and concealing—is superimposed on other images of Derek, standing in the front of the church, calling on members of the coalition, speaking calmly, assured and in control.

Others have been transformed in recent weeks. Across from us Arthur and Luke sit on the flagstones, their backs up against a bench. Luke's transformation is the most arresting: He seems expectant now, even curious about the future. Arthur is joyous, burning like a candle in a breeze. No one has taken photographs of us since Bernie died, but images are fixed in my mind, taken from the television screen: Mickey at Bernie's funeral, his tanned face, chin up, staring directly into the camera, his voice strong. *I am Mickey McNamara. I am a gay man. I was a friend of Bernie Mallett's.* I remember his earlier TV image: his face cast in shadow, lit from behind, his face down. There have been other images, some from today: on a television screen brilliant with sunshine and a crowd of shouting, angry, people, Suzanne, like an angry angel, leaping on a boy and carrying him down under her, while police blew whistles. Deborah in a red dress entering the Unitarian Church, turning and staring directly into the camera, her grief utterly open to the camera.

The transformation that occurs every evening in a theater dressing room as an actor puts on his makeup—surface disguise—is not what I mean. Everything Luke and Arthur say or do suggests they are aware of the tenuousness of gay existence. They are thirty-five years older than we are, and their perspective is pre-Stonewall, forties and fifties, McCarthy witchhunts, and the notion that homosexuality is both a sin and a sickness. They are certain there are boys behind the next tree, and while Luke and Arthur are novices at political organizing, they don't forget for a moment that every time a homosexual breathes, he performs a political act. They have been in therapy for thirty years.

Tonight in the play Derek's mask was torn from him. And this happened against a background as old and as ruined as a Piranesi view of eighteenth-century Rome: Every arch and column was half buried under the trash of centuries. It's not the grinning face of comedy under his mask of tragedy, it's another mask of tragedy, and what is driving him—he doesn't know this—is grief and mourning. Tonight he looked like he was going to a sacrifice when he led Viola off stage to be married.

I hunker down. Marcia's arm, lying along the wooden bench, provides a pillow for my head. The hard flagstones here, set in the ground, are half covered over by soft mosses and grass, and the benches and railings and tables set about under the trees are dark and sodden, split and curling, covered with lichen and moss. "I don't see how he can ignore the ruin all around him."

"He has his life to get on with. That's legitimate—" She touches my knee. "The Boston thing was only one of several possibilities, he told me. He could stay here. There was something on the West Coast, I believe—."

"His career. He's very good," Arthur says. "He told me this afternoon he had gotten the place with the repertory company in Cambridge. We can go down for weekends and see his play and go to symphony!"

"He's not the person they think they hired," I say, for I don't believe he can go on with his life. "How can he forget what he's seen?"

I watched Derek when he played the scene tonight: It was terrible to see his face while he tried to express joy at the moment he was also submitting to an overwhelming and inescapable force.

"I think that business in front of the court house today affected him deeply." Marcia speaks in the dark beside me. "It came as a shock." Then, "It's a sad play."

"Oh, yes!" It's Arthur. "Everything is in ruins. Her brother's dead, there's been the shipwreck, *Viola's* brother has drowned, all the talk is of funerals and mourning, of things coming apart—"

Our voices come out of the dark like the sounds made by the wind in the trees. Below us, I can hear the wavelets on the rocks, the sound of dry sand poured on tin.

"Yet it's beautiful," Marcia says. No one responds. "All sorrows do end—"

"Well, no." Luke's voice is dry and harsh. "Malvolio, Sir Andrew—"

"Luke—" Arthur puts his hand on Luke's knee. "It's meant to be beautiful—"

"Antonio."

"Ah, yes. *Antonio.*"

The moon provides just enough light for us to talk. The breeze off the lake cools us just enough. We have achieved a fragile balance. We are pulled in different directions. Something in our genes, our histories, makes us see different parts of what we share. I am struck by our delicate equilibrium. We are like dancers in a line who touch only at the tips of our fingers.

Then a voice comes to me, drifting through the dark: "Why did you say we wouldn't know what we were?"

My back is against the bench, my head rests on Marcia's arm. "I thought it was strange that the four of us—and Derek inside—have come to know one another. We differ so. We are here together because Bernie was murdered—"

"Where are you going with this?" Marcia asks at my ear.

"I don't know." I look at her. "All the way."

"I don't see why—"

"We wouldn't be here together if we didn't feel pressured in some way from outside, would we?—"

"But we share so much—"

"—and we come together to protect ourselves."

"I don't know why you need to look beyond the obvious—"

"We don't really know how we'd be if Bernie hadn't died. We wouldn't know each other, we wouldn't have this sense of purpose—. We don't know how we'd be if we lived in a world without bigotry. Our homosexual feelings would be expressed in a different way. *Why must it be in relationships?* Why must it be monogamous? Why must we form a community? Gay people are so embattled that we are afraid to look at ourselves. It is as if self-analysis will weaken us. This is an historic moment, but there was no need for things to work out this way—"

"What way?"

"The coalition, this division in town between the gays and the straights—bigotry makes us pick up sides, makes us define ourselves in ways—"

"Not me!"

"You, Arthur."

I am aware of Luke, sitting at right angles to me, his back against another bench. "Why do you work so hard for the coalition?"

The clearest statement would be this: It's a means of defining my own life. But by the time you come to consciousness at—what—age three or four, you have already become a creature of the culture you're born in. You've been branded by some historical necessity, scored all over with *their* signs and symbols, and you live the rest of your life baking someone else's bread. Bernie was murdered, and we were trapped. There was nothing else but work for the coalition. That or hide. From yourself.

We walk down the small path toward the lake. Marcia has folded her arms across her chest, and the sweater which she has carried all evening now hangs from her shoulders. It has become cool. We listen to the sound the small waves make in the gravel at our feet. The moon up behind us casts a platinum glow across the lake and the landscape. We stand there in the dark on the gravel and listen and take in the mysterious beauty of the scene.

At length she says how good things are. Everything goes well on its proper course as it should be. She speaks slowly in a low voice without turning to me, knowing I am listening to her, not needing a response. She talks of our years together, of the years of our schooling, of getting our first jobs, our house—the roots of our lives—and then of Marc, even Bernie's murder, the coalition—what she calls the "new work" we have before us—and the people we've met through the coalition, of Luke and Arthur sitting on the flagstones under the trees. She turns to me. She straightens the sweater which hangs from my shoulders and runs her fingers through my hair and down my cheek. "I have never been so happy. Thank you."

"Thank you," I respond. I feel stiff beside her. My part in her happiness mystifies me. We walk on along the lake, turned sideways toward the water so that the moon now comes from in front, a great false hope. The sound of the wind across the surface of the water is louder—a high-pitched whisper—than the wavelets when they fall on the gravel. I think more than she, or I think about the wrong things.

I have a strong hold on my own identity. I'm active, spirited, concentrated. But down in my psyche somewhere there lurk bits and pieces of their thoughts about what a woman should be, placed there long before I was able to know that I was being violated. And I suspect that these bits and pieces are not minor little things, evidence of some evolutionary deadend, genetic codes long since turned useless, but something central, my backbone or my central nervous system or my brain. I think my sense that I am a lesbian all my life long comes from them and not from me. I think my sense that I am exclusively lesbian comes from them and not from me. I think my commitment to an exclusive love for Marcia comes from them and not from me. I think if I had developed in a freedom-loving, nurturing culture, instead of in a sex-hating, woman-hating, homosexual-hating culture, I would be different from me.

Our culture manipulates us in trivial ways: Fashion leads us to want to cut our hair short or let it grow very long. We develop ideas of beauty in women and in men because of our historical moment. What I am talking about is profoundly deeper than that, at my root awareness of myself and at the way I feel my desire, the way it expresses itself. How can I know how my integrity has been violated? And how can I reclaim my integrity, which was violated so long ago and so deeply that I can't even feel it! I think that even my sense that I am a lesbian—that I am a person defined by my sexual feelings—comes from them and not from me. What have I lost—and I don't mean I want to lose the feelings—what have I lost by being defined by those feelings?

Now I know how I am going to look on the television screen tomorrow morning or on the news tonight. I am a discerning, perceptive, able lesbian woman. I have created myself as much as Derek when he puts on his makeup in the theater, but I am playing for someone else's benefit. Being gay is merely a role someone else has arranged. What I think I am doing out of my freedom is a consequence of my submitting to someone else's necessity. My integrity has been violated so horribly, so deeply and permanently, that the wound is mortal—not that I will die, but that my *self* has died, and I am left struggling against a role that someone else branded me with at birth, a sex-hating, woman-hating, freedom-hating lesbian in America at the end of the twentieth century.

We walk on through the cool night air to where the gravel ends and the large rocks begin. Then we turn back and leave the shore of the lake and walk back up onto the grass under the trees, out of the light of the moon, toward the lights and the theater and the clearing where Luke and Arthur wait. Marcia doesn't have a sense of falseness about what we are doing. She's an American lesbian in the twentieth century, and she doesn't pursue how she got here. Her work is cut out for her, she says, and she begins with a solid sense of self. Don't think, she says to me. That's what she's is always saying to me: Don't think. She takes my hand. Her fingers first enclose my hand and gently squeeze and then her fingers interlace my fingers. Our hands swing between us as we walk up the long slope.

I don't, actually, think very much, not as much or as effectively as I'd like. The pressure of events, of my duties, the needs of friends and the people I work with, of my child: I don't have the time for contemplation. It is late, and Derek has not appeared. "We don't really have time to wait much more for Derek. We should get home to Marc. The babysitter—."

Tomorrow late in the morning some of the women—Deborah and some others—are coming to talk about how the coalition can work more closely with women's groups in town. There's also the business of the school committee and its tolerance policy.

Luke and Arthur still sit on the flagstones in the clearing. We can hear Arthur's high pitched voice as we approach. He talks rapidly and with emphasis. They have known each other for twenty years or more, and it is a wonder that they have so much still to say to each other. Luke and he *listen* and find each other fascinating.

Derek hasn't come.

"Where have you been?"

"Down by the lake. It's beautiful. The moon—"

"Ah! Yes! How sweet the moonlight sleeps upon this bank!"

"Arthur!" Luke looks at him scornfully.

"We have to go home," I say. "We have a lot to do tomorrow."

"We have a lot to do, young lady!"

"Oh Luke, you're right." I must write letters. I received a package of materials from the Commission on Antigay Violence of the National Gay Task Force, and I have to respond. People are now sending money to the coalition to defray expenses of buttons and posters, and they need to be thanked. I get letters in the mail from men and women who have read about us and write to ask what they can do. A reporter is here from the West Coast and wants to talk to me and Derek.

They stand up. Marcia kisses both men on the cheek, and then I do also. Luke takes both my shoulders in his hands and pulls me toward him and presses his cheek against mine. "Into the trenches—"

"Not the First World War, Luke, dear! The Second! We fight against the Fascist Powers!"

We mill about for a moment, sorting ourselves out, and then Marcia moves off in the direction of the slope and the parking lot. Luke watches her back and then glances at me. "It's the First World War. We're all going to be covered with mud and live in the trenches for years—"

We move up the slope toward the parking lot where our cars are. The lights in the theater are being turned off. I wonder where Derek is. He has forgotten. Luke is right: life in the trenches.

Tonight we will make love. She has a long pale yellow silk nightgown, and she will come into the bedroom wearing it after she has brushed her hair. She will be standing by the bedside table waiting for me, taking off her rings one at a time and placing them on the table. She will ask me if Marc is sleeping. Her nightgown falls all the way to the floor, showing only her white arms and her toes and when I say he is sleeping, she will smile and turn off the light, and we will find our way to the bed by the glow of the moon through the window. Then we will make love.

At the cars, we say goodbye. They go to theirs, and we stand by ours. I look up toward the theater. Derek said he would join us by the lake. I am disappointed. He has been called away to something else. I feel like being called away to something else myself, a cottage on the coast, me and Marcia and Marc and a stack of books. I feel called away to friends who have maintained their freedom in the midst of this ruin. The last lights in the theater are turned off, and the entire landscape is lit now only by the cool platinum light of the moon.

Suddenly I hear their car behind me and, "Goodbye my dearest friends!" I turn around. It is Arthur, leaning out of their car window, waving, blowing kisses with both his hands. Luke waves also from the driver's side. They drive way, Arthur still leaning from the window, throwing out his arms blowing kisses, calling, "Goodbye, my dearest friends!" They drive to the end of the parking lot and enter the driveway to the road, their lights disappearing among the trees. I hear him call, "I love you!" the last long *ooooooo* sound diminishing into the dark distance.

We get in, and Marcia starts the car. We drive home through the deserted country. I slide down in the seat and rest my head. The Republican convention is next month. They will celebrate family values. The first woman candidate for a national office has been under continuous attack all week for her husband's finances. The boys are going to be tried as juveniles, and their harshest punishment will be confinement in a juvenile home until their twenty-first birthday. All around us are ruins. We are trapped in a moment in history which allows us almost no freedom, except the freedom to define ourselves inside an utterly oppressive culture.

Marc is five-and-a-half months old. He grows daily, discovering his body and Marcia and me, what he likes, what he doesn't. How will he grow to express himself? How would he be if he were free? How would we express ourselves if we were free? Would Marcia and I be as we are now, in love, committed to one another for all our lives?

The road winds up and down and from side to side among the evergreen trees, the moon sometimes on this side of the road, sometimes on Marcia's. I imagine perfect freedom. Would many women live as Marcia and I live, without a man at all, if they were able? Would many women live together happily and with purpose in communes? their children in common, the men somewhere else, there for the occasional coupling? Would some of us—or most of us—live with men in couples, sharing sex and affection and the raising of children? going to other men or women for primary affectional needs? Would the relationship with men be primarily economic and for the raising of children? Would we resort to serial monogamy? first women, then a man for children, then women again for spiritual values? And polygamy? one woman and many men? or the other way around, one man and many women, whose primary sexual and affectional needs would be met in each other?

If Marc were to grow up in perfect freedom, in a culture without fear of sex, a culture that celebrated all the diverse sexual and emotional and intellectual possibilities of men and women, wouldn't things be more fluid? less rigid? And wouldn't it be certain in such a community where anarchy ruled that there would be no rigidly defined groups who were constrained to limit their affections and their desire to members of only one other group? Wouldn't Marc be free? Would Marc have to define himself *straight* or *gay?*

What of Marc's feelings? Don't his feelings flow from object to object, person to person, occasion to occasion without break, a rich continuum of emotional life, flowing over and around and under whatever comes into his life? Don't we feel desire with one—or some or many—forever or for a little while, at the same time or at different times? And doesn't our desire take different forms and different intensities according to the moment and the object?

Look at what we have done to ourselves! Can anybody get to the end of the rules we have devised for controlling and limiting and defusing and destroying the integrity of the person and the richness of her emotional response to the world? And haven't we done all of this because we thought there was something dangerous in Marc that, if left to itself, would appall us?

And what have people with homosexual feelings done to protect ourselves from this obsessive elaboration of rules which kills everything it touches? We have devised our rules and have named our subgroups! We have agreed with them to set ourselves apart, have formed our coalitions and our committees. We have our gay fathers and our lesbian mothers, our bisexuals, leather groups, bondage and dominance groups, and sadomasochist groups. We have our queens and our femmes and our butches. By calling ourselves gay, we have played into a system already in place for a thousand years of western history and bought a place for ourselves as rigidly defined and confining as that which we say oppresses us.

The road comes over the crest of a hill, and the city lies below us, the cold bright lights spread out across the hills, and the broad dark stripe of the river like a great tear through their middle. We have blinded ourselves to our special vision of life, abandoned our special contribution, impoverished our souls, desiccated our spirit, built a wall around us and ensured that our only emotions would be anger and rage. And we ask why—

3

Craig

It's cool. The day looks the same as yesterday—flawless blue sky, the sun high overhead, sharp dark shadows under the trees—and it feels the same: sweat down your cheeks and on your back. Then you walk in under a tree, and you are a month ahead of yourself in the chill of the middle of September, where the cold and the warmth are dappled like sunlight. I got out of bed this morning and felt naked for the first time since the end of June, my body tingling.

The divided highway runs off ahead of us to a rise and then disappears and then appears again farther on, turning gently to the left. We are in a rented car going north, a few miles north of Cardiff, two hundred and fifty miles north of Boston. On either side of the highway, the woods run off to the horizon over hills and small valleys, unbroken by farms or houses. Boulders crop up through the undergrowth in the high ground, and in the low ground, we can see the shine of swampy water through the leaves. Occasionally we see a sign for one of the gas companies standing above the trees, indicating that hidden in the shade civilization hasn't completely petered out.

This highway—Interstate 95—begins in Miami and parallels the Atlantic seacoast to Maine. One time I drove the whole length, almost, at least up to where it turns into two lanes. It runs up the Florida peninsula through the southern forests and cotton fields, through Georgia, South Carolina, through the pinewoods and high-tech industry of North Carolina, through the tidewater of Virginia, into a city which stretches six hundred miles: Washington and Philadelphia and around New York and then through Connecticut and Rhode Island, and around Boston. I-95 is the Main Street of the East Coast, linking city to city to city, three thousand miles long through the thirteen original colonies, through the northeastern megalopolis, tying together the races of America—Cubans and Italians and Chinese and Irish and blacks and Jews and Anglo-Saxons and Puerto Ricans—and their intricate, stressed layering of economic and social classes.

Then at the Massachusetts-New Hampshire border, it enters the woods and leaves the people behind. There is a bridge at Kittery, a string of small Maine resorts—Ogunquit, Wells, Bath, Kennebunkport—and the inner harbor at Portland. The towns get smaller and smaller, farther and farther away from the highway—Lewiston, Augusta, Waterville, Cardiff—as if the culture were hunkering down. Between Portland and Cardiff, we enter what a friend calls "the long green tunnel" and hardly escape from it until we reach the turnoff to Millinocket, the end of the road for us, out in what Thoreau called the Great North Woods.

The highway poses a question. Wills says the end of the road—these woods, these fields, these small towns—is the "real" America. I think it left that behind at the last high-tech industry at Danvers, just south of the Massachusetts border. Some people, thinking like Wills, move back to the land, to tiny places in the Belgrade Lakes region where they dream they will be beyond the reach of urban sprawl and pollution and insistent public sex and the corrosive commercialization of American culture. Other people, thinking like me, pick up and leave these tiny, pretty little towns and move to cities where there is public transportation that runs underground, lottery tickets, trash and beggars in the streets, Titians in the museums, and the volatile mix of class and race, gender and sexuality, the sick and the well, and an intense energy born of the competition to survive. Why should anyone ever come back up here to live? When you drive north on Interstate 95, you are headed back into the American past. Whether that is a good thing is what divides Wills and me.

It's ten o'clock in the morning. Wills drives. He sits easily in the seat, his hands lightly on the wheel, content. He enjoys driving, usually chooses to drive when we rent a car, and seems unaffected by the hours on the road: He doesn't squint behind his dark glasses. I have slumped down in my seat, as far as the seat belt will allow, and rest my head, my eyes mere slits, seeing the white broken line come toward me, marking off our progress at seventy-five miles an hour.

We escape from the crowded city in summer to a place cool and empty and absolutely foreign. The map of the area north to the Canadian border—ten thousand square miles—has almost no roads, and most of the ones that do exist are privately owned across timber company lands. In Baxter you can hike back into the mountains and not meet anyone in a four-day outing. Governor Baxter, who gave all the land to make the park, said he wanted to keep it "forever wild," which suggests that if you go far enough north on 95 you can go too far beyond the northeastern magalopolis, too far beyond small town America, right back into chaos.

We left Boston yesterday at noon and spent last night in Cardiff, where the boy was murdered last month. We will stop for gas at some point, and coffee, and then drive through to Millinocket and Baxter and Katahdin. We'll get into the park after noon and have eight hours before dark. I was held up yesterday at the committee. A client needed to be hospitalized, and I went by his place and packed a bag for him and drove him over. I do work for them. I am a client advocate now. I've been a buddy, but my buddy died, and now I am taking a breather before I get another. Wills has a buddy, and so far he is OK. Wills says backpacking is a way of getting back to basics, but the city dust we're shaking off is basic too: Thirty-one gay men have died so far in Boston of AIDS, and people are scared to touch one another.

Wills looks over at me. He doesn't talk much, and there's nothing soft or affectionate—or needy, either—about his manner. I don't have to keep him awake. I speak to him, a question about a piece of our equipment, and he tells me without taking his eyes off the road where he put it in his backpack. I am satisfied. I made a list a week ago and checked everything off two days ago, stuff for my backpack and stuff for his, as well as a second list of things to buy in Millinocket just before we go into the park. This year we bought a new tent: a Moss tent we had been coveting for two years, light enough so that whoever is carrying it won't complain that he's getting a raw deal.

Wills and I share the same crowd in Boston. He's an engineer, I run a home for autistic clients on the South Shore, and we give our time to the same things: the AIDS Action Committee and the Gay and Lesbian Advocates and Defenders. He helps raise money for GLAD, and I work with support groups for the AAC. We share friends—once he passed a boyfriend on to me—and much of the same social life. During the time I have known him, he has had two lovers, and I have had three. Occasionally Wills and I have slept together, and we usually do when we come north. Sometimes we have sex. With the memory of that, I reach out and touch his knee as he drives. I stroke his thigh. He smiles, barely, and keeps his eye on the road. We make good friends: He is solid, and I am steady. I need the touch of Wills—of somebody like Wills—more than Wills does, and that suggests one way we differ. But we are alike in that we are both dutiful people. I accept the duty I owe to my community. I look into the eyes of a furiously angry client, and I know the benefits I have received and my privilege. Being a methodical person, I arrange things so I can fit it all in. In Baxter one's duty is limited mainly to eating when you're hungry.

Millinocket is a lumbering town. The principal odor—heavy, suffocating, sweet and bitter at the same time—comes from the paper mill. It is a classic town on the frontier—Indians everywhere—and while I've never had a drink there, there are many bars. Since we see it only driving through, it's easy to make generalizations: People are of a type. They dress alike, and they tend to look alike: beards and long hair. You see men on the street in groups coming from or going to work in the mill or out in the woods, and I noticed first thing how homogeneous the population is—loggers, millworkers, whites and Indians—and how few have the visual characteristics of gay men. The stereotypes are not true, of course: Franco-Americans are there too, who add a mysterious ingredient to the cultural stew, and there must be gay people there, but they are out of sight.

Wills first suggested we go backpacking six years ago. The idea was simple enough: get out of the city dirt and into the country dirt. But it was also to get out of town—where we are known by everybody and know everybody and the phone rings constantly—into the anonymity of the woods north of Millinocket. We wanted exactly to escape from the gay community into a terrain which has nothing to do with our communal values. You don't go to Millinocket and Baxter State Park and Mount Katahdin to have your gay values reinforced. You go to explore the line where your community stops and you begin. We both like the sense of distance and clarity; and we like being tested in a basic way different from the way we are tested the rest of the year. It is gratifying to carry all you need on your back, to make a camp with your tent and your stove and your sleeping bag, and to do your own cooking. We've been up here six times.

I can't imagine living a gay life here. We stopped in Kittery yesterday when we crossed the bridge into Maine and called ahead to see if we could get in touch with some of the coalition members. Cardiff is a dour little town on the Penobscot. Knowing that Mallett was killed there, I found it a grim, resentful, scared, place. We went out for drinks with some of the members of the coalition after we got to town, and there was nowhere for us to go but a chain restaurant off 95. The tone was set by families with small children and by heterosexual couples. There were no single women, no women together, no men in couples. There were two men together whose body language—the distance they kept between them, the lack of eye contact with each other, the inclination of the head—all declared they had no sexual awareness of one another. We found ourselves, as we talked about murder and the coalition, talking in lowered voices. I haven't done that in years.

From Kittery Wills got in touch with a woman named Deborah Elkins—her name had been in the paper and was in the phone book—and she steered us to a man named Derek, whom we had read about in the paper. We went by his place—he only had time for a drink and something quick to eat before he had to go to the theater—but he invited us to spend the night. He made some phone calls, and later we met some of his friends, members of the coalition they've started. And when Derek came back from the theater, we had a drink and talked.

Last night when we were going to bed, I told Wills the whole thing had the unreal quality of a timewarp. These people are dealing with issues the rest of us dealt with in 1970. When I was sixteen, I knew I was gay, and I knew that Colrain, Mass, was no place for being gay. When I graduated from high school, I made certain I went to college in a city where there was a gay community. I've been in Boston ever since. I never "came out." People who need to know know, the rest wonder or don't care. I've taken my place in my community, working for the good of all of us, supporting social services, raising funds, letting my legislators know I want them to support gay rights legislation. Our organizations are ten or fifteen years old.

It's all new to the people in Cardiff. One boy, a computer wizard, talked last night about his job. He wonders if he will be "allowed" to stay on now. If he keeps thinking like that, he'll go back in the closet. If my employer doesn't like me being gay, he has a problem, not me. I have never had to say it, but it is always ready in my mind to say, If you don't like it, you can find someone else: I won't change for you. You have to keep the power in your own hands.

Craig

I don't understand why any of them have stayed in Cardiff. The computer whiz went back after college. The boy who was murdered went there voluntarily two months ago. What in God's name for? Went there! There have been no organizations till now, there are no gay enclaves, no gay shopping centers, no churches that welcome gays, no gay newspaper, dances, bars. There are no gay politicians, no gay service organizations, no openly gay doctors, lawyers. Who would you go to when you had the clap? Where would you go when you wanted to buy a book or rent a gay porno? There's nothing that makes a community. It's as if they don't know that, elsewhere in the country, gay people have found a place in American society.

They're still reacting. Everything they've done so far—the formation of the coalition, the response to the media, the pickets at the court house—has been in response to actions taken by the other side. Derek admitted they have called no press conference to outline their agenda. They haven't called any public demonstration to dramatize their concerns, haven't published any leaflets, or made a public call for funds, and haven't made any move to make common cause with other groups which might have the same agenda.

Both of us noticed how obsessed they are with the boys who threw Mallett in the water. One of them mentioned something he had heard yesterday, and another picked it up and told something *he* had heard, and then it went around the table. Mainly they were talking about what the boys are doing now, out on bail. Apparently they are still harassing gay people. Gay people also have this profound anxiety about what is to happen to the three boys: *Will they be tried? Will they be charged with murder? Will they be convicted?* It is as if gays feel that everything will be made OK if the boys go to jail.

Wills said it is early yet. They're still angry and haven't gotten their act together. Later they'll start focusing on the future. He says the people in Cardiff are doing fine—finding each other. I don't know. The most obvious thing they've neglected to do is make common cause with other gay groups in other cities, particularly the big cities. They haven't asked anyone how to respond to an act of violence. They seem unaware that other gay communities have confronted murders before, and they feel they are moving across uncharted territory. They are recapitulating the response gay men and lesbians have to their first discovery of bigotry: I am the only person this has ever happened to. I think they have some idea of the extent of their injury, but I don't think they've been able to ask themselves yet what caused it—aside from the boys—and I think they have only a hazy notion of what they want now: revenge, healing, reparations, some alteration in society which will prevent a reoccurrence. They are reinventing the wheel.

Wills says, "Rest stop?" and I say, *sure*, and in a few miles he pulls off onto an exit, toward one of the giant gas signs standing above the trees. The gas station stands in a clearing in pine woods on a road which runs under 95. There is an expanse of white concrete marked by gas and oil stains around the pumps, and in the center stands the small concrete block one-story building—two bays, an office, two rest rooms—painted red, white and blue. Wills pulls up to the "unleaded, regular" pump and turns off the ignition. We release our seatbelts and open doors, sliding our feet outward. It is hot in the sun, and I feel the wave of heavy, warm air move over me. The station attendant walks toward us across the pavement. He is a young man, early twenties, closely cropped hair, t-shirt and overalls and work boots. He is wiping his hands on an oily cloth, which, when he is finished, he sticks into a rear pocket. I stand up beside the car and watch the boy move around the car toward Wills, who waits for him, standing by the open car door. The boy looks from Wills to me, waiting.

Wills tells him to fill it up and to check the oil. We go to the rest room and buy sodas, leaving the boy to the car. Wills drops coins in the machine and pulls the knob for peanuts, which he hands to me. Then he gets himself a package, and we stand on the concrete, watching the boy check the oil. A car comes down the road and pulls off onto the concrete, and the driver leans out of the window and asks the boy a question. He answers, and the driver pulls away again. The boy's manner has been sullen and hostile. I throw the cellophane wrapper from the peanuts in a trash bin, and we move toward the car. Wills pays the boy, and we get in. When we are pulling away, Wills looks over his shoulder and then down the road to see if it is clear. In the mirror, I can see the boy standing in the middle of the concrete, staring. Wills depresses the accelerator and crosses the road and enters the ramp up to 95.

Craig

Derek showed us the clippings from the paper, articles interviewing gay men and lesbians on their lifestyles, on the jobs gay men and lesbians hold, what they do with their time, and what their homes look like. There were pictures of smiling people stroking animals. I recognized Derek and Mickey and Mickey's lover in some of them. He pointed out Deborah Elkins and told us who the rest of them were. Wills pointed out the paper's treatment of the gay community. It has just discovered gay men and lesbians and doesn't know what to do with what it finds. The articles report the ordinariness of gay men and lesbians, but taken together they reinforce the sense one has of gay people being alien. Because the paper can't talk about sex and won't report what has caused these men and women to form a community, the nature of this alienness must remain a mystery to the paper's readers.

The paper reports the three boys are regular, normal members of the community in Cardiff, even if they are slow or difficult or dropouts. In contrast to the dead kid's flamboyance and his homelessness, and to the mysterious otherness of the gay community, the three boys live with their parents, play ball and go to the local high school. These ordinary boys threw the gay kid off the bridge. Much of what is meant is unsaid, and what is said is understandable only in the context of an unspoken xenophobia. Wills says the boys' place is to be offered up as sacrifices for the sins of the community. *That's what a scapegoat is.* When the scapegoat wandered away into the wilderness, the Israelites were free of sin once more.

We cross over a lake, the dark waters shining in the sun, the edge rimmed by fir trees. On the horizon Mt. Katahdin looms, solitary and imposing. Wills says it will not be long now before we reach Millinocket. I have asked this question: How do you be gay on the streets of Millinocket? There, amidst the lumbermen and the mill workers and the Indians? When we stop the car and step out into the street, the small town surrounded by the enclosing, wooded hills, how do we carry with us our sexuality? Wills says it is a question not to be asked. One is, or one isn't, wherever one is. Being gay is not a question of appearance, of the apparatus of gay life—the clothes, the style—and being out is not a question of being among people who know. Yet on the streets of Millinocket, as we go about buying the last few things we'll need to take with us, my sexuality will suddenly

374

have become my secret. My being gay suddenly will be reduced again to what it was when I was an adolescent—my secret desires—and all that has happened to me since I was eighteen, the flowering of my sexuality into a whole way of being, a selected style, a way of thinking about myself in a community of people, is left in Boston with my cats. I have no place in Millinocket.

I have also asked this question: If a gay man goes into the woods alone, *is he still gay?* The Roman Catholic Church, the Puritan fathers, the English Renaissance, the whole liberal middle-class, and Guy Hocquenghem would all say *no.* The fundamentalist right, the psychiatric profession, the gay community, the Democratic party and Michel Foucault would all say *yes.* Wills says yes, I say no. Where does being gay reside? Is it in the genitals and their use, in the heavy, charged operation of the organs, the rush of blood, the pressure of arteries, the sudden intake of breath, the rapid working of the hungry and thirsty mouth, the eyes' seizure on an object of desire? Or is it in the mind, the sudden apprehension by the memory of something seen? Is it in the sense of the totality of self, which sees its reflections in the mirror of other people and expresses itself in the complex public ceremonies of life?

Derek, I think, doesn't understand his appearance. I imagine all that male energy—he's a big handsome man—makes him think he can carry off being straight when he wants to appear straight while living a gay life. He's been around, that's clear, and knows how to make use of his looks. What is attractive about him is that his eyes give off a different signal from the rest of him—they suggest he's in pain—and he hasn't yet resolved his dilemma, caught somewhere between his acting and being gay. Even while he's in the midst of those people, he resists being one of them. He wanted to talk about moving to Boston!

Mickey, the computer whiz, on the other hand, is working toward something clean. He's a young man of about 25, I suppose, and has an engaging manner. His face is lopsided, and his grin is crooked. He's attractive rather than handsome, open and inviting. People gravitate toward him. I would imagine he would be good with children. He doesn't know yet what it's going to cost him to hang onto his integrity, but he's determined. He's not being helped much by his crowd.

Craig

This morning at Derek's the phone rang early. A few minutes later two older men came over and joined us for breakfast. I think one of them used to be very handsome, but now the lines in his forehead and around his mouth suggested an omnipresent bitterness. The other was cute, in his late sixties, even coquettish. I came to understand that they were a couple. The cute one spoke of the coalition as a power base. He kept saying over and over, *Things are changing now!* and laughing. He was exhilarated at the thought of coming out. The bitter one suspects betrayal, but he can't locate the direction it will come from, and he doesn't know what form it will take. They both want to go to the trial of the boys. "I can hardly *wait!*" the cute one said. I think they have been waiting for this moment for forty years—somebody to pay for all their hurts—and would be happy with a public hanging.

In the daytime I work with autistic clients who live in the house I run. The most visible characteristic of my clients is their anger. They bite me if they can and hit me with their hands and fists, and when members of the staff and I are not around, they will bite themselves until the blood comes. One client I have picks at his skin until it is raw. Science doesn't know why they are the way they are, and it can't do anything about it. It can't tell me what is going on in my client's brain. It is our job to provide a safe home for them and to care for them so they can't hurt themselves or other people. It is inescapable that what we do is provide a haven for them out of sight of the general population. I am paid to do this by the state, which contracts with private enterprise to maintain these homes. Most people never see humans like the ones I work with, and our society arranges things so that this is so. They are humans, and our society has made room for the autistic among the Jews and the Italians and the Puerto Ricans and the Cubans and the Anglo-Saxons and the Chinese, and their place is *out of sight*. It is their place in the community, and it is *out of sight*. What seems to be an act of spontaneous generosity is at the same time an act of stunning cruelty.

Wills and I drive north at seventy-five miles an hour into the woods, leaving our community behind, the whole enormously rich and complex culture of men and women who are known as the *gay community,* a name which includes but yields its smaller communities—whites, blacks, Chinese, Hispanic, the whole range of economic classes—which overlap and join and divide like live organisms. I move through my community from center of energy to center of energy, drawn by people and ideas and interests and activities: A moment in a bar for me or a bath or at work leads to a connection with a man and a trip to Glad Day to find a novel or a book on politics or on the German homophile movement or on sadomasochism, which leads to a conversation with a man reading a book on drag, which leads to an invitation to a party. He says, *Wear your best frock.* The man at the party I'm talking to is a recovering alcoholic—sober for nine-and-a-half years—and drinking seltzer, in full leather, talking about his buddy and the AIDS Action Committee. Somebody else is with the Gay and Lesbian Counselling Service, where he is on the Hotline, or the Bay State Lesbian and Gay Democratic Club, which is working to get gays to vote for the Democratic candidate for president. I have a close friend who is an anarchist, working to overthrow the whole political system and start again from chaos. He says to me, grinning, *Won't you join me?* The men at the party or at a bar or a meeting or in the bookstore or at my house on Sunday afternoon are all ages—sexual and political and social interests cross age barriers—and classes. My next door neighbors are a doctor and a waiter, who've been together seven years.

The variety of us suggests what we share with the rest of humanity. What is special for me is my sense of how conservative our community is, which is an odd notion, given the way we are perceived. My sense of my own past didn't come from my parents, who are kind and loving people. It came from the institutions of the gay community, the bookstores and the baths and the bars and the political groups, which, like churches and schools, have conserved the facts of homosexual history and taught us a way to be gay, and what to believe, and how to act as gay men and women.

Years ago at my first Gay Pride March, amid the volatile chemistry of the great stream of people moving up Cambridge Street behind signs indicating their loyalties, I first marched with a group from a bar, and we danced in the street from Copley Square to Boston Common. I've marched with the Batucada Belles, a lesbian rhythm band, with the alcoholics under the Gay, Sober and Proud banner, with Black and White Together the year I was living with a black man, and, when my sister joined me, I marched with Parents and Families of Gays and Lesbians. Lately I've marched with the

377

political groups, feeling beleaguered and angry. This year I wore a green t-shirt and marched with the AIDS Action Committee, carrying a sign with the date of death of someone from our community.

    Our Community. Wills puts out his hand and takes mine and clasps it in his, resting them on his thigh. Going into the woods, he is saying, is necessary to separate himself from his world and define who he is. He talks of the year since we last made this trip to Katahdin, of becoming absorbed by our friends who are sick and the one from our crowd who has died. Wills has a quiet, low voice, and I can barely hear him above the hum of the car. We were shocked when we first realized one of ours was dying, that the thing had invaded our shores, which had been our safe haven. We struggled between seeing the gay community as a safe place, when no where else was safe for gay people, and seeing our community eaten alive by a virus which seems to seek out our community alone. We are passing the disease on to each other, and it is difficult to remember that it is a virus and not our community which is destroying us. Through all of this, the president, a pleasant grandfatherly man, has smiled and looked at us through the medium of television, and has spoken of family values and the home, as if it were always Thanksgiving afternoon in America. His image has come to us as if beamed by satellite from another continent, and his message is this: *My community is not your community.*

    Along the highway, occasionally, there is a farm, or we pass over a road which opens up through the forest and gives a glimpse, before we pass on and the trees obscure the view, of a clump of white houses and a service station a mile or two down in the woods. Even here in this isolated wilderness, humans gather together and make their homes. I would suppose, I think idly as we pass, before the trees close in again, that they come together for the same reasons the rest of us do: need for support in the long winters, the loan of a snowplow or help with a sick child or with a stack of wood. I would suppose, too, they live together because in some basic way they must think alike, have similar ideas about politicians and preachers and sex and work and money. Love, here, among these people would be balanced, in the normal way, with hate, and gratitude with resentment, all of which would be adhesives to hold them together. The histories and beliefs these communities conserve are different from mine, and I wonder, as I confront the image of the three or four white houses on a road in the wood, the green lawns and the truck, inevitably, up on blocks, what is kept out of the picture, as well as what is presented, what is never spoken of in this little village, as well as what is spoken of.

When the highway passed Lewiston, you could see on the horizon the giant twin towers of a Gothic church and in Waterville, the English eighteenth century red brick and white-columned towers of Colby College. Near Augusta we passed the civic center and the chunky red brick modern campus of the University of Maine at Augusta. At Cardiff we passed between the town hidden down by the river and the commercial center which has grown up around the airport—a giant truck stop and a series of cutrate motels. Along this highway in September and early October, every second vehicle is a truck coming south out of the woods, and tied across the hood is a dead deer.

The old man this morning was thrilled by what has been happening in Cardiff. He says the memorial service for Bernie Mallett was the moment they all found each other, and so some meaning came out of Bernie's death. The first time I took part in a gay demonstration, I looked about me and saw the variety of us in what seemed to me our huge numbers. I was proud and grateful that I was among these people! I wanted to cry with joy. I've forgotten why we demonstrated—some injury we had sustained—but the demonstration was on Boston Common, called the "cradle of American democracy," "the burying ground of patriots," and I remember what I kept thinking over and over again: I am here, *in public*, with my people, being gay, protesting my injury. I looked at the old man this morning—How has he survived so long so cheerful!—and I wondered how much his injuries have defined him. The line between me and my community has long since dissolved, and *what I am* is impossible to be found under any microscope separate from the values I hold and the history I have sustained and the community which expresses them.

They are still in the middle of hand-to-hand combat around here, too busy staying alive to stop and take a breather and understand what they're really fighting for. The special vision of gay people. It is important that Stonewall is our great communing event. It has the same symbolic shape as the crucifixion and resurrection.

Craig

What happened on Christopher Street that night was that something in us died—and was reborn. Stonewall should be celebrated with high ceremony every week, not so much commemorating rebellion as symbolizing a way to transcend, reminding us continuously that sex is a mystery, that even gay people, so close to the heart of it, don't understand it, that gender is a mystery, and that what causes us to feel ourselves men and women is mysterious. We should celebrate Gay Pride every day because gay people, above all others, are in a position to know the mysterious multiplicity of life.

We go north deeper into the woods, crossing streams, running quicker now, and through thicker forests. Katahdin, which Indians used to worship, takes up half the sky now. We will be in Millinocket in ten or fifteen minutes. The hum of the tires on the pavement seems to have found a lower note: The car needs a muffler. I feel like Huck and Jim, free at last, going *south*, escaping deeper into slave territory. The prospect of five days in the woods with Wills is balanced by the fear I have always felt at leaving my home and my people behind and heading somewhere foreign. Everywhere about us, there is in this countryside, in the cool shadows, the possibility of figures lurking. I think of the three boys and the bridge in Cardiff, and the boy, a while ago, at the gas station pump who stared so impassively. Where does he live? What friends does he have? *People* live here, out there somewhere under those trees where you can't see them, and they might as well be an enemy tribe, naked, faces painted blue, carrying sticks and stones.

G ot it!" Then Claire heaves it to Suzanne, who grunts, "Got it!" and tosses it on to Cynthia, who whispers, "Got it!" and drops it in the splitter, whose low roar rises in pitch while it gathers in force. The shining steel plunger forces the log against the blade, and the machine groans as the log is torn apart and the pieces fall to the ground.

"Got it!" Claire says—she is hoarse with this shouting above the gasoline engine—and pitches it on to Suzanne, who tosses it to Cynthia, who drops it in the engine and pulls the lever and looks around at us, sweat and dust streaking her face. The engine's noise rises to a whine as the blade splits the log.

I stand at the top of the heap. The sun and wind are high and blow the limbs of the pine trees above us, blow our hair, and I make sweeping movements with my body as I pull a log from the pile and swing it over and drop it down to Claire, who catches one end and swings it in an arc to Suzanne.

"Got it!" from Suzanne. She throws it up, and Cynthia catches it and laughs.

Got it. Cynthia looks up at me and grimaces. She looks wonderful, dirt and sweat giving her skin a dark sheen. The sun flashes on everything—our hair, our earrings, pieces of the machinery.

Our house—an eighty-year-old cape—stands in a grove of pines, facing the road. It has an ell off the back, and the pile of logs is where the house joins the ell, in an area where the grass is worn away by cars and now in the late summer drought is dry and dusty. I watch my friends from my perch at the top of the heap. Each of them wears a green button the size of a half dollar, which says, *Another Friend of Bernie Mallett.* They are sweaty and dogged at their work. Beyond them I can see the shining river. I toss a log and then spread my legs and stand, my hands on my hips, and listen to the *got it!* down the line. The machine is a good one, simple and powerful, glistening in the sun, an air pump which increases pressure against an hydraulic plunger, which forces the log against a stationery blade. We have reduced what we are to arms and backs, throwing and catching logs. We have become a machine ourselves, glistening, simple, and powerful.

I am to go to the store and get food from Helen Demopoulos to feed us. I work at Dominic's later, and the others are going to the movies tonight. It is Saturday, three weeks tonight since Bernie died. The Summer Olympics start today in Los Angeles. The coalition meets for the third time Monday night in Cardiff. And the governor is going to hold a press conference Monday in Augusta. The Democratic Convention ended a week ago in San Francisco, and the Republican Convention starts in three weeks in Dallas. There haven't been any out-of-town reporters here all week. Then Eleanor came from Washington and plans to stay a while. She interviewed Dana, who told her to call me. Now she's staying with us.

Meanwhile I'm making my plans. There's a course this fall in the sociology department at the U on the rise of nineteenth century capitalism and its effect on gender roles in the family, which I want to take. The new woman is teaching it, and she's supposed to be good. I want to learn to write—really write, not just school papers—and for that, I need to learn how to do real research.

Since Bernie's death, I got the message: I'm not going to be safe anywhere. There are always going to be "boys" out there somewhere—in the bank, on a bridge, teaching at the U, wherever. And these boys are murderous. Time is not going to make anything better. It's not "getting better," it's getting worse. It's obvious it's getting worse, and I don't see anything on the horizon which looks like it's going to change things. I'm going to have to look after myself, and I'm going to have to assume from now on that I live in the camp of the enemy. Anything I can do to protect myself is OK. And lastly, traditional values are bullshit.

We take a break. Cynthia and I go into the house, and while we are in the kitchen, Cynthia puts her arms around my neck and draws me to her. She is exactly my height, but she is slightly heavier, more rounded, less bony, more giving. The sexual attraction I feel for her now in the height of summer is hot, damp, and compelling. When I feel her against my chest, I lose focus, and I fight that. "Cynthia." She won't release me. I take her shoulders and push her away and turn away to the counter. She holds the back of her hand to her mouth. I am intensely aware of the five of us, of my place in that loose chain, and I don't want now to lose my place there by turning inward to Cynthia.

I take out soft drinks and corn muffins. Cynthia stays in the house for a minute to make tea for Eleanor. Claire is sitting on the pile of logs, her hands on her knees. She looks at the sky. "It's too hot. We need rain."

"Your garden is droopy," Suzanne says, sitting on the ground.

"What have you done about your wood, Claire?"

"Nothing. Would you come help in a couple of weeks?"

We agree.

Claire talks about insulating her attic. I've done that here. "I'll show you how, when you want."

Eleanor is listening to all this. She is a heavy, dark woman, her curly hair pulled back in a braid. "It's work, isn't it, living here?"

We laugh, looking at each other, knowing the truth.

"In Washington you call a repair man or have it delivered."

"If you can afford it," Claire says.

"Anyway, getting it done is not the point."

"Sure it is."

"Being together is the point. We could hire somebody—"

"We can't afford that. If we don't do it ourselves, it won't be done, and we'll be cold this winter."

When Cynthia comes out with the tea, she puts the mugs down on the ground where Eleanor and she can reach them and then sits down herself. She brushes her hair away from her eyes. "Would you like to go swimming later? We can go in right here." She nods toward the river. Her eyes exclude me.

Suzanne and Claire are talking about Suzanne's latest discovery, a young woman in the coalition who works in the shoe factory.

Eleanor turns to me. "Are you and Cynthia monogamous?"

I can see Cynthia's face express hurt, just at the question.

"No." We are monogamous, but we are discussing giving that up, and what I have just done is speak it out loud, for the first time.

Later, they discuss whether they will watch the opening ceremonies of the Olympics in Los Angeles.

Helen Demopoulos presides at the cash register at the store. She wears the green button: *Another Friend of Bernie Mallett*. She is talking almost as soon as I walk in: "There're the divers and the swimmers and the runners and the gymnasts. And they look fresh—have you ever seen such beautiful people?—and new and innocent, brought to you by this brand of running shoe or that brand of swim suit." She looks at me as if for the first time. "How are you, dear?"

I get my things. We talk about the little American gymnast and how many gold medals she'll win. I tell Helen about Eleanor coming up from Washington to do a long story on Cardiff, and I invite her to come to supper later in the week. She knows I do not invite Constantine. Once I asked Helen how Constantine felt about her going off alone. She said, "He knows I love him. I like the way he thinks. He's interesting. He cares about the right things. Sex with him is like nothing on God's earth. And when I'm feeling down—or weak—it's reassuring having Constantine around to take up the slack. Honey," she said, "we've lived together so long—" She stopped and looked out the window, thinking, before she went on. "—we've got so much history between us that it's like a mountain. Two hours here, three hours there, a weekend with other people, men or women, wouldn't diminish that."

Sometimes sitting around the table after supper, there'll be me and Helen and Cynthia, and I have this weird feeling that Constantine is with us in one of the chairs, and I'm not seeing him. Her consciousness of him is so powerful it conjures him up, and he moves in on us, taking his seat, taking his part in what we're talking about, making his presence felt, even though I can't see him anywhere.

Late on Sunday afternoon before I go to work, I go by to see Mother. The others have been there for Sunday dinner, and I get there just after they have all left. She has something she wants to talk to me about, and she summons me. When I came home after I had been on the road, I wanted to see if there was anything left of our relationship. I looked for some part that was personal that survived my going on the road. To do that, we talked, but we don't get anywhere with our talk. We are tense and uneasy. She feels guilty about me—somehow me being a lesbian is her fault—and she has only a few ideas how to fix things between us. Me, I'm angry at that, and I don't tell her what I want her to know.

Now I see evidence of the children lying about, blocks on the floor and the books Frances and I used to read as kids, falling apart now, in a stack on the chair that used to be my father's before he died. There's a large bowl of cut flowers in the middle of the dining room table. Frances brought them. "Aren't they nice?" She is not sure they are nice.

"How is everybody?"

"Everybody watched the Olympics! It was so exciting! The wrestling—"

The TV is still on, its sound turned down, showing a picture of a blond woman selling shock absorbers, touching them delicately with long manicured fingernails.

Mother has on her apron from doing the kitchen duties, and now she gathers her thoughts. She takes it off and folds it and places it over the back of a chair. "Sit down, Marybeth, I have some things I want to talk to you about."

I sit at the end of the sofa, and she takes the stack of books and puts them on the floor and takes Dad's chair. The room—Dad's chair, the oak table with the brass bowl in front of the windows, the magazines—is as familiar as an old movie.

"I want to talk about money."

I wait for her to begin.

"I wish you'd been able to come today." She looks at me, waiting for me to say something, her fingers absently pulling at the striped fabric of Dad's chair.

"I was up in Hamlin with everybody." I am aware of how I sound. I would rather say nothing at all, but I feel compelled to fill the silence.

"But I wish you'd come."

I wait a moment, thinking. "What do you want me to say, Mother? I was up in Hamlin with everybody."

Now, she doesn't know what to say. Finally, she draws a breath: "We all wish you liked it here more."

It is my turn to draw a breath. What she wants me to say is I'm sorry I didn't come and that I'll come next time. What I want to say is I want you to accept my reason for not coming. "I told you I was going to be with my friends in Hamlin. What do you want me to say?"

"Arnold and Seth are doing right well for themselves—"

I nod. I can see the TV screen, where things are being sold.

"—getting established. That's what your dad and I wanted for you young ones. We worked hard to make it possible for you to have things easy. You've graduated from college—"

"I paid for that myself—" There's a picture of me in my robes on the wall in the hall.

"—and we're so proud of you, all of us. But Frances—" She leans forward a little in Dad's chair. "—feels that you don't care about the advantages you have. Waiting is all right for a little while, but—" She goes on to say that she wants me to get a more presentable job, something with a future, by which she means something that will pay more and allow me to dress better, get a car. "All of us want you to get on in life—" She looks at me brightly and waits.

"I don't want to dress better, and Cynthia and I have a car."

"Your friends—"

"None of my friends care much about the way I dress."

"I mean the ones you went to school with—"

"What are we talking about here, Mother?"

She seems surprised. "We're talking about you being happy!"

"I think you're talking about me living like Arnold and Seth and Frances. I think you're talking about me being married. I don't want to live like them." We've been over all this before.

She reaches out and puts a hand on my knee. The effort costs her something because Dad's chair is too large for her, and to reach out to me means rising from its low cushions. "What do you want?"

I don't forget the pain I went through before I came out to her, and I don't forget the fact that she wasn't aware of it. She wasn't aware that she didn't know how to teach me to grow up a lesbian. She wasn't even aware she had that responsibility. When I was ten, I knew even then I couldn't look to her to raise me, and it was two or three years before I made contact with a girl at the town swimming pool and learned that there was a lesbian community that would "raise" me. Now I listen to her running on about how I ought to live my life, and I think, she abandoned me when I was ten and left me to find my own way, and now she expects me to listen to her.

The conversation goes on aimlessly because what we are talking about is never clear. What I want is already settled. I tell her what I want, and she can't hear it, listening in her head so hard to what she wants. I tell her again.

"But," Mother says, "you can't spend all your life with women!"

This gets more difficult all the time. There was a time three years ago when all I wanted to do was cut loose. I did that, and it sometimes seems now that that was the easy part. This woman is my mother, and some part of me feels like her daughter. I know I want her to be something in my life, but I don't know how to make that happen. I'm afraid to give in to her. It'd mean giving up what I've gained, and yet the other thing seems hard. If I could hate her, it'd be easy. I think sometimes that loving her means hating myself.

Monday we are coming home from the coalition meeting. Cynthia and I have not seen each other since early yesterday afternoon, and when we got into the car together after the meeting, her hand groped for mine in the dark and closed on it, cool and transmitting sex. We are to drop Mickey off at his place. He sits in the back seat, talking about the gay rights bill as I drive through the dark city streets. It will be introduced again in the legislature this winter and will be voted on sometime during the next couple of months after that. It's been introduced in the last four legislative sessions and lost each time by a two-thirds majority. I stop for a light and shift and listen to him, and the noise jangles in my head. I'm tired, and I wish he wouldn't talk now, and I'm angry that he doesn't know that.

"The people in Portland and Augusta are working together."

"Have you joined up with them?" Cynthia asks, her fingers tighten on my forearm.

"We've been on the phone, and our task force is going to meet with them to divide up the list of legislators and go to see each one. That's what I want to talk to you about—"

Cynthia turns, her back to the door, to see Mickey in the back seat more clearly. We have entered Mickey's street.

"I need some help. I want to find people here to contact their senators and representatives—" He speaks in a low voice, calmly, reasonably.

"Sure," Cynthia says.

"Why don't we get together one night—"

Cynthia turns to me, her hand coming to rest on my shoulder, the tips of her fingers tiny claws scratching my neck. We are in front of Mickey's place. I double park and turn off the ignition.

"When would be good for you?"

I don't want to answer her. "I don't want to do that." I pull away from her hand.

She's surprised. "Why not?"

"The coalition should attend to ourselves. The gay rights bill isn't going to get at our issues, anyway—" Mickey has not gotten out. I reach forward and grasp the ignition key.

"It'll give us protection in housing and credit—"

"But not employment."

"That'll come later."

"Attitudes'll remain the same." I turn on the ignition. Cynthia stares at me.

"It's like the ERA or the civil rights bills of the sixties," Mickey says.

"Which, we all know, eradicated racism." I depress the gas pedal slightly, running the engine.

"OK. It's a start."

"I don't want to put my energies into this. We should look after ourselves—"

Cynthia stiffens. She has turned again in her seat so that now she is facing directly forward, her arms crossed over her chest.

"—develop our friendships, develop sources of energy among ourselves. Encourage each other. Build places for us to discover ourselves, away from them. *Be alone for a while.*"

"That's so inward turning—"

I wonder to what extent she is playing to Mickey. "That's what I mean it to be. This isn't about a gay rights bill. It's about us—"

"It's about getting together and wielding political and economic power."

"No, Mickey. It's about a corrupt, sexist, homophobic system. It's about change—"

"Power comes from using it," Mickey says decisively from the back seat.

The coalition has been at the edge of a split during the last two meetings. The women have a history of the women's movement. We've had our organizations and our meetings for years, and the men seem naive, unpracticed. Their issues have to do with the police and politics, and they've tried to override us and define the agenda of the coalition. They haven't really understood the issues we face, and Mickey has been a part of that. I am tired and impatient, and I don't feel like trying to undo Mickey's bad education sitting in a car at eleven at night double-parked in front of his house.

The governor, a Democrat, at his press conference today, was asked this question: *What will be the response of the state government to the murder of Bernard Mallett in Cardiff?* His answer had two parts. He said that he had always supported the gay rights bill now before the legislature, which would protect the civil rights of gay men and lesbians in matters of credit and housing. He was opposed to including employment because, he said, there were certain employers who, because of religious beliefs, should not be forced to employ homosexuals. He was talking about the Roman Catholic Church and the fundamentalist Christian right. Nobody pointed out that the national Democratic platform specifically included protecting gay rights in matters of employment.

The governor said the matter of the murder was in the hands of the criminal justice system—the police and the courts—and it would be inappropriate for him to comment further. He's like my mother: You can have this, and you can have that, but you can't have everything you want. And there are a certain number of things he won't even discuss.

Every day I come home from work and find Cynthia watching some sporting event from Los Angeles. I get in bed with her, run my hand up and down her body and cup her breasts, and then with the tips of my fingers, pull gently on her nipples. I pull her toward me and kiss them. The sound of the television set pulls me away. We watch athletic women running and jumping and heaving and swimming and diving before the huge crowds in the stadium. The color of the photography is unnaturally intense, and the red, white and blue of the athletes' uniforms is as unreal as technicolor. The image the screen presents is of a group of female athletes

competing before a stadium of men. Afterwards Cynthia responds to
my fingers' pressure on her nipples with rapid breathing, pushing her
pelvis toward me. Those women in Los Angeles are far away, and I
give up thinking and fall down the deep slope toward Cynthia's
vulva.

Cynthia is tearing the lettuce apart and washing it, and I am
cutting up the vegetables. Deborah and Sally are due here in about an
hour. We have rented half this house for two years, and the point of
it, for me, has been that, here on the river in Hamlin, above
Baskahegon and Staceyville, Cynthia and I have a safe home.

"Suzanne is looking for a place to live."

"What's she looking for?"

"A room. I don't think she can afford more than that."

"That's hard to find."

"There're plenty of rooms. She's looking for something with
other women."

She dries the lettuce on a paper towel.

"I've been thinking."

She waits.

"I've been thinking about getting more women here."

"Here?"

"Our place. Turning this into a women's house."

"Here! Where?" She stops with the lettuce and looks at me.
"What about us?"

"We have the extra room. In September, the apartment next
door is vacant and Mr. Clucker will be looking for a tenant. I've been
thinking we could rent it and then get two or three women to live
upstairs. A commune. Just women—"

"What about us!"

At the next coalition meeting, the task force on the bill
reports on the beginnings of the lobbying effort in Augusta. When
they ask for volunteers, hands rise all over the room. I sit on mine
and listen as Mickey speaks:

"This is what coming out means—letting them know we are
here and what our agenda is. That means door-to-door work,
lobbying each legislator. It means mailing lists and telephone calls. It
doesn't mean going back in the closet and nursing our wounds. If we

are not out there where they can see us—specifically, if we are not there in the legislature letting them know we want a gay rights bill— and if we are not militant about what we want, we won't get any of it. We have to get involved in the dogged work of politics."

I want to go home. I think of my bedroom. I am going to tell Cynthia tonight that I want separate beds. I want myself to myself. I listen to the discussion. They speak of ways to make our power effective. Someone else has defined the rules of this game we are about to play. My father, my brothers, and their big bodies and slow unthinking minds. Why should I fight, especially now, when I am twenty-two, have been on the road and come back and supported myself for the last five years and gotten a college degree and owe nobody anything? What good would this gay rights bill have done Bernie? Protect his credit!

I want an absolutely separate community. I want no men around me. No men.

Early in August we pass the tenth anniversary of Nixon's resignation, and the thirty-ninth anniversary of the bombing of Nagasaki. The Olympics are over finally. It was all about winning and losing. The major story of the Olympiad was the number of nations who boycotted the games this year for political reasons because America boycotted the games four years ago. There are stories speculating on who is going to boycott the games in Seoul in four years. In the middle of the month, there is a big story attacking the financial reporting of the man married to Geraldine Ferraro. The president, a good-natured, pleasant guy, makes a joke after a press conference, at a moment when he thought his microphone was turned off, that Russia has been abolished. "The bombing starts in five minutes."

On the eighteenth of August, the *New York Times* carries on its front page in the upper left two columns a story from Washington: "US Court Upholds Navy's Discharge of a Homosexual." The Cardiff *Sentinel* carries the same story from wire services under the headline, "US Court: Homosexuals Have No Right to Privacy." The navy, it seems, discharged a sailor for engaging in private homosexual activity with another consenting adult, and the sailor sued to be reinstated, saying his constitutionally protected right to privacy had been violated. The court ruled that "private, consensual homosexual conduct is not constitutionally protected."

On the same day, the lead story on the front page of the *Times* has to do with the Republican Convention, which starts in two days. The headline reads: "GOP Statement Says Voters Face Stark Fall Choice." Inside, editorials comment on the president's tendency to fall asleep during cabinet meetings, on his joke about bombing Russia, and on the poor, of whom the *Times* says there are more than there used to be and they are poorer than they used to be.

"I'm thinking of going to camp for the whole week," Helen says. "And just close the store. Can't bear it. Every time you turn on the tube, there is someone waving the flag and talking about patriotism." She sighs and lifts her arms up high and stretches. She takes out the huge plastic barrette in her hair and lets her hair fall down on her shoulders. Then she runs her fingers through it, like combs, and piles it back up again, rapidly, thoughtlessly, and fixes the barrette to hold it. "Such self-satisfaction!" She gazes out the window into the street. "My image of a patriot is of a man carrying a rifle at his hip."

I don't plan to watch. And yet it is impossible not to watch. It is difficult to turn on the tube without seeing either some politician live or a rerun of some politician live, talking about what it means to be an American. I turn off the sound and stare at their faces. They are white men, standing on a podium so large it looks like the front of an ocean liner about to run you down. They grip the sides of the podium and straighten their arms and tuck their chins in and pronounce. The day before the convention opens, the *Boston Globe*'s lead headline: "GOP Moves to Right, Conservatives in Control." Elsewhere on the front page: "Archbishop Vows to 'Teach' on Moral Issues." And, finally, a feature: "In Brassy, Booming Dallas, Success Counts."

Lying in bed one night, the room lit only by the moon, Cynthia said, "Look, I don't mind having people over all the time. I like that. I wouldn't even mind asking Suzanne to stay here for a while until she gets settled again. But I don't want her moving in." She was on her side facing me, and her fingers picked gently at me.

"You feel threatened."

She didn't like that. She closed her mouth firmly. Then she said, "Yes. I feel threatened."

"You're afraid that the commitment we have for one another will be diluted by the presence of another person in our house."

"Yes."

"You're afraid that means another person in our bed."

"Yes! Doesn't it? *Does* it?"

"I don't know." I don't know what it means. I don't understand people's fear. When things got really bad for me, I went on the road. I *changed*. I just went out one day with a pack on my back and stuck out my thumb, going west. And I survived and I'm better now, and I don't understand why people hang on so long until the only thing you can feel is pain in your knuckles because you're holding on so tight.

I watch the convention in Dallas and conclude that systems are amazing. They don't have a life of their own. They are not living organisms, but they are in a weird way self-perpetuating and act in predictable ways as if they were living organisms. The conservatives in our political system disapprove of homosexuality. The liberals are in favor of some sort of civil rights for homosexuals. The clear choice between Republicans and Democrats seems to be what we are looking at now in this election. Yet systems never act to self-destruct. There is a consensus on gender and sex which both Republicans and Democrats agree on. And whether our challenge is accepted or rejected, the system will remain intact, self-preserved, undisturbed. We may be given a little right here, a small right there by this court or that law—protection in housing and credit!—but the serious issues, Bernie's murder, the definition of the family, the proper uses of sex, what kind of sex is permissible, the whole range of gender issues, are beyond our reach, enclosed in society's consensus, or referred to the courts, where we don't have a voice. The men, Derek and Mickey and the others, because they are men and therefore privileged, don't see that.

"This is what love means," Cynthia said.

"What does love mean?"

"Loving only me. Only me. How can you love me if you say you don't want to commit yourself to me only?"

"I love you," I say. I say that, and I wonder how I can define what I mean by it. "I love what you are—"

"Sure, and sex—"

"And sex. I want to be with you."

"But not only with me—"

"I don't know. There is nobody else. I have no plans. I have no agenda."

"I am not enough for you—"

"I didn't say that. What I said was, I couldn't promise—"

"Why can't you promise? That's what love means!"

"Why does it mean that? Who said, 'Love means promising'?" I want to know that. Who said, *Love means promising?*

Jack and I stand on opposite sides of a table in the parish house of the Unitarian Church. We face one another across mounds of copies of our new newsletter. When he came in I saw him down the hall before he saw me. He walked tentatively, almost on tiptoes, looking for me in the rooms he passed.

"I didn't see you." He grins, and his face is open, waiting. He is relieved and in a good mood. Jack is wearing his uniform. He is a driver for a service that delivers packages, and his uniform is a green jumpsuit. He wears the button, *Another Friend of Bernie Mallett.* "What do we do?"

"We stuff. We fold first. Then we stuff."

I show him how to fold the newsletter to get it in the envelope. Now he asks what is in it. If he weren't a man, I might think he was a dear.

"Something on the memorial service for Bernie."

"The founding of the coalition?"

"Yes, and a description of the task forces—"

"What they do—?"

"One from each of them."

"Did anybody write anything personal about Bernie—"

"—yeah. There's a lot of politics—"

He frowns. "Was there anything about the fight at the court house?"

I laugh. "No, Jack." Then it occurs to me: "Why don't you write something about street violence, talk to other people, get a lot of stories—"

He is folding the newsletters. He's gotten the hang of it now, and his hands are moving quickly. "I can't write. Let somebody else do that—" He looks at me. "I wasn't good at English in school." He looks down at his work. While he works, his head is bent down, and when I look up from my side of the table, we are very close.

"I got something to ask you." He hesitates. He looks around the room, at the pile yet to go and the pile already folded.

"Well?" He seems so tough, and he is so innocent.

"Do you really not like men?"

That comes out of the blue! I can't think of anything to say.

"I mean, even gay men?"

Just beyond this room, through the door, I can see into the auditorium of the church, a great space whose light through the windows is colored by the stained glass: It's such an absurd idea. It's so exactly wrong.

I begin to laugh. "Jack!" I want to sit down.

He blushes and looks down at his work again, and I can't stop laughing. I am giggling and laughing.

Suddenly everything changes, and he drops a newsletter on the table, one-third folded, and turns away. He's moving away from the table and toward the door.

"Wait!" I try to stop him. "Where are you going?"

"Out of here." He turns away. "You can go fuck yourself."

I didn't mean to do this. "Wait." I reach out to him, try to reach him. I have stopped laughing. "Wait, Jack. Come back. I won't laugh anymore." I am confused because I care what Jack is feeling, and that surprises me.

He is standing by the door, looking at me, hurt and confusion all over his face.

"Come back, Jack. I didn't mean to laugh."

He hesitates.

"Please, Jack."

Slowly, he lowers his head and moves across the room again toward the table. He picks up a newsletter. He folds it over and runs his fingers down it to make a crease. His face is a confused scowl.

"I didn't mean to laugh—"

"Why do you laugh at me?"

"I didn't mean to. It was just that it was a funny question. It seemed so odd—" I run out of things to say, and I watch his face. He goes on folding the newsletters.

Marybeth

"I been thinking about all the people in the coalition and how you and I are the most alike." He looks up at me. "We're fighters—"

I stand here, my fingers to my lips, looking at him. He's right, of course. Who would have thought *Jack* and I—? But he's right: Everyone else wants to make some accommodation. Jack and I could end up on the same side of things. That's funny. That's a dangerous notion.

One of the good things about our society is that nothing is left to chance. It keeps reminding you, in case you had forgotten, where everybody stands on everything. And it does it in easy, clear language so there won't be any confusion: *Gays Have No Right To Privacy.* This morning in the paper, the Republican Party announced that the president has said, "Society has always regarded marital love as a sacred expression of the bond between a man and a woman. In the Judeo-Christian tradition, it is the means by which husband and wife participate with God in the creation of new human life. In part the erosion of those values has given way to a celebration of forms of expression most reject. We will resist the efforts of some to obtain government endorsement of homosexuality."

Since I brought up inviting Suzanne to share our apartment, Cynthia and I have become intensely sexual. Her eyes follow me wherever we are, even when we are in large groups, and when we are alone, our hands are all over each other. The intensity of our sex has to do with our splitting up, as if we could hold on with our mouths and tongues and fingers to what we can't retain with our hearts. Her soft wet lips and her slick fingers overwhelm and confuse me—as I think she wants to do—and muddy my thoughts.

Helen and Suzanne and Eleanor and Claire and Cynthia and I are sitting on the floor in our living room. It is Sunday evening late in August, a day the president has proclaimed Women's Equality Day. Cynthia sits directly across from me, the others are on the side.

Helen is talking: "The trouble is that it's her responsibility too. She signed the tax returns. And when she agreed to run for vice president, she should have known that they would go after every little flaw in her record. She can't escape him—"

"That's just it. If she were a man—" Suzanne stops and starts again. "How many men do you know in public life have wives who

396

have large businesses? Just because she is a woman, her circumstances are different, and she is being treated differently. *Her* taxes are OK. It's his that are a mess. Why is she being asked to defend him?"

"She's a woman, and that makes her vulnerable—"

"—responsible—"

"Why is she being held responsible for him?"

Helen heaves a sigh. "Look, you can see it all over her face. She wants to be loyal to him, but she wants her career too. *You know how Italian husbands are!* The woman is being torn apart—"

Cynthia looks at the floor, and then she looks up at me and rests her eyes on me. I told her last night again that I would not be monogamous with her.

I want to live in a woman's house with other women, and I would do that with her here, or without her in some other house. I said all this in a kind of rush. I knew that if she stopped me, I would forget what I was trying to say and get lost in trying to explain. I knew that if she kissed me—or touched me anywhere—I would lose my direction, a sense of what is important to me, myself.

"What," she asked, "has happened to us?"

Before I could stop her, she was before me, my neck enclosed by her hand and her moist soft lips. Involuntarily—because I have always done it instinctively—I threw my arms around her, and I couldn't think any more. She nibbled at my neck on one side and ran her hand up and down on the other, and I struggled, my hands on her shoulders, gripping them, holding her to me.

I said that day to Jack that I want to fight *for* something. He had developed the mechanical movements necessary to folding the newsletters quickly: picking up the paper, moving down the table with rapid arm movements, and dropping the folded newsletter in a pile at the end.

He stopped folding and looked at me. I suddenly thought, wildly, he can't fold and talk at the same time. "For what?"

"Me. When I am with you—"

He took one hand and made a fist and ground it into the heel of the other hand. "What happens—?"

"You remind me of things—" I looked at his green button.

"How?"

Before I could answer, he asked, "Why?"

"You remind me of being helpless—"

He was looking at me, listening, real hard.

"I don't think you mean to—"

"What do you mean *helpless*—?"

"When I am with you, I start thinking, the point is who's stronger."

"That's weird—"

"You don't listen to anybody else. You have your mind made up. You're so big. You bully people—"

"I don't mean to—"

"I don't think you mean to. You get excited—"

"What do I do?"

"You're a man." I shrugged. "You represent your privilege."

He stared down at me. "I don't know what that means." It'd been a long time since either of us had folded a newsletter. He squinted his eyes. "You want room for yourself—"

I shrugged, and then I nodded.

"That's what you want?"

I nodded. "I don't want to have to struggle for my place."

He picked up a newsletter and slowly folded it. "I like the way you take people on." We folded for a while. "You don't want to be friends."

"I don't know, Jack." In fact, at that moment, I did. All the feelings I was having suggested I did, in fact. I could see he was trying. But I also was aware that wasn't enough.

"I thought we were friends. Two fighters." That's it. Again.

"We'll have to see." I hurt him. Part of me said he deserved it. Still does. He needs to learn. But part of me saw him as an ally— Jack won't compromise on anything—and I don't want my principles to cause hurt. I saw that it was going to take a while to sort all this out.

He grunted. "Let me know when you decide."

I am all tangled up now.

Since Bernie died, it has become essential to think everything through again, but the difficulty is that *thought* is not what's effective. I keep forgetting that. What's needed is a clarification, a simplification, of feeling. I think I ought to be able to work with Jack. My feelings, still hurting, say *no*. But when I see

Jack trying so hard, they say yes. I'm thinking if he'll stay steady, if he'll keep offering and not get mad if I don't say yes, if I can have time to let this happen, then I can see—I don't know what I can see.

Then he said something else that surprised me: "You and me, we're different from Mickey and Dana and those folks. They got money. That makes them be careful." He grinned. "I got nothing to lose. I don't think you do either." He crossed his arms over his chest. "That makes us free."

We're sitting in the living room on the floor, Cynthia and I and Eleanor, our backs up against the sofa or a chair, drinking beer. It's 1:30 a.m.

"Marybeth wants to invite Suzanne to move in."

So. "That's sudden."

Cynthia looks at me. "What?"

"Your bringing that up." I look at them. "Have you two been talking about that?"

Cynthia shrugs. Eleanor looks awkward.

"I'm being set up." I look at them. "What were you saying?"

There is a long pause. I look from one to the other. I decide not to break the silence.

We wait.

I shrug. I drink my beer.

"I was saying that I don't believe you—"

"'bout what—"

"About Suzanne. I think you've fallen in love with her."

She waits for me to say something.

"I haven't." I want to be together with Cynthia. What I can no longer do is *promise* anything. I consider, from time to time, the possibility of giving up sex. Is it the glands that makes all this so difficult?

When I could, I would drive Eleanor around, show her the sights in the area. Other times she borrowed the car when we were at work. She wanted to see the bridge, of course, and the court house and the jail where the boys were brought in that Sunday morning, the graveyard. I took her to the church, where we had the dances and Bernie's memorial service and the coalition meetings. The weather was what it was supposed to be at the end of August, cloudless skies, warm breezy days, slightly cool nights, and Eleanor kept saying over and over again, "This place is paradise. You don't know what you have here." I showed her where the boys live, and she drew a map in her notebook so she could come back, which she did later, and talked to people in the neighborhood about hunting deer.

She was the first reporter to try to get to know people around here. She did the usual things—interviewed the principal and the police chief—but she said afterwards that she wasn't going to get anything out of either of them, since they were so programmed. So she started looking for high school boys. She was cool about it. She found out where they were hanging out and started hanging out there too. Then after she had gotten their confidence, she told them who she was. By that time, they were friends, and the boys kept on talking, about deer hunting and shooting squirrel, about drowning cats and about shooting bb guns at dogs, and about the high-pitched yelp the dog makes when you hit him. She used it in her piece, which she sent us later.

"It's paradise where Adam has a gun," she said. "Are you afraid of getting shot during season?"

"You don't go in the woods then—"

She went over the press clippings when she got here. She said, "The weird thing is how they concentrate on 'the boys' and 'the murder,' the court business, and ignore what is really going on.

I asked her what she thought was really going on.

"Why, how we are going to govern ourselves sexually. Of course."

We are in bed. I am on my back. My thigh is between Suzanne's legs, her leg between my thighs. What does it mean, *fall in love?* Why must it mean, at least, *keep you only to her, so long as you both shall live?* To whose purpose is it that we revere sexual monogamy? Isn't it that men are afraid they can't be sure they are the fathers of their children unless they make us be monogamous? And so they teach us, from the moment we are sucking our mothers' milk, that love and monogamy are synonymous, until we can't conceive of the one without the other? Why should I accept Judeo-Christian values, which make love so small and narrow?

Later we talk.

"There'd be no rules."

"Right."

"Nobody owning anybody else."

"Right."

"Everything by consensus."

"Right. No coercion."

"Right."

We have spoken to Suzanne's friend from the shoe factory, and to Claire, which makes five of us if Cynthia will come along.

On Friday before Labor Day, I am about to go to work when Frances calls. Her sugary voice needs no introduction: "We've missed you so!"

"Hi, Frances."

She tells me about Van in his new job and what a chore it is to keep his clothes looking nice, and she tells me about the children.

"I'm calling," she says, "to invite you to a picnic. It's going to be grand! We want you to come!" She tells me the picnic is to be Labor Day afternoon at Green Lake. Frances and Van and Arnold and Helen and Seth are going to be there, with children. There will be boating and a ball game and singing—everybody's going to bring guitars—and wonderful food. Frances is going to do a ham and a cake both, although she doesn't have to: Most people are only doing one or the other.

"Sure, I'll come," I say. "And I'll bring Cynthia. She's not doing anything either that afternoon."

There is a long pause. "Well, ah—"

Another long pause. "That might be awkward—"

Her voice, while it has lost its excitement, has not lost its mellifluousness. "I don't know if there will be enough—"

"Now Frances. You invited me, and you know there will be enough food and enough room—"

"Nobody knows her—"

"They can meet her. She's nice—"

There is another long pause. "I don't know. I'll have to ask Van. I don't think—" This time her voice has lost its melody and taken an edge. "I think her presence might be intrusive."

"Frances?"

"People will misunderstand."

"I think everybody will understand immediately that we are lovers. Nobody will misunderstand. You've invited me, and now I am coming, and I am going to bring my lover—"

She tries to back off: She is already thinking of how she can be sick Labor Day, but I am clear and at ease. I feel calm and sure, and when she hangs up, I gently replace the receiver, and I wonder, as I go back into the kitchen what I should cook to bring, should I go to her picnic, a cake, a ham, or both.

I am grateful to Frances. Like the president and the Republican Party and the boys, she clarifies things for me when I get wishy-washy. There's no such thing with any of those folks as a feeling. It's all principle and decency and traditional values and power and oppression. Her "traditional values" don't give me but one way to think about myself, and no matter how sweet she is, she doesn't offer me anything but a kind of suicide. I won't go to her picnic, because I'm a friend of Bernie Mallett's.

Cynthia lies on her stomach in the bed, her head on my stomach and her arms around me. It is very late—after one in the morning—and we are both very tired. She talks—it's almost a whisper—in long slow sentences with long pauses. She talks of how she loves me, what she loves about me—my feistiness, how scatterbrained I am, my courage—and how she hopes I love her too. She says she wants to spend the rest of her life with me. She talks of what we have built together—this apartment, our garden, the group of friends we've got around us, the work we do in the coalition, for the shelter, in NOW—and how sustaining that is. These are structures which we have built, she says, as extensions of ourselves, expressive of our goals and values, which must be honored as we honor ourselves. She says her love for me makes her want to be with me only. She could not imagine wanting to be with anyone else the way she is with me.

While she talks, I move my fingers in long slow figure-eights over her bare back, going into the valley of her backbone and then up and out again across the small hill of her waist and along the escarpment of her sides. The tips of my fingers move up out of her armpit and across the waving plain of her back and back into the small valley of her backbone. She tightens barely perceptibly, her arms around my body and snuggles her head down deeper into the soft pit of my stomach. She says she is afraid. I move my fingers down her side.

I love this moment, here in the bed in the dark, my fingers exploring this ground I need no light to know. There can't be any promises, no way to structure the future by mere will. We are in the dark. I can feel her tears wet on my skin. She says this feels like betrayal. I can now compare the feel of Suzanne's body with Cynthia's, and even though it doesn't feel like it to me, it is called "betrayal." I think of Cynthia and Suzanne and Claire and the woman from the shoe factory, of Deborah and Sally and Dana and Marcia. I think of Jack. I weigh these demands and needs, and mine, and, for an instant, I long for the moment when I was fifteen, when it seemed simple, and love was the same thing as lust and found its object in one body.

I think about what we do. I don't think it's clear to anybody. I think what people think is that if they give us our rights, we'll be OK. I think that's what *they* think too. Give them their "rights" and then the problem will be solved, and we can stop thinking about this and get on back to living. But if you carry all this down to its logical conclusion, if we get what is obviously ours, nothing in society will ever be the same again, and I mean the really deep things—the relationship between a man and a woman will never, ever be the same again, if we get what is ours. The relationship between a parent and a child will be *totally different* if we get what is ours. All they have to do is recognize that we exist, really accept that, and recognize where we came from—

The fundamentalists are right: We are incredibly dangerous to society. We're a time bomb. Moderates and liberals don't have any inkling.

On the Tuesday after Labor Day, I am at Dominic's. It is the supper crowd. We serve plain fare: roast beef and potatoes, roast chicken and rice, pork and apple sauce. And pies. I am going back and forth, back and forth to the kitchen, where Dominic, his head hunched over his enormous black stove, moves his pots and pans around with a giant clatter.

I stop at a booth near the back of the room. It is a man and a woman who have had two dinners—roast beef and chicken, two coffees, two pies—and are waiting for their check.

The man, thirty-five, short brushcut hair, a foreman somewhere, looks over the check and pulls out his wallet to look for bills.
The woman, her elbows on the table, her hands clasped in front of
her chin, lets her eyes wander from him to me. They come to rest on
my green button: *Another Friend of Bernie Mallett.*

He gives me the money, and I give him the change. He puts
it down on the table. Then he looks up at me.

"I've seen you on television." He squints against the lights in
his eyes.

I wait, not sure.

"You're a member of that coalition."

So. I don't say anything. It wasn't a question.

"You're a friend of that boy's." He stares at my button.

Then I say it slowly, "Yes—"

"People like you shouldn't be allowed in this town."
Suddenly he's grinning. "Scum of the earth." She's grinning too now.

They rise from the booth, almost trampling me.

I watch them leave. I think of my house. This weekend, we
are going to help Claire move into the apartment next door. She says
we ought to be able to do it in one morning, since she has so little
stuff. The weekend after that, Suzanne will move in. I think it would
be best if she moved in with Claire, and the new woman from the
shoe factory—her name is Wilma—moved in with us. We are going
to help each other paint. Our women's house.

Jack came by earlier. He offered to help us move the heavy
stuff. I told him I'd ask the other women to see if that was OK. Jack
is in a bad way about Derek. Derek's leaving this weekend. Jack says
he feels betrayed, and he wanted to know how you handled that. I
told him I didn't know, but we could talk. We will, and I don't look
forward to it. I'm standing here thinking, I guess I know something
about it, from both sides. I wonder how much courage he has. Is he
willing to give up all that power his maleness gives him? And about
myself: When will I stop wanting revenge?

I carry dishes back to the kitchen and dump them on the
counter. I take coffee to people, take orders, bring them checks. The
supper crowd thins out, the movie crowd starts drifting in. George
comes in, and I tell him how good he looks. Cynthia says she's
willing to try this new arrangement. I love her for that. Tonight she's
been helping Claire pack, and they will pick me up after work. It's a

full moon, and if it's bright enough out, we're going skinny-dipping in the river. We do that around here in the summertime when the moon is full and makes everything look like pale silver, except for where it shines on the water, which looks like gold.

Mickey

My house used to be a safe place. Two nights ago at one in the morning Robbie and I were inside the front door, and Jack stood just outside, holding the screen open while he said goodbye. A car came down the street, and a man leaned out of it and screamed, "Faggots!" The word echoed off the sides of the houses, and Jack took off like a bull—he jumped over all the steps down to the ground—and ran across the yard and down the street after the car, yelling, "Fight, you son of a bitch!" Robbie and I stood in the door, looking down the dark street, hearing the thud of his feet and his voice get fainter and fainter: "Fight, you son of a bitch! Come back and fight!" Finally, Robbie said, "I can't stand this," and took off down the stairs, and then I went too. We caught up with Jack—he had stopped running and was leaning on his arm against a tree, his breath coming in great heaves—but the car was long gone. This happens regularly, and it always ends the same way.

This morning it was a dead chicken: It says we are the garbage of their civilization. It was left hanging from the light beside the front door. It had been dead for a while, and it still had its head and feathers and claws. Its beak was open, and it was stiff and attracted flies. When Robbie and I tried to take it down, the knots in the cord were pulled tight, so we had to cut it down. One day it was a dead cat, and another time it was half a dog, so old it didn't smell, and the blood and the mess inside were dry. They must have found it on the highway somewhere. I've painted the door now six times, but they paint FAGGOT on it again while it is still wet.

I called the police because that is what you're supposed to do, but they make no effort to stop it or to catch the people doing it. They don't take me seriously, and they don't care. A reporter from the paper came by one day and talked, but they didn't print anything. Sometimes in the middle of the night, I hear noises outside. Jack has stayed up all night in the dark waiting. I know they're out there watching. They taunt me. Once I went out Saturday afternoon and found dead pigeons on the front steps when I came home, so they must watch even in the daytime. I am used to being watched by people I can't see and stared at by people I don't know. I am becoming hard, and I hadn't expected that.

Timothy is still here. He eats here, and when I go to bed, he's on the sofa in the living room, but he gets up and sneaks out—I know he goes to the hill—and that defeats the purpose of his living here. He's always high, or drunk, but I've never seen him drinking, and I don't know where he's getting the stuff. He has no money. When he's here, he sits in a corner and stares—*What does he see when he stares?*—and he won't, or can't, tell me where he's been or where he's getting it or who he's been with. Every article this summer on Bernie's murder has identified him. His picture has been on TV every time there's a demonstration at the court house—he seems to like the attention he gets at the demonstrations, and the reporters find him an easy mark for a crazy quote—so he's instantly identifiable. Whoever hung the dead chicken must know Timothy is here and goes out in the middle of the night alone. One night he won't come home. He'll be drunk and high and get beaten up, and when we find him he won't be able to tell us who did it, or he'll be dead. He's everybody's victim. I've given up thinking I can protect him, and that's another thing I feel hard about.

At work I sit at my terminal, the keys clicking as I program. Charles drops off papers on my desk. I speak, and he speaks, and then he leaves. His tone with me remains audibly the same as it has always been: casual, friendly, distant in the way that straight men are distant from one another. But since that day I told him I was gay, he has arranged things not to be alone with me. Occasionally when I invite him to lunch, he will come if others join us, but more often, he has an excuse. When I ask him, I watch his face for the flicker—it is almost not there—of discomfort and confusion. The others remain distant, friendly, hardworking. I find I am odd man out. This has happened so slowly over these two months that the change is almost imperceptible. The currents of friendship eddy around me but don't break over me any more in this clean sterile environment. Sometimes I find myself walking in on a group of my colleagues in the conference room or on the front steps of the building, laughing or talking among themselves. They see me and fall silent and then scatter. Yet if I ask one for help with an issue, or if I am given an assignment to work with one particular man, the work goes well and there seems to be nothing wrong. It is difficult to point to evidence of what is happening here, but I know something is happening, and I watch it develop.

407

It is Labor Day weekend, the beginning of the presidential election campaign. In Cardiff we have the school committee meetings to look forward to: This fall they are going to consider the tolerance policy proposed this past summer. Some of the preachers have been at every school committee meeting since July to speak against it, and some of us—Deborah, particularly—have been there to speak in favor. That will all come to a head this month or next.

The judge still hasn't made a judgment on whether to try the boys as adults. Every night at supper somebody says he's heard a rumor that the charges are going to be dropped. The attorney general in Augusta says he's treating this case extremely seriously, but they haven't decided how the boys are to be tried, and Jack says, "Shit, they're not going to try those boys at all." It's been almost two months since Bernie died, and nothing is resolved. First, there were psychiatric evaluations of the boys. Then there was a probable cause hearing. In the middle of September, the court is to decide whether to try them as adults. Most people think they're going to keep putting this off and putting it off until nobody cares anymore. Then they'll drop the charges. Jack says, "We'll be left here feeling like shit." I am waiting for the end of all of this, and the end I think I am waiting for is the boys' being convicted of murder. But that's not going to happen, and I have become very hard about that.

I have spent almost every night this last week with Dana and Arthur, making a list. Dana has the university phone book. Arthur has gotten a list of all the clergy in town and a list of the students at the seminary. He has also brought a phone book from the medical center. He says he stole it from his proctologist's office. We have a list of lawyers—a photocopy of the yellow pages listings—and of the teachers in the school system which Deborah got for us. Luke provided a list of the historical society members, and we are working on getting the Democratic Party mailing lists.

Dana and Marcia lend me books to read, and I keep a list in my notebook of the ones I've finished. The first was by John Boswell, a professor at Yale, and called *Christianity, Social Tolerance, and Homosexuality.* I've never read a book about homosexuality like this, aside from the Kinsey report. It has footnotes and a bibliography. And it doesn't say anywhere in it that we're sick—or anybody's *abomination.* It says it's the Christians who are fucked up.

Robbie and I are in shorts on the back steps, feeling the sun on our chests. It is Saturday afternoon of Labor Day weekend, about two. There's a wind blowing through the branches of the trees. The oaks rustle and click; they're getting dry because fall is coming on, and the hemlock at the bottom of the yard hisses. The weeds are higher than they were in July and more impenetrable. It's hot but the wind is cool on my bare skin. We've had lunch—sandwiches and some fruit—and tonight we're going to a going-away party for Derek. Now we're seized with lethargy, our bodies stretched out up and down the steps, our heads back, our eyes closed. After a time, I have a thought.

"Would you like a beer?"

"God, no."

We speak very slowly. There are long pauses. "What would you like?"

"Nothing."

I have my eyes closed, and I sense that Robbie does too. "Would you like to move in here?"

He laughs. "Yeah."

"Well?" I listen to the trees. "Will you?"

"Yes."

"When?"

"Now."

So. "Then we can get your things tomorrow and Monday."

"Yeah. Are you sure?"

My eyes are still closed, so I don't know whether he is looking at me. "Sure."

"I think I'd like a beer."

"Me too."

"What about a screwdriver?"

"That sounds better." I hear him get up off the steps, and I open my eyes and watch him move around me up to the door. He has beautiful legs, dancer's legs, almost hairless. We'll have drinks, and then we'll go to bed and have sex. Then we'll take a nap and get up and get something to eat and go to Derek's party. When he comes back, I am sitting up, watching him. He sits down next to me and hands me the cold glass, his eyes on me. I put the glass down, and then I take his away from him and set it next to mine. I put my arms around him and kiss him.

He puts his arms around me too. He pulls away. "Are you sure?" He smiles.

"Sure." I smile and kiss him again lightly.

"You're a weird one—" He smiles and runs his fingers through my hair.

I grimace, and then I shrug. "I'm slow. I'm sure."

"This is a weird place to want to move to—"

"It's just the place to be, now—" We kiss again. This time deeper. Then we take our drinks into the house.

I notice how my priorities change. My job has slipped down from number one to number two and then three—I don't know where it is now. I don't remember ever deciding, *Now* I'm going to make the coalition the most important thing in my life, but one morning I woke up and found my job didn't matter as much as, say, the books I have borrowed from Dana. I think about that sometimes, and wonder how it happened.

In bed Robbie runs his fingers over my back, up and down my backbone from my crack to my neck. It's hot in the late afternoon. The sun comes through the blinds and puts a lattice on the opposite wall. Robbie kisses the back of my neck, his finger searching for my anus.

"*Relax.*" He says it softly and draws out the vowels. *Relax.*

The tip of his finger circles my anus, and he kisses my neck again.

"*Relax.*"

My sphincter tightens against my will. The tension in my muscles runs all the way down the inside of my legs.

"*Relax.*"

My arms press down hard against the mattress, and my fingers, underneath my face, claw the sheet.

"Mickey. It's me." It's a whisper in my ear. *Mickey, it's me.*

We don't really have to get his "things." It was just a matter of a couple of trips to clean out his closet, since he has been living here half the time anyway since Bernie died. He moved in, and everything seems much the same. He takes up the same space in my life whether he is here or gone. We both think of us living together: It's our home now. It feels like a commitment of some sort too,

410

though we haven't mentioned that yet. And it feels safer, having him around. Oddly, now that Robbie has moved in, he doesn't seem to like having people around all the time, and we argue about that. He concentrates on us, and I concentrate on the things I have always concentrated on, my job, our gang, my family, and, now, the coalition. He wants me to give in to him—fall into his arms, I think is what he wants—and I want him around because I am ready to do battle, and I want support. We differ: I am dragged into responding to each attack, my attention diverted from him to this or that, while he remains calm, his focus inward, on his dance, on our sex, on his love for me.

In the first week after Labor Day, I get a call from my landlord, Mr. Fellowes. Since I rented the place three years ago, I haven't had much to do with him—a call now and then about plumbing or about a leak in the roof. I pay my rent on time, and our relationship has been distant and cordial, free of problems. It is early evening. Timothy lies on the sofa, his head in my lap.

"I want to speak to you about your door—"

His voice is soft, businesslike. I wait.

"It's an eyesore, the way it is, and I want you to paint it and keep it clean. Will you do that for me?"

I stroke Timothy's forehead, and I think how am I to respond to this.

"The neighbors complain."

"I have painted it, Mr. Fellowes. They keep coming back."

"Then you'll just have to paint it each time they come back. Will you do that for me?"

I wait a minute. I need to think. I don't want to rush into a commitment. "Mr. Fellowes?"

"Yes?"

"I will paint it one more time. If they paint FAGGOT on my door after that, it will have to stay there."

"Now, wait—"

"—or you will have to assume the responsibility for keeping the door clean."

He doesn't like my tone. "Now, Mickey, let's not get huffy. I've made a reasonable request—"

"I'm not defacing your door, Mr. Fellowes. I've called the police. They can't do anything. There's nothing more I can do."

"Well. Keep it clean, Mickey. I insist on that."

I stand at a booth in the middle of the main corridor at the Cardiff Mall, surrounded by indistinguishable music, the scraping and clicking noises people's feet make on the tiles and voices which can be heard but not listened to among the echoes. Behind me is the entrance to the department store, and in front of me is the record store and the pet store. I have my head down, my right ear in a device like a staple gun, and, just as I think I need to get ready, the girl pulls the trigger and drives a stud into my ear lobe.

It stings for a moment, and then I feel a small dull pain. I raise my head and smile at her—her face is emotionless, staring back—and look for the mirror. There. I look back at me out of the mirror. I have a gold stud in my ear lobe. While she stares at me, I stare at myself. The small globe of gold seems to leap out of the mirror at me, transforming, telling everything. I should grow a mustache and commit robberies to feed the poor. I grin and lift my chin. I am handsome, and I have admirers who worship me from afar. I have traveled widely, suffered much, and I know the secret of things.

The door has been painted again. I am struck by their energy and stamina. I know that this is the last time I will paint this door—the second Wednesday in September—but I don't know them and their plans. They are capable of painting my door every day or every week on into the fall and winter, till the paint freezes before it has a chance to dry. I think, when they get tired of doing this, they can call up reinforcements, fresh troops to paint my door, forever. The prospect hardens me to what's required. Stupid rage, helpless tears are not what's called for. I conserve my strength. I won't be like Jack and chase cars in the night. I will find a way to make the police respond. In the afternoon when I come home from work, I cover the letters with dark glossy green paint, and then I carry the paint out to the edge of the panel, making a neat job of it.

I am in the Discount Clothing Store on Columbia Street, and I see Marian in the next aisle. She is sorting through children's down jackets. Her American beauty is familiar and hurts, and I watch from my aisle as she concentrates on her thoughts of Sarah and Josh, their sizes, holding up jacket after jacket, thinking. After a time, I move around the end of my aisle to hers and speak.

She looks up and then back over her shoulder to me. She doesn't say anything immediately. Then, "Hello." She turns to face me. Her face is impassive.

"How are you?"

She shrugs. "OK." She stares, without giving anything away. "I'm OK."

"That's good." We run into one another like this everywhere in town, at least once a week, and we go through this exercise.

"Are Sarah and Josh OK?"

"They're OK."

She has her arms folded across her chest, and by now her face has hardened. We both are lit by harsh fluorescent light which reveals everything on the surface and conceals everything else. She stares at the gold stud in my ear and at the green button on my shirt. Her mouth is closed firmly.

"I would like to come by and see them this afternoon."

She colors. "That would not be good. I'm taking them out—"

"I won't hurt them, Marian."

"I am concerned about Josh—"

"You think I'll rape him?"

She winces. "Confuse him—"

"About what a man is supposed to be."

She hates this.

"That's absurd. Let me see them. They must miss me."

She opens her mouth to speak.

"When are you going to let me see them?"

She has gotten herself together. "Not now. I am not making any decisions now."

"When?"

"I don't know. Don't press me."

"Don't take too long, Marian. You don't have forever. I'm not going to give you forever." She drops the jacket she has had in her hand and walks past me to the front and to the doors. She doesn't return my calls. Once I went by, and Lloyd answered the door, his hand on the knob behind him, staring through the screen at me. He said she was not at home. I told him I wanted to come in. He said that that would not be OK. "I'll come back, Lloyd."

"Suit yourself," he said.

When the door is painted again, I don't repaint it. "*Paint it,*" Robbie tells me. "It's not worth the hassle with Fellowes." Then he says, "I'll do it." But that's not the point. I won't do it. I will not go to my basement and get a can of paint every time someone decides to express his hatred. Robbie and I argue, and he paints it and then we both sulk. Later, I get in the car and drive down to Dana's. We swap titles of books and pose questions the books raise. Dana's is a place to go when I need to get out of the house. She's teaching me.

Marybeth and I are sitting on a rock ledge on an island in the river in Baskahegon, halfway between her house and mine, in the middle of a Sunday in September. We wear the uniform of Maine: low boots, jeans, plaid shirts. She sits on the rock as if she has no weight, as if she were there first and the rock painted in afterward. She stares at me steadily, not blinking.

"I can't control him. I can't keep him safe unless I tie him down."

She gets reports from all over: People see him out alone almost every night, doing tricks. I tell her about his drinking.

"Drugs too?"

"Sure. I suppose so."

"Do you think he is an alcoholic?"

"I don't know. What does that mean? Isn't he too young?"

She laughs. "In a word, no." Here the river is deep, and the water black. It swirls and eddies around unseen objects, and on the surface occasional leaves bob and turn. We are lying on our backs, our torsos supported by our elbows, staring at the water. She says, "I'm thinking here's our solution."

"What?"

"We get the alcohol rehab unit at the hospital to take him. That'll keep him off the streets for 28 days. After that, if he's sober, he might be able to look after himself."

"How do we get him in?"

"We wait until he's drunk one day and then deliver him to the alcohol unit. They take over from there."

Marybeth says she will check it out for us, so we'll know what to do. She prepares to go, gathers herself together to stand up. I reach out to touch her, and I ask her to stay. Her body relaxes again against the rock.

We watch the water for a while. I ask her about the people who have moved in, Wilma, Suzanne, Claire. They are gradually becoming accustomed to one another. Cynthia, she says, is loosening up.

"You're not coming to the coalition meetings—"

She grimaces. "I just can't do that stuff right now. Later—"

"We need you—"

She pauses. "I need to be free of patriarchy."

There's nothing to say to that. What *am* I supposed to say to that? I don't try: "They're going to let the boys plea-bargain to manslaughter."

She looks over at me. "Where did you hear that?"

"Robbie."

"Are they going to try them as adults?"

"He doesn't know."

She stares at the water again. Finally, she speaks. "Well."

"Well, what."

"That's beside the point."

"What is?"

"Everything that happens to the boys. That has nothing to do with me." I feel a rush of anger. I could tell her what it has to do with her. Instead, I tell her what's been going on—the chicken and the cats.

"What about your landlord?"

"He's pissed about the door getting painted."

We watch the water for a while, listening to the gurgle along the shore. All of that seems very far away right now.

"You know, Mickey, you're very exposed. They all know where you live, and every time anybody gets irritated at queers, they go trash your place. Sooner or later, your landlord is going to get tired of it. And what I want to know is, How's your money? Can you handle getting thrown out? What about your job—?"

I have leaned back against the rocks and rested my head behind me and closed my eyes. I listen to her, but I don't want to hear what she is saying.

"—You live pretty well. Could you handle it if you got thrown out of your apartment and your boss fired you?"

That wouldn't happen.

"The only way you can be free, really, is to make certain you can support yourself, no matter what they do." She puts her hand on my knee. "What is it you do with computers? Is it easy to find a job?"

I sit up and look at her, about to answer.

"I mean, if you had to find a new job, could you do that? Without references?"

At home, I come in to find everybody here—Robbie in the kitchen cooking something, Timothy on the sofa staring at the TV, Jack on the phone, the stereo on loud. Suzanne and Claire sit at the table in the kitchen, watching Robbie and talking. I speak to everybody—run my fingers through Jack's hair while he is talking, and through Timothy's, who looks up at me and smiles before going back to the TV—and hug Robbie. His hands are wet. I sit down on the sofa at the other end from Timothy. I wonder what I would do if I were fired. I calculate the money in the savings account and add up my regular bills. I see my friends in every part of my apartment, and I consider how long I could live here, without a job, before I go broke. Gas usually runs $6, electricity $13 or so, my telephone bill $50 or $60—I can cut that back—cable TV is $19, and I don't owe anything on my credit cards. Total: $98.00.

Fellowes is angry about the door again—he left a message on the box yesterday—so I confront the possibility of having to move. I write down figures in my little notebook. I also jot down this: *What progress is being made in getting a meeting with the mayor of Cardiff?*

Claire comes in from the kitchen and drops herself into the sofa between me and Timothy. She squeezes my knee and grins. "You're a good dude."

I look at her—spiked hair, leathered studded wrist band, a tank top, and all the warmth of a furry dog—and grin back. "You're a good dude yourself."

"I wanta use your phone."

It is a funny thing to say, since they all use my phone all the time without asking me. "Go ahead."

"I mean, *use it*, honey. For the next two or three hours. Ya got any calls to make, you should make 'em now, cause I got fifty or sixty people to call—"

Claire is calling gay people for the task force, people who have been to a meeting of the coalition and then dropped out. Suzanne is using my typewriter to type up mailing labels for the newsletter. Cynthia is calling from their place, and other people are calling from other apartments, all over town. We don't want to lose anybody.

Jack hangs up the receiver and turns to all of us, talking loud over the stereo and the TV. "Hey, guys! Dana said we got another check today for $100!" He throws up his arms. "That means almost five hundred dollars in the bank, and that's enough for the mailing!" He stands up and throws himself up in the air like a cheerleader, coming down and shaking the whole house, "We're on the way!"

I move over to his chair by the phone while he is still jumping around shouting, and I dial.

"Guys!" I have to shout. "Cool it! I have to talk on the phone." I hear the dial tones and then Mr. Fellowes' voice. I tell him it's me.

"I drove by your house yesterday Mickey and I saw your door—" He is talking loud and fast and harshly. He goes on, and I run my hand up and down my thigh, smoothing out the material of my pants.

"—paint it!" he says.

"Mr. Fellowes, I was clear last time—"

"Paint it!"

I hang up. They're all quiet, watching me.

"What's he going to do?" Claire finally asks.

"I don't know."

"You going to paint it?" It's Jack.

"No. I'm not going to paint it. I told him I wouldn't the last time." I look around the room at the rest of them. Robbie is staring at me. I think: I have a gold stud in my ear.

"I guess I won't paint it either."

"Hot shit," Claire says. "Now, can I use the phone? Everybody through? I got some important calls to make."

I go back to my room and sit on my bed, my back against the headboard, my notebook on my knee, thinking. I write things.

Political Issue vs. Criminal Justice. Query: How many gay men and lesbians have reported antigay violence to the police in Cardiff? How many times did the police investigate? Do we have proof of complaints they have ignored? I jot down words: MAILING. MONEY. MAILING. MONEY. MONEY. MONEY. MONEY. I begin to write: *Dear Mother, I am sorry you have not been able to speak to me on the phone*—I strike through all of it. I tear the whole page out of the notebook and ball it up and throw it across the room. I start a new page, and I write, WORK, and underline it. CHARLES. I write down my salary, which I get every two weeks, subtract half my rent and $49. I draw circles and squares and Xs through everything until the whole page is dark purple from the ink of the pen.

Someone knocks on the door. It is Jack. He comes in. He's subdued for once. He sits down and then lies down across the foot of the bed. I hear the noise from the other room, the stereo, the TV, Claire talking loudly, rapidly, the typewriter from the kitchen, the whole buzz and clatter we make.

"I don't see how he could leave—" He is lying on his back, his arms over his head and hanging off one side of the bed, his legs bent at the knees and hanging off this side. "It was perfect, wasn't it? I mean, wasn't he doing a perfect job here?"

I say that Derek was doing a perfect job here. I watch Jack. His broad, handsome, simple face suggests uncomplicated emotions: sadness, bitterness.

"I mean, could anybody be a better moderator of the coalition than he was? He could do all this better than any of us, 'cept maybe Dana. Now he's left."

There's nothing to say.

"He was tough, you know? That's what we need, somebody tough—"

He slowly rolls over onto his stomach, his face toward the foot of the bed, away from me.

"Only he didn't want to fight. I told him that. He was just a faggot—" He doesn't say anything for a while.

"His job here was over."

"He didn't care about any of us. He cared more about being an actor than about fighting—"

"You have to work to live."

"He didn't care about me. I loved him——." He doesn't speak to me. "He made me think he cared. He held my hand the night of the march. I thought that was the most beautiful thing anybody ever did. I spent the night at his house, and we fucked, and I thought he was going to love me. He was a beautiful man." He doesn't say anything. He has slipped his hands under his crotch. "It didn't mean anything to him. It only meant something to me. I'm just a jerk."

"You're not a jerk. You're OK." I watch his long body at the foot of my bed.

He lies on the foot of my bed, and after a time his breathing becomes regular, and he is asleep. Jack is in pain. The surprising thing is that he knows it, and he's not trying to hit anybody. The other day Marybeth said she thought he was "interesting."

I turn over the page and start again: *Dear Mother, I want you to know that I am well and happy. I hope you are too, and that work is easy for you. I miss you, and when you are willing to see me, I'd like to see you. In the meantime, I want you to know I love you.* I sign it, *Mickey*, and I tear it out and fold it carefully and put it on the table beside my bed so I can mail it tomorrow.

Later Robbie comes in and looks at Jack and grins and shrugs. He lies across the foot of the bed too, parallel to Jack, and then I switch my position so I am lying next to Robbie. They are asleep, and I listen to the clatter of Suzanne's typewriter and the assertive rumble of Claire's voice. The Kinsey report says, "Twenty-five percent of the male population has more than incidental homosexual experience or reactions for *at least three years* between the ages of 16 and 55." Marcia and Dana also gave me *Sexual Politics, Sexual Communities* by John D'Emilio. It is about "the making of a homosexual minority in the United States 1940-1970." I used to think we just *were*. That is what we are doing in Cardiff, making a minority.

Later, when I lie in bed waiting for sleep, I think about what is happening to us. I notice the difference between Kinsey's 25 percent and the group of people who call themselves "gay." I think about the process of moving out of the one group into the other, what makes people take that journey, and I wonder what happens to the ones who choose not to take it.

When Derek left, the coalition asked me to co-moderate the meetings with Dana, and what I wouldn't do two months ago, I'll do now. Derek has left town to go to Boston to pursue his acting career. He left the message that he thinks there are more important things in his life than a fight for gay rights. Marybeth seems to have dropped out too. She's formed a commune for women up in Hamlin and is turning into an anarchist. I don't understand either one of them. The first step should be to change the laws.

After a coalition meeting on Monday toward the end of September, Jack and Robbie and I go to Dominic's for coffee. Marybeth is on duty. She is harried, and there is a sheen of perspiration on her forehead. She asks how it was, and we tell her about the plans to get out the vote—reaching all the gay people on our mailing lists—and to lobby the state legislature.

"Well, guys, good luck."

She is not impressed.

"It's important work, Marybeth."

"You're going to end up with a bill protecting us in credit so we can tie ourselves up in knots in our capitalist economic system."

But she has to deliver coffee to other people, and she doesn't come back for a time. She sounds like something out of the sixties— *Let's bring the whole system down around our ears.*

Later when she comes back, she says, "Look, guys, you're asking the wrong questions."

"And you've got the right ones?" It's Jack. "What are the right ones?"

She puts the coffee pot down on the table and then puts her hands on her hips. "Well, for one thing, you could ask yourself this: In a bigoted society, how many people are going to stand up and say, 'I'm gay,' just to protect their right to an *apartment*?"

"I would," Jack says. "Fucking A."

She laughs. "You would. The law leaves alone all the bigoted feelings people have, leaves alone the truth that our whole society is homophobic, and then says, *but the people who will come out and declare themselves gay in the face of all this have a right to an apartment.* Holy shit. What crap. Even if you could get this little law passed, you'd only protect the rights of one percent—or something like that—of all the people who're gay in this country."

"Marybeth, with a law protecting gays, more people would be able to come out—"

"You think so? Shit. There ought to be 3,000 gay people in Cardiff, if there are 10 percent of us. *Four hundred* came out! That's a little over 10 percent of the gay people! A murder couldn't make more than 10 percent of us come out! Why should a law protecting us in *housing*? And another thing. Suzanne told me there were about 30 people at the last coalition meeting. How many is that? You figure it out. What percentage of 3,000 is 30? *One percent*. After a murder. The more political the coalition has become, the fewer people come. And you're talking about protecting the rights of gays. If you get this little law passed down in Augusta, the ones whose rights you'll be protecting are those 30 people! One percent! They are the only ones who are out and politically active. The rest of them have gone back in their holes to hide because they can't live out in this country as gay people. And when they get fired—or evicted or beat up—they won't go claim their rights under this fatuous little law, because it'll mean they have to *come out*."

Later we are driving home. Jack speaks.

"What did you think of what she said?"

I think of the easy things. She's an angry dyke. All her ideas are left over from the sixties. She's a romantic. She doesn't understand the system, the way things work, or where the power is. I don't say them. "People have to come out. There are 3,000 gay people in Cardiff. And we have to make them all come out. There are 24,000,000—"

"*I'm* out," Jack says.

Robbie has been quiet. "I hate this," he says. "I hate the way we live now. This division. I *like* Marybeth. I think she's smart."

She is smart. She's wrong. There is no help for it. When we get home, Jack asks if he can spend the night, and we leave him in the living room on the sofa with Timothy. They'll work that out somehow. In bed, I hold Robbie. His breathing is irregular, and sometimes his chest heaves, and he exhales deeply. Marybeth wants the millennium now: perfect souls living in perfect harmony. But we don't have the millennium now, and we don't have the power to bring down the system. *Revolution Now!* The sixties were twenty years ago.

Mickey

The leaves begin to turn, the weather is growing cooler, and my suitcoat is comfortable outside of the office for the first time since June. One Saturday I drive by Mother's house. Today she is down the coast with Marian and Lloyd and the children, and I park in the driveway and use my key to let myself in the side door. The house has been closed up since morning. It is stuffy and silent.

On the counter in the kitchen is a pad and pencil. There are notes Mother has made to herself. Half the top sheet is blank: I have come, as she left, in the middle of things. She has left no other sign of things being unfinished. There is no sweater on the back of a chair, no bag half unpacked. Nothing put down and forgotten before it was put away. Nothing dropped into the sink to be washed later. The kitchen is immaculate—white appliances and fixtures—and shiny. I ate at the formica table, and I can remember her wiping up my spills as I made them. On the walls is the brown and yellow flowered wallpaper, whose tiny flowers I see in my dreams. There are pictures of us, exactly as it has been for all my life.

I wander through the house, the dining room and living room, and back down the hall through the bedrooms. In Mother's at the front of the house, the twin beds are covered with white and pink chenille bedspreads. I learned how to climb up on her bed by grabbing the knots in the chenille and putting my foot on the runner and pulling myself up. I must have been two or three. I can feel against my cheek the knots in the bedspread when you fall asleep on the bed. On her dresser are pictures in metal frames of Marian and me as children. I learned to climb up on that too by putting my foot on the knob of the drawer and pulling myself up so I could see over the top. I used to pull open the drawers before I was tall enough to see into them and reach up over the edge and pull things out and inspect them. Everywhere in the house are things I can taste and feel. I know what her comb feels like in my mouth, and what the carpet in her bedroom feels like against my cheek. I know what my naked bottom feels like on the bare cold tile floor of the bathroom. I have these memories even though I don't remember ever sitting on the floor in the bathroom. I know I've done it, and I know what it feels like.

The hall is long, low-ceilinged, and dark. The walls are lined with pictures of us growing up. Shorts, long pants, coats and ties, and me in track uniforms. My own bedroom is at the back, the smallest of the three, with one window looking out on the backyard. If I lay down on the bed, I could look out the window over my head and see the pattern of branches of the trees. It was the first thing I could see when I woke up in the morning. My chest of drawers stands against the wall by the door. I pull open the middle one. It is empty. I can remember climbing up on *this* drawer too. I inspect the wallpaper. It is a brown pattern, and when I stand very close to it, I can see that it is made up of very small daggers and shields. I look at the light maple bed. I can feel the pillow under my ear and taste my thumb.

My memories of my house go back before I can remember any particular thing or event. They are sensations and tastes and smells which I can't think about. Walking through this house, I can remember how Mother felt—her arms and her bosom and her lap— before I can remember who she was or what she did. I can feel the timbre of her voice through her chest before I can remember her words. I feel her arms around me here, just as I feel the house around me.

I am given my efficiency report at work. It is a printed form with spaces for my job description, a chart with the headings, "Knowledge," "Willing to Take on Responsibility," "Efficiency," "Works Well with Others," "Willing to Take Direction," and boxes in which the preparer can enter a digit from "1" to "10," and blank lines at the bottom of the form for "Comments." I run down the form to the boxes, the central fact. My manager has filled in all the boxes with "7." I can feel my face turning red: In my other evaluations, I have always gotten "9" and "10." Under "Comments" he has said, "McNamara fills the responsibilities of his position satisfactorily, but the level of his performance has fallen off since his last efficiency report. While his technical knowledge remains high, he has markedly slackened in his willingness to take on responsibility and in his ability to work with others. At times, he has seemed unfocused, and his manager has had to point out to him times when his work has required correction due to his own thoughtlessness or inattention. He is no longer the steady employee he was six months ago. It is to be hoped that McNamara will pull himself together before the next evaluation period. Otherwise, the future of what began as a promising career will be in question."

Mickey

I feel my face burning hot. My embarrassment alternates with anger. I say things in my head to justify me. Then I say things to attack my manager. I think I am an asshole, and then I think he is, and then my anger settles in, and I know it's him, not me, and I know what is going on. My performance at work has been the same over the last two years: I am thorough, focused, skillful, and experienced. I see the future: My next evaluation will be no higher than this, no matter what I do, and it will probably be worse. This will be the basis for my not getting a raise. Two, perhaps three of these in a row, and I will not be promoted. Then I will be asked to leave. I need to talk to someone: *Has* my work been satisfactory? But there is no gay person here, and no one else I trust. I call Robbie and tell him. He says he loves me. Ho, ho, ho! I see my boss passing in the hall. I will have to speak to him. I know now what he will say, and I will have no proof—nothing written down on paper—to defend me.

At home there is a message on my answering machine from Fellowes. I call him, and he says he is coming by this afternoon to talk. So. I am going to have to face this. I take deep breaths and walk around the living room, picking up things and throwing them back down the hall toward the bedroom. This apartment belongs to me. It has been my home for the last three years, where I have made a life for myself and my friends. Yet it's his, and he can do anything he wants. I must not get angry, and I must be calm. I clear everybody out of the living room, and half an hour later he arrives. He is a large man, heavyset, wiry hair in a halo around his skull, and he settles into my chair with an irrefutable finality.

"You've been a huge disappointment to me."

I wait.

"You know why I'm here."

I nod.

"Your door is a mess. It's been that way now, even after I asked you to clean it up. That—" He points toward the front of the house. "—shit has been out there now for two months—"

"I painted it a good many—"

"—but it's not painted *now*. And I want it painted every time. You've left that dead cat out there too. The neighbors have been calling me. I want to get more serious with you."

He leans forward in his chair, pulling himself up out of it so he can put his elbows on the arms.

"You are creating a public nuisance. You are damaging my property. You are causing the neighbors to complain. I have reason to evict you."

He stops, giving time for that to sink in.

"I have reasons to evict you that we haven't spoken about."

I know what he is going to say. It is a question of steeling myself against it.

"Your lease says you are the only occupant of this apartment." He leans back again and fumbles for something in his coat pocket. "How many people are living here?"

"Me. One other. He just moved in. His name is Robbie. I was going to call you—"

"The neighbors say there are at least three people living here and possibly four—"

"That's not so—"

"I think it *is* so, and I have reason to evict you for breaking your lease."

"I have been a good tenant, Mr. Fellowes—"

"In the past, you have been. Since this summer, no."

He pulls himself out of the chair and stands up. I stand up too and wait.

"If that door is not clean *every time* I see it. If I *ever* get another call about shit on your door or dead cats or *any* complaint about the outside of this house, I will serve eviction notice on you. And I want only one person living here, *you*. If I hear that there is more than one person here, I will serve notice on you. Is that clear?"

We stand in the middle of the living room, confronting one another. Both of us have our legs spread, as if we were ready to fight. The room seems very small, and I have no room to maneuver. I have to be clear. What I will do, and what I won't.

"Mr. Fellowes. I've told you about the door. I painted it until it was clear there was no point in painting it again. They will always come back. I'm not going to paint it again—"

"That's it!" he says, bringing his arm down, as if to cut off further discussion. He begins to turn away.

425

"As for Robbie. He is my lover. He is going to live with me permanently. I am willing to negotiate a new lease with you and new rent, if you insist—"

His face is red, and the muscles around his mouth are contorted. He looks as if he is about to scream. "I insist that you get him out of here!"

"No."

"I won't have two queers living together, flaunting it—"

"No."

His eyes widen, and he opens his mouth, about to speak.

"And if you try to evict me, you'll have to take me to court. I've called the police at least six or seven times about the door, and that will be in the police record, and if you try to evict me, I'll bring all that to court. I'll get a lawyer—"

"You little shit—"

"—and fight you every step of the way. I have money, I want you to know. I'll spread this all over the newspapers too. You'll come out of this looking like a bigot, Mr. Fellowes, because I know what this is about—"

He stands in front of me, his legs spread, his hands massaging a folded piece of paper—my lease, I think—his mouth quivering with rage.

"—this is about bigotry against a gay man, Mr. Fellowes. And I am going to fight you every fucking inch of the way and do it as publicly as I can, and I want you to make no mistake about me, Mr. Fellowes. I'm not afraid of you or anything you can do to me—"

And for days afterwards, I feel the irony. I have prided myself on developing qualities of leadership—the ability to think on my feet, to articulate my thoughts, to respond reasonably to other people in a discussion. I did this because I found, back in high school, that I liked being a "leader." I liked being the president of clubs. I liked it when people came to me for advice as to the next course of action. In college I set about developing these qualities in a conscious way. When there was a job to be done, I volunteered. And now, the irony: I am aware that I am using all these skills for this!

Mother would like to have Charles as a son. She would have preferred to have someone who grew up and married and had a nine-month-old child and a pretty wife with a nothing job to help with the mortgage. My boss would have preferred as an employee to have Mother's son, too, if he were Charles and not me. There's a system here, which I am discovering. Mr. Fellowes wants to rent to somebody quiet and steady who pays the rent on time—just the kind of person Mother wants her son to be and, as it happens, just the kind of person my boss wants his employees to be. My boss wants his employee to live in one place so he won't be spending his time moving from house to house to house, and he doesn't want anybody working for him who is out marching in front of the court house on his days off. On days off he ought to go fishing to clear his mind! Then he can bring some fish home to his mother! All these people want people who will play the role assigned to them. Mother wants a son who will recapitulate—and therefore validate—her own and my father's life, and Mr. Fellowes wants a renter who is so afraid of being thrown out in the street along with a wife and children that he will make it a religious vocation to pay his rent on time. And keep the goddamned porch clean of dead cats. My boss wants a man tied down to his job by a wife and children. They want decent young men, all of them.

On weekends I begin to make contingency plans. The first step is the want ads in the papers. I skip over the "household help" and "general help" and the want ads for waiters and hair stylists and dental ceramists, drivers and office assistants to "Professional Help." In each weekend paper, I find a couple of ads for "Systems Administrator" or "Systems Analyst" with big companies around Cardiff, the paper mills or the shoe manufacturers. I don't know anything about these jobs—whether they are entry level or what the salary is—but they're there, and that's reassuring. I have three thousand dollars—a little less—saved. My car is paid off. I don't have anything big on my credit cards. With my damage deposit and my last month's rent in my apartment, I have enough to move. I can go two months, maybe three, without a job.

Robbie and I pass the papers back and forth between us at breakfast. He has circled some apartments on the river south of here, down toward Dana. "Good location," he says.

They would have river views. Some of them might even be on land going down to the river. "But how would Jack come to see us?"

Robbie shrugs.

"We need two things: We have to be close to the main road and the buses because whatever we do we have to protect Timothy and not abandon Jack, who already feels abandoned enough. We need at least as much space as we have now." I show him the job lists. "There are two this weekend. There was one last weekend. I think those numbers will hold steady. They're not as good as the job I have, but they'll support us—"

"You. I have my own money." Robbie teaches dance classes, and none of this has touched him. His employer has been sympathetic about Bernie's death, his colleagues supportive, and his parents in touch and intact.

"There's Boston—"

"I don't want to move to Boston." Cardiff is my home. I won't be run out of it. If I am to fight Fellowes, I need money. I need to know how much a new apartment will cost and how much I can make if I have to get a new job. Right now our contributions to the apartment are unequal—I make more so I give more. Robbie may have to take on something to supplement his dancing job.

Sometimes I find myself staring out through the glass in the kitchen door at trees. They are brilliantly colored—flashy and domineering and demanding attention. How could this be happening to me? It is not happening to Dana or Marybeth, or even to Deborah, and I hear she has come out to the school committee. It is merely a random selection of numbers. Mine came up. Someone saw me on TV this summer who remembered that I was a guy who lived on German Street. And that someone was deeply bigoted, or mentioned me to someone who was deeply bigoted. The rest followed. Scores of us were on TV or in pictures in the newspaper who weren't recognized or placed in a street or neighborhood, and for them there has been no danger, no dead chickens.

My private life, centered on Robbie's body in my bed, on my sense of myself as I conceive myself in my mind and as I present myself to my close friends in my home, is now part of an enormous struggle carried out on the front pages of the paper, in the debates in the legislature and in Congress, in the pronouncements of the president, in the judgments of the courts. As long as I was closeted, the laws against homosexuality, the public condemnation of homosexuals, didn't reach me: I closed the door on them and pulled down the blinds. I shut my mind to them and searched for Robbie's lips in the dark. Then Bernie was murdered, and I had to go to the memorial service, past the television cameras. Why did I go? The world was suddenly divided between Bernie, dead in the water, and everybody else, and I had to choose where I would stand. It had to do with feeling cornered, with being righteously angry, with the affection I had for Bernie. He had slept on my sofa, and how could I not stand by him?

What I didn't understand—I understood so little of it then!—was that when I went, there would be the TV cameras and the people driving by. I was coming out to Mother and at work at the same time. It was either Bernie, dead in the water, or it was everybody else, and when I chose, I took on for the first time the public condemnation of homosexuals. I looked my boss—or Charles, or Mother or Marian—in the face and said, *I'm gay, and I know what you think about me, and I'm gay anyway.* Suddenly, I was in the middle of the thicket of laws against homosexuality and felt for the first time how vulnerable I was. Despite what I've said to my boss and to Fellowes, there isn't any protection from being fired or evicted for being gay. *I'm gay, and I know how vulnerable I am, and I know your condemnation of me, and I'm gay anyway.* I couldn't violate the obligation I have to my friends, Bernie on my sofa, Robbie in my bed, and this moral obligation—to my sense of myself as much as to Bernie—has transformed my most intimate feelings into the stuff of politics.

One night in the middle of October, I have a message on my box to call a reporter at the *Sentinel*. I have talked to her before, and she says she wants to meet me for a follow-up. We are having coffee at Dominic's. She is a stocky, short young woman, confident and certain of herself, and when she hears something she doesn't like, or doesn't understand, she laughs through her nose. She wants to know what has been happening.

"You see, I am doing a piece on the election, a background piece, on how different groups in the area feel about the candidates. The polls say the blacks are going for the Democrats. Women are going for the Democrats. Since there was a gay rights plank in the Democratic platform and nothing in the Republican platform, I assume gays are going strongly for the Democrats, because that's where their support is." She arranges a pad in front of her and picks up a pencil. "What do gays in town think?"

I feel an immense weariness. The president and the Democratic candidate talk at cross purposes. One speaks in generalities—his phrase is "Morning in America"—and the other speaks of the disposition of America's resources, the shift of income from the poor to the rich, the lack of access of great classes of American citizens to the American Dream. They don't engage one another. Geraldine Ferraro hasn't fulfilled anybody's hopes about the progress of humankind. She's turned into an honorary male at the same time she's being flogged for being female. The media trivializes the debates, and the election, which was to have presented a clear choice, is not about fundamentals. It is already lost.

I tell her what we are doing in the coalition, and about how we are trying to get gay men and lesbians to vote in the election.

"Do you think you can make a difference?"

I have to say we can. But I don't believe it. "We are in this for the long haul," I say, but what I am thinking is that we are now a recognized special interest—blacks, women, gays—in the American political system, and, at least as far as Cardiff is concerned, that has just happened this summer, since Bernie died.

"You know," I say, "that this is a less interesting and important story than what you could be writing about." She queries me with her eyes. "You could be writing about why we now have a gay community when we didn't four months ago."

She seems perplexed.

"I'm talking about murder. Why don't you write about murder!"

She snorts, and then she laughs. "We did that. Last summer!"

I confronted my boss about my evaluation. He stood up behind his desk and dropped his pencil on the desk top and looked at me. "Your performance has fallen off, Mickey. And I don't appreciate your telling me I'm wrong. I'm not wrong—"

"Tell me where my work has been inadequate—"

"—and I won't be grilled by you. I don't like your attitude—"

"I don't think you have any grounds for this evaluation—"

"It might be best if you thought about your future, young man."

I face the closing of doors. My job for the last three years has provided me the freedom to live a private life. Now that my life is no longer private—he knows now I won't have a female spouse—my boss brings his power to bear on me to go back in the closet. But I have a skill which is marketable, and I can find another job. There is a job in today's paper which is similar to mine. And if I can't get a reference letter from my boss, I can get a job that doesn't require a reference letter. There are a couple for programmers—less money, but they ask less about you. I can, if I have to, be a data entry clerk. There'll always be somebody who needs the kinds of skills I have, no questions asked, and I don't, in order to live, have to go back in the closet. I can be a waiter.

People active in the coalition are not the closeted ones living at home. They are the ones who can support themselves—Dana, Marybeth, Cynthia, Robbie, me—who are not threatened by the power of money to control behavior. They have jobs like Marybeth's or Robbie's, where no questions are ever asked, or they have jobs like Dana's at the university, where the bigotry itself is closeted and where one's job is not threatened, only the quality of one's life. The economic factor in bigotry is clearest when you look at the people who aren't here at the coalition meetings: no doctors, no lawyers, no people in the upper reaches of business. There aren't any union members, either, electricians, carpenters. These people all have too much to lose economically by coming out. It is predictable that virtually every member of the coalition has a job in a unisex industry. People with jobs which are strongly identified with males are either closeted or straight.

On Wednesday night late in October, I am driving down for another session with Dana and Marcia. On the way through town, I pass near Mother's street, and I take a turn off my route to drive by. When I get on her street, I discover Marian's car in the drive, and I pull in behind it and get out. I walk up to the door and knock, and then I push open the door and enter. Mother is standing at the sink, her hands in the water, and Marian sits at the formica table. They are both looking at me.

"Hi." I close the door behind me.

They don't respond for a moment. Then Mother pulls her hands out of the water and shakes them, and, without looking, reaches for the towel on the hook underneath the counter edge. She stares at me—she's afraid of me—and rubs her hands in the towel over and over.

"Mickey." Marian begins to rise from her chair.

I am standing at the door, my back against it, my hand behind me on the knob.

"Hi. I was driving by—"

"I don't think you ought to be here—"

"—and thought I would stop in—"

"—you're just going to upset us all."

"Well, I thought I would come in, since I saw your car." I move toward the table.

"Don't sit down, Mickey. Don't stay. This will just upset everybody."

"I'm going to sit down now, Marian. Mother is my mother too. I grew up here, just as you did—" I am at the table, and I sit down. Mother still has the towel around her hands, staring at me. Her eyes are wide.

"Hi, Mom."

She doesn't know what to say. She doesn't say anything.

"Mother, I'll call Lloyd—"

The name seems to wake her. "No. Don't do that." She speaks slowly, almost as if in a trance. She moves over to the table. "Why have you come?"

"I was just driving by—"

"Have you come to make peace?"

"I've missed you—"

"Mother, Mickey hasn't changed. He's still the same."

"Have you come to repent?" She is staring at me with enormous eyes as if she is frightened by a miracle.

"I came by to tell you I love you, Mom. I'm the same I've always been. I wanted to see how you were."

"Are you changed?"

"No, Mom."

"Are you still one of them?"

So. "Yes, Mom." She stands over me, staring down. I have to bend my neck to see up to her.

The muscles of her eyelids tense, and everything in the room is silent.

I laugh. "Mother. This is me. Mickey. I'm your son." She stands above me, looking like hell.

"Mickey, please go."

"No. I want to talk. I'm here now, and I want to talk."

"You're damned!"

"Mother, please." Marian stands up and moves toward Mother. She slides her arm along Mother's shoulder. "Let me take you to bed, to take a rest. Wouldn't that be nice!" She turns to me. "Please go."

"Holy shit!" I stand up.

"I told you, Mickey, it wouldn't do any good. Now why don't you go and leave us alone." She stands up. "Don't come back, hear?"

Marian leads Mother through the door into the dining room, and they pass out of my sight in the direction of the living room and the hall and the bedrooms. Boswell ended his book on homosexuality and Christian doctrine with the thirteenth century because, he said, there hasn't been any change in Christian doctrine since then. But I'm here, I'm a member of this family. I won't change. I'm not going to move away. I'm not going to avoid them. I'm not going to apologize or make excuses. I am an activist, militant homosexual. I am a man. And they are what they are. We are all in this cage together. Preachers and priests, Mother and Marian, Josh and Sarah, the fundamentalist right, the president, the Democratic candidate, lesbian separatists, and me and Robbie and Timothy, and dead Bernie's body lying in his grave. We snarl at each other and arch our backs and hiss, bare our fangs, strut, and claw each other. Our cage is littered with fur and dried blood.

Is this what always happens—this intimate, human pain bared in someone's kitchen—when the ideas we use to shape our lives don't fit reality? Did people weep in kitchens when sailors came back from Columbus's voyage and said the earth was round? Did people point and glare and say to them, "You're *damned*!" and then go crazy? I sit at the table. Eventually, I take the sugar bowl and tip it and pour a little sugar on the slick formica surface. I spread it around with my fingers. The grit is an affront to Mother's immaculate surfaces. I could have told them sometime years ago, when I was a teenager and first found out myself. Would it have been easier for them then? Wouldn't they have said, then, "You're *damned*!" and gone crazy? When would have been the right time? How would have been the right way to say, *The earth is round and revolves around the sun!* I smooth the sugar out and press my fingers into it and lick my fingers clean. I press my fingers again into the sugar. There is no sound from the front of the house. Mother is in her bedroom, lying on her chenille bedspread, and Marian will be standing—or sitting—beside the bed, holding her hand. I take the back of my hand and rake it across the table, through the sugar, and, with a swift spasm of my arm, send the sugar flying all over the room. There was no moment, no way to have done this better. I know why I am where I am at this moment: The Industrial Revolution, the Rise of Capitalism, Nineteenth Century Medicine, Freud, the Urbanization of America, the Sexual Revolution. Three boys and Bernie on a bridge. We are trapped by historical necessity. I am a militant homosexual. I am everything the preacher preaches against. Marian and Lloyd use me as an example for Josh. We exist as examples to be pointed at, whispered about, so that the other side may say, *We* are as God intended.

My feelings are the feelings I had when I first discovered computers—there was an enormous world which I had stumbled upon, about which no one had told me. Everything was new. And everything that didn't have to do with computers seemed suddenly old, limited, and confining. When I broke through those initial simple barriers into the interior world where information could be moved, transformed, simplified, extrapolated from, *achieved*, I felt immensely powerful, free, new. Now I sit on the floor in front of Dana's bookcase, pulling down books and reading and asking her and Marcia which I should read next. "Does this one agree, or disagree, with the essentialist theory?" I look for books on the law and homosexuality, and Dana tells me to go to Boston to Glad Day. I begin to do systematic research in the library that I have never done before. The power I feel from this new knowledge comes on me at unexpected moments and makes the hairs rise on my neck. I watch television ads and count the narrow spectrum of possibilities for male styles: working-class butch, college-educated intellectual, rich snob, family man. I think, this is not because there are so few styles among us. The ads homogenize us, and lie about us, and I know their secret. When I think of Mother or Marian, I am aware of their pain, but I am more aware of their ignorance. Mother and Marian don't know how they have been manipulated by their historical moment.

The freedom I feel at my discoveries—this summer, my reading—is exactly a liberation from my moment in history and allows me to wander over centuries of people who have felt the same union of body and mind and spirit as I have felt when I put my hand on Robbie. It is a liberation from my*self*, trapped in Cardiff in 1984, and it allows me to search for the roots of myself, free of the bigotry of my culture.

For this reason, I am unwilling to be understanding. Mr. Fellowes wanted his door clean, and Mother wanted her "faith." My boss wanted an employee who fits in. Everybody had some demand, some different small demand, to make of gay people. Paint my door. Don't hold hands. Don't wear your earring because it is offensive or shocking to my sensibilities. I can't say, any longer, *I will paint your door because you have been a good landlord, and I don't want to offend you.* I can't be polite or kind, or savvy.

Bernie's death taught me something about myself. It has also taught me about my place in America. After the boys threw Bernie off the bridge, I came to understand that in America, one's gender and sexuality are matters of life and death. I don't know what I would have been like in a time and place where gender and sex differences were not mortal, but in my time and place, they are mortal, and I have become vibrantly sensitive to each vicious assault. Mr. Fellowes says it's a matter of his door, but I know the truth. He's trying to kill me. You can't have Bernie without his earring. You can't live without holding hands. Life is seamless, things fuse into one another and cannot be separated. Each thing in its separate place! Bernie's earring. My gold stud. *Another friend of Bernie Mallett!* I know the people who surround me, and when they make their demands on me, I know their effect, and it is murder. When I go through the little events of my day—the grocery store, work, getting into my car on the street, walking to Dominic's to get a bagel—I have my eyes open and all around me. The little old lady with teary eyes and a shopping bag who jerks in disagreeable amazement at the sight of Robbie and me holding hands is really a sniper in disguise who carries a gun with a silencer and who wants *my life*.

Late in the afternoon on Thursday, the first of November, I drive across town to pick up Robbie at his dancing school. It is five-thirty, and he will be finished with his class at six. The skies are low.

Mickey

Silver clouds hang from horizon to horizon, blanketing us in an autumn chill, and the wind makes them churn and seethe. They glow from within. The trees are bare now, angular, inflexible and stiff, blown by the wind, and speak of the next stage of our lives, winter. The traffic is slow and irritable. People blow horns and cut me off at intersections. I have a stack of books on the back seat of the car, and my pad of paper with my notes is on my knee. I have no life now that is not about the movement.

The dance school is held in the gymnasium of an old grammar school, now unused—brick and high ceilings and high casement windows, and wood floors. I park in the small parking lot—there are two other cars there, parents coming to pick up their children—and walk across the cold ground to the door. It is very cold, and I wear a down coat. I will go inside and wait for Robbie's class to end.

Inside I walk down the short, dark hall past the office. Alice, the school secretary, is there and waves to me. She is just leaving.

"Mickey!" She has on her coat, a bag over her shoulder. She smiles and puts a hand on my arm. "Tell Robbie to be sure to turn off the lights, will you?"

"Sure. How are you?"

"Ah! Harried, dear, harried! You're a dear." Then, "I must run!" She goes toward the door I have just come from, and I walk on down the hall to the gym and push open the doors. I hear Mozart's music: a violin sonata. Down at the other end, Robbie has three kids. They stand in a little row in front of him, facing him and the mirrors on the wall, their arms over their heads. I climb up the bleachers beside me and then quietly walk down toward them. When I am about half way down, I climb up to the back row of the bleachers and sit down.

Above the low music, I hear Robbie's voice, counting, calling out the positions which he and the children take. His arm and hand, forming an arc to a point above his head, move down, opening up and out, followed by the children like images in water. He steps to the side and brings his other arm up, and the children follow, the music and his voice holding them together, breaking down the fluid movements of the ballet into its parts.

Only their end of the gym is lit, and even there, the lights being so high, deep shadows fall around them on the floor, on their

436

shoulders and under their cheekbones and brows. What can be seen of them—their chests and buttocks, their foreheads and noses and cheekbones—makes them seem formal and ceremonious as the music. Everything is slow, and their motions have the quality of a dream, or of an intensely exerted will. The children, going through this studied ritual, seem ageless. When it is over, Robbie claps, and they all laugh, a shrill sound against the high brick walls of the gym in the sudden absence of Mozart.

The brick wall behind me is softened by my down jacket. Robbie slides his arm along the shoulders of two of them, and then all four walk to the bleachers, chattering and laughing and the children sit down and start to pull on their winter leggings and down jackets. I watch all this in a dream, remembering the Mozart while I hear the chatter and the laughter, and above all, Robbie's voice.

"Hurry, Clara! Your Mother's waiting—"

"Seth! Your boots!"

"You were wonderful today."

"Chris, practice your posture, hear? Will you do that?"

"Goodbye, Robbie."

"Goodbye—"

"—bye."

The children make their way across the polished floor, two of them holding hands, moving through the vast cavern of the dark gym toward the two small hard squares of light which mark the doors into the hall. My eyes follow them. They are uncomfortable in the dark going away from Robbie and not yet at the safety of the lighted door. They have fallen silent.

Then I hear the same Mozart violin again. Robbie is down in front of the mirrors, alone in his pool of light. It is hardly a Robbie I know. He stands in fifth position, waiting for the measure of the music, absorbed, hardly there except in body and spirit. When the music begins an *adagio*, he performs deep *pliés*. Then, his body erect, his hands barely touching above his head, he begins a series of slow *chainé* turns, transcribing a small circle in the pool of light. He makes one circle and then another, his body the only thing moving in the vast gymnasium, self-absorbed, each tiny movement of his hand or ankle unchanged since the nineteenth century, handed down from dancer to dancer from Italian Renaissance courts to Medici France to

Mickey

Tzarist Russia to Diagilev to America and, improbably, here to Cardiff. I often come here early to watch Robbie dance.

I watch and don't move or cough. His concentration is not mental. It is an intense physical awareness of the measure of the music and of the floor and the light and the slow elegant movements of his body as he cuts a circumference around the circle of light, spinning just at the edge of the shadow. His turns seem to stitch the light and shadow together and to weld together the occupied and unoccupied space.

He performs a series of *grand fouetté* turns around the circle, using the line between light and dark to define the edge of his stage, dancing with the intense *adagio*. As he faces the center and turns and faces the center and turns and faces the center and turns—spinning rapidly but moving slowly—the harsh light from directly over his head casts all his features into shadow except his brows and his cheeks and nose. His face is a mask, and each foot almost transparent with speed moving through its complex elegant kicks.

At the moment the music, with a sudden crash, becomes *allegro*, Robbie, turning on his back, leaps into the air in a *grand jeté*—his body suspended in the air, followed by a turn, another *grand jeté*, another turn. Moving into the shadow, he makes a giant circle, encompassing half the gym floor, claiming it too, weightlessly, his white leotard glowing in reflected light against the dark, his legs almost invisible when they touch the ground, the walls of the gym passing behind him in a blur as he makes high long legged leaps exultantly around the edge of the gym.

Robbie stands still again in the middle of the circle of light and the music ends. In the silence, he makes a low dignified, respectful bow to himself in the mirror. He studies himself, and then he bows again, from the waist. I applaud, the sharp claps echoing in the vast dark empty room. He turns to me. He has known I have been watching him. The gym is not so dark that he wouldn't have caught sight of me as his head spun round and round and round in those fantastic turns. I get up from my seat on the bleachers and climb over the benches down to the floor of the gym, my sneakers making heavy clunking noises on the dry wood. I have been able to watch him, but I can't break the privacy of the dancer—the step and the music and the space. Even at our most intimate moments in bed in a dark room, his body in my hands, I don't reach this private place in him. He bows to me.

He has picked up a towel from the bench and wipes his shoulders. He buries his face in the cloth and scrubs. He pulls it over his head and rubs his wet hair. Then he comes over to me, his hands in front of his chest, holding the towel. He leans over them and kisses me. The judge is to announce tomorrow if he will try the boys as juveniles. On November 6, in five days, the country will hold the presidential election. Tonight we are to deliver Timothy to the alcohol rehab unit, if we can find him on the hill. This weekend we are to mail out the first batch of letters in our mailing. On Monday the school committee will vote on the tolerance policy. I have in my pocket a letter from Fellowes enclosing an eviction notice, effective at the end of November.

"How are you?" Robbie asks.

"Tired, happy."

He looks at me. "What's up?"

"Deborah has invited us for dinner."

"We going?"

"I told her yes. OK?"

"OK."

"You were beautiful."

He smiles.

I am tired. I envy him his dancing. My own work seems pedestrian and soulless by comparison. He pulls on jeans over his tights and then his down jacket and then his boots, and we walk across the polished floor to the door. He turns out the lights. I think of what I must do for tomorrow. When I get home I will make a list. I don't dance beautifully. My job is to make lists, make sure the groceries are in the cabinet so everyone will have food, pick up people, stroke their foreheads when they go to sleep, provide a *place*. My job is settled now. The coalition, work to change the laws, study and learn, protect, provide. My eyes on the immediate future, the nearest crime. Robbie takes my arm. We push through the outer doors into the hard night under the cold stars. I am very strong, and he is very handsome.

Deborah

How am I to say this? *I did it because I wanted to.* Who could believe that? Wouldn't she ask, in return, *Why did you want to?* What was there there so compelling that you were willing to give up the satisfaction of every other intimate feeling in order to gratify this one? She looks at me, waiting for my answer. I say this: "I wanted to do it, and it was the most natural thing in the world—"

"Of course, Deborah, of course. You may not have known your feelings—" She sits at angle from me at the table, her hands on the edge of the mahogany, her dark eyes resting on me, alive with interest and sympathy. She explores me. Her method is to agree, to urge, to express surprise, happiness, dismay, to reformulate my tentative thoughts into declarations.

"Of course I knew—" She has asked me about my marriage. She has waited to ask during these weeks of our courtship, for reasons of delicacy, depending on our unanticipated discovery of each other. We have been engaged in a kind of research in which there is no bibliography. Everything we have read leads to another part of the library. She was in New York from the newspaper strike in 1963 until a few months after the Stonewall riots, in 1969, studying at Columbia and working on the side: *What did you do with yourself when you were not in class? Civil rights demonstrations? Antiwar demonstrations? Beatles groupie?* A few moments ago I was speaking of a phone call from Rebecca—she has a new boyfriend—and I remarked that my life had been fortunate in that I have not stumbled down blind alleys. She began, *But your marriage—*, asking for the first time if I saw it as a false start or a self-deception. *Wasn't it*, she asked, *a violation of your feelings?*

"Feelings?"

"For women—"

I laugh. "But Sally, I didn't have feelings for *women*. I had feelings for this woman, for that woman. They were never violated. Never touched—"

"Oh please, tell me." Her seriousness is not disturbed by my laughter. "I should have thought they were the whole thing—"

"I don't know that that is true." She pressures me, and I am apprehensive standing up to her. "I didn't know that my feelings—

They were strong and deeply private. I didn't know that these feelings could resonate into the rest of my life, my waking life." I have difficulty explaining. We have feelings, some of which are affirmed: I saw my parents embracing. "Nothing I felt for women had echoes." I look at her. I wonder if she knows what I mean. "This was thirty-six years ago after all. I flushed with pleasure around certain women, was embarrassed and stammered, was awkward and childlike. Of course I knew what my feelings were. I didn't know what they meant! My dear—" I put out my hand and touch hers, lying there on the polished mahogany, my fingers closing across the strong back of her hand, her rings glinting in the candlelight. "And there was no one to tell me what they meant! What I was aware of were the pleasures of marriage, the natural, inevitable pleasures of marriage. Of course, you understand that—"

She looks away from me toward the cut glass bowl of brilliant orange oak leaves resisting, apparently with some difficulty, what I have asked her.

"—you understand that, don't you?"

She takes my hand and nods.

"And I understood what *pleasures* meant—a husband, children, a house, a family, part of my family's family. These pleasures are everywhere elaborated on. I wanted that. There is no doubt in my mind that I wanted to be made love to." I am aware I have used an odd phrase. I try again. "I knew what *sex* meant. And I saw that leading to my relationship with him—with Edmund—" I correct myself. "I am aware it may have been the other way around: My affection for Edmund led to the idea of sex with him."

"Did you feel sexual toward him?"

"Oh, certainly—"

"As distinct from all the mythology surrounding marriage—"

"But can you separate them?"

She smiles. "Of course not."

"Is it possible to separate one kind of feeling toward a person from all the other kinds of feelings you may have toward that person?" Edmund was tall and heavy and always wore white shirts and red bow ties and vested suits through all periods of fashion. He wore gold-rimmed glasses, and when I first saw him, I thought, *He is practicing to look like somebody's grandfather.* It was impossible to distinguish his body, which my hands came to know like my own, from his clothes, the one image always an afterimage of the other. "He would be the father of my child, and for a time he would help me look after my mother, and it is impossible to remember my attraction for him as Rebecca's father without feeling how erotically compelling he was in my bed—"

We have finished dinner and have taken the plates to the kitchen, and now I have brought the service to the table, and we dawdle over coffee, talking about ourselves. Later we will have the pastry—mocha chocolate and almonds, which now sits on a plate in front of us—and brandy. It is Sunday evening, and I have intense, mixed emotions. On Friday I told the superintendent that I was a lesbian. I was proud of that, but he limited his response to *Thank you for telling me.* Since the courts have ruled it illegal to hire a lesbian teacher, his *thank you* constituted a refusal to engage: *I have told you my knowledge of a crime. Thank you.* I will need to tell him again. Tomorrow night I have been chosen to speak when the school committee considers the tolerance policy. I am grateful that the school committee is considering this policy and grateful that the coalition has chosen me to defend it, but I am not confident that *tolerance* is what we want. I have a certain anxiety about being able to speak well for our side, and it is on my mind constantly. There is a rumor that the trial of the boys is going to be held within a few days, which makes me think things are coming to a head, but I wonder what outcome of the trial would dissipate my clotted feelings. We vote on Tuesday.

"He suited me then. I had a dream of my life—" I am afraid of Sally at moments. I am a plain woman, conventional and uninspiring, and I am afraid that at some moment, I will say something which is unintentionally too revealing, and she will be startled and suddenly scornful and say, *But we are not suited to each other, are we?* "You will laugh," I say, searching her face beforehand for reaction, "but I dreamt of being a mother and a wife—"

She looks away. "How seductive. That dream: Every madonna and child in a round frame—" She wanders off in her mind and seems to discover something of interest on the floor in the corner of the room. Finally, she comes back. "Did you ever think—"

"What?"

"—that this might not be for you?"

Deborah

"No. No, I didn't think that. And I don't mean to suggest that the culture simply directed me toward a conclusion unsuited for me. I wanted to get married, and I fell in love with Edmund when he presented himself. I loved him, and I was sexually attracted to him, and—"

"—and—?"

"I found fulfillment in my marriage to him." I can hear her disbelief. I can see it in her strong profile, and I am aware of the smallest note of defensiveness in my voice. "I made a home. I took an empty set of rooms, and I turned them into a home for the two of us and later, for Rebecca, when she was born. Our home was lovely. At first when we were first married, our energies were focused—we were ecstatically happy—focused on the future, our plans for our careers, for a house, for children. We used to spend hours discussing the kind of house we wanted and what it was to be like. We had a notion of Rebecca even before Rebecca was planned for, and we talked about how we wished to raise her, give her love and teach her discipline. It was a loving home, ordered and—. Do you know Yeats' 'Prayer for my daughter?'"

She smiles at me.

"—*ceremonious.* You see, I had feelings, and I knew what they were, but my feelings were not merely for this woman or for that woman. They were for Edmund too, the hardness—" which is not the right word "—the solidity of his body. How can you separate your feelings into this area and that area? How can you separate sexual feelings from other kinds? I had wonderful feelings about his integrity, his solid sense of himself. He was a kind man, kind to me and to Rebecca. He held her so she fell asleep immediately in his arms." How do you prove you were in love? "I liked being with him. For years, our marriage was everything I had dreamed of."

"—your feelings for women?—" Behind Sally is the dining room wall with its pale figured wallpaper and framed steel engravings.

"They were there. I dreamt of women when we were having sex. There were times when I had crushes on women at work, at the library. I made excuses to place myself where they might be, and sometimes I thought of nothing else. The problem was, until I married, my feelings were largely unfocused, and then after I was married, they became focused very strongly on Edmund on the one

443

hand and on women on the other. Marriage is a great organizer of feelings."

"Did you feel this was a denial?"

"Oh, no. It wasn't a denial." When I speak to Sally of my feelings for Edmund, even though they exist in my life separated by twenty-eight years of living, I sense that she feels a betrayal, as if to give him his due is to take something away from her. And yet she doesn't mind being in a house three quarters of whose furniture Edmund and I chose together. "When I spoke to Edmund, finally, about my feelings for a woman at school, he was stunned. He wanted to know whether we had had sex—"

"Had you?"

"But you see, having sex was so unimportant compared to what I felt for him and for our lives together, and when he asked me that, it was my turn to feel surprised—that his notion of infidelity was centered on sexual infidelity—"

"But—"

"I tried to tell him that I wasn't talking about infidelity at all. I was talking about *me* and *us*. He became very angry, and gradually after that everything changed in our marriage. It ceased, I think, to be a marriage, that is, a shared life, although we continued to live together and parent our child and to make love. He refused to let me open my emotional life to him—"

"Why did you want to talk to *him*? Why didn't you just file for divorce?"

It is here that she will find me boring, that the room we are in and the house around us, being expressions of myself—of myself and of Edmund—will not measure up, will be conventional and timid. "I didn't want a divorce. I told the woman at school I wouldn't leave Edmund for her. It was never a question of him or her. Edmund and I had made a home together and life together—"

"—on a basis of—"

"What was wrong with the basis for our marriage?" This is very daring. "I loved him. You make of sexual fidelity too important a thing—" I smile. I reach out and touch her. "You are like Edmund. I would try to talk to him about my feelings for women, and he said he felt betrayed—"

"You expected him to understand—"

"I did, you see. It was part of me. I was coming to understand what those feelings meant in our society. *This* was the resonance. I was a lesbian. But I couldn't be a lesbian, since I was—"

"—married—"

"—I was in love with Edmund."

"You are bisexual."

Suddenly the logic, the finality of our misunderstanding is depressing. I look about my dining room. My mahogany table will seat twelve. There is an oriental rug on the floor. On the walls are nineteenth century steel engravings of scenes from Shakespeare— Romeo and Juliet, Othello and Desdemona, Hamlet and Ophelia, Henry V and Katherine of France. Arthur says we won't have arrived until there are steel engravings of David and Jonathan, of Edward II and Gaveston. I want one, now, of Ruth and Naomi.

"What does that mean?"

Sally is increasingly disturbed. "I had not thought that you would be so unclear—"

"I am not unclear. I am not a bisexual: I don't know what that means. I am ready to call myself *lesbian*. I have organized a life now around my sexual feelings for women. My feelings resonate. At that time, though, I couldn't call myself a lesbian. Edmund said it made him feel useless. I suspect that what he was dimly aware of was that two women could love one another and that meant he wasn't *necessary*. Poor man. Men are never *necessary*. But they are nice to have around, wonderful to fall in love with."

"Are women necessary?"

My room around me. These old houses were of two kinds: those with absurdly high ceilings and those with ceilings so low they sometimes, at certain moments, make you feel you are not getting enough air. Mine is the second kind. *Are women necessary.* Is this the question? Necessary *how*? *Some*one is necessary. Women? I say it: "Wonderful to fall in love with." Her face registers disappointment. "Our marriage gradually dried up, and a great division opened up between us. Gradually, after I told Edmund about my feelings for women, sex became more and more important to us. We were defined by the way we had sex, and I became defined by these unnamed, undescribed, unshared feelings I had in my head. I couldn't live like that—"

"In a heterosexual marriage—"

445

"In a relationship in which a significant part of my emotional life was never to be acknowledged. He was insistent that our marriage was defined by sexual fidelity. He was unable to recognize all the ways in which we were devoted to each other, and he put everything into this one small corner of our lives together."

"Small!"

"Small. He made it all hang on the symbol of my devotion to his organ. If he felt I could get any emotional or spiritual satisfaction anywhere else in the cosmos, then I was being unfaithful to him, had lost respect for him. He wanted to control my mind. I didn't know that at first."

"What did you do?"

"I took Rebecca and left. Later I divorced him."

"Left for *her*!"

"Oh, no! There was no *her*. I've said that, Sally. I left for myself—"

"So that you would be free to explore relationships with women."

I touch her hand. "I left him out of respect for myself." She needs a moment to assimilate what I have told her. I touch her hand again. "Coffee?"

She nods, but she cannot answer.

I get up from the table and go to the kitchen and refill the coffee pot. I place it on a tray with the brandy and the glasses.

What she wants is for me to say, *I am a lesbian.* She wants me to say my feelings are now clear: My marriage was a mistake, and I am now ready to explore a relationship with her. I am discovering that Sally's strength is of a certain kind, deriving its power from the clarity of her perceptions. When we first began to see one another, she was certain that I would fill a space in her life and she in mine. Apparently it was a sudden revelation which has not lost its authority in the four months since. What she lacks, I have: an intuition of the incompleteness, the tentativeness, even the experimental nature of things. I might even call myself diffident.

When I get back to the table, I find that she has sliced the pastry. "Ah! Chocolate and coffee and brandy! We should get tipsy."

"Drunk, my dear. *Drunk.*"

We laugh. And then I take my seat again. I pass her the cream and sugar.

"The boys are going to say it was *homosexual panic*."

"Where did you hear that? That can't be right."

"Arthur."

"I don't see how that can work—"

"No. Timothy was there and can testify."

"He won't be a good witness—" Timothy has been interviewed everywhere. He insists that there were a gang of boys beating on Bernie, and the police seem satisfied that there were only three. "He has no credibility."

"I meant they can't justify murder just because they think Bernie came on to them—"

I am familiar with the notion of panic. The boys are said to have panicked when—if—Bernie came on to one of them. I tell Sally that Edmund's panic caused him to work harder, to be more insistently the male, to organize our lives more dogmatically into family activities—picnics, family meals, sporting events, the movies—until there was barely a moment any of us had to ourselves. He wanted to know the names of every person I had spoken to during my day, and he insisted that every friend of mine should be a friend of ours. His panic meant that no detail of our separate lives—mine or Rebecca's—escaped his eyes. He opened my mail and listened in on my phone calls. If I was in a room with the door closed, he contrived to walk by and to knock. Everything suddenly had to be out in plain view. He wanted to know everything about me but how I felt. *He read my books*.

"You were driven out—"

"Closed out. I thought I had said that."

"And all this because you told him of your gay feelings!"

"I must admit I told him again and again. You see, he wanted to ignore—or forget—what I had said, and I had to do it again, and each time I told him again, it grew worse—"

"It must have been a prison. You had to come out to him again and again—"

"I think what he wanted was to be able to act as if it hadn't happened, as if I didn't have the feelings I told him insistently that I did have. I think he would have tolerated his memory of what I had said to him if I had not insisted that the thing had not happened once. It was continuous. You see, I couldn't bear the imprisonment, the violation. You can't imagine my terror—"

The candles are burning low, and when I rise to replace them, Sally suggests we take the plate of pastries and the coffee into the living room. She leads, I follow with the brandy and glasses. Sally is to spend the night. She now leaves clothes here and brings only her makeup kit and whatever book she is reading. I have cleaned out a closet for her and a chest of drawers.

She puts her plate down on the coffee table and settles back against the cushions. We seat ourselves on the sofa, each at an end but our shoes lightly touching. Something bothers her. Her strength, which I admire, is no help for her in equivocal issues. She brings up the election: On my coffee table are two magazines with the candidates' pictures on the covers. "Are we to vote?"

The choices that we make are not about the issues that matter. We vote on Tuesday for the Democratic candidate—he seems to care about the transference of income from the poor to the rich, about our racial divisions, about the place of women in America—but his candidacy is doomed, and we face a landslide against us. To vote or not to vote, this candidate or that one. My frustration does not arise out of my sense that this candidate, whom I support, will lose or that candidate, whom I abhor, will win. Nor does it arise out of my belief that neither one of these men is addressing the issues of the country—

"Mickey has taken over the assault on the legislature. He's become quite single-minded."

He is finding his place. And he is very young and has time to discover ways of using his strength effectively. "He will discover that the coalition can be more than merely a power base."

"The only use he makes of the coalition is as a source of lists of people he can call on to help him—"

"He uses it, doesn't he?"

"Yes. He hasn't learned to work with it yet."

It's odd. Marybeth, who professes to have dropped out, is actually in touch daily and regularly with all of us. Mickey, who professes to be still active in the coalition, has gone off on his own, organizing a private army against the legislature. His anger prevents him from trusting us. Sally and I differ: She finds every need met among women. But for me, Arthur and Luke are special, and I could not do without them. I expect, over a period of time, Derek or Mickey will grow to have the same importance in my life, and I would not want to destroy that growth here at the beginning merely because of their gender.

Sally puts her hand on my arm. "What did Derek say?"

I get the letter, which I received yesterday from my desk: *I am settled here in Boston now, in rehearsals for Macbeth, which will open in early November. I am MacDuff, a survivor, which suits me, but, after the storm and stress of the summer, I might have wished for something more serene. You know, in the play, I lose everyone around me. I have sublet an apartment in the Back Bay and have what things I need here with me. My parents paid a visit—they were relieved to find me alive—and asked no questions about me, where I have been, what happened, where I am now.*

I find myself thinking of the tight little gang of you in Cardiff. The events of the summer seem far away and very much in the past. I am glad I am here, getting on with my life, but at moments Bernie's face comes back up through my memories. I can't get him out of my mind. Do you suppose he knew the risks he was taking and the effect he had on all of us? His death was a catastrophe.

My work goes well. I think the show will be well reviewed, but at the same time, I wonder if it can be escaped. I was walking down Boylston the other night headed back to the Fenway when a car slowed down and a kid yelled "Faggot!" at me. I am angry all the time now, and I don't know how to escape that. I think I lost something important last summer in Cardiff. Some equilibrium that I had always had, some sense of safety.

Looking back on you there, I think of you as very much be-leaguered. But I also remember you as being happy. Were we happy this summer, too, along with everything else? The election is upon us—fucking bad news—and I suppose by now the boys will have been tried, putting an end to things. Would you write me and tell me how you are and what has happened?

She takes the letter from me and runs her eyes over the scrawl. His handwriting is like Derek himself: large, emphatic, unclear.

She hands it back to me. "He can't escape all this. He will have to deal with it eventually." She reaches forward to sip her coffee and, finding it cold, grimaces, and resettles herself back against the cushions. "It would be better for him to do it now, rather than wait until it happens in the next crisis—"

449

Deborah

We have settled down more comfortably into the sofa, our arms along the back toward one another, our fingers touching and stroking each other's hands. As we talk, we communicate with our voices and our fingers at the same time. "Maybe he can. Maybe he can escape 'all this' and live his life in Boston."

"Do you think so? I should think he'd have to face it again. Someday some other young man will be beaten up or killed—or some other horror, which we can't even imagine."

I toss the letter onto the coffee table, where it lands just beyond our coffee cups, on the magazine with the president's face.

"He experienced a kind of panic, didn't he—"

"You could hardly blame him—"

She smiles. "Oh, Deborah! You are too sympathetic. You are maddening." She squeezes my hand. "I want to make you make judgments, divide the world between the sheep and the goats, and send the goats where they belong!"

It's my turn to smile. "But I can't, you see. I used to talk to Derek late in the summer. He was obsessed with the letters he was getting. They were from old men, and he used to say, *It's a whole world I didn't know about.* He'd say that these old men had had whole lives of oppression, and he hated that. They had survived with their integrity intact, but they were very different from him. I think they taught him that everything is political. He said, *I've been so privileged—*"

"People are really getting killed."

"Yes. He panicked at that."

"And ran to Boston. But I don't think his fear was of being killed—"

"What was it?"

"Oh, surely it was fear that he wasn't strong enough—"

We drift on into the evening, the living room lit by two lamps, one at the end of the sofa, one on the table against the wall in front of us. The two pools of light cast soft shadows, and the corners of the room are left dark. Half of Sally's face is in darkness. She rests her head back against the sofa, the tight curls of her hair brushing my fingers. I withdraw my hand and then slide it back under her head again so that my fingers, like combs, run through her curls and separate them. She smiles. Then she stops smiling. "I am

450

apprehensive. You don't know what you want. You are unwilling—unable—to commit to me—"

Two nights ago, Friday night, we were at a dinner party given by one of Sally's colleagues at the university. Arthur and Luke were there, and two other couples, and us. We were at a small table in the dining room of a small house overlooking the river, candles lighting our faces. We had talked of the university, of our children, of the election, and of whether the choice of a woman as vice presidential candidate had advanced the cause of women in our culture beyond the question of mere visual imagery. We explored the ways in which the "cause of women" differed from the problem of sexism and patriarchy. Arthur had much to say on this—*If we gave up the idea that women and men are different in any important way, neither women nor gays would have a "cause."* One of the women I have known for years watched Sally and me during the evening, and as it progressed, she began to tease us. "You two are like teenagers," she said, looking at our intertwined hands. She giggled. "You've just discovered sex." She looked at her husband and then around the room for support, and the two heterosexual couples smiled at us as if we *were* teenagers. Luke *smiled*—it took me a moment to understand why—and Arthur's eyes widened. "When you've grown accustomed to it—sex—you'll realize you can have it anytime, and you'll stop—" her eyes dropped to our hands "—flaunting it." I colored and squeezed Sally's hand. I didn't know what to do. Then the speaker laughed and turned and took in the table with a sweeping glance. Something shocking was happening. They were all smiling at us and glancing at our *hands*. "But Edna," I said, my voice trembling, "what an appalling thing to say—"

The table was suddenly still. Our hostess whispered, *We are all friends here*, and the heterosexual men looked embarrassed. Luke took a deep breath, Arthur looked from Sally to me, and the women tittered. Sally and I were perfectly still, and I was intensely aware of my fingers in her grip. Then Edna said something which astonished me but which I have come to understand perfectly. She looked around the table at everyone and said, this time not smiling, speaking as if she were being very scholarly, "It all depends on whether homosexuals are born that way or—"

Sally abruptly stood up. Our friends at the table looked up at her with amazement. Sally still held onto my hand, and in a fury she said, "Edna, you're an ignorant woman." Then she invited me to leave, and I did, there being no reason to stay. She stopped in the door just as we were leaving and turned to Edna: "You should read books." I was in a fury myself. Tolerance is a shallow virtue, superimposed on sins.

I found out Saturday morning that Luke and Arthur left almost immediately too, but not before Luke said to our hostess, *We're not all friends here. And you're a silly woman for thinking so.*

When I told Edmund again that I had erotic feelings for women, he said, *Then you've lied to me!* I sat at the kitchen table, and he walked up and down shaking his hands in front of him as if they were wet and he could shake off the water. *You've lied to me! No, Edmund*, I said, *I've always told the truth*. He stopped suddenly and turned to face me. He was sweating. It was heartbreaking to see him attempt to comprehend what it was I was saying, and to fail. *If you can love women*—here he brought his hands up in front of him, palms up, and slapped one in the other—*how could you love me?* I told him I didn't 'love women.' I had erotic feelings for them. Rebecca was in bed upstairs, and we were thrashing it out. He said, *What am I to do with myself?* And then he said, *What use do you have for me?*

It was futile to try to explain. I went over and over what was happening, and he could never say anything but *You have insulted me.* At the kitchen table, I reached out for his hand, and I tried to hold it. I reached out to him and said in as many ways as I could devise *I love you*, but his hand slipped away from me. His fear turned to anger, and that night in our bed he turned his back to me and whispered into his pillow: *You have ruined me.* His back was an accusation, and I was in turmoil between guilt and my self-respect.

I have turned myself on the sofa so that my back is to Sally, and I have leaned my head against her shoulder. She allows her arm to encircle me, to come to rest on my stomach underneath my breasts. She talks of the election. Underneath the president's campaign slogan, *It's morning in America*, is another issue: the unequal division of American resources. Underneath that is the deeper issue of personal dignity: How, in American materialistic society, can one respect oneself? And underneath that is the issue of freedom. Sally speaks of freedom.

While I listen, my eyes rest on the wall opposite me, on a framed photograph of Rebecca when she graduated from high school. She is leaning forward slightly, and she looks over her left shoulder at the camera, her brown hair partly veiling her face. She smiles as if sharing a stupendous secret. I am aware of all these things, the mahogany and linen of my well-appointed home, the sound of Sally's voice speaking of freedom, Rebecca and her secret, my own feelings and the memory of the insult they gave Edmund, the president's smiling face, Derek's charming, nostalgic, apprehensive letter, our cold coffee and the uneaten pastry. The brandy bottle sits, still capped, on the stack of magazines. I feel her arm around me and under my breasts, and I am aware of the richness of my life.

I hear Sally saying, "It must mean something more than the freedom to choose between candidates, or to choose between faiths, or even to choose between ideas. It must reach deeper than that—" She stops for a moment, and I listen to the silence.

I find that the rhythms of her voice match some deep rhythms of my own, a fact which is profoundly comforting. My house, so still since alone I am not force enough to fill it up with movement, settles down around me. Sally and I, entwined here on the sofa, are like a heart, beating. He said I was offensive to him, who loved him. He said I had made him a stranger to himself. I shift slightly in my place, turning so that my head is on her breast, my arms around her neck, and she settles her arms around me. I feel her voice through her chest as I hear her words. Beyond us are the sounds of an old house on an early November night in Maine—the wind in the trees outside, the creaking inside. I am alive to my senses, the silk of her blouse against my cheek, the soft sofa pillow, the quiet intimate odor of her soap, which lingers on her body, the soft circle of light on the ceiling.

The thing he held against me was not some vulgar prejudice, some crass bigotry learned in school or on the playground, or the street, in the army, a prejudice which age and education, gentle reproof, would train out of him. The thing he held against me he had learned before he had gone on any playground. It had started in the cradle, and his culture, at the same time it was teaching him what he was, was teaching him this message. I looked for evidence that he hated lesbians. I didn't find that: He was too well bred, too well educated to give in to a simple *hatred*. It had to do with something more than the sudden discovery that he was married to a person he disapproved of. It was deeper, too, than jealousy. There was no single person he had to be jealous of, unless he was jealous of the thoughts in my mind.

He was afraid, and I didn't know what it was he had to be afraid of, until suddenly there it was: What I had done had disturbed profoundly his *self*. The barrier between us was like the mark on Rappacini's daughter: It went to the root of what he was, and if I were to educate him out of it, I would have to educate him out of himself. What I had told him revealed great faults in his own geological constructions. It must have been exactly like experiencing an earthquake: What had been so solid you had never given it a thought, now seemed fragile, the source of great danger, of pain and death. Worse, even its appearance of solidity seemed now like a betrayal.

"—When I've been around the young people, I've felt overwhelmed by how beautiful they all are. It has something to do with their youthful beauty, physical beauty, but it has more to do with some interior spirit. Their excitement, their courage, their sense of discovery and the strength that comes from that. It takes my breath away. And us! Oh, Deborah, this summer I've felt the same breathless excitement that I felt when I first discovered girls. It has to do with the sense of possibilities." She moves her hand across my hair and strokes me.

I smile into her blouse. I speak, my mouth up against the silk, my words muffled: "Coming out." The idea is a funny one at our age. "Freedom to feel without constraint." This is seismic for young people, I think, moving the earth under their feet. Absolute freedom carries in its train—isn't this so?—absolute fear? Isn't the possibility that *anything* is possible absolutely terrifying? And don't we impose so many restraints on ourselves just because we can't live with no restraints at all?

It was years before I understood what Edmund was trying to say to me: My fear—the clangor in my head—prevented me from hearing him. He said: "My whole sense of myself is founded upon my being male and your being female and upon that meaning something." I recognized the manipulative, controlling element in all this: I had to go back to fulfilling his idea of me so that he could go on being what he had always been. But what I didn't recognize was something else: He didn't know how to *be* if I were not what he thought I was.

"Do you still love her?" On the table next to the framed photograph of Rebecca is a studio portrait of Betsey. I have not seen her for years.

Edmund tried to get Rebecca away from me when he found I was living with Betsey, and we spent years living a lie. "Oh yes, of course I do." I also love Rebecca. And Edmund, who loved the part of me he could love. And now, Sally. I needn't raise my head to look at her. All my loves. This proliferation is not what Sally would want. What she seeks in me is constancy and focus. Isn't that the answer to the question of the ballads? And then, to still the panic she feels, I say, "I love you."

She strokes my head and is silent. For a long time she is still. I listen to her heart. Finally, she speaks. "It is impossible to ask that you love me only."

She is like Edmund. Everything must be simplified into choices. They are like the Hebrew God, who divided everything: night and day, water and land, man and woman. I wonder how courageous she is. I wonder if her fear will overcome her desires. Her arms are around me again, and she kisses my forehead. Yes. I settle down deeper into her lap, my memories crowding on me like images of seasons: snow and flowers and green grass and orange leaves.

"You are incomprehensible!"

I laugh. So. I sit up and face her, supporting myself on the sofa with my arms. "I thought I would bore you!"

"You frighten me." She looks steadily into my eyes.

"Would you like brandy?"

"Oh, yes!"

I turn and stare at the uneaten pastry. "And chocolate?"

"Oh, yes!"

She holds on to me tightly, and I wonder what it is I am doing. Her grip on my shoulder tightens and could, if she holds it a moment longer, begin to hurt. It is a long time since I have allowed any person to grip me with such determination and such a sense of ownership. She has all but moved in, and I have gone so far toward a promise to her that it will be difficult now to retrace my steps. Sally

455

and I are right now at the point where freedom and chaos and terror and imprisonment all come together. How rigid is she? What is the source of her fear? I pull back from her and loosen her fingers on my shoulder. I slide my hands up on either side of her head and stare into her face. Her large dark eyes stare back at me. There is something in her—her solid sense of herself—that is in danger of breaking open. "Sally—" I say. It is a moment before she can answer me.

Luke

So much passion. We are in the final, bucking, sweaty throes of it. For the past four months, thought has been obliterated by sensation, by the thrill of self-righteousness, and every person I have spoken to has the wild-eyed look by which we recognize virtue. Virtue. It exists to tell us that—thank God—we are not as other men. If hypocrisy were liquid, all Cardiff, and not just Bernie Mallett, would have drowned. I am as guilty as the next man. I've been swept away on the tide of anger and victimization, have become passionate rather than thoughtful, believing if enough of us came together, carried enough candles down enough hills, that the worm would turn, virtue would triumph, that there would be *joy*. Feelings. I have believed that things changed when Mallett died. I have believed that since I was a victim, I must be virtuous. I have believed that suffering was synonymous with thought.

These last four months have pulled me from my accustomed manner. Arthur says his greatest disappointment in me is that I won't hug him *back*. I can feel my mother taking my shoulders in her hands, pinning my arms to my sides, pulling me toward her for her kiss. My rage was expressed in turning my cheek. He sits across from me, the light in the late afternoon a shade of lavender, his hair silver, reading Trollope, his eyes in his dark tan round with astonishment. His quiet demeanor, absorbed in his book, seems to grin at my agitation. He trusts that when I want to give in to him, I will give in. In the meantime, he reads. Tonight Deborah and Sally join us for supper. Afterward we will go to the school committee meeting to swell the numbers of our side in the debate over whether homosexuals should be tolerated.

There will be virtue aplenty to behold.

A city and its sins. The Cities of the Plain: scorched earth, white clay, dust, the cries and shouts of citizens heedless of the Lord. Every single person will be destroyed there, except one, and those who might have escaped turned to salt when they look back to see the horror. The Old Testament is a gloss on the phrase and teaches us how to understand it: It's a children's story. Everything depends upon obedience to the Lord. He kills every person who disobeys, without regard to degree or circumstance or strength or weakness, age or sex. Lot's wife is an emblem of God's anger. At nine I wondered what it was like, turning to salt, warm resilient flesh numbing, thickening and crystallizing. The eyes: liquid clear vision becoming milky and opaque, hard, crazed, and shattering. The story is designed to terrify.

A city and its sins. I hold in my lap a retrospective "think piece" on the murder of Bernie Mallett, published this week under this title. The theological metaphor is ubiquitous. Even a progressive weekly in Boston, with roots in the counterculture of the sixties, can't avoid the notion of sin when it comes to talk about Cardiff. The article lays out in detail for the Bronze Age the bigotry of this town. A leading Baptist minister in town says, "Homosexuals are perverts," and a girl, a student at Cardiff High, says, "If I were queer, I'd move somewhere away from around here, that's for sure." A homemaker says, "Cardiff is a quiet, hardworking, family-oriented little town. No violence to speak of." The Mayor says, "What happened to Mallett doesn't represent Cardiff at all." Murder in town hasn't made Cardiff stop and become introspective or reconsider its ways, or consider the possibility of guilt. The citizens are heedless of their danger, and this newspaper account is a report from the Cities of the Plain before Lot is told to pack his bags and head into the desert.

That's a convenient way to look at it, if you are a member of a Bronze Age tribe in the Levant. And as a paradigm, sin and guilt suit both the religious fundamentalists and the progressive left, who differ only in their judgment of who will be allowed to escape the gaudy brimstone. Arthur puts down his glass of sherry to turn the page of his book. He reads Trollope, detached from the current turmoil. The light comes in from behind him and glints on his glasses frames and casts his face in lavender shadow and his wispy hair in silver. He tilts his head back slightly to see through his bifocals. It is four-thirty or so on Monday afternoon, a time when my nerves are exposed and tight: It is the apogee of the afternoon. I sip my scotch. We sit in silence. Later in the descent into evening, picking up speed, Deborah and Sally will join us and we will have supper to fortify us, and then we will go out to the meeting. All of Cardiff promises to go down to influence the great debate, a gathering of the tribes for the great battle.

Sin. I have in my hand a note from the rector of my parish. I wrote him—Arthur asked me not to—commenting upon his silence on Bernie Mallett's death this summer and fall. His reply points out that of course he deplores murder and bigotry for any reason and that he shares the anguish and sorrow of his gay parishioners, but his "way" is not to be confrontational, his "way" is to work quietly behind the scenes for peace and justice. He won't speak out, and he won't stand with us, and he won't be at the meeting tonight. The armies are in place, the clouds gather, the lightning flashes, the atmosphere becomes operatic. Some are cowardly and turn from the battle. Some rush in. When I was nine I knew that there are sins of omission as well as sins of commission.

I toss the note onto the table. Arthur glances up at me, at the note, then back down again at his book, his head tilted back to see through the bottom of his glasses, a halo around his head, so content in his body and his mind that he has no anxiety about catastrophe. He reads serenely. The weak lavender and silver light of dusk tints my room. Arthur settles into my house and unpacks his bags. He has taken the front room upstairs for his own, and comes into my room every night in his dressing gown, trailing contentment like silk. According to him, the Forces of Righteousness will triumph. He only barely manages to restrain himself from saying, "Amen!" He has no irony. After Armageddon, he believes, in the end, we will be free at last. Free at last.

That speaks for itself. Arthur and I have much to talk about, but we get nowhere. He has faith, and I suspect betrayal, and we have no common language. He is absorbed in his book. I pick up the priest's note again and throw it away again and pick up the paper. An advantage to living in Cardiff is that you can see what is going on: The scale is small enough so that from certain places you can see the whole city—the river where the stream enters, the railroad tracks, the three hills fanning out from the basin, the church spires. Arthur and I can see the whole battle—troops on this hill, troops on that hill, the ravine between—and smell the powder. Any place in town is a first row seat, and like any good civil war, we're related to soldiers dying on all sides.

Proximity—the smoke of battle—means we don't agree on what we see. People don't know what *gay* is—an ethnic group, a gender, a category of sin, a new political label. The coalition exists, which seems to prove we exist, but the coalition doesn't explain itself, and what we're hearing now—I get it in the babel on all sides, in the letters to the editor in the *Sentinel*, from people in the historical society, at church—are the voices of people trying out explanations. The Boston paper tries out the Sodom story—in a new angle—in "A City and Its Sins." A woman at church, in an effort to be supportive, is earnest and picks at my sleeve. "It's *exactly* like them finding those three boys under that dam in Mississippi." She waits for confirmation, and I stare at her serious lined plain face in disbelief.

I am unsettled. I get up and walk around the coffee table and cross the room, wending my way through the furniture scattered here and there, a rosewood chair, a sewing table of Mother's, a standing lamp, to my desk, a hundred-and-twenty-year-old mahogany secretary I bought dirt cheap twenty years ago, and store the priest's letter in a cubbyhole. I plan to write about all this someday under the heading, *Comedy of Errors*. I can feel Arthur's eyes tracking me. I close up the secretary and go to the window to see. The light is almost gone. The *Sentinel*, the Bishop of Portland, the whispers of our rector, the governor, the mayor, the state representative, the coalition: You would think that there would be some unanimity about *What happened that night*.

Arthur and I argue. After the dinner party, when our friend asked, *It all depends on whether homosexuals are born that way or choose it as a lifestyle*, and Deborah and Sally walked out in a huff, our hostess made soothing sounds and said, "We are all friends here." I laughed. I said, "We are *not* all friends here."

I stand with my back to the window and feel Arthur staring at me. My agitation bothers him. All this has hung fire month after month. Suddenly, out of nothing, everybody has fastened on the school committee. It is an odd choice. The committee can't make the police force more responsive or the judicial system more even-handed. It can't prevent victimization of gays. It is powerless to reimpose the *status quo ante* and make gays go back in the closet or bring Bernie back from the dead. Today a preacher, writing in the *Sentinel*, defined what he thinks is the issue: "Homosexuals are perverts. If you feel as I do, then join me at the school committee tonight to register your rejection of this offense against God."

In the more open climate since Mallett's death, Arthur and I go everywhere together: to buy groceries, to church, to symphony. We went by to see Carole one Sunday afternoon. She has stopped going anywhere. We found her sitting in her parlor, a drink in her hand, the only light from outdoors. Her house is as clean and ordered as a tray of surgical tools, and her face has hardened behind her powder. We hear that she has resigned from all her committees. She is trapped in a moment of time, and her moment was already forty-eight hours past at the memorial service. We told her we are living together. Her eyes widened, but she didn't say anything, and after a few moments of strain, we left. She told Deborah after Mallett was murdered that she was going to Europe, but she didn't, and now she is paralyzed. I will miss Carole. We shared the conviction that we are surrounded by fools, and now she has let fear overtake her. I wouldn't have thought that of her. That giving up. We have put both of our names on my mailbox, and Arthur is selling his house. I make it clear that Arthur and I are together.

It seems better now than it was before Mallett died. I like going down to the church, publicly, to the coalition meetings. A week ago a man at the historical society invited me to an engagement on Monday night, and I said I never accept anything that conflicts with the meetings of the coalition of lesbians and gays. But this is a paradox. The violence is worse. We all know about what is happening to Mickey, driven out of his house and job. Both Arthur and I were yelled at on Main Street, walking home from a movie, and that has never happened before to me. It's more obvious on the street, it's uglier, it's more consistent and sustained. Every gay man I know who has anything to do with the coalition has had *faggot* yelled at him since Mallett died. Someone hung an inner tube on the door of the Unitarian Church last month—*Throw this to drowning faggots*, it said—and there was a sign on the bridge that said, *Launching ramp for fairies*. Fundamentalist ministers are on the radio every Sunday. *Queers are the abomination of the Lord.*

I have polled my friends: *Are things better now than before Mallett died?* "What a question! Of course, things are better." Arthur puts down his Trollope—he reads *The Eustace Diamonds*—, leans forward and takes a sip of his sherry, and then stares off across the room at the steel engraving of the nineteenth century war. "Of course, things are better." He has settled into a contentment which has come on him as gradually as the darkness across a sky at twilight. His voice is lower, his rhythms more slowly paced, his breath deeper, his eyes lingering longer. "I'm out. You're out. We're together." He looks at me. "We're beginning to arrive at a place we should have started from." He leans forward and places the Trollope on the coffee table.

"And where is that?"

"Why, where we don't have to look over our shoulders." He crosses his arms over his chest. "I am beyond fear."

The fundamentalists call the "openness" of gays *flaunting* it. We are out and that seems better, but being "better" seems identical with accepting our difference. *You will be left alone only if you go away into your own community.* We are invited to think this is progress. Only a fool would look at that without flinching. Arthur asks me why I think of it. He likes to touch me when he speaks to me, the tips of his fingers on my arm, or at the nape of my neck. We have each other, he says, and our health. That's enough for him, and sometimes I think it would be easier if it were enough for me. This pleasant room and he and I sitting in the near dark. But I have a voracious hunger, and I am unsatisfied.

Deborah and Sally have joined us and will attend the meeting with us. Like Arthur, they are not skeptical about what we do, so I am alone. We stand in the front hall gathering together our things before we face the cold, girding ourselves against the battle.

"Oh, Arthur, dear, my boots. What did you do with them?"

"Here, under the stairs—"

"What does this cold promise for the winter—"

"I *dread* the winter—"

I am not a part of this. I find my suit jacket in the hall closet behind the down things, and I hold it in one hand while I close the closet door.

"Let me help you, dear—" I consider refusing his help. He insinuates himself into my life, moment by moment, and I notice I am liable to become dependent upon the comfort he provides. He holds the jacket, and it is done. In my suit I wear the uniform of my gender and class and race. I feel fit and ready.

"Is my coat there?" Deborah stands at my shoulder, picking at my sleeve.

I open the closet and get it out for her.

She struggles into her long plain brown coat. It has a green button pinned to its collar: *Another friend of Bernie Mallett.* "The church people will be offensive. This will be ugly."

"But we have the votes on the committee. They can be as offensive as they want—" Sally squeezes Deborah's hand. "We're on the right side of this one. And this time, right means might."

I give Arthur his coat. The coalition has been busy all week. A group met over the weekend and chose a number of people who are to speak, Deborah and Arthur among them.

"It's thrilling. I love being on the side that's going to win." He turns to me. "Oh, do be cheerful."

His command has the quality of a plea and is gently delivered, but my irritation knows no bounds. "We will have to listen to them, and that will be painful."

"I can listen to them if I know I don't have to do what they say—"

"All over town, right now, they are getting ready to go forth to do battle for the Lord—" I imagine them, arms raised, holding swords and torches, a vision of Socialist Realism.

"Oh, Luke, how good of you! We must remember that they are sincere in their beliefs—"

"Deborah!" She is like my mother. She flees reality into a vague world of good intentions. My mother looked for the good side of every disaster and so never got the point.

"I was referring to the liberals."

"Why are you acting this way, Luke?"

"Luke cannot be satisfied!"

I cannot be satisfied. Cardiff lies beneath us, its lights strung up and down the river and the stream, and when my car goes over the edge of the hill down to the center of town, I contemplate the numbers into which we descend: Penobscot Indians, Franco-Americans, blacks, Anglo-Saxons, Jews, Hispanics, now Vietnamese, men and women, adults and children. There are thirty thousand citizens of Cardiff spread out over these hills, and even in this out-of-the-way corner of the country it is absurd to think we are a homogeneous population.

We face tonight streams of people going to the microphone, each proclaiming his or her own self-satisfaction. People from all sides will be united under their rhetoric in their belief that their virtue compels them to do what they do. It's the religious wars of the seventeenth century. Not one soul tonight will stand up and say,

Luke

What is the need for all this virtue? What are the conditions that require all this tolerance?

Despite the cold, the room is hot with bodies and the white television lights. Every chair is filled when we enter, and the four of us pause for a moment at the door to get our bearings. Marcia, on the back row, waves a hand, and I see Jack, near her, stand up and motion us toward them. People stand three or four deep around the edges, and we make our way to the back wall. The young people are immediately in front of us—Marybeth turns and grins: "It's a fight to the death!"—and near me is a neighbor, her gray hair in a ponytail, who whispers in my ear, "You don't usually come to these things!" And she usually doesn't speak to me. I smile and compliment her on her cotton dress.

We meet in the largest auditorium in the City Hall, a room sometimes used for court sessions, for city council meetings and, when the need for such space arises, for the school committee. It used to be an imposing space. Its ceiling has been lowered and fluorescent lights installed. The tops of the window arches are cut off by the lowered ceiling, and despite the room's height, it gives the impression of a lobotomized space. On the front wall is a carved wooden plaque with the seal of the State of Maine with its figures of woodsman and fisherman. Spotted brown carpeting covers the floor, and, near the doors, there are soda machines. In the front corners are camera crews, two or three men and women carrying cameras on their shoulders and cases of some sort and one, behind them, carrying lights on a pole high above his head.

There are preachers and clergymen standing among their parishioners. These are the religious folk. Christians. They whisper among themselves and glance around the room. One is a fat little man, and his cheeks are puffy, as if he had something in them, a mouthful of mashed potatoes, or chewing tobacco. He is superior to his followers and knows it and shows it. They squeeze up next to him as if it were cold and he were warm, and he doesn't return their looks and words.

Very quickly the chairman of the committee, in a dry, laconic voice, calls the meeting to order, announces the subject, and invites public participation. Suddenly a woman is speaking. She stands amid the chairs on the left side, away from me and facing forward, a paper in her hand. *As we all know*, she says, introducing

464

her style. She says, *It is perfectly clear*. And then she says, *All science is in agreement*. Her language is fat with phrases designed to intimidate.

Across the front of the room the seven members of the school committee sit unevenly at a line of folding tables. There is a microphone which is to be passed as they need to speak. The committee, some familiar to me, are a cross section of the community—a male university professor whose children are grown, a housewife with two small children, a construction foreman with several school aged children, a young female, and two men unfamiliar to me, and the owner of a convenience store on outer German Street. Ordinary people, they sit in relative darkness, the TV lights directed toward the audience, staring out at the rest of us. The chairman of the committee, the owner of the convenience store, is of a pale northern European race who listens to the self-assured woman with a pained attentiveness.

The woman reads off the charges against homosexuals: "Homosexuals are promiscuous, they spread venereal disease, they solicit children." Her manner speaks of self-evident truths. Her voice is emphatic and carries the sharp edge of her feelings to the limits of the room. She is carefully groomed, her clothes and hair fashionably done. Her trained and educated voice, her sense of her class, are like weapons, and they raise in me a militant response, until I breathe deeply and it subsides. She speaks of the old ways and of traditional values and of the need to draw a line before it is what she calls too late. She speaks confidently of "our own dear children"—her voice taking on a softer coloration—and of the need to provide proper role models "so they may grow up into decent young men and women." She goes on and on. Her minister watches her paternally, even fondly, smiling.

Marybeth turns to look at us and raises her eyebrows. I raise mine in return, and frown, for good measure. This is to be a debate on the dangers homosexuals pose to society.

"She is always well prepared for these things," the man next to me says. "She is very smart."

"Evidently," I say, gently. For the next ten or fifteen minutes, we hear three of these formidable middle-class ladies. The lights go off when one of them finishes and then come back on when another is recognized; the camera crews run up and down the side or center aisles to shoot the new speaker. They are realists, refer to studies and to statistical analyses, and their short speeches have the form of syllogisms. *If it is true that homosexuals have the highest rate of sexually transmitted disease, then—*

The members of the audience, in the seats and around the edge of the room, are alert and follow the debate, their heads turning from one to another corner of the room as in a tennis match. Occasionally members of the committee take notes or whisper among themselves. No one is angry yet, and the deep feelings in the room have not been tapped. I contemplate what will set them off. Jack, sitting in front of us, seems equally interested in the television crews, whose activities are producing a kind of subplot to the main thread.

Then a man is called upon, over on the left from among the Christians. The camera crews run up the left side aisle and crouch near him, a man holding the lights high above. He rises and half turns from the committee at its long table to speak more directly to the room at large: "How can you ask me to tolerate," his earnestness already making his face turn red, "what the Good Lord has said is intolerable?" For several minutes, his face screwed into a grimace made unnatural by the intense light, he tells us children's stories. "God destroyed the City of Sodom when its citizens turned to homosexuality," he says, and describes the fire and brimstone. "The great civilization of Greece—the culture that produced Socrates and Plato and the great tragedies of Aeschylus and Sophocles, and the art of Praxiteles—rotted away when its citizens turned to homosexuality." In a smaller, more strained voice—he is showing us his gentility—he touches delicately on the sexual practices of homosexuals.

Marcia raises her hand high, and waves it. She is an earnest young woman. I am surrounded by earnest people.

The chairman—another crew drops to the floor in front of him, and a second set of lights comes on—raps his gavel: "We are discussing whether students in the Cardiff school system would be improved by a tolerance policy, not the sexual practices of persons." A sibilant ripple of whispered sound, folding back on itself, sweeps the room, some in favor, some against the chairman's reproval. He is wrong, of course. We are debating whether we are a Bronze Age tribe.

"Sir! Sir!" All over the room people wave their arms and call.

"I think it's important," a woman says from near the front when she is called upon, "to point out that the interpretation of the Sodom story given by the last speaker is outdated. Twentieth century Biblical scholarship interprets the story as having to do with hospitality, not homosexuality—!"

People grin and laugh—the groups who are probably Christians and the groups of queers—and the laughter interrupts the Biblical scholar, and she sits down.

Interspersed throughout the room are little groups of "us"— young men and women sitting together with lavender armbands which show the wear from the summer and small green buttons: *Another friend of Bernie Mallett.* Jack and Mickey are with a crowd of young men. They have Timothy with them. Marybeth, Dana, Marcia, and Claire are with a group of women. They turn in their chairs, watch the speaker, glance at each other, laugh or frown.

They know that they are being talked about, glancing from the speaker to each other to the committee observing their reactions, and I expect this is causing them a certain thrill. I have observed this since July: Cardiff's homosexuals study themselves being characterized on TV or on the radio. This has the fascination of attending your own wake, the thrill of eavesdropping. Jack and Marybeth strain up out of their seats to see and hear, and they grin at each other at some absurdity. They laugh at what is going on, or they are angered by it, but I expect to some extent these young folks are playing the part already expected of them: They are being outrageous and disrespectful.

One of the Christians—a lady I noticed earlier, her hands clinging to the arm of a man next to her, who seemed, in her agitation and nervous glances around the room, to be ridden with fear—lurches to her feet and, following the lead of the red-faced man, in a short speech, cries out, "—*the anger of my God!*" What she said before that was lost. I think she started speaking before she had stood up, her voice still modulated to whispering to her husband. The effect was a kind of shriek: The anger of my God! "You see what these people are getting!" She has it now. Her voice is still shrill, and it trembles, but it carries. "They are dying of this dreadful new disease! They have brought it upon themselves! God is punishing

467

them! They are all going to die! And if we let them, they will give it to us!"

"That is simply not so!—" A woman shouts from the other side of the room, yelling across the crowd. "AIDS is caused by a virus—"

Lights go on and off, and crews rush noiselessly around the room.

"That *is* so. It is the judgment of God!"

"It's a disease—" Several people speak at the same time, without being called upon and without waiting for the cameras, and I catch only phrases.

"It is not according to nature—"

"—perverted—" I watch the preachers in the corner, while they allow their eyes to rest on one after another of these people.

"Unnatural acts—"

The chairman raps for order. It is St. Thomas Aquinas in the thirteenth century arguing about the natural end of sex. These earnest virtuous people are Baptist Thomists, and this horrible room is a great hall in a monastery in the Pyrenees. We are monks, and we debate this proposition: *All that is, is natural.* I am amused. We are dying of scurvy, and we debate.

The committee observes all this. They sit at their ease, slouched back in their chairs or leaning forward, chins propped in the heels of their hands. While it is rumored that we have a majority, it is even possible that they will be affected by this debate, and I wonder how deeply.

A woman with prominent angular bones and a midwestern voice rises and looks around the room calmly. "All men are created equal." The lights come on again, the cameras make their small hissing sounds, and I notice for the first time near the front left, a reporter writing in a notebook. Her words create memories for me, call up images from classrooms and textbooks and spiral notebooks. Define these terms: *the equal protection of the laws, citizens of the United States.* The room is transformed. Independence Hall and soft red brick. The eighteenth century Enlightenment, and the Age of Reason. I imagine the pale Scandinavian chairman in a powdered wig.

The woman with the midwestern voice, her left hand resting lightly on the back of the chair in front of her, turned a little away from the direction she speaks, says, "We have come so very far in achieving a real equality among the citizens of the United States. We are recognizing the injustices done to women in the past, and we are close now to enacting into the Constitution an Equal Rights Amendment which will guarantee the equality of women under the law. It is well known that the patriarchal system is built upon a rigidly defined sense of gender identity and upon homophobia to keep women in their place and men in theirs. It is time we moved beyond these old primitive beliefs—." Federal architecture, pilasters and cornices, swags and bas reliefs of Roman suicides. It is a dream of harmony, a Mozart symphony. I smile.

People applaud, and she sits down. One of the ministers has folded his arms across his chest, his cheeks puffy from drawing back his lips in his strained smile. I join the applause for the woman with the midwestern voice, and the next speaker rises: "It is terribly important to remember that these people are sick—" Marybeth groans in front of me, and I laugh.

I am bemused by this odd sense I have of roaming over history, stories from the Bronze Age, scholastic philosophical debate in the thirteenth century, the Enlightenment and the new scientific learning in the eighteenth, modern sociology and criminology and psychology. These discourses are layered on top of one another in this room, and sometimes someone from one debate wanders into the other and, instead of clarifying issues, leaves the room fogged with confusion: A very earnest woman is just sitting down after rising to say, "Michelangelo was gay."

I am pleased for Michelangelo, and I laugh. Jack cheers, and the Chairman raps his gavel.

I nudge Arthur. "It's like A History of Western Ideas." He doesn't laugh. He is one of the earnest ones tonight. Being happy, he has lost his sense of play. I insist. I whisper, "It is a course in Twelve Great Ideas of Western Civilization."

I amuse myself, imagining the scene in a thirteenth century monastery in the Alps, rats on the floor and the breath freezing on the beard, monks discussing the proper uses of sex, or in the seventeen-forties in Paris, everyone in powdered wigs and high heels, discussing the powers of the Reason. Then I imagine the monks and the Parisians getting mixed up, a Parisian wandering into the monastery, an abbot appearing in Independence Hall. Freud in the Lateran Palace! What language could he use!

What language would I use were I to speak? I would speak slowly, take a leisurely tour. I would take the whole hour allotted to this meeting. I would describe in minute, exquisite detail the sexual practices of Mesapotamia and Melanesia, linger on Stone Age tribes, pause over temple prostitutes. I would list every one of the seventy-six known cultures with institutionalized homosexuality, and I would say, I intend to describe each one in loving detail. I would speak at such length that my audience would jeer and boo and leave the hall throwing obscene gestures at me!

The lights illuminate this speaker and then leave him in darkness when they go on to illuminate that speaker. Statisticians speak of students molesting each other, of teachers molesting students, of rape and childhood innocence, of violence, and Thomists answer them by speaking of biblical exegesis and the question of the authorship of Genesis, of Nature and Unnatural Acts, and Modernists define ideas of psychopathology and crime, of the labeling theory, and the politics of victimization, their voices amplified and made somehow metallic by the lurid lights which illuminate this person or that person in what seems increasingly to be a darkened room and give a sense of theater, of dislocation of time, of the spatial arrangement of ideas. The constant turning on and off of the lights is like lightning or a continually repeated power failure. My irises fail to respond. This has been going on for half an hour.

The construction foreman on the committee takes the microphone—all the natural color of his face bleached by the TV lights which suddenly pick him out of darkness—and says, "I am a church-going Baptist." He speaks in a low, measured voice. "I have a God too, and my God is a loving God, and not angry." People nod. Others are angry. Jack elbows Marybeth with a grin. The man's comment, like most of what's been said, is beside the point. I try to focus on these events.

Deborah is raising her hand. For several minutes, the chairperson calls on other people—the pools of light illuminating this corner and then that row—before getting to her. I watch her rise in her place, separated absolutely from her background, as if she were a cutout, by the intense white light. She seems to have no blood.

"I am a lesbian." She has placed her hands on the back of the folding chair in front of her, and since most of the room is to her left, she turns slightly to her left, her hands to her side, and for a moment, she allows her eyes to rest on the floor. I can't conceive of what she is doing here among these people. One of the Christians smiles but his smile is cold and filled with hatred as he stares unblinking at her.

"My name is Deborah Elkins. I teach history at Cardiff High. I have been on the faculty there for twenty-seven years." I stare at her until my eyes hurt in the glare, and I have to blink and then close my eyes tightly against the image graven on my retina.

Deborah stands very erect. She looks at the chairman of the committee, only occasionally glancing around at the rest of the room. A camera crew has knelt down in the aisle beside her, its lights striking her from her left, but almost immediately another crew switches on its lights from the front, photographing her a second time, and she seems like a medieval woodcut of Bravery, facing down Monsters. She says she is a mother of a twenty-four-year-old daughter, and she speaks of her relationship with Betsey. She announces that she is in love with a woman with whom she expects to live the rest of her life, though God and Time will be the judges of that. She speaks of her experience in the high school, that it is like most, she supposes, in that the students are easily swayed by peer pressure, that students who are "different" in some way are easily singled out for torment, "faggot" is the worst thing a student can call another student. She speaks of the virtues of tolerance, of how a policy implemented from above, in the school committee, would give administrators and teachers a powerful tool to use when discussions arose in the classroom or on the playing field.

She says all these expected things. She says, "This is America."

She says it is appropriate for people in America to band together for mutual aid and comfort. The right was written into the Constitution. She hopes the school administration will understand this and will help gay and lesbian youths at the high school to form a club for their mutual benefit and to counter the bigotry and ignorance in the student body. At length, long after I have ceased to hear anything she has said—my mind wanders over our years together and how, for her, good will has continuously been substituted for clear thought—she finishes, and the lights go off. People burst into

471

applause. Several members of the committee smile. The cameras hold their focus on her and only leave her face to pan across the audience, which is still applauding. There are waves of it, and it seems to go on forever.

These are the words I suspect people wished to hear in July: a public proclamation that all—every single one—have a right to be in the streets of Cardiff. Involuntarily, I see Bernie moving down the hill swinging his purse. Inexplicably, I want to laugh. He was said to have said, *I am what I am.*

I scan the members of the committee, and I wonder which of them has known a homosexual. Can they understand what is being said and what is not being said? I assume that they are ignorant, that even if they know a homosexual, they know nothing about his life and therefore nothing about what it is they do here tonight.

A woman at the back of the room is saying, "If one of us is not safe here, then none of us is safe here." The debate takes on for a moment the quality of a cliché: For blacks or Irish or women, the word *gay* is substituted.

The time is running out. I notice, absently, the small red light on the camera indicating that taping is in progress. A woman to my left says bigotry is un-American. The lights go off and then on again, and the camera crews run silently, in a low crouch, around the edge of the room and up the center aisle and then back to the edge again, pointing the cameras this way and that. The points seem irrelevant and merely a waste of time, self-congratulatory and soothing.

A man rises. "I am told that young man carried a purse. I am told that young man wore earrings. I want to know what kind of normal man would wear earrings and carry a purse." The harsh white lights go off and on, and the little red light goes on and off. People are beginning to tire.

Another man rises. "It is a case of arrested development."

The violent shifts of the grounds of debate give one a sense of vertigo: The twentieth century. The thirteenth century. The eighteenth century. Thomas Aquinas. Thomas Jefferson. Allen Ginsburg and Praxiteles. Freud. Nineteenth century medicine. These truths are self-evident. *Michaelangelo was gay.* The earth spins.

The principal of Cardiff High School raises his hand, caught in the harsh glare, and is called upon. He speaks with a ponderous grasp of the obvious: "We are no more intolerant at Cardiff High han the town of Cardiff. We don't need a 'tolerance' policy." This is he man quoted in every out-of-town newspaper article on the murder: The boys are good boys. But the superintendent, a man of he Enlightenment—the lights are on him now—says, "Now that it has been raised, a vote against it would be a license to discriminate and to abuse those who are different. I don't understand who could be against tolerance."

Who can be against tolerance? The American question. You can vote against money for welfare or against the ERA or against housing, but you can't vote against tolerance. Arthur turns to me and mouths the words, as if he were lip-synching, *Who could be against me?* I have seen him do "Somewhere, Over the Rainbow."

Suddenly Arthur is speaking. He has a half smile, and he looks at the committee only to look away again, up at the ceiling or down at the floor. "I am a gay man," he says, his eyes coming up from the floor, closed, and then opening wide to make a circuit of the room. As he speaks, he tilts his head to emphasize points—"I've always been gay, since I was a tiny little baby in my momma's arms!"—and raises his eyebrows and purses his lips. He is charming. He shrugs, "There's no help for me!" and throws out his hands, palms up, in a gesture of surrender: "But I have such a wonderful life!" He is charming the members of the committee. They smile with him. "I have my friends, my wonderful new friends." I recognize his gestures. He uses the same ones when he seduces me. I expect he has used these gestures, the same pleading eyebrows, all his life, getting what he wants. Then he stops smiling. "The awful pain we all felt when young Bernie Mallett died is less now because we have each other."

I divide my attention between Arthur and the various Christians in their corner. They are unable to smile now. They are contemptuous, narrow, rigid, blind. It would be easier if they were the only opponents. I survey the room. I wonder if Arthur knows any more than the others what it is he is debating. The Christians stare at him with open malice. Arthur's is a masterful performance. The committee is mesmerized. They listen intently, their eyes steady on him. Perfect theater. I scan the panel—dull provincial people—and imagine what they must think. I wonder that everyone here is not privy to what he is doing. His tone is appalling. I suffer my embarrassment and don't look around the room. I can only imagine what Carole would have thought. The Christians will be baffled.

"So many kind people have spoken tonight," Arthur is saying. "I want to thank them all. Young Bernie Mallett, I am sure would have been grateful. And for those who are opposed to this action, I am sure it is because you have not yet learned—" He is going to say it! "—how wonderful—" I grit my teeth. "—gay people are!" He did. People burst into applause, and I find myself unable not to join in.

I need to say something. I must say something. I raise my hand. There is a field of hands, waving in the warm room.

"I don't think it is normal for a man to carry a purse." The speaker is a heavy-set male on the front row in a t-shirt. "Men carry their things in a wallet. I don't want to have my son have to see people like that—not even men—"

"Hey! Hey!" Men and women all over the room are waving their hands. People begin to shout at the same time.

"Men don't carry purses!"

"I don't carry a purse, asshole!"

A man jumps up. "How can you tell the difference—?"

"This is incredible!"

"How can we be expected to—"

So. Here is the deep feeling. Here is the heavy breathing.

"They act like women, that's what—"

"It's not normal, and I don't want my son going to school—"

"*Fuck you*!" It is Jack, in a loud whisper.

I raise my hand high. I think what I want to say. What is there to say? Who is it we propose to tolerate? The chairman's eyes scan the room. People continue to shout at one another. I stretch my arm so he can see me. His eyes pass me, and then reverse themselves and return, settling on me. He will call on me. I will have to shout to make myself heard above the din. *Whose children are these that we speak of here?*

But the clock on the debate has run out—it has lasted an hour—and the chairman turns to the members of the committee on his right and left and offers a chance to comment.

The microphone is passed down the table from member to member. The first one, the housewife, toys with it with her fingers as she speaks. "I am troubled that young people can be so cruel, and I m going to vote for this policy because I hate cruelty. I want every young person in Cardiff to feel he or she has a place in the schools of Cardiff—" One.

The university professor leans over the microphone. 'America is a melting pot. My parents came here after World War II as immigrants—" Two.

The construction foreman folds his arms on the table. "I would not have voted for this policy if it had been restricted solely to homosexuals. I feel we must be tolerant of many kinds of differences—religious, ethnic, racial, gender—" Three.

The microphone, with an electronic clatter, is passed back to the other end of the table. The young woman is nervous, her voice quivering, her eyes down. "I am unhappy having to make a decision like this. My religious background leads me to feel that homosexuals—I hate to say this here—" She looks up for a moment. "—I don't mean to offend anybody. But I have been taught that homosexuality is wrong. But I have also been taught to hate the sin, not the sinner, and so—" There. Four votes in favor.

"The American Psychological Association says that homosexuality is no longer a mental illness." It is a young man I don't know. Clean cut, middle-class professional type. "I am going to vote in favor."

The other young man I don't know drops the microphone, and for a moment there is a clatter and a whistling sound from the speakers. "I don't know any homosexuals, personally. And I am straight, of course. But I am impressed by—"

The microphone is back at the chairman, the pale blond owner of the convenience store. He is businesslike and scans the room. "I intend to vote in favor. Homosexuals are a minority like any other. No matter how much we may disagree with a certain lifestyle, those people who choose that lifestyle have a right to safety in our culture. No one deserves to be murdered—" He concludes, and then he announces, looking at me, that he will entertain a motion to close and to proceed to a vote, and, to a certain rise in the tension in the room, the housewife raises her little finger to indicate that she is prepared to make the motion. What would I have said? In a rapid order, the chairman asks, *Do I hear a second?*

People rise in their seats to see. The construction foreman, from the same end of the table, raises his arm. We glance at each other as the drama approaches its climax, and the camera crews and both men with lights focus on the committee.

Are we then prepared to vote on the motion?

So move.

Arthur takes my arm.

Second?

A gesture with a hand.

The chairman nods. All in favor? The fat lady is about to sing. He looks to his right and then to his left, counting hands. Arthur has narrowed his lids, and his lips are drawn into a thin line.

People in the audience crane their necks to count, and people standing around me at the back can see in an instant the vote—the cameramen pan their cameras up and down the table: Unanimous, in favor. Tomorrow we will all be saying, for lack of a clearer message of what was voted on tonight, that the vote was unanimous in favor of tolerance. A loving God. Charity. Twentieth century biblical exegesis. Eighteenth-century beliefs in the equality of man, the power of reason, the endless perfectibility of human nature. Kinsey. Arthur.

I feel ill.

The lights are turned on us now, and the cameramen sweep their cameras from one side of the room to the other. I raise my chin high. Then people are clapping all over the room. There is a release of tension, a huge increase in noise, and people are moving around in their chairs.

Jack has stood up and, seeing me, grins broadly, showing his canine teeth. He holds his arms above his head like a prize-fighter. They talk openly, no longer whispering. This is wonderful. Do you see how easy it is?

The chairman raps for order—no one at first hears him and the lights are gone now—and asks if there is any other business. It takes a few minutes and several raps of his gavel on the block of wood before he gets people's attention. Finally they turn back to him, distracted by him from their pleasure in each other and in themselves, and listen.

Is there any other business?

For a moment I wonder what he means. Other business. He casts his eyes around the room, up and down the table at the committee.

That having completed the agenda, do I hear a motion to adjourn?

A committee member languidly moves the motion.

All in favor.

Hands are raised. People grin again and the level of sound rises again. The committee members break into smiles and animated talk with one another, and the room is filled with noise, people rising, talking, pushing back chairs, gathering their coats.

Is this it?

The Christians begin to rise. They take their coats from the back of their chairs, and move into the aisle. I watch them closely. I consider, for a moment, what they think has happened here. Their smiles seem strained, and they look directly ahead. The gays and lesbians—those with lavender ribbons and green buttons—in the seats watch them go. I think I want them to suffer. I don't care so much about defeating them as causing them pain. I want *someone* to suffer.

"We beat back the forces of darkness."

I turn and discover it is a member of the historical society, Hammond Douglas. He is my age, early seventies, his arms crossed over his chest, his overcoat draped over his arms, a shy, sheepish look on his face. He is extremely thin, and the cords of his neck work furiously while he swallows his spit and works his jaws. He smiles, a great open-mouthed grin, showing very long yellow teeth in the midst of dry, lined skin. "We did the right thing—"

I wait to see what he is going to say.

Confused, he discovers that I don't respond. He has huge eyes, and in his stress, he slides his lids back so far and then brings them forward so as almost to close them. "The policy—"

"Yes—"

Another pause. He must feel trapped.

He opens his eyes again and then brings them close. "Gays will feel more secure now—"

"Yes," I say. "I am sure of that."

"I am glad of that—" Douglas looks at me as if he doesn't know my meaning.

I am sure of that.

He searches my face. He knows that I have been attending the coalition meetings, that I am a homosexual, that I am "out." He must know all this dreary information that homosexuals must put out about themselves that makes them different from heterosexuals. He must have expected that I would be happy with the results of tonight's debate and vote, that I would be in some way grateful. He turned to me—We ordinarily have little to say to one another beyond the weather—because he thought I would be grateful to *him*. I find him now, his face drawn back into a horrible, dry grin, a scar in his lined face, his teeth, yellow and individually splayed like those in a skull, his lids widened to show veins across the yellow whites of his eyes. This policy would tie me to him in a bondage of the tolerant and the tolerated. This is the closure, the political response of communal, political Cardiff to the murder of Barnard Mallett.

His hand is on my arm, clutching me, picking at the fabric of my jacket. "What do you want?"

In the car going home, the others want to stop off at Dominic's for pie. It is a clear early November night, every star distinguishable in the black sky, as if you could see through to the beginning. Arthur says, "Oh, Luke, please don't be this way." He pats my knee, and the skin across my skull draws tight.

"Don't patronize me, Arthur."

"What can be eating at you?" It is Sally from the back seat.

"I hate this."

"I don't mind it at all. Let's me go about my business—"

"There is no difference between what was done tonight and those boys throwing Mallett—"

"How *can* you say that? Oh, Luke! Bernie is dead!"

They think I am insane, an old man lost in resentment, corrupted by years of anger. I wonder how is it that they are able to take the nearer way? They are easily satisfied. I feel sick. I am moved to rage when I hear a woman say, "It is the American way." They don't know what they're doing, and they don't mean to do it. Nobody sees what I see and hears what I hear: The Lord is going to smite them. The Lord is going to destroy the Cities of the Plain! And those who regret, who look back and regret, will be turned to pillars of salt! I have fought for sixty years, and these people come in the morning and talk of toleration. What weak words. Where were they yesterday, and all the yesterdays back to the day I was born, when the battle was really hard?

It is necessary to know the name of the crime. I feel the way I always do when I am confronted with unctuous hypocrisy. There is nothing to say to those who presume to tolerate reality.

I drive toward Dominic's.

"Don't take us there. I want to go home."

"You said—"

"Not while you're in this mood!"

"Luke is tired."

"Oh, Arthur, is he terrible to live with?"

"A bear—"

"They determined the terms of the settlement—"

"Oh, Luke, how sad. Take me home."

I am pouring myself a drink when Arthur comes in.

"I should think you don't need that tonight."

We participate in one of the grand clichés of the American experience. I am moved to think of Bernie Mallett. I would like to have known him. They say he walked down Main Street like a proper Queen, swinging his purse and his bottom, smiling at people, saying, "Good morning!" to this laborer and "How are you!" to that one. I am told he asked nothing of anybody. Arthur watches me. I run the glass under the water for a second, then I turn the water off. I can tell he is still there.

"Come into the living room."

"What is the matter with you?"

"I am going to get drunk. Would you like to join me?" I raise my glass to the level of his eyes and nod my head. I do not like having him here. I may not keep him. He stares at me, disbelieving.

Since July we have become full with stories of Bernie's "flamboyance." He turned his face to the side and lowered his eyelids and then slowly raised his eyes to look at you. It was a parody of a woman seducing. He pursed his lips. What was he doing? I make my way around Arthur and through the dining room and past the portrait of my father to the living room. I settle into a corner of the sofa. Was it something he was? Was it something he did? Was he a parody of something or the thing itself? He challenged every notion of manhood—it is no wonder the laborers were threatened by his presence—and *I* know why he did it.

479

On the opposite wall is the steel engraving of a nineteenth century battle, soldiers in long lines stretched out across the undulating countryside, marching forward, their rifles fixed with bayonets, little puffs of smoke floating up from the crowd of woods, the occasional soldier falling in his place, the one army indistinguishable from the other. Arthur comes in and sits in the small rosewood rocker opposite, staring at me. What did Mallett feel, walking down the hill into town, nodding, smiling, acknowledging the stares, knowing what was being whispered, knowing what he was walking into? What is it to be tolerated?

Arthur stares at my drink, disapproving, like an old wife. The long days stretch out ahead of me: the marriage of old people. He tells me I have been drunk twice this week already. He tells me I am drinking more now. More than when? Than what? It is his role to disapprove. Mine to do disapproving things. I do the expected thing. I drain my scotch and swirl the ice. We face old age together, a parody of a marriage.

I have walked down hills in my time into the battle. I walked down stairs when I was seventeen, and told my parents I was a poof. They sat in the living room on this very sofa—it was covered in brocade then—and heard me out. Mother, who never allowed her back to touch the sofa, pressed her lips shut. He stared at another part of the room. They gave me the chance to make the first volley. I talked fast, my chin up, filling the space between us with my words. Afterwards when it was over, they pretended it hadn't happened. Things went on as they always had, as the years went by. Since I was young, I must have thought somewhere in my mind that telling them would change them. I thought that gradually they would come to speak of it with me. *What friends do you have?* I imagined them asking. Bring him to tea. I imagined Mother moving over on the sofa and making room.

When Arthur asks me what it was, I say, "I never spoke of it again, and they never referred to it. I was different—"

"Why weren't you satisfied?"

"How could I have been satisfied—?"

"Oh!"

I had two legs, the same as they. Two arms. Two eyes. I had been born from my mother's womb. I was their flesh. I had my mother's mouth and my father's forehead. I have my father's distance and fastidiousness and my mother's suppressed rage.

Arthur's head rests back against his chair. He has closed his eyes. "I performed acrobatics with my mind. When I was fifteen, eighteen, I remember vividly how it felt to be in the presence of a man who excited me, these uncontrollable things happening to my body. I breathed quickly and felt lightheaded, and I was sure I was blushing. I knew all that, and I loved it! I knew it was me—"

I take a sip of my scotch and watch him. Arthur, to my distaste, enjoys his interior life.

"—and at the same time, I knew there were men called *poofs* who wore makeup and women's clothes and did unspeakable things with other men. They were perverts. For several years, I knew both of these things—how I felt around men and what a queer was. But I managed through a kind of mental gymnastics—twisting myself into incredible shapes—not to recognize that the one was the other, that I was a queer. You see, when it came a glimmering, when the nasty thought presented itself to me sometimes like a shadow behind the door or mud left on the carpet, I resisted recognizing the mere truth because it meant I had be one of them. And I couldn't be one of them! I was one of us! Recognizing that I was queer required a displacement of my feelings. That's what coming out means, isn't it? Recognizing that you aren't one of us anymore? You're one of them?"

Occasionally he sits up straight and reaches for his drink and brings it to his lips in a movement more studied than I am capable of. I like the care with which he lives.

"I cut them off. I cut them out of my emotional life. They knew nothing of my feelings and didn't want to know—"

It is one thing for one's peers to tolerate one, this group of adults to tolerate that group of different adults: *We don't approve of makeup and earrings and carrying a purse, but you may if you want to.* But say that to a child. Say that to Bernie when he was a child— nine-, ten-, eleven-years old: *Your father doesn't approve of men wearing makeup and earrings and carrying a purse, but you may if you want to.*

"My mother thinks we have a wonderful relationship because I call her and send her cards and visit her three or four times a year—. That's the way it is with all mothers, isn't it? Do parents ever know what is in their children's hearts?"

I watch him across the coffee table. In my fatigue and my drunken state, he recedes from me as if I have lost my fingerhold on the edge of a cliff. We speak here merely of the alienation of humankind.

Bernie's mother didn't say that to him. What she would have said was, *You've hurt your daddy and me. You've done this just to hurt us.* And when Bernie was a teenager, the teachers in his school would have looked the other way when he was taunted on the schoolground. His principal would have said, *When you dress that way, you must expect people to respond.*

But what if Bernie had been tolerated? *We are the source of love and nurturing, and these are the values we hold, and you have violated them, but we respect your right to live your life as you choose.* Love and nurturing and the values they hold and one's sense that one has violated them, respect and freedom. *We are the source of love and nurturing. You have violated our values. We respect your right to do so. Respect. Right.* He would have weighed those against *love* and *nurturing,* weighed these against a mother's arms. *We respect your right to be different from us. We are love and nurturing. You are different from us.* I know what Mallett felt, though I never knew Bernie Mallett. I have been offered respect by someone who said, *I am love, You are different.*

"But we've come such a long way—" Arthur has gone to the kitchen and refilled our glasses. He has put mine down on the coffee table and now, gathering up his dressing gown about his knees, lowers himself onto the floor by the sofa, laying his arm along the cushion. "Stonewall. Gay Pride. GMHC. New York has a gay rights bill. Portland has a bar." He settles back against the sofa, lowering his head gently on his arm, closing his eyes. "The memorial service for Bernie. When we walked down the street with our candles. That was the most beautiful moment of my life. I was an angel! We were the heavenly host! Praising God!" He grins. "There is a gay community here in Cardiff now. We know who we are. We have a mailing list." He opens his eyes and looks into his drink. "Do you know how important a mailing list is? The beginnings of political power." He turns his head so he can look up at me. "We walk down Main Street together. I am here. We are in love. We will sleep together tonight, something for us to be grateful for, my arms around you." He smiles. "Handsome man."

I am love. You are different. You are love. I am different. You left me to find my own way at thirteen. You abandoned me to find a way to be. A way to walk and talk. I have found my way to walk and talk in my time, with a boy down behind the garage and then with the succession of boys down behind some garage when I was thirteen and all the years since. I found my way, to walk and talk and to have friends and make a living and go to church and even bury you. I found a way to feel about myself and what I did—and about you—and through it all, I knew I was different, because you had told me *We are love. You are different.* You never found another way to tell me you were love that didn't also say, *You are different.*

"You can't forget. You hang on to your pain."

Because it happened to me sixty-five years ago, I can forget. I've forgotten what my father looked like, aside from the stiff, studio portrait of him in the dining room. I used to remember how he smelled. You can forget anything except the way it felt. I can't remember my childhood. The pain isn't over simply because it is over for me. Arthur doesn't believe Bernie Mallett's mother told him, "Hey, it's a free country." What Arthur means to say is that he doesn't believe Bernie Mallett's mother cut him off from her. All over town right now, some kid is telling his mother, and she's saying, *We are the source of love and nurturing and these are the values we hold, and you have violated them. But we respect your right to live your life as you choose.* She is saying *I am love, you are different.* And that's the best he can hope for.

"I'm so sorry for you, Luke."

Are things getting better, Arthur? You tolerate people who're different from you, not the same, and you tolerate people who're wrong, not right. I wonder if he remembered what it was like when he began to realize he was different from his mother, and he didn't know what he was like because he had never seen or read or heard ever before of anything like what he was. Does he remember the panic? At nine or ten, you are just old enough to know how much you need to learn, just at the moment when you are suddenly told that there is no one around to help you learn it, especially not your parents, not anyone in school, no one at church or in the neighborhood. You're fourteen, and you've never seen this in a book

Luke

or a magazine or on television, except as a joke which you didn't understand or a curse, which you did. The shifting of the ground throws you suddenly into a void which opens up under your feet which goes right to the center of the earth.

At the best, with the best and most progressive of teachers, and with the students most receptive and most secure in themselves, but *never, never, will there be a classroom like that*, a boy like Bernie will be offered "tolerance" for a few hours five days a week. Where will he get the strength to go through his life "tolerated"? Where will he find the lap on which he can lay his head? At just the moment when he needs a culture, a society to form him, he is forced out of the only one he has ever known. A gay person, every one of them, is born into a straight family. Where in the discussion tonight was that acknowledged?

Arthur has joined me on the sofa. He lies down, his head in my lap, his face buried in the silk folds of my dressing gown. I have placed my hand on his neck, and my finger explores the recesses of his ear. I feel an immeasurable tenderness toward him. The relationship we have begun takes for its model the late twentieth century relationship between men and women. Whose purposes do we serve here? Capitalism, Christianity, the State. We are trapped in systems of thought, and we don't find our way to the core of things.

"What they achieved served our purposes, too," Arthur murmurs.

They are secure against everything except the prospect that one of their children might be gay. Those with homosexual feelings, after tonight's action, remain securely "other," as decisively outside the realm of the normal as the Baptists and those three boys would have it, still to be treated as another race, let into America by some lax immigration law, tolerated but unassimilated, Chinese to work the railroad and to populate Chinatowns on the coasts. The progressive majority tonight may go home satisfied with the achievement of their illiberal purposes.

"What difference would it make?"

I dislike Arthur. I suspect all this comfort, his lying in my lap and our enjoying each other. Something must be wrong. I have never not been lied to. He pleaded for acceptance tonight. He should have used his talent to make a case for revolution. Betrayal is the mode by which we express our sexual desires. I look for it under the

484

softness of his body like change under sofa cushions, hard lumps of it. He patronizes me. He sweeps his arm across the horizon expansively and says, Look what we have! We have betrayed ourselves.

It is a matter of regret that I was born here and now. I live out my life—At seventy, how much longer do I have!—at an epoch when touching between persons brings forth feelings of fear and loathing. I should have been born in Sparta and at ten had an oiled and armed warrior take me away from my parents to teach me the male arts of love and war. I am surrounded by these little fools with mean and paltry emotions and even more trivial courage. *What difference would it make!* If one of those persons in that room tonight had had a child who was gay and had dared to speak of it, the "debate" would have been transformed, no monstrous lies about the sin of Sodom, no silly demeaning chatter about tolerance. God! If it had been my child, I would have thundered like Yahweh from the roof of Sinai, *Rewrite the course in human sexuality! Hang pictures of naked men! Institute a course in the anatomy of bigotry! Study the berdache and the shaman! Write essays on transgenderal and transgenerational and egalitarian homosexuality! Buy textbooks on famous queers!* Tolerance! My burning ass! *Start seminars in cult prostitution, symposia on historic lies. And every day give each boy and girl time and quiet space for sex in his or her own way.* Blood of Christ. I don't want to change men's minds, I want to destroy the earth.

I am seized with the knowledge of an historic outrage. What makes us gay? This unholy dialogue. A button lies on the coffee table: *Another friend of Bernie Mallett.* We define ourselves by this chatter back and forth. We are friends of Bernie's. We—all of us—lack courage. We are afraid of liberty, afraid of what our bodies are capable of, afraid of where our feelings lead us. Our sexuality is defined by fear and denial. *Toleration!* Why doesn't the Lord strike! Why doesn't the thunder sound and the city explode in flames! Like primitive peoples, we seek to govern our sexuality with taboo and fetishes.

Arthur shifts in my lap and extends his arms to my neck. He rises up slightly, his eyes closed, his mouth pursed: His goal is a kiss, and I give it to him, my thin lips on his. *What is the need for all this virtue?* I stood in my bare feet, my bare back against the refrigerator

485

door, my thumbs in my pockets, and stared at her. I was fifteen. She had something in the oven and was leaning over to inspect it, huge mittens on her hands, the hair about her face. She was tired. She squinted, and she didn't want to deal with me. She said, *I don't want to know,* looking directly into the oven. *You keep the details of your life private.*

No one tonight said, *We're talking about my kid, here.*

Arthur has no sense of privacy. He listens, and then he asks probing questions. He wants to know about me. He loves everything about me. I unfold to him. It is instinctive, involuntary, and spontaneous. I am being opened up, unforced. My gratitude to him seeps through me like a scotch on a cold night, and I stumble toward him like a man groping toward the only hut in the forest. I raise him up in my arms and touch my lips to his neck. I clutch him to me, my arms tight around his chest. We two. What drives me to him? Fear. Love. Love. Fear. Am I still capable? His arms are around my neck. Am I a fool? I am equal parts joy and grief. He hugs me tight, hard.

Dana

O h, isn't he beautiful!" It is an unfamiliar voice, and it envelops me in a soft intimacy which was unlooked for, and I turn, surprised. It is a neighbor whom I haven't met. I smile. People do this to mothers and babies, smile and say, *What a beautiful child.* Babies are everybody's connection with everybody else. I thank her. She moves closer to me and leans over him to see directly into his eyes. I can smell the odor of her powder. He chooses this moment to blink, slowly. "Such a beautiful child!" Her voice is so soft and full with feeling that I must lean over closer to hear her words.

I smile again, and she looks at me and smiles.

People can't help it. They see you, and they need to say, *Ah! It's happened again.* Since we were all babies once, I think it's an affirmation of the race. She glances at me, and then around the room and then back at us. We stare at Marc's face, concern for this tiny human shutting out for a moment the rest of the world and making me feel like a sharer in a stupendous and delightful secret.

"So late for him to be up!" Her face crinkles into a question mark and a suspicion. She is in her forties, married, with teenaged children, and lives up the river from us in one of the few modern houses on the main road with her family. She wears a down jacket and boots—we heard it was to snow tonight—and her hair is in a long braid, wrapped around the back of her head.

"He's half asleep now."

"Does he," she asks, smiling, full of hope but doubting, looking directly into my eyes, "get to see his father much?" She was at the school committee meeting last night and attends the Baptist church, and the rent in our intimacy is almost not there, so softly does she speak. But it is there nonetheless, our casual intimacy rent by her attempt at an invasion of our privacy.

Her question exposes the distance between us. "Enough." I will say no more than that, and I wonder if she arrived at the question by plan—she sees Marcia and me in the yard with Marc and no man—or merely by stumbling. *Enough.* Last summer I held him in my arms for most of the parade, and men and women both said, *What a beautiful kid!* But there was no doubt then and no suspicion, and the comments we heard on all sides—*What a beautiful child!*—

melted into *What a beautiful day!* Our gladness turned everything into beauty.

We stand in line to vote. It is a little after six-thirty in the evening. The school gymnasium echoes with the sounds of people's shoes walking across the polished wood floor from the line to the registration desk to the voting machines and the low murmur of voices. Every few minutes there is the pneumatic clank of the machine when someone pulls back the lever to record her vote. The windows above are dark, and the vast room is lit by harsh lights which leave the ceiling above the steel girders in deep shadows. There is a businesslike air to what we do. The registrars speak softly to one another, and the air extends to the people in the line, who wait quietly.

In the dark on the walk outside near the parking lot, people carry signs for the candidates, the president and vice president, and the Democratic presidential and vice presidential candidates.

"You knew him?" My neighbor looks at my green button, *Another Friend of Bernie Mallett*, and then at me, her smile open-mouthed and wide-eyed.

"Oh, yes. I knew him well," which was not so but is now. I brace myself against what is to come next.

She seems uncertain, pauses, unclear what to do.

But it doesn't come. "Such sadness. Such sadness." She brightens. "Well, we must do our civic duty!" She laughs. She makes a helpless gesture with her head, indicating the privacy of the voting machines. She turns away from me and shows me her shoulder.

Civic duty. All the way down from Maine, the sky had been overcast, an even silver-gray cover from horizon to horizon. As we crossed the Massachusetts line, the clouds grew lacy, and it was possible to see bits of blue, which became more and more pronounced as we crossed the Tobin Bridge, and then, as we left the car behind the library and rounded the corner from Boylston into Copley Square just at noon, the clouds disappeared—the silver had thinned and thinned until it evaporated—and we were drenched in warm bright sunlight, as if nothing should be allowed to cast shadows on what we were about.

Right there, at the intersection of Dartmouth and Boylston, the police had blocked off the street, and we entered a crowd of people who stood so close together that their bodies formed a solid mass and we couldn't get through. We stood on tiptoe, and I held Marc high above my head to see. The only thing missing to make us form connections was music to make our pulses beat in rhythm, and we heard music coming toward us. Under the new blue skies, the crowds parted like an opera curtain, and we saw a band coming through toward us, twenty or thirty women in a formation held together by the music but already unraveling in the sheer expressive joy of it, playing on rhythm instruments, drums and castenets and cymbals. People on the sidewalk and in the street around us cheered, and my heart beat faster and my breath came quicker, a complex, compelling rhythm. I wanted to dance. People cheered again, and the women laughed. They carried a banner that said *Batucada Belles* and did a slow shuffle dance out into the middle of the thousands of people toward Marcia and Marc and me.

Marc reached out his hand toward them as if he could touch them.

There were two women standing beside us. One of them said, "Oh, look!" and they both turned to look at Marc. "What a beautiful child!"

The whole square between the public library and Trinity Church and all the streets around it were crowded with noisy exuberant people carrying banners. The sharp edge of the Hancock building was an elegant jade knife slicing the sky, and the Copley Plaza was a florid beaux arts beauty smiling across all of us. On the other side of the square, the ragged line of buildings which house a florist shop and Copley Flair and Montillios gave a pedestrian and human-scaled note to a scene dominated by the exalted, ponderous strength of Trinity Church. High up and too far away to cast shadows on our day were great cumulus clouds, solid enough for a god to recline on, which made the whole scene into a baroque glory. It took my breath away, these thousands of people out in this brilliant sun under these immense white clouds in the middle of this huge city. It had the clarity of a Handel opera. And at that moment my world suddenly became hugely, inexplicably enlarged. I felt lightheaded and giddy.

That was in June. This is now. The woman in the line in front of me taps her toe in impatience. Our line stops at a table where registrars check our names against lists of eligible voters. We will then be allowed, one at a time, to proceed to the machines. Tonight at some point, our part in all this done, the networks will project a winner, and we can get on to something new, pick up our lives again where we left them, like a dropped sweater, when we learned Bernie was dead. Only you don't begin, or even begin again. *Morning in America.* The Gay Rights bill will be brought up again in January. Mickey has prepared folders on each person running for the legislature in this election, and tomorrow morning he will be able to say who our friends are and who are enemies. His campaign will go on and on. Whatever the outcome tonight, national elections have been transformed by the presence of a woman vice presidential candidate. The NOW Convention was held two weeks after the parade, in Miami, and now we see the end of the organizing and the street demonstrations and meetings and speeches and conventions.

The parade started slowly, and we had time to enter the square, threading our way through the people. Floating above the crowd, like hope, were thousands of lavender balloons and green balloons. Men and women were grouped around banners—*Old Cambridge Baptist Church, All God's People, Boston Gay Men's Chorus, Dorchester GALA*—and called out to one another.

"—Helen! Over here!"

"Join us!"

"I'm going to walk with the Tufts people!" a young man called out and pointed, joining a group of college students under the banner *Tufts Lesbian and Gay Community.*

Marcia and I and Marc walked among them, like a small boat among big ones, looking for a group to attach ourselves to. We passed *Lesbian Sober and Proud* next to *Gay Sober and Proud*, recovering alcoholics.

"Oh, look." A young slender gay man carried a sign with *Bill Erwin* and a date earlier in June with the legend *Sober and Free*.

"He's only been dead 13 days." We paused and watched. I searched his face for his feelings. He was talking to friends.

There were other banners—*Church of the Covenant*, and *Boston Unitarian-Universalist* under a rainbow, a single man carrying a boom box saturating his surroundings with driving rock music and a sign *Rock Against Heterosexism*, and *Dignity Boston*, the organization for gay and lesbian Catholics.

We passed a group of slightly older men and women under the banner *Parents and Friends of Gays and Lesbians*. Mother would not be here today even if she knew. She would have disapproved of what she would see as a public display of private feeling.

"Look. There's another." A young man and a young woman carried a sign *We miss John*.

I looked for the difference.

"There are supposed to be twenty thousand of us—"

"Do we look different?" After all that has been said, gay men and lesbians might have given an immediate assault on the visual sense of what men and women look like.

Marcia takes my arm. "You can't see it."

I saw a cityscape in summer where the people had taken possession of the streets for their music and dancing and for their cause. There was an air of holiday, of people released from chores and day-to-day routine. The square under the great church gave the air of a medieval fair—jesters and maypoles. "Young people have acne, and the older ones wrinkles." She laughed. We were dressed somewhere between streetwise kids and college students.

"Some of us look like social workers on a picnic."

Ordinary Americans. It is a little past six-thirty on Tuesday evening, November 6, 1984. The polls closed here ten minutes ago and have three hours to go on the West Coast.

I hold Marc in my arms, where he has grown almost too large. He is alert now, looking about and blinking his slow blink. Marcia and I take him everywhere in our arms or in a car bed, introducing him to our lives, which will be his. I know we give off the air of those who have just bought an expensive and delicate new possession, but what is hidden is our sense of him as a gift, and what shows on our faces—it seems like pride—is a strong blend of joy and gratitude. I think surely I am like other parents in believing that he will vote, in his time, for our values, that he will reject racism and sexism and homophobia and greed, and that he won't be afraid to be different.

"Yes," Marcia has laughed when she has heard me talk like that. "Despite their devotion, you grew up to reject every significant value your parents held." It is a chilling reminder—shade on a September day—and I face already, even as I am only just beginning to possess him, the pain of letting him go.

We followed the Batucada Belles, joining a hundred people dancing with a slow shuffle step into the street, past the ragged row of buildings on the left and the brown and beige parish house of Trinity Church. The crowd was now on the sidewalks on each side of us, and as we walked past, we divided into *us* and *them*, those in the parade and those not in it. The distinguishing mark seemed to be this: They had no sense of being special, of having come through fire.

I saw a middle-aged man in need of a shave, a white t-shirt and work boots who raised his arms and clapped and cheered loudly, a lady shopper in suit and heels, laughing and clapping politely, whose eyes met mine and twinkled for a moment, and a young woman in jeans and a t-shirt who saw me and cheered and straightened her arms above her head over and over. It was exhilarating to feel the wave of applause start up just ahead of us and die down for a moment behind before the next group came by, when it started up again. The sound was a greeting and a welcome and a celebration, and we walked through it—their applause suggested their affection for us—as though we were receiving a continuous benediction.

I looked ahead up Boylston Street, and the view toward the Common between the buildings on both sides was stopped by thousands of lavender and green balloons, bouncing just above the heads of the parade. We passed the wall of buildings on the left between Dartmouth and Clarendon, the great cumulus clouds piling high in the sky above the skyline. Behind us was a large banner saying *G.L.A.D.* and another *Dyke Doctors*. Farther back, *Nova Scotia Gay and Lesbian Alliance* and *Gay and Lesbian Labor Activists*, and one held by a single man in a tank top, *Come Out, Come Out of the Closet/And Into the Universe*. Much further back was *Gay Fathers*. The wave of applause from bystanders swelled and receded, and we cheered and clapped too, answering them, and, as we walked up Boylston under the blue sky and the high clouds, there was a wordless dialogue between us in the parade and those on the sidewalk, these cheers and claps answering cheers and claps, affection answering affection, and laughter everywhere.

Last night after Marcia had taken the babysitter home, we sat in the living room by the stove talking. We have two wonderful old wood rockers which we have given new cushions and have placed near the stove for warmth and comfort. Marcia was still thinking about the school committee meeting.

"What were they saying to us?" She had leaned back in her rocker, her head resting against the high back, staring at the ceiling. Then she swung forward and put her feet on the floor and her elbows on her knees and clasped her hands. "What was that all about?"

"They were telling us who they were—"

"And gays—"

"No. Nothing about us—"

"Do you suppose we had some part in that dialogue?"

"Oh, no. It was about them—"

The propositions on the ballot will only marginally affect us: There is one to authorize a bond issue for the University of Maine system, another for the prison system, and a third for the state vocational/technical school system. There are amendments to the state constitution—one having to do with benefits for veterans, one changing rules on state bond issues, and Question 6: the state ERA. The voter in the booth pulls the lever, and it clanks. My neighbor glances back at me, but her eyes don't linger, and she doesn't acknowledge me or Marc this time.

The effect of the propositions and questions and even the presidential race will be determined by forces which we can't foresee—the makeup of the legislature, the Senate and House races, the amount of money available, the cast of the judicial appointments over the next two years. The simplicity of the national ballot—this man or that man—suggests we have a power of choice which doesn't exist.

Behind me the line grows longer. I shift Marc in my arms—he puts his head on my shoulder—and turn and look and recognize some of them. Holly Simpson, who also works at the university, and Pamela McCrae, who works at the Medical Center, Peter Healey, a man who will come and trim your trees. I imagine Pamela and Holly are liberals and Peter, probably, a conservative, but there is no way to tell. I haven't seen any of them at a political meeting. Just at the door coming in is David Alfieri. He's married and has children, and I saw him at the memorial service for Bernie last summer. What does that say about him? I consider the possibilities—closeted gay, straight member of the U-U church, conservative humanitarian, liberal, radical—and abandon the effort. His hair is long and bushy, which says nothing. At a point each one of them will stand in the booth and pull the lever and vote for one of the major party candidates, but his votes on the other offices and the propositions will blur the distinction between *this* and *that*.

Behind us I saw the sign, *Lesbians Choosing Parenting*. It was the group I was looking for. That's where we can tie up our dinghy.

"Let's wait for them!"

"Let's go back—"

We moved out of the parade toward the sidewalk, into the crowd watching and cheering. We moved behind a male and female couple with a camera—she pointed and told him what to take a picture of—into a group of straight teenaged boys and turned and watched the first groups who were behind us, people under the banner *G.L.A.D.* and the dyke doctors, their arms in the air, applauding the bystanders.

"What is it?" It was one of the boys beside me, a boy with spiked hair.

"Gay and Lesbian Advocates and Defenders," another one said, one with a row of rings in his ear. "They're lawyers. They go to court and fight for gays—" I had been wrong.

The boys were clapping for the dyke doctors, and everybody laughed when the doctors applauded back. We began walking back along the parade route. I recognized some of the bystanders cheering. They had been in the parade with us a moment ago, and I saw now people in the parade who we had passed—they had been on the sidewalk—when we were in the parade. The gays and lesbians from Nova Scotia passed by and the labor activists and the Gay Fathers, men carrying babies and pushing strollers and walking with teenaged boys and girls. Then there were the *Lesbians Choosing Parenting*, some pushing strollers, some with babies in their arms or in seats on their backs.

We moved through the crowd on the sidewalk and joined them, walking among them. I felt we had found where we belonged, and I looked around me and saw the people on the sidewalk cheering us. I noticed one, the man in a tank top, who carried the sign *Come out, come out*—, who had been in the parade before. The bystanders, who seemed to be clearly *them* and not *us*, were some of us too. And we were some of them. I liked this. We were welcomed into the group of women, and I lost my sense of being different, which I didn't know I had, when I was carrying Marc before. The flip side of being out on the street in the middle of the city is the sense of being exposed, of being unsupported, and Marcia and I found our way to the center of the group of lesbians, at once refuge and liberation.

Marybeth and Cynthia vote in one of the Hamlin precincts. Marybeth feels to vote is to take part in and validate an oppressive system. With the lesbian parents we covered the same ground again, the first block of the parade, past Montillios on one side and Trinity Church on the other, under the blue sky and the jade blade of the Hancock building in which were reflected the proud clouds, past the stodgy solid New England Life and soigné Louis buildings, heading toward the Arlington Street Church at the corner of Boylston and Arlington, where we could hear great shouts.

"Hi—" It was a thin woman with a little girl walking beside us. She asked us where we were from. "Welcome to Boston!"

Marcia and I noticed that many of the women were holding hands, and we did too.

"Are you from Maine?" another asked—then, "I am too. Portland—"

We got into a conversation with a woman—red-haired, round-faced, freckles—from Texas, and we compared dates, and then I found she was working in Augusta, and I got her name and address.

We heard the shouts a long time before we got there. At first I couldn't tell what they were, and then it began to seem like a deep roar which rose and subsided and rose and subsided. The Batucada Belles were way in front of us, and all around us were lesbian mothers pushing strollers or carrying infants—there were also some little girls and boys and teenagers, holding their mothers' hands—and we acknowledged the shouts and cheers of the crowd by clapping. We crossed Berkeley, moving toward the roars of the people ahead of us.

It was a flag. As each new contingent of the parade drew close enough to see through the trees, we discovered that an old man was hanging out of a clerestory window in the tower of the Arlington Street Church, waving a pole with an enormous banner which carried a rainbow, a symbol during the campaign of the Rainbow Coalition of people of all colors, and it was being waved now, jubilantly, high on the elegant dark brown stone of the tower of the church. People broke out into a roar of shouts. Women all around me were holding

495

their free arms high—most of them were like me, carrying a baby in one arm—and shouting in response to the great banner waving back and forth high up against the wall of the building.

The image was explicitly revolutionary—the flag of the people hanging from the neoclassical church—and stirring.

"It's like the Marseillaise!"

It was Marianne carrying the Tricolor over the ramparts, and I raised my arm and shouted over and over again, and Marc, unable to focus on the flag, touched his fingers to my mouth and gurgled and giggled.

Marcia put her arm around my neck and squeezed and then slid it down to my waist, and all around us men and women hugged and kissed and shouted and grinned.

"Look, Marcia! Look at her." Ahead of me was a young woman with her long luxuriant brown hair piled on her head in a Gibson style, wearing a nineteenth century full-length dress. It was the style a woman might have worn in the eighteen seventies. She had a tiny waist and high, muttonchop sleeves, and lace high around her collar. I was struck by her fastidious beauty. She seemed out of time. And then as we moved past the church, she turned back to see the tower and the banner which we were passing, and I could see her face. She had a full mustache and beard—

"It's a man—"

—long and curly, covering even his throat, though I could see under the beard a cameo pin attached to his high lacy collar. His beard was so full that it covered all of his face, except his eyes, which were large and brown and moist and surrounded by long lashes.

"Isn't he beautiful!" Marcia reached out to him—he had stopped in the middle of the street to watch the flag while the crowd parted around him—and spoke, "You're beautiful!"

He didn't hear, and then when she repeated herself, he turned and looked directly at us, this tall slender young man in a full beard, his hair piled up in a knot on top of his head, wearing a full-length gingham dress, and grinned.

All of us in line have seen, in the last ten days, a large picture of two young men in jeans and t-shirts standing in the middle of a street, their arms around one another, embracing, caught by the camera at the moment of a full mouth-to-mouth kiss. It was in an advertisement which ran in all the Maine papers, including the *Sentinel*. The ad said, *Do you want this to happen in Maine? Vote against the ERA.* The majority for the ERA, which ran two to one in August, has now reversed itself and is a majority two to one against.

This suggests something about politics: It is partial, tentative, limited, tangential, roughhewn, inefficient and provisional and only occasionally does one's vote result directly in the resolution of the issue you are voting on. The machine *clanks* again across the polished gym floor. The voter is a man, slender, grayhaired, who wears a gray suit with polished black shoes and seems terribly satisfied, sending off his votes toward their targets like a bunch of roman candles toward the moon. He comes back across the gym smiling at us.

"That should do it!" he says to my neighbor standing in front of me.

I laugh.

"Give my love to Sylvia!"

He looks at me. "Beautiful baby!"

And then he is gone.

We turned, hearing voices behind us.

"Dana! Marcia! Over here!"

On the sidewalk under the trees of the Public Garden were Marybeth and Cynthia, waving. Behind them in the garden was the heroic bronze statute of Kosciuszko.

"You came! How wonderful!"

We dropped back and made our way to the crowd on the side to Marybeth and Cynthia. General Tadeusz Kosciuszko, on his pedestal among the trees in the garden, was said to be a Champion of Liberty and the Rights of Man.

"I wondered where you'd be!"

"With lesbian mothers, where else!"

We hugged all around.

"We were with Batucada Belles for a little bit."

"So were we. Then we walked with the New Alliance Party—"

"He's beautiful!"

Cynthia took Marc for a moment, and he looked back at me and at Marcia and then blinked slowly at Cynthia. We stood with them beside the Public Garden. Wendell Phillips, who said,

"Whether in chains or in laurels, Liberty knows nothing but victories," overlooked our conversation. We talked about going back to Maine that night.

"I want to stay to hear the speeches—"

"What do you want to do, Marcia?"

"I think we need to get home as soon as we can—"

Marcia and I agreed to leave immediately after the parade. We both have work to do.

"We're going to stay." Marybeth gave the political speeches more weight than Marcia or I.

While we talked, we watched the parade. Lesbian Mothers— their children in tow—went on without us, and we watched as a marching band went by playing the overture of *La Cage aux Folles*, and a group of older gay men under the banner *Prime Timers*, who were followed by *Gay and Lesbian Jews*, the *Alliance of Massachusetts Asian Lesbian and Gay Men*, *Gay Men Together from New Hampshire*, *The United Church of Christ* and *Northeastern University Law School*.

"Oh, come on," Marybeth said. "Don't let's wait. Let's walk. I want to be in it, not watching—"

The group going by at that moment carried a banner, *From Stonewall to Soweto*, and we stepped in behind them. Behind us was *The Alliance of Gays and Lesbians*, New Bedford, and the *Chiltern Mountain Club*, who all wore hiking boots and seemed about to climb Mount Katahdin.

The parade had become very ragged. There was a great open space between us and the Northeastern University Law School group, and the groups behind us were of different sizes, some taking up the whole space from sidewalk to sidewalk, and others just a few walkers. We turned onto Charles Street, between the Common and the Public Garden, and moved toward the gap in the wall of small red brick buildings that line Beacon Street. When we moved off Boylston Street into Charles, we began a giant circle around Beacon Hill, the curve tightening and forming itself into a giant reversed question mark, to end at the State House and the Common.

Charles Street, being narrow, caused the parade to funnel into a smaller space, and the sound of the applause on both sides reverberated off the red brick buildings. Some people in the apartments on the second and third floors above the shops were having parties. Men and women were hanging out the windows and calling to us, and all around us people in the parade were calling back, and the dialogue of applause, to which we had become accustomed by now, took on an added energy in the confined space, coming at us from street level and from two and three stories up too.

In our group, a woman began to chant, "What do we want!" And the group shouted, "Gay Rights!"

"When do we want them!"

"Now!"

Marcia and I and Marybeth and Cynthia looked at one another and laughed. It sounded rebellious, this chant, but in the soft air of a June day in Boston, rebellion seemed goodnatured and easygoing. Yet we had that day a sense of taking part in some momentous event which would change our lives, and as we walked—strolled—with our baby along the bend in Charles past the soft rose brick buildings, there was about everything we did an air of expectation, as if we were approaching a vantage from which we would be able to see our whole lives and were about to discover the secret of our birth.

"What do we want!"

"Gay Rights!"

"When do we want them?"

"*Now!*" hearing our voices reverberate off the nearby buildings.

Our leader kept up her cheer, *What do we want?* and we answered, *Gay Rights! When do we want them?* and it seemed the whole narrow street, the shoppers and the residents and the passersby and the walkers in the parade, carrying green and lavender balloons, all joined in a thunderous *Now!*

Above us, hanging from a window, a man in a blond wig threw out handfuls of confetti on the parade below. He would lean out with an armload of it and suddenly throw his arms straight out to the side, sending a cascade of confetti down on the street, turning his head to the side as he did, giving us his profile, his arms extended straight out to his side. We cheered and people who knew him called to him—"Carlos! Get your ass down here and stop showing off!"— to more laughter.

At that time we hadn't known Marybeth and Cynthia long. I had met Marybeth in the spring on campus—she was there for a class—and I met them both again at the end of the spring term at a Women-in-the-Curriculum symposium. They are younger than we, and at the time it wasn't predictable that we would become such good friends.

"I like that," Cynthia said, nodding toward a sign, *Pride, Fightback, Victory.* Marybeth said, this past week when we met for coffee at Dominic's, "I'm not going to vote. I won't participate in a charade." Marcia pointed out that there were issues that mattered to us that the candidates had addressed—there is a difference between them—and that it was nihilistic to refuse to participate. "It represents a refusal to fight," Marcia said. "How can you not fight?" It is difficult, standing in this long line in this cavernous gymnasium, to accept that the pneumatic clanking of the voting machine is a sign of a fight going on.

We moved through Cambridge Circle into the bottom of Cambridge Street, the great sweep of the road up to Government Center ahead of us, and Marybeth and Cynthia dropped out. They were going into a market for cokes for all of us. "What would you do instead?" I had asked her. "I'd never stop saying their laws are unjust, and I won't participate in enacting them, and I won't obey them—!" There is a part of me that I must suppress if I am to vote, she's right about that. When I stand in the booth, it is inescapable that I am an impostor. There is a thicket of laws in Maine excluding gays and lesbians from communal life, and the court has ruled that we have no right to privacy. I pretend, standing in this line, that I am a law-abiding citizen and not the potential felon that in fact I am. This government of straight men repudiates me, and when I vote, I must pretend that *that* doesn't matter. Or pretend, like most of us, that it hasn't happened.

Marcia took Marc on her shoulder, and we moved from the middle of Cambridge Street to the side, walking slowly, allowing the groups to pass us, waiting for Marybeth and Cynthia to catch up. Marybeth called my office late this morning to say that the trial has been held. Apparently no notice was given, and it was over in an hour. There were no witnesses called on either side, and almost no public witnesses—certainly no gay people—were there to observe. The judge announced that the boys would be tried as juveniles. Then the assistant attorney general announced the charge, which was manslaughter, reduced from murder, and the attorneys stood up one after another with the boys, and they pleaded guilty. Then the judge sentenced them to an indeterminate stay in the juvenile detention home. And then they were led away. Marybeth told me they cried. One of them will be out in eighteen months.

The pneumatic clank sounds again, and another voter crosses the polished floor toward us and the door. The line moves forward. What do we do when we vote? Do we express our faith in the goodwill of the government? That, in the long succession of national issues, eventually attention will be paid to ours? In the shifting alliances that go to make up a majority on any question, do we express our belief that eventually there will be a majority on our question? Signs passed us in the crowd: *RESIST: American Ignorance, Lesbian and Gay Pagans, The New Alliance Party, Gay and Lesbian Political Caucus, National Bisexual Network, Men of All Colors Together.* Unprotected by trees or tall buildings, we began to feel the heat intensely. Marc fretted a little, and men all around us were taking off their shirts.

"Oh, look," Marcia said, laughing. "Why didn't we think of that!"

Near the middle of the street were four women who had removed their tops, their nipples covered by circular stickers which read—I recognized them even from this distance, because they were ubiquitous in the parade—*Gay Pride.* They were doing an exuberant cancan. One of them saw me staring and laughed.

"Come on! Join us!"

I laughed back at her and waved.

The parade had become a mob—friendly, casual, anarchic, the divisions between groups gone now, groups marching without banners, banners without groups, enormous, undisciplined, in love with itself. We had the air of an immense family gathering, and my sense of discovery had to do with the discovery of relatives. All around us men were holding hands. Marcia and I held hands. Two women ahead of us walked up the hill to Government Center, their arms around each other's waists.

Marybeth and Cynthia arrived back with the cokes just as a contingent of *Dykes on Bikes* roared by, their motorcycles drowning out all human speech. They were in leather and had tattoos. I saw one of them looking at me. She pulled over and winked. "Can I give the mother and child a ride?" I laughed, thanked her, and raised my fist, and she roared off, a clinched fist above her head and a grin on her face.

Cynthia told us about a group of radical lesbians she encountered earlier who are going to start a program of street demonstrations.

We rejoined the crowd in the middle of the street behind a woman with white makeup, black lips and a maroon wig, who carried a sign that read, *That Cute Girl*. We had passed Mass General and Old West Church and were even with the Lindemann Mental Health Center.

We were surrounded by green balloons and by persons in green t-shirts. "It's the AIDS Action Committee," Cynthia said. "The people in green t-shirts are volunteers—"

They carried signs, small rectangular sheets of green cardboard, each of which had a date.

"—the date of someone's death—"

The presence of the committee struck a different—and darker—note from the many others struck during the parade. Their signs reminded us how many have died already and suggested the seeds of the disaster. The AAC is a source of pride, but also—and this was inescapable—of defiance.

Marybeth said something to a young man walking near her.

He laughed. "I want to live to see the Second Coming!"

It was so unexpected that I turned to see who could say such a thing. He was handsome—beautiful would be a better word—and thin and tall, and he had blond hair which hung down in his face, and he wore a thin silver chain in his ear. He attracted attention—I saw people turn and glance at him—even though there was no visible reason why. People turned to him and smiled, and he smiled back without stopping talking. He must have come back with Marybeth and Cynthia from the market when they went to get the cokes. He seemed to accept the attention without wondering. His eyes rested briefly on me.

"I just know there's going to be a better day. We weren't put here in this awful time just to suffer, dear, I know. You can tell people I said that." Then he looked at the others. He spread his arm out in a crescent, his palm up, gesturing toward all the men and women in green t-shirts carrying their signs and their dates, gathering to himself their eyes. He groped with his left hand hanging down at his side until he connected with the hand of a smaller, slighter boy who, I realized, was walking with him. They held hands. "How are you doing?" He smiled down at him, and then he hugged him.

"Dana, Marcia—" It was Marybeth speaking. "This is Bernie. And this is Timothy. They're from Cardiff."

That was when I met him.

It was the only time I met him, and that Sunday when Marcia heard the news on her walkman when I was out sailing, Marybeth called and said, "Do you remember—" That boy. Of course. That one I never forgot. The pretty one who attracted attention and said, oddly, *We were not born to suffer*. I just forgot his name and the fact that he was going to be murdered in two weeks.

Walking ahead of us was a man in a long silver lamé evening gown, too short and tight for him—he had a hard, angular body—and silver lamé shoes which had platform soles. His thin hair was silvered and spiked up, and when he turned around and we could see, his face was pockmarked, covered in thick white pancake makeup and dark maroon lipstick. He carried a sign: *Gay Pride Means Revolting Queens, and Don't You Forget It!*

Bernie whispered to us, "I like to be pretty myself. How is he going to get a boyfriend with his hair a mess like that?"

I remember laughing.

"And that dress!" Bernie narrowed his eyes. "Couldn't she have found something prettier at the Mall? If she had *tried?"*

And this morning, they allowed his murderers to plea bargain to manslaughter and sent them off to the juvenile detention home for eighteen months.

What ends today began when I met Bernie. Today I have returned in my mind to the Pride parade and to the moment when I met him and walked with him up Cambridge Street toward the seat of government, and my memory of the silken beauty of that day is rent by regret and anger and grief. The choices that brought us there were profound and costly and didn't brook reversal. But once made, they produced a strength in us which we brought to the parade and gave to all of us. We had dived into the great river of humanity and had come up swimming. It is only in memory that the promise of that day is betrayed, that I wonder what we did there on Cambridge hill before Government Center.

Dana

We were walking slowly. The climb up Cambridge Stree was hard, and the sun was hot. Things had taken on the sheen o brass, and we stopped at Joy Street and rested from the glare in th shade of buildings. We were high enough on the back side of Beacon Hill to see the shining Charles River basin below us and the salt and pepper bridge and, on the right, the white dome of the science museum.

"I've never been in such a big city."

"Oh, you must have," Marcia said.

"No—" Bernie dragged it out into several syllables. "My mommy and daddy brought me to Boston, but I wasn't gay then so wasn't here—"

A group of parents passed with their signs. *All gays and lesbians are somebody's children.* My father died still refusing to meet Marcia, and Mother did not come for Marc's birth. We reentered the parade behind one of the floats paid for by a gay bar. I was a flat bed truck, and on the back was a sound system and six or eight young men dancing in bikinis. The music covered the whole hill. Behind us the parade stretched all the way back to the foot of Cambridge Street. We had dropped out so many times I had thought we must be near the end, but from up on the shoulder of the hill, I could see all Cambridge Street filled with lesbians and gay persons, and the sidewalks packed to the foot of the buildings. It was a continuous, unbroken mass of us for half a mile. It was impossible to tell how much of the parade was still on Charles and couldn't be seen from here and how much of it was in front of us. We must have gathered people all along the route, like tributaries to a great river. We had become a flood, spilling over our banks and watering the earth.

"Come on, boy," Bernie said. He bumped his hip into Timothy. "This is too good to miss. Let's dance!"

Timothy hadn't spoken since they joined us, but he stared at Bernie and worshipped him. He smiled. And they began to dance.

We laughed at the two of them, they were so happy. Bernie noticed.

"I am what I am," Bernie said to us, "and I am not revolting!"

He waved at the people on the sidewalk with their shopping bags and their cameras. He waved at the men and women moving in

nd out of the parade. Some waved back. He kept on dancing,
hrowing his pelvis out to Timothy and his shoulders back in time to
he music, his whole body a slinky boneless marvel. Passing us, a
group of men and women carried a banner, *Parents and Friends of
Gays and Lesbians*. One hears now in the gay community, people
referring to "family-by-birth" and "family-by-choice."

"He's cute, isn't he?" There was that. What else was there?
Did I ask that then? Or is it only now that I require there be
something "else"? Marcia and I held hands and watched. Marc was
fascinated.

"That's a political statement the government can't ignore!"
Marybeth swung her arm in an arc to encompass the whole hill
beneath us back to the bottom of Cambridge and all the tens of
thousands of people walking up toward us.

"Is that what you see here?" It was Marcia.

"Militant, out gays and lesbians. Thirty thousand of us—"
Her arm took in the crowd, the green t-shirts and the banners.

Bernie danced. He waved again, and people watched,
laughing and smiling, and waved back. The parents seemed all
around us, carrying individual signs: *My Daughter is a Lesbian and I
love her*. One man's sign said, *My Son Has Died of AIDS*. The light
and the shadow. The applause started up again, the wordless
dialogue between us and—us. We could see a corner of City Hall
ahead of us, and behind us the vast panorama—Cambridge across the
river in the distance, the Charles basin slicing from left to right, the
tangle of expressways around the foot of the hill, and then the city
climbing up toward us on either side of Cambridge Street. The
parade filled Cambridge from the bottom of Beacon Hill, our view
foreshortened by the angle, the thousands of bodies—we seemed like
all of Boston—moving up and down under a blue sky where giant
cumulus clouds that piled up in sumptuous gaiety to forty thousand
feet moved at a stately pace across our path to the west, our
happiness softening every harsh shadow and sharp edge, and
everywhere the thousands of balloons, lavender for us, green for the
dead.

Pneumatic clank. The election. Thanksgiving. Christmas.
The New Year. The Inauguration. Winter. I will vote for the bond
issues for the university and the voc-tech system and against the
bond issue for the prison system. I will vote for the constitutional

question on the issuance of bonds, against the question of the bond issue for veterans, and for the ERA. I will vote for the Democratic candidates for the House from my district for the state legislature and the national House of Representatives. I will vote for the New Alliance Party candidate for president. He is black. He has a black lesbian vice presidential candidate on the ticket with him. His party is for the ERA, for a national gay rights bill, for nuclear disarmament. Pneumatic clank. I stand at the registration table, and the registrar searches for my name.

"There you are!" She smiles at me.

"Here I am." I walk toward the booth. I will send my roman candles to the moon. Tonight, when it is all over, I will pick up the sweater I dropped in July. I have a book to write.

At some point, rounding Cambridge Street into Government Center, Bernie and Timothy disappeared. Vanished. I never saw him again. And when I saw Timothy in Cardiff after Bernie was dead, we had to meet one another all over again. Timothy's drying out, they say. It seems Mickey took him in at the end of last week. At least he'll be off the street for a while, where somebody can look after him.

What was Bernie like? Every reporter has asked that question. I didn't pay attention when I had my chance, and most of what I saw and heard, I forgot. But in my grief at my loss and my anger at losing him, I remember one thing. When he first joined us, he took Marc from Marcia and carried him for us up the hill. He talked in a low voice—too low for us to hear—and pointed out things along the way, the telephone building and the Beacon Hill Grill and the McCormack building and the JFK Federal Building. He put his finger to Marc's nose each time after he had pointed something out, and Marc began to giggle, to wait for the finger and then to giggle when it came to his face. He pointed to us—to Marcia and me—and Marc reached out toward us, and then he put his finger to Marc's nose, and Marc tried to look at it, and giggled when he couldn't. It was a kid playing with a kid.

But when he handed him back to me, he said something that startled me because it wasn't the voice of a kid. He tilted his head down a little so he was looking at me from under his brows. He spoke, and then he closed his mouth and pursed his lips, as if he didn't expect me to argue with him.

He said, "Make sure he has a choice, hear, honey?"

Epilogue

Derek

A head of me on the corner of Commonwealth, a witch and a warlock discuss directions in Spanish. A man, balding, pot-bellied, in a nylon windbreaker, walks a dog. He has his hands in his jacket pockets, the loop of the leash over his wrist. I nod and grin. "Happy Halloween."

He grumbles, "Faggot!" and turns away.

In Boston I laugh it off. It is midnight. The show is over, I was terrific, the applause was long, loud, and sustaining, and I am in street clothes again, headed home to an efficiency on Beacon Street I sublet for the fall. I go to dress for a party in the South End. At the party there will be more applause, and I will find Malcolm, this fall's beauty.

I go down Essex toward Beacon, across the Back Bay, through the laughter and the shouts of "Trick or Treat!" echoing off the red brick walls of the houses under a yellow moon. I step aside to let groups pass: men and women dressed up to look like some gaudy thing they're not—or to expose what they really are underneath their everyday disguise. It's hard to tell, and it means appearance may suggest reality—or not—and you don't know. The man's windbreaker is a case in point and raises the question whether you can trust anything and suggests how high the stakes are.

"Malcolm" is in *Macbeth*, and we connected on the first read-through. We are two of the few left alive at the end of the play, which seems symbolic. What is compelling about him is his arrangement of opposites. His size, his musculature, and his powerful presence, all male qualities, contrast with a remarkable femininity, his long hair and the way he tosses it, his full sensuous mobile lips, his lowered eyelids. This tension in him between the male and female—he could play the extremes of either equally well—disturbs me and raises in me a narrow focus, a powerful singleness of mind about his body. When I make love to him, it is unclear whether I am fucking a man or a woman, and I want to make him choose.

On the opposite side of Commonwealth, Marie Antoinette and a page appear, coming toward me. A policeman passes in black leather chaps. A sliver of a cloud crosses the moon and darkens the scene. I wear leather pants and a leather jacket and black construction boots. The page, with a liquid androgyny, smokes a cigarette—he narrows his eyes against the smoke—and talks animatedly in Italian to Marie Antoinette. They have it right, Marie and her little boy page: The queen is 6 feet with a thick waist, has a beard under her makeup, and the page is 5 feet 6 inches, with full red lips. I come up upon a woman in a hooded black mink coat, walking quickly toward the corner. As I pass her I see her hands are crossed at her neck, holding closely the dark shimmering fur of the hood and completely hiding her face.

This has been my life since returning to Boston from Maine: rehearsals, the show, the bars, Malcolm's body, driven by a sensuality intensified by a play about clothes and sex: *I dare do anything that may become a man* and by a sexual hunger so deep it seems life threatening. I have returned to the gay community after my sojourn in the straight world, and I am no longer exposed. The stigma we took on ourselves in Cardiff—*Another Friend of Bernie Mallett*—in Boston is a badge of entry, and I search the shadows of the city in an effort to recapture the effortless, thoughtless, moment before I woke up and found Bernie was dead, his long hair across his eyes in his slow dance under the water.

I step into a dark entryway for a group of revelers to pass. Halloween, like Mardi Gras and New Year's Eve, expands the freedom of the city and the anonymity of night. "Halloween" used to suggest the spiritual world, but now what you meet on the street is secret fantasy, the eruption of suppressed reality, amateurish—yards of cheap tulle and fake eyelashes—but real. What did Bernie know when he said, *I am what I am*? What seemed then to be a shifting collection of quirks, his melodrama, his drag, his earring, his courage, his attitude, seems now to have been an absolute—he was absolute about it—which I can't define, but which seems now to be at the center of what's missing in my life.

I hear them cry, "Trick or Treat!"—threat and promise—and move along Essex toward Marlboro.

A towering courtesan comes toward me at the corner. She smiles and hides the lower half of her face behind a fan and, in a *basso profundo*, whispers, "Hmmm. Do you have somewhere to go, fella?"

"Yeah. Home—"

"Can a girl go with you?"

512

She implores me with her eyes.

I smile. "You're beautiful. But not tonight."

"Some other night, then?"

I used to think men wear pants and do men's things and women wear skirts and do women's things, and there is no reason to wonder what makes all this difference. My leather suggests an extreme of maleness—it pulls across my thighs and shoulders. I am comfortable with my manhood. Being gay doesn't make me less a man, but I am aware of the disturbing potential, inside me, which Bernie insisted on, of opposing forces. My male swagger alternates with the possibility that my strength may be insufficient or inappropriate or beside the point. Bernie knew something of this: Everything he was questioned my whole notion of maleness, and the more he recedes in my memory, the more insistent, the clearer his challenge to me becomes.

I have always liked a boy who gives in to me. I have liked to exercise my maleness by spreading his legs and exposing his ass and entering him, dominating him with my dick, riding him, feeling my body contract as I thrust hard into him. Coming toward me under the streetlights down Beacon Street is one: a boy in girl's clothes. He is all in white, a pale dress with no waist whose hem is above his knees, pale stockings, low white shoes. He wears a cloche hat, and when he passes me, his large round dark eyes cruise me from the side. I don't know now whether it is the boy or the girl I am after. His glance is an invitation, and I smile. I turn and watch him go on down the street, opportunity receding. When I am making love, whether to a man or a woman, I am concentrated in my dick. That is an irreducible minimum. But I turn over on the bed and bury my face in the pillow, dissatisfied, still charged with a sensuality that has grown more demanding, not less, and which, except for the shimmering iridescent image of Bernie in my mind, is unable to find a focus.

I have showered and shaved for the second time today. I shaved my legs and my arms up to my elbows, under my arms, and my chest down to my sternum. I took each nipple and pulled the tit to make the skin tight while I stroked the razor inward, removing the hair. I stand in front of the mirror, spreading foundation makeup on my face. It is like stage makeup, like fine clay, smooth, slick, and has a faint fragrance. I touch my fingers lightly to its squat jar and spread it across my forehead, a streak down each cheek, across my upper lip and my chin. Then I work it in, beyond my hairline and back to the base of my ears and down my throat, until gradually my face takes on the pale color of the creme. I put on an extra layer on my upper and lower lips and my lower cheeks to hide my beard. Steam soaks my body and covers the mirror, and I wipe it clear so I can see. I do all this deliberately, clinically, waiting to see what I am going to look like when I am through and how I will feel when I see myself. The heavy creme gradually covers my beard—my first sign that I was going to be a man—and hides the bristle, and the shadows of my face disappear under a mask. I cover the lines at the end of my eyes and mouth.

Gretchen, who is Lady Macbeth in our play, and who takes her breasts in her hands and speaks of the milk of human kindness and of killing her children, tells me I deal in stereotypes. Last month we sat in a cafe on Newbury Street.

"Drag, for you," she said, "is merely a matter of putting on clothes—" I saw Bernie in his dress once. He appeared at my door, standing in the shadows beyond the circle of light, a tall thin young woman in a black dress, his eyes down. I stood there for a moment watching him, my arm holding open the screen, and then he climbed the steps toward me and put his arm around my neck and leaned up and kissed me.

"How do you like this?"

I didn't like it. The thing was a shock to see the boy I was making it with suddenly dressed this way. I ran my arm down his back and found his bottom and kissed him, *a man in women's clothes*, and felt a confusion in my mind.

Flamboyant Bernie. But I discovered his dress made me feel profoundly male—bigger, stronger, immensely powerful—by comparison. It confirmed me, and when I found him in a dress, I wanted to fuck him, hard. I never knew why he wanted to do it, or why it was such a turn-on for me. It was dangerous—he was violating a primal taboo and doing it in public and exposing himself to ridicule and scorn and the hatred of every bigot in the shadows—and I never knew what there was so powerful about cross-dressing that he thought was worth the danger.

"You're gay, Derek. You don't know anything about women," Gretchen said, sipping a beer. "You're only putting on our clothes—"

What are women like? I open the door from the bathroom to let the steam out. I stand in front of the mirror, naked, the cold enamel of the sink pressed up against my scrotum, my dick flopping on the chilled edge. As the room cools and dries, I wipe the stick of deodorant across my armpit, raising first the left and then the right. I remember the first wisps of hair under my arm—they were light brown—which appeared when I was thirteen, and the smear of deodorant goes on unnaturally on my smooth skin.

I had asked Gretchen for help in getting this together. We went shopping, and she advised me, in secret, because this is to be a surprise. We went to shops, giggling, but underneath my laughter I felt a deep tension: My father said one time, when I was a kid and had come in from the yard crying about something, *Be a man*, and I thought, going from shop to shop with Gretchen looking for shoes big enough to fit me, braving the stares of the shop girls, how much cleaner it would be if it were a question of clothes, jeans for me, a skirt for her. And that would be the end of it. *Be a man*. Take charge. Be strong. Look after those less strong. Don't be victimized. Don't show fear. Don't show weakness. Get what you want. Women are not in charge, are weak, are victimized, show fear, don't get what they want. Buying a girdle and high heel shoes and a dress, I savor the tension in my mind as I step down from male eminence. I wonder: Which do I savor more, the danger? Or the breaking loose?

In my bedroom, the girdle lies on the bed. It is a full girdle and bra. I hold it across my belly, and then I slide my hands around to the back and—holding my breath and sucking in my stomach—I hook the stiff fabric, first in the middle of the row of hooks, and then work my way to the top. I am not limber enough to do this easily, and the muscles at the back of my arms and on my back—enlarged from lifting weights—bunch up and prevent me from getting easily at the tiny hooks. I fumble at them and strain to get the work done. Then I work my way down to the bottom. Men are clumsy.

I check myself in the mirror on the back of my closet door. What I do is, in itself, provocative, and I feel a heightened awareness. I study the person who looks back at me. Half this and half that. My torso is now an hourglass shape. The rest of me, except my white face, is the same. They would say I don't know what I am.

In my top drawer I find the garter belt. I tear open the package of stockings and sit down, cross my legs, and, bunching the filmy stuff on my fingers, begin to work my toes and feet into the sheath. My legs are not quite dry. I nicked one of them in shaving. The nylon sticks and pulls. When I have gotten one leg in up to the knee, I put that one on the floor and work on the other one. Then, standing up, I reach down—it is difficult to bend over in the corset— and pull up the stockings over my knees and stretch them to get over my thighs. I attach them to the garter belt. I walk around on the carpet for a moment, feeling the slick, tough nylon between my thighs. In this reversal of the usual—my waist and legs are tightly wrapped in fabric, my crotch exposed—there is something crazily erotic, and my dick stirs.

In the bathroom on the back of the toilet is a small box of loose powder. I pat the soft puff on my forehead and cheeks and chin and, throwing back my head, around my throat. My skin begins to look soft—I have always been proud that I looked rugged—and the face staring back at me from the mirror is still incomplete, half done: My eyes and mouth are still my own.

What I know about is strength, that and dominance, and with each step of this dressing, I move farther from what I know. I take one part after another of me—my skin or my legs or my waist—and hide my maleness to reveal—what? To look like a female? A man in women's clothes? I wonder if I want to be a woman. I am intensely aware of the step-by-step progression of this transformation and of how deliberately I am going into a place I don't know. I hear my father saying insistently, *Be a man*, and feel a chill of fear and the sleek nylon on my legs and a surge of sexual excitement.

With the heel of my thumb, I smear a streak of pale gold on my eyelids, and, trying to hold my hand steady, I draw a thin line of eyeliner just inside my eyelashes from the inside to the outside on the top and bottom lids, joining them together at the outer end. Then I brush mascara on my eyelashes, which are normally thick and black. My eyes are enlarged and expressive. I have never learned to use my eyelids.

The lipstick is in a new gold tube, deep red, and I begin at the middle of my lips and draw it out to the end on each side. I close my lips, purse them, relax them. My lips are strong and expressive: I can curl them in anger when I draw swords with Macbeth. Now I purse them and, leaning forward over the sink, kiss my image in the mirror.

My erection hangs heavy between my legs and flops as I walk. Back in the bedroom I take the dress out of the closet, and its soft folds hang on my fingers weightlessly. It is silk, a sheath, pale lavender, and has three-quarter length sleeves. I step into it, pushing my dick aside, and pull up the slinky fabric and slide my arms into the sleeves. I have a hook, which I use to pull up the zipper in the back. Black leather and denim: now all this unfamiliar, filmy, slick material sliding on my body. I transform myself body part by body part.

I check the effect in the mirror: It is incomplete. My face, which could be the face of a woman, is on the head of a man: The thickness of my neck can't be disguised, and my close-cropped hair is undeniably male. The dress features breasts—my pecs provide cleavage—but my legs are heavy and muscular. My forearms, showing from beneath the sleeves of the dress, are thick and veined. I stand with my pelvis thrust forward and my weight distributed evenly on each foot, my arms hanging down. I need to control my unquiet dick. Since it is too late for jockey shorts, I pull up the skirt of the dress and step into a jock strap from my gym bag.

The wig is on the post of the bed. The skirt forces me to take shorter steps and to bend at the waist to lean over. The wig is long and fluffy and dark brown, the color of my own hair, and I return to the mirror to put it on. After a quick toss from side to side—the long, loose curls swing out and around across my eyes, and I glimpse a seductive woman—I attach the earrings. They are large clusters of small pink pearls attached loosely, like a bunch of grapes hanging from my ears, and they tinkle when I toss my head. I purse my lips as I observe my reflection. That's her. I lift my chin and look at myself from the side and grin, openmouthed, feeling a strong sexual urgency. Then I laugh: I don't know what would be more satisfying right now: To fuck, or be fucked.

And then I step into the shoes. They are spike heeled, pointed toe black patent-leather pumps. I tower over the room. I am 5 feet 11 inches in my bare feet, and the shoes have 5-inch heels, so I stand 6 feet 4 inches, enough to get attention. I check the mirror. I pivot on the heels, cock my hip, stand on one leg and brace the other and watch the woman facing me do everything I do. This is what I was going for. I pose, checking myself from the side, and she poses, checking herself from the side, this large good-looking woman, sexy and sure of herself. Her legs are curvy and strong. The wig hides my neck, and I toss my head and see her hair streaming out across her face as if a wind had blown it. She tosses it again. I am beautiful. I stand on one leg and turn my other toe and knee in. She's even bashful. My basket shows. I am exhilarated. My eyes, in the mirror, are bright and flashing. I am beautiful and courageous, new and free, soft and strong.

I thought I would remain untouched, the me under the skirt. I feel like a girl. I walk around the room, catching glimpses of myself in mirrors, turning, posing. The skirt tells me how to feel, how to act. I walk a certain way and hold my legs a certain way, and I sit down a certain way. This is easy. I am a man, wear pants, have a dick, do men's things, and now I discover how easy it is to pass through to the other side, to run my hands down the back of my skirt and spread it out before sitting down, and to admire myself. I lounge on the sofa like the clothed Maja and let the tips of my fingers almost touch my breasts. Instead of sweat and the gym and ballgames and torn jeans, there is this other world of pretty, frilly dresses, things that smell good, a soft world of feeling. What do women feel? What do I know of women but stereotypes?

I have the same sense, less profound and less disturbing—at the same time liberating—every time I dress for a part. In the process of putting on the clothes, I find something in me that I hadn't known was there before. Tonight, like every night, the messenger tells me my wife and children have been murdered. The grief I express raises in me the question, *Am I acting this?* Is this a question of technique and skill, or have I found something in me that I never knew was there before? What grief do I have for wife and children when I don't have either one? Is being a man or a woman so inconsequential that you can put it on or take it off? Is it something you can learn? The size of my world has doubled, and I possess this immense, secret freedom. I could do this all the time. I could go in drag three days out of every week, all of December, say, in jeans in alternate seasons. I can be Don Giovanni and Donna Elvira.

I wonder what I say about women. Gretchen, a woman of harsh laughter, I think, staring at the triumphant woman in the mirror, didn't understand. This isn't about women. Seeing myself, my feminine self, in my spike heels and lavender, clingy dress, staring back at me, I see that this, I am finally beginning to understand, is about men.

I fling open the door and stand for a moment, my hip cocked out, my arm on the door jamb above my head, ready. Below me on the street couples pass, hanging on each other's arms, intensely self-aware. Large men in leather, women in tuxedos and masks, a druid priest and an acolyte, three youths in jeans and t-shirts wearing rubber faces of the president's wife, a man with a crown and scepter. All the cast of the play is here and ready. Finally, I step through the door into the outside: *Enter Queen*.

On the stairs down to the street, I turn slightly to the side to navigate the steps in my skirt and heels. My heels click on the stone. It is almost one. Fifteen minutes across the Back Bay into the South End. There is a breeze which causes the limbs of the trees to rattle. I feel the nylon between my legs, and the breeze on my face reminds me of my makeup, which is my mask. I walk with my back straight and my head up, and I am aware of every single thing: of the breeze in my hair and up my skirt, of the sounds of the branches of the trees, the huge yellow moon, the lights of the high houses along the street, and of the attention I'm getting. It's better than being in a show. I am intensely alive, charged by these unfamiliar soft slick fabrics sliding over my skin and by how I look. I think I want to be a woman. Gretchen, when I told her I was going to wear drag to the party and that I was going to *walk* to the South End, rolled her eyes and said, *That'll take balls*. I've got balls.

The moon is high now, straight above, a deep yellow, and there are slips of dark clouds against the dark silver sky. I turn to the left and go toward Dartmouth, passing revelers. Dartmouth, Marlborough, Commonwealth, Newbury, Boylston, then Copley Square. I stride across the Back Bay as if the Amazons have won, or better, as if a man has finally come out. I hear bursts of laughter from the dark hole of the square under the dark striped bulk of Trinity Church. Two people in black shrouds sit on the concrete parapet of the square and embrace, murmuring words I can't hear.

Derek

In the soft night under the high moon people call out to one another. Around me on the steps of the library leaning against the plinths of Art and Science, under the legend FREE TO ALL, are all sorts of men and women in various stages of costumes. Bernie walked like this through the streets of Cardiff, carrying his purse. I consider the uses of strength. I have been a football player, and I lift weights. I have traded on my rough Italian good looks since I was sixteen. My biceps stretch the fabric of my dress. My strength is an essential part of me. I have not dismantled step by step my whole conception of myself, but my self includes this too—these earrings, shoes, dress. I run my tongue over my lips and taste the lipstick. It's like saying I'm no longer a virgin. *I've been fucked.* A policeman stands at the far corner of the square. He watches me as I approach. High heels are a powerful thing! I feel invincible. He wears the drag of exaggerated masculinity—tight leather boots, tight pants that exhibit his ass and his crotch, leather belt, pistol holder, leather gloves. His bike is propped on the street. I consider what he is thinking, and when I am close enough, I see the lower part of his face under the visor of his cap. He observes me in my dress and mascara and high heels. I want him to see that I am beautiful. He grins as I come up to him.

I want him to see that I am this wonderful, new, unexpected, powerful thing, *a woman.* I know something he doesn't know: He wants there to be an unclimbable barrier between men and women, and I have just discovered that you can climb it. *Has this been inside me all along?* Trinity Church is lit. High reliefs of St. John and Isaiah and The Peaceable Kingdom way up on the red stone facade look down like blind judges on us all. People move in and out of its shadows, all the anarchic, vital, variety of us. The city is most alive at night: We are most free in the dark. The cop's drag weighs on him like chains. I consider my ass and know that the heels of my shoes make my buttocks sway, and when I pass him, I feel his laughter, burning in them. It doesn't much matter whether he sees me as a man or a woman. What matters is that he sees me as I am: powerful and free.

I kept photocopies of the letters I received this summer from the old men. They lived through years of being told they were not quite *men,* that they were failed men, impotent, weak, sick, that they were *women with dicks,* and their letters suggested an agony of shame. I know, when I am honest, I feel shame too. I didn't know that before this summer, before I had a chance to think about what Bernie's death meant. I wrote Deborah. *I feel shame. What am I supposed to do?* What is a guy supposed to do when a guy is a handsome muscular Italian actor, queer, and feels shame?

I feel the soft slick fabric pull across my shoulders and bind my thighs. I feel the cluster of tiny pearls clinking on my earlobes. My stockings whisper between my legs. The old men wrote, *They said we were like women.* Boys used to play Lady Macbeth and my wife. All of us actors here, the whole cast of characters on stage and off from all the plays, moving in and out of our roles. I wonder if it is possible to forget who I was before. Is it possible to go back once you have been here? I wonder how you get back your virginity.

There is a band somewhere inside the Copley Plaza playing Tommy Dorsey, and couples in evening dress are entering and leaving. The doorman in a crimson overcoat with brass trimming whistles for a cab and opens the doors: *Good evening, Madam.* He bows to the patrons with a barely perceptible nod of his head. *Thank you, sir.* He sees me approach. I know that I walk in a long-legged stride exaggerated by my heels and my skirt.

"Have a good evening, *Ma'am!*" He shows his teeth.

Like women. I smile.

As I walk past him, I throw my ass at him, and then I cross the bridge into the South End and, in a few blocks, turn into a side street. A block, a turn, a block, a turn, and I will be there. In the South End there are fewer revelers on the street, and more gangs of kids. In a crazy way tottering along the pavement in my high heels, the constraints of the dress and the girdle, the closeness of the wig, and the jangle of the earrings around my face make me more aware of my body, bound in this thin fabric. I am sexy, my body wrapped up in this absurdly thin filmy material. It's like gauze. Its delicate texture makes me feel pretty, weak, *willing*, dependent. Is this what women feel? God, I want to give in to a strong man. I imagine Malcolm fucking me, my legs up.

A tall man is leaning against a railing. He wears jeans and a jean jacket, and he watches me approach. I wonder if he will come on to me, as I am. I am aware of how odd the question is, from me. I hear the sound my heels make on the pavement. They are like hammers, and the shock of them hitting the pavement reverberates up my legs. The man fumbles for a cigarette and then a match, and I avert my eyes and look at the stone curb. I draw near to him. I want him to find me beautiful. I want to show him what I feel in myself— my courage, my freedom, which make me beautiful. Without meaning to, I slow down and let him see me. I want him to find me overwhelming.

I glance at him and meet his eye, and I am about to speak when I see him shake out the match and flick it away with his finger and thumb. He stares at me, up and down.

I stare back. He has a weatherbeaten face, and his eyes squint against the smoke from his cigarette.

"Fucking fairy."

Asshole. I look away, my face stinging underneath the heavy makeup, and go on, moving as fast as I can in my skirt and high heels. I'll be damned if I am going to feel shame for him.

I hear him behind me.

"You want to get fucked?"

The street is dark. The lights are far between. The revelers have suddenly disappeared.

"That it? Ya wanta get fucked?"

My heels catch on the pavement and scrape. I am alone on this street.

"Ya want me to fuck ya?" I hear this crazy laughter behind me.

He is following me. I am at the end of the block, and I turn. I think. I force myself to think. I am as big as he is. I can handle him. I think: That's the way a man thinks. He is only a man. Then I am confused. *Can* I handle him? I look around. Is there someone to help me?

He is running behind me.

I run too, a dozen yards, but I can't run in my heels. I am at the intersection with the avenue. There are cars. More lights. I am safe.

"Hey, faggot!"

He's still there, behind me, and closer.

"Ya wanta be a girl?"

Is it safer to cross, to make it to my friend's house in the dark, narrow streets on the other side of the avenue or to stay here, where it is light and there are cars? I can't think.

"Ya want me to cut ya nuts off?"

I can fight him. I am going to have to fight him. I stumble, and I think I have broken a heel. I turn and face him. He's drunk.

"Ya want me to show ya what a man is?"

But it's not just him.

"Yeah! Cut his nuts off!"

There are two more men. They are in a crouch, their legs spread, their arms out, making a circle around me.

I am going to have to fight.

"Lookit the lady!"

They are laughing at me. At my dress. My hair. The shame I feel—it's an old taste—flows and catches in my throat and chokes me. The long hair from my wig blows across my eyes.

"Ain't she pretty!"

"What she needs is a real man—"

I am in a crouch, turning, looking over my shoulder, trying to keep track of each one of them.

I think: *They are not going to hurt me.*

One of them behind me lunges. I hear his feet first on the pavement, and I whirl to meet him, throwing out my leg to keep my balance. I hear my skirt rip. Before I can see where he is, I feel it hit my side, under my arm: He has a board. It knocks me sideways, and I almost go down. I catch my balance. I feel cold. The pain erupts. I suck in air.

There's another behind me—

I can't think. I can't see. I feel like I can't see. Everything hurts. Every time I turn, I leave two behind me. I have to breathe, but each intake feels like an ice pick through my ribs.

I hear the feet behind me, the whoosh of air as it swings, and it hits me again. I lurch, lose my balance, regain it. Is it one board? Two?

They are laughing. My breath comes in sharp, jagged, intakes. The pain in my ribs—. The scene goes and comes with nausea.

"Lookit the lady now!"

I whirl to face him.

"Look at her jump!"

"Let's cut off her nuts!"

Two of them have two-by-fours, and I see another, out of the corner of my eye, coming back to the circle with more. Where do they get them? They circle me, and whenever I stumble toward an opening, they close it and stop me. I can't focus. There's something in my eye. There's an empty lot—a construction site—on the corner.

I hear one running from behind, and before I can turn, I am hit on both sides. I stagger. I can't stop myself. I am on my knees. I fall forward—

"Lookit 'er! I think she wants us to fuck 'er!"

That was when it happened. The thing struck me on the back of my head and went on striking me around my head, wrapping itself around my skull, round and round, my nose, my eyes, my ears—. I am screaming.

I can't see. I scream. It's a chain. One of them has the other end and jerks it, and it pulls my head in a circle, wrenches my neck, pulls me off my knees, pulls me up. It's blood. I taste it.

I wipe the blood from my eyes. Has it pulled all the skin off the bone? I am on my feet. I lurch. They circle me, jeering.

"He wants to be a girl!"

I stagger around in the middle of their circle, caught like a bear. Who has the chain?

Then I hear it first, whistling through the air at me. I throw up my arm, and it catches my wrist, wraps itself around the bone and hits my face again, across the bridge of my nose.

I jerk the chain, and I see who has it, the Marlboro man. I jerk hard, and he screams as it pulls through his fingers.

I've got the whole thing, and I swing it hard above my head. They move back to keep out of its way.

I circle to keep them all in view.

"OK, faggot." It's the Marlboro man. His eyes squint. He speaks in a low voice to the other men. "Let's take him—"

But I have the chain. It whistles above my head. It makes a great circle, whistling. I rise to my full height, my arm raised, whipping the chain, hard, above my head, dipping it down toward this man or that, my legs spread wide in my high heels.

They circle. They can't get close enough in to me to use their boards.

"He's a big mother—"

I *am* a big mother, me in my dress, swinging my chain.

524

A car passes, its lights sweeping us before it goes on down the avenue.

"You wanta be a woman—"

My chain whistles—the street light glints on it as it goes around—and I hear them smacking their palms with their boards. I can keep them away, but I can't get away. Another car passes and disappears. I can't see. There's the blood.

One of them behind me says, "Let's fuck him—"

My earring—it is a clip, a cluster of pearls—falls to the pavement. It lies on the stone between my legs, shining in the moonlight. I whirl my chain above it. It is mine, and in my pain, I have a sudden, clear, absurd, obsessive conviction that I must defend it. I think of Bernie. I didn't know until after he was dead that I loved him. Blood mats my hair and runs down my face from my broken nose. I taste it—mixed with the odd waxy taste of lipstick. The sharp points of pain in my ribs and skull mix with the dull ache all over. I dance this way and that in my heels, lurching to face this one or that one, my arm high above my head, whipping the chain. They grin, taunt me, mock me, above my little cluster of pink pearls on the concrete.

The whistle of my chain above my head, the smack of boards in their palms, the shuffle of our feet on the stones, my staggered breathing: These are the sounds of the night, under the bright moon and the sliver of dark cloud.

I can take one, maybe two. I hear behind me tires of a car on the avenue, passing. It comes to this. This is the way it is. I'm smart, not quick. It's taken me time. I am what I am. You led. Now I follow.

The End